CHARLOTTE LENNOX, née Ramsay, was born in or before ————, possibly in Gibraltar. She spent part of her youth in New York, where her father, Captain James Ramsay, was sent in 1739. Before 1747 she travelled to England and tried to make her own living; her marriage to the impecunious Alexander Lennox in 1747 was not to afford her financial or emotional support. Her first novel, *The Life of Harriot Stuart*, was published in 1750. Lennox's best-known and most celebrated work, *The Female Quixote*, appeared in 1752, and attracted the attention and approval of both Henry Fielding and Samuel Richardson; Samuel Johnson applauded it and Jane Austen was to read it more than once. Lennox's other novels, *Henrietta* (1758), *The History of Harriot and Sophia* (1760–1), and *Euphemia* (1790), display intelligence and wit; each novel is a different exploration of the patterns a contemporary woman's life might take. Lennox was a pioneer of Shakespeare criticism with her *Shakespeare Illustrated* (1753–4), the first work to trace Shakespeare's sources. Lennox supported herself with hack writing and translating, and also attempted drama; her first play *The Sister* (with an epilogue by Oliver Goldsmith) appeared for only one night at Covent Garden, but *Old City Manners* had a good run at Drury Lane in 1775–6. Lennox had two children; her daughter predeceased her and she seems to have separated from her husband. Her latter years were weighed down by illness and poverty; she died in a poor lodging on 4 January 1804.

MARGARET DALZIEL was Professor of English at the University of Otago, New Zealand, until her retirement in 1981.

MARGARET ANNE DOODY is the John and Barbara Glynn Family Professor of Literature at the University of Notre Dame. Her publications include *A Natural Passion: A Study of the Novels of Samuel Richardson*, *The Daring Muse: Augustan Poetry Reconsidered*, *Frances Burney: The Life in the Works*, and *The True Story of the Novel*, as well as two novels, *Aristotle Detective* and *The Alchemists*.

OXFORD WORLD'S CLASSICS

*For over 100 years Oxford World's Classics have brought
readers closer to the world's great literature. Now with over 700
titles—from the 4,000-year-old myths of Mesopotamia to the
twentieth century's greatest novels—the series makes available
lesser-known as well as celebrated writing.*

*The pocket-sized hardbacks of the early years contained
introductions by Virginia Woolf, T. S. Eliot, Graham Greene,
and other literary figures which enriched the experience of reading.
Today the series is recognized for its fine scholarship and
reliability in texts that span world literature, drama and poetry,
religion, philosophy and politics. Each edition includes perceptive
commentary and essential background information to meet the
changing needs of readers.*

OXFORD WORLD'S CLASSICS

CHARLOTTE LENNOX

The Female Quixote

OR

The Adventures of Arabella

Edited by
MARGARET DALZIEL

With an Introduction by
MARGARET ANNE DOODY

Chronology and Appendix by
DUNCAN ISLES

OXFORD
UNIVERSITY PRESS

OXFORD

UNIVERSITY PRESS

Great Clarendon Street, Oxford OX2 6DP

Oxford University Press is a department of the University of Oxford.
It furthers the University's objective of excellence in research, scholarship,
and education by publishing worldwide in

Oxford New York

Auckland Bangkok Buenos Aires Cape Town Chennai
Dar es Salaam Delhi Hong Kong Istanbul Karachi Kolkata
Kuala Lumpur Madrid Melbourne Mexico City Mumbai Nairobi
São Paulo Shanghai Taipei Tokyo Toronto

Oxford is a registered trade mark of Oxford University Press
in the UK and in certain other countries

Published in the United States
by Oxford University Press Inc., New York

Text, Chronology, Note on the Text, Select Bibliography,
Textual and Explanatory Notes © Oxford University Press 1970
Introduction © Margaret Anne Doody 1989

The moral rights of the author have been asserted

Database right Oxford University Press (maker)

First published as a World's Classic paperback 1989
Select Bibliography revised 1989 and
1997 with the assistance of J. David Macey Jr.
Reissued as an Oxford World's Classics paperback 1998
Reissued 2008

British Library Cataloguing in Publication Data

Data available

Library of Congress Cataloging in Publication Data
Lennox, Charlotte, ca. 1729–1804.
The female Quixote, or, The Adventures of Arabella / edited by
Margaret Dalziel; with an introduction by Margaret Anne Doody;
chronology and appendix by Duncan Isles.
p. cm.—(Oxford world's classics)
I. Dalziel, Margaret. II. Title. III. Title: The adventures of Arabella. IV. Series
PR3541 I.27A66 1989 823'.6—dc19 89–3021

ISBN 978–0–19–954024–2

17

Printed in Great Britain by
Clays Ltd, Elcograf S.p.A.

CONTENTS

THE FEMALE QUIXOTE

VOLUME I

BOOK I

CONTENTS

BOOK IV

VOLUME II

BOOK V

BOOK VI

BOOK VII

INTRODUCTION

And when I tell you, pursued she with a Smile, that I was born and
christen'd, had a useful and proper Education, receiv'd the Addresses of
my Lord —— through the Recommendation of my Parents, and marry'd
him with their Consents and my own Inclination, and that since we have
liv'd in great Harmony together, I have told you all the material Passages
of my Life . . .

IN the passage of Charlotte Lennox's novel here quoted as
epigraph, the virtuous and nameless Countess is trying to persuade
the heroine that good women have neither history nor adventures
(p. 327). Charlotte Lennox herself, however, had both history and
adventures: her life was nothing like that passive and unruffled
sequence of sub-events that acts as an ironically presented ideal in
the novel.

Charlotte Lennox's date and place of birth are obscure. She was
born between 1720 and 1730, perhaps in Gibraltar, to which her
father James Ramsay, an army officer, was sent in 1727.[1] In 1739
James Ramsay was appointed Captain of an Independent Company of Foot at New York, and the whole family moved to New
York. Travel across the Atlantic was itself an adventure in the
eighteenth century, and the American experience was to be of
importance to the novelist; she drew upon it for *The Life of Harriot
Stuart* (1750), and for *Euphemia*, her last novel (1790).

[1] Biographical information is partly based on that furnished in the study by
Miriam Rossiter Small, *Charlotte Ramsay Lennox: An Eighteenth-Century Lady of
Letters* (1935), but I have also consulted Jerry C. Beasley's entry in the *Dictionary of
Literary Biography* (1985). I am also indebted to Edith Larson's paper, 'Charlotte
Lennox and the Importance of Reputation, Marriage and Money in her Life and
Fiction', presented at the conference of the North-East Association of the Society
for Eighteenth-Century Studies in Syracuse, New York, in October 1983; I am
grateful to Dr. Larson for sending me a copy of this unpublished paper. There has
been much controversy over the date of Lennox's birth. Miriam Small, contradict-
ing Samuel Richardson, states flatly that Lennox must have been thirty-two when
The Female Quixote was published. But, as Larson points out, the dates of the birth
of Lennox's children (in 1765 and 1771) make it highly unlikely that the author was
born much before 1730. We may take it that Richardson was correct when he told a
correspondent in 1753 that the author of *The Female Quixote* was 'hardly twenty-
four'; see *Selected Letters of Samuel Richardson*, ed. John Carroll (1964), p. 223.

We do not know what education Charlotte Ramsay had in Fort New York, and whether it was 'useful and proper'. It is pleasant to imagine her reading the romances of Scudéry by the green banks of the wide Hudson. Lennox has been termed 'the first American novelist',[2] although her sojourn in America was fairly short. Her father died (c. 1743), and Charlotte returned to England alone, apparently in the unfulfilled expectation that she would be able to place herself under the protection of a female relative. She found two female patrons, the Lady Cecilia Isabella Finch and the Countess of Rockingham, but she was unprovided for, and practically in the position of the woman who has to live by her wits. She published her writing, and she married. Her book *Poems on Several Occasions* (By a Young Lady) was published in November 1747, about a month after Charlotte Ramsay had married Alexander Lennox.

Alexander Lennox had two things to recommend him: he was a fellow Scot, and he was connected with the literary market, as he worked for the printer William Strahan. Unfortunately, he never made any money, and Charlotte seems to have found him highly disagreeable to live with. Surviving letters by her show her in conflict with him, especially over their chlidren, which were not born to them until late in her life (a daughter in 1765, a son in 1771). Lennox complains about her son's ill-treatment 'by a most unnatural father'.[3] The Lennoxes seem to have split up in the early 1790s. By 1793 Charlotte Lennox was living with Sir Joshua Reynolds's sister Frances Reynolds, and trying to support herself on an income of £40 a year. She appealed to the Royal Literary Fund, which gave her son the desired thirteen guineas for his passage to America in 1793; in January 1802 the Fund supplied Charlotte Lennox with twenty pounds because of urgent distress, and in 1803 established an allowance out of the Fund of one guinea a week for life. She was not long to enjoy this humble pension; she died in 1804, poverty-stricken.

The early years of her married life were sufficiently exiguous to convince Charlotte Lennox that marriage alone was hardly a

---

[2] By Gustavus Howard Maynadier, in *The First American Novelist?* (1940); cf. Philippe Séjourné, *The Mystery of Charlotte Lennox, First Novelist of Colonial America (1727?–1804)* (1967).

[3] Lennox's application to the Royal Literary Fund, asking for help to send her son to America, 22 August 1793; printed in full in Small, op. cit., p. 59.

preservative against want. Whatever the conduct books might say to recommend retiring and submissive behaviour on the part of young ladies, the economic facts of life might dictate that a young lady should put herself forward and make an effort, entering the adventurous bustle of the world. Lennox was for a brief while an actress (Horace Walpole bestows an unfavourable comment upon her performance),[4] and in 1750 her first novel, *Harriot Stuart*, was published. The novelist had already made herself known to fellow writers, and secured the patronage of Samuel Johnson. Sir John Hawkins has left a slightly sneering account of the all-night party at the Devil Tavern which Johnson arranged in her honour:

Johnson had directed that a magnificent hot apple-pye should make a part of it, and this he would have stuck with bay-leaves, because, forsooth, Mrs. Lenox [*sic*] was an authoress, and had written verses; and further, he had prepared for her a crown of laurel, with which, but not till he had invoked the muses by some ceremonies of his own invention, he encircled her brows.[5]

This affair seems a good piece of advertising, as well as a pleasant festivity. Charlotte Lennox was not shy about public relations. She secured, through Johnson, an introduction to Samuel Richardson, one of the most famous novelists in Europe, fresh from the triumphant appearance of his *Clarissa.* Richardson was to act as her agent and adviser in the preparation of *The Female Quixote* for the press (see Appendix). Lennox seems also to have gained an acquaintance with Henry Fielding; Fielding's *Covent-Garden Journal* gave a surprisingly favourable notice of *The Female Quixote*.[6] In the period in which she wrote that novel, Lennox was anxiously securing access to the press, and beginning her career as a writer— some might say a hack writer. She translated *The Memoirs of the Duke of Sully* (1751), and produced a translation of Voltaire's history *Le Siècle de Louis XIV* (1752). The period of production of her best-known novel is also the period of Charlotte Lennox's determined entry into *professional* work. The heroines of the other

---

[4] 'I am just come from the play at Richmond ... we had a new actress, a Miss Clough ... very handsome ... and a Miss Charlotte Ramsay, a poetess, and a deplorable actress.' Horace Walpole to George Montagu, 3 Sept. 1748, *Horace Walpole's Correspondence*, ed. W. S. Lewis *et al.*, 42 vols. (1937–83), 9: 74.

[5] Sir John Hawkins, *The Life of Samuel Johnson, LL.D.* (1787), p. 286.

[6] Henry Fielding, *The Covent-Garden Journal*, no. 24, 24 Mar. 1752; see *The Covent-Garden Journal*, ed. Gerard Edward Jensen, 2 vols. (1915), 1: 279–82.

novels of Lennox's middle period are all hard up; Henrietta and Sophia are shown earning their living. (In the later *Euphemia* the heroine is at least provided for, but only in the confines of a dismally unhappy marriage.) Arabella in *The Female Quixote* is the most sheltered of Lennox heroines, and her protected life is part of what the heroine is reacting against. Arabella wishes to experience joy, sorrow, and activity—all those things which the Countess's vision of a woman's ideal history would deny her.

The title of *The Female Quixote* is of course an allusion to Miguel de Cervantes' great novel *Don Quixote* (1605; 1615). Cervantes' hero insists on believing entirely and literally in the chivalric romances (and Arcadian pastorals) he has read. He also insists on acting out the role of the knight errant, the adventurous hero he has encountered in his books. This first modern study of the nature and effects of novel-reading is profound and paradoxical. Some have read Cervantes' work as reflecting a simple intention, to ridicule and thus get rid of that absurd genre, romance. Such a reading vastly oversimplifies the book itself, and pays no heed to the fact that, as well as having written an extensive pastoral romance, *La Galatea* (1584), Cervantes in his last work *Persiles y Sigismunda* (1617) created a new romance. *Persiles* springs from the romance tradition derived ultimately from the Greeks, in works like Heliodorus' *Aethiopica* (*c.* AD 250). From this same romance tradition (rather than from the chivalric branch of it) emerged the works of which Arabella is so enamoured, such as the fiction by Madeleine de Scudéry, who wrote *Artamène, ou le grand Cyrus* (1649–53) and *Clélie* (1654–60).

The Female Quixote, like Cervantes' great model, has often been treated as a very simple work, exhibiting only its author's 'desire to ridicule the French heroic romances, and to point out their potentially harmful effects on the minds of inexperienced readers', as Duncan Isles says (Appendix, p. 419). Such summaries forget to enquire how the author became so knowledgeable about the French romances as to employ them in such detail. It is certainly an error to assume that the author 'mugged up' the French romances, as it were, for the purposes only of ridicule. Rather, this must be the work of an author already well-versed in the sources that the central character finds so addictive. The likeliest explanation is that Charlotte Lennox in her youth (and she was still in her youth when *The Female Quixote* appeared) read and re-read the works in question. The French romances of the early-to-mid-seventeenth century supplied the fiction read by English young people of both sexes in the early eighteenth century. Pope in *The Rape of the Lock* has the young Baron create his altar 'Of twelve vast *French Romances*, neatly gilt'.[7] (Twelve of the romances could create a substantial altar of nearly a hundred volumes.) The construction of his altar to Love tells us much about the Baron: that he has read a number of stories, and that he is at the point of male adolescence where he cannot reconcile his idealism about love (as an involvement characterized by sacrifice and constancy) and his sexual drive, which is also complicated by a need to engage in fraternal boasting (he keeps garters as trophies to prove his prowess).

We need not, however, turn to other fictions for examples of devoted romance-reading. Real people read the French works; they were still a literary presence in the 1730s. Mary Delany (née Granville), at the time still the young widow Mrs. Pendarves, records the reading aloud of *Clélie* at a house party in Killala, Ireland, in the summer of 1732: 'We have begun Clelia, she is a much better French lady than an English one.' The future Mrs. Delany had evidently read 'the English one' in her youth. She recalls the novels at odd moments: the Princess Royal's wedding dress in 1734 'puts me in mind of De Scudery's descriptions'.[8] Horace Walpole, a younger contemporary, was also likely to recall the works of Scudéry and others. His friend Henry Seymour Conway teased Walpole about his early reading at Eton: 'I remember you buried in romances and novels; I really believe you could have said all the *Grand Cyrus*'s, the *Cleopatra*'s, and the *Amadis*'s in the world by heart.'[9] Walpole himself offers a fascinating glimpse of his youthful reading in the 1730s, very much in the style of Lennox's Arabella; the landscape of Eton College was coloured for him by his quixotic reception of his reading matter:

[7] Alexander Pope, *The Rape of the Lock*, Canto II, 1.161. (In 1712 version, in Canto I, 1.53.)

[8] Mary Pendarves (later Delany) to Ann Granville (later Dewes), 28 June 1732, in *The Autobiography and Correspondence of Mary Granville, Mrs. Delany*, ed. Lady Llanover, 3 vols. (1861), 1: 362; 442. The autobiography that Mary Delany wrote privately for her friend the Duchess of Portland employs pseudonyms and tropes adapted from the romances (ibid., pp. 1–112).

[9] Henry Seymour Conway to Horace Walpole, 18 Apr. 1745 O.S., *Horace Walpole's Correspondence*, 37: 189.

were not the playing fields at Eton food for all manner of flights? No old maid's gown ... ever underwent so many transformations, as those poor plains have in my idea. At first I was contented with tending a visionary flock, and sighing some pastoral name to the echo of the cascade under the bridge: how happy should I have been to have had a kingdom, only for the pleasure of being driven from it, and living disguised in an humble vale. As I got farther into Virgil and *Clelia*, I found myself transported from Arcadia, to the garden of Italy, and saw Windsor Castle in no other view than the *capitoli immobile saxum*.[10]

In this letter of 1736 the 18-year-old Walpole, who had left Eton only two years previously, is looking down with lofty amusement upon his former tastes and imaginings; at the same time, he is still close to what he describes, and wishes to celebrate both the power of his reading matter and the power of his own imagination. After all, the landscape around the Marquis's castle, the abode of Lennox's heroine, seems a less unlikely scene for a replay of *Clélie* than do the playing fields of Eton.

In the later seventeenth century the French romances had seemed to offer a literary world common to men and women. Walpole could read both Virgil and *Clélie*; the classical works were jealously guarded as a male preserve, but women could read the romances and both men and women could discuss and allude to them. The salons of the *précieuses*, scenes of the first literary movement involving both sexes, made constant allusions to the works of the writers these same salons fostered. The prose romance was virtually the only extensive genre which women had successfully practised.

The first major critical discussion of the history of the modern novel, Bishop Huet's *Traité de l'origine des romans*, appeared in 1670 as a lengthy preface to *Zayde*, a novel (or romance) by a woman author.[11] Huet praises the women writers and emphasizes

---

[10] Horace Walpole to George Montagu, 6 May 1736, *Correspondence*, 9: 3.

[11] *Zayde* is by Mme de Lafayette, better known to us for *La Princesse de Clèves* (1678). The treatise of Pierre Daniel Huet, Bishop of Avranches, *Traité de l'origine des romans* (1670), was published separately, and was variously translated into English: *A Treatise of Romances and their Original* (1672) and *The History of Romances: An Enquiry into their Original; Instructions for Composing them; an Account of the most Eminent Authors* ... (1715). The translator of the latter, Stephen Lewis, comments in his Preface that '*Romance* has of late ... become the Principal Diversion of the Retirement of People of all Conditions', and he hopes that we will not have to rely solely upon the French supply 'but that some *English*

the fact that the important novels (*romans*) of Scudéry were written
by a woman, Madeleine de Scudéry, and not, despite the claims of
early title-pages, by her brother Georges. As Huet's treatise was
quickly translated and often republished, anyone interested in prose
fiction would have known his views and would certainly have been
fully aware (as Walpole was) of the fact that the author of *Artamène*
and *Clélie* was female. We may take it that Lennox knew this fact,
and expected her more sophisticated readers to know it, although
she makes no statement about it within *The Female Quixote*.

The history of the novel as established by Huet offers much encouragement to women writers of prose fiction, and it is noticeable
that a number of English women writers of prose fiction emerged
and flourished in the decades after 1670. The influence of writers
like Scudéry and others can be felt in non-fictional works such as the
poems of 'the Matchless Orinda' (Katherine Philips); in Charlotte
Lennox's early poems we can hear the same strain. It is noticeable
that Huet refers to all the works of prose fiction he discusses as
romans and makes no heavy distinction between romances and
novels. He begins to apply the neo–classical standard of 'probability', but it extends no further than a reluctance to read of
dragons, etc.: the spacious historical story of love and adventure,
battle and shipwreck, constancy, conversation, passion, and travel
is perfectly acceptable as *roman*—as novel—and delightful to read
and re-read.

Mary Granville and Horace Walpole could make similar
assumptions in their youth. So too could Charlotte Ramsay, but
she was half a generation younger than they were. Brought up
under the old habits of reading, she was destined to receive a shock.
She came into her own as a novelist in a period when the idea of
prose fiction was undergoing a decided change, a change that in
England took place with remarkable speed. From the time of the
early 1750s, the novel was to be circumscribed into what we know
as 'formal realism'. The new standards demanded an application of
a revised notion of probability, extending far beyond the meaning
of that term in the seventeenth century. The repudiation of the
romance can be felt in novelistic works themselves in the 1740s,

Genius will *dare* to Naturalize *Romance* into our Soil. . . .' (pp. viii–ix). Joan Dejean
offers a valuable discussion of the place Huet's treatise gave to women in the new
tradition of novel-writing: 'No Man's Land: The Novel's First Geography', *Yale
French Studies*, 73 (1987), 175–89.

especially the late 1740s, and by the mid-1750s a whole genre of prose fiction is officially dead.

Why this should have happened is a large and puzzling question and answers can only be suggested. The new standards applied to fiction might be seen as possessing a political dimension, even if those who applied these standards were unconscious of any political influence or bias. It is worth pointing out that the Whig government in power might have felt stronger if the stories that people told themselves acknowledged the essential power of the market-place and denied any potency to such engaging mythical historical plots as those offered by the too-romantic cause of the Jacobites. One may note in passing that an insistence that a novel show nothing beyond what is 'real' and 'probable' can operate as a subtle censorship, favouring the renewed recognition of and obedience to the powers already in place, and a humble silence or graceful acquiescence on the part of the powerless. (For the powerless to imagine a route to power is indeed 'romancing' on their part.) The change of taste is no abstract matter; it operates in the interest of some, and at the expense of others. A 'real' reflection of eighteenth-century society will have to acknowledge the power of institutions, hierarchies, and arrangements, especially the new power of money as the middle class knows about it. In the English-speaking world in particular, the novel since the mid-eighteenth century has been most heavily dissociated from 'romance', and Continental literature and practice became similarly affected in the nineteenth century. Still, the extreme wariness of 'romance' has remained an English characteristic, as linguistic use reflects; the French, Germans, and Italians make no equivalent effort to find another word, and *le roman*, *Der Roman*, etc., may cover many types of fiction. In our time, the post-modernist novel, in the English-speaking world as elsewhere, has cast off the restrictions of realism in favour of 'magic realism' and literary experiment. Readers now will not feel constrained to divide the literature of the past according to previous criteria.

But Charlotte Lennox was born as a novelist at a time when standards were changing, and had to accommodate herself to that revolution. Her first novel shows her unaware that such a change is in the offing. *Harriot Stuart* is open about its generic relationship to romance. Harriot, an avid reader of romance by the time she is eleven years old, interprets her own life in terms of what she has

read. In her precocious first sentimental attachment she reads her
experience in romance terms:

I compared my adventure with some of those I had read in novels and
romances, and found it full as surprising. In short, I was nothing less than
a Clelia or a Statira. These reflections had such an effect on my looks and
air next day, that it was very visible I thought myself of prodigious
importance.[12]

Harriot's youthful self-importance may be comical, but she is not
wrong, for her life has indeed all the perils and vicissitudes of
romance. At an unsuccessful lover's behest, she is abducted by a
party of Indians and taken up the Hudson. When she is returning
to England, her ship is captured by a Spanish privateer, then
recaptured by an English ship with a lascivious captain who tries to
rape Harriot; she saves herself by stabbing him, and the crew
threaten her with death. Later, she is abducted by members of her
lover's hostile Catholic family, and forcibly immured in a convent,
whence she must make her escape. Harriot Stuart would have been
surprised to hear the Countess's version of the truth, that nice
women do not have 'Adventures', and that 'the History of a
Woman of Honour' is composed of but 'few and natural' (and dull)
incidents.

The association of Charlotte Lennox and Harriot Stuart was
evidently close. The heroine with the Scottish surname is also a
poet, and some of the pieces composed by Harriot Stuart are verses
which had already appeared in Miss Ramsay's *Poems*; Lennox
allowed others to believe that the novel was autobiographical.
Romance was not thought altogether absurd by either author or
readers—including a reader as eminent as Johnson. It was for the
romantic *Harriot Stuart* and not for the satiric *Female Quixote* that
Johnson hosted the supper party of the 'apple pye' and the bay
leaves.

Lennox, however, had to realize that the old era of the romance
had gone. Women, who had formerly been able to believe that they
had a tradition behind them on which they could rely, and a body
of lore upon which they could draw, had to recognize that this
inheritance was to be entirely discounted. In the new phase of
Augustanism, that old tradition was disappearing, as if the women

[12] [Charlotte Lennox], *The Life of Harriot Stuart*. Written by Herself. 2 vols.
(1751), 1: 8.

writers had pitched their tents on islands of floating ice now melting in the sun. Both as reader and as writer, Lennox had to say farewell to the literature that had nourished her and her imagination and her hopes. The bitterness she felt about this farewell and about the mid-eighteenth century's views of the literary canon can be felt in her next major work, *Shakespeare Illustrated*.[13] In this important critical treatise, the first to trace Shakespeare's sources, she attacks Shakespeare and his Augustan admirers for misusing and misunderstanding older kinds of fiction in which women were of importance. Meanwhile, however, she had to deal with her own attraction to romance and her necessary but not willing relinquishment of it. The resulting complexity of thought and vivacity of emotion that went into *The Female Quixote* have given it its depth and lasting value, so that it has had its appeal even to those who wish to simplify its subject. The wit and lightness of touch of the novel are the more admirable as the whole is the result of such personal engagement. The novel's grace is a grace under pressure.

The Female Quixote begins with a character who is a slave to imagination—but that character is Arabella's father, not Arabella herself. In a fantasy of power born of frustration, the Marquis has retired to his remote castle, there creating in solitude an 'Epitome of *Arcadia*' (p. 6). He 'imagined he triumphed . . . over the Malice of his Enemies' (p. 5), and his egotistical romanticism is also expressed in what appears to be his first serious erotic impulse. Although advanced in years, he marries a young woman after 'a very short Courtship' (p. 6), and immures her in his castle in the wilds of the country. Arabella's mother (in some sense abducted and imprisoned) is not consulted as to plan of life, or even choice of décor. It is no wonder that she whiles away her boredom in his sulky Arcadia by reading romances, nor that she should die so promptly after giving birth to Arabella.

Arabella, tougher than her mother, and sharing her father's stubborn capacity for prolonged and wilful fantasy, survives the experience of childhood entrapment in her father's pastoral creation. Her mode of survival in adolescence is to make a fantasy of her own that will not subordinate her to her father's story. She discovers her mother's 'Store of Romances', books which the

[13] See my article, 'Shakespeare's Novels; Charlotte Lennox Illustrated', *Studies in the Novel*, 19 (Fall 1987), 296–307.

deceased Marchioness had purchased 'to soften a Solitude which she found very disagreeable' (p. 7). The Marquis had 'removed them from her Closet into his Library', a statement summarizing a movement in literary history; for a brief while the romances had seemed to be canonical, worthy of a place in the gentleman's library. Arabella reads them in the belief that they are canonical, and thus true 'histories'. The volumes of romances are Arabella's only inheritance from her mother, and the female inheritance is customarily presented by women in their novels as dangerous or double-edged. What is needed is the paternal inheritance, but that is usually surrounded by entail, prohibition, or conditional restrictions. The woman is never the proper inheritor, the truly desirable inheritor, of a paternal legacy. And paternal inheritance, composed of all aspects of public existence including name, home, and property, is in an oblique and unfavourable relation to the daughter.

Through reading her romances Arabella frees herself from fearing, or even seeing, the dangers of her position in relation to the paternal inheritance. She conceals from herself the sad truth, that she is a pawn in the game of property, by reading books in which women are of great importance. After her father's death, the discovery of the arranged marriage with her cousin is a disagreeable surprise. As a daughter, her lot is not to be one who is served (like Mandane or Clélie) but to serve. If Arabella does not marry her cousin Glanville, then she will lose part of the estate, as her cousin's father, Sir Charles, points out with crass succinctness. Even young Glanville, although he tells his father (Arabella's guardian) not to compel the girl, wishes himself that 'the Marquis had laid a stronger Injunction upon her in his Will to marry him' (p. 65).

Surrounded by such incestuous and greedy demands, Arabella retains the presence of mind that her reading inculcates. Strong in her conviction that she herself is supremely of importance, she resists the hectoring and the bribery, disconcerting her cousin and her uncle by wishing them joy of the third of her father's estate. She uses her mourning for her father and her chastity (inculcated alike by romances and by Christian conduct books) as weapons. She cannot marry, she says, until she has mourned her father for a year, and she haughtily withdraws from any conversation about marriage. Like her favourite heroines, she is to be served with long

and ardent devotion. Her female cousin is horrified: 'do you resolve
to be Ten Years a courting? Or rather, will you be loved in Silence
Ten Years, and be courted the other Ten; and so marry when you
are an old Woman?' Arabella evades the question, merely
retorting upon its style: 'I must really find Fault with the
Coarseness of your Language. Courting, and Old Woman! What
strange Terms!' (p. 112). But Arabella might prefer to wait until
twenty-eight, if not thirty-eight, rather than find herself thrust into
a marriage she did not choose at the age of eighteen. Eliza
Haywood's Betsy Thoughtless voices a contemporary objection to
the zeal of male relatives in marrying off young girls:

'One has no sooner left off one's bib and apron, than people cry,—"Miss
will soon be married."—And this man, and that man, is presently picked
out for a husband.—Mighty ridiculous!—they want to deprive us of all the
pleasures of life, just when one begins to have a relish for them.'[14]

In finding herself thus threatened, through the Glanvilles' determination, it is perhaps no wonder that Arabella's imaginings turn
upon rapes and ravishings, and that she fears 'the worst kind of
Robbers; Robbers who do not prey upon Gold and Jewels; but,
what is infinitely more precious, Liberty and Honour' (p. 92). Her
scenarios become more and more complex, emphatic, and violent.

   There were a number of literary precedents for comic presentation of ladies (rather than a gentleman like Don Quixote) who got
carried away into absurdity by their reading. The précieuses, the
first group of literary ladies in the West, were mocked, most
famously by Molière. The French produced parodies of the French
romances. It is highly likely that Charlotte Lennox knew La Fausse
Clélie (1670) by Adrien Thomas Perdou de Subligny, translated
into English in 1678 with the running title 'Mock-Clelia, or
Madam Quixote'. The heroine or anti-heroine of this novel, Juliette
d'Arvianne, is crazed enough to identify herself literally with the
Clélie of Scudéry's romance. Juliette's insanity is chronic and
periodic: each 'Fit', explains the kinsman who wishes to marry her,
'never holds her above ten or twelve hours, and then for two days
[sic] space there appears not the least alteration in her mind; she is
as rational as any other'. 'Perhaps,' he adds, 'if no body should ever
speak to her of Rome or the Romans, her Cure might be more

---

[14] Eliza Haywood, The History of Miss Betsy Thoughtless, 4 vols. (1751), 4: 24.

easie. . . .'[15] People do bring the Romans into conversation, however. Juliette-Clélie fires up in protest against the old judge who jokes that even Lucretia 'yielded before she killed herself'. Juliette indignantly bursts out, 'that's an infamous Calumny, and no body but an old corrupted Senator like your self, who hath always been in the Faction of the Kings, and is an enemy to the Liberty of the People, would have in that manner dishonoured the memory of Chastity itself.'[16] This episode seems to be reflected in Lennox's scene in which Arabella defends the chastity of Cleopatra (p. 105). Likewise, as Margaret Dalziel has pointed out, Arabella's imitation of Clélie in her leaping into the Thames, 'intending to swim over it, as *Clelia* did the *Tyber*' (p. 363), may have been drawn from the French satire, in which the heroine, mistaking the camp at Fontainebleau 'for that of King *Porsenna*, where she was detained as an Hostage', with heroic resolution 'rode at full speed towards the great Canal which she took for the *Tyber*, and whereinto she threw herself, that she might swim over in imitation of *Clelia* whom she believed her self to be'.[17] The emphasis of de Subligny does not fall very heavily upon the evils of female reading, however, and he seems primarily concerned with recognizing the romances' relationship to French contemporary life. The contemporary significance of the romances had been widely acknowledged. The first English translator of *Le grand Cyrus* says: 'the Intrigues and Miscarriages of War and Peace are better, many times, laid open and Satyriz'd in a *Romance*, than in a downright History, which being oblig'd to name the Persons, is often forc'd . . . to be too partial and sparing . . .'[18] 'Downright history' is often forced to lie and prevaricate, while romances can tell the truth. Perdou de Subligny undercuts the simple parodic nature of his tale by endowing his mad Clélie with a personal history that gives her only too much cause for identifying herself with a heroine. The civil wars of France and England support the

---

[15] Adrien Thomas Perdou de Subligny, *The Mock-Clelia: Being a Comical History of French Gallantries, and Novels, in Imitation of Don Quixote* (1678), p. 14. Margaret Dalziel proposes *The Mock-Clelia* as an influence upon *The Female Quixote* in her Introduction to the novel (1973), p. xvi.

[16] Perdou de Subligny, op. cit., pp. 178–9.

[17] Ibid., pp. 267–8.

[18] 'To the Reader', prefaced to *Artamenes; or, The Grand Cyrus, That Excellent Romance. In Ten Parts*. Written by that Famous Wit of France, Monsieur de Scudéry, Governour of *Notre-Dame*. Englished by F. G. Esq: (1691), pp. A4ᵛ–A5ʳ.

historical truth of romance events. Given the turbulent times she lives in, it is not wonderful that young Juliette should read herself into the one kind of historical narrative she knows that seems to make sense of her experience.

Other satirists dealing with mock-heroines whose heads are turned by their reading emphasize, as Lennox does, the dullness rather than the eventfulness of the girls' lives. Or rather, the young women are supposed to believe that the world they live in is sensible, safe, and orderly—that is, that any sense of unhappiness or threat they feel is the nonsensical product of their own silly heads. Even those who satirize these young women feel some sympathy for the boredom thrust upon them. Biddy Tipkin in Steele's *The Tender Husband* (1705) rebels against her lot, and against her own commonplace name. Her aunt decries the 'Idle Romances' that have turned Biddy's head, and wishes they had all been burned. Biddy cries in horror, 'What to burn *Philocles*, *Artaxerxes*, *Oroondates*, and the rest of the Heroick Lovers, and take my Country-Booby, Cousin *Humphry*, for an Husband!'[19] The unromantic hero, Clerimont, more interested in the girl's fortune than in the girl herself, complains about her: 'A perfect *Quixot* [sic] in Petticoats! . . . she governs herself wholly by Romance.' It is romance alone that has taught Biddy to be proud, critical, and demanding: 'How am I bound to Curse the cold Constitutions of the *Philocleas* and *Statiras*!'[20] A few crafty manipulations and romantic posturings on the part of Clerimont are, however, sufficient to deceive Biddy.

Steele, like other male creators of female Quixotes, emphasizes the folly of the girl's delusion, and in such male works the girl is customarily humiliated or tamed by some man more informed, worldly, or socially skilled. Lennox teases us with the prospect of these familiar satisfactions, while making us focus on other matters. Her Arabella is truly strong-minded, and deceiving or humouring her is more difficult than her would-be instructors or deceivers can foresee. Instead of their teaching Arabella, we see her trying to teach them. At first, young Mr. Glanville is slow in picking up the cues:

[19] Richard Steele, *The Tender Husband; or, The Accomplish'd Fools*, in *The Plays of Richard Steele*, ed. Shirley Strum Kenny (1971), II. ii, 233, 235.
[20] Ibid., II. iii, 241.

she made a Sign to him to retire; for he had walked up with her to her Chamber: But, finding he did not obey her, for really he was quite unacquainted with these Sorts of dumb Commands, she hastily retired to her Closet . . . (pp. 36–7)

But by unwavering effort and unyielding consistency, Arabella is able to make him learn her signs. Officially she has no power; when she tries to send her unwanted suitor packing, the Marquis brusquely overrides her command. Arabella, however, perseveres in the use of the 'dumb Commands' that institute her self-created power, and Glanville begins to learn to comply (see, for example, p. 57). By the time Glanville's father arrives to visit the now-orphaned Arabella, young Glanville can act as interpreter of Arabella's 'Signs', and even persuade his father to fall into line with them. Sir Charles expresses displeasure at the imperious conduct of his niece: 'does she so little understand the Respect that is due to me as her Uncle, that she, so peremptorily, desired me to leave her Room? . . . she is quite a Rustic! (p. 63). Sir Charles's displeasure underlines the fact that according to conventional rules of conduct the young woman, even if newly bereaved, has no right to ask to be left to herself. It is through assuming the powers the romances offer that Arabella can command a space, assert a woman's right to 'a room of one's own', and take upon herself the power to control the movements and behaviour of others. She succeeds amazingly in making her male kinsmen pay attention to her wishes and not assume that she is automatically under their control. Arabella educates them so they do not in fact treat her as patronizingly as they might otherwise have done, and she is allowed her own way—and her own words—a surprising amount of the time. She speaks, emphatically and at length, when according to conduct books and contemporary rules a young unmarried woman should remain totally silent. Her uncle at one point expresses 'much Admiration of her Wit', telling her that 'if she had been a Man, she would have made a great Figure in Parliament, and that her Speeches might have come perhaps to be printed in time' (p. 311). Of course, Arabella's 'Speeches' are printed—by Lennox— but the meta-fictional joke reminds us not only of the limitations placed on women in Arabella's world, but of the limits Arabella has already overleaped. Arabella cannot enter Parliament, and to dream of that would be *too* fantastic for any quixotic female to consider— but she has given herself full leave to speak.

Arabella in her dauntless self-fashioning is also successful in designing and wearing her own fashion of dress. She appears always *en costume*, highlighting the fact that she acts a self, invents her self, has consciously chosen a part. Others must adjust their more commonplace expectations to her striking and unusual appearance. Personality is a role, as the novel illustrates. It is as if Arabella is constantly at a masquerade; indeed, Harriet Byron's masquerade costume of an Arcadian Princess in Richardson's *Sir Charles Grandison*[21] may owe something to the extraordinary ball dress in which Arabella makes her appearance at the ball in Bath (p. 271). Instead of looking ridiculous, as malicious gossips expect, Arabella is capable of drawing 'the Admiration of the whole Assembly' (p. 272). Originality is sometimes rewarded, even in a world of conformity.

Arabella may attract admiration, but she is never successful in her attempts to draw others into her world, or to make them acquainted with the rich source of her imaginings. She tries to persuade young Glanville to read the books she so loves. He will not open the texts she sets, and fails miserably to pass the test of subsequent conversation, showing that he has only been pretending to have read the works in question (pp. 50–1). Glanville absolutely refuses to read the books—he knows *without reading them* that they are valueless. (Perhaps he should have gone to Eton.) Glanville's closed-mindedness makes him a more suspect censor than the priest and the barber in *Don Quixote*, who have read the books that they apparently condemn, and rescue a good number of romances and pastorals from their own inquisitorial bonfire. Glanville merely rejects the books, on the vague grounds of fashion and hearsay. If he wishes to marry Arabella, and is sincerely in love with her, should he not be willing to share some of her interests— or at least to try to find out what affects her so strongly? Glanville

---

[21] Samuel Richardson, *The History of Sir Charles Grandison* (1753–4); ed. Jocelyn Harris, 3 vols. (1972), 1: 115–16. The demise of romance is a subject in this novel. The heroine's grandmother, Mrs. Shirley, sixty years old (and thus Richardson's almost exact contemporary), tells the young ladies 'The reading in fashion when I was young, was Romances', adding, 'You, my children, have in that respect, fallen into happier days.' At sixteen she had been so taken with ideal love and heroes that she was in danger of not appreciating her suitor, Mr. Shirley: 'what was a good sort of man to an Oroondates?' (3: 398). This discussion in *Grandison* may owe something to Lennox's recent novel, in which Richardson had taken so keen an interest (see Appendix, pp. 418–27).

keeps himself pure of the dangerous contamination of the romances, which might confuse the clear lines that he (and his family) can draw between appropriate and inappropriate behaviour, sanity and insanity, sense and nonsense. Acquaintance with Arabella itself forms young Glanville's one inescapably 'romantic' experience, and he begins to experience unanticipated emotions. The novel in which he appears blurs the lines of which he and those like him wish to be confident.

The novel displays a generic struggle, focused on the question: 'How shall a woman's life be told?' Romances offer one way of interpreting and allegorizing a woman's life. The novel is full of parodic and self-referential explications of narration itself, and the power that narration provides. Arabella tells her maid Lucy how to relate her 'History'—a task which, as Lucy rightly sees, is formidable and intricate (pp. 121–3). To control modes of narration, the novel suggests, is to control the world. The novelist, of course, employs various modes of narration, placing within her story an abundance of approaches to representing a life, from the most vulgar and gossiping to the most elaborately romantic—as well as incorporating the inarticulate blunderings of Glanville and his father.

In contrast to Glanville's often tongue-tied and inadequate sincerity, the smooth visitor Sir George maintains a glib power over language. For a large central section of the novel, Sir George seizes the narrative in his own parodic mock-history. He is himself 'well read in Romances', and 'had actually employed himself some Weeks in giving a new version of the *Grand Cyrus* . . . he was perfectly well acquainted with the chief Characters in most of the *French* Romances' (p. 129). He is learned enough in the matter to criticize Dryden for want of invention in having borrowed plots and characters from the romances. (Lennox thus points out *en passant* the romances' real influence upon major Augustan litera-ture.) Sir George, with all his knowledge, seems well qualified to bamboozle Arabella. We may expect him to fool her to the top of her bent, in order to humiliate her or to get her to accept him as her husband. Her beauty, rank, and fortune incline him strongly to take the suitor's role with some seriousness, though he has a double game to play in hiding his intentions from the Glanvilles. He seems, in short, to be in the commanding position of Steele's Captain Clerimont, who can claim: 'I have been a great Traveller in Fairy-land my self, I know *Oroondates*, *Cassandra*, *Astraea*, and *Clelia*, are my intimate Acquaintance.'[22] Steele's hero makes his court to Biddy in impressive heroic style, reciting the names and deeds of her favourite characters, and mockingly wins the weak-minded Biddy in his fake whirlwind romantic courtship. Sir George seems to us at first (as he seems to himself) to be another in the line of witty deluders of romantic females. He spins his long story with the utmost confidence, enjoying his own elaborate parodic attention to style, and certain that so much literary skill must win the day, as well as the narrative laurels. The upshot of his verbal adventure disconcerts him completely. Arabella crisply interprets his story in a manner unfavourable to him. Sir George has told a disgraceful tale in which he has abandoned various mistresses; he is no miracle of romantic love but a hideous example of shameful inconstancy.

Sir George did not get the measure of Arabella's foot at all. He misjudged her altogether, thinking she would be pleased that he had fallen under her sway after 'adventures' with other lovely women. But Arabella does not wish to see a man faithless to the woman who should be his 'true love'. The romances uphold the central importance of Woman—and of women. The duty of the male lover is to be constant. Sir George has, unconsciously, reflected in his fiction his real attitude to women. His genuine faithlessness comes through his farrago which is a kind of allegory of his real love-life. Arabella does not see through the falsehood of the vehicle, but she correctly interprets the falsity and false-heartedness of the tenor. Sir George, in her judgement, is unworthy to be a character in a romance, as he had missed the point of Romance. He has certainly not understood the ideals the romances raise for female emotional behaviour; the heroine of romance is generous to other women, and is not meanly motivated to steal their lovers. Arabella has always wished other women to share the glory, strength, and beauty of their place in romantic fiction; she keeps trying to give commonplace young women (like Miss Glanville) or even disgraced young women (like the shady Miss Groves) access to the language of glory and power. It is one of Arabella's points of finer moral understanding that women are to complement each other, not compete.

<hr>

[22] Steele, op. cit., I. i, 223.

It is scarcely surprising that Arabella has such an antipathy to Sir George's reading of romance, in which the man is an adventurous wanderer, roving from woman to woman. Arabella wishes the male to remain dutifully fixed. But her imaginings appear to permit some roving on the part of the female. A woman is to have a multitude of suitors, even if she gives her heart to one alone, and she is to move around a good deal. Arabella claims mobility in terms of physical movement. All her moments of running away are moments of active escape from a fixity wished upon her. She is physically energetic; she hunts. She seems emotionally as well as physically mobile. Some mental experiments with sexuality are decorously concealed beneath her self-chosen veil; the romance plot she consistently adopts allows her to veil her own desires from herself while taking the liberty of imagining the male libidos around her. The most daring moment in the novel is that in which Arabella imagines that her uncle is in love with her, and 'was become the Rival of his own Son'. Her reading has taught her that various incestuous passions are possible (p. 164). Her fantasy about the 'impious Flame' she has raised in her uncle may reflect a certain attraction on her part to this older male, or at least a wish that young Glanville had more of the strength of his father. Her imagining her uncle's wicked passion is also a form of revenge upon him, and underlines the incestuous cosiness of the familial arrangement by which Arabella is to marry young Glanville. Yet the decorous innocence of Arabella's chosen posture as heroine allows her an unrivalled opportunity for sexual fantasies without guilt. By the end of the novel she has run through a number of adorers.

Charlotte Lennox's chief problem with her novel was how to bring it to closure. The same problem faced Cervantes, who chose to create disturbing and unhappy endings. At the end of the first *Don Quixote*, the crazed knight is tricked and humiliated and brought home in a cage. At the end of Cervantes' sequel, the hero dies after confessing the error of his ways. Quixotes must be brought back within the pale, tamed, made to recant. Certainly a young woman must find out that she cannot order the world in which she lives. The novelist, like the reader, knows that Arabella's illusions won't work, that she is on holiday and must be brought back to what the world acknowledges as reality. For a woman, that reality means the end of all story, and a cessation of all power.

Lennox in her story puts to mocking use and then discards several possible modes of untying the knot. Anna Laetitia Barbauld objected that the solution finally hit upon, the 'grave moralizing of a clergyman', did not work, and thought the heroine should have been 'cured of her reveries' by finding herself the prey of a 'romantic footman' or other low fellow, the method used by Molière to bring his *précieuse* to heel in *Les Précieuses ridicules*.[23] But the motif of the low fellow is exhausted early in Lennox's novel, in the sequence regarding the young gardener. In Lennox's variation of the motif, the woman invents the man's untrue high status, his pretensions, and his interest in her; the gardener is merely an object of her plot-creating gaze. Arabella's libido is always well guarded; she creates her hidden admirer in order to flee from him. She is after all right in suspecting he had designs, though they are only designs on the carp. Sir George, the deliberate and crafty masquerader, proves, as we have seen, incapable of acting the part of a Clerimont; he can neither cure nor entrap Arabella with his parody. Arabella emerges superior from an encounter which might have been expected to tame or humiliate her. Arabella is not easy to deceive. In many respects she is discerning about men, especially once she has heard them discourse. Lennox makes most of the men around Arabella rather stupid and ill-educated; despite their pretences to the classical education denied to her, they flounder amid references to the Vale of Tempe, or Thermopylae.

At length Lennox summons up a serious and intelligent male in the strange figure of the elderly clergyman who scolds and contradicts Arabella, making her see at last that her beloved 'Histories' are mere fictions, bearing no relation to reality. The novelist pays the heroine the compliment of having her converted by reason and discourse, by philosophy rather than by trickery. But the conversion scene—whether written by Johnson (see pp. 414–15) or Lennox—is not without its problems. In relation to the novel as a whole it appears perhaps more problematic and ironic than intended. After all, it is nonsense to tell a young woman that rape and abduction are only fictions. The novel itself has presented such dangers as distinctly possible in contemporary real life, and

---

[23] Anna Laetitia Barbauld, 'Mrs. Lennox', introduction to *The Female Quixote* in the British Novelists series, vol. 24 (1820), p. iii.

they were so, as the newspapers of the period will confirm. Other
novelists of the 1740s and 1750s were using stories of rape and
abduction in their fiction—most notably, but not only, in
Richardson's *Clarissa* (1747–8).

The nameless clergyman takes Arabella to task for her nearly
suicidal act of leaping into the river to escape an imaginary sexual
danger. But what if the threat had not been imaginary? If a rape
really had been menaced, would not the leap into the river have
been justified? Or even necessary, considering the high value
placed on physical virginity in well-born marriageable girls? The
clergyman never deals with that moral issue. Arabella's hysterical
proud leap seems the product of mores inculcated both by
seventeenth-century romances and by eighteenth-century conduct
books—all preach the high value of intact chastity. We may read in
all of Arabella's movements the theatricalized frenzy of a hetero-
sexual woman who would unconsciously prefer a fuller sexual life,
while recognizing not only that chastity is demanded but also that
sexual relations both outside and inside marriage are likely to
involve denigration and degradation. In acting according to the
romances, Arabella has supplied the lack of an emotional life,
created some room for libido, and taken upon herself the role of
heroic protector of her own chastity. But the proper protector of a
woman's chastity in the eighteenth century (as traditionally) is
assumed to be not herself but a male. Arabella's hyper-reaction in
defence of her honour is absurd in a society which wishes only to
marry her off without further ado. The novel leaves unsolved the
problem of whether a woman ought or ought not to risk death in
order to escape rape. For the *woman* to pose such a question with
any eagerness of interest is to take upon herself a position of sexual
centrality which verges on the aggressive. (Arabella's predecessor,
Harriot Stuart, we may remember, efficiently fires a pistol at the
sea-captain who wants to rape her.) Heroic females are aggressive
females. Arabella must exist quietly under the protection of others,
relinquishing the imaginings that made her important. The
conversion scene represents a brainwashing session as a sexual
taming.

Authority remoulds Arabella, abruptly, and Glanville speaks
thankfully of 'the Miracle'. At least her lover is not guilty of taming
her, but Arabella is humbled into penitence for past folly, losing
her haughtiness and her playfulness together. The ending may be

taken as a 'happy' ending because Glanville has been presented as likeable, if rather weak, and we have been assured that he really loves the girl. Arabella, however, must give herself away—as her significant last speech says (p. 383). She now forgoes her own control of the world, renounces narrative power, and submits to the role of object of the paternal authority which also claims the name of reason.

Charlotte Lennox's anger at the necessity that overtakes Arabella emerges in the author's bout with Shakespeare and the Augustans in her next work, the energetic and caustic *Shakespeare Illustrated*. Lennox's next novels are in a deliberately realistic mode, but never entirely forsake romance motifs. In Lennox's last novel *Euphemia*, closer to *Harriot Stuart* in action and setting, young Clara Bellenden is rebuked by her mother for reading romances, but is defended by the heroine—and the author:

I perceived the book was lettered on the back, it was Sidney's Arcadia; I smiled. 'That is a romance, is it not, Madam?' said Mrs. Bellenden; 'Clara is very fond of those sort of books, too fond I think.' Clara blush'd, and seemed apprehensive of more rebukes on this subject. 'It is a romance, Madam,' said I, 'but it is a very ingenious work, and contains excellent lessons of morality....'[24]

Lennox will not present 'more rebukes on this subject', but defends the genre of prose romance, implicitly reminding us that romance has an English as well as a French tradition, and that Sidney's *Arcadia* is one of the cornerstones of the English novel. Romances are both ingenious *and* moral—as the erring Arabella knew.

MARGARET ANNE DOODY

Princeton University, 1988

[24] Charlotte Lennox, *Euphemia*, 4 vols. (1790), 1: 185–6.

NOTE ON THE TEXT

The text is printed from the Bodleian Library copy of the first edition (two volumes 12°, 1752), collated with the second edition, 'Revised and Corrected' (also two duodecimo volumes) and published in the same year. Both editions were printed for Andrew Millar. For Volume I they share the same make-up (A⁸ B–M¹² N⁴; pp. [iii] + iv–vi + [x] + 271). Volume II of the first edition is made up [A] 1 B–O¹² P⁶ [Q] 1; pp. [ii] + 325; Volume II of the second edition, [A] 1 B–O¹² P⁶ (−P6); pp. [ii] + 322.

The revisions include substantive alterations, as well as changes in spelling, punctuation and typography. Many of the errors in the first edition were corrected, but some new ones were introduced. The changes in substance, including as they do two passages of some length and many altered phrases and words, can safely be attributed to Mrs. Lennox. Among them are expansions, such as an extra example of romance conduct, a fuller description of a place, or a few additional words to strengthen or elucidate meaning; and contractions arising from the omission of unnecessary detail or words. Some alterations avoid ugly repetition of words or sounds; some mistakes in grammar are corrected. Except for the few cases where a change introduces a new mistake, these substantial corrections are incorporated in this edition; changes in accidentals are not. Obvious misprints are silently corrected.

Other editions of *The Female Quixote* published during Mrs. Lennox's lifetime (Dublin 1752 and 1763, London 1783 and 1799) are reprints of either the first or the second edition, and show no sign of any revision.

All substantial differences between the first and second editions are recorded on p. 385.

SELECT BIBLIOGRAPHY

Barreca, Regina, 'Dearly Loving a Good Laugh Humor in Charlotte Lennox and Jane Austen.' Ch. 2 of *Untamed and Unabashed: Essays on Women and Humor in British Literature* (1994), pp. 34–60.

Beasley, Jerry C., 'Charlotte Lennox', in *Dictionary of Literary Biography*, vol. 39, pt. 1 (1985), pp. 306–12.

Craft, Catherine A, 'Reworking Male Models: Aphra Behn's *Fair Vow-Breaker*, Eliza Haywood's *Fantomina*, and Charlotte Lennox's *Female Quixote*,' *Modern Language Review* 86 (October 1991): 821–38.

Doody, Margaret Anne, 'Shakespeare's Novels: Charlotte Lennox Illustrated', *Studies in the Novel*, 19 (Fall 1987), pp. 296–307.

Fyvie, John, *Some Famous Women of Wit and Beauty* (1905), pp. 165–87.

Gallagher, Catherine, *Nobody's Story: The Vanishing Acts of Women Writers in the Marketplace*, 1670–1820 (1994).

Gardiner, Ellen, 'Writing Men Reading in Charlotte Lennox's *The Female Quixote*,' *Studies in the Novel* 28 (Spring, 1996): 1–11.

Isles, Duncan, 'Unpublished Johnson Letters', *Times Literary Supplement*, 29 July 1965, p. 666.

——, 'Other Letters in the Lennox Collection', *Times Literary Supplement*, 5 August 1965, p. 685.

——, 'Johnson and Charlotte Lennox', *The New Rambler*, serial C, no. 3 (June 1967), pp. 34–48.

Kauvar, Elaine, M., 'Jane Austen and *The Female Quixote*', *Studies in the Novel*, 2 (Summer 1970), pp. 211–21.

Langbauer, Laurie, 'Romance Revised: Charlotte Lennox's *The Female Quixote*', *Novel*, 18 (Fall 1984), pp. 29–49.

Langbauer, Laurie, *Women and Romance: The Consolations of Gender in the English Novel* (1990).

Lynch, James L. 'Romance and Realism in Charlotte Lennox's *The Female Quixote*,' *Essays in Literature* 14 (Spring, 1987): 51–63.

MacCarthy, B. G., *The Female Pen: The Later Women Novelists 1744–1818*, 2 vols. (1947).

Malina, Debra, 'Rereading the Patriarchal Text: *The Female Quixote, Northanger Abbey*, and the Trace of the Absent Mother,' *Eighteenth-Century Fiction* 8 (January, 1996): 271–92.

Marshall, David, 'Writing Masters and "Masculine Exercises" in *The Female Quixote*,' *Eighteenth-Century Fiction* 5 (January, 1993): 105–35.

Maynadier, Gustavus Howard, *The First American Novelist?* (1940).

Ross, Deborah, 'Mirror, Mirror: The Didactic Dilemma of *The Female Quixote*', *Studies in English Literature*, 27 (Summer 1987), pp. 455–73.

Schofield, Mary Anne, 'Charlotte Lennox,' Ch. 10 of *Masking and Unmasking the Female Mind: Disguising Romances in Feminine Fiction, 1713–1799* (1990), pp. 128–45.

Séjourné, Philippe, *The Mystery of Charlotte Lennox, First Novelist of Colonial America (1727?–1804)*, Publications des Annales de la Faculté des Lettres Air-en-Provence, Nouvelle Série No 62 (1967).

Small, Miriam Rossiter, *Charlotte Ramsay Lennox: An Eighteenth Century Lady of Letters* (1935). (Still the standard biography.)

Spacks, Patricia Meyer, 'The Subtle Sophistry of Desire: *The Female Quixote*,' Ch. 1 of *Desire and Truth: Functions of Plot in Eighteenth-Century Fiction* (1990), pp. 12–33.

Spencer, Jane, *The Rise of the Women Novelist from Aphra Behn to Jane Austen* (1986).

Spencer, Jane. 'Not Being a Historian: Women Telling Tales in Restoration and Eighteenth-Century England,' in *Contexts of Pre-Novel Narrative: The European Tradition*. Ed. Roy Eriksen. (1994), pp. 319–40.

Staves, Susan, 'Don Quixote in Eighteenth-Century England', *Comparative Literature*, 24 (1972), pp. 193–215.

Warren, Leland, 'Of the Conversation of Women: *The Female Quixote* and the Dream of Perfection', *Studies in Eighteenth-Century Culture*, 11 (1982), pp. 367–80.

Wolpers, Theodor, 'Der weibliche Quijote in England: Charlotte Lennox' *The Female Quixote* und die literarische Tradition,' in *Gelebte Literatur in der Literatur: Studien zu Erscheinungsformen und Geschichte eines literarischen Motivs*. Ed. Theodor Wolpers (1986), pp. 135–62.

PREPARED WITH THE ASSISTANCE OF J. DAVID MACEY JR.

A CHRONOLOGY OF
CHARLOTTE LENNOX

DUNCAN ISLES

TO THE
RIGHT HONOURABLE
THE
EARL OF MIDDLESEX[1]

My Lord,

Such is the Power of Interest over almost every Mind, that no one is long without Arguments to prove any Position which is ardently wished to be true, or to justify any Measures which are dictated by Inclination.

By this subtil Sophistry of Desire, I have been persuaded to hope, that this Book may, without Impropriety, be inscribed to Your Lordship; but am not certain, that my Reasons will have the same Force upon other Understandings.

The Dread which a Writer feels of the public Censure; the still greater Dread of Neglect; and the eager Wish for Support and Protection, which is impressed by the Consciousness of Imbecillity; are unknown to those who have never adventured into the World; and I am afraid, my Lord, equally unknown to those, who have always found the World ready to applaud them.

'Tis, therefore, not unlikely, that the Design of this Address may be mistaken, and the Effects of my Fear imputed to my Vanity: They who see Your Lordship's Name prefixed to my Performance, will rather condemn my Presumption, than compassionate my Anxiety.

But, whatever be supposed my Motive, the Praise of Judgment cannot be denied me; for, to whom can Timidity so properly fly for Shelter, as to him who has been so long distinguished for Candour and Humanity? How can Vanity be so completely gratified, as by the allowed Patronage of him whose Judgment has so long given a Standard to the National Taste? Or by what other means could I so powerfully suppress all Opposition, but that of Envy, as by declaring myself,

MY LORD,
YOUR LORDSHIP'S
Obliged and most Obedient Humble Servant,
THE AUTHOR?

THE
FEMALE QUIXOTE

BOOK I

CHAPTER I

*Contains a Turn at Court, neither new nor surprising—Some
useless Additions to a fine Lady's Education—The bad
Effects of a whimsical Study, which some will say is borrowed
from* Cervantes

THE Marquis of —— for a long Series of Years, was the first and
most distinguished Favourite at Court: He held the most honourable Employments under the Crown, disposed of all Places of
Profit as he pleased, presided at the Council, and in a manner
governed the whole Kingdom.

This extensive Authority could not fail of making him many
Enemies: He fell at last a Sacrifice to the Plots they were continually
forming against him; and was not only removed from all his Employments, but banished the Court for ever.

The Pain his undeserved Disgrace gave him, he was enabled to
conceal by the natural Haughtiness of his Temper; and, behaving
rather like a Man who had resigned, than been dismissed from his
Posts, he imagined he triumphed sufficiently over the Malice of his
Enemies, while he seemed to be wholly insensible of the Effects it
produced. His secret Discontent, however, was so much augmented by the Opportunity he now had of observing the Baseness and
Ingratitude of Mankind, which in some Degree he experienced
every Day, that he resolved to quit all Society whatever, and
devote the rest of his Life to Solitude and Privacy. For the Place of
his Retreat he pitched upon a Castle he had in a very remote
Province of the Kingdom, in the Neighbourhood of a small Village,

and several Miles distant from any Town. The vast Extent of Ground which surrounded this noble Building, he had caused to be laid out in a Manner peculiar to his Taste: The most laborious Endeavours of Art had been used to make it appear like the beautiful Product of wild, uncultivated Nature. But if this Epitome of *Arcadia* could boast of only artless and simple Beauties, the Inside of the Castle was adorned with a Magnificence suitable to the Dignity and immense Riches of the Owner.

While Things were preparing at the Castle for his Reception, the Marquis, though now advanced in Years, cast his Eyes on a young lady, greatly inferior to himself in Quality, but whose Beauty and good Sense promised him an agreeable Companion. After a very short Courtship, he married her, and in a few Weeks carried his new Bride into the Country, from whence he absolutely resolved never to Return.

The Marquis, following the Plan of Life he had laid down, divided his Time between the Company of his Lady, his Library, which was large and well furnished, and his Gardens. Sometimes he took the Diversion of Hunting, but never admitted any Company whatever; and his Pride and extreme Reserve rendered him so wholly inaccessible to the Country Gentry about him, that none ever presumed to solicit his Acquaintance.

In the Second Year of his Retirement, the Marchioness brought him a Daughter, and died in Three Days after her Delivery. The Marquis, who had tenderly loved her, was extremely afflicted at her Death; but Time having produced its usual Effects, his great Fondness for the little *Arabella* intirely engrossed his Attention, and made up all the Happiness of his Life. At Four Years of Age he took her from under the Direction of the Nurses and Women appointed to attend her, and permitted her to receive no Part of her Education from another, which he was capable of giving her himself. He taught her to read and write in a very few Months; and, as she grew older, finding in her an uncommon Quickness of Apprehension, and an Understanding capable of great Improvements, he resolved to cultivate so promising a Genius with the utmost Care; and, as he frequently, in the Rapture of paternal Fondness, expressed himself, render her Mind as beautiful as her Person was lovely.

Nature had indeed given her a most charming Face, a Shape easy and delicate, a sweet and insinuating Voice, and an Air so full of

Dignity and Grace, as drew the Admiration of all that saw her. These native Charms were improved with all the Heightenings of Art; her Dress was perfectly magnificent; the best Masters of Music and Dancing were sent for from *London* to attend her. She soon became a perfect Mistress of the *French* and *Italian* Languages, under the Care of her Father; and it is not to be doubted, but she would have made a great Proficiency in all useful Knowlege, had not her whole Time been taken up by another Study.[1]

From her earliest Youth she had discovered a Fondness for Reading, which extremely delighted the Marquis; he permitted her therefore the Use of his Library, in which, unfortunately for her, were great Store of Romances, and, what was still more un-- fortunate, not in the original *French*, but very bad Translations.[2]

The deceased Marchioness had purchased these Books to soften a Solitude which she found very disagreeable; and, after her Death, the Marquis removed them from her Closet into his Library, where *Arabella* found them.

The surprising Adventures with which they were filled, proved a most pleasing Entertainment to a young Lady, who was wholly secluded from the World; who had no other Diversion, but ranging like a Nymph through Gardens, or, to say better, the Woods and Lawns in which she was inclosed; and who had no other Conversation but that of a grave and melancholy Father, or her own Attendants.

Her Ideas, from the Manner of her Life, and the Objects around her, had taken a romantic Turn; and, supposing Romances were real Pictures of Life, from them she drew all her Notions and Expectations. By them she was taught to believe, that Love was the ruling Principle of the World; that every other Passion was subordinate to this; and that it caused all the Happiness and Miseries of Life. Her Glass, which she often consulted, always shewed her a Form so extremely lovely, that, not finding herself engaged in such Adventures as were common to the Heroines in the Romances she read, she often complained of the Insensibility of Mankind, upon whom her Charms seemed to have so little Influence.

The perfect Retirement she lived in, afforded indeed no Opportunities of making the Conquests she desired; but she could not comprehend, how any Solitude could be obscure enough to conceal a Beauty like hers from Notice; and thought the Reputation of her Charms sufficient to bring a Croud of Adorers to demand her of her Father. Her Mind being wholly filled with the most extravagant Expectations, she was alarmed by every trifling Incident; and kept in a continual Anxiety by a Vicissitude of Hopes, Fears, Wishes, and Disappointments.[1]

CHAPTER II

Contains a Description of a Lady's Dress in Fashion not much above Two thousand Years ago.—The Beginning of an Adventure which seems to promise a great deal

Arabella had now entered into her Seventeenth Year with the Regret of seeing herself the Object of Admiration to a few Rustics only, who happened to see her; when, one *Sunday*, making use of the Permission the Marquis sometimes allowed her, to attend Divine Service at the Church belonging to the Village near which they lived, her Vanity was flattered with an Adorer not altogether unworthy of her Notice.

This Gentleman was young, gay, handsome, and very elegantly dressed; he was just come from *London* with an Intention to pass some Weeks with a Friend in that Part of the Country; and at the time *Arabella* entered the Church, his Eyes, which had wandered from one rural Fair to another, were in an Instant fixed upon her Face. She blushed with a very becoming Modesty; and, pleased with the unusual Appearance of so fine a Gentleman, and the particular Notice he took of her, passed on to her Seat thro' a double Row of Country People, who, with a Profusion of aukward Bows and Courtesies, expressed their Respect.

Mr. *Hervey*, for that was the Stranger's Name, was no less surprised at her Beauty, than the Singularity of her Dress; and the odd Whim of being followed into the Church by three Women-Attendants, who, as soon as she was seated, took their Places behind her.[2]

Her Dress, tho' singular,[3] was far from being unbecoming. All the Beauties of her Neck and Shape were set off to the greatest Advantage by the Fashion of her Gown, which, in the Manner of a Robe, was made to fit tight to her Body; and fastened on the Breast with a Knot of Diamonds. Her fine black Hair, hung upon her Neck in Curls, which had so much the Appearance of being artless, that all but her Maid, whose Employment it was to give them that Form, imagined they were so. Her Head-dress was only a few Knots advantageously disposed, over which she wore a white Sarsenet Hood, somewhat in the Form of a Veil, with which she sometimes wholly covered her fair Face, when she saw herself beheld with too much Attention.

This Veil had never appeared to her so necessary before. Mr. *Hervey's* eager Glances threw her into so much Confusion, that, pulling it over her Face as much as she was able, she remained invisible to him all the time they afterwards stayed in the Church. This Action, by which she would have had him understand that she was displeased at his gazing on her with so little Respect, only increased his Curiosity to know who she was.

When the Congregation was dismissed, he hastened to the Door, with an Intention to offer her his Hand to help her to her Coach; but seeing the magnificent Equipage that waited for her, and the Number of Servants that attended it, he conceived a much higher Idea of her Quality than he had at first; and, changing his Design, contented himself with only bowing to her as she passed; and as soon as her Coach drove away, inquired of some Persons nearest him, who she was?

These Rustics, highly delighted with the Opportunity of talking to the gay *Londoner*, whom they looked upon as a very extraordinary Person, gave him all the Intelligence they were able, concerning the Lady he inquired after; and filled him with an inconceivable Surprize at the strange Humour of the Marquis, who buried so beautiful a Creature in Obscurity.

At his Return home he expressed his Admiration of her in Terms that persuaded his Friend, she had made some Impression on his Heart; and, after raillying him a little upon this Suspicion, he assumed a more serious Air, and told him, If he really liked Lady *Bella*, he thought it not impossible but he might obtain her. The poor Girl, added he, has been kept in Confinement so long, that I believe it would not be difficult to persuade her to free herself by Marriage. She never had a Lover in her Life; and therefore the first Person who addresses her has the fairest Chance for succeeding.

Mr. *Hervey*, tho' he could not persuade himself his Cousin was in Earnest when he advised him to court the only Daughter of a Man of the Marquis's Quality, and Heiress to his vast Estates; yet relished the Scheme, and resolved to make some Attempt upon her before he left the Country. However, he concealed his Design from his Cousin, not being willing to expose himself to be ridiculed, if he did not succeed; and, turning the Advice he had given him into a Jest, left him in the Opinion, that he thought no more of it.

CHAPTER III

In which the Adventure goes on after the accustomed Manner

Arabella, in the mean time, was wholly taken up with the Adventure, as she called it, at Church: The Person and Dress of the Gentleman who had so particularly gazed on her there, was so different from what she had been accustomed to see, that she immediately concluded, he was of some distinguished Rank. It was past a Doubt, she thought, that he was excessively in Love with her; and as she soon expected to have some very extraordinary Proofs of his Passion, her Thoughts were wholly employed on the Manner in which she should receive them.

As soon as she came home, and had paid her Duty to the Marquis, she hurried to her Chamber, to be at Liberty to indulge her agreeable Reflections; and, after the Example of her Heroines, when any thing extraordinary happened to them, called her favourite Woman; or, to use her own Language, her, 'in whom she confided her most secret Thoughts.'

Well, *Lucy*, said she, did you observe that Stranger who ey'd *us**1 so heedfully To-day at Church?

This Girl, notwithstanding her Country-Simplicity, knew a Compliment was expected from her on this Occasion; and therefore replied, 'That she did not wonder at the Gentleman's staring at her; for she was sure he had never seen any body so hándsome as her Ladyship before.'

I have not all the Beauty you attribute to me, said *Arabella*, smiling a little: And, with a very moderate Share of it, I might well

* The Heroines always speak of themselves in the Plural Number.

fix the Attention of a Person who seemed to be not overmuch pleased with the Objects about him. However, pursued she, assuming a more serious Air, if this Stranger be weak enough to entertain any Sentiments more than indifferent for me; I charge you, upon Pain of my Displeasure, do not be accessary to the Conveying his presumptuous Thoughts to me either by Letters or Messages; nor suffer him to corrupt your Fidelity with the Presents he will very probably offer you.

Lucy, to whom this Speech first gave a Hint of what she ought to expect from her Lady's Lovers, finding herself of more Importance than she imagined, was so pleased at the Prospect which opened to her, that it was with some Hesitation she promised to obey her Orders.

Arabella, however, was satisfied with her Assurances of observing her Directions; and dismissed her from her Presence, not without an Apprehension of being too well obeyed.

A whole Week being elapsed without meeting with the Importunities she expected, she could hardly conceal her Surprize at so mortifying a Disappointment; and frequently interrogated *Lucy*, concerning any Attempts the Stranger had made on her Fidelity; but the Answers she received, only increased her Discontent, as they convinced her, her Charms had not had the Effect she imagined.

Mr. *Hervey*, however, had been all this time employed in thinking of some Means to get acquainted with the Marquis; for, being possessed with an extraordinary Opinion of his Wit, and personal Accomplishments, he did not fear making some Impression on the Heart of the young Lady; provided he could have an Opportunity of conversing with her.

His Cousin's Advice was continually in his Mind, and flattered his Vanity with the most agreeable Hopes: But the Marquis's Fondness for Solitude, and that Haughtiness which was natural to him, rendered him so difficult of Access, that *Hervey*, from the Intelligence he received of his Humour, despaired of being able to prosecute his Scheme; when, meeting with a young Farmer in one of his Evening-Walks, and entering into Conversation with him upon several Country Subjects, the Discourse at last turned upon the Marquis of —— whose fine House and Gardens were within their View; upon which the young Fellow informed him, he was Brother to a young Woman that attended the Lady *Arabella*; and,

being fond of lengthening out the Conversation with so fine a
Gentleman, gave him, without being desired, the domestic History
of the whole Family, as he had received it from *Lucy*, who was the
Sister he mentioned.

Hervey, excessively delighted at this accidental Meeting with a
Person so capable of serving his Design, affected a great Desire of
being better acquainted with him; and, under Pretence of acquiring
some Knowledge in rural Affairs, accustomed himself to call so
often at *William's* Farm, that at last he met with the Person whom
the Hopes of seeing had so often carried him thither.

Lucy, the Moment she saw him enter, knowing him again,
blushed at the Remembrance of the Discourse which had passed
between her Lady and herself concerning him; and was not at all
surprised at the Endeavours he used to speak to her apart: But, as
soon as he began a Conversation concerning *Arabella*, she interrupted him by saying, I know, Sir, that you are *distractedly* in Love
with my Lady; but she has forbid me to receive any Letters or
Messages from you; and therefore I beg you will not offer to bribe
me; for I dare not disobey her.

Mr. *Hervey* was at first so astonished at her Speech, that he knew
not what to think of it; but, after a little Reflection, attributing to an
Excess of aukward Cunning what, in Reality, was an Effect of her
Simplicity, he resolved to make use of the Hint she had given him;
and, presenting her with a Couple of Guineas, intreated her to
venture displeasing her Lady, by bearing a Letter from him;
promising to reward her better, if she succeeded.

Lucy made some Difficulty to comply; but, not being able
absolutely to refuse the first Bribe that ever was offered to her, she,
after some Intreaties, consented to take the Letter; and, receiving
the Money he presented her, left him at Liberty to write, after she
had got her Brother to furnish him with Materials for that Purpose.

CHAPTER IV

A Mistake, which produces no great Consequences—An extraordinary Comment upon a Behaviour natural enough— An Instance of a Lady's Compassion for her Lover, which the Reader may possibly think not very compassionate

Hervey, who was Master of no great Elegance in Letter-writing, was at first at some Loss, how to address a Lady of her Quality, to whom he was an absolute Stranger, upon the Subject of Love; but, conceiving there was no great Occasion for much Ceremony in declaring himself to one who had been educated in the Country, and who, he believed, could not be displeased with a Lover of his Figure, he therefore, in plain Terms, told her, how *deeply* he was enamoured of her; and conjured her to afford him some Opportunity of paying his Respects to her.

Lucy received this Letter from him with a worse Grace than she did the Gold; and, tho' she promised him to deliver it to her Lady immediately, yet she kept it a Day or two before she had the Courage to attempt it: At last, drawing it out of her Pocket, with a bashful Air, she presented it to her Lady, telling her it came from the fine Gentleman whom she saw at Church.

Arabella blushed at the Sight of the Letter; and tho', in Reality, she was not displeased, yet, being a strict Observer of romantic Forms, she chid her Woman severely for taking it. Carry it back, added she, to the presumptuous Writer of it; and let him know how greatly his Insolence has offended me.

Lucy, however, suffered the Letter to remain on the Toilet, expecting some Change in her Lady's Mind; for she traversed the Chamber in great seeming Irresolution, often stealing a Glance to the Letter, which she had a strong Inclination to open; but, searching the Records of her Memory for a Precedent, and not finding, that any Lady ever opened a Letter from an unknown Lover, she reiterated her Commands to *Lucy* to carry it back, with a Look and Accent so very severe, that the Girl, extremely apprehensive of having offended her, put the Letter again in her Pocket, resolving to return it the first Opportunity.

Mr. *Hervey*, who had his Thoughts wholly taken up with the flattering Prospect of Success, no sooner saw *Lucy*, who gave him his Letter without speaking a Word, than, supposing it had been the Answer he expected, he eagerly snatched it out of her Hand, and, kissing it first in a Rapture of Joy, broke it open; but his Surprize and Confusion, when he saw it was his own Letter returned, was inexpressible. For some Moments he kept his Eyes fastened upon the tender Billet, as if he was really reading it. His Disappointment, and the ridiculous Figure he knew he must make in the Eyes of his Messenger, filled him with so much Confusion, that he did not dare to look up; but, recovering himself at last, he affected to turn it into a Jest; and, laughing first himself, gave *Lucy* the Liberty of laughing also, who had with much Difficulty been able to prevent doing it before.

The Curiosity he felt to hear how she had acquitted herself of the Trust he had reposed in her, made him oblige her to give a Truce to her Mirth, in order to satisfy him; and *Lucy*, who was extremely exact in her Relations, told him all that had passed, without omitting the smallest Circumstance.

Though it was impossible to draw any favourable Omen from what he heard, yet he determined to make another Effort, before he set out for *London*; and, taking Leave of his Confident, after he had appointed her to meet him again the next Day, at her Brother's, he went home to consider upon Means to effect his Designs, which the ill Success of his first Attempt had not forced him to abandon.

Arabella, who expected to hear, that the Return of his Letter would make her Lover commit some very extravagant Actions; and having impatiently waited for an Account of them from *Lucy*; finding she seemed to have no Intention to begin a Discourse concerning him; asked her, at last, If she had executed her Commission, and returned the Letter to the insolent Unknown?

The Girl answered, Yes.

Which not being all that her Lady expected, And how did he receive it? resumed she, peevishly.

Why Madam, replied *Lucy*, I believe he thought your Ladyship had sent him an Answer; for he kissed the Letter several times.

Foolish Wench! replied *Arabella*, How can you imagine he had the Temerity to think I should answer his Letter? A Favour, which, though he had spent Years in my Service, would have been infinitely greater than he could have expected. No, *Lucy*, he kissed the Letter, either because he thought it had been touched at least by my Hands, or to shew the perfect Submission with which he received my Commands; and it is not to be doubted, but his Despair will force him to commit some desperate Outrage against himself, which I do not hate him enough to wish, though he has mortally offended me.

Arabella was possessed of great Sensibility and Softness; and, being really persuaded, that her Lover would entertain some fatal Design, seemed so much affected with the Thoughts of what might happen, that *Lucy*, who tenderly loved her, begged her not to be so much concerned for the Gentleman: There is no Fear, added she, that he will do himself a Mischief; for when he discovered his Mistake, he laughed heartily, as well as myself.

How! replied *Arabella*, extremely surprised, Did he laugh?

Which *Lucy* confirming, Doubtless, resumed she, having taken a little Time to consider of so strange a Phænomenon, he laughed, because his Reason was disturbed at the sudden Shock he received: Unhappy Man! his Presumption will be severely enough punished, though I do not add Anger to the Scorn which I have expressed for him: Therefore, *Lucy*, you may tell him, if you please, that, notwithstanding the Offence he has been guilty of, I am not cruel enough to wish his Death; and that I command him to live, if he can live without Hope.

CHAPTER V

In which one would imagine the Adventure concluded, but for a Promise, that something else is to come

Lucy now began to think there was something more, than she imagined, in this Affair. Mr. *Hervey* indeed, in her Opinion, had seemed to be very far from having any Design to attempt his own Life; but her Lady, she thought, could not possibly be mistaken; and therefore she resolved to carry her Message to him immediately, though it was then late in the Evening.

Accordingly she went to her Brother's, where she had some Hope of meeting with him; but not finding him there, she obliged him to go to the House where he lived, and tell him she desired to speak with him.

William, being let into the Secret of his Sister's frequent Meetings with Mr. *Hervey*, imagined she had some agreeable News to acquaint him with; and therefore ran immediately to his Relation's House, which was but at a small Distance; but he was told Mr. *Hervey* was in Bed, very much indisposed, and could not be seen.

This News put *Lucy* in a terrible Fright: She told her Apprehensions to her Brother; which being such as her Lady had put into her Head, and were now confirmed by Mr. *Hervey's* Illness, the young Farmer stood amazed, not being able to comprehend her Meaning; and she, without staying to explain herself any further, went home to the Castle, and told her Lady, That what she feared was come to pass; the Gentleman would certainly die; for he was very ill in Bed.

This being no more than what *Arabella* expected, she discovered no Surprize; but only asked *Lucy*, If she had delivered her Message to him?

Would you have me, Madam, replied she, go to his House? I am afraid the Marquis will hear of it.

My Father, replied *Arabella*, can never be offended with me for doing a charitable Action.

Ah! Madam, interrupted *Lucy*, let me go then immediately, for fear the poor Gentleman should grow worse.

If he be sick almost to Death, resumed *Arabella*, he will recover, if I command him to do so: When did you hear of a Lover dying through Despair, when his Mistress let him know it was her Pleasure he should live? But as it will not be altogether so proper for you to go to his House, as it may be suspected you come from me; I'll write a few Lines, which you shall copy, and your Brother may carry them to him To-morrow, and I'll engage he shall be well in a few Hours.

Saying this, she went into her Closet, and, having written a short Note, made *Lucy* write it over again. It was as follows:

Lucy, *To the Unfortunate Lover of her Lady*.

MY Lady, who is the most generous Person in the World, has commanded me to tell you, that, presumptuous as you are, she does not desire your Death; nay more, she commands you to live, and permits you, in case you obey her, to hope for her Pardon,

provided you keep within the Bounds she prescribes to you.
Adieu.

This Letter *Lucy* copied, and *Arabella*, examining it again, thought it rather too kind; and, seeming desirous of making some Alteration in it, *Lucy*, who was extremely anxious for Mr. *Hervey's* Life, fearing lest she should alter it in such a manner, that the Gentleman might be at Liberty to die, if he chose it, conjured her Lady in such pressing Terms to let it remain as it was, that *Arabella* suffered herself to be prevailed upon by her Intreaties; and, remembring that it was not uncommon for the Ladies in Romances to relax a little in their Severity through the Remonstrances of their Women, told her, with an inchanting Smile, that she would grant her Desire; and went to Bed with that pleasing Satisfaction, which every generous Mind experiences at the Consciousness of having done some very benevolent Action.

In the Morning, this life-restoring Billet was dispatched by *Lucy* to her Brother, inclosed in one to him, charging him to carry it to the sick Gentleman immediately.

William, having a strong Curiosity to see what his Sister had written, ventured to open it; and, not being able to imagine Lady *Bella* had really given her Orders to write what appeared to him the most unintelligible Stuff in the World, resolved to suppress this Letter till he had questioned her a little concerning it.

A few Hours after, Mr. *Hervey*, who expected to meet *Lucy* at her Brother's, came in. His Illness having been only a violent Headach, to which he was subject, being now quite off, he remembred the Appointment he had made; but, having waited some time, and she not coming, he returned again to his Cousin's, leaving word for her, that he would see her the next Day.

Scarce was he gone out, when *Lucy*, who longed to know what Effect her Letter had produced in his Health, came in; and eagerly inquiring of her Brother how Mr. *Hervey* was, received for Answer, that he had been there a Moment before she came.

Well, cried she, clasping her Hands together, with Surprize, my Lady said, her Letter would cure him, if he was ever so sick; but I did not imagine he would have been well enough to come abroad so soon.

Your Lady! interrupted *William*, why was it not yourself that wrote the Letter you gave to me?

No, truly, Brother, resumed she: How was it possible I should write so fine a Letter? My Lady *made* every Word of it, and I only wrote it after her.

William, hearing this, would not own the Indiscretion he now thought he had been guilty of, in keeping the Letter; but suffered his Sister to return to her Lady, in the Belief that he had delivered it, resolving, when he saw her next, to say he had lost it; for he knew not what Excuse to make to Mr. *Hervey* for not giving it him when he saw him.

Arabella received the Account of her Lover's Recovery as a Thing she was absolutely sure of before; and thinking she had now done all that could be expected from her Compassion, resumed her usual Severity, and commanded *Lucy* to mention him no more. If he loves me with that Purity he ought to do, pursued she, he will cease to importune me any further: And though his Passion be ever so violent, his Respect and Submission to my Commands will oblige him to Silence. The Obedience he has already shewn, in recovering at the first Intimation I gave, that it was my Will he should do so, convinces me, I need not apprehend he will renew his Follies to displease me.

Lucy, who found by this Discourse of her Lady's, that her Commission was at an End with regard to Mr. *Hervey*, followed her Directions so exactly, that she not only spoke no more of him to her, but also, in order to avoid him, neglected to go to her Brother's.

His Impatience at not seeing her made him prevail upon her Brother to go the Castle, and intreat her to give him another Interview: But *Lucy* positively refused; and, to make a Merit with her Lady of her Obedience, informed her what he had requested.

Arabella, resenting a Boldness which argued so little Respect to her Commands, began now to repent of the Compassion she had shewn him; and, commending *Lucy* for what she had done, bid her tell the insolent Unknown, if he ever sent to her again, that she was resolved never to pardon the Contempt he had shewn for her Orders.

Mr. *Hervey*, finding himself deserted by *Lucy*, resolved to give over his Attempts, congratulating himself for his Discretion in not acquainting his Cousin with what he had already done: His Heart not being very much engaged, he found no great Difficulty in consoling himself for his bad Success. In a few Days he thought of Lady *Bella* no more, than if he had never seen her; but an Accident bringing her again in his Way, he could not resist the Inclination he felt to speak to her; and by that means drew upon himself a very sensible Mortification.

In which the Adventure is really concluded; tho', possibly, not as the Reader expected

THE Marquis sometimes permitting his Daughter to ride out, and this being the only Diversion she was allowed, or ever experienced, she did not fail to take it as often as she could.

She was returning from one of these Airings one Day, attended by two Servants, when Mr. *Hervey*, who happened to be at some Distance, observing a Lady on Horseback, who made a very graceful Figure, he rode up to her, in order to have a nearer View; and, knowing Lady *Bella* again, resolved to speak to her: But while he was considering how he should accost her, *Arabella* suddenly seeing him, and observing he was making up to her, her Imagination immediately suggested to her, that this insolent Lover had a Design to seize her Person; and this Thought terrifying her extremely, she gave a loud Shriek; which Mr. *Hervey* hearing, rode eagerly up to her to inquire the Reason of it, at the same time that her two Attendants, as much amazed as himself, came galloping up also.

Arabella, upon his coming close to her, redoubled her Cries. If you have any Valour, said she to her Servants, defend your unfortunate Mistress, and rescue her from this unworthy Man.

The Servants, believing him to be a Highwayman, by this Exclamation, and dreading lest he should present his Pistol at their Heads, if they offered to make any Resistance, recoiled a few Paces back, expecting he would demand their Purses when he had robbed their Lady: But the extreme Surprize he was in, keeping him motionless, the Fellows not seeing any Pistols in his Hand, and animated by *Arabella's* Cries, who, calling them Cowards and Traitors, urged them to deliver her; they both, in a Moment, laid hold of Mr. *Hervey*, and forced him to alight; which they did also themselves, still keeping fast hold of him, whom Surprize, Shame, and Rage, had hitherto kept silent.

Rascals! cried he, when he was able to speak, what do you mean by using me in this manner? Do you suppose I had any Intention to hurt the Lady?—What do you take me for?

For a Ravisher, interrupted *Arabella*, an impious Ravisher, who, contrary to all Laws both human and divine, endeavour to possess yourself by Force of a Person whom you are not worthy to serve; and whose Charity and Compassion you have returned with the utmost Ingratitude.

Upon my Word, Madam, said Mr. *Hervey*, I don't understand one Word you say: You either mistake me for some other Person, or are pleased to divert yourself with the Surprize I am in: But I beseech you carry the Jest no farther, and order your Servants to let me go; or, by Heaven—cried he struggling to get loose, if I can but free one of my Hands, I'll stab the Scoundrels before your Face.

It is not with Threats like these, resumed *Arabella* with great Calmness, that I can be moved. A little more Submission and Respect would become you better; you are now wholly in my Power; I may, if I please, carry you to my Father, and have you severely punished for your Attempt: But to shew you, that I am as generous as you are base and designing, I'll give you Freedom, provided you promise me never to appear before me again: But, in order to secure my own Safety, you must deliver up your Arms to my Servants, that I may be assured you will not have it in your Power to make a second Attempt upon my Liberty.

Mr. *Hervey*, whose Astonishment was increased by every Word she spoke, began now to be apprehensive, that this might prove a very serious Affair, since she seemed resolved to believe he had a Design to carry her off; and, knowing that an Attempt of that Nature upon an Heiress might have dangerous Consequences, he resolved to accept the Conditions she offered him: But while he delivered his Hanger[1] to the Servant, he assured her in the strongest Terms, that he had no other Design in riding up to her, but to have a nearer View of her Person.

Add not Falshood, said *Arabella* sternly, to a Crime already black enough; for tho', by an Effect of my Generosity, I have resolved not to deliver you up to the Resentment of my Father, yet nothing shall ever be able to make me pardon this Outrage. Go then, pursued she, go, base Man, unworthy of the Care I took of thy Safety; go to some distant Country, where I may never hear of thee more; and suffer me, if possible, to lose the Remembrance of thy Crimes,

Saying this, she ordered her Servants, who had got the Hanger in their Possession, to set him at Liberty, and mount their Horses; which they did immediately, and followed their Lady, who rode with all imaginable Speed to the Castle.

Mr. *Hervey*, not yet recovered from his Surprize, stood some Moments considering the strange Scene he had been Witness to; and in which he had, much against his Will, appeared the principal Character. As he was not acquainted with Lady *Bella's* Foible, he concluded her Fears of him were occasioned by her Simplicity, and some Misrepresentations that had been made her by *Lucy*, who, he thought, had betrayed him; and, fearing this ridiculous Adventure would be soon made public, and himself exposed to the Sneers of his Country Acquaintance, he resolved to go back to *London* as soon as possible.

The next Day, pretending he had received a Letter which obliged him to set out immediately, he took Leave of his Cousin, heartily glad at the Escape he should make from his Raillery; for he did not doubt but the Story would very soon be known, and told greatly to his Disadvantage.

But *Arabella*, in order to be completely generous, a Quality for which all the Heroines are famous, laid a Command upon her two Attendants not to mention what had passed, giving them, at the same time, Money to secure their Secrecy; and threatening them with her Displeasure, if they disobeyed.

Arabella, as soon as she had an Opportunity, did not fail to acquaint her faithful *Lucy* with the Danger from which she had so happily escaped, thanking Heaven at the same time with great Devotion, for having preserved her from the Hands of the Ravisher.

Two or three Months rolled away, after this Accident, without offering any new Adventure to our fair Visionary; when her Imagination, always prepossessed with the same fantastic Ideas, made her stumble upon another Mistake, equally absurd and ridiculous.

CHAPTER VII

In which some Contradictions are very happily reconciled

THE Marquis's head Gardener had received a young Fellow into his Master's Service, who had lived in several Families of Distinction. He had a good Face; was tolerably genteel; and, having an Understanding something above his Condition, join'd to a great deal of *secondhand* Politeness, which he had contracted while he lived at *London*, he appeared a very extraordinary Person among the Rustics who were his Fellow-Servants.

Arabella, when she walked in the Garden, had frequent Opportunities of seeing this young Man, whom she observed with a very particular Attention. His Person and Air had something, she thought, very distinguishing. When she condescended to speak to him about any Business he was employed in, she took Notice, that his Answers were framed in a Language vastly superior to his Condition; and the Respect he paid her had quite another Air from that of the aukward Civility of the other Servants.

Having discerned so many Marks of a Birth far from being mean, she easily passed from an Opinion that he was a Gentleman, to a Belief that he was something more; and every new Sight of him adding Strength to her Suspicions, she remained, in a little time, perfectly convinced that he was some Person of Quality, who, disguised in the Habit of a Gardener, had introduced himself into her Father's Service, in order to have an Opportunity of declaring a Passion to her, which must certainly be very great, since it had forced him to assume an Appearance so unworthy of his noble Extraction.

Wholly possessed with this Thought, she set herself to observe him more narrowly; and soon found out, that he went very aukwardly about his Work; that he sought Opportunities of being alone; that he threw himself in her Way as often as he could, and gazed on her very attentively: She sometimes fansied she saw him endeavour to smother a Sigh when he answered her any Question about his Work; once saw him leaning against a Tree with his Hands crossed upon his Breast; and, having lost a String of small Pearls, which she remembered he had seen her threading as she sat in one of the Arbours, was persuaded he had taken it up, and kept it for the Object of his secret Adoration.

She often wondered, indeed, that she did not find her Name carved on the Trees, with some mysterious Expressions of Love; that he was never discovered lying along the Side of one of the little Rivulets, increasing the Stream with his Tears; nor, for three Months that he had lived there, had ever been sick of a Fever caused by his Grief, and the Constraint he put upon himself in not declaring his Passion: But she considered again, that his Fear of being discovered kept him from amusing himself with making the Trees bear the Records of his secret Thoughts, or of indulging his Melancholy in any Manner expressive of the Condition of his Soul; and, as for his not being sick, his Youth, and the Strength of his Constitution, might, even for a longer time, bear him up against the Assaults of a Fever: But he appeared much thinner and paler than he used to be; and she concluded, therefore, that he must in time sink under the Violence of his Passion, or else be forced to declare it to her; which she considered as a very great Misfortune; for, not finding in herself any Disposition to approve his Love, she must necessarily banish him from her Presence, for fear he should have the Presumption to hope, that Time might do any thing in his Favour: And it was possible also, that the Sentence she would be obliged to pronounce, might either cause his Death, or force him to commit some extravagant Action, which would discover him to her Father, who would, perhaps, think her guilty of holding a secret Correspondence with him.

These Thoughts perplexed her so much, that, hoping to find some Relief by unburdening her Mind to *Lucy*, she told her all her Uneasiness. Ah! said she to her, looking upon *Edward*, who had just passed them, how unfortunate do I think myself in being the Cause of that Passion which makes this illustrious Unknown wear away his Days in so shameful an Obscurity! Yes, *Lucy*, pursued she, that *Edward*, whom you regard as one of my Father's menial Servants, is a Person of *sublime Quality*, who submits to this Disguise only to have an Opportunity of seeing me every Day. But why do you seem so surprised? Is it possible, that you have not suspected him to be what he is? Has he never unwittingly made any Discovery of himself? Have you not surprised him in Discourse with his faithful 'Squire, who, certainly, lurks hereabouts to receive his Commands, and is haply the Confident of his Passion? Has he never entertained you with any Conversation about me? Or have you never seen any valuable Jewels in his Possession by which you suspected him to be not what he appears?

Truly, Madam, replied *Lucy*, I never took him for any body else but a simple Gardener; but now you open my Eyes, methinks I can find I have been strangely mistaken; for he does not look like a Man of low Degree; and he talks quite in another Manner from our Servants. I never heard him indeed speak of your Ladyship, but once; and that was, when he first saw you walking in the Garden, he asked our *John*, If you was not the Marquis's Daughter? And he said, You was as beautiful as an Angel. As for fine Jewels, I never saw any; and I believe he has none; but he has a Watch, and that looks as if he was something, Madam: Nor do I remember to have seen him talk with any Stranger that looked like a 'Squire.

Lucy, having thus, with her usual Punctuality, answered every Question her Lady put to her, proceeded to ask her, What she should say, if he should beg her to give her a Letter, as the other Gentleman had done?

You must by no means take it, replied *Arabella*: My Compassion had before like to have been fatal to me. If he discovers his Quality to me, I shall know in what manner to treat him.

They were in this Part of their Discourse, when a Noise they heard at some Distance, made *Arabella* bend her Steps to the Place from whence it proceeded; and, to her infinite Amazement, saw the head Gardener, with a Stick he had in his Hand, give several Blows to the concealed Hero, who suffered the Indignity with admirable Patience.

Shocked at seeing a Person of sublime Quality treated so unworthily, she called out to the Gardener to hold his Hand; who immediately obeyed; and *Edward*, seeing the young Lady advance, sneaked off, with an Air very different from an *Oroondates*.[1]

For what Crime, pray, said *Arabella*, with a stern Aspect, did you treat the Person I saw with you so cruelly? He whom you take such unbecoming Liberties with, may possibly—But again I ask you, What has he done? You should make some Allowance for his want of Skill in the abject Employment he is in at present.

It is not for his want of Skill, Madam, said the Gardener, that I corrected him; he knows his Business very well, if he would mind it; but, Madam, I have discovered him—

Discovered him, do you say? interrupted *Arabella*: And has the Knowledge of his Condition not been able to prevent such Usage? or rather, Has it been the Occasion of his receiving it?

His Conditions are very bad, Madam, returned the Gardener; and I am afraid are such as will one Day prove the Ruin of Body and Soul too. I have for some time suspected he had evil Designs in his Head; and just now watched him to the Fish-pond, and prevented him from——

O dear! interrupted *Lucy*, looking pitifully on her Lady, whose fair Bosom heaved with Compassion, I warrant he was going to make away with himself.

No, resumed the Gardener, smiling at the Mistake, he was only going to make away with some of the Carp, which the Rogue had caught, and intended, I suppose, to sell; but I threw them into the Water again; and if your Ladyship had not forbid me, I would have drubbed him soundly for his Pains.

Fye! fye! interrupted *Arabella*, out of Breath with Shame and Vexation, tell me no more of these idle Tales.

Then, hastily walking on to hide the Blushes which this strange Accusation of her illustrious Lover had raised in her Face, she continued for some time in the greatest Perplexity imaginable.

Lucy, who followed her, and could not possibly reconcile what her Lady had been telling her concerning *Edward*, with the Circumstance of his stealing the Carp, ardently wished to hear her Opinion of this Matter; but, seeing her deeply engaged with her own Thoughts, she would not venture to disturb her.

Arabella indeed, had been in such a terrible Consternation, that it was some Time before she even reconciled Appearances to herself; but, as she had a most happy Facility in accommodating every Incident to her own Wishes and Conceptions, she examined this Matter so many different Ways, drew so many Conclusions, and fansied so many Mysteries in the most indifferent Actions of the supposed noble Unknown, that she remained, at last, more than ever confirmed in the Opinion, that he was some great Personage, whom her Beauty had forced to assume an Appearance unworthy of himself: When *Lucy*, no longer able to keep Silence, drew off her Attention from those pleasing Images, by speaking of the Carp-stealing Affair again.

Arabella, whose Confusion returned at that disagreeable Sound, charged her, in an angry Tone, never to mention so injurious a Suspicion any more: For, in fine, said she to her, do you imagine a Person of his Rank could be guilty of stealing Carp? Alas! pursued she, sighing, he had, indeed, some fatal Design; and, doubtless, would have executed it, had not this Fellow so luckily prevented him.

But Mr. *Woodbind*, Madam, said *Lucy*, saw the Carp in his Hand: I wonder what he was going to do with them.

Still, resumed *Arabella*, extremely chagrined, still will you wound my Ears with that horrid Sound? I tell you, obstinate and foolish Wench, that this unhappy Man went thither to die; and if he really caught the Fish, it was to conceal his Design from *Woodbind*: His great Mind could not suggest to him, that it was possible he might be suspected of a Baseness like that this ignorant Fellow accused him of; therefore he took no Care about it, being wholly possessed by his despairing Thoughts.

However, Madam, said *Lucy*, your Ladyship may prevent his going to the Fishpond again, by laying your Commands upon him to live.

I shall do all that I ought, answered *Arabella*; but my Care for the Safety of other Persons must not make me forget what I owe to my own.

As she had always imputed Mr. *Hervey's* fansied Attempt to carry her away, to the Letter she had written to him, upon which he had probably founded his Hopes of being pardoned for it, she resolved to be more cautious for the future in giving such Instances of her Compassion; and was at a great Loss in what manner to comfort her despairing Lover, without raising Expectations she had no Inclination to confirm: But she was delivered from her Perplexity a few Days after by the News of his having left the Marquis's Service; which she attributed to some new Design he had formed to obtain her; and *Lucy*, who always thought as her Lady did, was of the same Opinion; tho' it was talked among the Servants, that *Edward* feared a Discovery of more Tricks, and resolved not to stay till he was disgracefully dismissed.

CHAPTER VIII

In which a Mistake, in point of Ceremony, is rectified

Arabella had scarce done thinking of this last Adventure, when the Marquis communicated a Piece of Intelligence to her, which opened a Prospect of an infinite Number of new ones.

His Nephew, having just returned from his Travels, was preparing to come and pay him a Visit in his Retreat; and, as he always designed to marry *Arabella* to this Youth, of whom he was extremely fond, he told his Daughter of the intended Visit of her Cousin, whom she had not seen since she was eight Years old; and, for the first time, insinuated his Design of giving him to her for an Husband.

Arabella, whose Delicacy was extremely shocked at this abrupt Declaration of her Father, could hardly hide her Chagrin; for, tho' she always intended to marry some time or other, as all the Heroines had done, yet she thought such an Event ought to be brought about with an infinite deal of Trouble; and that it was necessary she should pass to this State thro' a great Number of Cares, Disappointments, and Distresses of various Kinds, like them; that her Lover should purchase her with his Sword from a Croud of Rivals; and arrive to the Possession of her Heart by many Years of Services and Fidelity.

The Impropriety of receiving a Lover of a Father's recommending appeared in its strongest Light. What Lady in Romance ever married the Man that was chose for her? In those Cases the Remonstrances of a Parent are called Persecutions; obstinate Resistance, Constancy and Courage; and an Aptitude to dislike the Person proposed to them, a noble Freedom of Mind which disdains to love or hate by the Caprice of others.

Arabella, strengthening her own Resolutions by those Examples of heroic Disobedience, told her Father, with great Solemnity of Accent, that she would always obey him in all just and reasonable Things; and, being persuaded that he would never attempt to lay any Force upon her Inclinations, she would endeavour to make them conformable to his, and receive her Cousin with that Civility and Friendship due to so near a Relation, and a Person whom he honoured with his Esteem.

The Marquis, having had frequent Occasions of admiring his

Daughter's Eloquence, did not draw any unpleasing Conclusion from the nice Distinctions she made; and, being perfectly assured of her Consent whenever he demanded it, expected the Arrival of his Nephew with great Impatience.

Arabella, whose Thoughts had been fully employed since this Conversation with her Father, was indulging her Meditations in one of the most retired Walks in the Garden; when she was informed by *Lucy*, that her Cousin was come, and that the Marquis had brought him into the Garden to look for her.

That Instant they both entered the Walk, when *Arabella*, prepossessed, as she was, against any favourable Thoughts of the young *Glanville*, could not help betraying some Surprize at the Gracefulness of his Figure.

It must be confessed, said she to her Attendant, with a Smile, that this Lover my Father has brought us, is no contemptible Person: Nevertheless I feel an invincible Repugnance in myself against receiving him in that Character.

As she finished these Words, the Marquis came up, and presented Mr. *Glanville* to her; who, saluting[1] her with the Freedom of a Relation, gave her a Disgust that shewed itself immediately in her fair Face, which was overspread with such a Gloom, that the Marquis was quite astonished at it. Indeed *Arabella*, who expected he would hardly have presumed to kiss her Hand, was so surprised at his Freedom, in attempting her Lips, that she not only expressed her Indignation by Frowns, but gave him to understand he had mortally offended her.

Mr. *Glanville*, however, was neither surprised nor angry at her Resentment; but, imputing it to her Country Education, endeavoured to railly her out of her ill Humour; and the Marquis, being glad to find a Behaviour, which he thought proceeded from her Dislike of her Cousin, was only an Effect of an over-scrupulous Modesty, told her that Mr. *Glanville* had committed no Offence by saluting her, since that was a Civility which was granted to all Strangers at the first Interview, and therefore could not be refused to a Relation.

Since the World is so degenerate in its Customs from what it was formerly, said *Arabella*, with a Smile full of Contempt upon her Cousin, I am extremely happy in having lived in a Solitude which has not yet exposed me to the Mortification of being a Witness to Manners I cannot approve; for if every Person I shall meet with for the future be so deficient in their Respects to Ladies, as my Cousin is, I shall not care how much I am secluded from Society.

But, dear Lady *Bella*, interrupted Mr. *Glanville* gaily, tell me, I beseech you, how I must behave to please you; for I should be extremely glad to be honoured with your good Opinion.

The Person, resumed she, whom I must teach how to acquire my good Opinion, will, I am afraid, hardly recompense me by his Docility in learning, for the Pains I should be at in instructing him.

But, resumed *Glanville*, that I may avoid any more Occasions of offending you, only let me know how you would be approached for the future.

Since, answered she, there is no Necessity to renew the Ceremony of introducing you again to me, I have not a second Affront of that Kind to apprehend; but I pray tell me, If all Cavaliers are as presuming as yourself; and if a Relation of your Sex does not think a modest Embrace from a Lady a Welcome sufficiently tender?*

Nay, Cousin, cried *Glanville* eagerly, I am now persuaded you are in the Right; an Embrace is certainly to be preferred to a cold Salute. What would I give, that the Marquis would introduce me a second time, that I might be received with so delightful a Welcome?

The Vivacity with which he spoke this was so extremely disagreeable to *Arabella*, that she turned from him abruptly, and, striking into another Walk, ordered *Lucy* to tell him she commanded him not to follow her.

Mr. *Glanville*, however, who had no Notion of the exact Obedience which was expected from him, would have gone after her, notwithstanding this Prohibition, which *Lucy* delivered in a most peremptory Manner, after her Lady's Example: But the Marquis, who had left the two young People at Liberty to discourse, and had walked on, that he might not interrupt them, turning about, and seeing *Glanville* alone, called him to have some private Discourse with him; and, for that time, spared *Arabella* the Mortification of seeing her Commands disobeyed.

---

* The Heroines, tho' they think a Kiss of the Hand a great Condescention to a Lover, and never grant it without Blushes and Confusion; yet make no Scruple to embrace him upon every short Absence.[1]

CHAPTER IX

In which a Lover is severely punished for Faults which the
Reader never would have discovered, if he had not been told

THE Marquis, tho' he had resolved to give *Arabella* to his Nephew, was desirous he should first receive some Impressions of Tenderness for her, before he absolutely declared his Resolution; and ardently wished he might be able to overcome that Reluctance which she seemed to have for Marriage: But, tho' *Glanville* in a very few Days became passionately in Love with his charming Cousin, yet she discovered so strong a Dislike to him, that the Marquis feared it would be difficult to make her receive him for an Husband: He observed she took all Opportunities of avoiding his Conversation; and seemed always out of Temper when he addressed any thing to her; but was well enough pleased, when he discoursed with him; and would listen to the long Conversations they had together with great Attention.

The Truth is, she had too much Discernment not to see Mr. *Glanville* had a great deal of Merit; his Person was perfectly handsome; he possessed a great Share of Understanding, an easy Temper, and a Vivacity which charmed every one, but the insensible *Arabella*.

She often wondered, that a Man, who, as she told her Confident, was Master of so many fine Qualities, should have a Disposition so little capable of feeling the Passion of Love, with the Delicacy and Fervour she expected to inspire; or, that he, whose Conversation was so pleasing on every other Subject, should make so poor a Figure when he entertained her with Matters of Gallantry. However, added she, I should be to blame to desire to be beloved by Mr. *Glanville*; for I am persuaded that Passion would cause no Reformation in the Coarseness of his Manners to Ladies, which makes him so disagreeable to me, and might possibly increase my Aversion.

The Marquis, having studied his Nephew's Looks for several Days, thought he saw Inclination enough in them for *Arabella*, to make him receive the Knowlege of his Intention with Joy: He, therefore, called him into his Closet, and told him in few Words, that, if his Heart was not pre-engaged, and his Daughter capable of making him happy, he resolved to bestow her upon him, together with all his Estates.

Mr. *Glanville* received this agreeable News with the strongest
Expressions of Gratitude; assuring his Uncle, that Lady *Bella*, of
all the Women he had ever seen, was most agreeable to his Taste;
and that he felt for her all the Tenderness and Affection his Soul
was capable of.

I am glad of it, my dear Nephew, said the Marquis, embracing
him: I will allow you, added he smiling, but a few Weeks to court
her: Gain her Heart as soon as you can, and when you bring me her
Consent, your Marriage shall be solemnized immediately.

Mr. *Glanville* needed not a Repetition of so agreeable a Command: He left his Uncle's Closet, with his Heart filled with the
Expectation of his approaching Happiness; and, understanding
Arabella was in the Garden, he went to her with a Resolution to
acquaint her with the Permission her Father had given him to
make his Addresses to her.

He found his fair Cousin, as usual, accompanied with her
Women; and, seeing that, notwithstanding his Approach, they
still continued to walk with her, and impatient of the Restraint they
laid him under, I beseech you, Cousin, said he, let me have the
Pleasure of walking with you alone: What Necessity is there for
always having so many Witnesses of our Conversation? You may
retire, said he, speaking to *Lucy*, and the other Woman; I have
something to say to your Lady in private.

Stay, I command you, said *Arabella*, blushing at an Insolence so
uncommon, and take Orders from no one but myself.—I pray you,
Sir, pursued she frowning, What Intercourse of Secrets is there
between you and me, that you expect I should favour you with a
private Conversation? An Advantage which none of your Sex ever
boasted to have gained from me; and which, haply, you should be
the last upon whom I should bestow it.

You have the strangest Notions, answered *Glanville*, smiling at
the pretty Anger she discovered: Certainly you may hold a private
Conversation with any Gentleman, without giving Offence to
Decorum; and I may plead a Right to this Happiness, above any
other, since I have the Honour to be your Relation.

It is not at all surprising, resumed *Arabella* gravely, that you and
I should differ in Opinion upon this Occasion: I don't remember
that ever we agreed in any thing; and, I am apt to believe, we never
shall.

Ah! don't say so, Lady *Bella*, interrupted he: What a Prospect of

Misery you lay before me! For, if we are always to be opposite to each other, it is necessary you must hate me as much as I admire and love you.

These Words, which he accompanied with a gentle Pressure of her Hand, threw the astonished *Arabella* into such an Excess of Anger and Shame, that, for a few Moments, she was unable to utter a Word.

What a horrid Violation this, of all the Laws of Gallantry and Respect, which decree a Lover to suffer whole Years in Silence before he declares his Flame to the divine Object that causes it; and then with awful Tremblings, and submissive Prostrations at the Feet of the offended Fair!

Arabella could hardly believe her Senses when she heard a Declaration, not only made without the usual Forms, but also, that the presumtuous Criminal waited for her Answer, without seeming to have any Apprehension of the Punishment to which he was to be doomed; and that, instead of deprecating her Wrath, he looked with a smiling Wonder upon her Eyes, as if he did not fear their Lightenings would strike him dead.

Indeed, it was scarce possible for him to help smiling, and wondering too, at the extraordinary Action of *Arabella*; for, as soon as he had pronounced those fatal Words, she started back two or three Steps; cast a Look at him full of the highest Indignation; and, lifting up her fine Eyes to Heaven, seemed, in the Language of Romance, to accuse the Gods for subjecting her to so cruel an Indignity.

The Tumult of her Thoughts being a little settled, she turned again towards *Glanville*; whose Countenance expressing nothing of that Confusion and Anxiety common to an Adorer in so critical a Circumstance, her Rage returned with greater Violence than ever.

If I do not express all the Resentment your Insolence has filled me with, said she to him, affecting more Scorn than Anger, 'tis because I hold you too mean for my Resentment; but never hope for my Pardon for your presumptuous Confession of a Passion I could almost despise myself for inspiring. If it be true that you love me, go and find your Punishment in that Absence to which I doom you; and never hope I will suffer a Person in my Presence, who has affronted me in the manner you have done.

Saying this, she walked away, making a Sign to him not to follow her.

Mr. *Glanville*, who was at first disposed to laugh at the strange Manner in which she received his Expressions of Esteem for her, found something, so extremely haughty and contemptuous in the Speech she had made, that he was almost mad with Vexation.

As he had no Notion of his Cousin's heroic Sentiments, and had never read Romances, he was quite ignorant of the Nature of his Offence; and, supposing the Scorn she had expressed for him was founded upon the Difference of their Rank and Fortune, his Pride was so sensibly mortified at that Thought, and at her so insolently forbidding him her Presence, that he was once inclined to shew his Resentment of such ungenteel Usage, by quitting the Castle without taking Leave even of the Marquis, who, he thought, could not be ignorant of the Reception he was likely to meet with from his Daughter; and ought to have guarded him against it, if he really meant him so well as he seemed to do.

As he was extremely violent and hasty in his Resolutions, and nicely sensible of the least Affront, he was not in a Condition to reason justly upon the Marquis's Conduct in this Affair; and while he was fluctuating with a thousand different Resolutions, *Lucy* came to him with a Billet from her Lady, which she delivered without staying till he opened it; and was superscribed in this Manner:

Arabella, *To the most presumptuous Man in the World*—

YOU seem to acknowledge so little Respect and Deference for the Commands of a Lady, that I am afraid it will be but too necessary to reiterate that, which, at parting, I laid upon you: Know then, that I absolutely insist upon your repairing, in the only manner you are able, the Affront you have put upon me; which is, by never appearing before me again. If you think proper to confine me to my Chamber, by continuing here any longer, you will add Disobedience to the Crime by which you have already mortally offended

Arabella.

The Superscription of this Letter, and the uncommon Style of it, persuaded Mr. *Glanville*, that what he had been foolish enough to resent as an Affront, was designed as a Jest, and meant to divert him as well as herself: He examined her Behaviour again, and wondered

at his Stupidity in not discovering it before. His Resentment
vanishing immediately, he returned to the House; and went, without Ceremony, to *Arabella's* Apartment, which he entered before
she perceived him, being in a profound Musing at one of the Windows: The Noise he made, in approaching her, obliged her at last
to look up; when, starting, as if she had seen a Basilisk, she flew to
her Closet, and, shutting the Door with great Violence, commanded
him to leave her Chamber immediately.

· Mr. *Glanville*, still supposing her in Jest, intreated her to open
the Door; but, finding she continued obstinate, Well, said he,
going away, I shall be revenged on you some time hence, and make
you repent the Tricks you play me now.

Arabella not being able to imagine any thing, by these Words he
spoke in Raillery, but that he really, in the Spite and Anguish of his
Heart, threatened her with executing some terrible Enterprize;
she did not doubt, but he either intended to carry her away; or,
thinking her Aversion to him proceeded from his having a Rival
happy enough to be esteemed by her, those mysterious Words he
had uttered related to his Design of killing him; so that as she
knew, he could discover no Rival to wreak his Revenge upon, she
feared, that, at once to satisfy that Passion as well as his Love, he
would make himself Master of her Liberty: For, in fine, said she
to *Lucy*, to whom she communicated all her Thoughts, have I not
every thing to apprehend from a Man, who knows so little how to
treat my Sex with the Respect which is our Due; and who, after
having, contrary to the timorous Nature of that Passion, insulted
me with a free Declaration of Love, treated my Commands with
the utmost Contempt by appearing before me again; and even
threatens me with the Revenge he is meditating at this Moment?

Had Mr. *Glanville* been present, and heard the terrible Misfortunes which she presaged from the few Words he had jestingly
spoke, he would certainly have made her quite furious, by the
Diversion her Mistake would have afforded him. But the more she
reflected on his Words, the more she was persuaded of the terrible
Purpose of them.

'Twas in vain to acquaint her Father with the Reasons she had
for disliking his Choice: His Resolution was fixed, and if she did
not voluntarily conform to it, she exposed herself to the Attempts of
a violent and unjust Lover, who would either prevail upon the
Marquis to lay a Force upon her Inclinations, or make himself

Master of her Person, and never cease persecuting her, till he had obliged her to give him her Hand.

Having reasoned herself into a perfect Conviction that all these things must necessarily happen, she thought it both just and reasonable to provide for her own Security, by a speedy Flight: The Want of a Precedent, indeed, for an Action of this Nature, held her a few Moments in Suspense; for she did not remember to have read of any Heroine that voluntarily left her Father's House, however persecuted she might be; but she considered, that there was not any of the Ladies in Romances, in the same Circumstances with herself who was without a favoured Lover, for whose sake it might have been believed she had made an Elopement, which would have been highly prejudicial to her Glory; and, as there was no Foundation for any Suspicion of that Kind in her Case, she thought there was nothing to hinder her from withdrawing from a tyrannical Exertion of parental Authority, and the secret Machinations of a Lover, whose Aim was to take away her Liberty, either by obliging her to marry him, or by making her a Prisoner.

CHAPTER X

Contains several Incidents, in which the Reader is expected to be extremely interested

Arabella had spent some Hours in her Closet, revolving a thousand different Stratagems to escape from the Misfortune that threatened her, when she was interrupted by *Lucy*, who, after desiring Admittance, informed her, that the Marquis, having rode out to take the Air that Evening, had fallen from his Horse and received some Hurt; that he was gone to Bed, and desired to see her.

Arabella, hearing her Father was indisposed, ran to him, excessively alarmed; and reflecting on the Resolution she had just before taken, of leaving him, which aggravated her Concern, she came to his Bedside with her Eyes swimming in Tears. Mr. *Glanville* was sitting near him; but, rising at her Appearance to give her his Chair, which she accepted without taking any Notice of him, he stood at some Distance contemplating her Face, to which Sorrow had given so many Charms, that he gazed on her with an Eagerness and Delight that could not escape her Observation.

She blushed excessively at the passionate Looks he gave her; and, finding the Marquis's Indisposition not considerable enough to oblige her to a constant Attendance at his Bed-side, she took the first Opportunity of returning to her Chamber; but, as she was going out, *Glanville* presented his Hand to lead her up Stairs: Which she scornfully refusing;

Sure, Cousin, said he, a little piqued, you are not disposed to carry on your ill-natured Jest any further?

If you imagined I jested with you, said *Arabella*, I am rather to accuse the Slowness of your Understanding, for your persisting in treating me thus freely, than the Insolence I first imputed it to: But, whatever is the Cause of it, I now tell you again, that you have extremely offended me; and, if my Father's Illness did not set Bounds to my Resentment at present, I would make you know, that I would not suffer the Injury you do me, so patiently.

Since you would have me to believe you are serious, replied *Glanville*, be pleased to let me know what Offence it is you complain of; for I protest I am quite at a Loss to understand you.

Was it not enough, resumed *Arabella*, to affront me with an insolent Declaration of your Passion, but you must also, in Contempt of my Commands to the contrary, appear before me again, pursue me to my Chamber, and use the most brutal Menaces to me?

Hold, pray, Madam, interrupted *Glanville*, and suffer me to ask you, If it is my Presumption, in declaring myself your Admirer, that you are so extremely offended at?

Doubtless it is, Sir, answered *Arabella*; and such a Presumption, as, without the aggravating Circumstances you have since added to it, is sufficient to make me always your Enemy.

I beg Pardon, returned Mr. *Glanville* gravely, for that Offence; and also, for staying any longer in a House, which you have, so genteelly, turned me out of.

My Pardon, Mr. *Glanville*, resumed she, is not so easily gained: Time, and your Repentance, may, indeed, do much towards obtaining it.

Saying this, she made a Sign to him to retire; for he had walked up with her to her Chamber: But, finding he did not obey her, for really he was quite unacquainted with these Sorts of dumb

Commands, she hastily retired to her Closet, lest he should attempt to move her Pity, by any Expressions of Despair for the cruel Banishment she had doomed him to.

Mr. *Glanville*, seeing she had shut herself up in her Closet, left her Chamber, and retired to his own, more confounded than ever at the Behaviour of his Cousin.

Her bidding him so peremptorily to leave the House, would have equally persuaded him of her Ignorance and Ill-breeding, had not the Elegance of her Manners, in every other respect, proved the contrary: Nor was it possible to doubt she had a great Share of Understanding; since her Conversation, singular as some of her Sentiments seemed to him, was far superior to most other Ladies. Therefore, he concluded, the Affront he had received, proceeded from her Disdain to admit the Addresses of any Person, whose Quality was inferior to hers; which, probably, was increased by some particular Dislike she had to his Person.

His Honour would not permit him to make Use of that Advantage her Father's Authority could give him; and, wholly engrossed by his Resentment of the Usage he had received from her, he resolved to set out for *London* the next Day without seeing the Marquis, from whom he was apprehensive of some Endeavours to detain him.

Having taken this Resolution, he ordered his Servant to have the Horses ready early in the Morning; and, without taking any Notice of his Intention, he left the Castle, riding, as fast as possible, to the next Stage, from whence he wrote to his Uncle; and, dispatching a Messenger with his Letter, held on his Way to *London*.

The Marquis, being pretty well recovered from his Indisposition by a good Night's Rest, sent for Mr. *Glanville* in the Morning, to walk with him, as was his Custom, in the Garden; but, hearing he had rode out, tho' he imagined it was only to take the Air, yet he could not help accusing him, in his own Thoughts, of a little Neglect; for which he resolved to chide him, when he returned: But his long Stay filling him with some Surprize, he was beginning to express his Fears that something had befallen him, to *Arabella*, who was then with him; when a Servant presented him the Letter, which Mr. *Glanville's* Messenger had that Moment brought.

The Marquis casting his Eyes on the Direction, and knowing his Nephew's Hand, Bless me, cried he, extremely surprised, What can this mean? *Bella*, added he, here's a Letter from your Cousin.

Arabella, at these Words, started up; and, preventing her Father, with a respectful Action, from opening it, I beseech you, my Lord, said she, before you read this Letter, suffer me to assure you, that, if it contains any thing fatal, I am not at all accessary to it: 'Tis true I have banished my Cousin, as a Punishment for the Offence he was guilty of towards me; but, Heaven is my Witness, I did not desire his Death; and if he has taken any violent Resolution against himself, he has greatly exceeded my Commands.

The Marquis, whose Surprize was considerably increased by these Words, hastily broke open the Letter, which she perceiving, hurried out of the Room; and, locking herself up in her Closet, began to bewail the Effect of her Charms, as if she was perfectly assured of her Cousin's Death.

The Marquis, however, who, from Lady *Bella*'s Exclamation, had prepared himself for the Knowlege of some very extra-ordinary Accident, was less surprised, than he would otherwise have been, at the Contents; which were as follow:

My Lord,

As my leaving your House so abruptly will certainly make me appear guilty of a most unpardonable Rudeness, I cannot dispense with myself from acquainting your Lordship with the Cause; though, to spare the Reproaches Lady *Bella* will probably cast on me for doing so, I could wish you knew it by any other Means.

But, my Lord, I value your Esteem too much to hazard the Loss of it by suffering you to imagine, that I am capable of doing any thing to displease you. Lady *Bella* was pleased to order me to stay no longer in the House; and menaced me with some very terrible Usage, if I disobeyed her: She used so many other contemptuous Expressions to me, that, I am persuaded, I shall never be so happy as to possess the Honour you designed for,

My Lord,

Your most obedient, &c.
Charles Glanville.

When the Marquis had read this Letter, he went to his Daughter's Apartment with an Intention to chide her severely for her Usage of his Nephew; but, seeing her come to meet him with her Eyes bathed in Tears, he insensibly lost some Part of his Resentment.

Alas! my Lord, said she, I know you come prepared to load me
with Reproaches, upon my Cousin's Account; but, I beseech your
Lordship, do not aggravate my Sorrows: Tho' I banished Mr.
Glanville, I did not desire his Death; and, questionless, if he knew
how I *resent*[1] it, his Ghost would be satisfied with the Sacrifice I
make him.

The Marquis, not being able to help smiling at this Conceit,
which he saw had so strongly possessed her Imagination, that she
had no sort of Doubt but that her Cousin was dead, asked her, If
she really believed Mr. *Glanville* loved her well enough to die with
Grief at her ill Usage of him?

If, said she, he loves me not well enough to die for me, he certainly loves me but little; and I am the less obliged to him.

But I desire to know, interrupted the Marquis, For what Crime
it was you took the Liberty to banish him from my House?

I banished him, my Lord, resumed she, for his Presumption in
telling me he loved me.

That Presumption, as you call it, tho' I know not for what
Reason, said the Marquis, was authorized by me: Therefore,
know, *Bella*, that I not only permit him to love you, but I also
expect you should endeavour to return his Affection; and look
upon him as the Man whom I design for your Husband: There's his
Letter, pursued he, putting it into her Hand. I blush for the Rudeness you have been guilty of; but endeavour to repair it, by a more
obliging Behaviour for the future: I am going to send after him
immediately to prevail upon to return: Therefore, write him an
Apology, I charge you; and have it done by the Time my Messenger is ready to set out.

Saying this, he went out of the Room; and *Arabella* eagerly
opened the Letter; and, finding it in a Style so different from what
she expected, her Dislike of him returned with more Violence
than ever.

Ah! the Traitor! said she aloud, Is it thus that he endeavours to
move my Compassion? How greatly did I over-rate his Affection,
when I imagined his Despair was capable of killing him? Disloyal
Man! pursued she, walking about, Is it by Complaints to my
Father that thou expectest to succeed? And dost thou imagine the
Heart of *Arabella* is to be won by Violence and Injustice?

In this manner she wasted the Time allotted for her to write;
and, when the Marquis sent for her Letter, having no Intention to

comply, she went to his Chamber, conjuring him not to oblige her to a Condescension so unworthy of her.

The Marquis, being now excessively angry with her, rose up in a Fury, and, leading her to his Writing-Desk, ordered her, instantly, to write to her Cousin.

If I must write, my Lord, said she, sobbing, pray be so good as to dictate what I must say.

Apologize for your rude Behaviour, said the Marquis; and desire him, in the most obliging manner you can, to return.

Arabella, seeing there was a necessity for obeying, took up the Pen, and wrote the following Billet:

The unfortunate Arabella, *to the most ungenerous* Glanville.

IT is not by the Power I have over you, that I command you to return, for I disclaim any Empire over so unworthy a Subject; but, since it is my Father's Pleasure I should invite you back, I must let you know, that I repeal your Banishment, and expect you will immediately return with the Messenger who brings this; however, to spare your Acknowlegements, know, that it is in Obedience to my Father's absolute Commands, that you receive this Mandate from

Arabella.

Having finished this Billet, she gave it to the Marquis to read; who, finding a great deal of his own Haughtiness of Temper in it, could not resolve to check her for a Disposition so like his own: Yet he told her, her Stile was very uncommon: And pray, added he, smiling, who taught you to superscribe your Letters thus, 'The unfortunate *Arabella*, to the most ungenerous *Glanville?*' Why, *Bella*, this Superscription is wholly calculated for the Bearer's Information: But come, alter it immediately; for I don't choose my Messenger should know, that you are unfortunate, or that my Nephew is ungenerous.

Pray, my Lord, replied *Arabella*, content yourself with what I have already done in Obedience to your Commands, and suffer my Letter to remain as it is: Methinks it is but reasonable I should express some little Resentment at the Complaint my Cousin has been pleased to make to you against me; nor can I possibly make my Letter more obliging, without being guilty of an unpardonable Meanness.

You are a strange Girl, replied the Marquis, taking the Letter, and inclosing it in one from himself; in which he earnestly intreated his Nephew to return, threatening him with his Displeasure, if he disobeyed; and assuring him, that his Daughter would receive him as well as he could possibly desire.

The Messenger being dispatched, with Orders to ride Post, and overtake the young Gentleman, he obeyed his Orders so well, that he came up with him at —, where he intended to lodge that Night.

Mr. *Glanville*, who expected his Uncle would make use of some Methods to recal him, opened his Letter without any great Emotion; but seeing another inclosed, his Heart leaped to his Mouth, not doubting but it was a Letter from *Arabella*; but the Contents surprised him so much, that he hardly knew whether he ought to look upon them as an Invitation to return, or a new Affront, her Words were so distant and haughty. The Superscription being much the same with a Billet he had received from her in the Garden, which had made him conclude her in Jest, he knew not what to think of it: One would swear this dear Girl's Head is turned, said he to himself, if she had not more *Wit* than her whole Sex besides.

After reading *Arabella*'s Letter several times, he at last opened his Uncle's; and, seeing the pressing Instances he made him to return, he resolved to obey; and the next Morning set out for the Castle.

Arabella, during the time her Cousin was expected, appeared so melancholy and reserved, that the Marquis was extremely uneasy: You have never, said he to her, disobeyed me in any one Action of your Life; and I may with reason expect you will conform to my Will in the Choice I have made of a Husband for you, since it is impossible to make any Objection either to his Person or Mind; and, being the Son of my Sister, he is certainly not unworthy of you, tho' he has not a Title.

My first Wish, my Lord, replied *Arabella*, is to live single, not being desirous of entering into any Engagement which may hinder my Solicitude and Cares, and lessen my Attendance, upon the best of Fathers, who, till now, has always most tenderly complied with my Inclinations in every thing: But if it is your absolute Command, that I should marry, give me not to one who, tho' he has the Honour to be allied to you, has neither merited your Esteem, or my Favour, by any Action worthy of his Birth, or the Passion he pretends to have for me; for, in fine, my Lord, by what Services has he de-

served the Distinction with which you honour him? Has he ever
delivered you from any considerable Danger? Has he saved your
Life, and hazarded his own, for you, upon any Occasion whatever?
Has he merited my Esteem, by his Sufferings, Fidelity, and
Respect; or, by any great and generous Action, given me a Testimony of his Love, which should oblige me to reward him with my
Affection? Ah! my Lord, I beseech you, think not so unworthily
of your Daughter, as to bestow her upon one who has done so little
to deserve her: If my Happiness be dear to you, do not precipitate
me into a State from whence you cannot recal me, with a Person
whom I can never affect.

She would have gone on, but the Marquis interrupted her
sternly: I'll hear no more, said he, of your foolish and ridiculous
Objections: What Stuff is this you talk of? What Service am I to
expect from my Nephew? And by what Sufferings is he to merit
your Esteem? Assure yourself, *Arabella*, continued he, that I will
never pardon you, if you presume to treat my Nephew in the
Manner you have done: I perceive you have no real Objection to
make to him; therefore I expect you will endeavour to obey me
without Reluctance; for, since you seem to be so little acquainted
with what will most conduce to your own Happiness, you must
not think it strange, if I insist upon directing your Choice in the
most important Business of your Life.

Arabella was going to reply; but the Marquis ordered her to be
silent; and she went to her own Apartment in so much Affliction,
that she thought her Misfortunes were not exceeded by any she had
ever read.

CHAPTER XI

In which a logical Argument is unseasonably interrupted

THE Marquis was also extremely uneasy at her Obstinacy: He
desired nothing more ardently than to marry her to his Nephew;
but he could not resolve to force her Consent; and, however
determined he appeared to her, yet, in Reality, he intended only to
use Persuasions to effect what he desired; and, from the natural

Sweetness of her Temper, he was sometimes not without Hopes, that she might, at last, be prevailed upon to comply.

His Nephew's Return restored him to Part of his usual Tranquillity: After he had gently chid him for suffering himself to be so far transported with his Resentment at the little Humours of a Lady, as to leave his House, without acquainting him, he bid him go to *Arabella*, and endeavour to make his Peace with her.

Mr. *Glanville* accordingly went to her Apartment, resolving to oblige her to come to some Explanation with him concerning the Offence she complained of; but that fair incensed Lady, who had taken Shelter in her Closet, ordered *Lucy* to tell him she was indisposed, and could not see him.

Glanville, however, comforted himself for this Disappointment by the Hopes of seeing her at Supper; and accordingly she came, when the Supper-Bell rung, and, making a very cool Compliment to her Cousin, placed herself at Table: The soft Languor that appeared in her Eyes, gave such an additional Charm to one of the loveliest Faces in the World, that *Glanville*, who sat opposite to her, could not help gazing on her with a very particular Attention; he often spoke to her, and asked her trifling Questions, for the sake of hearing the Sound of her Voice, which Sorrow had made inchantingly sweet.

When Supper was over, she would have retired; but the Marquis desired her to stay and entertain her Cousin, while he went to look over some Dispatches he had received from *London*.

Arabella blushed with Anger at this Command; but, not daring to disobey, she kept her Eyes fixed on the Ground, as if she dreaded to hear something that would displease her.

Well, Cousin, said *Glanville*, tho' you desire to have no Empire over so unworthy a Subject as myself, yet I hope you are not displeased at my returning, in Obedience to your Commands.

Since I am not allowed any Will of my own, said she, sighing, it matters not whether I am pleased, or displeased; nor is it of any Consequence to you to know.

Indeed but it is, Lady *Bella*, interrupted he; for if I knew how to please you, I would never, if I could help it, offend: Therefore, I beg you, tell me how I have disobliged you; for, certainly, you have treated me as harshly as if I had been guilty of some very terrible Offence.

You had the Boldness, said she, to talk to me of Love; and you well know that Persons of my Sex and Quality are not permitted to listen to such Discourses; and if, for that Offence, I banished you my Presence, I did no more than Decency required of me; and which I would yet do, were I Mistress of my own Actions.

But is it possible, Cousin, said *Glanville*, that you can be angry with any one for loving you? Is that a Crime of so high a Nature as to merit an eternal Banishment from your Presence?

Without telling you, said *Arabella*, blushing, whether I am angry at being loved, 'tis sufficient you know, that I will not pardon the Man who shall have the Presumption to tell me he loves me.

But, Madam, interrupted *Glanville*, if the Person who tells you he loves you, be of a Rank not beneath you, I conceive you are not at all injured by the favourable Sentiments he feels for you; and, tho' you are not disposed to make any Returns to his Passion, yet you are certainly obliged to him for his good Opinion.

Since Love is not voluntary, replied *Arabella*, I am not obliged to any Person for loving me; for, questionless, if he could help it, he would.

If it is not a voluntary Favour, interrupted *Glanville*, it is not a voluntary Offence; and, if you do not think yourself obliged by the one, neither are you at Liberty to be offended with the other.

The Question, said *Arabella*, is not whether I ought to be offended at being loved, but whether it is not an Offence to be told I am so.

If there is nothing criminal in the Passion itself, Madam, resumed *Glanville*, certainly there can be no Crime in declaring it.

However specious your Arguments may appear, interrupted *Arabella*, I am persuaded it is an unpardonable Crime to tell a Lady you love her; and, tho' I had nothing else to plead, yet the Authority of Custom is sufficient to prove it.

Custom, Lady *Bella*, said *Glanville*, smiling, is wholly on my Side; for the Ladies are so far from being displeased at the Addresses of their Lovers, that their chiefest Care is to gain them, and their greatest Triumph to hear them talk of their Passion: So, Madam, I hope you'll allow that Argument has no Force.

I don't know, answered *Arabella*, what Sort of Ladies there are who allow such unbecoming Liberties, but I am certain, that *Statira*, *Parisatis*, *Clelia*, *Mandana*,[1] and all the illustrious Heroines of Antiquity, whom it is a Glory to resemble, would never admit of such Discourses.

Ah for Heaven's sake, Cousin, interrupted *Glanville*, endeavouring to stifle a Laugh, do not suffer yourself to be governed by such
antiquated Maxims! The World is quite different to what it was in
those Days; and the Ladies in this Age would as soon follow the
Fashions of the *Greek* and *Roman* Ladies, as mimick their Manners;
and I believe they would become one as ill as the other.

I am sure, replied *Arabella*, the World is not more virtuous now
than it was in their Days, and there is good Reason to believe it is
not much wiser; and I don't see why the Manners of this Age are to
be preferred to those of former ones, unless they are wiser and
better: However, I cannot be persuaded, that Things are as you
say, and that when I am a little better acquainted with the World, I
shall find as many Persons who resemble *Oroondates, Artaxerxes,*
and the illustrious Lover of *Clelia*,[1] as those who are like *Tiribases,
Artaxes*,[2] and the presuming and insolent *Glanville*.

By the Epithets you give me Madam, said *Glanville*, I find you
have placed me in very bad Company: But pray, Madam, if the
illustrious Lover of *Clelia* had never discovered his Passion, how
would the World have come to the Knowlege of it?

He did not discover his Passion, Sir, resumed *Arabella*, till, by
the Services he did the noble *Clelius,* and his incomparable
Daughter, he could plead some Title to their Esteem: He several
times preserved the Life of that renowned *Roman*; delivered the
beautiful *Clelia* when she was a Captive; and, in fine, conferred so
many Obligations upon them, and all their Friends, as he might
well expect to be pardoned by the divine *Clelia* for daring to love
her. Nevertheless, she used him very harshly, when he first
declared his Passion, and banished him also from her Presence;
and it was a long time before she could prevail upon herself to
compassionate his Sufferings.

The Marquis coming in interrupted *Arabella*; upon which she
took Occasion to retire; leaving *Glanville* more captivated with her
than ever.

He found her Usage of him was grounded upon Examples she
thought it her Duty to follow; and, strange as her Notions of Life
appeared, yet they were supported with so much Wit and Delicacy,
that he could not help admiring her, while he foresaw, the Oddity
of her Humour would throw innumerable Difficulties in his Way,
before he should be able to obtain her.

However, as he was really passionately in Love with her, he

resolved to accommodate himself, as much as possible, to her Taste, and endeavour to gain her Heart by a Behaviour most agreeable to her: He therefore assumed an Air of great Distance and Respect; never mentioned his Affection, nor the Intentions of her Father in his Favour; and the Marquis, observing his Daughter conversed with him with less Reluctance than usual, leaving to Time, and the Merit of his Nephew, to dispose her to comply with his Desires, resolved not to interpose his Authority in an Affair upon which her own Happiness so much depended.

CHAPTER XII

In which the Reader will find a Specimen of the true Pathetic, in a Speech of Oroondates. — *The Adventure of the Books*

Arabella saw the Change in her Cousin's Behaviour with a great deal of Satisfaction; for she did not doubt but his Passion was as strong as ever; but that he forbore, thro' Respect, from entertaining her with any Expressions of it: Therefore she now conversed with him with the greatest Sweetness and Complaisance: She would walk with him for several Hours in the Garden, leaning upon his Arm; and charmed him to the last Degree of Admiration by the agreeable Sallies of her Wit, and her fine Reasoning upon every Subject he proposed.

It was with the greatest Difficulty he restrained himself from telling her a Thousand times a Day that he loved her to Excess, and conjuring her to give her Consent to her Father's Designs in his Favour: But, tho' he could get over his Fears of offending her, yet it was impossible to express any Sentiments of this Nature to her, without having her Women Witnesses of his Discourse; for, when he walked with her in the Garden, *Lucy,* and another Attendant, always followed her: If he sat with her in her own Chamber, her Women were always at one End of it: And, when they were both in the Marquis's Apartment, where her Women did not follow her, poor *Glanville* found himself embarrassed by his Presence; for, conceiving his Nephew had Opportunities enough of talking to his Daughter in private, he always partook of their Conversation.

He passed some Weeks in this Manner, extremely chagrined at the little Progress he made; and was beginning to be heartily weary of the Constraint he laid upon himself, when *Arabella*, one Day, furnished him, without designing it, with an Opportunity of talking to her on the Subject he wished for.

When I reflect, said she, laughing, upon the Difference there was between us some Days ago, and the Familiarity in which we live at present, I cannot imagine by what means you have arrived to a good Fortune you had so little Reason to expect; for, in fine, you have given me no Signs of Repentance for the Fault you committed, which moved me to banish you; and I am not certain whether, in conversing with you in the manner I do, I give you not as much Reason to find Fault with my too great Easiness, as you did me to be displeased with your Presumption.

Since, returned *Glanville*, I have not persisted in the Commission of those Faults which displeased you, what greater Signs of Repentance can you desire, than this Reformation in my Behaviour?

But Repentance ought to precede Reformation, replied *Arabella*; otherwise, there is great room to suspect it is only feigned: And a sincere Repentance shews itself in such visible Marks, that one can hardly be deceived in that which is genuine. I have read of many indiscreet Lovers, who not succeeding in their Addresses, have pretended to repent, and acted as you do; that is, without giving any Signs of Contrition for the Fault they had committed, have eat and slept well, never lost their Colour, or grew one bit thinner, by their Sorrow; but contented themselves with saying they repented; and, without changing their Disposition to renew their Fault, only concealed their Intention, for fear of losing any favourable Opportunity of committing it again: But true Repentance, as I was saying, not only produces Reformation, but the Person who is possessed of it voluntarily punishes himself for the Faults he has been guilty of. Thus *Mazares*, deeply repenting of the Crime his Passion for the divine *Mandana* had forced him to commit; as a Punishment, obliged himself to follow the Fortune of his glorious Rival; obey all his Commands; and, fighting under his Banners, assist him to gain the Possession of his adored Mistress.[1] Such a glorious Instance of Self-denial was, indeed, a sufficient Proof of his Repentance; and infinitely more convincing than the Silence he imposed upon himself with respect to his Passion.

Oroondates, to punish himself for his Presumption, in daring to tell the admirable *Statira*, that he loved her, resolved to die, to expiate his Crime; and, doubtless, would have done so, if his fair Mistress, at the Intreaty of her Brother, had not commanded him to live.[1]

But pray, Lady *Bella*, interrupted *Glanville*, were not these Gentlemen happy at last in the Possession of their Mistresses?

Doubtless they were, Sir, resumed she; but it was not till after numberless Misfortunes, infinite Services, and many dangerous Adventures, in which their Fidelity was put to the strongest Trials imaginable.

I am glad, however, said *Glanville*, that the Ladies were not insensible; for, since you do not disapprove of their Compassion for their Lovers, it is to be hoped you will not be always as inexorable as you are now.

When I shall be so fortunate, interrupted she, to meet with a Lover who shall have as pure and perfect a Passion for me, as *Oroondates* had for *Statira*; and give me as many glorious Proofs of his Constancy and Affection, doubtless I shall not be ungrateful: But, since I have not the Merits of *Statira*, I ought not to pretend to her good Fortune; and shall be very well contented if I escape the Persecutions which Persons of my Sex, who are not frightfully ugly, are always exposed to, without hoping to inspire such a Passion as that of *Oroondates*.

I should be glad to be better acquainted with the Actions of this happy Lover, Madam, said *Glanville*; that, forming myself upon his Example, I may hope to please a Lady as worthy of my Regard as *Statira* was of his.

For Heaven's sake, Cousin, resumed *Arabella*, laughing, how have you spent your Time; and to what Studies have you devoted all your Hours, that you could find none to spare for the Perusal of Books from which all useful Knowlege may be drawn; which give us the most shining Examples of Generosity, Courage, Virtue, and Love; which regulate our Actions, form our Manners, and inspire us with a noble Desire of emulating those great, heroic, and virtuous Actions, which made those Persons so glorious in their Age, and so worthy Imitation in ours? However, as it is never too late to improve, suffer me to recommend to you the reading of these Books, which will soon make you discover the Improprieties you have been guilty of; and will, probably, induce you to avoid them for the future.

I shall certainly read them, if you desire it, said *Glanville*; and I have so great an Inclination to be agreeable to you, that I shall embrace every Opportunity of becoming so; and will therefore take my Instructions from these Books, if you think proper, or from yourself; which, indeed, will be the quickest Method of teaching me.

Arabella having ordered one of her Women to bring *Cleopatra*,[1] *Cassandra*, *Clelia*, and the Grand *Cyrus*, from her Library, *Glanville* no sooner saw the Girl return, sinking under the Weight of those voluminous Romances, but he began to tremble at the Apprehension of his Cousin laying her Commands upon him to read them; and repented of his Complaisance, which exposed him to the cruel Necessity of performing what to him appeared an *Herculean* Labour, or else incurring her Anger by his Refusal.

Arabella, making her Women place the Books upon a Table before her, opened them, one after another, with Eyes sparkling with Delight; while *Glanville* sat rapt in Admiration at the Sight of so many huge Folio's, written, as he conceived, upon the most trifling Subjects imaginable.

I have chosen out these few, said *Arabella* (not observing his Consternation) from a great many others, which compose the most valuable Part of my Library; and, by that time you have gone thro' these, I imagine you will be considerably improved.

Certainly, Madam, replied *Glanville*, turning over the Leaves in great Confusion, one may, as you say, be greatly improved; for these Books contain a great deal: And, looking over a Page of *Cassandra*, without any Design, read these Words, which were Part of *Oroondates*'s Soliloquy when he received a cruel Sentence from *Statira*:

'Ah cruel! says this Miserable Lover, and what have I done to merit it? Examine the Nature of my Offence, and you will see I am not so guilty, but that my Death may free me from Part of that Severity: Shall your Hatred last longer than my Life? And can you detest a Soul that forsakes its Body only to obey you? No, no, you are not so hard-hearted; that Satisfaction will, doubtless, content you: And, when I shall cease to be, doubtless I shall cease to be odious to you.'

Upon my Soul, said *Glanville*, stifling a Laugh with great Difficulty, I cannot help blaming the Lady this sorrowful Lover complains of, for her great Cruelty; for here he gives one Reason to suspect, that she will not even be contented with his dying in Obedience to her Commands, but will hate him after Death; an Impiety quite inexcusable in a Christian!

You condemn this illustrious Princess with very little Reason, interrupted *Arabella*, smiling at his Mistake; for, besides that she was not a Christian, and ignorant of those Divine Maxims of Charity and Forgiveness, which Christians, by their Profession, are obliged to practise, she was very far from desiring the Death of *Oroondates*; for, if you will take the Pains to read the succeeding Passages, you will find that she expresses herself in the most obliging Manner in the World; for when *Oroondates* tells her he would live, if she would consent he should, the Princess most sweetly replies, 'I not only consent, but also intreat it; and, if I have any Power, command it.' However, lest you should fall into the other Extreme, and blame this great Princess for her Easiness (as you before condemned her for her Cruelty), 'tis necessary you should know how she was induced to this favourable Behaviour to her Lover: Therefore pray read the whole Transaction. Stay! here it begins, continued she; turning over a good many Pages, and marking where he should begin to read.

Glanville, having no great Stomach to the Task, endeavoured to evade it, by intreating his Cousin to relate the Passages she desired he should be acquainted with: But she declining it, he was obliged to obey; and began to read where she directed him: And, to leave him at Liberty to read with the greater Attention, she left him, and went to a Window at another End of the Chamber.

Mr. *Glanville*, who was not willing to displease her, examined the Task she had set him, resolving, if it was not a very hard one, to comply; but, counting the Pages, he was quite terrified at the Number, and could not prevail upon himself to read them: Therefore, glancing them over, he pretended to be deeply engaged in reading, when, in Reality, he was contemplating the surprising Effect these Books had produced in the Mind of his Cousin; who, had she been untainted with the ridiculous Whims they created in her Imagination, was, in his Opinion, one of the most accomplished Ladies in the World.

When he had sat long enough to make her believe he had read what she had desired, he rose up, and, joining her at the Window, began to talk of the Pleasantness of the Evening, instead of the Rigour of *Statira*.

Arabella coloured with Vexation at his extreme Indifference in a Matter which was of such prodigious Consequence, in her Opinion; but disdaining to put him in mind of his Rudeness, in quitting a Subject they had not thoroughly discussed, and which she had taken so much Pains to make him comprehend, she continued silent; and would not condescend to afford him an Answer to any thing he said.

Glanville, by her Silence and Frowns, was made sensible of his Fault; and, to repair it, began to talk of the inexorable *Statira*, though, indeed, he did not well know what to say.

Arabella, clearing up a little, did not disdain to answer him upon her favourite Topic: I knew, said she, you would be ready to blame this Princess equally for her Rigour and her Kindness; but it must be remembred that, what she did in Favour of *Oroondates*, was wholly owing to the Generosity of *Artaxerxes*.

Here she stopped, expecting *Glanville* to give his Opinion; who, strangely puzzled, replied at random, To be sure, Madam, he was a very generous Rival.

Rival! cried *Arabella*; *Artaxerxes* the Rival of *Oroondates*! Why certainly you have lost your Wits: He was *Statira*'s Brother; and it was to his Mediation that *Oroondates*, or *Orontes*, owed his Happiness.

Certainly, Madam, replied *Glanville*, it was very generous in *Artaxerxes*, as he was Brother to *Statira*, to interpose in the Behalf of an unfortunate Lover; and both *Oroondates*, and *Orontes*, were extremely obliged to him.

Orontes, replied *Arabella*, was more obliged to him than *Oroondates*; since the Quality of *Orontes* was infinitely below that of *Oroondates*.

But, Madam, interrupted *Glanville* (extremely pleased at his having so well got over the Difficulty he had been in), which of these two Lovers did *Statira* make happy?

This unlucky Question immediately informed *Arabella*, that she had been all this time the Dupe of her Cousin; who, if he had read a single Page, would have known that *Orontes* and *Oroondates* was the same Person; the Name of *Orontes* being assumed by *Oroondates*, to conceal his real Name and Quality.

The Shame and Rage she conceived at so glaring a Proof of his Disrespect, and the Ridicule to which she had exposed herself, were so great, that she could not find Words severe enough to express her Resentment; but, protesting that no Consideration whatever should oblige her to converse with him again, she ordered him instantly to quit her Chamber; and assured him, if he ever attempted to approach her again, she would submit to the most terrible Effects of her Father's Resentment, rather than be obliged to see a Person who had, by his unworthy Behaviour, made himself her Scorn and Aversion.

Glanville, who saw himself going to be discarded a second time, attempted, with great Submission, to move her to recal her cruel Sentence; but *Arabella*, bursting into Tears, complained so pathetically of the Cruelty of her Destiny, in exposing her to the hated Importunities of a Man she despised, and whose Presence was so insupportable, that *Glanville*, thinking it best to let her Rage evaporate a little before he attempted to pacify her, quitted her Chamber; cursing *Statira* and *Orontes* a thousand times, and loading the Authors of those Books with all the Imprecations his Rage could suggest.

CHAPTER XIII

The Adventure of the Books continued

In this Temper he went to the Gardens to pass over the Chagrin this unfortunate Accident had given him; when, meeting the Marquis, who insisted upon knowing the Cause of that ill Humour, so visible in his Countenance, *Glanville* related all that had passed; but, in Spite of his Anger, it was impossible for him to repeat the Circumstances of his Disgrace without laughing, as well as the Marquis; who thought the Story so extremely diverting, that he would needs hear it over again.

However, *Charles*, said he, though I shall do what I can to gain your Pardon from *Bella*, yet I shall not scruple to own you acted extremely wrong, in not reading what she desired you; for, besides losing an Opportunity of obliging her, you drew yourself into a terrible Dilemma; for how was it possible for you to evade a Discovery of the Cheat you put upon her, when she began to talk with you upon those Passages she had desired you to read?

I acknowlege my Error, my Lord, answered *Glanville*; but if you restore me to my Cousin's Favour again, I promise you to repair it by a different Behaviour for the future.

I'll see what I can do for you, said the Marquis; leaving him, to go to *Arabella*'s Apartment, who had retired to her Closet, extremely afflicted at this new Insult she had received from her Cousin: Her Grief was the more poignant, as she was beginning to imagine, by the Alteration in his Behaviour, that he would prove such a Lover as she wished; for Mr. *Glanville*'s Person and Qualifications had attracted her particular Notice: And, to speak in the Language of Romance, she did not hate him; but, on the contrary, was very much disposed to wish him well: Therefore, it was no Wonder she extremely resented the Affront she had received from him.

The Marquis, not finding her in her Chamber, proceeded to her Closet, where her Women informed him she was retired; and, knocking gently at the Door, was admitted by *Arabella*, whom he immediately discerned to have been weeping very much; for her fine Eyes were red and swelled, and the Traces of her Tears might still be observed on her fair Face; which, at the Sight of the Marquis, was overspread with a Blush, as if she was conscious of her Weakness in lamenting the Crime her Cousin had been guilty of.

The Marquis drew a favourable Omen for his Nephew from her Tears and Confusion; but, not willing to increase it, by acknowleging he had observed it, he told her he was come, at Mr. *Glanville*'s Request, to make up the Quarrel between them.

Ah! my Lord, interrupted *Arabella*, speak no more to me of that unworthy Man, who has so grossly abused my Favour, and the Privilege I allowed him: His baseness and Ingratitude are but too manifest; and there is nothing I so much regret as my Weakness in restoring him to Part of my good Opinion, after he had once forfeited it, by an Insolence not to be paralleled.

Indeed, *Bella*, said the Marquis, smiling, you resent too deeply these slight Matters: I can't think my Nephew so guilty as you would have me believe he is; and you ought neither to be angry or surprised, that he preferred your Conversation before reading in a foolish old-fashioned Book that you put in his Hands.

If your Lordship had ever read these Books, replied *Arabella*, reddening with Vexation, 'tis probable you would have another Opinion of them; but, however that may be, my Cousin is not to be excused for the Contempt he shewed to my Commands; and for daring, by the Cheat he put on me, to expose me to the Shame of seeing myself so ridiculously imposed upon.

However, you must forgive him, said the Marquis; and I insist upon it, before I quit your Apartment, that you receive him into Favour.

Pardon me, my Lord, replied *Arabella*; this is what I neither can, nor ought to do; and I hope you will not wrong me so much as to continue to desire it.

Nay, *Bella*, said he, this is carrying Things too far, and making trifling Disputes of too great Consequence: I am surprised at your Treatment of a Man whom, after all, if ever you intend to obey me, you must consent to marry.

There is no Question, my Lord, replied she, but it would be my Glory to obey you in whatever is possible; but this you command me now to do, not being so, I conceive you will rather impute my Refusal to Necessity, than Choice.

How! returned the Marquis, will you endeavour to persuade me, that it is not possible Mr. *Glanville* should be your Husband?

'Tis impossible he should be so with my Consent, resumed *Arabella*; and I cannot give it without wounding my own Quiet in a most sensible manner.

Come, come, *Bella*, said the Marquis (fretting at her extreme Obstinacy), this is too much: I am to blame to indulge your Foibles in this Manner: Your Cousin is worthy of your Affection, and you cannot refuse it to him without incurring my Displeasure.

Since my Affection is not in my own Power to bestow, said *Arabella*, weeping, I know not how to remove your Displeasure; but, questionless, I know how to die, to avoid the Effects of what would be to me the most terrible Misfortune in the World.

Foolish Girl! interrupted the Marquis, how strangely do you talk? Are the Thoughts of Death become so familiar to you, that you speak of dying with so little Concern?

Since, my Lord, resumed she, in an exalted Tone, I do not yield, either in Virtue or Courage, to many others of my Sex, who, when persecuted like me, have fled to Death for Relief, I know not why I should be thought less capable of it than they; and if *Artimisa*, *Candace*, and the beautiful Daughter of *Cleopatra*,[1] could brave the Terrors of Death for the sake of the Men they loved, there is no Question but I also could imitate their Courage, to avoid the Man I have so much Reason to hate.

The Girl is certainly distracted, interrupted the Marquis, excessively enraged at the strange Speech she had uttered: These foolish Books my Nephew talks of have turned her Brain! Where are they? pursued he, going into her Chamber: I'll burn all I can lay my Hands upon.[1]

Arabella, trembling for the Fate of her Books, followed her Father into the Room; who seeing the Books which had caused this woful Adventure lying upon the Table, he ordered one of her Women to carry them into his Apartment, vowing he would commit them all to the Flames.

Arabella not daring, in the Fury he was in, to interpose, he went out of the Room, leaving her to bewail the Fate of so many illustrious Heroes and Heroines, who, by an Effect of a more cruel Tyranny than any they had ever experienced before, were going to be cast into the merciless Flames; which would, doubtless, pay very little Regard to the divine Beauties of the admirable *Clelia*, or the heroic Valour of the brave *Orontes*;[2] and the rest of those great Princes and Princesses, whose Actions *Arabella* proposed for the Model of hers.

Fortune, however, which never wholly forsook these illustrious Personages, rescued them from so unworthy a Fate, and brought Mr. *Glanville* into the Marquis's Chamber just as he was giving Orders to have them destroyed.

END of the FIRST BOOK.

BOOK II

CHAPTER I

In which the Adventure of the Books is happily concluded

THE Marquis, as soon as he saw Mr. *Glanville*, told him he was resolved to cure *Arabella* of her Whims, by burning the Books that had put them into her Head: I have seized upon some of them, pursued he, smiling; and you may, if you please, wreak your Spite upon these Authors of your Disgrace, by burning them yourself.

Though I have all the reason in the World to be enraged with that Incendiary *Statira*, said *Glanville* laughing, for the Mischief she has done me; yet I cannot consent to put such an Affront upon my Cousin, as to burn her favourite Books: And now I think of it, my Lord, pursued he, I'll endeavour to make a Merit with Lady *Bella* by saving them: Therefore spare them, at my Request, and let me carry them to her. I shall be quite unhappy till we are Friends again.

You may do as you will, said the Marquis; but I think it encouraging her in her Follies to give them to her again.

Glanville, without replying, eagerly took up the Books, for fear the Marquis should change his Mind; and, highly delighted with the Opportunity he had got of making his Peace with Lady *Bella*, ran to her Apartment, loaded with these kind Intercessors; and, making his Way by *Lucy*, who would have opposed him, penetrated even into the Closet of the melancholy Fair-one, who was making bitter Reflections on the Cruelty of her Destiny, and bewailing her Loss with a Deluge of Tears.

As ridiculous as the Occasion of these Tears was, yet *Glanville* could not behold them without being affected: Assuming, therefore, a Countenance as sad as he was able, he laid the Books before her; and told her, he hoped she would excuse his coming into her Presence without her Permission, since it was only to restore her those Books, whose Loss she seemed so greatly to lament; and

added, that it was with much Difficulty he prevailed upon the
Marquis not to burn them immediately; and his Fears, that he
might really do as he threatened, made him snatch them up, and
bring them, with so little Ceremony, into her Closet.

Arabella, whose Countenance brightened into a Smile of pleasing
Surprize at the Sight of her recovered Treasure, turned her bright
Eyes upon *Glanville* with a Look of Complacency that went to his
Heart.

I well perceive, said she, that, in exaggerating the Merit of this
little Service you have done me, you expect I should suffer it to
cancel your past Offences: I am not ungrateful enough to be insensible of any Kindness that is shewn me; and, tho' I might be
excused for suspecting it was rather Policy than Friendship, that
induced you to seek my Satisfaction, by saving these innocent
Victims of my Father's Displeasure, nevertheless I pardon you
upon the Supposition, that you will, for the future, avoid all
Occasion of offending me.

At these Words, she made a Sign to him to be gone, fearing the
Extravagance of his Joy would make him throw himself at her Feet
to thank her for the infinite Favour she had conferred upon him;
but, finding he seemed disposed to stay longer, she called one of
her Women into the Closet; and, by some very significant Frowns,
gave *Glanville* to understand his Stay was displeasing; so that he
left her, with a very low Bow, highly pleased at her having repealed
his Banishment; and, assured the Marquis, that nothing could have
happened more fortunate for him, than his intended Disposal of his
Daughter's Books, since it had proved the Means of restoring him
to her Favour.

CHAPTER II
Which contains a very natural Incident

FROM this Time Mr. *Glanville*, tho' he was far from coming up to
Lady *Bella's* Idea of a Lover, yet, by the Pains he apparently
seemed to be at in obliging her, made every Day some Progress in
her Esteem. The Marquis was extremely pleased at the Harmony
which subsisted between them; tho' he could have wished to have

seen their Marriage advance a little faster; but *Glanville*, who was better acquainted with *Arabella*'s Foible than the Marquis, assured him, he would ruin all his Hopes, if he pressed her to marry; and intreated him to leave it intirely to him, to dispose her to consent to both their Wishes.

The Marquis was satisfied with his Reasons, and, resolving not to importune his Daughter, upon that Subject, any more, they lived for some Months in a perfect Tranquillity; to which an Illness the Marquis was seized with, and which was, from the first, thought to be dangerous gave a sad Interruption.

Arabella's extreme Tenderness upon this Occasion, her anxious Solicitude, her pious Cares, and never-ceasing Attendance at the Bedside of her sick Father, were so many new Charms, that engaged the Affection of *Glanville* more strongly. As the Marquis's Indisposition increased, so did her Care and Assiduity: She would not allow any one to give him any thing but herself; bore all the pettish Humours of a sick Man with a surprising Sweetness and Patience; watched whole Nights, successively, by his Bedside; and when, at his Importunity, she consented to take any Rest, it was only upon a Couch in his Chamber, from whence no Intreaties could make her remove. Mr. *Glanville* partook with her in these Fatigues; and, by his Care of her Father, and Tenderness for her, confirmed her in the Esteem she had entertained of him.

The Marquis, who had struggled with the Violence of his Distemper for a Fortnight, died on the Fifteenth Day in the Arms of *Arabella*, who received his last Looks; his Eyes never removing themselves from her Face, till they were closed by Death. Her Spirits, which the Desire she had of being useful to him, had alone supported, now failed her at once; and she fell upon the Bed, without Sense or Motion, as soon as she saw him expire.

Mr. *Glanville*, who was kneeling on the other Side, and had been holding one of his Uncle's Hands, started up in the most terrible Consternation, and, seeing the Condition she was in, flew to her Relief: Her Women, while he supported her, used all the Endeavours they could think of to recover her; but she continued so long in her Swoon, that they apprehended she was dead; and *Glanville* was resigning himself up to the most bitter Sorrow, when she opened her Eyes; but it was only to close them again. Her Faintings continued the whole Day; and the Physicians declaring she was in great Danger, from her extreme Weakness, she was

carried to Bed in a Condition that seemed to promise very little
Hopes of her Life.

The Care of the Marquis's Funeral devolving upon Mr. *Glanville*, he sent a Messenger express for his Father, who was appointed Guardian to Lady *Bella*; the Marquis having first asked
her if she was willing it should be so. This Gentleman arrived Time
enough to be Witness of that sad Ceremony, which was performed
with a Magnificence suitable to the Birth and Fortune of the
Marquis.

Lady *Bella* kept her Bed several Days, and her Life was thought
to be in Danger; but her Youth, and the Strength of her Constitution, overcame her Disease; and, when she was so well recovered as
to be able to admit of a Visit from her Uncle, Mr. *Glanville* sent for
Permission to introduce him: The afflicted *Arabella* granted his
Request; but, being then more indisposed than usual, she intreated they would defer their Visit for an Hour or two, which they
complied with; and, returning at the appointed Time, were conducted into her Dressing-Room by *Lucy*, who informed them her
Lady was just fallen into a Slumber.

Mr. *Glanville*, who had not seen her for some Days, expected her
waking with great Impatience; and pleased himself with describing
her, with a Lover's Fondness, to his Father, when the Sound of her
Voice in the next Room interrupted him.

CHAPTER III

Which treats of a consolatory Visit, and other grave Matters

Arabella, being then awaked from her Slumber, was indulging her
Grief by Complaints, which her Women were so used to hear, that
they never offered to disturb her. Merciless Fate! said she, in the
most moving Tone imaginable, Cruel Destiny! that, not contented
with having deprived my Infancy of the soft Cares, and tender
Indulgences, of a Mother's Fondness, has robbed me of the only
Parent I had left, and exposed me, at these early Years, to the Grief
of losing him, who was not only my Father, but my Friend, and
Protector of my Youth!

Then, pausing a Moment, she renewed her Complaints with a

deep Sigh: Dear Relics of the best of Fathers! pursued she, Why
was it not permitted me to bathe you with my Tears? Why were
those sacred Remains of him, from whom I drew my Life, snatched
from my Eyes, ere they had poured their Tribute of Sorrow over
them? Ah! pitiless Women! said she to her Attendants, you prevented me from performing the last pious Rites to my dear Father!
You, by your cruel Care, hindered me from easing my sad Heart,
by paying him the last Duties he could receive from me! Pardon, O
dear and sacred Shade of my loved Father! pardon this unwilling
Neglect of thy afflicted Child, who, to the last Moment of her
wretched Life, will bewail thy Loss!

Here she ceased speaking; and Mr. *Glanville*, whom this Soliloquy had much less confounded than his Father, was preparing to
go in, and comfort her; when the old Gentleman stopping him with
a Look of great Concern: My Niece is certainly much worse than
we apprehend, said he: She is in a Delirium: Our Presence may,
perhaps, discompose her too much.

No, Sir, replied *Glanville*, extremely confused at this Suspicion;
my Cousin is not so bad as you suppose: It is common enough for
People in any great Affliction to ease themselves by Complaints.

But these, replied the Knight, are the strangest Complaints I
ever heard, and favour so much of Phrensy, that I am persuaded
her Head is not quite right.

Glanville was going to reply, when *Lucy*, entering, told them her
Lady had ordered their Admission: Upon which they followed her
into *Arabella*'s Chamber, who was lying negligently upon her Bed.

Her deep Mourning, and the black Gawfe, which covered Part
of her fair Face, was so advantageous to her Shape and Complexion,
that Sir *Charles*, who had not seen her since she grew up, was
struck with an extreme Surprize at her Beauty, while his Son was
gazing on her so passionately, that he never thought of introducing
his Father to her, who contemplated her with as much Admiration
as his Son, though with less Passion.

Arabella, rising from her Bed, saluted her Uncle with a Grace
that wholly charmed him; and, turning to receive Mr. *Glanville*,
she burst into Tears at the Remembrance of his having assisted her
in her last Attendance upon her Father. Alas! Sir, said she, when
we saw each other last, we were both engaged, in a very melancholy
Office: Had it pleased Heaven to have spared my Father, he would,
doubtless, have been extremely sensible of your generous Cares;

nor shall you have any Reason to accuse me of Ingratitude, since I shall always acknowlege your Kindness as I ought.

If you think you owe me any Obligation, returned *Glanville*, pay me, dearest Cousin, by moderating your Sorrow: Indeed you suffer yourself to sink too much under an Affliction which is impossible to be remedied.

Alas! answered *Arabella*, my Grief is very slight, compared to that of many others upon the Death of their Relations: The Great *Sysigambis*, who, questionless, wanted neither Fortitude nor Courage, upon the News of her Grand-daughter's Death, wrapt herself up in her Veil; and, resolving never more to behold the Light, waited for Death in that Posture.[1]

Menecrates, upon the Loss of his Wife, built a magnificent Tomb for her; and, shutting himself up in it, resolved to pass away the Remainder of his Life with her Ashes.[2] These, indeed, were glorious Effects of Piety and Affection, and unfeigned Signs of an excessive Sorrow: What are the few Tears I shed to such illustrious Instances of Grief and Affection, as these?

Glanville, finding his Cousin upon this Strain, blushed extremely, and would have changed the Subject; but the old Gentleman, who had never heard of these two Persons she mentioned, who expressed their Sorrow for their Losses in so strange a Manner, was surprised at it; and was resolved to know more about them.

Pray, Niece, said he, were you acquainted with these People, who could not submit to the Dispensation of Providence, but, as one may say, flew in the Face of Heaven by their Impatience?

I am very well acquainted with their History, resumed *Arabella*; and I can assure you, they were both very admirable Persons.

Oh! Oh! their History! interrupted the Knight! What, I warrant you, they are to be found in the *Fairy Tales*, and those sort of Books! Well, I never could like such Romances, not I; for they only spoil Youth, and put strange Notions into their Heads.

I am sorry, resumed *Arabella*, blushing with Anger, that we are like to differ in Opinion upon so important a Point.

Truly, Niece, said Sir *Charles*, if we never differ in any thing else, I shall be very easy about this slight Matter; tho' I think a young Lady of your fine Sense (for my Son praises you to the Skies for your *Wit*) should not be so fond of such ridiculous Nonsense as these Story-Books are filled with.

Upon my Word, resumed *Arabella*, all the Respect I owe you

cannot hinder me from telling you, that I take it extremely ill you
should, in my Presence, rail at the finest Productions in the World:
I think, we are infinitely obliged to these Authors, who have, in so
sublime a Style, delivered down to Posterity the heroic Actions of
the bravest Men, and most virtuous of Women: But for the inimitable Pen of the famous *Scudery*,[1] we had been ignorant of the Lives
of many great and illustrious Persons: The warlike Actions of
Oroondates, Aronces, Juba, and the renowned *Artaban,* had, haply,
never been talked of in our Age; and those fair and chaste Ladies,
who were the Objects of their pure and constant Passions, had still
been buried in Obscurity; and neither their divine Beauties, or
singular Virtue, been the Subject of our Admiration and Praise.
But for the famous *Scudery,* we had not known the true Cause of
that Action of *Clelia*'s, for which the Senate decreed her a Statue;
namely, Her casting herself, with an unparalleled Courage, into the
Tyber, a deep and rapid River, as you must certainly know, and
swimming to the other Side. It was not, as the *Roman* Historians
falsly report, a Stratagem to recover herself, and the other Hostages, from the Power of *Porsena*; it was to preserve her Honour
from Violation by the impious *Sextus,* who was in the Camp.[2] But
for *Scudery,* we had still thought the inimitable Poetess *Sappho* to
be a loose Wanton, whose Verses breathed nothing but unchaste
and irregular Fires: On the contrary, she was so remarkably chaste,
that she would never even consent to marry; but, loving *Phaon,*
only with a Platonic Passion, obliged him to restrain his Desires
within the Compass of a Brother's Affection.[3] Numberless are the
Mistakes he has cleared up of this Kind; and I question, if any
other Historian, but himself, knew that *Cleopatra* was really
married to *Julius Caesar*;[4] or that *Caesario,* her Son by this Marriage, was not murdered, as was supposed, by the Order of *Augustus,* but married the fair Queen of *Ethiopia,* in whose Dominions he
took Refuge.[5] The prodigious Acts of Valour, which he has recounted of those accomplished Princes, have never been equalled
by the Heroes of either the *Greek* or *Roman* Historians: How poor
and insignificant are the Actions of their Warriors to *Scudery*'s,
where one of those admirable Heroes would put whole Armies into
Terror, and with his single Arm oppose a Legion!

    Indeed, Niece, said Sir *Charles,* no longer able to forbear inter-
rupting her, these are all very improbable Tales. I remember,
when I was a Boy, I was very fond of reading the History of *Jack the*

Giant killer,[1] and *Tom Thumb*; and these Stories so filled my Head, that I really thought one of those little Fellows killed Men an hundred Feet high; and that the other, after a great many surprising Exploits, was swallowed up by a Cow.

You was very young, Sir, you say, interrupted *Arabella* tartly, when those Stories gained your Belief: However, your Judgment was certainly younger, if you ever believed them at all; for as credulous as you are pleased to think me, I should never, at any Age, have been persuaded such Things could have happened.

My Father, Madam, said *Glanville*, who was strangely confused all this Time, bore Arms in his Youth; and Soldiers, you know, never trouble themselves much with reading.

Has my Uncle been a Soldier, said *Arabella*, and does he hold in Contempt the Actions of the bravest Soldiers in the World?

The Soldiers you speak of, Niece, said Sir *Charles*, were indeed the bravest Soldiers in the World; for I don't believe, they ever had their Equals.

And yet, Sir, said *Arabella*, there are a great Number of such Soldiers to be found in *Scudery*.

Indeed, my dear Niece, interrupted Sir *Charles*, they are to be found no-where else, except in your Imagination, which, I am sorry to see, is filled with such *Whimsies*.

If you mean this to affront me, Sir, resumed *Arabella*, hardly able to forbear Tears, I know how far, as my Uncle, I ought to bear with you: But, methinks, it is highly unkind to aggravate my Sorrows by such cruel Jests; and, since I am not in an Humour to suffer them, don't take it ill, if I intreat you to leave me to myself.

Mr. *Glanville*, who knew nothing pleased his Cousin so much as paying an exact Obedience to her Commands, rose up immediately; and, bowing respectfully to her, asked his Father, If he should attend him into the Gardens?

The Baronet, who thought *Arabella*'s Behaviour bordered a good deal upon Rudeness, took his Leave with some Signs of Displeasure upon his Countenance; and, notwithstanding all his Son could say in Excuse for her, he was extremely offended.

What, said he, to Mr. *Glanville*, does she so little understand the Respect that is due to me as her Uncle, that she, so peremptorily, desired me to leave her Room? My Brother was to blame to take so little Care of her Education; she is quite a Rustic!

Ah! don't wrong your Judgment so much, Sir, said *Glanville*;

my Cousin has as little of the Rustic as if she had passed all her Life in a Court: Her fine Sense, and the native Elegance of her Manners give an inimitable Grace to her Behaviour; and as much exceed the studied Politeness of other Ladies I have conversed with, as the Beauties of her Person do all I have ever seen.

She is very handsome, I confess, returned Sir *Charles*; but I cannot think so well of her *Wit* as you do; for methinks she talks very oddly, and has the strangest Conceits! Who, but herself, would think it probable, that one Man could put a whole Army to Flight; or commend a foolish Fellow for living in a Tomb, because his Wife was buried in it? Fie, fie! these are silly and extravagant Notions, and will make her appear very ridiculous.

Mr. *Glanville* was so sensible of the Justness of this Remark, that he could not help sighing; which his Father observing, told him, That, since she was to be his Wife, it was his Business to produce a Reformation in her; for, added he, notwithstanding the immense Fortune she will bring you, I should be sorry to have a Daughter-in-law, for whom I should blush as often as she opens her Mouth.

I assure you, Sir, said Mr. *Glanville*, I have but very little Hopes, that I shall be so happy as to have my Cousin for a Wife; for, tho' it was my Uncle's Command I should make my Addresses to her, she received me so ill, as a Lover, that I have never dared to talk to her upon that Subject since.

And pray, resumed Sir *Charles*, upon what Terms are you at present?

While I seem to pretend nothing to her, as a Lover, replied Mr. *Glanville*, she is very obliging, and we live in great Harmony together; but I am persuaded, if I exceed the Bounds of Friendship in my Professions, she will treat me extremely ill.

But, interrupted Sir *Charles*, when she shall know, that her Father has bequeathed you one Third of his Estate, provided she don't marry you, 'tis probable her Mind may change; and you may depend upon it, since your Heart is so much set upon her, that, as I am her Guardian, I shall press her to perform the Marquis's Will.

Ah! Sir, resumed Mr. *Glanville*, never attempt to lay any Constraint upon my Cousin in an Affair of this Nature: Permit me to tell you, it would be an Abuse of the Marquis's generous Confidence, and what I would never submit to.

Nay, nay, said the old Gentleman, you have no Reason to fear any Compulsion from me: Tho' her Father has left me her Guardian, till she is of Age, yet it is with such Restriction, that my Niece is quite her own Mistress in that Respect; for tho' she is directed to consult me in her Choice of an Husband, yet my Consent is not absolutely necessary. The Marquis has certainly had a great Opinion of his Daughter's Prudence; and I hope, she will prove herself worthy of it by her Conduct.

Mr. *Glanville* was so taken up with his Reflections upon the State of his Affairs, that he made but little Reply; and, as soon as he had disengaged himself, retired to his Chamber, to be at more Liberty to indulge his Meditations. As he could not flatter himself, with having made any Impression upon the Heart of *Arabella*, he foresaw a thousand Inconveniences from the Death of the Marquis; for, besides that he lost a powerful Mediator with his Cousin, he feared that, when she appeared in the World, her Beauty and Fortune would attract a Croud of Admirers, among whom, it was probable, she would find some one more agreeable to her Taste than himself. As he loved her with great Tenderness, this Thought made him extremely uneasy; and he would sometimes wish the Marquis had laid a stronger Injunction upon her in his Will to marry him; and regretted the little Power his Father had over her: But he was too generous, to dwell long upon these Thoughts, and contented himself with resolving to do all that was honourable to obtain her, without seeking for any Assistance from unjustifiable Methods.

CHAPTER IV

Which contains some common Occurrences, but placed in a new Light

Arabella, in a few Days, leaving her Chamber, had so many Opportunities of charming her Uncle by her Conversation, which, when it did not turn upon any Incident in her Romances, was perfectly fine, easy, and entertaining, that he declared, he should quit the Castle with great Regret; and endeavoured to persuade her to accompany him to Town: But *Arabella*, who was determined to pass the Year of her Mourning, in the Retirement she had always lived in, absolutely refused, strong as her Curiosity was, to see *London*.

Mr. *Glanville* secretly rejoiced at this Resolution, tho' he seemed desirous of making her change it; but she was unalterable; and, therefore, the Baronet did not think proper to press her any more.

Her Father's Will being read to her, she seemed extremely pleased with the Articles in favour of Mr. *Glanville*, wishing him Joy of the Estate that was bequeathed to him, with a most inchanting Sweetness.

Mr. *Glanville* sighed, and cast his Eyes on the Ground, as he returned her Compliment, with a very low Bow; and Sir *Charles*, observing his Confusion, told *Arabella*, that he thought it was a very bad Omen for his Son, to wish him Joy of an Estate, which he could not come to the Possession of, but by a very great Misfortune.

Arabella, understanding his Meaning, blushed; and, willing to change the Discourse, proceeded to consult her Uncle upon the Regulation of her House. Besides the Legacies her Father had bequeathed to his Servants, those, who were more immediately about his Person, she desired, might have their Salaries continued to them: She made no other Alteration, than discharging these Attendants, retaining all the others; and submitting to her Uncle the Management of her Estates, receiving the Allowance he thought proper to assign her, till she was of Age, of which she wanted three Years.

Every Thing being settled, Sir *Charles* prepared to return to Town. Mr. *Glanville*, who desired nothing so much as to stay some time longer with his Cousin in her Solitude, got his Father to intreat that Favour for him of *Arabella*: But she represented to her Uncle the Impropriety of a young Gentleman's staying with her, in her House, now her Father was dead, in a manner so genteel and convincing, that Sir *Charles* could press it no further; and all that Mr. *Glanville* could obtain, was, a Permission to visit her some time after, provided he could prevail upon his Sister, Miss *Charlotte Glanville*, to accompany him.

The Day of their Departure being come, Sir *Charles* took his Leave of his charming Niece, with many Expressions of Esteem and Affection; and Mr. *Glanville* appeared so concerned, that *Arabella* could not help observing it; and bade him adieu with great Sweetness.

When they were gone, she found her Time hung heavy upon her Hands; her Father was continually in her Thoughts, and made her extremely melancholy: She recollected the many agreeable Conversations she had had with *Glanville*; and wished it had been consistent with Decency to have detained him. Her Books being the only Amusement she had left, she applied herself to reading with more Eagerness than ever; but, notwithstanding the Delight she took in this Employment, she had so many Hours of Solitude and Melancholy to indulge the Remembrance of her Father in, that she was very far from being happy.

As she wished for nothing more passionately than an agreeable Companion of her own Sex and Rank, an Accident threw a Person in her Way, who, for some Days, afforded her a little Amusement. Stepping one Day out of her Coach, to go into Church, she saw a young Lady enter, accompanied with a middle-aged Woman, who seemed to be an Attendant. As *Arabella* had never seen any one, above the Rank of a Gentleman Farmer's Daughter, in this Church, her Attention was immediately engaged by the Appearance of this Stranger, who was very magnificently dressed: Tho' she did not seem to be more than eighteen Years of Age, her Stature was above the ordinary Size of Women; and, being rather too plump to be delicate, her Mien was so majestic, and such an Air of Grandeur was diffused over her whole Person, joined to the Charms of a very lovely Face, that *Arabella* could hardly help thinking she saw the beautiful *Candace* before her, who, by *Scudery*'s Description, very much resembled this Fair one.

Arabella, having heedfully observed her Looks, thought she saw a great Appearance of Melancholy in her Eyes, which filled her with a generous Concern for the Misfortunes of so admirable a Person; but, the Service beginning, she was not at Liberty to indulge her Reflections upon this Occasion, as she never suffered any Thoughts, but those of Religion, to intrude upon her Mind, during these pious Rites.

As she was going out of Church she observed the young Lady, attended only with the Woman who came with her, preparing to walk home, and therefore stept forward, and, saluting her with a Grace peculiar to herself, intreated her to come into her Coach, and give her the Pleasure of setting her down at her own House: So obliging an Offer from a Person of *Arabella*'s Rank could not fail of being received with great Respect by the young Lady, who was not ignorant of all the Forms of Good-breeding; and, accepting her Invitation, she stepped into the Coach; *Arabella* obliging her

Woman to come in also, for whom, as she had that Day only *Lucy* along with her, there was Room enough.

As they were going home, *Arabella*, who longed to be better acquainted, intreated the fair Stranger, as she called her, to go to the Castle, and spend the Day with her; and she consenting, they passed by the House where she lodged, and alighted at the Castle, where *Arabella* welcomed her, with the most obliging Expressions of Civility and Respect. The young Lady, tho' perfectly versed in the Modes of Town-Breeding, and *nothing-meaning* Ceremony, was at a Loss how to make proper Returns to the Civilities of *Arabella*: The native Elegance and Simplicity of her Manners were accompanied with so much real Benevolence of Heart, such insinuating Tenderness, and Graces so irresistible, that she was quite oppressed with them; and, having spent most of her Time between her Toilet and Quadrille,[1] was so little qualified for partaking a Conversation so refined as *Arabella*'s, that her Discourse appeared quite tedious to her, since it was neither upon Fashions, Assemblies, Cards, or Scandal.

Her Silence, and that Absence of Mind, which she betrayed, made *Arabella* conclude, she was under some very great Affliction; and, to amuse her after Dinner, led her into the Gardens, supposing a Person, whose Uneasiness, as she did not doubt, proceeded from Love, would be pleased with the Sight of Groves and Streams, and be tempted to disclose her Misfortunes, while they wandered in that agreeable Privacy. In this, however, she was deceived; for, tho' the young Lady sighed several times, yet, when she did speak, it was only of indifferent Things, and not at all in the manner of an afflicted Heroine.

After observing upon a thousand Trifles, she told *Arabella* at last, to whom she was desirous of making known her Alliance to Quality, that these Gardens were extremely like those of her Father's-in-Law, the Duke of —— at ——.

At this Intimation, she expected *Arabella* would be extremely surprised; but that Lady, whose Thoughts were always familiarized to Objects of Grandeur, and would not have been astonished, if she had understood her Guest was the Daughter of a King, appeared so little moved, that the Lady was piqued by her Indifference; and, after a few Moment's Silence, began to mention going away.

Arabella, who was desirous of retaining her a few Days, in-

treated her so obligingly to favour her with her Company, for some
time, in her Solitude, that the other could not refuse; and, dispatching her Woman to the House where she lodged, to inform
them of her Stay at the Castle, would have dispensed with her
coming again to attend her, had not *Arabella* insisted upon the
contrary.

The Reserve, which the Daughter-in-Law of the Duke of ——
still continued to maintain, notwithstanding the repeated Expressions of Friendship *Arabella* used to her, increased her Curiosity to
know her Adventures, which she was extremely surprised, she had
never offered to relate; but, attributing her Silence, upon this
Head, to her Modesty, she was resolved, as was the Custom in those
Cases, to oblige her Woman, who, she presumed, was her Confidante, to relate, her Lady's History to her; and sending for this
Person one Day, when she was alone, to attend her in her Closet,
she gave Orders to her Women, if the fair Stranger came to inquire
for her, to say she was then busy, but would wait on her as soon as
possible.

After this Caution, she ordered Mrs. *Morris* to be admitted; and,
obliging her to sit down, told her, she sent for her in order to hear
from her the History of her Lady's Life, which she was extremely
desirous of knowing.

Mrs. *Morris*, who was a Person of Sense, and had seen the World,
was extremely surprised at this Request of *Arabella*, which was
quite contrary to the Laws of Good-breeding; and, as she thought,
betrayed a great deal of impertinent Curiosity: She could not tell
how to account for the free Manner in which she desired her to
give up her Lady's Secrets, which, indeed, were not of a Nature to
be told; and appeared so much confused, that *Arabella* took
Notice of it; and, supposing it was her Bashfulness which caused
her Embarrassment, she endeavoured to re-assure her by the most
affable Behaviour imaginable.

Mrs. *Morris*, who was not capable of much Fidelity for her Lady,
being but lately taken into her Service, and not extremely fond of
her, thought she had now a fine Opportunity of recommending
herself to *Arabella*, by telling her all she knew of Miss *Groves*, for
that was her Name; and, therefore, told her, since she was pleased
to command it, she would give her what Account she was able of her
Lady; but intreated her to be secret, because it was of great Consequence to her, that her Affairs should not be known.

I always imagined, said *Arabella*, that your beautiful Mistress had some particular Reason for not making herself known, and for coming in this private Manner into this Part of the Country: You may assure yourself therefore, that I will protect her as far as I am able, and offer her all the Assistance in my Power to give her: Therefore you may acquaint me with her Adventures, without being apprehensive of a Discovery that would be prejudicial to her.

Mrs. *Morris*, who had been much better pleased with the Assurances of a Reward for the Intelligence she was going to give her, looked a little foolish at these fine Promises, in which she had no Share; and *Arabella*, supposing she was endeavouring to recollect all the Passages of her Lady's Life, told her, She need not give herself the Trouble to acquaint her with any thing that passed during the Infancy of her Lady, but proceed to acquaint her with Matters of greater Importance: and since, said she, you have, no doubt, been most favoured with her Confidence you will do me a Pleasure to describe to me, exactly, all the Thoughts of her Soul, as she has communicated them to you, that I may the better comprehend her History.

CHAPTER V

The History of Miss Groves, *interspersed with some very curious Observations*

THOUGH, Madam, said Mrs. *Morris*, I have not been long in Miss *Groves*'s Service, yet I know a great many Things by the means of her former Woman, who told them to me, tho' my Lady thinks I am ignorant of them; and I know that this is her second Trip into the Country.

Pray, interrupted *Arabella*, do me the Favour to relate Things methodically: Of what Use is it to me to know that this is your Lady's second Trip, as you call it, into the Country, if I know not the Occasion of it? Therefore begin with informing me, who were the Parents of this admirable young Person.

Her Father, Madam, said Mrs. *Morris*, was a Merchant; and, at his Death, left her a large Fortune, and so considerable a Jointure to his Wife, that the Duke of ——, being then a Widower, was tempted to make his Addresses to her. Mrs. *Groves* was one of the proudest Women in the World; and, this Offer flattering her Ambition more than ever she had Reason to expect, she married the Duke after a very short Courtship; and carried Miss *Groves* down with her to ——, where the Duke had a fine Seat, and where she was received by his Grace's Daughters, who were much about her own Age, with great Civility. Miss *Groves*, Madam, was then about twelve Years old, and was educated with the Duke's Daughters, who, in a little time, became quite disgusted with their new Sister; for Miss *Groves*, who inherited her Mother's Pride, tho' not her Understanding, in all things affected an Equality with those young Ladies, who, conscious of the Superiority of their Birth, could but ill bear with her Insolence and Presumption. As they grew older, the Difference of their Inclinations caused perpetual Quarrels amongst them; for his Grace's Daughters were serious, reserved, and pious. Miss *Groves* affected noisy Mirth, was a great Romp, and delighted in masculine Exercises.

The Duchess was often reflected on for suffering her Daughter, without any other Company than two or three Servants, to spend great Part of the Day in riding about the Country, leaping over Hedges and Ditches, exposing her fair Face to the Injuries of the Sun and Wind; and, by those coarse Exercises, contracting a masculine and robust Air not becoming her Sex, and tender Years: Yet she could not be prevailed upon to restrain her from this Diversion, till it was reported, she had listened to the Addresses of a young Sportsman, who used to mix in her Train, when she went upon those Rambles, and procured frequent Opportunities of conversing with her.

There is a great Difference, interrupted *Arabella*, in suffering Addresses, and being betrayed into an involuntary Hearing of them, and this last, I conceive to have been the Case of your Lady; for it is not very probable, she would so far forget what she owed to her own Glory, as to be induced to listen quietly to Discourses like those you mention.

However, Madam, resumed Mrs. *Morris*, the Duchess thought it necessary to keep her more at home; but, even here, she was not without meeting Adventures, and found a Lover in the Person who taught her to write.

That, indeed, was a very notable Adventure, said *Arabella*; but it is not strange, that Love should produce such Metamorphoses:

'Tis not very long ago, that I heard of a Man of Quality, who disguised himself in a poor Habit, and worked in the Gardens of a certain Nobleman, whose Daughter he was enamoured with: These things happen every Day.

The Person I speak of, Madam, said Mrs. *Morris*, was never discovered to be any thing better than a Writing-master; and yet, for all that, Miss was *smitten* with his fine Person, and was taking Measures to run away with him, when the Intrigue was discovered, the Lover dismissed, and the young Lady, whose faulty Conduct had drawn upon her her Mother's Dislike, was sent up to *London*, and allowed to be her own Mistress at Sixteen; to which unpardonable Neglect of her Mother she owes the Misfortunes that have since befallen her.

Whatever may be the common Opinion of this Matter, interrupted *Arabella* again, I am persuaded the Writing-master, as you call him, was some Person of Quality, who made use of that Device to get Access to his beautiful Mistress. Love is ingenious in Artifices: Who would have thought, that, under the Name of *Alcippus*, a simple Attendant of the fair *Artemisa* Princess of *Armenia*, the gallant *Alexander* Son of the great and unfortunate *Antony*, by Queen *Cleopatra*, was concealed, who took upon himself that mean Condition for the sake of seeing his adored Princess?[1] Yet the Contrivance of *Orontes*, Prince of the *Massagetes*, was far more ingenious, and even dangerous; for this valiant and young Prince, happening to see the Picture of the beautiful *Thalestris*, Daughter of the Queen of the *Amazons*, he fell passionately in Love with her; and, knowing that the Entrance into that Country was forbid to Men, he dressed himself in Womens Apparel; and, finding means to be introduced to the Queen, and her fair Daughter, whose Amity he gained by some very singular Services in the Wars, he lived several Years undiscovered in their Court:[2] I see, therefore, no Reason to the contrary, but that this Writing-master might have been some illustrious Person, whom Love had disguised; and, I am persuaded, added she, smiling, that I shall hear more of him anon, in a very different Character.

Indeed, Madam, said Mrs. *Morris*, whom this Speech of *Arabella* had extremely surprised, I never heard any thing more about him, than what I have related; and, for what I know, he continues still to teach Writing; for I don't suppose the Duchess's Displeasure could affect him.

How is it possible, said *Arabella*, that you can suppose such an Offence to Probability? In my Opinion, 'tis much more likely, that this unfortunate Lover is dead thro' Despair; or, perhaps, wandering over the World in Search of that Fair one, who was snatched from his Hopes.

If it was his Design to seek for her, Madam, resumed Mrs. *Morris*, he need not have gone far, since she was only sent to *London*, whither he might easily have followed her.

There is no accounting for these Things, said *Arabella*: Perhaps he has been imposed upon, and made to believe, that it was she herself that banished him from her Presence: 'Tis probable too, that he was jealous, and thought she preferred some one of his Rivals to him. Jealousy is inseparable from true Love; and the slightest Matters imaginable will occasion it: And, what is still more wonderful, this Passion creates the greatest Disorders in the most sensible and delicate Hearts. Never was there a more refined and faithful Passion, than that of the renowned *Artamenes* for *Mandana*; and yet this Prince was driven almost to Distraction by a Smile, which, he fansied, he saw in the Face of his Divine Mistress, at a time when she had some Reason to believe he was dead; and he was so transported with Grief and Rage, that, tho' he was a Prisoner in his Enemy's Camp, where the Knowlege of his Quality would have procured him certain Death, yet he determined to hazard all Things for the sake of presenting himself before *Mandana*, and upbraiding her with her Infidelity; when, in Reality, nothing was farther from the Thoughts of that fair and virtuous Princess, than the Lightness he accused her of.[1] So that, as I said before, it is not at all to be wondered at, if this disguised Lover of your Lady was driven to Despair by Suspicions as groundless, perhaps, as those of *Artamenes*, yet not the less cruel and tormenting.

Mrs. *Morris*, finding *Arabella* held her Peace at these Words, went on with her History in this manner:—Miss *Groves*, Madam, being directed by her Woman in all things, took up her Lodgings in her Father's House, who was a broken Tradesman, and obliged to keep himself concealed for fear of his Creditors: Here she formed her Equipage, which consisted of a Chair, one Footman, a Cook, and her Woman: As she was indulged with the Command of what Money she pleased, her Extravagance was boundless: She lavished away large Sums at Gaming, which was her favourite Diversion;

kept such a Number of different Animals for Favourites, that their
Maintenance amounted to a considerable Sum every year: Her
Woman's whole Family were supported at her Expence; and, as
she frequented all public Places, and surpassed Ladies of the first
Quality in Finery, her Dress alone consumed great Part of her
Income. I need not tell you, Madam, that my Lady was a celebrated
Beauty: You have yourself been pleased to say, that she is very
handsome. When she first appeared at Court, her Beauty, and the
uncommon Dignity of her Person, at such early Years, made her
the Object of general Admiration. The King was particularly
struck with her; and declared to those about him, that Miss
Groves was the finest Woman at Court. The Ladies, however,
found means to explain away all that was flattering in this Distinction: They said, Miss *Groves* was clumsy; and it was her Resemblance to the *unwieldy German* Ladies that made her so much admired by his Majesty. Her Pride, and the Quality Airs she affected,
were the Subject of great Ridicule to those that envied her Charms:
Some Censures were maliciously cast on her Birth; for, as she was
always styled the Duchess of ——'s Daughter, a Custom she introduced herself, she seemed to disclaim all Title to a legal Father.
Miss *Groves*, as universally admired as she was, yet made but very
few particular Conquests. Her Fortune was known to be very considerable, and her Mother's Jointure was to descend to her after
her Death: Yet there was no Gentleman, who would venture upon
a Wife of Miss *Groves*'s Taste for Expence, as very few Estates, *to
which she could pretend*, would support her Extravagance.—The
Honourable Mr. *L* ——, Brother to the Earl of ——, was the only
one, amidst a Croud of Admirers, who made any particular Address
to her. This Gentleman was tolerably handsome, and had the Art of
making himself agreeable to the Ladies, by a certain Air of Softness
and Tenderness, which never failed to make some Impression upon
those he desired to deceive.

Miss *Groves* was ravished with her Conquest, and boasted of it so
openly, that People, who were acquainted with this Gentleman's
Character, foreseeing her Fate, could not help pitying her.

A very few Months Courtship completed the Ruin of poor Miss
Groves: She fell a Sacrifice to Oaths which had been often prostituted for the same inhuman Purposes; and became so fond of her
Betrayer, that it was with great Difficulty he could persuade her not
to give him, even in public, the most ridiculous Proofs of her

Tenderness. Her Woman pretends, that she was ignorant of this Intrigue, till *Miss Groves* growing big with Child, it could no longer be concealed; it was at length agreed, she should lie-in at her own Lodgings, to prevent any Suspicions from her retreating into the Country; but that Scheme was over-ruled by her Woman's Mother, who advised her to conceal herself in some Village, not far from Town, till the Affair was over.

Miss *Groves* approved of this second Proposal, but took Advantage of her Shape, which, being far from delicate, would not easily discover any growing Bigness, to stay in Town as long as she possibly could. When her Removal was necessary, she went to the Lodgings provided for her, a few Miles distant from *London*: And, notwithstanding the Excuses which were framed for this sudden Absence, the true Cause was more than suspected by some busy People, who industriously inquired into her Affairs.

Mr. *L* —— saw her but seldom during her Illness: The Fear of being discovered was his Pretence: But her Friends easily saw through this Disguise, and were persuaded Miss *Groves* was waning in his Affections.

As she had a very strong Constitution, she returned to Town at the End of three Weeks: The Child was dead, and she looked handsomer than ever. Mr. *L* —— continued his Visits; and the Town to make Remarks of them. All this time the Duchess never troubled herself about the Conduct of this unfortunate young Creature: And the People she was with had not the Goodness to give her any Hint of her Misconduct, and the Waste of her Fortune: On the contrary, they almost turned her Head with their Flatteries, preyed upon her Fortune, and winked at her Irregularities.

She was now a second time with Child: Her Character was pretty severely handled by her Enemies: Mr. *L* —— began openly to slight her: And she was several thousand Pounds in Debt. The Mother and Sisters of her Woman, in whose House she still was, were base enough to whisper the Fault she had been guilty of to all their Acquaintances. Her Story became generally known: She was shunned and neglected by every body; and even Mr. *L* ——, who had been the Cause of her Ruin, intirely abandoned her, and boasted openly of the Favours he had received from her.

Miss *Groves* protested to her Friends, That he had promised her Marriage; but Mr. *L* —— constantly denied it, and never scrupled to say, when he was questioned about it, That he found Miss *Groves* too easy a Conquest to make any Perjury necessary. Her Tenderness, however, for this base Man, was so great, that she never could bear to hear him railed at in her Presence; but would quarrel with the only Friends she had left, if they said any thing to his Disadvantage. As she was now pretty far advanced with Child, she would have retired into the Country; but the bad Condition of her Affairs made her Removal impossible: In this Extremity she had Recourse to her Uncle, a rich Merchant in the City, who, having taken all the necessary Precautions for his own Security; paid Miss *Groves*'s Debts, carrying on, in her Name, a Law-suit with the Duchess, for some Lands, which were to be put into her Hands, when she was of Age, and which that great Lady detainèd. Miss *Groves*, being reduced to live upon something less than an Hundred a Year, quitted *London*, and came into this Part of the Country, where she was received by Mrs. *Barnett*, one of her Woman's Sisters, who is married to a Country Gentleman of some Fortune: In her House she lay-in of a Girl, which Mr. *L——* sent to demand, and will not be persuaded to inform her how, or in what manner, he has disposed of the Child.

Her former Woman leaving her, I was received in her Place, from whom I learnt all these Particulars: And Miss *Groves* having gained the Affections of Mr. *Barnett*'s Brother, her Beauty, and the large Fortune which she has in Reversion, has induced him, not-withstanding the Knowlege of her past unhappy Conduct, to marry her. But their Marriage is yet a Secret, Miss *Groves* being apprehensive of her Uncle's Displeasure for not consulting him in her Choice.

Her Husband is gone to *London*, with an Intention to acquaint him with it; and, when he returns, their Marriage will be publicly owned.

CHAPTER VI

Containing what a judicious Reader will hardly approve

MRS. *Morris* ending her Narration, *Arabella*, who had not been able to restrain her Tears at some Parts of it, thanked her for the Trouble she had been at; and assured her of her Secrecy: Your Lady's Case, said she, is much to be lamented; and greatly resembles the unfortunate *Cleopatra*'s, whom *Julius Caesar* privately marrying, with a Promise to own her for his Wife, when he should be peaceable Master of the *Roman* Empire, left that great Queen big with Child, and, never intending to perform his Promise, suffered her to be exposed to the Censures the World has so freely cast upon her; and which she so little deserved.

Mrs. *Morris*, seeing the favourable Light in which *Arabella* viewed the Actions of her Lady, did not think proper to say any thing to undeceive her; but went out of the Closet, not a little mortified at her Disappointment: For she saw she was likely to receive nothing for betraying her Lady's Secrets, from *Arabella*: Who seemed so little sensible of the Pleasure of Scandal, as to be wholly ignorant of its Nature; and not to know it when it was told her.

Miss *Groves*, who was just come to Lady *Bella*'s Chamber-door, to inquire for her, was surprised to see her Woman come out of it; and who, upon meeting her, expressed great Confusion. As she was going to ask her some Questions concerning her Business there, *Arabella* came out of the Closet; and, seeing Miss *Groves* in her Chamber, asked her Pardon for staying so long from her.

I have been listening to your History, said she, with great Frankness, which your Woman has been relating: And I assure you I am extremely sensible of your Misfortunes.

Miss *Groves*, at these Words, blushed with extreme Confusion; and Mrs. *Morris* turned pale with Astonishment and Fear. *Arabella*, not sensible that she had been guilty of any Indiscretion, proceeded to make Reflections upon some Part of her Story; which, though they were not at all disadvantageous to that young Lady, she received as so many Insults: And asked Lady *Bella*, If she was not ashamed to tamper with a Servant to betray the Secrets of her Mistress?

Arabella, a little surprised at so rude a Question, answered, however, with great Sweetness; and protested to her, that she would make no ill Use of what she had learned of her Affairs: For, in fine, Madam, said she, do you think I am less fit to be trusted with your Secrets, than the Princess of the *Leontines* was with those of *Clelia*;[1] between whom there was no greater Amity and Acquaintance, than with us? And you must certainly know, that the Secrets which that admirable Person entrusted with *Lysimena*, were of a Nature to be more dangerous, if revealed, than yours. The Happiness of *Clelia* depended upon *Lysimena*'s Fidelity: And the Liberty, nay, haply, the Life, of *Aronces*, would have been in Danger, if she had betrayed them. Though I do not intend to arrogate to myself the Possession of those admirable Qualities which adorned the Princess of the *Leontines*, yet I will not yield to her, or any one else, in Generosity and Fidelity: And if you will be pleased to repose as much Confidence in me, as those illustrious Lovers did in her, you shall be convinced I will labour as earnestly for your Interest, as that fair Princess did for those of *Aronces* and *Clelia*.

Miss *Groves* was so busied in reflecting upon the Baseness of her Woman in exposing her, that she heard not a Word of this fine Harangue (at which Mrs. *Morris*, notwithstanding the Cause she had for Uneasiness, could hardly help laughing); but, assuming some of that Haughtiness in her Looks, for which she used to be remarkable, she told Lady *Bella*, that she imputed her impertinent Curiosity to her Country Ignorance, and ill Breeding: And she did not doubt but she would be served in her own kind, and meet with as bad Fortune as she had done; and, perhaps, deserve it *worse* than she did: For there are more false Men in the World besides Mr. *L* ——; and she was no handsomer than other People.

Saying this, she flung out of the Room, her Woman following, leaving *Arabella* in such Confusion at a Behaviour of which she had never before had an Idea, that for some Moments she remained immoveable.

Recollecting herself, at last, and conceiving, that Civility required she should endeavour to appease this incensed Lady, she went down Stairs after her; and, stopping her just as she was going out of the House, intreated her to be calm, and suffer her to vindicate herself from the Imputation of being impertinently curious to know her Affairs.

Miss *Groves*, quite transported with Shame and Anger, refused absolutely to stay.

At least, Madam, said *Arabella*, stay till my Coach can be got ready; and don't think of walking home, so slightly attended.

This Offer was as sullenly answered as the other: And *Arabella*, finding she was determined to venture home, with no other Guard than her Woman, who silently followed her, ordered two of her Footmen to attend her at a small Distance; and to defend her, if there should be Occasion.

For who knows, said she to *Lucy*, what Accident may happen? Some one or other of her insolent Lovers may take this Opportunity to carry her away; and I should never forgive myself for being the Cause of such a Misfortune to her.

Mrs. *Morris* having found it easy to reconcile herself to her Lady, by assuring her, that Lady *Bella* was acquainted with great Part of her Story before; and that what she told her, tended only to justify her Conduct, as she might have been convinced by what Lady *Bella* said; they both went home with a Resolution to say nothing of what had passed, with relation to the Cause of the Disgust Miss *Groves* had received: But only said, in general, that Lady *Bella* was the most ridiculous Creature in the World; and was so totally ignorant of good Breeding, that it was impossible to converse with her.

CHAPTER VII

Which treats of the Olympic *Games*

WHILE *Arabella* was ruminating on the unaccountable Behaviour of her new Acquaintance, she received a Letter from her Uncle, informing her (for she had expressly forbid Mr. *Glanville* to write to her), that his Son and Daughter intended to set out for her Seat in a few Days.

This News was received with great Satisfaction by *Arabella*, who hoped to find an agreeable Companion in her Cousin; and was not so insensible of Mr. *Glanville*'s Merit, as not to feel some kind of Pleasure at the Thought of seeing him again.

This Letter was soon followed, by the Arrival of Mr. *Glanville*, and his Sister; who, upon the Sight of *Arabella*, discovered some

Appearance of Astonishment and Chagrin; for, notwithstanding all her Brother had told her of her Accomplishments, she could not conceive it possible for a young Lady, bred up in the Country, to be so perfectly elegant and genteel as she found her Cousin.

As Miss *Charlotte* had a large Share of Coquetry in her Composition, and was fond of Beauty in none of her own Sex but herself, she was sorry to see Lady *Bella* possessed of so great a Share; and, being in Hopes her Brother had drawn a flattering Figure of her Cousin, she was extremely disappointed at finding the Original so handsome.

Arabella, on the contrary, was highly pleased with Miss *Glanville*; and, finding her Person very agreeable, did not fail to commend her Beauty: A sort of Complaisance mightily in Use among the Heroines, who knew not what Envy or Emulation meant.

Miss *Glanville* received her Praises with great Politeness, but could not find in her Heart to return them: And, as soon as these Compliments were over, Mr. *Glanville* told Lady *Bella*, how tedious he had found the short Absence she had forced him to, and how great was his Satisfaction at seeing her again.

I shall not dispute the Truth of your last Assertion, replied *Arabella*, smiling, since I verily believe, you are mighty well satisfied at present; but I know not how you will make it appear, that an Absence, which you allow to be short, has seemed so tedious to you; for this is a manifest Contradiction: However, pursued she, preventing his Reply, you look so well, and so much at Ease, that I am apt to believe, Absence has agreed very well with you.

And yet I assure you, Madam, said Mr. *Glanville*, interrupting her, that I have suffered more Uneasiness during this Absence, than I fear you will permit me to tell you.

Since, replied *Arabella*, that Uneasiness has neither made you thinner, nor paler, I don't think you ought to be pitied: For, to say the Truth, in these Sort of Matters, a Person's bare Testimony has but little Weight.

Mr. *Glanville* was going to make her some Answer; when Miss *Glanville*, who, while they had been speaking, was adjusting her Dress at the Glass, came up to them, and made the Conversation more general.

After Dinner, they adjourned to the Gardens, where the gay Miss *Glanville*, running eagerly from one Walk to another, gave her Brother as many Opportunities of talking to Lady *Bella* as he could wish: However, he stood in such Awe of her, and dreaded so much another Banishment, that he did not dare, otherwise than by distant Hints, to mention his Passion; and *Arabella*, well enough pleased with a Respect that in some measure came up to her Expectation, discovered no Resentment at Insinuations she was at Liberty to dissemble the Knowlege of: And if he could not, by her Behaviour, flatter himself with any great Hopes, yet he found as little Reason, in *Arabella's* Language, to despair.

Miss *Glanville*, at the End of a few Weeks, was so tired of the magnificent Solitude she lived in, that she heartily repented her Journey; and insinuated to her Brother, her Inclination to return to Town.

Mr. *Glanville*, knowing his Stay was regulated by his Sister's, intreated her not to expose him to the Mortification of leaving *Arabella* so soon; and promised her he would contrive some Amusements for her, which should make her relish the Country better than she had yet done.

Accordingly, he proposed to *Arabella* to go to the Races, which were to be held at —— a few Miles from the Castle: She would have excused herself, upon account of her Mourning; but Miss *Glanville* discovered so great an Inclination to be present at this Diversion, that *Arabella* could no longer refuse to accompany her.

Since, said she to Miss *Glanville*, you are fond of public Diversions, it happens very luckily, that these Races are to be held at the Time you are here: I never heard of them before, and I presume 'tis a good many Years since they were last celebrated. Pray, Sir, pursued she, turning to *Glanville*, do not these Races, in some Degree, resemble the *Olympic* Games? Do the candidates ride in Chariots?[1]

No, Madam, replied *Glanville*; the Jockeys are mounted upon the fleetest Coursers they can procure; and he who first reaches the Goal obtains the Prize.

And who is the fair Lady that is to bestow it? resumed *Arabella*: I dare engage one of her Lovers will enter the Lists; she will, doubtless, be in no less Anxiety than he; and the Shame of being overcome, will hardly affect him with more Concern, than herself; that is, provided he be so happy as to have gained her Affections. I cannot help thinking the fair *Elismonda* was extremely happy in this Particular: For she had the Satisfaction to see her secret Admirer Victor in all the Exercises at the *Olympic* Games, and carry away the Prize from many Princes, and Persons of rare Quality, who were Candidates with him; and he had also the Glory to receive three Crowns in one Day, from the Hands of his adored Princess; who, questionless, bestowed them upon him with an infinite deal of Joy.

What Sort of Races were those, Madam? said Miss *Glanville*; whose Reading had been very confined.

The *Olympic* Games, Miss, said *Arabella*, so called from *Olympia*, a City near which they were performed, in the Plains of *Elis*, consisted of Foot and Chariot-Races; Combats with the Cestus; Wrestling, and other Sports. They were instituted in Honour of the Gods and Heroes; and were therefore termed sacred, and were considered as a Part of Religion.

They were a kind of School, or military Apprenticeship; in which the Courage of the Youth found constant Employment: And the Reason why Victory in those Games was attended with such extraordinary Applause, was, that their Minds might be quickened with great and noble Prospects, when, in this Image of War, they arrived to a Pitch of Glory, approaching, in some respects, to that of the most famous Conquerors. They thought this Sort of Triumph one of the greatest Parts of Happiness of which Human Nature was capable: So that when *Diagoras* had seen his Sons crowned in the *Olympic* Games, one of his Friends made him this Compliment, Now, *Diagoras*, you may die satisfied; since you can't be a God. It would tire you, perhaps, was I to describe all the Exercises performed there: But you may form a general Notion of them, from what you have doubtless read of Justs and Tournaments.[1]

Really, said Miss *Glanville*, I never read about any such Things.

No! replied *Arabella*, surprised: Well, then, I must tell you, that they hold a middle Place, between a Diversion and a Combat; but the *Olympic* Games were attended with a much greater Pomp and Variety: And not only all *Greece*, but other neighbouring Nations, were in a manner drained, to furnish out the Appearance.

Well, for my Part, said Miss *Glanville*, I never before heard of these Sort of Races; those I have been at were quite different. I know the Prizes and Bets are sometimes very considerable.

And, doubtless, interrupted *Arabella*, there are a great many Heroes who signalize themselves at these Races; not for the sake of the Prize, which would be unworthy of great Souls, but to satisfy

that burning Desire of Glory, which spurs them on to every
Occasion of gaining it.

As for the Heroes, or Jockeys, said Miss *Glanville*, call them what
you please, I believe they have very little Share, either of the Profit
or Glory: For their Masters have the one, and the Horses the
other.

Their Masters! interrupted *Arabella :* What, I suppose, a great
many foreign Princes send their Favourites to Combat, in their
Name? I remember to have read, that *Alcibiades* triumphed three
times successively at the *Olympic* Games, by means of one of his
Domestics, who, in his Master's Name, entered the Lists.[1]

Mr. *Glanville*, fearing his Sister would make some absurd
Answer, and thereby disoblige his Cousin, took up the Discourse:
And, turning it upon the *Grecian* History, engrossed her Conversation, for two Hours, wholly to himself; while Miss *Glanville* (to
whom all they said was quite unintelligible) diverted herself with
humming a Tune, and tinkling her Cousin's Harpsichord; which
proved no Interruption to the more rational Entertainment of her
Brother and *Arabella*.

CHAPTER VIII

Which concludes with an excellent moral Sentence

THE Day being come on which they designed to be present at the
Races (or, as *Arabella* called them, the *Games*), Miss *Glanville*,
having spent four long Hours in dressing herself to the greatest
Advantage, in order, if possible, to eclipse her lovely Cousin, whose
Mourning, being much deeper, was less capable of Ornaments,
came into her Chamber; and, finding her still in her Morning
Dress, For Heaven's sake, Lady *Bella*, said she, when do you purpose to be ready? Why it is almost time to be gone, my Brother says,
and here you are not a bit dressed!

Don't be uneasy, said *Arabella*, smiling; and, going to her
Toilet, I shan't make you wait long.

Miss *Glanville*, seating herself near the Table, resolved to be
present while her Cousin was dressing, that she might have an
Opportunity to make some Remarks to her Disadvantage: But she

was extremely mortified, to observe the Haste and Negligence she made her Women use in this important Employment; and that, notwithstanding her Indifference, nothing could appear more lovely and genteel.[1]

Miss *Glanville*, however, pleased herself with the Certainty of seeing her Cousin's Dress extremely ridiculed, for the peculiar Fashion of her Gown: And the Veil, which, as becoming as it was, would, by its Novelty, occasion great Diversion among the Ladies, helped to comfort her for the Superiority of her Charms; which, partial as she was to her own, she could not help secretly confessing.

Arabella being dressed in much less time than her Cousin, Mr. *Glanville* was admitted, who led her down Stairs to her Coach. His Sister (secretly repining at the Advantage *Arabella* had over her, in having so respectful an Adorer) followed: And, being placed in the Coach, they set out with great Appearance of Good-humour on all Sides.

They got to —— but just time enough to see the Beginning of the first Course: *Arabella*, who fansied the Jockeys were Persons of great Distinction, soon became interested in the Fate of one of them, whose Appearance pleased her more than the others. Accordingly, she made Vows for his Success, and appeared so extremely rejoiced at the Advantage he had gained, that Miss *Glanville*, maliciously told her, People would make Remarks at the Joy she expressed, and fansy she had a more than ordinary Interest in that Jockey, who had first reached the Goal.

Mr. *Glanville*, whom this impertinent Insinuation of his Sister had filled with Confusion and Spite, sat biting his Lips, trembling for the Effect it would produce in *Arabella*: But she, giving quite another Turn to her Cousin's Words, I assure you, said she, with a Smile, I am not any further interested in the Fate of this Person, who has hitherto been successful, than what the Handsomeness of his Garb, and the Superiority of his Skill, may demand, from an unprejudiced Spectator: And, though I perceive you imagine he is some concealed Lover of mine, yet I don't remember to have ever seen him: And I am confident it is not for my sake that he entered the Lists; nor is it my Presence which animates him.

Lord bless me, Madam! replied Miss *Glanville*, Who would ever think of such strange things as these you talk of? No-body will pretend to deny that you are very handsome, to be sure; but yet, thank Heaven, the Sight of you is not so dangerous, but that such sort of People, as these are, may escape your Chains.

Arabella was so wholly taken up with the Event of the Races, that she gave but very little Heed to this sarcastic Answer of Miss *Glanville*; whose Brother, taking Advantage of an Opportunity which *Arabella* gave him by putting her Head quite out of the Coach, chid her very severely for the Liberty she took with her Cousin. *Arabella*, by looking earnestly out of the Window, had given so full a View of her fine Person to a young Baronet, who was not many Paces from the Coach, that, being struck with Admiration at the Sight of so lovely a Creature, he was going up to some of her Attendants to ask who she was, when he perceived Mr. *Glanville*, with whom he was intimately acquainted, in the Coach with her: Immediately he made himself known to his Friend, being excessively rejoiced at having got an Opportunity of beginning an Acquaintance with a Lady whose Sight had so charmed him.

Mr. *Glanville*, who had observed the profound Bow he made to *Arabella*, accompanied with a Glance that shewed an extreme Admiration of her, was very little pleased at this Meeting; yet he dissembled his Thoughts well enough in his Reception of him. But Miss *Glanville* was quite overjoyed, hoping she would now have her Turn of Gallantry and Compliment: Therefore, accosting him in her free Manner, Dear Sir *George*, said she, you come in a lucky Time to brighten up the Conversation: Relations are such dull Company for one another, 'tis half a Minute since we have exchanged a Word.

My Cousin, said *Arabella* smiling, has so strange a Disposition for Mirth, that she thinks all her Moments are lost, in which she finds nothing to laugh at: For my Part, I do so earnestly long to know, to which of these Pretenders Fortune will give the Victory, that I can suffer my Cares for them to receive no Interruption from my Cousin's agreeable Gaiety.

Mr. *Glanville*, observing the Baronet gazed upon *Arabella* earnestly while she was speaking those few Words, resolved to hinder him from making any Reply, by asking him several Questions concerning the Racers, their Owners, and the Bets which were laid; to which *Arabella* added, And pray, Sir, said she, do me the Favour to tell me, if you know who that gallant Man is, who has already won the first Course.

I don't know really, Madam, said Sir *George*, what his Name is, extremely surprised at her Manner of asking.

The Jockey had now gained the Goal a Second time; and *Arabella* could not conceal her Satisfaction. Questionless, said she, he is a very extraordinary Person; but I am afraid we shall not have the Pleasure of knowing who he is; for if he has any Reason for keeping himself concealed, he will evade any Inquiries after him, by slipping out of the Lists while this Hurry and Tumult lasts, as *Hortensius* did at the *Olympic* Games; yet, notwithstanding all his Care, he was discovered by being obliged to fight a single Combat with one of the Persons whom he had worsted at those Games.[1]

Mr. *Glanville*, who saw his Sister, by her little Coquetries with Sir *George*, had prevented him from hearing great Part of this odd Speech, proposed returning to the Castle; to which *Arabella* agreed: But, conceiving Civility obliged her to offer the Convenience of a Lodging to a Stranger of Sir *George's* Appearance, and who was an Acquaintance of her Cousins, You must permit me, said she to Mr. *Glanville*, to intreat your noble Friend will accompany us to the Castle, where he will meet with better Accommodations than at any Inn he can find; for I conceive, that, coming only to be a Spectator of these Games, he is wholly unprovided with a Lodging.

The Baronet, surprised at so uncommon a Civility,[2] was at a Loss what Answer to make her at first; but, recollecting himself, he told her that he would, if she pleased, do himself the Honour to attend her home; but, as his House was at no great Distance from ——, he would be put to no Inconveniency for a Lodging.

Miss *Glanville*, who was not willing to part so soon with the Baronet, insisted, with her Cousin's Leave, upon his coming into the Coach; which he accordingly did, giving his Horse to the Care of his Servant; and they proceeded together to the Castle; *Arabella* still continuing to talk of the Games, as she called them, while poor *Glanville*, who was excessively confused, endeavoured to change the Discourse, not without an Apprehension, that every Subject he could think of, would afford *Arabella* an Occasion of shewing her Foible; which, notwithstanding the Pain it gave him, could not lessen his Love.

Sir *George*, whose Admiration of Lady *Bella* increased the longer he saw her, was extremely pleased with the Opportunity she had given him of cultivating an Acquaintance with her: He therefore lengthened out his Visit, in hopes of being able to say some fine Things to her before he went away; but Miss *Glanville*, who strove by all the little Arts she was Mistress of, to engage his Conversation wholly to herself, put it absolutely out of his Power; so that he was obliged to take his Leave without having the Satisfaction of even pressing the fair Hand of *Arabella*; so closely was he observed by her Cousin. Happy was it for him, that he was prevented by her Vigilance from attempting a Piece of Gallantry, which would, undoubtedly, have procured him a Banishment from her Presence; but, ignorant, how kind Fortune was to him in balking his Designs, he was ungrateful enough to go away in a mighty ill Humour with this fickle Goddess: So little capable are poor Mortals of knowing what is best for them!

CHAPTER IX

Containing some curious Anecdotes

LADY *Bella*, from the Familiarity with which Miss *Glanville* treated this gay Gentleman, concluding him her Lover, and one who was apparently well received by her, had a strong Curiosity to know her Adventures;[1] and as they were walking the next Morning in the Garden, she told her, that she thought it was very strange they had hitherto observed such a Reserve to each other, as to banish mutual Trust and Confidence from their Conversation: Whence comes it, Cousin, added she, being so young and lovely as you are, that you, questionless, have been engaged in many Adventures, you have never reposed Trust enough in me to favour me with a Recital of them?

Engaged in many Adventures, Madam! returned Miss *Glanville*, not liking the Phrase: I believe I have been engaged in as few as your Ladyship.

You are too obliging, returned *Arabella*, who mistook what she said for a Compliment; for since you have more Beauty than I, and have also had more Opportunities of making yourself beloved, questionless you have a greater Number of Admirers.

As for Admirers, said Miss *Charlotte* bridling, I fancy I have had my Share! Thank God, I never found myself neglected; but, I assure you, Madam, I have had no Adventures, as you call them, with any of them.

No, really! interrupted *Arabella*, innocently.

No, really, Madam, retorted Miss *Glanville*; and I am surprised you should think so.

Indeed, my Dear, said *Arabella*, you are very happy in this respect, and also very singular; for I believe there are few young Ladies in the World, who have any Pretensions to Beauty, that have not given Rise to a great many Adventures; and some of them haply very fatal.

If you knew more of the World, Lady *Bella*, said Miss *Glanville* pertly, you would not be so apt to think, that young Ladies engage themselves in troublesome Adventures: Truly the Ladies that are brought up in Town are not so ready to run away with every Man they see.

No, certainly, interrupted *Arabella*; they do not give their Consent to such Proceedings; but for all that, they are, doubtless, run away with many times; for truly there are some Men, whose Passions are so unbridled, that they will have recourse to the most violent Methods to possess themselves of the Objects they love. Pray do you remember how often *Mandana* was run away with?[1]

Not I indeed, Madam, replied Miss *Glanville*; I know nothing about her; but I suppose she is a *Jew*, by her outlandish Name.

She was no *Jew*, said *Arabella*, tho' she favoured that People very much; for she obtained the Liberty of great Numbers of them from *Cyrus*, who had taken them Captives, and could deny her nothing she asked.[2]

Well, said Miss *Glanville*; and I suppose she denied *him* nothing he asked; and so they were even.

Indeed but she did tho', resumed *Arabella*; for she refused to give him a glorious Scarf which she wore, tho' he begged it on his Knees.[3]

And she was very much in the right, said Miss *Glanville*; for I see no Reason why a Lover should expect a Gift of any Value from his Mistress.

Doubtless, said *Arabella*, such a Gift was worth a Million of Services; and, had he obtained it, it would have been a glorious Distinction for him: However, *Mandana* refused it; and, severely virtuous as you are, I am persuaded you can't help thinking, she was a little too rigorous in denying a Favour to a Lover like him—

Severely virtuous, Lady *Bella*! said Miss *Glanville*, reddening with Anger: Pray what do you mean by that? Have you any Reason to imagine, I would grant any Favour to a Lover?

Why, if I did, Cousin, said *Arabella*, would it derogate so much from your Glory, think you, to bestow a Favour upon a Lover worthy your Esteem, and from whom you had received a thousand Marks of a most pure and faithful Passion, and also a great Number of very singular Services?

I hope, Madam, said Miss *Glanville*, it will never be my Fate to be so much obliged to any Lover, as to be under a Necessity of granting him Favours in Requital.

I vow, Cousin, interrupted *Arabella*, you put me in mind of the fair and virtuous *Antonia*, who was so rigid and austere, that she thought all Expressions of Love were criminal; and was so far from granting any Person Permission to love her, that she thought it a mortal Offence to be adored even in private.[1]

Miss *Glanville*, who could not imagine *Arabella* spoke this seriously, but that it was designed to sneer at her great Eagerness to make Conquests, and the Liberties she allowed herself in, which had probably come to her Knowlege, was so extremely vexed at the malicious Jest, as she thought it, that, not being able to revenge herself, she burst into Tears.

Arabella's Good-nature made her be greatly affected at this Sight; and, asking her Pardon for having undesignedly occasioned her so much Uneasiness, begged her to be composed, and tell her in what she had offended her, that she might be able to justify herself in her Apprehensions.

You have made no Scruple to own, Madam, said she, that you think me capable of granting Favours to Lovers, when, Heaven knows, I never granted a Kiss without a great deal of Confusion.

And you had certainly much Reason for Confusion, said *Arabella*, excessively surprised at such a Confession: I assure you I never injured you so much in my Thoughts, as to suppose you ever granted a Favour of so criminal a Nature.

Look you there now! said Miss *Glanville*, weeping more violently than before: I knew what all your round-about Speeches would come to: All you have said in Vindication of granting Favours, was only to draw me into a Confession of what I have done: How ungenerous was that!

The Favours I spoke of, Madam, said *Arabella*, were quite of another Nature, than those it seems you have so liberally granted: Such as giving a Scarf, a Bracelet, or some such Thing, to a Lover, who had haply sighed whole Years in Silence, and did not presume to declare his Passion, till he had lost best Part of his Blood in Defence of the Fair one he loved: It was when you maintained, that *Mandana* was in the right to refuse her magnificent Scarf to the illustrious *Cyrus*, that I took upon me to oppose your Rigidness; and so much mistaken was I in your Temper, that I foolishly compared you to the fair and wise *Antonia*, whose Severity was so remarkable; but really, by what I understand from your own Confession, your Disposition resembles that of the inconsiderate[1] *Julia*, who would receive a Declaration of Love without Anger from any one; and was not over-shy, any more than yourself, of granting Favours almost as considerable as that you have mentioned.

While *Arabella* was speaking, Miss *Glanville*, having dried up her Tears, sat silently swelling with Rage, not knowing whether she should openly avow her Resentment for the injurious Language her Cousin had used to her, by going away immediately, or, by making up the Matter, appear still to be her Friend, that she might have the more Opportunities of revengeing herself. The Impetuosity of her Temper made her most inclined to the former; but the Knowlege that Sir *George* was to stay yet some Months in the Country, made her unwilling to leave a Place, where she might often see a Man whose fine Person had made some Impression upon her Heart; and, not enduring to leave such a charming Conquest to *Arabella*, she resolved to suppress her Resentment for the present; and listened, without any Appearance of Discomposure, to a fine Harangue of her Cousin upon the Necessity of Reserve, and distant Behaviour, to Men who presumed to declare themselves Lovers, enforcing her Precepts with Examples drawn from all the Romances she had ever read; at the End of which she embraced her; and assured her, if she had said any thing harsh, it proceeded from her great Regard to her Glory, of which she ardently wished to see her as fond as herself.

Miss *Glanville* constrained herself to make a Reply that might not appear disagreeable: And they were upon these Terms, when Mr. *Glanville* came up to them, and told Lady *Bella*, Sir *George* had sent to intreat their Company at his House that Day: But, added he, as I presume you will not think proper to go, on account of your Mourning, neither my Sister nor I will accept the Invitation.

I dare say, interrupted Miss *Glanville* hastily, Lady *Bella* will not expect such a needless Piece of Ceremony from us; and, if she don't think proper to go, she won't confine *us*.

By no means, Cousin, said *Arabella*, smiling; and, being persuaded Sir *George* makes the Entertainment purely for your Sake, it would not be kind in me to deprive him of your Company.

Mr. *Glanville*, being pleased to find his Cousin discovered no Inclination to go, would have persuaded his Sister not to leave Lady *Bella*: But Miss *Glanville* looked so much displeased at his Request, that he was obliged to insist upon it no more; and, both retiring to dress, Lady *Bella* went up to her Apartment, and betook herself to her Books, which supplied the Place of all Company to her.

Miss *Glanville*, having taken more than ordinary Pains in dressing herself, in order to appear charming in the Eyes of Sir *George*, came in to pay her Compliments to Lady *Bella* before she went, not doubting but she would be chagrined to see her look so well: But Lady *Bella*, on the contrary, praised the Clearness of her Complexion, and the Sparkling of her Eyes.

I question not, said she, but you will give Fetters to more Persons than one To-day; but remember, I charge you, added she smiling, while you are taking away the Liberty of others, to have a special Care of your own.

Miss *Glanville*, who could not think it possible, one Woman could praise another with any Sincerity, cast a Glance at the Glass, fearing it was rather because she looked but indifferently, that her Cousin was so lavish in her Praises; and, while she was settling her Features in a Mirror which every Day represented a Face infinitely more lovely than her own, Mr. *Glanville* came in, who, after having very respectfully taken Leave of Lady *Bella*, led his Sister to the Coach.

Sir *George*, who was extremely mortified to find Lady *Bella* not in it, handed Miss *Glanville* out with an Air so reserved, that she raillied him upon it; and gave her Brother a very unpleasing Emotion, by telling Sir *George*, she hoped Lady *Bella*'s not coming along with them, would not make him bad Company.

As he was too gallant to suffer an handsome young Lady, who spread all her Attractions for him, to believe he regretted the absence of another when she was present; he coquetted with her so much, that Mr. *Glanville* was in hopes his Sister would wholly engage him from Lady *Bella*.

CHAPTER X

In which our Heroine is engaged in a very perilous Adventure

IN the mean time, that solitary Fair one was alarmed by a Fear of a very unaccountable Nature; for, being in the Evening in her Closet, the Windows of which had a Prospect of the Gardens, she saw her illustrious concealed Lover, who went by the Name of *Edward*, while he was in her Father's Service, talking with great Emotion to her House-Steward, who seemed earnestly to listen to some Propositions he was making to him. Her Surprize at this Sight was so great, that she had not Power to observe them any longer; but, seating herself in her Chair, she had just Spirits enough to call *Lucy* to her Assistance; who, extremely frighted at the pale Looks of her Lady, gave her a Smelling-bottle, and was preparing to cut her Lace, when *Arabella*, preventing her, told her in a low Voice, that she feared she should be betrayed into the Hands of an insolent Lover, who was come to steal her away. Yes, added she with great Emotion, I have seen this presumptuous Man holding a Conversation with one of my Servants; and tho' I could not possibly, at this Distance, hear their Discourse, yet the Gestures they used in speaking, explained it too well to me; and I have Reason to expect, I shall suffer the same Violence that many illustrious Ladies have done before me; and be carried away by Force from my own House, as they were.

Alas! Madam! said *Lucy*, terrified at this Discourse, who is it that intends to carry your Ladyship away? Sure no Robbers will attempt any Mischief at such a time as this!

Yes, *Lucy*, replied *Arabella*, with great Gravity, the worst kind of Robbers; Robbers who do not prey upon Gold and Jewels; but, what is infinitely more precious, Liberty and Honour. Do you know that Person who called himself *Edward*, and worked in these Gardens like a common Gardener, is now in the House, corrupting my Servants; and, questionless, preparing to force open my Chamber, and carry me away? And Heaven knows when I shall be delivered from his Chains.

God forbid, said *Lucy*, sobbing, that ever such a Lady should have such hard Hap! What Crime, I wonder, can you be guilty of, to deserve to be in Chains?

My Crime, resumed *Arabella*, is to have Attractions which ex-

pose me to these inevitable Misfortunes, which even the greatest
Princesses have not escaped.—But, dear *Lucy*, can you not think of
some Methods by which I may avoid the Evil which waits me?
Who knows but that he may, within these few Moments, force a
Passage into my Apartment? These slight Locks can make but a
poor Resistance to the Violence he will be capable of using.

Oh dear Madam! cried *Lucy*, trembling, and pressing near her,
what shall we do?

I asked your Advice, said she; but I perceive you are less able
than myself to think of any thing to save me.—Ah! *Glanville*, pursued she, sighing, would to Heaven thou wert here now!

Yes, Madam, said *Lucy*, Mr. *Glanville*, I am sure, would not
suffer any one to hurt your Ladyship.

As thou valuest my Friendship, said *Arabella*, with great Earnestness, never acquaint him with what has just now escaped my
Lips: True, I did call upon him in this Perplexity; I did pronounce
his Name; and that, haply, with a Sigh, which involuntarily forced
its Way: And, questionless, if he knew his good Fortune, even
amidst the Danger of losing me for ever, he would resent some
Emotions of Joy: But I should die with Shame at having so indiscreetly contributed to his Satisfaction: And, therefore, again I
charge you, conceal, with the utmost Care, what I have said.

Indeed, Madam, said *Lucy*, I shall tell him nothing but what
your Ladyship bids me; and I am so frighted, that I can think of
nothing but that terrible Man, that wants to carry you away. Mercy
on us! added she, starting, I think I hear somebody on the Stairs!

Do not be alarmed, said *Arabella*, in a majestic Tone: It is I who
have most Reason to fear: Nevertheless, I hope the Grandeur of
my Courage will not sink under this Accident. Hark, somebody
knocks at the Door of my Antechamber:—My own Virtue shall
support me:—Go, *Lucy*, and ask who it is.

Indeed I can't, Madam, said she, clinging to her: Pray pardon
me: Indeed I am so afraid, I cannot stir.

Weak-souled Wench! said *Arabella*, How unfit art thou for
Accidents like these! Ah! had *Cylenia* and *Martesia* been like thee,
the fair *Berenice*, and the Divine Princess of *Media*, had not so
eagerly intreated their Ravishers to afford them their Company in
their Captivity.[1] But go, I order you, and ask who it is that is at the
Door of my Apartment: They knock again: Offer at no Excuses;
but do your Duty.

Lucy, seeing her Lady was really angry, went trembling out of the Closet; but would go no farther than her Bedchamber, from whence she called out to know who was at the Door.

I have some Business with your Lady, said the House-Steward (for it was he that knocked): Can I speak with her at present?

Lucy, a little reassured by his Voice, made no Answer; but, creeping softly to the Door of the Antechamber, double-locked it; and then cried out in a Transport, No, I will take Care you shall not come to my Lady.

And why, pray, Mrs. *Lucy*? said the Steward: What have I done, that you are so much my Enemy?

You are a Rogue, said *Lucy*, growing very courageous, because the Door was locked between them.

A Rogue! said he, What Reason have you for calling me a Rogue? I assure you I will acquaint my Lady with your Insolence. I came to speak to her Ladyship about *Edward*; who prayed me to intercede for him, that he may be taken again into her Service: For he says, my Lady never believed any thing against him; and that was my Business: But, when I see her, I'll know whether you are allowed to abuse me in this manner.

Arabella, by this time, was advanced as far as the Bedchamber, longing to know what sort of Conference *Lucy* was holding with her intended Ravisher: When that faithful Confidante, seeing her, came running to her, and whispered her, that the House-Steward was at the Door, and said he wanted to intercede for *Edward*.

Ah! the Traitor! said *Arabella*, retiring again: Has he, then, really bargained with that disloyal Man, to deliver up his Mistress? I am undone, *Lucy*, said she, unless I can find a Way to escape out of the House. They will, questionless, soon force the Doors of my Apartment.

Suppose, said *Lucy*, your Ladyship went down the Stairs that lead from your Dressing-room into the Garden; and you may hide yourself in the Gardener's House till Mr. *Glanville* come.

I approve, said *Arabella*, of one Part of your Proposal: But I shall not trust myself in the Gardener's House; who, questionless, is in the Plot with the rest of my perfidious Servants, since none of them have endeavoured to advertise me of my Danger. If we can gain the Gardens undiscovered, we may get out by that Door at the Foot of the Terrace, which leads into the Fields; for you know I always keep the Key of that private Door: So, *Lucy*, let us commend ourselves to the Direction of Providence, and be gone immediately.

But what shall we do, Madam, said *Lucy*, when we are got out?

Why, said *Arabella*, you shall conduct me to your Brother's; and, probably, we may meet with some generous Cavalier by the Way, who will protect us till we get thither: However, as I have as great a Danger to fear within Doors, as without, I will venture to make my Escape, though I should not be so fortunate as to meet with any Knight who will undertake to protect me from the Danger which I may apprehend in the Fields.

Saying this, she gave the Key of the Door to *Lucy*, whose Heart beat violently with Fear; and, covering herself with some black Cypress, which she wore in the Nature of a Veil, went softly down the little Staircase to the Terrace, followed by *Lucy* (who looked eagerly about her every Step that she went); and, having gained the Garden-door, hastily unlocked it, and fled, as fast as possible, cross the Fields, in order to procure a Sanctuary at *William*'s House: *Arabella*, begging Heaven to throw some generous Cavalier in her Way, whose Protection she might implore, and, taking every Tree at a Distance for a Horse and Knight, hastened her Steps to meet her approaching Succour; which, as soon as she came near, miserably balked her Expectations.

Though *William*'s Farm was not more than two Miles from the Castle; yet *Arabella*, unused to such a rude Way of Travelling, began to be greatly fatigued: The Fear she was in of being pursued by her apprehended Ravisher, had so violent an Effect upon her Spirits, that she was hardly able to prosecute her Flight; and, to complete her Misfortunes, happening to stumble over a Stump of a Tree that lay in her Way, she strained her Ancle; and the violent Anguish she felt, threw her into a Swoon.

Lucy, upon whose Arm she leaned, perceiving her fainting, screamed out aloud, not knowing what to do with her in that Condition: She placed her upon the Ground; and, supporting her Head against that fatal Stump, began to rub her Temples, weeping excessively all the time. Her Swoon still continuing, the poor Girl was in inconceivable Terror: Her Brother's House was now but a little Way off; but it being impossible for her to carry her Lady thither without some Help, she knew not what to resolve upon.

At length, thinking it better to leave her for a few Moments, to run for Assistance, than to sit by her and see her perish for want of it, she left her, though not without extreme Agony; and flew, with the utmost Eagerness, to her Brother's. She was lucky enough to meet him just coming out of his Door; and, telling him the Condition in which she left her Lady, he, without asking any Questions about the Occasion of so strange an Accident, notwithstanding his Amazement, ran with all Speed to the Place where *Lucy* had left her: But, to their Astonishment and Sorrow, she was not to be found:[1] They walked a long time in Search of her; and *Lucy*, being almost distracted with Fear lest she had been carried away, made Complaints that so puzzled her Brother he knew not what to say to her: But, finding their Search fruitless, they agreed to go home to the Castle, supposing, with some Appearance of Reason, that they might hear of her there.

Here they found nothing but Grief and Confusion. Mr. *Glanville* and his Sister were just returned, and had been at Lady *Bella*'s Apartment; but, not finding her there, they asked her Women where she was, who, not knowing any thing of her Flight, concluded she was in the Garden with *Lucy*. Mr. *Glanville*, surprised at her being at that Hour in the Garden, ran eagerly to engage her to come in, being apprehensive she would take Cold, by staying so late in the Air: But, not finding her in any of her usual Walks, he ordered several of the Servants to assist him in searching the whole Garden, sending them to different Places: But they all returned without Success; which filled him with the utmost Consternation.

He was returning, excessively uneasy, to the House, when he saw *Lucy*; who had been just told, in answer to her Inquiries about her Lady, that they were gone to look for her in the Garden; and running up to Mr. *Glanville*, who hoped to hear News of Lady *Bella* from her, Oh! Sir, said she, is my Lady found?

What! *Lucy*, said Mr. *Glanville* (more alarmed than before), do not you know where she is? I thought you had been with her.

Oh! dear, cried *Lucy*, wringing her Hands; for certain my poor Lady was stolen away while she was in that fainting Fit. Sir, said she to *Glanville*, I know who the Person is that my Lady said (and almost broke my Heart) would keep her in Chains: He was in the House not many Hours ago.

Mr. *Glanville*, suspecting this was some new Whim of *Arabella*'s, would not suffer *Lucy* to say any more before the Servants, who stood gaping with Astonishment at the strange Things she uttered;

but bid her follow him to his Apartment, and he would hear what she could inform him concerning this Accident. He would, if possible, have prevented his Sister from being present at the Story; but, not being able to form any Excuse for not suffering her to hear every thing that related to her Cousin, they all three went into his Chamber; where he desired *Lucy* to tell him what she knew about her Lady.

You must know, Sir, said *Lucy*, sobbing, that there came a Man here to take away my Lady: A great Man he is, though he worked in the Gardens; for he was in Love with her: And so he would not own who he was.

And pray, interrupted Miss *Glanville*, Who told you he was a great Man, as you say?

My Lady told me, said *Lucy*: But, *howsomever*, he was turned away; for the Gardener says he catched him stealing Carp.

A very great Man, indeed, said Miss *Glanville*, that would steal Carp!

You must know, Madam, said she, that was only a Pretence: For he went there, my Lady says, to drown himself.

Bless me! cried Miss *Glanville*, laughing; the Girl's distracted, sure. Lord! Brother, don't listen to her nonsensical Tales; we shall never find my Cousin by her.

Leave her to me, said Mr. *Glanville*, whispering: Perhaps I may discover something by her Discourse, that will give us some Light into this Affair.

Nay, I'll stay, I am resolved, answered she; for I long to know where my Cousin is: Tho', do you think what this Girl says is true, about a great Man disguised in the Gardens? Sure my Cousin could never tell her such Stuff: But, now I think of it, added she, Lady *Bella*, when we were speaking about the Jockey, talked something about a Lover: I now believe it is as the Girl says. Pray let's hear her out.

Mr. *Glanville* was ready to die with Vexation, at the Charmer of his Soul's being thus exposed; but there was no Help for it.

Pray, said he to *Lucy*, tell us no more about this Man: But, if you can guess where your Lady is, let me know.

Indeed I can't, Sir, said she; for my Lady and I both stole out of the House, for fear *Edward* should break open the Doors of her Apartment; and we were running as fast as possible to my Brother's House (where she said she would hide herself till you came); but my poor dear Lady fell down and hurt herself so much, that she fainted away: I tried what I could to fetch her again; but she did not open her Eyes: So I ran like Lightning to my Brother, to come and help me to carry her to the Farm; but, when we came back, she was gone.

What do you say? cried Mr. *Glanville*, with a distracted Look: Did you leave her in that Condition in the Fields? And was she not to be found when you came back?

No, indeed, Sir, said *Lucy*, weeping, we could not find her, though we wandered about a long time.

Oh! Heavens! said he, walking about the Room in a violent Emotion, Where can she be? What is become of her? Dear Sister, pursued he, order somebody to saddle my Horse: I'll traverse the Country all Night in quest of her.

You had best inquire, Sir, said *Lucy*, if *Edward* is in the House: He knows, may be, where my Lady is.

Who is he? cried *Glanville*.

Why the great Man, Sir, said *Lucy*, whom we thought to be a Gardener, who came to carry my Lady away; which made her get out of the House as fast as she could.

This is the strangest Story, said Miss *Glanville*, that ever I heard: Sure nobody would be so mad to attempt such an Action; my Cousin has the oddest Whims!

Mr. *Glanville*, not able to listen any longer, charged *Lucy* to say nothing of this Matter to any one; and then ran eagerly out of the Room, ordering two or three of the Servants to go in Search of their Lady: He then mounted his Horse in great Anguish of Mind, not knowing whither to direct his Course.

CHAPTER XI

In which the Lady is wonderfully delivered

BUT to return to *Arabella*, whom we left in a very melancholy Situation: *Lucy* had not been gone long from her before she opened her Eyes; and, beginning to come perfectly to herself, was surprised to find her Woman not near her: The Moon shining very bright, she looked round her, and called *Lucy* as loud as she was able; but not seeing her, or hearing any Answer, her Fears became so powerful, that she had like to have relapsed into her Swoon.

Alas! unfortunate Maid that I am! cried she, weeping excessively, questionless I am betrayed by her on whose Fidelity I
relied, and who was acquainted with my most secret Thoughts:
She is now with my Ravisher, directing his Pursuit, and I have no
Means of escaping from his Hands! Cruel and ungrateful Wench,
thy unparalleled Treachery grieves me no less than all my other
Misfortunes: But why do I say, Her Treachery is unparalleled?
Did not the wicked *Arianta* betray her Mistress into the Power of
her insolent Lover?[1] Ah! *Arabella*, thou art not single in thy
Misery, since the divine *Mandana* was, like thyself, the Dupe of a
mercenary Servant.

Having given a Moment or two to these sad Reflections, she rose
from the Ground with an Intention to walk on; but her Ancle was
so painful, that she could hardly move: Her Tears began now to
flow with greater Violence: She expected every Moment to see
Edward approach her; and was resigning herself up to Despair,
when a Chaise, driven by a young Gentleman, passed by her.
Arabella, thanking Heaven for sending this Relief, called out as
loud as she could, conjuring him to stay.

The Gentleman, hearing a Woman's Voice, stopped immediately, and asked what she wanted.

Generous Stranger, said *Arabella*, advancing as well as was she
able, do not refuse your Assistance to save me from a most terrible
Danger: I am pursued by a Person whom, for very urgent Reasons,
I desire to avoid. I conjure you, therefore, in the Name of her you
love best, to protect me; and may you be crowned with the Enjoy-
ment of all your Wishes, for so charitable an Action!

If the Gentleman was surprised at this Address, he was much
more astonished at the Beauty of her who made it: Her Stature;
her Shape, her inimitable Complexion; the Lustre of her fine
Eyes, and the thousand Charms that adorned her whole Person,
kept him a Minute silently gazing upon her, without having the
Power to make her an Answer.

Arabella, finding he did not speak, was extremely disappointed.
Ah! Sir, said she, What do you deliberate upon? Is it possible you
can deny so reasonable a Request, to a Lady in my Circumstances?

For God's sake, Madam, said the Gentleman, alighting, and
approaching her, let me know who you are, and how I can be of any
Service to you.

As for my Quality, said *Arabella*, be assured it is not mean; and let this Knowlege suffice at present: The Service I desire of you is, to convey me to some Place where I may be in Safety for this Night: To-morrow I will intreat you to let some Persons, whom I shall name to you, know where I am; to the end they may take proper Measures to secure me from the Attempts of an insolent Man, who has driven me from my own House, by the Designs he was going to execute.

The Gentleman saw there was some Mystery in her Case, which she did not choose to explain; and, being extremely glad at having so beautiful a Creature in his Power, told her she might command him in all she pleased; and, helping her into the Chaise, drove off as fast as he could; *Arabella* suffering no Apprehensions from being alone with a Stranger, since nothing was more common to Heroines than such Adventures; all her Fears being of *Edward*, whom she fansied every Moment she saw pursuing them: And, being extremely anxious to be in some Place of Safety, she urged her Protector to drive as fast as possible; who, willing to have her at his own House, complied with her Request; but was so unlucky in his Haste, as to overturn the Chaise. Though neither *Arabella* nor himself were hurt by the Fall, yet the Necessity there was to stay some time to put the Chaise in a Condition to carry them any farther, filled her with a thousand Apprehensions, lest they should be overtaken.

In the mean time, the Servants of *Arabella*, among whom *Edward*, not knowing how much he was concerned in her Flight, was resolved to distinguish himself by his Zeal in searching for her, had dispersed themselves about in different Places: Chance conducted *Edward* to the very Spot where she was: When *Arabella*, perceiving him while he was two or three Paces off, Oh! Sir, cried she, behold my Persecutor! Can you resolve to defend me against the Violence he comes to offer me?

The Gentleman, looking up, and seeing a Man in Livery approaching them, asked her, If that was the Person she complained of; and if he was her Servant?

If he is my Servant, Sir, replied she, blushing, he never had my Permission to be so: And, indeed, no one else can boast of my having granted them such a Liberty.

Do you know whose Servant he is, then, Madam? replied the Gentleman, a little surprised at her Answer; which he could not well understand.

You throw me into a great Embarrassment, Sir, resumed *Arabella*, blushing more than before: Questionless, he appears to be mine; but, since, as I told you before, he never discovered himself to me, and I never permitted him to assume that Title, his Services, if ever I received any from him, were not at all considered by me, as Things for which I was obliged to him.

The Gentleman, still more amazed at Answers so little to the Purpose, was going to desire her to explain herself upon this strange Affair; when *Edward*, coming up close to *Arabella*, cried out in a Transport, Oh! Madam! thank God you are found.

Hold, impious Man! said *Arabella*, and do not give Thanks for that which, haply, may prove thy Punishment. If I am found, thou wilt be no better for it: And, if thou continuest to persecute me, thou wilt probably meet with thy Death, where thou thinkest thou hast found thy Happiness.

The poor Fellow, who understood not a Word of this Discourse, stared upon her like one that had lost his Wits; when the Protector of *Arabella*, approaching him, asked him, with a stern Look, What he had to say to that Lady, and why he presumed to follow her?

As the Man was going to answer him, Mr. *Glanville* came galloping up; and *Edward*, seeing him, ran up to him, and informed him, that he had met with Lady *Bella*, and a Gentleman, who seemed to have been overturned in a Chaise, which he was endeavouring to refit; and that her Ladyship was offended with him for coming up to her; and also, that the Gentleman had used some threatening Language to him upon that Account.

Mr. *Glanville*, excessively surprised at what he heard, stopped; and, ordering a Servant who came along with him, to run back to the Castle, and bring a Chaise thither to carry Lady *Bella* home, he asked *Edward* several more Questions relating to what she and the Gentleman had said to him: And, notwithstanding his Knowlege of her ridiculous Humour, he could not help being alarmed by her Behaviour, nor concluding that there was something very mysterious in the Affair.

While he was thus conversing with *Edward*, *Arabella*, who had spied him almost as soon, was filled with Apprehension to see him hold so quiet a Parly with her Ravisher: The more she reflected upon this Accident, the more her Suspicions increased; and, persuading herself at last, that Mr. *Glanville* was privy to his Designs, this Belief, however improbable, wrought so powerfully upon her Imagination, that she could not restrain her Tears.

Doubtless, said she, I am betrayed, and the perjured *Glanville* is no longer either my Friend or Lover: He is this Moment concerting Measures with my Ravisher, how to deliver me into his Power; and, like *Philidaspes*, is glad of an Opportunity, by this Treachery, to be rid of a Woman whom his Parents and hers had destined for his Wife.[1]

Mr. *Glanville*, having learned all he could from *Edward*, alighted; and, giving him his Horse to hold, came up to *Arabella*: And, after expressing his Joy at meeting with her, begged her to let him know what Accident had brought her, unattended, from the Castle, at that time of Night.

If by this Question, said the incensed *Arabella*, you would persuade me you are ignorant of the Cause of my Flight, know, your Dissimulation will not succeed; and that, having Reason to believe you are equally guilty with him from whose intended Violence I fled, I shall have recourse to the Valour of this Knight you see with me, to defend me, as well against you, as that Ravisher, with whom I see you leagued.—Ah! unworthy Cousin, pursued she, What dost thou propose to thyself by so black a Treachery? What is to be the Price of my Liberty, which thou so freely disposest of? Has thy Friend there, said she (pointing to *Edward*), a Sister, or any Relation, for whom thou barterest, by delivering me up to him? But, assure thyself, this Stratagem shall be of no Use to thee: For, if thou art base enough to oppress my valiant Deliverer with Numbers, and thinkest, by Violence, to get me into thy Power, my Cries shall arm Heaven and Earth in my Defence. Providence may, haply, send some generous Cavaliers to my Rescue; and, if Providence fails me, my own Hand shall give me Freedom; for that Moment thou offerest to seize me, that Moment shall be the last of my Life.

While *Arabella* was speaking, the young Gentleman and *Edward*, who listened to her, eagerly, thought her Brain was disturbed: But Mr. *Glanville* was in a terrible Confusion, and silently cursed his ill Fate, to make him in Love with a Woman so ridiculous.

For Heaven's sake, Cousin, said he, striving to repress some Part of his Disorder, Do not give way to these extravagant Notions: There is nobody intends to do you any Wrong.

What! interrupted she, would you persuade me, that that Im-

'Rascals! . . . what do you mean by using me in this
manner?' (p. 20)

poster there, pointing to *Edward*, has not a Design to carry me away; which you, by supporting him, are not equally guilty of?

Who? I! Madam! cried out *Edward*: Sure your Ladyship does not suspect me of such a strange Design! God knows I never thought of such a Thing!

Ah! Dissembler! interrupted *Arabella*, do not make use of that sacred Name to mask thy impious Falshoods: Confess with what Intent you came into my Father's Service disguised.

I never came disguised, Madam, returned *Edward*.

No! said *Arabella*: What means that Dress in which I see you, then?

'Tis the Marquis's Livery, Madam, said *Edward*, which he did not order to be taken from me when I left his Service.

And with what Purpose didst thou wear it? said she, Do not your Thoughts accuse you of your Crime?

I always hoped, Madam —— said he.

You hoped! interrupted *Arabella*: frowning, Did I ever give you Reason to hope? I will not deny but I had Compassion on you; but even That you was ignorant of.

I know, Madam, you had Compassion on me, said *Edward*; for your Ladyship, I always thought, did not believe me guilty.

I was weak enough, said she, to have Compassion on you, though I *did* believe you guilty.

Indeed, Madam, returned *Edward*, I always hoped, as I said before (but your Ladyship would not hear me out), that you did not believe any malicious Reports; and therefore you had Compassion on me.

I had no Reports of you, said she, but what my own Observation gave me; and that was sufficient to convince me of your Fault.

Why, Madam, said *Edward*, did your Ladyship see me steal the Carp then, which was the Fault unjustly laid to my Charge?

Mr. *Glanville*, as much Cause as he had for Uneasiness, could with great Difficulty restrain Laughter at this Ludicrous Circumstance; for he guessed what Crime *Arabella* was accusing him of: As for the young Gentleman, he could not conceive what she meant, and longed to hear what would be the End of such a strange Conference. But poor *Arabella* was prodigiously confounded at his mentioning so low an Affair; not being able to endure that *Glanville* and her Protector should know a Lover of her's could be suspected of so base a Theft.

The Shame she conceived at it, kept her silent for a Moment: But, recovering herself at last, No, said she, I knew you better than to give any Credit to such an idle Report: Persons of your Condition do not commit such paltry Crimes.

Upon my Soul, Madam, said the young Gentleman, Persons of his Condition often do worse.

I don't deny it, Sir, said *Arabella*; and the Design he meditated of carrying me away was infinitely worse.

Really, Madam, returned the Gentleman, if you are such a Person as I apprehend, I don't see how he durst make such an Attempt.

It is very possible, Sir, said she, that I might be carried away, though I was of greater Quality than I am: Were not *Mandana, Candace, Clelia*,[1] and many other Ladies who underwent the same Fate, of a Quality more illustrious than mine?

Really, Madam, said he, I know none of these Ladies.

No, Sir! said *Arabella*; extremely mortified.

Let me intreat you, Cousin, interrupted *Glanville* (who feared this Conversation would be very tedious), to expose yourself no longer to the Air at this time of Night: Suffer me to conduct you home.

It concerns my Honour, said she, that this generous Stranger should not think I am the only one that was ever exposed to these insolent Attempts. You say, Sir, pursued she, that you don't know any of these Ladies I mentioned before: Let me ask you, then, If you are acquainted with *Parthenissa*, or *Cleopatra*?[2] who were both, for some Months, in the Hands of their Ravishers.

As for *Parthenissa*, Madam, said he, neither have I heard of her; nor do I remember to have heard of any more than one *Cleopatra*: But she was never ravished, I am certain; for she was too willing.

How! Sir, said *Arabella*: Was *Cleopatra* ever willing to run away with her Ravisher?

Cleopatra was a Whore, was she not, Madam? said he.

Hold thy Peace, unworthy Man, said *Arabella*; and profane not the Memory of that fair and glorious Queen, by such injurious Language: That Queen, I say, whose Courage was equal to her Beauty; and her Virtue surpassed by neither. Good Heavens! What a black Defamer have I chosen for my Protector!

Mr. *Glanville*, rejoicing to see *Arabella* in a Disposition to be offended with her new Acquaintance, resolved to sooth her a little, in hopes of prevailing upon her to return home. Sir, said he to the

Gentleman, who could not conceive why the Lady should so
warmly defend *Cleopatra*, you were in the Wrong to cast such
Reflections upon that great Queen (repeating what he had heard
his Cousin say before): For all the World, pursued he, knows she
was married to *Julius Caesar*.

Though I commend you, said *Arabella*, for taking the Part of a
Lady so basely vilified; yet let not your Zeal for her Honour induce
you to say more than is true for its Justification; for thereby you
weaken, instead of strengthening, what may be said in her Defence.
One Falshood always supposes another, and renders all you can say
suspected: Whereas pure, unmixed Truth, carries Conviction
along with it, and never fails to produce its desired Effect.

Suffer me, Cousin, interrupted *Glanville*, again to represent to
you, the Inconveniency you will certainly feel, by staying so late in
the Air: Leave the Justification of *Cleopatra* to some other Opportunity; and take care of your own Preservation.

What is it you require of me? said *Arabella*.

Only, resumed *Glanville*, that you would be pleased to return to
the Castle, where my Sister, and all your Servants, are inconsolable
for your Absence.

But who can assure me, answered she, that I shall not, by returning home, enter voluntarily into my Prison? The same Treachery
which made the Palace of *Candace* the Place of her Confinement,
may turn the Castle of *Arabella* into her Jayl.[1] For, to say the Truth,
I still more than suspect you abet the Designs of this Man; since I
behold you in his Party, and ready, no doubt, to draw your Sword
in his Defence: How will you be able to clear yourself of this
Crime? Yet I will venture to return to my House, provided you will
swear to me, you will offer me no Violence, with regard to your
Friend there: and also I insist, that he, from this Moment, disclaim
all Intentions of persecuting me, and banish himself from my Presence for ever. Upon this Condition I pardon him, and will likewise
pray to Heaven to pardon him also. Speak, presumptuous Unknown, said she to *Edward*, Wilt thou accept of my Pardon upon
the Terms I offer it thee? And wilt thou take thyself to some Place
where I may never behold thee again?

Since your Ladyship, said *Edward*, is resolved not to receive me
into your Service, I shan't trouble you any more: But I think it hard
to be punished for a Crime I was not guilty of.

'Tis better, said *Arabella*, turning from him, that thou shouldst complain of my Rigour, than the World tax me with Lightness and Indiscretion. And now, Sir, said she to *Glanville*, I must trust myself to your Honour, which I confess I do a little suspect: But, however, 'tis possible you have repented, like the poor Prince *Thrasybulus*, when he submitted to the Suggestions of a wicked Friend, to carry away the fair *Alcionida*, whom he afterwards restored.[1] Speak, *Glanville*, pursued she, are you desirous of imitating that virtuous Prince, or do you still retain your former Sentiments?

Upon my Word, Madam, said *Glanville*, you will make me quite mad, if you go on in this manner: Pray let me see you safe home; and then, if you please, you may forbid my Entrance into the Castle, if you suspect me of any bad Intentions towards you.

'Tis enough, said she; I will trust you. As for you, Sir, speaking to the young Gentleman, you are so unworthy, in my Apprehensions, by the Calumnies you have uttered against a Person of that Sex which merits all your Admiration and Reverence, that I hold you very unfit to be a Protector of any of it: Therefore I dispense with your Services upon this Occasion; and think it better to trust myself to the Conduct of a Person, who, like *Thrasybulus*, by his Repentance, has restored himself to my Confidence, than to one, who, though, indeed, he has never betrayed me, yet seems very capable of doing so, if he had the Power.

Saying this, she gave her Hand to *Glanville*, who helped her into the Chaise that was come from the Castle; and the Servant, who brought it, mounting his Horse, Mr. *Glanville* drove her Home, leaving the Gentleman, who, by this time, had refitted his Chaise, in the greatest Astonishment imaginable at her unaccountable Behaviour.

END of the SECOND BOOK

BOOK III

CHAPTER I

Two Conversations, out of which the Reader may
pick up a great deal

Arabella, continuing to ruminate upon her Adventure during their little Journey, appeared so low-spirited and reserved, that Mr. *Glanville*, tho' he ardently wished to know all the Particulars of her Flight, and Meeting with that Gentleman, whose Company he found her in, was obliged to suppress his Curiosity for the present, out of a Fear of displeasing her. As soon as they alighted at the Castle, her Servants ran to receive her at the Gates, expressing their Joy to see her again, by a thousand confused Exclamations.

Miss *Glanville*, being at her Toilet when she heard of her Arrival, ran down to welcome her, in her Hurry forgetting, that as her Woman had been curling her Hair, she had no Cap on.

Arabella received her Compliments with a little Coolness; for, observing that her Grief for her Absence had not made her neglect any of her usual Solicitude about her Person, she could not conceive it had been very great: Therefore, when she had made some slight Answer to the hundred Questions she asked in a Breath, she went up to her Apartment; and, calling *Lucy*, who was crying with Joy for her Return, she questioned her strictly concerning her leaving her in the Fields, acknowleging to her, that she suspected her Fidelity, tho' she wished, at the same time, she might be able to clear herself.

Lucy, in her Justification, related, after her punctual Way, all that had happened: By which, *Arabella* was convinced she had not betrayed her; and was also in some Doubt, whether Mr. *Glanville* was guilty of any Design against her.

Since, said she to *Lucy*, thou art restored to my good Opinion, I will, as I have always done, unmask my Thoughts to thee. I confess then, with Shame and Confusion, that I cannot think of Mr.

Glanville's assisting the Unknown to carry me away, without *resenting* a most poignant Grief: Questionless, my Weakness will surprise thee; and could I conceal it from myself, I would from thee; but, alas! it is certain, that I do not hate him; and I believe I never shall, guilty as he may be in my Apprehensions.

Hate him! Madam, said *Lucy*: God forbid you should ever hate Mr. *Glanville*, who, I am sure, loves your Ladyship as well as he does his own Sister!

You are very confident, *Lucy*, said *Arabella* blushing, to mention the Word Love to me: If I thought my Cousin had bribed thee to it, I should be greatly incensed: However, tho' I forbid you to talk of his Passion, yet I permit you to tell me the Violence of his Transports when I was missing; the Threats he uttered against my Ravishers; the Complaints he made against Fortune; the Vows he offered for my Preservation; and, in fine, whatever Extravagances the Excess of his Sorrow forced him to commit.

I assure you, Madam, said *Lucy*, I did not hear him say any of all this.

What! interrupted *Arabella*: And didst thou not observe the Tears trickle from his Eyes, which, haply, he strove to conceal? Did he not strike his Bosom with the Vehemence of his Grief; and cast his accusing and despairing Eyes to Heaven, which had permitted such a Misfortune to befal me?

Indeed, Madam, I did not, resumed *Lucy*; but he seemed to be very sorry; and said, He would go and look for your Ladyship.

Ah! the Traitor! interrupted *Arabella* in a Rage: Fain would I have found out some Excuse for him, and justified him in my Apprehensions; but he is unworthy of these favourable Thoughts: Speak of him no more, I command you; he is guilty of assisting my Ravisher to carry me away; and therefore merits my eternal Displeasure: But tho' I could find Reasons to clear him even of that Crime, yet he is guilty of Indifference and Insensibility for my Loss, since he neither died with Grief at the News of it; nor needed the Interposition of his Sister, or the Desire of delivering me, to make him live.

Arabella, when she had said this, was silent; but could not prevent some Tears stealing down her fair Face: Therefore, to conceal her Uneasiness, or to be at more Liberty to indulge it, she ordered *Lucy* to make haste and undress her; and, going To-bed, passed the small Remainder of the Night, not in Rest, which she very much needed, but, in Reflections on all the Passages of the preceding Day: And, finding, or imagining she found, new Reasons for condemning Mr. *Glanville*, her Mind was very far from being at Ease.

In the Morning, lying later than usual, she received a Message from Mr. *Glanville*, inquiring after her Health; to which she answered, That he was too little concerned in the Preservation of it, to make it necessary to acquaint him.

Miss *Glanville* soon after sent to desire Permission to drink her Chocolate by her Bedside; which as she could not in Civility refuse, she was very much perplexed how to hide her Melancholy from the Eyes of that discerning Lady, who, she questioned not, would interpret it in favour of her Brother.

Upon Miss *Glanville*'s Appearance, she forced herself to assume a chearful Look, asking her Pardon, for receiving her in Bed; and complaining of bad Rest, which had occasioned her lying late.

Miss *Glanville*, after answering her Compliments with almost equal Politeness, proceeded to ask her an hundred Questions concerning the Cause of her Absence from the Castle: Your Woman, pursued she, laughing, told us a strange Medley of Stuff about a great Man, who was a Gardener; and wanted to carry you away: Sure there was nothing in it! Was there?

You must excuse me, Cousin, said *Arabella*, if I do not answer your Questions precisely now: 'Tis sufficient that I tell you, Certain Reasons obliged me to act in the Manner I did, for my own Preservation; and that, another time, you shall know my History; which will explain many things you seem to be surprised at, at present.

Your History, said Miss *Glanville*! Why, will you write your own History then?

I shall not write it, said *Arabella*; tho', questionless, it will be written after my Death.

And must I wait till then for it, resumed Miss *Glanville*, gaily?

No, no, interrupted *Arabella*: I mean to gratify your Curiosity sooner; but it will not be yet a good time; and, haply, not till you have acquainted me with yours.

Mine! said Miss *Glanville*: It would not be worth your hearing; for really I have nothing to tell, that would make an History.

You have, questionless, returned *Arabella*, gained many Vic-

tories over Hearts; have occasioned many Quarrels between your
Servants, by favouring some one, more than the others: Probably,
you have caused some Bloodshed; and have not escaped being
carried away once or twice: You have also, I suppose, undergone
some Persecution, from those who have the Disposal of you, in
Favour of a Lover whom you have an Aversion to; and lastly, there
is haply some one among your admirers, who is happy enough not
to be hated by you.

I assure you, interrupted Miss *Glanville*, I hate none of my
Admirers; and I can't help thinking you very unkind to use my
Brother as you do: I am sure, there is not one Man in an hundred,
that would take so much from your Hands as he does.

Then there is not one Man in an hundred, resumed *Arabella*,
whom I should think worthy to serve me: But, pray, Madam, What
ill Usage is it your Brother complains of? I have treated him with
much less Severity than he had Reason to expect; and, notwithstanding he had the Presumption to talk to me of Love, I have
endured him in my Sight; an Indulgence, for which I may haply
be blamed in After-ages.

Why, sure, Lady *Bella*, said Miss *Glanville*, it would be no such
Crime for my Brother to love you!

But it was a mortal Crime to tell me so, interrupted *Arabella*.

And why was it such a mortal Crime to tell you so, said Miss
Glanville? Are you the first Woman by Millions, that has been
told so?

Doubtless, returned *Arabella*, I am the first Woman of my
Quality, that ever was told so by any Man, till after an infinite
Number of Services, and secret Sufferings: And truly, I am of the
illustrious *Mandana*'s Mind; for she said, That she should think
it an unpardonable Presumption, for the greatest King on Earth to
tell her he loved her, tho' after Ten Years of the most faithful
Services, and concealed Torments.[1]

Ten Years! cried out Miss *Glanville*, in Amazement; Did she
consider what Alterations ten Years would make in her Face, and
how much older she would be at the End of Ten Years, than she
was before?

Truly, said *Arabella*, it is not usual to consider such little
Matters so nicely; one never has the Idea of an Heroine older than
Eighteen, tho' her History begins at that Age; and the Events,
which compose it, contain the Space of Twenty more.

But, dear Cousin, resumed Miss *Glanville*, do you resolve to be Ten Years a courting? Or rather, will you be loved in Silence Ten Years, and be courted the other Ten; and so marry when you are an old Woman?

Pardon me, Cousin, resumed *Arabella*; I must really find Fault with the Coarseness of your Language. Courting, and Old Woman! What strange Terms! Let us, I beseech you, end this Dispute: If you have any thing to say in Justification of your Brother, which, I suppose, was the chief Intention of your Visit, I shall not be rude enough to restrain you; tho' I could wish you would not lay me under the Necessity of hearing what I cannot persuade myself to believe.

Since, returned Miss *Glanville*, I know of no Crime my Brother has been guilty of, I have nothing to say in his Justification: I only know, that he is very much mortified at the Message you sent him this Morning; for I was with him when he received it: But pray, What has he done to offend you?

If Mr. *Glanville*, interrupted *Arabella*, hopes for my Pardon, he must purchase it by his Repentance, and a sincere Confession of his Fault; which you may much better understand from himself, than from me: And, for this Purpose, I will condescend to grant him a private Audience, at which I desire you would be present; and also, I should take it well, if you will let him know, that he owes this Favour wholly to your Interposition.

Miss *Glanville*, who knew her Brother was extremely desirous of seeing *Arabella*, was glad to accept of these strange Terms; and left her Chamber, in order to acquaint him with that Lady's Intentions.

CHAPTER II

A solemn Interview

IN the mean time, that Fair-one, being risen, and negligently dressed, as was her Custom, went into her Closet, sending to give Miss *Glanville* Notice, That she was ready to see her. This Message immediately brought both the Brother and the Sister to her Apartment: And Miss *Glanville*, at her Brother's Request, staying in the Chamber, where she busied herself in looking at her

Cousin's Jewels, which lay upon the Toilet, he came alone into the Closet, in so much Confusion at the Thoughts of the ridiculous Figure he made in complying with *Arabella*'s fantastical Humours, that his Looks persuading her, there was some great Agitation in his Mind, she expected to see him fall at her Feet, and endeavour to deprecate her Wrath by a Deluge of Tears.

Mr. *Glanville* however disappointed her in that respect; for, taking a Seat near her, he began to intreat her, with a smiling Countenance, to tell him in what he had offended her; protesting, that he was not conscious of doing or saying any thing to displease her.

Arabella was greatly confused at this Question, which she thought she had no Reason to expect; it not being possible for her to tell him she was offended, that he was not in absolute Despair for her Absence, without, at the same time, confessing she looked upon him in the Light of a Lover, whose Expressions of a violent Passion would not have displeased her: Therefore, to disengage herself from the Perplexity his Question threw her into, she was obliged to offer some Violence to her Ingenuousness; and, contrary to her real Belief, tax him again with a Design of betraying her into the Power of the Unknown.

Mr. *Glanville*, tho' excessively vexed at her persisting in so ridiculous an Error, could hardly help smiling at the stern Manner in which she spoke; but, knowing of what fatal Consequence it would be to him, if he indulged any Gaiety in so solemn a Conference, he composed his Looks to a Gravity suitable to the Occasion; and asked her, in a very submissive Tone, What Motive she was pleased to assign for so extraordinary a Piece of Villainy, as that she supposed him guilty of?

Truly, answered she, blushing, I do not pretend to account for the Actions of wicked and ungenerous Persons.

But, Madam, resumed *Glanville*, if I must needs be suspected of a Design to seize upon your Person, methinks it would have been more reasonable to suppose, I would rather use that Violence in Favour of my own Pretensions, than those of any other whatever; for, tho' you have expressly forbid me to tell you I love you, yet I hope, you still continue to think I do.

I assure you, returned *Arabella*, assuming a severe Look, I never gave myself the Trouble to examine your Behaviour with Care enough to be sensible, if you still were guilty of the Weakness, which displeased me; but, upon a Supposition, that you repented of your Fault, I was willing to live with you upon Terms of Civility and Friendship, as became Persons in that Degree of Relationship in which we are: Therefore, if you are wise, you will not renew the Remembrance of those Follies I have long since pardoned; nor seek Occasions of offending me by new ones of the same kind, lest it produce a more severe Sentence than that I formerly laid upon you.

However, Madam, returned Mr. *Glanville,* you must suffer me to assure you, That my own Interest, which was greatly concerned in your Safety, and my Principles of Honour, would never allow me to engage in so villainous an Enterprize, as that of abetting any Person in stealing you away: Nor can I conceive, how you possibly could imagine a Fellow, who was your menial Servant, could form so presumptuous and dangerous a Design.

By your Manner of speaking, resumed *Arabella,* one would imagine you were really ignorant, both of the Quality of that presumptuous Man, as well as his designed Offence: But yet, 'tis certain, I saw you in his Company; and saw you ready to draw your Sword in his Defence, against my Deliverer. Had I not the Evidence of my own Senses, for your Guilt, I must confess, I could not be persuaded of it by any other Means: Therefore, since Appearances are certainly against you, it is not strange, if I cannot consent to acquit you in my Apprehensions, till I have more certain Confirmation of your Innocence, than your bare Testimony only; which, at present, has not all the Weight with me it had some time ago.

I protest, Madam, said Mr. *Glanville,* who was strangely perplexed, I have Reason to think my Case extremely hard, since I have brought myself to be suspected by you, only through my Eagerness to find you, and Solicitude for your Welfare.

Doubtless, interrupted *Arabella,* if you are innocent, your Case is extremely hard; yet it is not singular; and therefore you have less Reason to complain: The valiant *Coriolanus,* who was the most passionate and faithful Lover imaginable, having, by his admirable Valour, assisted the Ravishers of his adored *Cleopatra,* against those who came to rescue her; and, by his Arm alone, opposed to great Numbers of their Enemies, facilitated the Execution of their Design, had the Mortification afterwards to know, that he had, all that time, been fighting against that Divine Princess, who loaded him with the most cruel Reproaches for the Injury he had

done her: Yet Fortune was so kind, as to give him the Means of
repairing his Fault, and restoring him to some Part of her good
Opinion; for, covered with Wounds as he was, and fatigued with
fighting, before, yet he undertook, in that Condition, to prevent her
Ravishers from carrying her off; and, for several Hours, continued
fighting alone with near Two hundred Men, who were not able to
overcome him, notwithstanding his extreme Weariness, and the
Multitude of Blows which they aimed at him:[1] Therefore, *Glanville*, considering you, as *Cleopatra* did that unfortunate Prince,
who was before suspected by her, as neither guilty nor innocent, I
can only, like her, wish you may find some Occasion of justifying
yourself, from the Crime laid to your Charge: Till then, I must be
under a Necessity of banishing you from my Presence, with the
same consolatory Speech she used to that unfortunate Prince:—
'Go, therefore, *Glanville*, go, and endeavour your own Justification;
I desire you should effect it, no less than you do yourself; and, if
my Prayers can obtain from Heaven this Favour for you, I shall not
scruple to offer some *in your behalf*.'[2]

CHAPTER III

*In which the Interview is ended, not much to the Lover's
Satisfaction, but exactly conformable to the Rules of Romance*

Arabella, when she had pronounced these Words, blushed
excessively, thinking she had said too much: But, not seeing any
Signs of extreme Joy in the Face of *Glanville*, who was silently
cursing *Cleopatra*, and the Authors of those Romances, that had
ruined so noble a Mind; and exposed him to perpetual Vexations,
by the unaccountable Whims they had raised—Why are you not
gone, said she, while I am in an Humour not to repent of the
Favour I have shewn you?

You must excuse me, Cousin, said Mr. *Glanville*, peevishly, if I
do not think so highly as you do of the Favour. Pray how am I
obliged to you for depriving me of the Pleasure of seeing you, and
sending me on a Wild-goose Chace, after Occasions to justify
myself of a Crime I am wholly innocent of, and would scorn to
commit?

Though, resumed *Arabella*, with great Calmness, I have Reason
to be dissatisfied with the cool and unthankful manner in which you
receive my Indulgence, yet I shall not change the favourable
Disposition I am in towards you, unless you provoke me to it by
new Acts of Disobedience: Therefore, in the Language of *Cleopatra*, I shall tell you.——

Upon my Soul, Madam, interrupted *Glanville*, I have no
Patience with that rigorous Gipsy, whose Example you follow so
exactly, to my Sorrow: Speak in your own Language, I beseech
you; for I am sure neither hers, nor any one's upon Earth, can
excel it.

Yet, said *Arabella*, striving to repress some Inclination to smile
at this Sally, notwithstanding your unjust Prohibitions, I shall
make use of the Language of that incomparable Lady, to tell you my
Thoughts; which are, That 'tis possible you might be sufficiently
justified in my Apprehensions, by the Anxiety it now appears
you had for my Safety, by the Probability which I find in your
Discourse, and the good Opinion I have of you, were it not
requisite to make your Innocence apparent to the World, that so
it might be lawful for *Arabella* to readmit you, with Honour, into
her former Esteem and Friendship.

Mr. *Glanville*, seeing it would be in vain to attempt to make her
alter her fantastical Determination at this time, went out of the
Closet without deigning to make any Reply to this Sentence,
though delivered in the Language of the admirable *Cleopatra*:
But his ill Humour was so visible in his Face, that *Arabella*, who
mistook it for an Excess of Despair, could not help feeling some
kind of Pity for the Rigour which the Laws of Honour and Romance obliged her to use him with. And, while she sat meditating
upon the Scene which had just passed, Mr. *Glanville* returned to his
own Room, glad that his Sister, not being in *Arabella*'s Chamber,
where he had left her, had no Opportunity of observing his Discontent, which she would not fail to inquire the Cause of.

Here he sat, ruminating upon the Follies of *Arabella*, which he
found grew more glaring every Day: Every thing furnished Matter
for some new Extravagance; her Character was so ridiculous, that
he could propose nothing to himself but eternal Shame and Dis-
quiet, in the Possession of a Woman, for whom he must always
blush, and be in Pain. But her Beauty had made a deep Impression
on his Heart: He admired the Strength of her Understanding;

her lively Wit; the Sweetness of her Temper; and a Thousand amiable Qualities which distinguished her from the rest of her Sex: Her Follies, when opposed to all those Charms of Mind and Person, seemed inconsiderable and weak; and, though they were capable of giving him great Uneasiness, yet they could not lessen a Passion which every Sight of her so much the more confirmed.

As he feared it was impossible to help loving her, his Happiness depended upon curing her of her romantic Notions; and, though he knew not how to effect such a Change in her as was necessary to complete it, yet he would not despair, but comforted himself with Hopes of what he had not Courage to attempt. Sometimes he fansied Company, and an Acquaintance with the World, would produce the Alteration he wished: Yet he dreaded to see her exposed to Ridicule by her fantastical Behaviour, and become the Jest of Persons who were not possessed of half her Understanding.

While he traversed his Chamber, wholly engrossed by these Reflections, Miss *Glanville* was entertaining Sir *George*, of whose coming she was informed while she was in *Arabella's* Chamber.

CHAPTER IV

In which our Heroine is greatly disappointed

MISS *Glanville*, supposing her Brother would be glad not to be interrupted in his Conference with Lady *Bella*, did not allow any one to acquaint them with Sir *George's* Visit; and, telling the Baronet her Cousin was indisposed, had, by these means, all his Conversation to herself.

Sir *George*, who ardently wished to see Lady *Bella*, protracted his Visit, in hopes that he should have that Satisfaction before he went away. And that fair Lady, whose Thoughts were a little discomposed by the Despair she apprehended Mr. *Glanville* was in, and fearful of the Consequences, when she had sat some time after he left her, ruminating upon what had happened, quitted her Closet, to go and inquire of Miss *Glanville*, in what Condition his Mind seemed to be when he went away; for she never doubted but that he was gone, like *Coriolanus*, to seek out for some Occasion to manifest his Innocence.

Hearing, therefore, the Voice of that Lady, who was talking and laughing very loud in one of the Summer-parlours, and being terrified with the Apprehension, that it was her Brother with whom she was thus diverting herself, she opened the Door of the Room precipitately; and, by her Entrance, filled Sir *George* with extreme Pleasure; while her unexpected Sight produced a quite contrary Effect on Miss *Glanville*.

Arabella, eased of her Fear, that it was Mr. *Glanville*, who, instead of dying with Despair, was giving Occasion for that noisy Laugh of his Sister, saluted the Baronet with great Civility; and, turning to Miss *Glanville*, I must needs chide you, said she, for the Insensibility with which it appears you have parted with your Brother.

Bless me, Madam, interrupted Miss *Glanville*, what do you mean? Whither is my Brother gone?

That, indeed, I am quite ignorant of, resumed *Arabella*; and I suppose he himself hardly knows what Course he shall take: But he has been with you, doubtless, to take his Leave.

Take his Leave! repeated Miss *Glanville*: Has he left the Castle so suddenly then, and gone away without me?

The Enterprize upon which he is gone, said *Arabella*, would not admit of a Lady's Company: And, since he has left so considerable an Hostage with me as yourself, I expect he will not be long before he return; and, I hope, to the Satisfaction of us both.

Miss *Glanville*, who could not penetrate into the Meaning of her Cousin's Words, began to be strangely alarmed: But, presently, supposing she had a mind to divert herself with her Fears, she recovered herself, and told her she would go up to her Brother's Chamber, and look for him.

Arabella did not offer to prevent her, being very desirous of knowing, whether he had not left a Letter for her upon his Table, as was the Custom in those Cases: And, while she was gone, Sir *George* seized the Opportunity of saying an hundred gallant Things to her, which she received with great Indifference; the most extravagant Compliments being what she expected from all Men: And, provided they did not directly presume to tell her they loved her, no Sort of Flattery or Adulation could displease her.

In the mean time, Miss *Glanville*, having found her Brother in his Chamber, repeated to him what Lady *Bella* had said, as she supposed, to fright her.

Mr. *Glanville*, hearing this, and that Sir *George* was with her, hastened to them as fast as possible, that he might interrupt the foolish Stories he did not doubt she was telling.

Upon Miss *Glanville*'s Appearance with her Brother, *Arabella* was astonished.

I apprehended, Sir, said she, that you were some Miles from the Castle by this time: But your Delay and Indifference convince me, you neither expect nor wish to find the means of being justified in my Opinion.

Pray, Cousin, interrupted *Glanville* (speaking softly to her), let us leave this Dispute to some other time.

No, Sir, resumed she, aloud, my Honour is concerned in your Justification: Nor is it fit I should submit to have the Appearance of Amity for a Person who has not yet sufficiently cleared himself of a Crime, with too much Reason laid to his Charge. Did *Coriolanus*, think you, act in this manner? Ah! if he had, doubtless, *Cleopatra* would never have pardoned him: Nor will I any longer suffer you to give me repeated Causes of Discontent.

Sir *George*, seeing Confusion in Mr. *Glanville*'s Countenance, and Rage in *Arabella*'s, began to think, that what he had at first took for a Jest, was a serious Quarrel between them, at which it was not proper he should be present; and was preparing to go: When *Arabella*, stopping him with a graceful Action——

If, noble Stranger, said she, you are so partial to the Failings of a Friend, that you will undertake to defend any unjustifiable Action he may be guilty of, you are at Liberty to depart: But, if you will promise to be an unprejudiced Hearer of the Dispute between Mr. *Glanville* and myself, you shall know the Adventure which has given Rise to it; and will be Judge of the Reasonableness of the Commands I have laid on him.

Though, Madam, said Sir *George* (bowing very low to her), Mr. *Glanville* is my Friend, yet there is no Likelihood I shall espouse his Interest against yours: And a very strong Prepossession I feel in Favour of you, already persuades me, that I shall give Sentence on your Side, since you have honoured me so far, as to constitute me Judge of this Difference.

The solemn Manner in which Sir *George* (who began to suspect Lady *Bella*'s peculiar Turn) spoke this, pleased her infinitely; while Mr. *Glanville*, vexed as he was, could hardly forbear laughing: When *Arabella*, after a Look of Approbation to Sir *George*, replied;

I find I have unwillingly engaged myself to more than I first intended: For, to enable you to judge clearly of the Matter in Dispute, 'tis necessary you should know my whole History.

Mr. *Glanville*, at this Word, not being able to constrain himself, uttered a Groan, of the same Nature with those which are often heard in the Pit at the Representation of a new Play. Sir *George* understood him perfectly well; yet seemed surprised: And *Arabella*, starting up,

Since, said she, I have given you no new Cause of Complaint, pray, from whence proceeds this Increase of Affliction?

I assure you, Cousin, answered he, my Affliction, if you please to term it so, increases every Day; and I believe it will make me mad at last: For this unaccountable Humour of yours is not to be borne.

You do not seem, replied *Arabella*, to be far from Madness already: And if your Friend here, upon hearing the Passages between us, should pronounce you guilty, I shall be at a Loss, whether I ought to treat you as a Madman, or a Criminal. Sir, added she, turning to Sir *George*, you will excuse me, if, for certain Reasons, I can neither give you my History myself, nor be present at the Relation of it: One of my Women, who is most in my Confidence, shall acquaint you with all the Particulars of my Life: After which I expect Mr. *Glanville* will abide by your Decision, as, I assure myself, I shall be contented to do.

Saying this, she went out of the Parlour, in order to prepare *Lucy* for the Recital she was to make.

Mr. *Glanville*, resolving not to be present at this new Absurdity, ran out after her; and went into the Garden, with a strong Inclination to hate the lovely Visionary who gave him such perpetual Uneasiness; leaving his Sister alone with the Baronet, who diverted herself extremely with the Thoughts of hearing her Cousin's History, assuring the Baronet, that he might expect something very curious in it, and find Matter sufficient to laugh at; for she was the most whimsical Woman in the World.

Sir *George*, who resolved to profit by the Knowlege of her Foible, made very little Reply to Miss *Glanville*'s Sneers; but waited patiently for the promised History, which was much longer coming than he imagined.

CHAPTER V

Some curious Instructions for relating an History

Arabella, as soon as she left them, went up to her Apartment; and, calling *Lucy* into her Closet, told her that she had made Choice of her, since she was best acquainted with her Thoughts, to relate her History to her Cousins, and a Person of Quality who was with them.

Sure your Ladyship jests with me, said *Lucy*: How can I make a History about your Ladyship?

There is no Occasion, replied *Arabella,* for you to make a History: There are Accidents enough in my Life to afford Matter for a long one: All you have to do is to relate them as exactly as possible. You have lived with me from my Childhood, and are instructed in all my Adventures; so that you must be certainly very capable of executing the Task I have honoured you with.

Indeed, said *Lucy,* I must beg your Ladyship will excuse me: I never could tell how to repeat a Story when I have read it; and I know it is not such simple Girls as I can tell Histories: It is only fit for Clerks, and such Sort of People, that are very learned.

You are learned enough for that Purpose, said *Arabella*; and, if you make so much Difficulty in performing this Part of your Duty, pray how came you to imagine you were fit for my Service, and the Distinction I have favoured you with? Did you ever hear of any Woman that refused to relate her Lady's Story, when desired? Therefore, if you hope to possess my Favour and Confidence any longer, acquit yourself handsomely of this Task, to which I have preferred you.

Lucy, terrified at the Displeasure she saw in her Lady's Countenance, begged her to tell her what she must say.

Well! exclaimed *Arabella*: I am certainly the most unfortunate Woman in the World! Every thing happens to me in a contrary manner from any other Person! Here, instead of my desiring you to soften those Parts of my History where you have greatest room to flatter; and to conceal, if possible, some of those Disorders my Beauty has occasioned; you ask me to tell you what you must say; as if it was not necessary you should know as well as myself, and be able, not only to recount all my Words and Actions, even the smallest and most inconsiderable, but also all my Thoughts, however instantaneous; relate exactly every Change of my Countenance; number all my Smiles, Half-smiles, Blushes, Turnings pale, Glances, Pauses, Full-stops, Interruptions; the Rise and Falling of my Voice; every Motion of my Eyes; and every Gesture which I have used for these Ten Years past; nor omit the smallest Circumstance that relates to me.

Lord bless me! Madam, said *Lucy*, excessively astonished, I never, till this Moment, it seems, knew the hundredth thousandth Part of what was expected from me: I am sure, if I had, I would never have gone to Service; for I might well know I was not fit for such Slavery.

There is no such great Slavery in doing all I have mentioned to you, interrupted *Arabella*: It requires, indeed, a good Memory, in which I never thought you deficient; for you are punctual to the greatest Degree of Exactness in recounting every thing one desires to hear from you.

Lucy, whom this Praise soothed into good Humour, and flattered with a Belief, that she was able, with a little Instruction, to perform what her Lady required, told her, if she pleased only to put her in a Way how to tell her History, she would engage, after doing it once, to tell it again whenever she was desired.

Arabella, being obliged to comply with the odd Request, for which there was no Precedent in all the Romances her Library was stuffed with, began to inform her in this manner:

First, said she, you must relate my Birth, which you know is very illustrious; and, because I am willing to spare you the Trouble of repeating Things, that are not absolutely necessary, you must apologize to your Hearers for slipping over what passed in my Infancy, and the first Eight or Ten Years of my Life; not failing, however, to remark, that, from some sprightly Sallies of Imagination, at those early Years, those about me conceived marvellous Hopes of my future Understanding: From thence you must proceed to an accurate Description of my Person.

What! Madam, interrupted *Lucy*, must I tell what Sort of Person you have, to People who have seen you but a Moment ago?

Questionless you must, replied *Arabella*; and herein you follow the Examples of all the 'Squires and Maids who relate their Masters and Ladies Histories: For, though it be to a Brother, or near Relation, who has seen them a thousand times, yet they never omit an exact Account of their Persons.

Very well, Madam, said *Lucy*: I shall be sure not to forget that

Part of my Story. I wish I was as perfect in all the rest.

Then, *Lucy*, you must repeat all the Conversations I have ever held with you upon the Subjects of Love and Gallantry, that your Audience may be so well acquainted with my Humour, as to know exactly, before they are told, how I shall behave, in whatever Adventures befal me.—After that, you may proceed to tell them, how a noble Unknown saw me at Church; how prodigiously he was struck with my Appearance; the tumultuous Thoughts that this first View of me occasioned in his Mind.——

Indeed, Madam, interrupted *Lucy* again, I can't pretend to tell his Thoughts: For how should I know what they were? None but himself can tell that.

However that may be, said *Arabella*, I expect you should decypher all his Thoughts, as plainly as he himself could do; otherwise my History will be very imperfect: Well, I suppose you are at no loss about that whole Adventure, in which you yourself bore so great a Share; so I need not give you any further Instructions concerning it: Only you must be sure, as I said before, not to omit the least Circumstance in my Behaviour, but relate every thing I did, said, and thought, upon that Occasion. The disguised Gardener must appear next in your Story: Here you will of necessity be a little deficient, since you are not able to acquaint your Hearers with his true Name and Quality; which, questionless, is very illustrious. However, above all, I must charge you not to mention that egregious Mistake about the Carp; for, you know how——

Here Miss *Glanville*'s Entrance put a Stop to the Instructions *Lucy* was receiving: For she told *Arabella*, that Sir *George* was gone.

How! returned she, is he gone? Truly I am not much obliged to him for the Indifference he has shewed to hear my Story.

Why, really, Madam, said Miss *Glanville*, neither of us expected you would be as good as your Word, you were so long in sending your Woman down: And my Brother persuaded Sir *George* you were only in Jest; and Sir *George* has carried him home to Dinner.

And is it at Sir *George*'s, replied *Arabella*, that your Brother hopes to meet with an Occasion of clearing himself? He is either very insensible of my Anger, or very conscious of his own Innocence.

Miss *Glanville*, having nothing to say in Answer to an Accusa-

tion she did not understand, changed the Discourse: And the two
Ladies passed the rest of the Day together, with tolerable Good-
humour on Miss *Glanville*'s Side; who was in great hopes of
making a Conquest of the Baronet, before whom *Arabella* had
made herself ridiculous enough: But that Lady was far from being
at Ease; she had laid herself under a Necessity of banishing Mr.
Glanville, if he did not give some convincing Proof of his Innocence; which, as Matters stood, she thought would be very hard
for him to procure; and, as she could not absolutely believe him
guilty, she was concerned she had gone so far.

CHAPTER VI

A very Heroic Chapter

MR. *Glanville*, coming home in the Evening, a little elevated with
the Wine, of which he had drank too freely at Sir *George*'s, being
told the Ladies were together, entered the Room where they were
sitting; and, beholding *Arabella*, whose Pensiveness had given an
inchanting Softness to her Face, with a Look of extreme Admiration——

Upon my Soul, Cousin, said he, if you continue to treat me so
cruelly, you'll drive me mad. How I could adore you this Moment,
added he, gazing passionately at her, if I might but hope you did
not hate me!

Arabella, who did not perceive the Condition he was in, was
better pleased with this Address than any he had ever used; and,
therefore, instead of chiding him, as she was wont, for the Freedom
of his Expressions, she cast her bright Eyes upon the Ground, with
so charming a Confusion, that *Glanville*, quite transported, threw
himself on his Knees before her; and, taking her Hand, attempted
to press it to his Lips: But she, hastily withdrawing it——

From whence is this new Boldness? said she: And what is it you
would implore by that prostrate Posture? I have told you already
upon what Conditions I will grant you my Pardon. Clear yourself
of being an Accomplice with my designed Ravisher, and I am
ready to restore you to my Esteem.

Let me perish, Madam, returned *Glanville*, if I would not die to please you, this Moment!

It is not your Death that I require, said she: And, though you should never be able to justify yourself in my Opinion, yet you might, haply, expiate your Crime, by a less Punishment than Death.

What shall I do, then, my Angelic Cousin? resumed he.

Truly, said she, the Sense of your Offence ought so mortally to afflict you, that you should invent some strange kind of Penance for yourself, severe enough to prove your Penitence sincere.—You know, I suppose, what the unfortunate *Orontes* did, when he found he had wronged his adored *Thalestris* by an injurious Suspicion.[1]

I wish he had hanged himself, said Mr. *Glanville*, rising up in a Passion, at seeing her again in her Altitudes.

And why, pray, Sir, said *Arabella*, are you so severe upon that poor Prince? who was, haply, infinitely more innocent than yourself.

Severe, Madam! said *Glanville*, fearing he had offended her: Why, to be sure, he was a sad Scoundrel, to use his adored *Thalestris* as he did: And I think one cannot be too severe upon him.

But, returned *Arabella*, Appearances were against her; and he had some Shadow of Reason for his Jealousy and Rage: Then, you know, amidst all his Transports, he could not be prevailed upon to draw his Sword against her.

What did that signify? said *Glanville*: I suppose he scorned to draw his Sword upon a Woman: That would have been a Shame indeed.

That Woman, Sir, resumed *Arabella*, was not such a contemptible Antagonist as you think her: And Men, as valiant, possibly, as *Orontes* (though, questionless, he was one of the most valiant Men in the World), have been cut in Pieces by the Sword of that brave *Amazon*.

Lord bless me! said Miss *Glanville*, I should be afraid to look at such a terrible Woman: I am sure she must be a very masculine Sort of Creature.

You are much mistaken, Miss, said *Arabella*: For *Thalestris*, tho' the most stout and courageous of her Sex, was, nevertheless, a perfect Beauty; and had as much Harmony and Softness in her Looks and Person, as she had Courage in her Heart, and Strength in her Blows.

Indeed, Madam, resumed Miss *Glanville*, you can never persuade me, that a Woman who can fight, and cut People to Pieces with her Blows, can have any Softness in her Person: She must needs have very masculine Hands, that could give such terrible Blows: And I can have no Notion of the Harmony of a Person's Looks, who, by what you say, must have the Heart of a Tyger. But, indeed, I don't think there ever could be such a Woman.

What! Miss, interrupted *Arabella*: Do you pretend to doubt, that there ever was such a Person as *Thalestris*, Queen of the *Amazons*? Does not all the World know the Adventures of that illustrious Princess; her Affection for the unjust *Orontes*, who accused her of having a scandalous Intrigue with *Alexander*, whom she went to meet, with a very different Design, upon the Borders of her Kingdom? The injurious Letter he wrote her, upon this Suspicion, made her resolve to seek for him all over the World, to give him that Death he had merited, by her own Hand: And it was in those Rencounters that he had with her, while she was thus incensed, that he forebore to defend himself against her, though her Sword was often pointed to his Breast.

But, Madam, interrupted Mr. *Glanville*, pray what became of this Queen of the *Amazons*? Was she not killed at the Siege of *Troy*?[1]

She never was at the Siege of *Troy*, returned *Arabella*: But she assisted the Princes who besieged *Babylon*, to recover the Liberty of *Statira* and *Parisatis*: And it was in the opposite Party that she met with her faithless Lover.

If he was faithless, Madam, said Mr. *Glanville*, he deserved to die: And I wish, with all my Soul, she had cut him in Pieces with that famous Sword of hers that had done such Wonders.

Yet this faithless Man, resumed *Arabella*, whom you seem to have such an Aversion to, gave so glorious a Proof of his Repentance and Sorrow, that the fair Queen restored him to her Favour, and held him in much dearer Affection than ever: For, after he was convinced of her Innocence, he was resolved to punish himself with a Rigour equal to the Fault he had been guilty of; and, retiring to the Woods, abandoned for ever the Society of Men; dwelling in a Cave, and living upon bitter Herbs, passing the Days and Nights in continual Tears and Sorrow for his Crime: And here he proposed to end his Life, had not the fair *Thalestris* found him out in this Solitude; and, struck with the Sincerity of his Repentance, pardoned him; and, as I have said before, restored him to her Favour.

And, to shew you, said *Glanville*, that I am capable of doing as much for you; I will, if you insist upon it, seek out for some Cave, and do Penance in it, like that *Orontes*, provided you will come and fetch me out of it, as that same fair Queen did him.

I do not require so much of you, said *Arabella*; for I told you before, that, haply, you are justified already in my Opinion; but yet it is necessary, you should find out some Method of convincing the World of your Innocence; otherwise it is not fit I should live with you upon Terms of Friendship and Civility.

Well, well, Madam, said *Glanville*, I'll convince you of my Innocence, by bringing that Rascal's Head to you, whom you suspect I was inclined to assist in stealing you away.

If you do that, resumed *Arabella*, doubtless you will be justified in my Opinion, and the World's also; and I shall have no Scruple to treat you with as much Friendship as I did before.

My Brother is much obliged to you, Madam, interrupted Miss *Glanville*, for putting him upon an Action, that would cost him his Life!

I have so good an Opinion of your Brother's Valour, said *Arabella*, that I am persuaded he will find no Difficulty in performing his Promise; and I make no question but I shall see him covered with the Spoils of that Imposter, who would have betrayed me; and I flatter myself, he will be in a Condition to bring me his Head, as he bravely promises, without endangering his own Life.

Does your Ladyship consider, said Miss *Glanville*, that my Brother can take away no Person's Life whatever, without endangering his own?

I consider, Madam, said *Arabella*, your Brother as a Man possessed of Virtue and Courage enough to undertake to kill all my Enemies and Persecutors, though I had ever so many; and I presume, he would be able to perform as many glorious Actions for my Service, as either *Juba*,[1] *Caesario*, *Artamenes*, or *Artaban*,[2] who, though not a Prince, was greater than any of them.

If those Persons you have named, said Miss *Glanville*, were Murderers, and made a Practice of killing People, I hope my Brother will be too wise to follow their Examples: A strange kind of Virtue and Courage indeed, to take away the Lives of one's

Fellow-Creatures! How did such Wretches escape the Gallows, I wonder?

I perceive, interrupted *Arabella*, what kind of Apprehensions you have: I suppose you think, if your Brother was to kill my Enemy, the Law would punish him for it: But pray undeceive yourself, Miss: The Law has no Power over Heroes;[1] they may kill as many Men as they please, without being called to any Account for it; and the more Lives they take away, the greater is their Reputation for Virtue and Glory. The illustrious *Artaban*, from the Condition of a private Man, raised himself to the sublimest Pitch of Glory by his Valour; for he not only would win half a dozen Battles in a Day; but, to shew that Victory followed him where-ever he went, he would change Parties, and immediately the Vanquished became Conquerors; then, returning to the Side he had quitted, changed the Laurels of his former Friends into Chains. He made nothing of tumbling Kings from their Thrones, and giving away half a dozen Crowns in a Morning; for his Generosity was equal to his Courage; and to this Height of Power did he raise himself by his Sword. Beginning at first with petty Conquests, and not disdaining to oppose his glorious Arm to sometimes less than a Score of his Enemies; so, by degrees, ensuring himself to conquer inconsiderable Numbers, he came at last to be the Terror of whole Armies, who would fly at the Sight of his single Sword.

This is all very astonishing indeed, said Miss *Glanville*: However, I must intreat you, not to insist upon my Brother's quarrelling and fighting with People, since it will be neither for your Honour, nor his Safety; for I am afraid, if he was to commit Murder to please you, the Laws would make him suffer for it; and the World would be very free with its Censures on your Ladyship's Reputation, for putting him upon such shocking Crimes.

By your Discourse, Miss, replied *Arabella*, one would imagine, you knew as little in what the good Reputation of a Lady consists, as the Safety of a Man; for certainly the one depends intirely upon his Sword, and the other upon the Noise and Bustle she makes in the World. The Blood that is shed for a Lady, enhances the Value of her Charms;[2] and the more Men a Hero kills, the greater his Glory, and, by Consequence, the more secure he is. If to be the Cause of a great many Deaths, can make a Lady infamous; certainly none were ever more so, than *Mandana, Cleopatra,* and *Statira,* the most illustrious Names in Antiquity; for each of

whom, haply, an hundred thousand Men were killed: Yet none
were ever so unjust, as to profane the Virtue of those Divine
Beauties, by casting any Censures upon them for these glorious
Effects of their Charms, and the heroic Valour of their Admirers.

I must confess, interrupted Miss *Glanville*, I should not be sorry
to have a Duel or Two fought for me in *Hyde-park*; but then I
would not have any Blood shed for the World.

Glanville here interrupting his Sister with a Laugh, *Arabella*
also could not forbear smiling at the harmless Kind of Combats
her Cousin was fond of.

But to put an End to the Conversation, and the Dispute which
gave Rise to it, she obliged Mr. *Glanville* to promise to fight with
the Impostor *Edward*, whenever he found him; and either take
away his Life, or force him to confess, he had no Part in the
Design he had meditated against her.

This being agreed upon, *Arabella*, conducting Miss *Glanville* to
her Chamber, retired to her own; and passed the Night with much
greater Tranquillity, than she had done the preceding; being
satisfied with the Care she had taken of her own Glory, and
persuaded that *Glanville* was not unfaithful; a Circumstance,
that was of more Consequence to her Happiness, than she was yet
aware of.

CHAPTER VII

In which our Heroine is suspected of Insensibility

WHILE these things passed at the Castle, Sir *George* was meditating
on the Means he should use to acquire the Esteem of Lady *Bella*,
of whose Person he was a little enamoured, but of her Fortune a
great deal more.

By the Observations he had made on her Behaviour, he discovered her peculiar Turn: He was well read in Romances himself,
and had actually employed himself some Weeks in giving a new
Version of the *Grand Cyrus*; but the prodigious Length of the
Task he had undertaken, terrified him so much, that he gave it
over: Nevertheless, he was perfectly well acquainted with the
chief Characters in most of the *French* Romances; could tell every

thing that was borrowed from them, in all the new Novels that came out; and, being a very accurate Critic, and a mortal Hater of *Dryden*, ridiculed him for want of Invention, as it appeared by his having recourse to these Books for the most shining Characters and Incidents in his Plays. *Almanzor*, he would say, was the Copy of the famous *Artaban* in *Cleopatra*, whose Exploits *Arabella* had expatiated upon to Miss *Glanville*, and her Brother: His admired Character of *Melantha* in Marriage *à-la-mode*, was drawn from *Berissa* in the *Grand Cyrus*; and the Story of *Osmyn* and *Bensayda*, in his Conquest of *Granada*, taken from *Sesostris* and *Timerilla* in that Romance.[1]

Fraught therefore with the Knowlege of all the Extravagances and Peculiarities in those Books, he resolved to make his Addresses to *Arabella* in the Form they prescribed; and, not having Delicacy enough to be disgusted with the Ridicule[2] in her Character, served himself with her Foible, to effect his Designs.

It being necessary, in order to his better Acquaintance with *Arabella*, to be upon very friendly Terms with Miss *Glanville* and her Brother, he said a thousand gallant Things to the one, and seemed so little offended with the Gloom he observed upon the Countenance of the other, who positively assured him, that *Arabella* meant only to laugh at him, when she promised him her History, that he intreated him, with the most obliging Earnestness, to favour him with his Company at his House, where he omitted no sort of Civility, to confirm their Friendship and Intimacy; and persuaded him, by several little and seemingly unguarded Expressions, that he was not so great an Admirer of Lady *Bella*, as her agreeable Cousin Miss *Glanville*.

Having thus secured a Footing in the Castle, he furnished his Memory with all the necessary Rules of making Love in *Arabella*'s Taste, and deferred his next Visit no longer than till the following Day; but Mr. *Glanville* being indisposed, and not able to see Company, he knew it would be in vain to expect to see *Arabella*, since it was not to be imagined, Miss *Glanville* could admit of a Visit, her Brother being ill; and Lady *Bella* must be also necessarily engaged with her.

Contenting himself, therefore, with having inquired after the Health of the Two Ladies, he returned home, not a little vexed at his Disappointment.

Mr. *Glanville*'s Indisposition, increasing every Day, grew at last dangerous enough to fill his Sister with extreme Apprehensions. *Arabella*, keeping up to her Forms, sent regularly every Day, to inquire after his Health; but did not offer to go into his Chamber, though Miss *Glanville* was almost always there.

As she conceived his Sickness to be occasioned by the Violence of his Passion for her,[1] she expected some Overture should be made by his Sister, to engage her to make him a Visit; such a Favour being never granted by any Lady to a sick Lover, till she was previously informed, her Presence was necessary to hinder the Increase of his Distemper.

Miss *Glanville* would not have failed to represent to her Cousin the Incivility and Carelessness of her Behaviour, in not deigning to come and see her Brother in his Indisposition, had not Mr. *Glanville*, imputing this Neglect to the Nicety of her Notions, which he had upon other Occasions experienced, absolutely forbid her to say any thing to her Cousin upon this Subject.

Miss *Glanville* being thus forced to Silence, by the Fear of giving her Brother Uneasiness, *Arabella* was extremely disappointed to find, that, in Five Days Illness, no Application had been made to her, either by the sick Lover, or his Sister, who she thought interested herself too little in his Recovery; so that her Glory obliging her to lay some Constraint upon herself, she behaved with a Coolness and Insensibility, that increased Miss *Glanville*'s Aversion to her, while, in Reality, she was extremely concerned for her Cousin's Illness; but not supposing it dangerous, since they had not recourse to the usual Remedy, of beseeching a Visit from the Person whose Presence was alone able to work a Cure, she resolved to wait patiently the Event.

However, she never failed in her Respect to Miss *Glanville*, whom she visited every Morning, before she went to her Brother; and also constantly dined with her in her own Apartment, inquiring always, with great Sweetness, concerning her Brother's Health; when perceiving her in Tears one Day, as she came in, as usual, to dine with her, she was extremely alarmed; and asked with great Precipitation, If Mr. *Glanville* was worse?

He is so bad, Madam, returned Miss *Glanville*, that I believe it will be necessary to send for my Papa, for fear he should die, and he not see him.

Die, Miss! interrupted *Arabella* eagerly: No, he must not die; and shall not, if the Pity of *Arabella* is powerful enough to make

him live. Let us go then, Cousin, said she, her Eyes streaming with
Tears; let us go and visit this dear Brother, whom you lament:
Haply my Sight may repair the Evils my Rigour has caused him;
and since, as I imagine, he has forborn, through the profound
Respect he has for me, to request the Favour of a Visit, I will
voluntarily bestow it on him, as well for the Affection I bear you,
as because I do not wish his Death.

You do not wish his Death, Madam! said Miss *Glanville*,
excessively angry at a Speech, in her Opinion, extremely insolent:
Is it such a mighty Favour, pray, not to wish the Death of my
Brother, who never injured you? I am sure, your Behaviour has
been so extremely inhuman, that I have repented a thousand
times, we ever came to the Castle.

Let us not waste the time in idle Reproaches, said *Arabella*: If
my Rigour has brought your Brother into this Condition, my
Compassion can draw him out of it: It is no more than what all do
suffer, who are possessed of a violent Passion; and few Lovers ever
arrive to the Possession of their Mistresses, without being several
times brought almost to their Graves, either by their Severity, or
some other Cause: But nothing is more easy, than to work a Cure,
in these Cases; for the very Sight of the Person beloved sometimes
does it, as it happened to *Artamenes*, when the Divine *Mandana*
condescended to visit him:[1] A few kind Words, spoken by the
fair Princess of *Persia* to *Oroondates*, recalled him from the Gates of
Death;[2] and one Line from *Parisatis*'s Hand, which brought a
Command to *Lysimachus* to live, made him not only resolve, but
even able, to obey her.[3]

Miss *Glanville*, quite out of Patience at this tedious Harangue,
without any Regard to Ceremony, flounced out of the Room; and
ran to her Brother's Chamber, followed by *Arabella*, who imputed
her rude Haste to a Suspicion, that her Brother was worse.

CHAPTER VIII

By which we hope the Reader will be differently affected

AT their Entrance into the Room, Miss *Glanville* inquired of the Physician, just going out, How he found her Brother? Who replied, that his Fever was increased since last Night; and that it would not (seeing *Arabella* preparing to go to his Bedside) be proper to disturb him.

Saying this, he bow'd, and went out; and Miss *Glanville*, repeating what the Physician had said, begged her to defer speaking to him till another time.

I know, said she, that he apprehends, the Sight of me will cause so many tumultuous Motions in the Soul of his Patient, as may prove prejudicial to him: Nevertheless, since his Disorder is, questionless, more in his Mind than Body, I may prove, haply, a better Physician than he; since I am more likely, than he, to cure an Illness I have caused——

Saying this, she walked up to Mr. *Glanville*'s Bedside, who, seeing her, thanked her, with a weak Voice, for coming to see him; assuring her, he was very sensible of the Favour she did him——

You must not, said she, blushing, thank me too much, lest I think the Favour I have done you, is really of more Consequence than I imagined, since it merits so many Acknowlegements: Your Physician tells us, pursued she, that your Life is in Danger; but I persuade myself, you will value it so much from this Moment, that you will not protract your Cure any longer.

Are you mad, Madam, whispered Miss *Glanville*, who stood behind her, to tell my Brother, that the Physician says he is in Danger? I suppose you really wish he may die, or you would not talk so.

If, answered she, whispering again to Miss *Glanville*, you are not satisfied with what I have already done for your Brother, I will go as far as Modesty will permit me: And gently pulling open the Curtains;

Glanville, said she, with a Voice too much raised for a sick Person's Ear, I grant to your Sister's Solicitations, what the fair *Statira* did to an Interest yet more powerful, since, as you know, it was her own Brother, who pleaded in Favour of the dying *Orontes*: Therefore, considering you in a Condition haply no less dangerous, than that of that passionate Prince, I condescend, like her, to tell you, that I do not wish your Death; that I intreat you to live; and, lastly, by all the Power I have over you, I command you to recover.

Ending these Words, she closed the Curtain, that her transported Lover might not see her Blushes and Confusion, which were so great, that, to conceal them, even from Miss *Glanville*, she hurried out of the Room, and retired to her own Apartment, expecting, in a little time, to receive a Billet, under the sick Man's Hand, importing, that, in Obedience to her Commands, he was recovered, and ready to throw himself at her Feet, to thank her for that Life she had bestowed upon him, and to dedicate the Remains of it to her Service.

Miss *Glanville*, who stayed behind her, in a strange Surprize at her ridiculous Behaviour; though she longed to know what her Brother thought of it, finding he continued silent, would not disturb him. The Shame he conceived at hearing so absurd a Speech from a Woman he passionately loved; and the Desire he had, not to hear his Sister's Sentiments upon it; made him counterfeit Sleep, to avoid any Discourse with her upon so disagreeable a Subject.

That Day his Fever increased; and the next, the Physician pronouncing him in great Danger, a Messenger was dispatched to Town, to hasten the Coming of Sir *Charles*; and poor Miss *Glanville* was quite inconsoleable, under the Apprehensions of losing him.

Arabella, not to derogate from her Character, affected great Firmness of Mind upon this Occasion; she used the most persuasive Eloquence to moderate her Cousin's Affliction, and caused all imaginable Care to be taken of Mr. *Glanville*: While any one was present, her Looks discovered only a calm and decent Sorrow; yet when she was alone, or had only her dear *Lucy* with her, she gave free Vent to her Tears; and discovered a Grief for Mr. *Glanville's* Illness, little different from that she had felt for her Father's.

As she now visited him constantly every Day, she took an Opportunity, when she was alone by his Bedside, to chide him for his Disobedience, in not recovering, as she had commanded him.

Dear Cousin, answered he faintly, Can you imagine, Health is not my Choice? And do you think, I would suffer these Pains, if I could possibly ease myself of them?

'I do not wish your Death: . . . I entreat you to live; and . .
I command you to recover'

Those Pains, replied *Arabella*, mistaking his Complaint, ought to have ceased, when the Cause of them did; and when I was no longer rigorous, you ought no longer to have suffered: But tell me, since you are, questionless, one of the strangest Men in the World, and the hardest to be comforted; nay, and I may add, the most disobedient of all, that ever wore the Fetters of Love; Tell me, I say, what must I do to content you?

If I live, Cousin, said *Glanville*—

Nay, interrupted *Arabella*, since my Empire over you is not so absolute as I thought; and since you think fit to reserve to yourself the Liberty of dying, contrary to my Desire; I think I had better resolve, not to make any Treaty with you: However, as I have gone thus far, I will do something more; and tell you, since I have commanded you to live, I will also permit you to love me, in order to make the Life I have bestowed on you, worthy your Acceptance. Make me no Reply, said she, putting her Hand on his Mouth; but begin from this Moment to obey me.

Saying this, she went out of the Room—

A few Hours after, his Fever being come to a Height, he grew delirious, and talked very wildly; but a favourable Crisis ensuing, he fell into a sound and quiet Sleep, and continued in it for several Hours: Upon his waking, the Physician declared, his Fever was greatly abated; and the next Morning, pronounced him out of Danger—

Miss *Glanville*, transported with Joy, ran to Lady *Bella*, and informed her of this good News; but as she did not make her the Acknowlegements she expected, for being the Cause of his Recovery, she behaved with more Reserve than Miss *Glanville* thought was necessary: Which renewed her former Disgusts; yet, dreading to displease her Brother, she concealed it from the Observation of her Cousin—

Arabella, being desirous of completing her Lover's Cure by some more favourable Expressions, went to his Chamber, accompanied by Miss *Glanville*.

I see, said she, approaching to his Bedside, with an inchanting Smile, that you know how to be obedient, when you please; and I begin to know, by the Price you set upon your Obedience, that small Favours will not content you.

Indeed, my dearest Cousin, said *Glanville*, who had found her more interested in his Recovery than he expected, you have been very obliging, and I will always most gratefully own it.

I am glad, interrupted *Arabella*, that Gratitude is not banished from all your Family; and that that Person in it, for whom I have the most Sensibility, is not intirely divested of it—

I hope, said Mr. *Glanville*, my Sister has given you no Cause to complain of her.

Indeed but she has, replied *Arabella*; for, notwithstanding she is obliged to me for the Life of a Brother, whom questionless she loves very well; nevertheless, she did not deign to make me the least Acknowlegement for what I have done in your Favour: However, *Glanville*, provided you continue to observe that Respect and Fidelity towards me, which I have Reason to hope for from you; your Condition shall be never the worse for Miss *Glanville's* unacknowleging Temper; and I now confirm the Grant I Yesterday made you, and repeat it again; That I permit you to love me, and promise you not to be displeased at any Testimonies you will give me of your Passion, provided you serve me with an inviolable Fidelity.

But, Madam, returned Mr. *Glanville*, to make my Happiness complete, you must also promise to love me; or else what signifies the Permission you give me to love you?

You are almost as unacknowleging as your Sister, resumed *Arabella*, blushing; and if your Health was perfectly re-established, questionless, I should chide you for your Presumption; but since something must be allowed to sick Persons, whose Reason, one may suppose, is weakened by their Indisposition, I will pardon your Indiscretion at this time, and counsel you to wait patiently for what Heaven will determine in your Favour: Therefore endeavour to merit my Affection by your Respect, Fidelity, and Services; and hope from my Justice, whatever it ought to bestow—

Ending this Speech, with a Solemnity of Accent, that gave Mr. *Glanville* to understand, any Reply would offend her, he silently kissed her fair Hand, which she held out to him; a Favour, his Sickness, and the Terms upon which they now were, gave him a Right to expect—And, finishing her Visit for that time, left him to his Repose; being extremely pleased at the Prospect of his Recovery, and very well satisfied at having so gracefully got over so great a Difficulty, as that of giving him Permission to love her: For by the Laws of Romance, when a Lady has once given her Lover that Permission, she may lawfully allow him to talk to her upon the

Subject of his Passion, accept all his Gallantries, and claim an
absolute Empire over all his Actions; reserving to herself the Right
of fixing the Time when she may own her Affection: And when
that important Step is taken, and his Constancy put to a few Years
more Trial; when he has killed all his Rivals, and rescued her from
a thousand Dangers; she at last condescends to reward him with her
Hand; and all her Adventures are at an End for the future.

END of the THIRD BOOK.

BOOK IV

CHAPTER I

In which our Heroine discovers her Knowlege in Astronomy

SIR *George*, who had never missed a Day, during Mr. *Glanville*'s Illness, in sending to the Castle, now he was able to see Company, visited him very frequently; and sometimes had the Happiness to meet with *Arabella* in his Chamber: But, knowing the Conditions of her Father's Will, and Mr. *Glanville*'s Pretensions, he was obliged to lay so much Constraint upon himself, in the Presence of Miss *Glanville*, and her Brother, that he hardly durst trust his Eyes, to express his Admiration of her, for Fear of alarming them with any Suspicion of his Designs: However, he did not fail to recommend himself to her Esteem, by a Behaviour to her full of the most perfect Respect; and very often, ere he was aware, uttered some of the extravagant Compliments, that the Gallants in the *French* Romances use to their Mistresses.

If he walked with her in the Gardens, he would observe, that the Flowers, which were before languishing and pale, bloomed with fresh Beauty at her Approach; that the Sun shined out with double Brightness, to exceed, if possible, the Lustre of her Eyes; and that the Wind, fond of kissing her celestial Countenance, played with her fair Hair; and, by gentle Murmurs, declared its Happiness—

If Miss *Glanville* happened to be present, when he talked to her in this Strain, she would suppose he was ridiculing her Cousin's fantastical Turn; and when she had an Opportunity of speaking to him alone, would chide him, with a great deal of good Humour, for giving her so much Diversion at her Cousin's Expence.

Sir *George*, improving this Hint, persuaded Miss *Glanville* by his Answers, that he really laughed at *Arabella*; and, being now less fearful of giving any Suspicion to the gay Coquet, since she assisted him to deceive her, he applied himself, with more Assiduity than ever, to insinuate himself into *Arabella*'s Favour.

However, the Necessity he was under of being always of *Arabella*'s Opinion, sometimes drew him into little Difficulties with Miss *Glanville*. Knowing that young Lady was extremely fond of Scandal, he told her, as a most agreeable Piece of News, one Afternoon when he was there, that he had seen Miss *Groves*, who, he supposed, had come into the Country upon the same Account as she had done a Twelve-month before: Her Marriage being yet a Secret, the complaisant Baronet threw out an Hint or two, concerning the Familiarity and Correspondence there was between her and the Gentleman to whom she was really secretly married.

Miss *Glanville*, making the most of this Intelligence, said a thousand severe Things against the unfortunate Miss *Groves*; which *Arabella*, always benevolent and kind, could not bear.

I persuade myself, said she to her Cousin, that you have been misinformed concerning this Beauty, whose Misfortunes you aggravate by your cruel Censures; and whoever has given you the History of her Life, has, haply, done it with great Injustice—

Why, Madam, interrupted Miss *Glanville*, do you think you are better acquainted with her History, as you call it, who have never been in Town, where her Follies made her so remarkable, than Persons who were Eye-witnesses of all her ridiculous Actions?

I apprehend, said *Arabella*, that I, who have had a Relation made to me of all the Passages of her Life, and have been told all her most secret Thoughts, may know as much, if not more, than Persons who have lived in the same Place with her, and have not had that Advantage; and I think, I know enough to vindicate her from many cruel Aspersions.

Pray, Madam, returned Miss *Glanville*, will your Ladyship pretend to defend her scandalous Commerce with Mr. *L*——?

I know not, Miss, said *Arabella*, why you call her Intercourse with that perjured Man by so unjust an Epithet. If Miss *Groves* be unchaste, so was the renowned *Cleopatra*, whose Marriage with *Julius Caesar* is controverted to this Day.

And what Reasons, Madam, said Miss *Glanville*, have you for supposing, Miss *Groves* was married to Mr. *L*——, since all the World knows to the contrary?

Very sufficient ones, said *Arabella*; since it is hardly possible to suppose, a young Lady of Miss *Groves*'s Quality would stain the Lustre of her Descent by so shameful an Intrigue; and also, since there are Examples enough to be found of Persons, who suffered under the same unhappy Circumstances as herself; yet were perfectly innocent, as was that great Queen I have mentioned; who questionless, you, Sir, are sufficiently convinced, was married to that illustrious Conqueror; who, by betraying so great and so fair a Queen, in great measure tarnished the Glory of his Laurels—

Married, Madam! replied Sir *George*: Who presumes to say, that fair Queen was not married to that illustrious Conqueror?

Nay, you know, Sir, interrupted *Arabella*, many People did say, even while she was living, that she was not married; and have branded her Memory with infamous Calumnies, upon Account of the Son she had by *Caesar*, the brave *Caesario*, who, under the Name of *Cleomedon*, performed such Miracles of Valour in *Ethiopia*.[1]

I assure you, Madam, said Sir *George,* I was always a great Admirer of the famous *Cleomedon*, who was certainly the greatest Hero in the World.

Pardon me, Sir, said *Arabella*; *Cleomedon* was, questionless, a very valiant Man; but he, and all the Heroes that ever were, must give place to the unequalled Prince of *Mauritania*;[2] that illustrious, and for a long time unfortunate, Lover of the Divine *Cleopatra*, who was Daughter, as you questionless know, of the great Queen we have been speaking of—

Dear Heart! said Miss *Glanville*, What is all this to the Purpose? I would fain know, whether Sir *George* believes, Miss *Groves* was ever married to Mr. *L——*.

Doubtless, I do, said he; for, as Lady *Bella* says, she is in the same unhappy Circumstance with the great *Cleopatra*; and if *Julius Caesar* could be guilty of denying his Marriage with that Queen, I see no Reason to suppose, why Mr. *L——* might not be guilty of the same kind of Injustice.

So then, interrupted Miss *Glanville*, reddening with Spite, you will really offer to maintain, that Miss *Groves* was married? Ridiculous! How such a Report would be laughed at in *London*!

I assure you, replied *Arabella*, if ever I go to *London*, I shall not scruple to maintain that Opinion to every one, who will mention that Fair-one to me; and use all my Endeavours to confirm them in it.

Your Ladyship would do well, said Miss *Glanville*, to persuade People, that Miss *Groves*, at Fifteen, did not want to run away with her Writing-master.

As I am persuaded myself, said *Arabella*, that Writing master was some noble Stranger in Disguise, who was passionately in Love with her, I shall not suffer any body, in my Hearing, to propagate such an unlikely Story; but since he was a Person worthy of her Affection, if she had run away with him, her Fault was not without Example, and even Excuse: You know what the fair *Artemisa* did for *Alexander*, Sir, pursued she, turning to Sir *George*. I would fain know your Sentiments upon the Action of that Princess, which some have not scrupled to condemn—

Whoever they are, Madam, said Sir *George*, who condemn the fair *Artemisa* for what she did for *Alexander*,[1] are Miscreants and Slanderers; and though that beautiful Princess has been dead more than Two thousand Years, I would draw my Sword in Defence of her Character, against all who should presume, in my Presence, to cast any Censures upon it.

Since you are so courageous, said Miss *Glanville*, laughing excessively at this Sally, which, she thought, was to ridicule her Cousin; it is to be hoped, you will defend a living Lady's Character, who may thank you for it; and make the World believe, that her Correspondence with Mr. *L——* was intirely innocent; and that she never had any Design to run away with her Writing-master.

Are you resolved, Cousin, said Lady *Bella*, to persist in that ridiculous Mistake, and take a Nobleman for a Writing-master only because his Love put him upon such a Stratagem to obtain his Mistress?

Indeed, Lady *Bella*, said Miss *Glanville*, smileing, you may as well persuade me, the Moon is made of a Cream Cheese, as that any Nobleman turned himself into a Writing-master, to obtain Miss *Groves*—

Is it possible, Miss, said *Arabella*, that you can offer such an Affront to my Understanding, as to suppose, I would argue upon such a ridiculous System; and compare the Second glorious Luminary of the Heavens to so unworthy a Resemblance? I have taken some Pains to contemplate the Heavenly Bodies; and, by Reading and Observation, am able to comprehend some Part of their Excellence: Therefore it is not probable, I should descend to such trivial Comparisons; and liken a Planet, which, haply, is not much less than our Earth, to a thing so inconsiderable, as that you name—

Pardon me, dear Cousin, interrupted Miss *Glanville*, laughing louder than before, if I divert myself a little with the Extravagance of your Notions. Really I think, you have no Reason to be angry, if I supposed you might make a Comparison between the Moon and a Cream Cheese; since you say, that same Moon, which don't appear broader than your Gardener's Face, is not much less than the whole World: Why, certainly, I have more Reason to trust my own Eyes, than such whimsical Notions as these.

Arabella, unwilling to expose her Cousin's Ignorance, by a longer Dispute upon this Subject, begged her to let it drop for the present; and, turning to Sir *George*, I am very glad, said she, that having always had some Inclination to excuse, and even defend, the Flight of *Artemisa* with *Alexander*, my Opinion is warranted by that of a Person so generous as yourself: Indeed, when we consider, that this Princess forsook her Brother's Dominions, and fled away with a Lover whom she did not hate; questionless, her Enemies accuse her, with some Appearance of Reason, of too great Imbecillity.[1]

But, Madam, replied Sir *George*, her Enemies will not take the Pains to examine her Reasons for this Conduct—

True, Sir, resumed *Arabella*; for she was in Danger of seeing a Prince, who loved her, put to a cruel and infamous Death upon a public Scaffold; and she did not resolve to fly with him, till all her Tears and Prayers were found ineffectual to move the King her Brother to Mercy.

Tho', replied Sir *George*, I am extremely angry with the indiscreet *Cepio*, who discovered *Alexander* to the *Armenian* King; yet what does your Ladyship think of that gallant Action of his, when he saw him upon the Scaffold, and the Executioner ready to cut off his Head? How brave it was of him, to pass undauntedly thro' the prodigious Number of Guards that environed the Scaffold; and, with his drawn Sword, run the Executioner through the Body, in the Sight of them all! Then giving the Prince another Sword, engage more than Two thousand Men in his Defence!

Questionless, replied *Arabella*, it was a glorious Action; and when I think, how the King of *Armenia* was enraged to see such a Multitude of Soldiers fly from the Swords of Two Men, I cannot choose but divert myself with the Consternation he was in: Yet that was nothing to the horrible Despair, which tormented him afterwards, when he found, that *Alexander*, after being again taken and imprisoned, had broken his Chains, and carried away with him the Princess *Artimesa* his Sister.

CHAPTER II

In which a very pleasing Conversation is left unfinished

As *Arabella* was in this Part of her Discourse, a Servant came to inform her, that Sir *Charles Glanville* was just alighted. Upon which, Miss *Glanville* flew to receive her Father; and *Arabella*, walking a little slower after her, gave Sir *George* an Opportunity of holding a little longer Conversation with her.

I dare believe, Madam, said he, when you read the Story of the unfortunate *Alexander*, your fair Eyes did not refuse to shed some Tears at the barbarous and shameful Death he was going to suffer: Yet I assure you, melancholy as his Situation was, it was also very glorious for him, since he had the sublime Satisfaction of dying for the Person he adored; and had the ravishing Pleasure to know, that his Fate would draw Tears from that lovely Princess, for whom he sacrificed his Life: Such a Condition, Madam, ought to be envied rather than pitied; for, next to the Happiness of possessing the Person one adores, certainly the Glory of dying for her is most to be coveted.

Arabella, pleasingly surprised to hear Language so conformable to her own Ideas, looked for a Moment upon the Baronet, with a most inchanting Complaisancy in her Eyes—

It must be confessed, Sir, says she, that you speak very rationally upon these Matters; and by the Tenderness and Generosity of your Sentiments, you give me Cause to believe, that your Heart is prepossessed with some Object worthy of inspiring them.

Sir *George* seeming, as if he struggled to suppress a Sigh; You are in the right, Madam, said he, to suppose, that if my Heart be prepossessed with any Object, it is with one, who is capable of inspiring a very sublime Passion; and I assure you, if ever it submits to any Fetters, they shall be imposed on me by the fairest Person in the World—

Since Love is not voluntary, replied *Arabella*, smiling, it may happen, that your Heart may be surprised by a meaner Beauty, than such a one as you describe: However, as a Lover has always an extraordinary Partiality for the beloved Object, 'tis probable, what you say may come to pass; and you may be in Love with the fairest Person in the World, in your own Opinion.

They were now so near the House, that Sir *George* could reply no other ways, than by a very passionate Glance, which *Arabella* did not observe, being in haste to pay her Respects to her Uncle, whom she met just going to Mr. *Glanville*. Her Looks were directed to him. Sir *Charles* saluting her with great Affection, they all went into Mr. *Glanville*'s Chamber, who received his Father with the utmost Respect and Tenderness; extremely regretting the Trouble he had been at in taking a Journey to the Castle upon his Account; and gently blaming his Sister for her Precipitancy in alarming him so soon.

Sir *Charles*, extremely overjoyed to find him so well recovered, would not allow him to blame Miss *Glanville* for what she had done; but, addressing himself to his Niece, he thanked her for the Care she had taken of Mr. *Glanville*, in very obliging Terms.

Arabella could not help blushing at her Uncle's Compliment, supposing he thanked her for having restored her Cousin to his Health.

I assure you, Sir, said she, Mr. *Glanville* is less obliged to my Commands, than to the Goodness of his Constitution, for his Recovery; and herein he was not so obedient, as many Persons I could name to him.

Mr. *Glanville*, willing to prevent the Company's Observation upon this Speech, began to acquaint his Father with the Rise and Progress of his Distemper: But though the old Gentleman listened with great Attention to his Son, while he was speaking; yet not having lost a Word of what *Arabella* had said, as soon as he was done, he turned to his Niece, and asked her, how she could be so unjust, to accuse his Son of Disobedience, because he did not recover, when she commanded him? Why, Madam, added he, you want to carry your Power farther then ever any Beauty did before you; since you pretend to make People sick and well, whenever you please.

Really, Sir, replied *Arabella*, I pretend to no more Power, than what I presume all others of my Sex have upon the like Occasions; and since nothing is more common, than for a Gentleman, though ever so sick, to recover in Obedience to the Commands of that

Person, who has an absolute Power over his Life, I conceive, I have a Right to think myself injured, if Mr. *Glanville*, contrary to mine, had thought proper to die—

Since, said the old Gentlemen, smiling, my Son has so well obeyed your Commands in recovering his Health, I shall tremble, lest, in Obedience to a contrary Command of yours, he should die, and deprive me of an Heir; a Misfortune, which, if it should happen, I should place to your Account.

I assure you, Sir, said *Arabella*, very gravely, I have too great an Esteem for Mr. *Glanville*, to condemn him to so severe a Punishment as Death for light Offences: And since it is not very probable, that he will ever commit such Crimes against me, as can be only expiated by his Death; such as Infidelity, Disobedience, and the like; you have no Reason to fear such a Misfortune by my means—

Alas! replied Sir *George*, you Beauties make very nice Distinctions in these Cases; and think, if you do not directly command your Lovers to die, you are no-ways accountable for their Death: And when a Lover, as it often happens, dies through Despair of ever being able to make himself beloved; or, being doomed to Banishment or Silence, falls into a Fever, from which nothing but Kindness can recover him; and, that being denied, he patiently expires; I say, when these Things happen, as they certainly do every Day; How can you hold yourselves guiltless of their Deaths, which are apparently occasioned, either by your Scorn or Insensibility?

Sir *Charles* and Miss *Glanville* were extremely diverted at this Speech of Sir *George*'s; and Mr. *Glanville*, though he would have wished he had been raillying any other Person's Follies than his Cousin's, yet could not help smiling at the solemn Accent, in which he delivered himself—

Arabella, mightily pleased with his Manner of talking, was resolved to furnish him with more Occasions of diverting the Company at her Expence.

I see, answered she, you are one of those Persons, who call a just Decorum, which all Ladies, who love Glory as they ought to do, are obliged to preserve, by the Name of Severity: But pray, what would you have a Lady do, whom an importunate Lover presumes to declare his Passion to? You know it is not permitted us to listen to such Discourses; and you know also, whoever is guilty of such an

Offence, merits a most rigorous Punishment: Moreover, you find, that when a Sentence of Banishment or Silence is pronounced upon them, these unhappy Criminals are so conscious of the Justice of their Doom, that they never murmur against their Judge who condemns them; and therefore, whatever are their Fates, in Consequence of that Anger they have incurred, the Ladies, thus offended, ought not to be charged with it, as any cruel Exertion of their Power.

Such Eloquence as yours, Madam, replied Sir *George*, might defend Things yet more unjustifiable: However, you must give me Leave, as being interested in the Safety of my Sex, still to be of Opinion, that no Man ought to be hated, because he adores a beautiful Object, and consecrates all his Moments to her Service.

Questionless, resumed *Arabella*, he will not be hated, while, out of the Respect and Reverence he bears her, he carefully conceals his Passion from her Knowlege; but as soon as ever he breaks through the Bounds, which that Respect prescribes him, and lets her understand his true Sentiments, he has Reason to expect a most rigorous Sentence, since her certainly, by that Presumption, has greatly deserved it.

If the Ladies, replied Sir *George*, were more equitable, and would make some Distinction between those who really love them in a passionate and respectful Silence, and others who do not feel the Power of their Charms, they might spare themselves the Trouble of hearing what so mortally offends them: But when a Lady sees a Man every Day, who by his Looks, Sighs, and Solicitude to please her, by his numberless Services and constant Attendance of her, makes it evident, that his Soul is possessed with a violent Passion for her; I say, when a Lady sees, and yet will not see, all this, and persists in using a passionate Adorer with all the Indifference due to a Man wholly insensible of the Power of her Charms; what must he do in such a mortifying Situation, but make known his Torments to her that occasions them, in order to prevail upon her to have some Sense of what he does and feels hourly for her sake?

But since he gains nothing by the Discovery of his Passion, resumed *Arabella*; but, on the contrary, loses the Advantages he was before possessed of, which were very great, since he might see and discourse with his Mistress every Day; and, haply, have the Honour to do her a great many petty Services, and receive some of her Commands; all these Advantages he loses, when he declares he

loves: And truly, I think, a Man who is so unwise as to hazard a
certain Happiness for a very improbable Hope, deserves to be
punished, as well for his Folly as Presumption; and, upon both
these Accounts, Banishment is not too rigorous a Sentence.

CHAPTER III

Definition of Love and Beauty.—The necessary Qualities of a Hero and Heroine

THOUGH, replied Mr. *Glanville*, you are very severe in the Treatment you think it necessary our Sex should receive from yours;
yet I wish some of our Town Beauties were, if not altogether of your
Opinion, yet sufficiently so, as to make it not a Slavery for a Man
to be in their Company; for unless one talks of Love to these fair
Coquets the whole time one is with them, they are quite displeased, and look upon a Man who can think any thing, but
themselves, worthy his Thoughts or Observation, with the utmost
Contempt. How often have you and I, Sir *George*, pursued he,
pitied the Condition of the few Men of Sense, who are sometimes
among the Croud of Beaux, who attend the Two celebrated
Beauties[1] to all Places of polite Diversion in Town? For those
Ladies think it a mortal Injury done to their Charms, if the Men
about them have Eyes or Ears for any Object but their Faces, or any
Sound but that of their Voices: So that the Connoisseurs in Music,
who attend them to *Ranelagh*, must stop their Ears, like *Ulysses*,
when the *Siren Frasi*[2] sings; and the Wits, who gallant them to the
Side box, must lay a much greater Constraint upon themselves, in
order to resist the Soul-moving *Garrick*; and appear insensible,
while he is upon the Stage.

Upon my Soul, added Sir *George* (forgetting the Character he
assumed) when I have seen some Persons of my Acquaintance
talking to the eldest of these Ladies, while one of *Congreve*'s
Comedies has been acting; his Face quite turned from the Stage,
and hers overspread with an eternal Smile; her fine Eyes sometimes
lifted up in a beautiful Surprize, and a little inchanting Giggle
half-hid with her Fan; in spite of their Inattention, I have been
ready to imagine, he was entertaining her with Remarks upon the
Play, which she was judicious enough to understand; and yet I have

afterwards been informed by himself, that nothing was less in their Thoughts; and all that Variety in her Face, and that extreme seeming Earnestness in his Discourse, was occasioned by the most trifling Subjects imaginable: He perhaps had been telling her, how the Sight of her Squirrel, which peeped out of her Pocket, surprised some Ladies she was visiting; and what they said upon her Fondness for it, when she was gone; blaming them at the same time for their want of Delicacy, in not knowing how to set a right Value upon such pleasing Animals: Hence proceeded her Smiles, the lifting up of her Eyes, the half-stifled Laugh, and all the pretty Gestures that appeared so wonderfully charming to all those who did not hear their Discourse: And it is upon such Trifles as these, or else on the inexhaustible Subject of their Charms, that all who are ambitious of being near these Miracles, are under a Necessity of talking.

And pray, interrupted *Arabella*, What Subjects afford Matter for a more pleasing Variety of Conversation, than those of Beauty and Love? Can we speak of any Object so capable of delighting as Beauty, or of any Passion of the Mind more sublime and pleasing than Love?

With Submission, Madam, said *Glanville*, I conceive, all that can be said, either of Beauty, or of Love, may be comprised in a very few Words: All who have Eyes, and behold true Beauty, will be ready to confess it is a very pleasing Object; and all that can be said of it, may be said in very few Words; for when we have run over the Catalogue of Charms, and mentioned fine Eyes, fine Hair, delicate Complexion, regular Features, and an elegant Shape, we can only add a few Epithets more, such as Lovely, Dangerous, Inchanting, Irresistible and the like; and every thing that can be said of Beauty is exhausted. And so likewise it is with Love; we know that Admiration precedes it, that Beauty kindles it, Hope keeps it alive, and Despair puts an End to it; and that Subject may be as soon discussed as the other, by the judicious Use of proper Words; such as Wounds, Darts, Fires, Languishings, Dyings, Torture, Rack, Jealousy, and a few more of no Signification, but upon this Subject.

Certainly, Sir, said *Arabella*, you have not well considered what you say, since you maintain, that Love and Beauty are Subjects easily and quickly discussed: Take the Pains, I beseech you, to reflect a little upon those numerous and long Conversations,[1] which these Subjects have given Rise to in *Clelia*, and the *Grand Cyrus*, where the most illustrious and greatest Personages in the World manage the Disputes; and the agreeable Diversity of their Sentiments on those Heads affords a most pleasing and rational Entertainment: You will there find, that the greatest Conquerors, and Heroes of invincible Valour, reason with the most exact and scrupulous Nicety upon Love and Beauty; the Superiority of fair and brown Hair controverted by Warriors, with as much Eagerness as they dispute for Victory in the Field; and the different Effects of that Passion upon different Hearts defined with the utmost Accuracy and Eloquence.

I must own, interrupted Sir *Charles*, I should have but a mean Opinion of those Warriors, as you call them, who could busy themselves in talking of such Trifles; and be apt to imagine such insignificant Fellows, who could wrangle about the Colour of their Mistresses Hair, would be the first to turn their Backs upon the Enemy in Battle.

Is it possible, Sir, resumed *Arabella*, glowing with Indignation, that you can entertain such unworthy Thoughts of Heroes, who merit the Admiration and Praise of all Ages for their inestimable Valour, whom the Spears of a whole Army opposed to each of their single Swords would not oblige to fly? What think you, Sir, pursued she, looking at Sir *George*, of the injurious Words my Uncle has uttered against those heroic Princes, whose Courage, I believe, you are as well acquainted with as myself? The great *Oroondates*, the invincible *Artaban*, the valiant and fortunate *Artamenes*, the irresistible *Juba*, the incomparable *Cleomedon*, and an hundred other Heroes I could name, are all injured by this unjust Assertion of my Uncle; since certainly they were not more famous for their noble and wonderful Actions in War, than for the Sublimity and Constancy of their Affections in Love.

Some of these Heroes you have named, replied Sir *George*, had the Misfortune, even in their Lives, to be very cruelly vilified: The great *Oroondates* was a long time accused of Treachery to his Divine Princess;[1] the valiant and unfortunate *Artamenes* was suspected of Inconstancy;[2] and the irresistible *Juba* reproached with Infidelity and Baseness, by both his Mistress and Friend.[3]

I never knew you was so well acquainted with these Persons, interrupted Mr. *Glanville*; and I fansy it is but very lately that you have given yourself the Trouble to read Romances.

I am not of your Opinion, said *Arabella*. Sir *George*, questionless, has appropriated great Part of his Time to the Perusal of those Books, so capable of improving him in all useful Knowlege; the Sublimity of Love, and the Quintessence of Valour; which Two Qualities, if possessed in a superlative Degree, form a true and perfect Hero, as the Perfection of Beauty, Wit, and Virtue, make a Heroine worthy to be served by such an illustrious Personage; and I dare say, Sir *George* has profited so much by the great Examples of Fidelity and Courage he has placed before his Eyes, that no Consideration whatever could make him for one Moment fail in his Constancy to the Divine Beauty he adores; and, inspired by her Charms, he would scorn to turn his Back, as my Uncle phrases it, upon an Army of an hundred thousand Men.

I am extremely obliged to you, Madam, said Sir *George*, bowing his Head to the Ground, to hide a Smile he could not possibly restrain, for the good Opinion you have of my Courage and Fidelity.

As for Sir *George*'s Courage, Cousin, said Mr. *Glanville* laughing, I never disputed it: And though it be indeed a very extraordinary Exertion of it, to fight singly against an Army of an hundred thousand Men; yet since you are pleased to think it probable, I am as willing to believe Sir *George* may do it as any other Man; but, as for his Fidelity in Matters of Love, I greatly suspect it, since he has been charged with some very flagrant Crimes of that Nature.

How, Sir! resumed *Arabella*, Have you ever been faithless then? and, after having sworn, haply, to devote your whole Life to the Service of some Beauty, have you ever violated your Oaths, and been base enough to forsake her?

I have too much Complaisance, Madam, said Sir *George*, to contradict Mr. *Glanville*, who has been pleased positively to assert, that I have been faithless, as you most unkindly phrase it.

Nay, Sir, replied *Arabella*, this Accusation is not of a Nature to be neglected; and though a King should say it, I conceive, if you are innocent, you have a Right to contradict him, and clear yourself: Do you consider how deeply this Assertion wounds your Honour and Happiness for the future? What Lady, think you, will receive your Services, loaded as you are with the terrible Imputation of Inconstancy?

Oh! as for that, Madam, said Miss *Glanville*, I believe no Lady will think the worse of Sir George for being faithless: For my Part, I declare, nothing pleases me so much, as gaining a Lover from another Lady; which is a greater Compliment to one's Beauty, then the Addresses of a Man that never was in Love before—

You may remember, Cousin, replied *Arabella*, that I said once before, your Spirit and Humour resembled a certain great Princess very much; and I repeat it again, never was there a greater Conformity in Tempers and Inclinations.[1]

My Daughter, said Sir *Charles*, is mightily obliged to you, Lady *Bella*, for comparing her to a great Princess: Undoubtedly you mean it as a Compliment.

If you think, said *Arabella*, that barely comparing her to a Princess be a Compliment, I must take the Liberty to differ from you: My Cousin is not so many Degrees below a Princess, as that such a Comparison should be thought extraordinary; for if her Ancestors did not wear a Crown, they might, haply, have deserved it; and her Beauty may one Day procure her a Servant, whose Sword, like that of the great *Artaban*, may win her a Sceptre;[2] who, with a noble Confidence, told his Princess, when the Want of a Crown was objected to him, I wear a Sword, Madam, that can perform things more difficult, than what you require; and if a Crown be all that I want to make me worthy of you, tell me what Kingdom in the World you choose to reign in, and I will lay it at your Feet.

That was a Promise, replied Sir *George*, fit only for the great *Artaban* to make: But, Madam, if you will permit me to make any Comparison between that renowned Warrior and myself, I would venture to tell you, that even the great *Artaban* was not exempted from the Character of Inconstancy any more than myself, since, as you certainly know, he was in Love with Three great Princesses successively.

I grant you, replied *Arabella*, that *Artaban* did wear the Chains of Three Princesses successively:[3] But it must also be remembred in his Justification, that the Two First of these Beauties refused his Adorations, and treated him with Contempt, because he was not a Prince: Therefore, recovering his Liberty, by those Disdains they cast on him, he preserved that illustrious Heart from Despair, to tender it with more passionate Fidelity to the Divine Princess of the *Parthians*; who, though greatly their Superior in Quality and Beauty, did permit him to love her. However, I must confess, I find something like Levity in the Facility he found in breaking his Fetters so often; and when I consider, that among all those great

Heroes, whose Histories I have read, none but himself ever bore, without dying, the Cruelties he experienced from those Princesses, I am sometimes tempted to accuse him myself of Inconstancy: But indeed every thing we read of that Prodigy of Valour is wholly miraculous; and since the Performance of Impossibilities was reserved for him, I conclude this Miracle also, among many others, was possible to him, whom nothing was ever able to resist upon Earth. However, pursued she, rising, I shall not absolutely condemn you, till I have heard your Adventures from your own Mouth, at a convenient Time, when I shall be able to judge how far you merit the odious Appellation of Inconstancy.

Saying this, she saluted her Uncle, who had for some time been conversing in a low Voice with his Son, with a Grace wholly charming, and retired to her Apartment. Miss *Glanville* following her a few Moments after (the Compliment, extravagant as it was, which she had paid her, having procured her some Good-will from the vain and interested Miss *Glanville*), they conversed together with a great deal of good Humour till Dinner-time, which, because Mr. *Glanville* was not absolutely recovered, was served in his Chamber.

CHAPTER IV

In which our Heroine is engaged in a new Adventure

As Mr. *Glanville* took a great deal of Pains to turn the Discourse upon Subjects, on which the charming *Arabella* could expatiate, without any Mixture of that Absurdity, which mingled itself in a great many others; the rest of that Day and several others, were passed very agreeably: At the End of which, Mr. *Glanville* being perfectly recovered, and able to go abroad; the Baronet proposed to take the Diversion of Hunting; which *Arabella*, who was used to it, consented to partake of; but being informed, that Miss *Glanville* could not ride, and chose to stay at home, she would have kept her Company, had not Sir *Charles* insisted upon the contrary.

As Sir *George*, and some other Gentlemen, had invited themselves to be of the Party; *Arabella*, on her coming down to mount her Horse, found a great many young Gallants, ready to offer her their Assistance upon this Occasion: Accepting therefore, with great Politeness, this Help from a Stranger, who was nearest her, she mounted her Horse, giving Occasion to every one that was present, to admire the Grace with which she sat and managed him. Her Shape being as perfect as any Shape could possibly be, her Riding-habit discovered all its Beauties: Her Hat, and the white Feather waving over Part of her fine black Hair, gave a peculiar Charm to her lovely Face: And she appeared with so many Advantages in this Dress and Posture, that Mr. *Glanville*, forgetting all her Absurdities, was wholly lost in the Contemplation of so many Charms, as her whole Person was adorned with.

Sir *George*, though he really admired *Arabella*, was not so passionately in Love as Mr. *Glanville*; and, being a keen Sportsman, eagerly pursued the Game, with the rest of the Hunters; but Mr. *Glanville* minded nothing but his Cousin, and kept close by her.

After having rode a long time, *Arabella*, conceiving it a Piece of Cruelty, not to give her Lover an Opportunity of talking to her, as, by his extreme Solicitude, he seemed ardently to desire, coming to a delightful Valley, she stopped; and told Mr. *Glanville*, that, being weary of the Chace, she should alight, and repose herself a little under the Shade of those Trees.

Mr. *Glanville*, extremely pleased at this Proposition, dismounted; and, having helped her to alight, seated himself by her on the Grass.

Arabella, expecting he would begin to talk to her of his Passion, could not help blushing at the Thoughts of having given him such an Opportunity; and Mr. *Glanville*, endeavouring to accommodate himself to her Ideas of a Lover, expressed himself in Terms extravagant enough to have made a reasonable Woman think he was making a Jest of her: All which, however, *Arabella* was extremely pleased with; and she observed such a just Decorum in her Answers, that, as the Writers of Romance phrase it, if she did not give him any absolute Hopes of being beloved, yet she said enough to make him conclude she did not hate him.

They had conversed in this manner near a Quarter of an Hour, when *Arabella*, perceiving a Man at a little Distance, walking very composedly, shrieked out aloud; and, rising with the utmost Precipitation, flew from Mr. *Glanville*, and went to untie her Horse; while his Astonishment being so great at her Behaviour, that he could not, for a Moment or two, ask her the Cause of her Fear—

Do you not see, said she, out of Breath with the Violence of her Apprehensions, the Person who is coming towards us? It is the same, who, some Months ago, attempted to carry me away, when I was riding out with only Two Attendants: I escaped, for that time, the Danger that threatened me; but, questionless, he comes now to renew his Attempts: Therefore can you wonder at my Fear?

If it should be as you say, Madam, interrupted *Glanville*, What Reason have you to fear? Do you not think I am able to defend you?

Ah! without Doubt, you are able to defend me, answered she; and though, if you offer to resist the Violence he comes to use against me, he will, haply, call Two or Three Dozen armed Men to his Assistance, who are, I suppose, concealed hereabouts, yet I am not apprehensive, that you will be worsted by them: But as it happened to the brave *Juba*, and *Cleomedon*, while they were fighting with some hundred Men, who wanted to carry away their Princesses before their Faces; and were giving Death at every Blow, in order to preserve them; the Commander of these Ravishers, seeing the Two Princesses sitting, as I was, under a Tree, ordered them to be seized by Two of his Men, and carried away, while the Two Princes were losing best Part of their Blood in their Defence;[1] therefore, to prevent such an Accident happening, while you are fighting for my Rescue, I think it will be the safest Way for me to get on Horseback, that I may be in a Condition to escape; and that you may not employ your Valour to no Purpose.

Saying this, having, with Mr. *Glanville*'s Assistance, loosed her Horse from the Tree, he helped her to mount, and then remounted his own.

Your Antagonist, said *Arabella*, is on Foot; and therefore, though I prize your Life extremely, yet I cannot dispense with myself from telling you, that 'tis against the Laws of Knighthood to take any Advantage of that kind over your Enemy; nor will I permit your Concern for my Safety to make you forget what you owe to your own Reputation.

Mr. *Glanville*, fretting excessively at her Folly, begged her not to make herself uneasy about things that were never likely to happen.

The Gentleman yonder, added he, seems to have no Designs to make any Attempt against you: If he should, I shall know how to deal with him: But, since he neither offers to assault me, nor affront you, I think we ought not to give him any Reason to imagine we suspect him, by gazing on him thus; and letting him understand by your Manner, that he is the Subject of our Conversation: If you please, Madam, we will endeavour to join our Company.

Arabella, while he was speaking, kept her Eyes fixed upon his Face, with Looks which expressed her Thoughts were labouring upon some very important Point: And, after a Pause of some Moments, Is it possible, said she, with a Tone of extreme Surprize, that I should be so mistaken in you? Do you really want Courage enough to defend me against that Ravisher?

Oh Heavens! Madam, interrupted *Glanville*, try not my Temper thus: Courage enough to defend you! 'Sdeath! you will make me mad! Who, in the Name of Wonder, is going to molest you?

He whom you see there, replied *Arabella*, pointing to him with her Finger: For know, cold and insensible as thou art to the Danger which threatens me, yonder Knight is thy Rival, and a Rival, haply, who deserves my Esteem better than thou dost; since, if he has Courage enough to get me by Violence into his Power, that same Courage would make him defend me against any Injuries I might be offered from another: And since nothing is so contemptible in the Eyes of a Woman, as a Lover who wants Spirit to die in her Defence; know, I can sooner pardon him, whom thou would cowardly fly from, for the Violence which he meditates against me, than thyself for the Pusillanimity thou hast betrayed in my Sight.

With these Words, she galloped away from her astonished Lover; who, not daring to follow her, for fear of increasing her Suspicions of his Cowardice, flung himself off his Horse in a violent Rage; and, forgetting that the Stranger was observing, and now within Hearing, he fell a cursing and exclaiming against the Books, that had turned his Cousin's Brain; and railing at his own ill Fate, that condemned him to the Punishment of loving her. Mr. *Hervey* (for it really was he, whom an Affair of Consequence had brought again into the Country), hearing some of Mr. *Glanville*'s last Words, and observing the Gestures he used, concluded he had been treated like himself by *Arabella*, whom he knew again at a Distance: Therefore coming up to Mr. *Glanville*, laughing—

Though I have not the Honour of knowing you, Sir, said he, I must beg the Favour you will inform me, if you are not disturbed at the ridiculous Folly of the Lady I saw with you just now? She is the most fantastical Creature that ever lived, and, in my Opinion, fit for a Mad-house: Pray, are you acquainted with her?

Mr. *Glanville*, being in a very ill Humour, could not brook the Freedom of this Language against his Cousin, whose Follies he could not bear any one should rail at but himself; and, being provoked at his Sneers, and the Interruption he had given to their Conversation, he looked upon him with a disdainful Frown, and told him in an haughty Tone, That he was very impertinent to speak of a Lady of her Quality and Merit so rudely.

Oh! Sir, I beg your Pardon, replied Mr. *Hervey*, laughing more than before; What, I suppose, you are the Champion of this fair Lady! But, I assure myself, if you intend to quarrel with every one that will laugh at her, you will have more Business upon your Hands than you can well manage.

Mr. *Glanville*, transported with Rage at this Insolence, hit him such a Blow with the But-End of his Whip, that it stunned him for a Moment; but recovering himself, he drew his Sword, and, mad with the Affront he had received, made a Push at *Glanville*; who, avoiding it with great Dexterity, had recourse to his Hanger for his Defence.

Arabella, in the mean time, who had not rid far, concealing herself behind some Trees, saw all the Actions of her Lover, and intended Ravisher; and, being possessed with an Opinion of her Cousin's Cowardice, was extremely rejoiced to see him fall upon his Enemy first, and that with so much Fury, that she had no longer any Reason to doubt his Courage: Her Suspicions, therefore, being removed, her Tenderness for him returned; and when she saw them engaged with their Swords (for, at that Distance, she did not plainly perceive the Difference of their Weapons), her Apprehensions for her Cousin were so strong, that, though she did not doubt his Valour, she could not bear to see him expose his Life for her: And, without making any Reflections upon the Singularity of her Design, she was going to ride up to them, and endeavour to part them; when she saw several Men come towards them, whom she took to be the Assistants of her Ravisher, though they were, in reality, Haymakers; who, at a Distance, having seen the Beginning of their Quarrel, had hastened to part them.

Terrified, therefore, at this Reinforcement, which she thought would expose her Cousin to great Danger, she galloped, with all

Speed, after the Hunters, being directed by the Sound of the Horn. Her Anxiety for her Cousin made her regardless of her own Danger, so that she rode with a surprising Swiftness; and, over-taking the Company, she would have spoken, to tell them of her Cousin's Situation; when her Spirits failing her, she could only make a Sign with her Hand, and sunk down in a Swoon, in the Arms of Sir *George*, who eagerly galloped up to her; and, support-ing her as well as he was able till some others came to her Relief, they took her off her Horse, and placed her upon the Ground; when, by the Help of some Water they brought from a Spring near them, in a little time she came to herself.

Sir *Charles*, who, seeing her come up to them without his Son, and by her fainting, concluded some Misfortune had happened to him, the Moment she opened her Eyes, asked her eagerly, Where he was?

Your Son, said *Arabella*, sighing, with a Valour equal to that of the brave *Cleomedon*, is this Moment fighting in my Defence against a Croud of Enemies; and is, haply, shedding the last Drop of his Blood in my Quarrel.

Shedding the last Drop of his Blood, *haply!* repeated Sir *Charles*, excessively grieved; and, not a little enraged at *Arabella*, supposing she had introduced him into some Quarrel, It may be *happy* for you, Madam; but I am sure it will make me very miser-able, if my Son comes to any Harm.

If it be the Will of Heaven he should fall in this Combat, resumed *Arabella*, he can never have a more glorious Destiny: And as that Consideration will, doubtless, sweeten his last Moments, so it ought to be your Consolation: However, I beg you'll lose no time, but haste to his Assistance; for since he has a considerable Number of Enemies to deal with, 'tis not improbable but he may be over-powered at last.

Where did you leave my Son, Madam? cried Sir *Charles*, eagerly.

He is not far off, replied *Arabella*: And you will, doubtless, be directed to the Place, by the Sight of the Blood of his Enemies, which he has spilt. Go that way, pursued she, pointing with her Finger towards the Place where she had left her Cousin: There you will meet with him, amidst a Croud of Foes, which he is sacrificing to my Safety, and his just Resentment.

Sir *Charles*, not knowing what to think, galloped away, followed by most Part of the Company; Sir *George* telling Lady *Bella*, that he would stay to defend her against any Attempts that might be made on her Liberty, by any of her Ravisher's Servants, who were, probably, straggling about. *Arabella*, however, being perfectly recovered, insisted upon following her Uncle.

There is no Question, said she, but Mr. *Glanville* is victorious: I am only apprehensive for the dangerous Wounds he may have received in the Combat, which will require all our Care and Assistance.

Sir *George*, who wanted to engross her Company a little to himself, in vain represented to her, that, amidst the Horrors of a Fight so bloody as that must certainly be, in which Mr. *Glanville* and his Friends would be now engaged, it would be dangerous for her to venture her Person: Yet she would not be persuaded; but, having mounted her Horse, with his Assistance, she rode as fast as she was able after the rest of the Company.

CHAPTER V

Being a Chapter of Mistakes

SIR *Charles*, who, by this Time, had got to the Place she directed him to, but saw no Appearance of fighting, and only a few Haymakers in Discourse together, inquired, If there had been any Quarrel between two Gentlemen in that Place?

One of them, at this Question, advancing, told Sir *Charles*, that two Gentlemen had quarrelled there, and were fighting with Swords; but that they had parted them; and that one of them, having an Horse tied to a Tree, mounted him, and rode away: That the other, they believed, was not far off; and that there had been no Bloodshed, they having come time enough to prevent it.

Sir *Charles* was extremely satisfied with this Account; and, giving the Haymakers some Money for the good Office they did in parting the two Combatants, rode up to meet Lady *Bella*; and informed her, that his Son was safe.

I cannot imagine he is safe, replied she, when I see some of his Enemies (pointing to the Haymakers) still alive: It is not customary, in those Cases, to suffer any to escape: And, questionless, my Cousin is either dead, or a Prisoner, since all his Adversaries are not vanquished.

Why, you dream, Madam, replied Sir *Charles*: Those Fellows yonder are Haymakers: What should make them Enemies to my Son? They were lucky enough to come in time to prevent him and another Gentleman from doing each other a Mischief. I cannot imagine for what Reason my Son quarrelled with that Person they speak of: Perhaps you can inform me.

Certainly, Sir, said *Arabella*, I can inform you, since I was the Cause of their Quarrel. The Story is too long to tell you now; and, besides, it is so connected with the other Accidents of my Life, that 'tis necessary you should be acquainted with my whole History, in order to comprehend it: But, if those Persons are what you say, and did really part my Cousin and his Antagonist, truly I believe they have done him a very ill Office: For, I am persuaded, my Cousin will never be at Rest, till, by his Rival's Death, he has freed himself from one, capable of the most daring Enterprizes to get me into his Power: And, since I cannot be in Security while he lives, and persists in the Resolution he has taken to persecute me, it had been better if he had suffered all the Effects of my Cousin's Resentment at that time, than to give him the Trouble to hunt him through the World, in order to sacrifice him to the Interest of his Love and Vengeance.

Sir *Charles*, no less astonished than alarmed at this Discovery of his Niece's sanguinary Sentiments, told her, he was sorry to see a Lady so far forget the Gentleness of her Sex, as to encourage and incite Men to such Extremities, upon her Account. And, for the future, added he, I must intreat you, Niece, to spare me the Affliction of seeing my Son exposed to these dangerous Quarrels: For, though his Life is so little regarded by you, yet it is of the utmost Consequence to me.

Arabella, who found Matter sufficient in the Beginning of this Speech, to be offended with her Uncle, yet, mistaking the latter Part of it for a pathetic Complaint of her Cruelty, replied very gravely, That her Cousin's Safety was not so indifferent to her as he imagined: And that she did not hate him so much, but that his Death would affect her very sensibly.

Arabella, in speaking these Words, blushed with Shame, as thinking they were rather too tender: And Sir *Charles*, who coloured likewise, from a very different Motive, was opening his Mouth, to tell her, that he did not think his Son was much obliged to her for not hating him; when *Arabella*, supposing he designed to press her to a further Explanation of the favourable Sentiments she felt for Mr. *Glanville*, stopped him with Precipitation: Press me no more, said she, upon this Subject: And, as I have already spoken too much, haply, before so many Witnesses, seek not to enhance my Confusion, by prolonging a Discourse that at present must needs be disagreeable to me.

I shall readily agree with you, Madam, replied Sir *Charles*, that you have spoken too much: And, if I had thought you capable of speaking in the manner you have done, I would have been more cautious in giving you an Occasion for it.

I should imagine, Sir, said *Arabella*, blushing with Anger, as she before did with Shame, that you would be the last Person in the World who could think I had spoken too much upon this Occasion: And, since you are pleased to tell me so, I think it fit to let you know, that I have not, in my Opinion, transgressed the Laws of Decency and Decorum, in what I have said in my Cousin's Favour: And I can produce many Examples of greater Freedom of Speech, in Princesses, and Ladies of the highest Quality: However, I shall learn such a Lesson of Moderation in this respect, from your Reproof, that I promise you, neither yourself, or Mr. *Glanville*, shall have any Cause, for the future, to complain of my want of Discretion.

Sir *Charles*, who was very polite and good-natured, was half angry with himself, for having obliged his Niece to such a Submission, as he thought it; and, apologizing for the Rudeness of his Reprehension, assured her, that he was perfectly convinced of her Discretion in all things; and did not doubt but her Conduct would be always agreeable to him.

Arabella, who, from what her Uncle had said, began to entertain Suspicions, that would never have entered any Imagination but hers, looked earnestly upon him for half a Moment, as if she wished to penetrate into the most secret Recesses of his Heart: But, fansying she saw something in his Looks that confirmed her Apprehensions, she removed her Eyes from his Face, and, fastening them on the Ground, remained for some Moments in Confusion.—Sir *Charles*, whom her apparent Disturbance made very uneasy, proposed returning to the Castle; telling Lady *Bella* he expected to find his Son already there.

'Tis more than probable, said she, turning to Sir *George*, that my

Cousin is gone in Pursuit of my Ravisher; and the Interruption
that has been given to his designed Vengeance, making him more
furious than before, 'tis not likely he will return till he has punished
his Insolence by that Death he so justly merits.

Mr. *Glanville* is already so happy in your Opinion, said Sir
George, with a very profound Sigh, that there is no need of his
rendering you this small Service, to increase your Esteem: But, if
my Prayers are heard, the Punishment of your Ravisher will be
reserved for a Person less fortunate, indeed, than Mr. *Glanville*,
tho' not less devoted to your Interest, and concerned in your
Preservation.

Sir *George* counterfeiting a Look of extreme Confusion and Fear,
as he ended these Words;

Arabella, who perfectly comprehended the Meaning they were
designed to convey, thought herself obliged to take no Notice of
them: And, therefore, without making any Reply to the young
Baronet, who ventured slowly to lift his Eyes to her Face, in order
to discover if there were any Signs of Anger in it, she told Sir
Charles she inclined to go home: And Sir *George*, with the rest of
the Company, attended them to the Castle; where, as soon as they
arrived, they took their Leave.

Sir *George*, notwithstanding *Arabella*'s Care to deprive him of an
Opportunity of speaking to her, told her, in a Whisper, having
eagerly alighted to help her off her Horse,

I am going, Madam, to find out that insolent Man, who has
dared to offer Violence to the fairest Person in the World: And, if I
am so happy as to meet with him, he shall either take my Life, or I
will put him into a Condition never to commit any more Offences
of that Nature.

Saying this, he made a low Bow; and, being desirous to prevent
her Answer, remounted his Horse, and went away with the rest of
the Company.

Arabella, who, upon this Occasion, was to be all Confusion,
mixed with some little Resentment, discovered so much Emotion
in her Looks, while Sir *George* was whispering to her, that her
Uncle, as he was handing her into the House, asked her, If she was
offended at any thing Sir *George* had said to her?

Arabella, construing this Question as she had done some other
things her Uncle had said to her, replied, in a reserved manner,
Since my Looks, contrary to my Intention, have betrayed my

Thoughts to you, I will not scruple to confess, that I have some Cause to be offended with Sir *George*; and that, in two Instances To-day, he has seemed to forget the Respect he owes me.

Sir *Charles* was fired at this Account: Is it possible, said he, that Sir *George* has had the Assurance to say any thing to offend you, and that before my Face too? This Affront is not to be borne.

I am sorry, replied *Arabella*, eying him heedfully, to see you so much concerned at it.

Don't be uneasy, interrupted Sir *Charles*: There will be no bad Consequences happen from it: But he shall hear of it, added he, raising his Voice with Passion: I'll force him this Night to explain himself.

You must pardon me, Sir, said *Arabella*, more and more confirmed in her Notions, if I tell you, that I am extremely offended at your uncommon Zeal upon this Occasion: And also I must assure you, that a little more Calmness would be less liable to Suspicion.

Miss *Glanville* coming to meet them, Sir *Charles*, who did not take much Notice of what *Arabella* said, eagerly inquired for his Son; and, hearing he was not come home, was apprehensive of his meeting again with the Person he had quarrelled with: But his Fears did not last long; for Mr. *Glanville* came in, having purposely avoided the Company, to hide the Uneasiness Lady *Bella's* tormenting Folly had given him.

CHAPTER VI

In which the Mistakes are continued

As soon as Mr. *Glanville* appeared, the two Ladies retired; Miss *Glanville* asking *Arabella* a hundred Questions concerning their Diversion, the Drift of which was, to know how Sir *George* behaved to her: But that fair Lady, whose Thoughts were wholly employed on the strange Accidents which had happened to her that Day, longed to be at Liberty to indulge her Reflections; and, complaining of extreme Weariness, under Pretence of reposing herself till Dinner, got quit of Miss *Glanville's* Company, which, at that time, she thought very tedious.

As soon as she was left to herself, her Imagination running over

all that had happened, she could not help confessing, that few
Women ever met with such a Variety of Adventures in one Day: In
Danger of being carried off by Violence, by one Lover; delivered by
another; Insinuations of Love from a Third, who, she thought,
was enamoured of her Cousin; and, what was still more surprising
a Discovery, that her Uncle was not insensible of her Charms, but
was become the Rival of his own Son.

As extravagant as this Notion was, *Arabella* found Precedents in
her Romances of Passions full as strange and unjustifiable; and
confirmed herself in that Opinion, by recollecting several Examples
of unlawful Love. Why should I not believe, said she, that my
Charms can work as powerful Effects as those of *Olympia*, Princess
of *Thrace*, whose Brother was passionately enamoured of her?[1]

Did not the Divine *Clelia* inspire *Maherbal* with a violent Passion
for her, who, though discovered to be her Brother, did not, nevertheless, cease to adore her?[2] And, to bring an Instance still nearer
to my own Case, was not the Uncle of the fair *Alcyone* in Love with
her? And did he not endeavour to win her Heart by all the Methods
in his Power?[3]

Ah! then, pursued she, let us doubt no more of our Misfortune:
And, since our fatal Beauty has raised this impious Flame, let us
stifle it with our Rigour, and not allow an ill-timed Pity, or Respect,
to encourage a Passion which may, one Day, cast a Blemish upon
our Glory.

Arabella, having settled this Point, proceeded to reflect on the
Conquest she had made of Sir *George*: She examined his Words
over and over, and found them so exactly conformable to the
Language of an *Oroondates* or *Orontes*, that she could not choose
but be pleased: But, recollecting that it behoved her, like all other
Heroines, to be extremely troubled and perplexed at an Insinuation
of Love, she began to lament the cruel Necessity of parting with an
agreeable Friend; who, if he persisted in making her acquainted
with his Thoughts, would expose himself to the Treatment Persons
so indiscreet always meet with; nor was she less concerned, lest, if
Mr. *Glanville* had not already dispatched her Ravisher, Sir *George*,
by wandering in Search of him, and, haply, sacrificing him to his
eager Desire of serving her, should, by that means, lay her under
an Obligation to him, which, considering him as a Lover, would be
a great Mortification.

Sir *George*, however, was gone home to his own House, with no

Thoughts of pursuing *Arabella*'s Ravisher: And Mr. *Glanville*, being questioned by his Father concerning his Quarrel, invented some trifling Excuse for it; which not agreeing with the Account the Baronet had received from *Arabella*, he told his Son, that he had concealed the Truth from him; and that there was more in that Affair than he had owned. You quarrelled, added he, upon *Arabella*'s Account; and she did not scruple to affirm it before all the Company.

Mr. *Glanville*, who had vainly flattered himself with an Hope, that his Cousin had not acquainted the Company with her whimsical Apprehensions, was extremely vexed when he found she had exposed herself to their Ridicule, and that it was probable even he had not escaped: But, willing to know from her own Mouth how far she had carried her Folly, he went up to her Chamber; and, being immediately admitted, she began to congratulate him upon the Conquest he had gained, as she supposed, over his Enemy; and thanked him very solemnly for the Security he had procured for her.

Mr. *Glanville*, after assuring her, that she was in no Danger of ever being carried away by that Person whom she feared, proceeded to inquire into all that had passed between her and the Company whom she had joined, when she left him; and *Arabella*, relating every Particular, gave him the Mortification to know, that her Folly had been sufficiently exposed: But she touched upon her Fears for him with so much Delicacy, and mentioned her Fainting in such a manner, as insinuated a much greater Tenderness than he before had Reason to hope for; and this Knowlege destroying all his Intentions to quarrel with her for what she had said, he appeared so easy and satisfied, that *Arabella*, reflecting upon the Misfortune his Father's new-born Passion would probably be the Occasion of to him, could not help sighing at the Apprehension; looking on him, at the same time, with a kind of pitying Complacency; which did not escape Mr. *Glanville*'s Notice.

I must know the Reason of that Sigh, Cousin, said he, smiling, and taking her Hand.

If you are wise, replied *Arabella*, gravely, you will be contented to remain in the pleasing Ignorance you are at present; and not seek to know a thing which will, haply, afford you but little Satisfaction.

You have increased my Curiosity so much by this Advice,

resumed he, accommodating his Looks to *Arabella*'s, that I shall
not be at Rest till I know what it is you conceal from me: And,
since I am so much concerned in it, even by your own Confession, I
have a Right to press you to explain yourself.

Since you are so importunate, replied *Arabella*, I must tell you,
that I will not do you so great a Diskindness, as to explain myself;
nor will I be the first who shall acquaint you with your Misfortune,
since you will, haply, too soon arrive at the Knowlege of it, by
other means.

Glanville, who imagined this was some new Whim that had got
into her Head, was but little perplexed at an Insinuation, which,
had he been ignorant of her Foible, would have given him great
Uneasiness: But, being sensible that she expected he would press
her to disclose herself, and appear extremely concerned at her
refusing him that Satisfaction, he counterfeited so well, that she
was at a loss how to evade the Arguments he used to make her un-
fold the terrible Mystery; when the Dinner-bell ringing, and
relieving her for the present, Mr. *Glanville* led her down to the
Parlour; where Sir *Charles* and his Daughter attended their coming.

CHAPTER VII

In which the Mistakes are not yet cleared up

THE Baronet, who had been put into a bad Humour by *Arabella*'s
Insinuations, that Sir *George* had affronted her, appeared reserved
and uneasy; and, being resolved to question her about it, was
willing first to know exactly what it was his Niece had been offended
at: But as he feared, if it came to his Son's Knowlege, it would
produce a Quarrel between the young Gentlemen, that might have
dangerous Consequences, he was desirous of speaking to her alone;
and, as soon as Dinner was over, asked her to take a Walk with him
upon the Terrace, telling her he had something to say to her in
private. *Arabella*, whose Fears had been considerably increased by
the Pensiveness which appeared in her Uncle's Looks during
Dinner, and supposing he wanted a private Conversation, only to
explain himself more clearly to her, than he had yet done, was
excessively alarmed at this Request; and, casting her Eyes down

to the Ground, blushed in such a manner as betrayed her Confusion; and made Miss *Glanville* and her Brother believe, that she suspected her Uncle had a Design to press her soon to give her Hand to Mr. *Glanville*, which occasioned her apparent Disorder.

Sir *Charles*, however, who had not so heedfully observed her Behaviour, repeated his Request; adding, with a Smile, upon her giving him no Answer, Sure, Lady *Bella*, you are not afraid to be alone with your Uncle.

No, Sir, replied *Arabella*, giving him a piercing Look; I am not afraid of being alone with my Uncle; and, as long as he pretends to be no more than my Uncle, I shall not scruple to hear what he has to say to me.

Sir *Charles*, a little vexed at an Answer which insinuated, as he thought, a Complaint of his having pretended to more Authority over her than he ought, told her, he hoped she had no Cause to believe he would displease her, by any improper Exertion of that Power over her, with which her Father had instrusted him: For I assure you, added he, I would rather you should follow my Advice as an Uncle, than obey me as a Guardian; and, since my Affection for you is, perhaps, greater than what many People have for a Niece, my Solicitude ought to be imputed to that Motive.

I have all the Sense I ought to have of that Affection you honour me with, replied *Arabella*; and since I hope it will be always what it should be, without wishing for its Increase, I am contented with those Testimonies I have already received of it; and do not desire any other.

Sir *Charles*, a little puzzled to understand the Meaning of these Words, which the grave Looks of *Arabella* made yet more mysterious, rose from his Seat with an Air of Discontent: I should have been glad to have spoken a Word in private to you, Niece, said he; but, since you think proper to make so much Ceremony in such a Trifle, I'll defer it till you are in a better Humour.

Miss *Glanville*, seeing her Father going out of the Room, stepped before him: Nay, Papa, said she, if you want to speak with my Cousin, my Brother and I will go out, and leave you to yourselves.

You will do me a very great Displeasure, said *Arabella*; for, I am sure, my Uncle has not any thing of Consequence to say to me: However, added she, seeing Miss *Glanville* go away, I am resolved, I will not be left alone; and therefore, Mr. *Glanville*, since I can pretend to some Power over you, I command you to stay.

You may remember, Madam, said Mr. *Glanville*, with a Smile, you refused to gratify my Curiosity, with regard to something you hinted to me some time ago; and, to punish you, added he, going out of the Room, I am resolved you shall listen to what my Father has to say to you; for, by your Unwillingness to hear it, I imagine you suspect already what it is.

Arabella, finding she had no way to avoid hearing what she dreaded so much, and observing her Uncle had resumed his Chair, prepared to give him Audience; but, in order to deprive him of all Hope, that she would receive his Discourse favourably, she assumed the severest Look she was capable of; and, casting her Eyes on the Ground, with a Mixture of Anger and Shame, waited with a kind of Fear and Impatience for what he had to say.

I see, Madam, said the Baronet, observing her Confusion, that you apprehend what I am going to say to you; but, I beseech you, do not fear I have any Intentions, but such as you'll approve.

You are certainly in the right, Sir, said *Arabella*, in the Interpretation you have put on my Looks: I am really in Pain about the Purport of your Discourse: And you would particularly oblige me, if you would dispense with me from hearing it.

I see, replied Sir *Charles*, that, out of a mistaken Fear, you are unwilling to hear me, in order to avoid coming to the Explanation I desire: But I tell you, once again, you have nothing to apprehend.

I have every thing to apprehend, Sir, resumed *Arabella*, tartly, while you persist in your Design of disobliging me; and you cannot give me a greater Proof of the Badness of your Intentions, than by thus forcing me to listen to Discourses I ought to avoid.

Since my Word has no Weight with you, replied Sir *Charles*, I'll condescend to assure you, by the most sacred Oath, That I do not mean to come to any Extremities with Sir *George*, concerning what you already told me: All I desire to know is, If you think you had any Reason to be offended with him for any thing he said? And, in that Case, I cannot dispense with myself from expostulating with him about it.

You would do me a Favour, Sir, resumed *Arabella*, if you would interest yourself a little less in what Sir *George* said to me: The Offence was committed against me only; and none but myself has any Right to resent it.

'Tis enough, Niece, said Sir *Charles*, rising: You acknowlege sufficient to make me resolve to oblige him to ask Pardon for the

Affront you have received: However, I beg you may make yourself easy; no ill Consequences will happen from this Affair, provided my Son does not know it: And I know you have too much Discretion to acquaint him with it.

Saying this, he went out of the Room, leaving *Arabella* in great Confusion at what he had said; which, in her Opinion, had amounted almost to a plain Declaration of his Passion; and his Design of putting an End to Sir *George*'s Pretensions, whom, it was probable, he looked upon as a more dangerous Rival than his Son, confirmed her in the Opinion of his Resolution to persecute her.

Full of the Reflections this Accident had occasioned, she went to walk in the Garden, where Mr. *Glanville*, his Sister having just left him, joined her.

As he imagined, his Father's Design, in speaking to her alone, was to prevail upon her to consent to marry him before she left the Country, which was what he most earnestly wished, he drew a bad Omen from the Discontent which appeared in her Eyes.

Is it with me, Cousin, said he, or with what my Father has been saying to you, that you are angry?

With both, replied *Arabella*, hastily; for if you had staid in the Room, as I commanded you, I should not have been exposed to the Pain of hearing Things so disagreeable.

Since I knew what would be the Purport of my Father's Discourse, said Mr. *Glanville*, you ought not to be surprised I could not resolve to give any Interruption to it, by my Presence: And, being so much interested in the Success of his Solicitations, I could not choose but give him an Opportunity of speaking to you alone, as he desired.

It seems then, resumed *Arabella*, you know what was the Subject of his Conversation.

I believe I can guess, interrupted Mr. *Glanville*, smiling.

Is it possible, cried *Arabella*, starting back in great Surprize, that, knowing, as you say you do, your Father's Intentions, you would resolve to furnish him with an Opportunity of disclosing them?

Can you blame me, said Mr. *Glanville*, for suffering him to undertake what I durst not myself? I know your Delicacy, or rather your Severity, so well, that I am sensible, if I had taken the Liberty to say what my Father has said, you would have been extremely offended; and punished me, as you have often done,

with a Banishment from your Presence: Nay, pursued he, seeing
Astonishment and Anger in her Countenance, I perceive you are,
at this Moment, going to pronounce some terrible Sentence against
me.

You are deceived, said *Arabella*, with a forced Calmness; I am so
far from being offended with you, that I am ready to acknowlege,
you merit very extraordinary Praises for the perfect Resignation
you shew to the Will, and, for your Credit, I will suppose, the
Commands, of your Father: But I would advise you to be contented with the Reputation of being a dutiful Son; and, for the
future, never aspire to that of being a faithful Lover.

Speaking these Words, which were wholly unintelligible to her
amazed Admirer, she left him, and went to her own Apartment,
strangely surprised at the Indifference of Mr. *Glanville*; who, as
she understood what he had said, was not only willing to resign her
to his Father, but also took upon him to mediate in his behalf.

As she was unwilling to acknowlege, even to herself, that the
Grief she felt at this Discovery, proceeded from any Affection for
her Cousin, she imputed it to the Shame of seeing herself so basely
forsaken and neglected; and, not being able to find a Precedent for
such an Indignity offered to the Charms of any Lady in her
Romances, the Singularity of her Fate, in this respect, seemed to
demand all her Uneasiness.

CHAPTER VIII

Which contains some necessary Consequences of the foregoing
Mistakes.—A Soliloquy on a Love-Letter

WHILE *Arabella* passed her Time in her Closet, in the most
disagreeable Reflections, *Glanville* was racking his Brain to find out
the Meaning of those mysterious Words she had uttered at leaving
him: He examined them twenty times over, but could not possibly
penetrate into their Sense: But, supposing at last, that they really
meant nothing at all, or were occasioned by some new Flight of her
Imagination, he went to find out his Father, in order to know what
had passed between him and *Arabella*.

Sir *Charles*, however, was not to be found; he had ordered his

Horse to be made ready, under Pretence of taking a little Ride after
Dinner; and, passing by Sir *George's* House, alighted to pay him a
Visit.

The young Baronet, being at home, received him with great
Politeness: And Sir *Charles*, whose peculiar Disposition was, to be
nicely tenacious of every thing which, he imagined, had any
Relation to the Honour of his Family, took the first Opportunity
to question him, concerning the Confusion his Whisper had occasioned in Lady *Bella*; adding, That she had confessed, he had
given her Reason to take ill what he had said to her.

Sir *George*, who was by no means willing to quarrel with the
Uncle of *Arabella*, received the old Gentleman's Remonstrances
with a great deal of Calmness; and, finding *Arabella* had not discovered the Purport of that Whisper which had offended her, he
told Sir *Charles*, That the Confusion he saw in her Countenance,
was occasioned by his raillying her upon the Fright she had been
in upon Mr. *Glanville's* Account: He added some other Particulars
that intirely taking away all Inclination in Sir *Charles* to pursue the
Matter any farther, they parted upon very good Terms; Sir *George*
promising, very soon, to return his Visit at the Castle.

Mr. *Glanville*, upon his Father's Return, being impatient to
know what he had said to *Arabella*, inquired with so much Precipitation, concerning the Conversation they had had together, that
Sir *Charles*, unwilling to tell him the Truth, and not having time to
consider of an Answer, evaded his Question in such a manner, that
Mr. *Glanville* could not help making some Observation upon it;
and, comparing this Circumstance with what *Arabella* had said,
tho' he could not comprehend the Meaning that seemed to be concealed under their Behaviour, he immediately concluded, there was
some Mystery, which it concerned him to find out.

Possessed with this Opinion, he longed for an Opportunity to
talk with *Arabella* alone; but he was not so happy to obtain one;
for, tho' that Fair-one presided at the Tea-table, as usual, and also
appeared at Supper, yet she so industriously avoided all Occasions
of being alone with him, tho' but for a Moment, and appeared so
reserved and uneasy, that it was impossible for him to speak to her
upon that Subject.

As soon as it was time to retire, having resolved to request the
Favour of a few Moments Conversation with her, in her own
Apartment; and when he had, as was his Custom, handed her up

Stairs; instead of wishing her a good Night, at her Chamber door, he was going to desire Permission to enter it with her; when *Lucy*, coming to meet her Lady, whispered her in the Ear; upon which, *Arabella*, turning towards him, gave him an hasty Salute, and hurried into her Apartment.

Glanville, no less vexed at this Disappointment, than perplexed at that Whisper, which had caused such a visible Emotion in *Arabella*, retired to his own Room, tormented with a thousand uneasy Suspicions, for which he could not exactly assign a Cause; and wishing impatiently for the next Day, in which he hoped to procure some Explanation of what at present greatly perplexed him.

In the mean time, *Arabella*, who had been informed by *Lucy*, in that Whisper, who was eager to let her know it, that a Messenger had brought a Letter from Sir *George*, and, late as it was at Night, waited for an Answer, was debating with herself, whether she should open this Billet or not: She had a strong Inclination to see what it contained; but, fearful of transgressing the Laws of Romance, by indulging a Curiosity not justifiable by Example, she resolved to return this Letter unopened.

Here, said she to *Lucy*, give this Letter to the Messenger that brought it, and tell him, I was excessively offended with you, for receiving it from his Hands.

Lucy, taking the Letter, was going to obey her Orders; when, recollecting herself, she bid her stay.

Since Sir *George*, said she to herself, is no declared Lover of mine, I may, without any Offence to Decorum, see what this Letter contains: To refuse receiving it, will be to acknowlege, that his Sentiments are not unknown to me; and, by consequence, to lay myself under a Necessity of banishing him: Nor is it fit, that I should allow him to believe, I am so ready to apprehend the Meaning of every gallant Speech, which is used to me; and to construe such Insinuations, as he took the Liberty to make me, into Declarations of Love.

Allowing, therefore, the Justice of these Reasons, she took the Letter out of *Lucy's* Hand; and, being upon the Point of opening it, a sudden Thought controuled her Designs: She threw it suddenly upon her Toilet; and, looking very earnestly upon it,

Presumptuous Paper! said she, speaking with great Emotion to the Letter: Bold Repository of thy Master's daring Thoughts!

Shall I not be blamed by all, who hereafter will hear, or read, my History, if, contrary to the Apprehensions I have, that thou containest a Confession that will displease me, I open thy Seal, and become accessary to thy Writer's Guilt, by deigning to make myself acquainted with it? And thou, too indiscreet and unwary Friend, whose Folds contain the Acknowlegement of his Crime! What will it advantage thee or him, if, torn by my resenting Hand, I make thee suffer, for the Part thou bearest in thy Master's Fault; and teach him, by thy Fate, how little Kindness he has to expect from me! Yet, to spare myself the Trouble of reading what will, questionless, displease me, I will return thee, uninjured, into thy Master's Hands; and, by that Moderation, make him repent the Presumption he has been guilty of!

CHAPTER IX

Containing a Love-Letter in the Heroic Stile ; with some occasional Reasonings by Lucy, *full of Wit and Simplicity*

OUR fair Heroine, having ended the foregoing Soliloquy, took up the Letter, and gave it to *Lucy*, who had, all the time she was speaking, observed a profound Silence, mixed with a most eager Attention.

Here, pursued she, carry it to the Person who brought it; and bid him tell his Master, that, lest I should find any thing in it, which may offend me, I have chosen not to read it: And, if he is wise, he will profit by my Concern for him, and take care how he hazards displeasing me a Second time by an Importunity of this kind, which I shall not so easily pardon him.

Lucy, who had taken particular Notice of this Speech, in order to remember every Word of it, when she repeated it again, went conning her Lesson to the Place where she had desired the Servant to wait her coming: But he was gone; such being indeed his Master's Orders; for he was apprehensive, that, following the Custom of the Ladies in Romances, *Arabella* would return his Letter; and therefore, to deprive her of an Opportunity of sending it back that Night, he ordered his Man to say, he waited for an Answer; but, as soon as he conveniently could, to come away without one.

Lucy, in a great Surprize at the Servant's going away, returned to her Lady with the Letter in her Hand, telling her she must needs read it now, since the Person, who brought it, was gone.

It must be confessed, said *Arabella*, taking the Letter from her, with a Smile, he has fallen upon an ingenious Device, to make me keep it for this Night; and, since, haply, I may be mistaken in the Contents, I have a mind to open it.

Lucy did not fail to confirm her Lady in this Design: And *Arabella*, making as if she yielded to the Importunities of her Confidante, opened the Letter; which she found as follows:

The unfortunate and despairing Bellmour, *to
the Divine* Arabella.

Madam,

SINCE it is, doubtless, not only with your Permission, but even by your Commands, that your Uncle, Sir *Charles Glanville*, comes to pronounce the Sentence of my Death, in the Denunciation of your Anger, I submit, Madam, without repining at the Rigour of that Doom you have inflicted on me. Yes, Madam, this Criminal, who has dared to adore you, with the most sublime and perfect Passion that ever was, acknowleges the Justice of his Punishment; and, since it is impossible to cease loving you, or to live without telling you he does so, he is going, voluntarily, to run upon that Death your Severity makes him wish for, and the Greatness of his Crime demands. Let my Death then, O Divine *Arabella*, expiate the Offence I have been guilty of! And let me hope those fair Eyes, that have beheld me with Scorn when alive, will not refuse to shed some Tears upon my Tomb! And that, when you remember my Crime of loving you, you will also be pleased to remember, that I died for that Crime; and wish for no other Comfort in Death, but the Hope of your not hating, when he is no more,

The unhappy Bellmour.

Arabella, who had read this Letter aloud, sighed gently at the Conclusion of it; but poor *Lucy*, who was greatly affected at so dolorous an Epistle, could not restrain her Tears; but sobbed so often, and with so much Violence, as, at length, recalled her Lady from the Reverie, into which she was plunged.

What ails you? said she to her Confidante, greatly surprised: What is the Cause of this unseemly Sorrow?

Oh! Madam! cried *Lucy*, her Sobs making a frequent and un-pleasing Interruption in her Words; I shall break my Heart to be sure: Never was such a sad mournful Letter in the World: I could cry my Eyes out for the poor Gentleman. Pray excuse me, Madam; but, indeed, I can't help saying, You are the most hard-heartedest Lady I ever knew in my born Days: Why, to be sure, you don't care, if an hundred fine Gentlemen should die for you, tho' their Spirits were to haunt you every Night! Well! I would not have what your Ladyship has to answer for, for all the World!

You are a foolish Wench! replied *Arabella*, smiling at her Sim-plicity: Do you think I have any Cause to accuse myself, tho' Five thousand Men were to die for me? 'Tis very certain, my Beauty has produced very deplorable Effects: The unhappy *Hervey* has ex-piated, by his Death, the Violence his too desperate Passion forced him to meditate against me: The no less guilty, the noble Unknown, *Edward*, is wandering about the World, in a tormenting Despair; and stands exposed to the Vengeance of my Cousin, who has vowed his Death. My Charms have made another Person, whose Character ought to be sacred to me, forget all the Ties of Consanguinity; and become the Rival of his Son, whose Interest he once endeavoured to support: And, lastly, the unfortunate *Bellmour* consumes away in an hopeless Passion; and, conscious of his Crime, dooms himself, haply, with more Severity than I desire, to a voluntary Death; in hopes, thereby, of procuring my Pardon and Compassion, when he is no more. All these, *Lucy*, as I said before, are very deplorable Effects of my Beauty; but you must observe, that my Will has no Part in the Miseries, that unfortunate Beauty occasions; and that, tho' I could even wish myself less fair, in order to avoid giving so much Unhappiness to others, yet these Wishes would not avail; and since, by a fatal Necessity, all these Things will happen, whether I would or no, I must comfort myself under the Uneasi-ness, which the Sensibility of my Temper makes me feel, by the Reflection, that, with my own Consent, I contribute nothing to the Misfortune of those who love me.

Will your Ladyship then let poor Sir *George* die? said *Lucy*, who had listened very attentively to this fine Harangue, without under-standing what it meant.

Questionless, he must die, replied *Arabella*, if he persists in his Design of loving me.

But, pray, Madam, resumed *Lucy*, cannot your Ladyship command him to live, as you did Mr. *Hervey*, and Mr. *Glanville*, who both did as you bid them?

I may command him to live, said *Arabella*; and there is no Question but he would obey me, if I likewise permit him to love me; but, this last not being fit for me to do, I see no way to prevent the sad Resolution he has taken.

To be sure, Madam, returned *Lucy*, your Ladyship knows what you ought to do better than I can advise your Ladyship, being that you are more learned than me: But, for all that, I think it's better to save Life than to kill, as the Bible-Book says; and, since I am sure your Ladyship is a good Christian, if the Gentleman dies for the Want of a few kind Words, or so, I am sure you will be troubled in Mind about it.

It must be confessed, said *Arabella*, smiling, that, tho' your Solicitations are not very eloquent, they are very earnest and affecting; and I promise you, I will think about it; and, if I can persuade myself, I am doing no wrong Thing, by concerning myself about his Preservation, I will dispatch you To-morrow Morning, with my Orders to him, to live, or, at least, to proceed no further in his Design of dying, till he has further Cause.

Lucy, being extremely glad she had gained her Point, called in her Lady's other Women, who, having assisted her to undress, left her in her Closet, to which she always retired for an Hour, before she went to Bed.

END of the FIRST VOLUME.

VOLUME II

VOLUME II

BOOK V

CHAPTER I

A Dispute very learnedly handled by two Ladies, in which the Reader may take what Part he pleases

MR. *Glanville*, who was too much in Love to pass the Night with any great Degree of Tranquillity, under the Apprehensions he felt; it being the Nature of that Passion, to magnify the most inconsiderable Trifles into Things of the greatest Importance, when they concern the beloved Object; did not fail to torment himself with a thousand different Fears, which the mysterious Behaviour of his Father, and the more mysterious Words of his Mistress, gave Rise to. Among many various Conjectures, all equally unreasonable, he fixed upon one, no way advantageous to Sir *Charles*; for, supposing that the Folly of *Arabella* had really disgusted him, and made him desirous of breaking off the designed Match between them; he was, as he thought, taking Measures to bring this about, knowing, that if Lady *Bella* refused to fulfil her Father's Desire in this Particular, a very considerable Estate would descend to him.

Upon any other Occasion, Mr. *Glanville* would not have suspected his Father of so ungenerous an Action; but Lovers think every thing possible, which they fear; and being prepossessed with this Opinion, he resolved the next Morning to sound his Father's Inclinations, by intreating him to endeavour to prevail upon Lady *Bella* to marry him before her Year of Mourning for the Marquis was expired.

Attending him, therefore, at Breakfast, in his own Chamber, he made his designed Request, not without heedfully observing his Countenance at the same time; and trembling, lest he should make him an Answer, that might confirm his uneasy Suspicion.

Sir *Charles*, however, agreeably surprised him, by promising to comply with his Desire that Day; for, added he, tho' my Niece has some odd ways, yet, upon the Whole, she is a very accomplished

Woman; and when you are her Husband, you may probably find
the Means of curing her of those little Follies, which at present are
conspicuous enough; but, being occasioned by a Country Education, and a perfect Ignorance of the World, the Instruction, which
then you will not scruple to give her, and which, from a Husband,
without any Offence to her Delicacy, she may receive, may reform
her Conduct; and make her Behaviour as complete, as, it must be
confessed, both her Person and Mind now are.

Mr. *Glanville* having acquiesced in the Justice of this Remark,
as soon as Breakfast was over, went to visit the two Ladies, who
generally drank their Chocolate together.

Miss *Glanville* being then in Lady *Bella's* Apartment, he was
immediately admitted, where he found them engaged in a high
Dispute; and, much against his Will, was obliged to be Arbitrator
in the Affair, they having, upon his Entrance, both appealed to him.

But, in order to place this momentous Affair in a true Light, 'tis
necessary to go back a little, and acquaint the Reader with what had
passed in the Apartment; and also, following the Custom of the
Romance and Novel-Writers, in the Heart, of our Heroine.

No sooner were her fair Eyes open in the Morning, than the
unfortunate Sir *George* presenting himself to her Imagination, her
Thoughts to use *Scudery's* Phrase, were at a cruel War with each
other: She wished to prevent the Death of this obsequious Lover;
but she could not resolve to preserve his Life, by giving him that
Hope he required; and without which, she feared, it would be
impossible for him to live.

After pondering a few Hours upon the Necessity of his Case, and
what a just Regard to her own Honour required of her, Decorum
prevailed so much over Compassion, that she resolved to abandon
the miserable Sir *George* to all the Rigour of his Destiny; when,
happily for the disconsolate Lover, the History of the fair *Amalazontha*[1] coming into her Mind, she remembred, that this haughty
Princess, having refused to marry the Person, her Father recommended to her, because he had not a Crown upon his Head;
nevertheless, when he was dying for Love of her, condescended to
visit him, and even to give him a little Hope, in order to preserve
his Life: She conceived it could be no Blemish to her Character, if
she followed the Example of this most glorious Princess; and
suffered herself to relax a little in her Severity, to prevent the
Effects of her Lover's Despair.

Fear not, *Arabella*, said she to herself; fear not to obey the Dictates of thy Compassion, since the glorious *Amalazontha* justifies, by her Example, the Means thou wilt use to preserve a noble Life, which depends upon a few Words thou shalt utter.

When she had taken this Resolution, she rung her Bell for her Women; and as soon as she was dressed, she dismissed them all but *Lucy*, whom she ordered to bring her Paper and Pens, telling her, she would write an Answer to Sir *George's* Letter.

Lucy obeyed with great Joy; but by that time she had brought her Lady all the Materials for Writing, her Mind was changed; she having reflected, that *Amalazontha*, whose Example, in order to avoid the Censure of future Ages, she was resolved exactly to follow, did not write to *Ambiomer*, but paid him a Visit, she resolved to do the like; and therefore bid *Lucy* take them away again, telling her: She had thought better of it, and would not write to him.

Lucy, extremely concerned at this Resolution, obeyed her very slowly, and with great seeming Regret.

I perceive, said *Arabella*, you are afraid, I shall abandon the unfortunate Man you solicit for, to the Violence of his Despair; but tho' I do not intend to write to him, yet I'll make use of a Method, perhaps as effectual; for, to speak truly, I mean to make him a Visit; his Fever I suppose being violent enough by this time to make him keep his Bed.

And will you be so good, Madam, said *Lucy*, to go and see the poor Gentleman? I warrant you, he will be ready to die for Joy, when he sees you.

'Tis probable what you say may happen, replied *Arabella*, but there must be proper Precautions used to prevent those Consequences, which the sudden and unexpected Sight of me may produce. Those about him, I suppose, will have Discretion enough for that: Therefore give Orders for the Coach to be made ready, and tell my Women, they must attend me; and be sure you give them Directions, when I enter Sir *George's* Chamber, to stay at a convenient Distance, in order to leave me an Opportunity of speaking to him, without being heard: As for you, you may approach the Bed-side with me; since, being my Confident, you may hear all we have to say.

Arabella, having thus settled the Ceremonial of her Visit, according to the Rules prescribed by Romances, sat down to her

Tea-table, having sent to know, if Miss *Glanville* was up, and received for Answer, that she would attend her at Breakfast.

Arabella, who had at first determined to say nothing of this Affair to her Cousin, could not resist the Desire she had of talking upon a Subject so interesting; and, telling her with a Smile, that she was about to make a very charitable Visit that Morning, asked her, if she was disposed to bear her Company in it.

I know you Country Ladies, said Miss *Glanville*, are very fond of visiting your sick Neighbours: For my Part, I do not love such a grave kind of Amusement; yet, for the sake of the Airing, I shall be very willing to attend you.

I think, said *Arabella*, with a more serious Air than before, it behoves every generous Person to compassionate the Misfortunes of their Acquaintance and Friends, and to relieve them as far as lies in their Power; but those Miseries we ourselves occasion to others, demand, in a more particular Manner, our Pity; and, if consistent with Honour, our Relief.

And pray, returned Miss *Glanville*, who is it you have done any Mischief to, which you are to repair by this charitable Visit, as you call it?

The Mischief I have done, replied *Arabella*, blushing, and casting down her Eyes, was not voluntary, I assure you: Yet I will not scruple to repair it, if I can; tho', since my Power is confined by certain unavoidable Laws, my Endeavours may not haply have all the Success I could wish.

Well, but, dear Cousin, interrupted Miss *Glanville*, tell me in plain *English*, what this Mischief is, which you have done; and to what Purpose you are going out this Morning?

I am going to pay a Visit to Sir *George Bellmour*, replied *Arabella*; and I intreat you, fair Cousin, to pardon me for robbing you of so accomplished a Lover. I really always thought he was in Love with you, till I was undeceived by some Words he spoke Yesterday; and a Letter I received from him last Night, in which he has been bold enough to declare his Passion to me, and, through the Apprehension of my Anger, is this Moment dying with Grief; and 'tis to reconcile him to Life, that I have prevailed upon myself to make him a Visit; in which charitable Design, as I said before, I should be glad of your Company.

Miss *Glanville*, who believed not a Word Lady *Bella* had said, burst out a laughing, at a Speech, that appeared to her so extremely false and ridiculous.

I see, said *Arabella*, you are of a Humour to divert yourself with the Miseries of a despairing Lover; and in this Particular, you greatly resemble the fair and witty *Doralisa*,[1] who always jested at such Maladies as are occasioned by Love: However, this Insensibility does not become you so well as her, since all her Conduct was conformable to it, no Man in the World being bold enough to talk to her of Love; but you, Cousin, are ready, even by your own Confession, to listen to such Discourses from any body; and therefore this Behaviour, in you, may be with more Justice termed Levity, than Indifference.

I perceive, Cousin, said Miss *Glanville*, I have always the worst of those Comparisons you are pleased to make between me and other People; but, I assure you, as free and indiscreet as you think me, I should very much scruple to visit a Man, upon any Occasion whatever.

I am quite astonished, Miss *Glanville*, resumed *Arabella*, to hear you assume a Character of so much Severity; you, who have granted Favours of a Kind in a very great Degree criminal.

Favours! interrupted Miss *Glanville*, criminal Favours! Pray explain yourself, Madam.

Yes, Cousin, said *Arabella*, I repeat it again; criminal Favours, such as allowing Persons to talk to you of Love; not forbidding them to write to you; giving them Opportunities of being alone with you for several Moments together; and several other Civilities of the like Nature, which no Man can possibly merit, under many Years Services, Fidelity, and Pains: All these are criminal Favours, and highly blameable in a Lady, who has any Regard for her Reputation.

All these, replied Miss *Glanville*, are nothing in Comparison of making them Visits; and no Woman, who has any Reputation at all, will be guilty of taking such Liberties.

What! Miss, replied, *Arabella*, will you dare, by this Insinuation, to cast any Censures upon the Virtue of the divine *Mandana*,[2] the haughty *Amalazontha*,[3] the fair *Statira*,[4] the cold and rigid *Parisatis*,[5] and many other illustrious Ladies, who did not scruple to visit their Lovers, when confined to their Beds, either by the Wounds they received in Battle, or the more cruel and dangerous ones they suffered from their Eyes? These chaste Ladies, who never granted a Kiss of their Hand to a Lover, till he was upon the

Point of being their Husband,[1] would nevertheless most charitably condescend to approach their Bed-side, and speak some compassionate Words to them, in order to promote their Cure, and make them submit to live; nay, these divine Beauties would not refuse to grant the same Favour to Persons whom they did not love, to prevent the fatal Consequences of their Despair.

Lord, Madam! interrupted Miss *Glanville*, I wonder you can talk so blasphemously, to call a Parcel of confident Creatures divine, and such terrible Words.

Do you know, Miss, said *Arabella*, with a stern Look, that 'tis of the greatest Princesses that ever were, whom you speak in this irreverent Manner? Is it possible, that you can be ignorant of the sublime Quality of *Mandana*, who was the Heiress of Two powerful Kingdoms?[2] Are you not sensible, that *Amalazontha* was Queen of *Turringia*? And will you pretend to deny the glorious Extraction of *Statira* and *Parisatis*, Princesses of *Persia*?

I shall not trouble myself to deny any thing about them, Madam, said Miss *Glanville*; for I never heard of them before; and really I do not choose to be always talking of Queens and Princesses, as if I thought none but such great People were worthy my Notice: It looks so affected, I should imagine every one laughed at me, that heard me.

Since you are so very scrupulous, returned *Arabella*, that you dare not imitate the Sublimest among Mortals, I can furnish you with many Examples, from the Conduct of Persons, whose Quality was not much superior to yours, which may reconcile you to an Action, you at present, with so little Reason, condemn: And, to name but One among some Thousands, the fair *Cleonice*, the most rigid and austere Beauty in all *Sardis*, paid several Visits to the passionate *Ligdamis*, when his Melancholy, at the ill Success of his Passion, threw him into a Fever, that confined him to his Bed.[3]

And pray, Madam, who was that *Cleonice*? said Miss *Glanville*; and where did she live?

In *Sardis*, I tell you, said *Arabella*, in the Kingdom of *Lydia*.

Oh! then it is not in our Kingdom, said Miss *Glanville*: What signifies what Foreigners do? I shall never form my Conduct, upon the Example of Outlandish People; what is common enough in their Countries, would be very particular here; and you can never persuade me, that it is seemly for Ladies to pay Visits to Men in their Beds.

A Lady, said *Arabella*, extremely angry at her Cousin's Obstinacy, who will suffer Men to press her Hand, write to her, and talk to her of Love, ought to be ashamed of such an affected Niceness, as that you pretend to.

I insist upon it, Madam, said Miss *Glanville*, that all those innocent Liberties you rail at, may be taken by any Woman, without giving the World room to censure her: but, without being very bold and impudent, she cannot go to see Men in their Beds; a Freedom that only becomes a Sister, or near Relation.

So then, replied *Arabella*, reddening with Vexation, you will persist in affirming the divine *Mandana* was impudent?

If she paid such indiscreet Visits as those, she was, said Miss *Glanville*.

Oh Heavens! cried *Arabella*, have I lived to hear the most illustrious Princess, that ever was in the World, so shamefully reflected on?

Bless me, Madam! said Miss *Glanville*, what Reason have you to defend the Character of this Princess so much? She will hardly thank you for your Pains, I fancy.

Were you acquainted with the Character of that most generous Princess, said *Arabella*, you would be convinced, that she was sensible of the smallest Benefits; but it is not with a View of acquiring her Favour, that I defend her against your inhuman Aspersions, since it is more than Two thousand Years since she died; yet common Justice obliges me to vindicate a Person so illustrious for her Birth and Virtue; and were you not my Cousin, I should express my Resentment in another Manner, for the Injury you do her.

Truly, said Miss *Glanville*, I am not much obliged to you Madam, for not downright quarrelling with me for one that has been in her Grave Two thousand Years: However, nothing shall make me change my Opinion, and I am sure most People will be of my Side of the Argument.

That Moment Mr. *Glanville* sending for Permission to wait upon *Arabella*, she ordered him to be admitted, telling Miss *Glanville*, she would acquaint her Brother with the Dispute: To which she consented.

CHAPTER II

*Which inculcates by a very good Example, that a Person
ought not to be too hasty in deciding a Question he does not
perfectly understand*

YOU are come very opportunely, Sir, said *Arabella*, when he
entered the Room, to be Judge of a great Controversy between Miss
Glanville and myself. I beseech you therefore, let us have your
Opinion upon the Matter.

Miss *Glanville* maintains, that it is less criminal in a Lady to hear
Persons talk to her of Love, allow them to kiss her Hand, and permit
them to write to her, than to make a charitable Visit to a Man who
is confined to his Bed through the Violence of his Passion and
Despair; the Intent of this Visit being only to prevent the Death of
an unfortunate Lover, and, if necessary, to lay her Commands
upon him to live.

And this latter is your Opinion, is it not Madam? said Mr.
Glanville.

Certainly, Sir, replied *Arabella*, and in this I am justified by all
the Heroines of Antiquity.

Then you must be in the Right, Madam, returned Mr. *Glanville*,
both because your own Judgment tells you so, and also the Example
of these Heroines you mention.

Well, Madam, interrupted Miss *Glanville* hastily, since my
Brother has given Sentence on your Side, I hope you will not delay
your Visit to Sir *George* any longer.

How! said Mr. *Glanville*, surprised, is Lady *Bella* going to visit
Sir *George*? Pray, Madam, may I presume to inquire the Reason for
your doing him this extraordinary Favour?

You are not very wise, said *Arabella*, looking gravely upon Miss
Glanville, to discover a Thing, which may haply create a Quarrel
between your Brother, and the unfortunate Person you speak of:
Yet since this Indiscretion cannot be recalled, we must endeavour
to prevent the Consequences of it.

I assure you, Madam, interrupted Mr. *Glanville*, extremely impatient to know the Meaning of these Hints, you have nothing to
fear from me: Therefore you need not think yourself under any
Necessity of concealing this Affair from me.

You are not, haply, so moderate as you pretend, said *Arabella*, (who would not have been displeased to have seen him in all the jealous Transports of an enraged *Orontes*);[1] but whatever ensues, I can no longer keep from your Knowlege, a Truth your Sister has begun to discover; but, in telling you what you desire to know, I expect you will suppress all Inclinations to Revenge, and trust the Care of your Interest to my Generosity.

You are to know then, that in the Person of your Friend Sir *George*, you have a Rival, haply the more to be feared, as his Passion is no less respectful than violent: I possibly tell you more than I ought, pursued she, blushing, and casting down her Eyes, when I confess, that for certain Considerations, wherein perhaps you are concerned, I have received the first Insinuation of this Passion with Disdain enough; and I assure myself, that you are too generous to desire any Revenge upon a miserable Rival, of whom Death is going to free you.

Then, taking Sir *George*'s Letter out of her Cabinet, she presented it to Mr. *Glanville*.

Read this, added she; but read it without suffering yourself to be transported with any violent Motions of Anger: And as in Fight, I am persuaded you would not oppress a fallen and vanquished Foe; so in Love, I may hope, an unfortunate Rival will merit your Compassion.

Never doubt it, Madam, replied Mr. *Glanville*, receiving the Letter, which Miss *Glanville*, with a beating Heart, earnestly desired to hear read. Her Brother, after asking Permission of *Arabella*, prepared to gratify her Curiosity; but he no sooner read the first Sentence, than, notwithstanding all his Endeavours, a Smile appeared in his Face; and Miss *Glanville*, less able, and indeed less concerned to restrain her Mirth at the uncommon Stile, burst out a laughing, with so much Violence, as obliged her Brother to stop, and counterfeit a terrible Fit of Coughing, in order to avoid giving *Arabella* the like Offence.

The Astonishment of this Lady, at the surprising and unexpected Effect her Lover's Letter produced on Miss *Glanville*, kept her in a profound Silence, her Eyes wandering from the Sister to the Brother; who, continuing his Cough, was not able, for some Moments, to go on with his Reading.

Arabella, during this Interval, having recovered herself a little, asked Miss *Glanville*, if she found any thing in a Lover's Despair, capable of diverting her so much, as she seemed to be with that of the unfortunate Sir *George*?

My Sister, Madam, said Mr. *Glanville*, preventing her Reply, knows so many of Sir *George's* Infidelities, that she cannot persuade herself he is really in such a dangerous Way as he insinuates: Therefore you ought not to be surprised, if she is rather disposed to laugh at this Epistle, than to be moved with any Concern for the Writer, who, though he is my Rival, I must say, appears to be in a deplorable Condition.

Pray, Sir, resumed *Arabella*, a little composed by those Words, finish the Letter: Your Sister may possibly find more Cause for Pity than Contempt, in the latter Part of it.

Mr. *Glanville*, giving a Look to his Sister, sufficient to make her comprehend, that he would have her restrain her Mirth for the future, proceeded in his Reading; but every Line increasing his strong Inclination to laugh, when he came to the pathetic Wish, that her fair Eyes might shed some Tears upon his Tomb, no longer able to keep his assumed Gravity, he threw down the Letter in a counterfeited Rage.

Curse the stupid Fellow! cried he, is he mad, to call the finest Black Eyes in the Universe, fair. Ah! Cousin, said he to *Arabella*, he must be little acquainted with the Influence of your Eyes, since he can so egregiously mistake their Colour.

And it is very plain, replied *Arabella*, that you are little acquainted with the sublime Language in which he writes, since you find Fault with an Epithet, which marks the Beauty, not the Colour, of those Eyes he praises; for, in fine, Fair is indifferently applied, as well to Black and Brown Eyes, as to Light and Blue ones, when they are either really lovely in themselves, or by the Lover's Imagination created so: And therefore, since Sir *George's* Prepossession has made him see Charms in my Eyes, which questionless are not there; by calling them fair, he has very happily expressed himself, since therein he has the Sanction of those great Historians, who wrote the Histories of Lovers he seems to imitate, as well in his Actions as Stile.

I find my Rival is very happy in your Opinion, Madam, said Mr. *Glanville*; and I am apt to believe, I shall have more Reason to envy than pity his Situation.

If you keep within the Bounds I prescribe you, replied *Arabella*, you shall have no Reason to envy his Situation; but, considering the Condition to which his Despair has by this Time certainly reduced him, Humanity requires that we should take some Care of him; and, to shew you how great my Opinion of your Generosity is, I will even intreat you to accompany me in the Visit I am going to make him.

Mr. *Glanville*, being determined, if possible, to prevent her exposing herself, affected to be extremely moved at this Request; and, rising from his Chair in great seeming Agitation, traversed the Room for some Moments, without speaking a Word: Then suddenly stopping;

And can you, Madam, said he, looking upon *Arabella*, suppose, that I will consent to your visiting my Rival; and that I will be mean enough to attend you myself to his House? Do you think, that *Orontes* you have often reproached me with, would act in such a Manner?

I don't know how *Orontes* would have acted in this Case, said *Arabella*, because it never happened that such a Proof of his Submission was ever desired of him; but, considering that he was of a very fiery and jealous Disposition, it is probable he might act as you do.

I always understood, Madam, said Mr. *Glanville*, that *Orontes* was a Favourite of yours, but it seems I was mistaken.

You will be very unjust, said *Arabella*, to draw any unfavourable Conclusion from what I have said, to the Prejudice of that valiant Prince, for whom I confess I have a great Esteem; and truly whoever reflects upon the great Actions he did in the Wars between the *Amazons* and the fierce *Naobarzanes* King of the *Cilicians*,[1] must needs conceive a very high Idea of his Virtue; but if I cannot bring the Example of *Orontes* to influence you in the present Case, I can mention those of other Persons, no less illustrious for their Birth and Courage, than him. Did not the brave *Memnon*, when his Rival *Oxyatres* was sick, intreat the beautiful *Barsina* to favour him with a Visit?[2] And the complaisant Husband of the divine *Parisatis* was not contented with barely desiring her to visit *Lysimachus*, who was dying with Despair at their Marriage, but would many times bring her himself to the Bed-side of this unfortunate Lover, and, leaving her there, give him an Opportunity of telling her what he suffered for her sake.[3]

I am afraid, Madam, said Mr. *Glanville*, I shall never be capable of imitating either the brave *Memnon*, nor the complaisant *Lysimachus*, in this Case, and the Humour of *Orontes* seems to me the most commendable.

Nevertheless, said *Arabella*, the Humour of *Orontes* cost him an infinite Number of Pains; and it may happen, you will as near resemble him in his Fortune as you do in his Disposition: But pray let us end this Dispute at present. If you are not generous enough to visit an unfortunate Rival, you shall not put a Stop to the Charity of my Intentions; and since Miss *Glanville* is all of a sudden become so severe, that she will not accompany me in this Visit, I shall be contented with the Attendance of my Women.

Saying this, she rose from her Seat, calling *Lucy*, and ordered her to bid her Companions attend.

Mr. *Glanville*, seeing her thus determined, was almost mad with Vexation.

Upon my Soul, Madam, said he, seizing her Hand, you must not go.

How, Sir! said *Arabella*, sternly.

Not without seeing me die first, resumed he, in a languishing Tone.

You must not die, replied *Arabella*, gravely, nor must you pretend to hinder me from going.

Nay, Madam, said *Glanville*, one of these two Things will certainly happen: Either you must resolve not to visit Sir *George*, or else be contented to see me die at your Feet.

Was ever any Lady in so cruel a Dilemma? said *Arabella*, throwing herself into the Chair in a languishing Posture: What can I do to prevent the Fate of two Persons, one of whom I infinitely pity, and the other, obstinate as he is, I cannot hate? Shall I resolve to let the miserable *Bellmour* die, rather than grant him a Favour the most rigid Virtue would not refuse him? or shall I, by opposing the impetuous Humour of a Lover, to whom I am somewhat obliged, make myself the Author of his Death? Fatal Necessity! which obliges me either to be cruel or unjust; and, with a Disposition to neither, makes me, in some Degree, guilty of both!

CHAPTER III

In which our Heroine is in some little Confusion

WHILE *Arabella* was uttering this pathetic Complaint, Mr.
Glanville, with great Difficulty, kept himself from smiling; and, by
some supplicating Looks to his Sister, prevented her laughing out;
yet she gigled in secret behind her Fan: But *Arabella* was so lost
in her melancholy Reflections, that she kept her Eyes immoveably
fixed on the Ground for some Moments: At last, casting an upbraiding Glance at *Glanville*;

Is it possible, cruel Person that you are! said she to him, that you
can, without Pity, see me suffer so much Uneasiness; and, knowing
the Sensibility of my Temper, can expose me to the Grief of being
accessary to the Death of an unfortunate Man, guilty indeed of a
too violent Passion, which merits a gentler Punishment, than that
you doom him to?

Don't be uneasy, dear Cousin, interrupted Miss *Glanville*; I dare
assure you Sir *George* won't die.

It is impossible to think that, said *Arabella*, since he has not so
much as received a Command from me to live; but tell me truly,
pursued she, do you believe it probable, that he will obey me, and
live?

Indeed, Madam, said Miss *Glanville*, I could swear for him that
he will.

Well, replied *Arabella*, I will content myself with sending him
my Commands in Writing; but it is to be feared they will not have
so much Efficacy upon his Spirit.

Mr. *Glanville*, extremely pleased that she had laid aside her
Design of visiting Sir *George*, did not oppose her writing to him,
though he was plotting how to prevent the Letter reaching his
Hands; and while she went into her Closet to write, he conferred
with his Sister upon the Means he should use, expressing, at the
same time, great Resentment against Sir *George*, for endeavouring
to supplant him in his Cousin's Affection.

What then, said Miss *Glanville*, do you really imagine Sir *George*
is in Love with Lady *Bella*?

He is either in Love with her Person or Estate, replied Mr.
Glanville, or perhaps with both; for she is handsome enough to
gain a Lover of his Merit, though she had no Fortune; and she has

Fortune enough to do it, though she had no Beauty.

My Cousin is well enough, to be sure, said Miss *Glanville*; but I never could think her a Beauty.

If, replied Mr. *Glanville*, a most lovely Complection, regular Features, a fine Stature, an elegant Shape, and an inexpressible Grace in all her Motions, can form a Beauty, Lady *Bella* may pretend to that Character, without any Dispute.

Though she was all that you say, returned Miss *Glanville*, I am certain Sir *George* is not in Love with her.

I wish I was certain of that, replied Mr. *Glanville*; for 'tis very probable you are mistaken.

You may see by his Letter, interrupted Miss *Glanville*, what a Jest he makes of her; and if you had heard how he talked to her the other Day in the Garden, you would have died with Laughing; yet my poor Cousin thought he was very serious, and was so foolishly pleased!

I assure you *Charlotte*, said Mr. *Glanville*, gravely, I shall take it very ill, if you make so free with your Cousin's little Foibles; and if Sir *George* presumes to make a Jest of her, as you say, I shall teach him better Manners.

You are the strangest Creature in the World! said Miss *Glanville*: A Minute or two ago, you was wishing to be sure he was not in Love with her; and now you are angry, when I assure you he is only in Jest.

Arabella, that Moment coming out of her Closet, broke off their Discourse. I have written to Sir *George*, said she, addressing herself to Mr. *Glanville*; and you are at Liberty, if you please, to read my Letter, which I propose to send away immediately.

Mr. *Glanville*, taking the Letter out of her Hand, with a low Bow, began to read it to himself; but *Arabella*, willing his Sister should also be acquainted with the Contents, obliged him, much against his Will, to read it aloud. It was as follows:

Arabella, *To* Bellmour.

WHATEVER Offence your presumptuous Declaration may have given me, yet my Resentment will be appeased with a less Punishment than Death: And that Grief and Submission you have testified in your Letter, may haply have already procured you Pardon for your Fault, provided you do not forfeit it by Disobedience.

I therefore command you to live, and command you by all that Power you have given me over you.

Remember I require no more of you, than *Parisatis* did of *Lysimachus*, in a more cruel and insupportable Misfortune:[1] Imitate then the Obedience and Submission of that illustrious Prince; and tho' you should be as unfortunate as he, let your Courage also be equal to his; and, like him, be contented with the Esteem that is offered you, since it is all that can be bestowed, by

Arabella.

Mr. *Glanville*, finding by this Epistle, that *Arabella* did not design to encourage the Addresses of Sir *George*, would not have been against his receiving it, had he not feared the Consequence of his having such a convincing Proof of the Peculiarity of her Temper in his Possession; and while he kept the Letter in his Hand, as if he wanted to consider it a little better, he meditated on the Means to prevent its being ever delivered; and had possibly fixed upon some successful Contrivance, when a Servant coming in, to inform the Ladies, that Sir *George* was come to wait on them, put an End to his Schemes; and he immediately ran down to receive him, not being willing to increase, by his Stay, the Astonishment and Confusion, which appeared in the Countenance of *Arabella*, at hearing a Man, whom she had believed and represented to be dying, was come to pay her a Visit.

CHAPTER IV

Where the Lady extricates herself out of her former Confusion, to the great Astonishment, we will suppose, of the Reader

MISS *Glanville*, not having so much Delicacy as her Brother, could not help exulting a little upon this Occasion.

After the terrible Fright you have been in, Madam, said she, upon Sir *George's* Account, I wonder you do not rather think it is his Ghost than himself, that is come to see us.

There is no Question, but it is himself that is come, said *Arabella*, (who had already reconciled this Visit, to her first Thoughts of him;) and it is, haply, to execute his fatal Design in my Presence, that has brought him here; and, like the unfortunate *Agilmond*, he means to convince me of his Fidelity and Love, by falling upon his Sword before my Eyes.[1]

Bless me, Madam, said Miss *Glanville*, what horrid Things come into your Head! I vow, you terrify me out of my Wits, to hear you.

There is no Occasion for your Fears, interrupted *Arabella*: Since we already suspect his Designs, it will be very easy to prevent them: Had the Princess of the *Sarmatians* known the fatal Intentions of her despairing Lover, doubtless, she would have used some Precautions to hinder him from executing them; for want of which, she saw the miserable *Agilmond* weltering in his Blood at her Feet; and with Reason accused herself of being the Cause of so deplorable a Spectacle.

The Astonishment Miss *Glanville* was in, to hear her Cousin talk in this Manner, kept her from giving her any Interruption, while she related several other terrible Instances of Despair.

In the mean time, Sir *George*, who was impatient to go up to Lady *Bella's* Apartment, having flattered himself into a Belief, that his Letter was favourably received; and that he should be permitted to *hope* at least; made a short Visit to Sir *Charles* in his own Room; and, accompanied by Mr. *Glanville*, who was resolved to see in what manner *Arabella* received him, went to her Apartment.

As he had taken care, at his Entrance, to accommodate his Looks to the Character he had assumed of an humble despairing Lover, *Arabella* no sooner saw him, but her Countenance changed; and, making a Sign to Mr. *Glanville*, who could not comprehend what she meant, to seize upon the Guard of his Sword, she hastily stept forward to meet him.

I am too well convinced, said she to Sir *George*, that the Intent of your coming hither To-day, is to commit some Violence against yourself before my Eyes: But listen not, I beseech you, to the Dictates of your Despair: Live; I command you, live; and since you say, I have the absolute Disposal of your Life, do not deprive yourself of it, without the Consent of her, on whom you profess to have bestowed it.

Sir *George*, who did not imagine *Arabella* would communicate his Letter to her Cousins, and only expected some distant Hints from her concerning it, was so confounded at this Reception before them, that he was not able to reply: He blushed, and turned pale alternately; and, not daring to look, either upon Miss *Glanville*, or her Brother, or to meet the Eyes of the fair Visionary, who, with great Impatience, expected his Answer, he hung down his Head in a very silly Posture; and, by his Silence, confirmed *Arabella* in her Opinion.

As he did not want for Wit and Assurance, during that Interval of Silence, and Expectation from all Parties; his Imagination suggested to him the Means of extricating himself out of the ridiculous Perplexity he was in; and as it concerned him greatly to avoid any Quarrel, with the Brother and Sister, he determined to turn the whole Matter into a Jest; but, if possible, to manage it so, that *Arabella* should not enter into his Meaning.

Raising therefore his Eyes, and looking upon *Arabella* with a melancholy Air;

You are not deceived, Madam, said he: This Criminal, with whom you are so justly offended, comes with an Intention to die at your Feet, and breathe out his miserable Life, to expiate those Crimes of which you accuse him: But since your severe Compassion will oblige me to live, I obey, oh! most divine, but cruel *Arabella*! I obey your harsh Commands; and, by endeavouring to live, give you a more convincing Proof of that Respect and Submission I shall always have for your Will.

I expected no less from your Courage and Generosity, said *Arabella*, with a Look of great Complacency; and since you so well know how to imitate the great *Lysimachus* in your Obedience, I shall not be less acknowleging then the fair *Parisatis*;[1] but will have for you an Esteem equal to that Virtue I have observed in you.

Sir *George*, having received this gracious Promise, with a most profound Bow, turned to Mr. *Glanville*, with a kind of chastened Smile upon his Countenance.

And, you, fortunate and deserving Knight, said he, happy in the Affections of the fairest Person in the World! grudge me not this small Alleviation of my Misfortunes; and envy me not that Esteem, which alone is able to make me suffer Life, while you possess, in the Heart of the divine *Arabella*, a Felicity that might be envied by the greatest Monarchs in the World.

As diverting as this Scene was, Mr. *Glanville* was extremely uneasy: For though Sir *George's* Stratagem took, and he believed he was only indulging the Gaiety of his Humour, by carrying on this Farce; yet he could not endure, he should divert himself at

Arabella's Expence. The solemn Speech he had made him, did indeed force him to smile; but he soon assumed a graver Look, and told Sir *George*, in a low Voice, that when he had finished his Visit, he should be glad to take a Turn with him in the Garden.

Sir *George* promised to follow him, and Mr. *Glanville* left the Room, and went into the Gardens; where the Baronet, having taken a respectful Leave of *Arabella*, and, by a sly Glance, convinced Miss *Glanville*, he had sacrificed her Cousin to her Mirth, went to join her Brother.

Mr. *Glanville*, as soon as he saw him, walked to meet him with a very reserved Air: Which Sir *George* observing, and being resolved to keep up his Humour;

What, inhuman, but too happy Lover, said he, what, am I to understand by that Cloud upon your Brow? Is it possible, that thou canst envy me the small Comfort I have received; and, not satisfied with the glorious Advantages thou possessest, wilt thou still deny me that Esteem, which the divine *Arabella* has been pleased to bestow upon me?

Pray, Sir *George*, said Mr. *Glanville*, lay aside this pompous Style: I am not disposed to be merry at present, and have not all the Relish for this kind of Wit, that you seem to expect. I desired to see you here, that I might tell you without Witnesses, I take it extremely ill, you should presume to make my Cousin the Object of your Mirth. Lady *Bella*, Sir, is not a Person, with whom such Liberties ought to be taken; nor will I, in the double Character of her Lover and Relation, suffer it from any one whatever.

Cruel Fortune! said Sir *George*, stepping back a little, and lifting up his Eyes, shall I always be exposed to thy Persecutions? And must I, without any apparent Cause, behold an Enemy in the Person of my Friend; who, though, without murmuring, I resign to him the adorable *Arabella*, is yet resolved to dispute with me, a Satisfaction, which does not deprive him of any Part of that glorious Fortune to which he is destined? Since it is so, unjust and cruel Friend, pursued he, strike this Breast, which carries the Image of the divine *Arabella*; but think not, that I will offer to defend myself, or lift my Sword, against a Man beloved by her.

This is all very fine, returned Mr. *Glanville*, hardly able to forbear laughing; but 'tis impossible, with all your Gaiety, to hinder me from being serious upon this Business.

Then be as serious as thou wilt, dear *Charles*, interrupted Sir

George, provided you will allow me to be gay; and not pretend to infect me with thy unbecoming Gravity.

I have but a few Words to say to you, then, Sir, replied Mr. *Glanville*: Either behave with more Respect to my Cousin; or prepare to give me Satisfaction, for the Insults you offer her.

Oh! I understand you, Sir, said Sir *George*; and because you have taken it into your Head to be offended at a Trifle of no Consequence in the World, I must give you a fair Chance to run me through the Body! There is something very foolish, faith, in such an extravagant Expectation: But since Custom has made it necessary, that a Man must venture his Soul and Body upon these important Occasions; because I will not be out of the Fashion, you shall command me whenever you think fit; though I shall fight with my Schoolfellow with a very ill Will, I assure you.

There is no Necessity for fighting, said Mr. *Glanville*, blushing at the ludicrous Light, in which the gay Baronet had placed his Challenge: The Concession I have required, is very small, and not worth the contesting for, on your Side. Lady *Bella's* Peculiarity, to which you contribute so much, can afford you, at best, but an ill-natured Diversion, while it gives me a real Pain; and sure, you must acknowlege, you are doing me a very great Injury, when you endeavour to confirm a Lady, who is to be my Wife, in a Behaviour that excites your Mirth, and makes her a fit Object for your Ridicule, and Contempt.

You do Lady *Bella*, a much greater Injury than I do, replied Sir *George*, by supposing, she can ever be an Object of Ridicule and Contempt: I think very highly of her Understanding; and though the Bent of her Studies has given her Mind a romantic Turn, yet the Singularity of her Manners is far less disagreeable, than the lighter Follies of most of her Sex.

But to be absolutely perfect, interrupted Mr. *Glanville*, I must cure her of that Singularity; and therefore I beg you will not persist in assuming a Behaviour conformable to her romantic Ideas; but rather help me to banish them from her Imagination.

Well, replied Sir *George*, since you no longer threaten, I'll do what I can to content you; but I must quit my Heroics by Degrees, and sink with Decency into my own Character; otherwise she will never endure me in her Presence.

Arabella and Miss *Glanville*, appearing in the Walk, broke off the Conversation. The Baronet and Mr. *Glanville* walked forward to meet them; but *Arabella*, who did not desire Company, struck into another Walk, whither Mr. *Glanville* following, proposed to join her; when he saw his Father, who had been taking a Turn there alone, make up to *Arabella*; and, supposing he would take that Opportunity to talk to her concerning him, he went back to his Sister and Sir *George*, whose Conversation he interrupted, to the great Regret of Miss *Glanville*.

CHAPTER V

In which will be found one of the former Mistakes pursued, and another cleared up, to the great Satisfaction of Two Persons; among whom, the Reader, we expect, will make a Third

Arabella no sooner saw Sir *Charles* advancing towards her, when, sensible of the Consequence of being alone with a Person whom she did not doubt, would make use of that Advantage, to talk to her of Love, she endeavoured to avoid him, but in vain; for Sir *Charles*, guessing her Intentions, walked hastily up to her; and, taking hold of her Hand,

You must not go away, Lady *Bella*, said he: I have something to say to you.

Arabella, extremely discomposed at this Behaviour, struggled to free her Hand from her Uncle; and, giving him a Look, on which Disdain and Fear were visibly painted,

Unhand me, Sir, said she, and force me not to forget the Respect I owe you, as my Uncle, by treating you with a Severity such uncommon Insolence demands.

Sir *Charles*, letting go her Hand in a great Surprize, at the Word Insolent, which she had used, asked her, If she knew to whom she was speaking?

Questionless, I am speaking to my Uncle, replied she; and 'tis with great Regret I see myself obliged to make use of Expressions no way conformable to the Respect I bear that sacred Character.

And, pray, Madam, said Sir *Charles*, somewhat softened by this Speech, who is it that obliges you to lay aside that Respect you seem to acknowlege is due to your Uncle?

You do, Sir, replied she; and 'tis with infinite Sorrow, that I beheld you assuming a Character unbecoming the Brother of my Father.

This is pretty plain, indeed, interrupted Sir *Charles*: But pray, Madam, inform me, what is it you complain of.

You, questionless, know much better than I can tell you, replied *Arabella*, blushing, the Offence I accuse you of; nor is it proper for me to mention, what it would not become me to suffer.

Zounds! cried Sir *Charles*, no longer able to suppress his growing Anger, this is enough to make a Man mad.

Ah! I beseech you, Sir, resumed *Arabella*, suffer not an unfortunate and ill-judged Passion to be the Bane of all your Happiness and Virtue: Recall your wandring Thoughts; reflect upon the Dishonour you will bring upon yourself, by persisting in such unjustifiable Sentiments.

I do not know how it is possible to avoid it, said Sir *Charles*; and, notwithstanding all this fine Reasoning, there are few People but would fly into greater Extremities; but my Affection for you makes me.——

Hold, hold, I conjure you, Sir, interrupted *Arabella*; force me not to listen to such injurious Language; carry that odious Affection somewhere else; and do not persecute an unfortunate Maid, who has contributed nothing to thy Fault, and is only guilty of too much Compassion for thy Weakness.

Good God, cried Sir *Charles*, starting back, and looking upon *Arabella* with Astonishment; how I pity my Son! What would I not give, if he did not love this Girl?

Think not, replied *Arabella*, that the Passion your Son has for me, makes your Condition a bit the worse; for I would be such as I am, with respect to you, were there no Mr. *Glanville* in the World.

I never thought, Niece, said Sir *Charles*, after a little Pause, that any Part of my Behaviour, could give you the Offence you complain of, or authorize that Hatred and Contempt you take the Liberty to express for me: But since it is so, I promise you, I will quit your House, and leave you to your self; I have always been solicitous for your Welfare; and, ungrateful as you are—

Call me not ungrateful, interrupted *Arabella* again: Heaven is my Witness, that had you not forgot I was your Niece, I would have always remembred you was my Uncle; and not only have regarded you as such, but have looked upon you as another Father, under whose Direction Providence had placed me, since it had deprived me of my real Father; and whose Tenderness and Care, might have in some measure supplied the Loss I had of him: But Heaven has decreed it otherwise; and since it is its Will, that I should be deprived of the Comfort and Assistance my Orphan State requires, I must submit, without murmuring, to my Destiny. Go then, unfortunate and lamented Uncle, pursued she, wiping some Tears from her fine Eyes; go, and endeavour by Reason and Absence to recover thy Repose; and be assured, whenever you can convince me you have triumphed over these Sentiments which now cause both our Unhappiness, you shall have no Cause to complain of my Conduct towards you.

Finishing these Words, she left him with so much Speed, that it would have been impossible for him to have stopped her, though he had intended it: But indeed, he was so lost in Wonder and Confusion at a Behaviour for which he was not able to assign any other Cause than Madness, that he remained fixed in the same Posture of Surprize, in which she had left him; and from which he was first interrupted by the Voice of his Son, who, seeing *Arabella* flying towards the House in great seeming Emotion, came to know the Result of their Conversation.

Sir, said Mr. *Glanville*, who had spoken to his Father before, but had no Answer, will you not inform me, what Success you have had with my Cousin? How did she receive your Proposal.

Speak of her no more, said Sir *Charles*, she is a proud ungrateful Girl, and unworthy the Affection you have for her.

Mr. *Glanville*, who trembled to hear so unfavourable an Answer to his Inquiries, was struck dumb with his Surprize and Grief; when Sir *Charles* taking Notice of the Alteration in his Countenance;

I am sorry, said he, to find you have set your Heart upon this fantastic Girl: If ever she be your Wife, which I very much doubt, she will make you very unhappy: But, *Charles*, pursued he, I would advise you to think no more of her; content yourself with the Estate you gain by her Refusal of you: With that Addition to your own Fortune, you may pretend to any Lady whatever; and you will find many that are full as agreeable as your Cousin, who will be proud of your Addresses.

Indeed, Sir, said Mr. *Glanville*, with a Sigh, there is no Woman upon Earth whom I would choose to marry, but Lady *Bella*: I flattered myself, I had been happy enough to have made some

Progress in her Affection; but it seems, I was mistaken; however, I should be glad to know, if she gave you any Reasons for refusing me.

Reasons! said Sir *Charles*: There is no making her hear Reason, or expecting Reason from her; I never knew so strange a Woman in my Life: She would not allow me to speak what I intended concerning you; but interrupted me, every Moment, with some highflown Stuff or other.

Then I have not lost all Hopes of her, cried Mr. *Glanville* eagerly; for since she did not hear what you had to say, she could not possibly deny you.

But she behaved in a very impertinent Manner to me, interrupted Sir *Charles*; complained of my harsh Treatment of her; and said several other Things, which, because of her uncommon Style, I could not perfectly understand; yet they seemed shocking; and, upon the Whole, treated me so rudely, that I am determined to leave her to herself, and trouble my Head no more about her.

For God's sake, dear Sir, said Mr. *Glanville*, alarmed at this Resolution, suspend your Anger, till I have seen my Cousin: There is some Mistake, I am persuaded, in all this. I know she has some very odd Humours, which you are not so well acquainted with, as I am. I'll go to her, and prevail upon her to explain herself.

You may do so, if you please, replied Sir *Charles*; but I fear it will be to very little Purpose; for I really suspect her Head is a little turned: I do not know what to do with her: It is not fit she should have the Management of herself; and yet 'tis impossible to live upon easy Terms with her.

Mr. *Glanville*, who did not doubt but *Arabella* had been guilty of some very ridiculous Folly, offered nothing more in her Justification; but, having attended his Father to his own Chamber went to *Arabella's* Apartment.

He found the pensive Fair-one, in a melancholy Posture, her Head reclined upon one of her fair Hands; and though her Eyes were fixed upon a Book she held in the other, yet she did not seem to read, but rather to be wholly buried in Contemplation.

Mr. *Glanville* having so happily found her alone (for her Women were not then in her Chamber) seated himself near her; having first asked Pardon for the Interruption he had given to her Studies; and *Arabella*, throwing aside her Book, prepared to listen to his Discourse; which by the Agitation, which appeared in Looks, she imagined, would be upon some extraordinary Subject.

I left my Father just now, said he, in a great deal of Uneasiness, on account of something you said to him, Lady *Bella*: He apprehends you are disobliged, and he would willingly know how.

Has your Father then acquainted you with the Subject of our Conversation? interrupted *Arabella*.

I know what would have been the Subject of your Conversation, replied Mr. *Glanville*, if you had been pleased to listen to what Sir *Charles* intended to say to you on my Behalf.

On your Behalf? interrupted *Arabella*: Ah poor deceived *Glanville*! how I pity thy blind Sincerity! But it is not for me to undeceive thee: Only thus much I must say to you, Beware of committing your Interests to a Person, who will be a much better Advocate for another than for you.

Mr. *Glanville*, rejoiced to find by these Words, that her Resentment against his Father was occasioned by a Suspicion so favourable for him, assured her, that Sir *Charles* wished for nothing more earnestly, than that he might be able to merit her Esteem; and that it was to dispose her to listen to his Addresses, that he wanted to discourse with her that Morning.

Mr. *Glanville*, being obliged, through his Knowlege of his Cousin's Temper, to speak to her in this distant Manner, went on with his Assurances of his Father's Candour in this Respect; and *Arabella*, who would not declare her Reasons for doubting it, only replied, That she wished Sir *Charles* meant all that he had said to him; but that she could not persuade herself to believe him sincere, till his future Actions had convinced her he was so.

Mr. *Glanville*, impatient to let his Father know, how greatly he had been mistaken in the Cause of *Arabella's* Behaviour, made his Visit shorter than he would otherwise have done, in order to undeceive him.

Is it possible, said Sir *Charles*, when his Son had repeated the Conversation he had just had with *Arabella*, that she could be so foolish, as to imagine, I had a Design to propose any one else to her but you? What Reason have I ever given her, to think I would not be glad to have her for my Daughter-in-law? Indeed, she has some odd Ways that are very disagreeable; but she is one of the best Matches in *England* for all that: Poor Girl! pursued he, she had Reason to be angry, if that was the Case; and now I remember, she cried, when I told her I would leave the House; yet her Spirit was so great, that she told me, I might go. Well, I'll go and make it up with her; but who could have imagined, she would have been so foolish? Sir *Charles*, at the Repetition of these Words, hurried away to *Arabella's* Apartment.

Niece, said he at his Entrance, I am come to ask you Pardon, for having led you into a Belief, that I meant—

'Tis enough, Sir, interrupted *Arabella*; I grant you my Pardon for what is past; and as it does not become me to receive Submissions from my Uncle, while he remembers he is so, I will dispense with your Acknowlegements at present: Only to convince me, that this sudden Alteration is sincere, avoid, I beseech you, for the future, all Occasions of displeasing me.

I protest, cried Sir *Charles*, that I never intended—

I will not hear you say a Word more of your past Intentions, interrupted *Arabella* again: I have forgot them all; and, while you continue to regard me as your Niece, I will never remember them to your Disadvantage.

Then I may hope, said Sir *Charles*—

Oh! Heavens! cried *Arabella*, not suffering him to proceed; do you come to insult me thus, with a mock Repentance? And has my Easiness, in being so ready to forget the Injury you would have done me, made you presumptuous enough to cherish an insolent Hope that I will ever change my Resolution?

How vexatious is this! replied Sir *Charles*, fretting to see her continually mistaking him. I swear to you, by all that is sacred, that 'tis my Son, for whom I would solicit your Consent.

How! said *Arabella*, astonished, Will you then be just at last? And can you resolve to plead for that Son, whose Interest, but a Moment ago, you would have destroyed?

I see, said Sir *Charles*, it is impossible to convince you.

No, no interrupted *Arabella*, hastily; it is not impossible but my own ardent Wishes that it may be so, will help to convince me of the Truth of what you say: For in fine, do you think, I shall not be as glad as yourself, to find you capable of acting honourably by your Son; and to see myself no longer the Cause of the most unjustifiable Conduct imaginable?

Sir *Charles* was opening his Mouth, to press her in Favour of Mr. *Glanville*; whom, notwithstanding her strange Behaviour, he was glad to find, she loved; when *Arabella* preventing him,

Seek not, I beseech you, said she, to destroy that Belief I am willing to give your Words, by any more Attempts at this time to persuade me; for truly, I shall interpret your Solicitude no way in your Favour; therefore, if you desire I should be convinced you are sincere, let the Silence I require of you, be one Proof of it.

Sir *Charles*, who looked excessively out of Countenance at such a peremptory Command from his Niece, was going out of her Chamber in a very ill Humour, when the Dinner-bell ringing, she gave him her Hand, with a very gracious Air; and permitted him to lead her into the Dining-room, where they found Mr. *Glanville*, his Sister, and Sir *George*, who had been detained to Dinner by Miss *Glanville*, expecting their coming.

CHAPTER VI

Containing some Account of Thalestris, *Queen of the*
Amazons, *with other curious Anecdotes*

LADY *Bella* having recovered her usual Chearfulness, thro' the Satisfaction she felt at her Uncle's returning to Reason, and the Abatement she perceived in Sir *George*'s extreme Melancholy, mixed in the Conversation with that Wit and Vivacity which was natural to her, and which so absolutely charmed the whole Company, that not one of them remembred any of her former Extravagancies.

Mr. *Glanville* gazed on her with a passionate Tenderness, Sir *George* with Admiration, and the old Baronet with Wonder and Delight.

But Miss *Glanville*, who was inwardly vexed at the Superiority her Cousin's Wit gave her over herself, wished for nothing more than an Opportunity of interrupting a Conversation in which she could have no Share; and, willing to put them in mind of some of *Arabella's* strange Notions, when she observed them disputing concerning some of the Actions of the antient *Romans*, she very innocently asked Sir *George*, Whether in former times Women went to the Wars, and fought like Men? For my Cousin, added she, talks of one *Thaltris*, a Woman, that was as courageous as any Soldier whatever.

Mr. *Glanville*, horridly vexed at a Question that was likely to engage *Arabella* in a Discourse very different from that she had

been so capable of pleasing in, frowned very intelligibly at his
Sister; and, to prevent any Answer being given to her absurd
Demand, directed some other Conversation to *Arabella*: But she,
who saw a favourite Subject started, took no Notice of what Mr.
Glanville was saying to her; but, directing her Looks to Sir
George,

Though Miss *Glanville*, said she, be a little mistaken in the Name
of that fair Queen she has mentioned; yet I am persuaded you know
whom she means; and that it is the renowned *Thalestris*, whose
Valour staggers her Belief, and of whom she wants to be informed.

Ay, ay, *Thalestris*, said Miss *Glanville*: It is such a strange Name
I could not remember it; but, pray, was there ever such a Person?

Certainly, Madam, there was, replied Sir *George*: She was
Queen of the *Amazons*, a warlike Nation of Women, who possessed
great Part of *Cappadocia*, and extended their Conquests so far,
that they became formidable to all their Neighbours.

You find, Miss, said *Arabella*, I did not attempt to impose upon
you, when I told you of the admirable Valour of that beautiful
Queen; which indeed was so great, that the united Princes, in
whose Cause she fought, looked upon her Assistance to be equal to
that of a whole Army; and they honoured her, accordingly, with
the most distinguishing Marks of their Esteem and Acknowlegement, and offered her the chief Command of their Forces.[1]

O shameful! cried Sir *Charles*, offer a Woman the Command of
an Army! Brave Fellows indeed, that would be commanded by a
Woman! Sure you mistake, Niece; there never was such a thing
heard of in the World.

What, Sir, said *Arabella*, will you contradict a Fact attested by
the greatest Historians that ever were? You may as well pretend to
say, there never were such Persons as *Oroondates* or *Juba*, as dispute
the Existence of the famous *Thalestris*.

Why, pray, Madam, said Sir *Charles*, who were those?

One of them, replied *Arabella*, was the great King of *Scythia*;
and the other, Prince of the Two *Mauritanias*.

Ods-heart! interrupted Sir *Charles*, I believe their Kingdoms
are in the Moon: I never heard of *Scythia*, or the Two *Mauritanias*,
before.

And yet, Sir, replied *Arabella*, those Kingdoms are doubtless as
well known, as *France* or *England*; and there is no Question, but
the Descendants of the great *Oroondates*, and the valiant *Juba*, sway
the Sceptres of them to this Day.

I must confess, said Sir *George*, I have a very great Admiration for those Two renowned Princes, and have read their beautiful Exploits with infinite Pleasure; notwithstanding which, I am more inclined to esteem the great *Artaban*, then either of them.

Though *Artaban*, replied *Arabella*, is without Question, a Warrior equal to either of them, and haply no Person in the World possessed so sublime a Courage as his was; yet, it may be, your Partiality proceeds from another Cause; and you having the Honour to resemble him in some little Infidelities he was accused of,[1] with less Justice than yourself perhaps, induces you to favour him more than any other.

Arabella blushed when she ended these Words: And Sir *George* replied, with a Sigh;

I have, indeed, the Honour, Madam, to resemble the great *Artaban*, in having dared to raise my Thoughts towards a Divine Person, who, with Reason, condemns my Adorations.

Hey-day! cried Sir *Charles*, are you going to speak of Divine Things, after all the Fables you have been talking of? Troth, I love to hear young Men enter upon such Subjects: But pray, Niece, who told you Sir *George* was an infidel?

Mr. *Glanville*, replied *Arabella*: And I am inclined to think he spoke Truth; for Sir *George* has never pretended to deny it.

How! interrupted Sir *Charles*; I am sorry to hear that. I hope you have never, added he, looking at the young Baronet, endeavoured to corrupt my Son with any of your Free-thinking Principles: I am for every body having Liberty of Conscience; but I cannot endure to hear People of your Stamp endeavouring to propagate your mischievous Notions; and because you have no Regard for your own future Happiness, disturbing other People in the laudable Pursuit of theirs.

We will not absolutely condemn Sir *George*, said *Arabella*, till we have heard his History from his own Mouth, which he promised, some time ago, to relate when I desired it.

I do not imagine his History is fit to be heard by Ladies, said Sir *Charles*; for your Infidels live a strange kind of Life.

However that may be, replied *Arabella*, we must not dispense with Sir *George* from performing his Promise: I dare say there are no Ladies here, who will think the worse of him for freely confessing his Faults.

You may answer for yourself, if you please, Madam, said Sir *Charles*; but I hope my Girl there, will not say as much.

I dare say my Cousin is not so rigid, said *Arabella*: She has too much the Spirit of *Julia* in her, to find Fault with a little Infidelity.[1]

I am always obliged to you for your Comparisons, Cousin, said Miss *Glanville*: I suppose this is greatly to my Advantage too.

I assure you, Madam, said Sir *George*, Lady *Bella* has done you no Injury by the Comparison she has just now made; for *Julia* was one of the finest Princesses in the World.

Yet she was not free from the Suspicion of Infidelity, replied *Arabella*; but though I do not pretend to tax my Cousin with that Fault, yet it is with a great deal of Reason that I say she resembles her in her volatile Humour.

I was never thought to be ill-humoured in my Life, Madam, said Miss *Glanville*, colouring; and I cannot imagine what Reason I have given you for saying I am.

Nay, Cousin, said *Arabella*, I am not condemning your Humour; for, to say the Truth, there are a great many Charms in a volatile Disposition; and, notwithstanding the admirable Beauty of *Julia*, it is possible she made as many Slaves by her light and airy Carriage, as she did by her Eyes, though they were the fairest in the World, except the divine *Cleopatra's*.

Cleopatra! cried Sir *Charles*: Why she was a Gypsey, was she not?

I never heard her called so, said *Arabella*, gravely; and I am apt to believe you are not at all acquainted with her: But pray, pursued she, let us wave this Discourse at present, and prepare to listen to Sir *George*'s Relation of his Life; which, I dare say, is full of very extraordinary Events: However, Sir, added she, directing her Speech to the young Baronet, I am afraid your Modesty will induce you to speak with less Candour than you ought, of those great Actions, which questionless you have performed: Therefore we shall hear your History, with greater Satisfaction, from the Mouth of your faithful 'Squire, who will not have the same Reasons that you have, for suppressing what is most admirable in the Adventures of your Life.

Since it is your Pleasure, Madam, replied Sir *George*, to hear my Adventures, I will recount them as well as I am able myself, to the end that I may have an Opportunity of obliging you by doing some Violence to my natural Modesty, which will not suffer me to relate

Things the World have been pleased to speak of to my Advantage, without some little Confusion.

Then, casting down his Eyes, he seemed to be recollecting the most material Passages in his Life. Mr. *Glanville*, though he could have wished he had not indulged *Arabella* in her ridiculous Request, was not able to deny himself the Diversion of hearing what Kind of History he would invent; and therefore resolved to stay and listen to him.

Miss *Glanville* was also highly delighted with the Proposal; but Sir *Charles*, who could not conceive there could be any thing worth listening to, in a young Rake's Account of himself, got up with an Intention to walk in the Garden; when, perceiving it rained, he changed his Resolution, and, resuming his Seat, prepared to listen, as every one else did, to the expected Story.

When Sir *George*, after having paused a Quarter of an Hour longer, during which all the Company observed a profound Silence, began his Relation in this Manner, addressing himself to *Arabella*.

End of the Fifth BOOK.

BOOK VI

Containing the Beginning of Sir George's *History ; in which the ingenious Relater has exactly copied the Stile of Romance*

THOUGH at present, Madam, you behold me in the Quality of a private Gentleman, in the Possession only of a tolerable Estate; yet my Birth is illustrious enough: My Ancestors having formerly worn a Crown; which, as they won by their Valour, so they lost by their Misfortune only.

How, interrupted Sir *Charles*, are you descended from Kings? Why, I never heard you say so before: Pray, Sir, how far are you removed from Royal Blood? and which of your Forefathers was it that wore a Crown?

Sir, replied Sir *George*, it is not much more than Eight hundred Years since my Ancestors, who were *Saxons*, swayed the Sceptre of *Kent*; and from the first Monarch of that mighty Kingdom, am I lineally descended.

Pray where may that Kingdom of *Kent* lie? said Sir *Charles*.

Sir, replied Sir *George*, it is bounded by *Sussex* on the South-West; *Surry* on the West; the *English* Channel on the South; *Dover* Streights on the South East; and the *Downs* on the East; and it is divided from *Middlesex* and *Essex* on the North by the *Thames*.

A mighty Kingdom indeed! said Sir *Charles*: Why, it makes but a very small Part of the Kingdom of *Britain* now: Well, if your Ancestors were Kings of that County as it is now called, it must be confessed their Dominions were very small.

However that may be, said *Arabella*, it raises Sir *George* greatly in my Esteem, to hear he is descended from Kings; for, truly, a Royal Extraction does infinitely set off noble and valiant Actions, and inspires only lofty and generous Sentiments: Therefore, illustrious Prince (for in that Light I shall always consider you), be assured, though Fortune has despoiled you of your Dominions, yet since she cannot deprive you of your Courage and Virtue, Providence will one Day assist your noble Endeavours to recover your Rights, and place you upon the Throne of your Ancestors, from whence you have been so inhumanly driven: Or, haply, to repair that Loss, your Valour may procure you other Kingdoms, no less considerable than that to which you was born.

For Heaven's sake, Niece, said Sir *Charles*, How come such improbable Things into your Head? Is it such an easy Matter, think you, to conquer Kingdoms, that you can flatter a young Man, who has neither Fleets nor Armies, with such strange Hopes?

The great *Artaban*, Sir, resumed *Arabella*, had neither Fleets nor Armies, and was Master only of a single Sword; yet he soon saw himself greater than any King, disposing the Destinies of Monarchs by his Will, and deciding the Fates of Empires by a single Word: But pray let this Dispute rest where it is, and permit Sir *George* to continue his Relation.

It is not necessary, Madam, resumed Sir *George*, to acquaint you with the Misfortunes of my Family, or relate the several Progressions it made towards the private Condition in which it now is: For, besides that reciting the Events of so many Hundred Years may haply, in some measure, try your Patience, I should be glad if you would dispense with me from entering into a Detail of Accidents that would sensibly afflict me: It shall suffice, therefore, to inform you, that my Father, being a peaceable Man, fond of Retirement and Tranquillity, made no Attempts to recover the Sovereignty from which his Ancestors had been unjustly expelled; but quietly beheld the Kingdom of *Kent* in the Possession of other Masters, while he contented himself with the Improvement of that small Pittance of Ground, which was all that the unhappy Prince *Veridomer*, my Grandfather, was able to bequeath to him.

Hey-day! cried Sir *Charles*, Will you new-christen your Grandfather, when he has been in his Grave these Forty Years? I knew honest Sir *Edmard Bellmour* very well, though I was but a Youth when he died; but I believe no Person in *Kent* ever gave him the Title of Prince *Veridomer*: Fie! fie! these are idle Brags.

Sir *George*, without taking Notice of the old Baronet's Heat, went on with his Narration in this manner:

Things were in this State, Madam, when I was born. I will not trouble you with the Relation of what I did in my Infancy.

No, pray skip over all that, interrupted Sir *Charles*; I suppose your Infancy was like other Peoples? What can there be worth hearing in that?

You are deceived, Sir, said *Arabella*: The Infancy of illustrious Personages has always something very extraordinary in it; and from their childish Words and Actions there have been often Presages drawn of their future Greatness and Glory.

Not to disoblige Sir *Charles*. however, said the young Prince of *Kent*, I will not repeat many things, which I said and did in the first Years of my Life, that those about me thought very surprising; and from them prognosticated, that very strange Accidents would befal me.

I have been a Witness of some very unfavourable Prognostics of you, said Sir *Charles*, smiling; for you was the most unlucky bold Spark, that ever I knew in my Life.

'Tis very certain, pursued Sir *George*, that the Forwardness of my Spirit gave great Uneasiness to my Father; who, being, as I said before, inclinable to a peaceable and sedentary Life, endeavoured as much as possible to repress that Vivacity in my Disposition, which he feared might involve me in dangerous Enterprizes. The Pains he took in my Education, I recompensed by a more than ordinary Docility; and, before I was Thirteen, performed all my Exercises with a marvelous Grace; and, if I may dare say so, was, at those early Years, the Admiration and Wonder of all that saw me.

Lady *Bella* had some Reason to fear your Modesty, I find, said Sir *Charles*, smiling; for, methinks you really speak too slightly of your Excellencies.

However that may be, resumed Sir *George*; my Father saw these early Instances of a towering Genius in me, with a Pleasure, chastened by his Fears, that the Grandeur of my Courage would lead me to attempt something for the Recovery of that Kingdom, which was my Due; and which might haply occasion his losing me.

Possessed with these Thoughts, he carefully avoided saying any thing to me concerning the glorious Pretences, to which my Birth gave me a Right; and often wished it had been possible for him to conceal from me, that I was the true and lawful Heir of the Kingdom of *Kent*; a Circumstance he never chose to mention to any Person, and would have been glad, if it had always remained a Secret.

And so it was a Secret, interrupted Sir *Charles*; for, till this Day,

I never heard of it; and it might still have been a Secret, if you had pleased; for nobody, I dare say, would suspect such a Thing; and very few, I believe, will be inclined to think there is any thing in such an improbable Tale.

Notwithstanding all my Father's Endeavours to the contrary, Madam, pursued Sir *George*, I cherished those towering Sentiments, the Knowlege of my Birth inspired me with; and it was not without the utmost Impatience, that I brooked the private Condition, to which I found myself reduced.

Cruel Fate! would I sometimes cry; was it not enough to deprive me of that Kingdom, which is my Due, and, subject me to a mean, and inglorious State; but, to make that Condition infinitely more grievous, must thou give me a Soul, towering above my abject Fortune? A Soul, that cannot but disdain the base Submission, I must pay to those, who triumph in the Spoils of my ruined House? A Soul, which sees nothing above its Hopes and Expectations? And, in fine, a Soul, that excites me daily to attempt Things worthy of my Birth, and those noble Sentiments I inherit from my great Forefathers? Ah, pursued I, unhappy *Bellmour*; what hinders thee from making thyself known and acknowleged for what thou art? What hinders thee from boldly asserting thy just and natural Rights; and from defying the Usurper, who detains them from thee? What hinders thee, I say?

What? Interrupted Sir *Charles*, why the Fear of a Halter, I suppose: There is nothing more easy than to answer that Question.

Such, Madam, said Sir *George*, were the Thoughts, which continually disturbed my Imagination; and, doubtless, they had not failed to push me on to some hazardous Enterprize, had not a fatal Passion interposed; and by its sweet, but dangerous Allurements, stifled for a while that Flame, which Ambition, and the Love of Glory, kindled in my Soul.

Sir *George* here pausing, and fixing his Eyes with a melancholy Air on the Ground, as if prest with a tender Remembrance;

Mr. *Glanville* asked him, smiling, If the Thoughts of poor *Dolly* disturbed him? Pray, added he, give us the History of your first Love, without any Mixture of Fable; or shall I take the Trouble off you? For you know, I am very well acquainted with your Affair with the pretty Milk-maid, and can tell it very succinctly.

'Tis true, Sir, said Sir *George*, sighing, I cannot recall the Idea of *Dorothea*, into my Remembrance, without some Pain; That fair, but unfaithful Shepherdess, who first taught me to sigh, and repaid my Tenderness with the blackest Infidelity: Yet I will endeavour to compose myself, and go on with my Narration.

Be pleased to know then, Madam, pursued Sir *George*, that having my Thoughts, in this manner, wholly employed with the Disasters of my Family, I had arrived to my seventeenth Year, without being sensible of the Power of Love; but the Moment now arrived, which was to prove fatal to my Liberty. Following the Chace one Day with my Father, and some other Gentlemen, I happened to lag a little behind them; and, being taken up with my ordinary Reflections, I lost my Way, and wandered a long time, without knowing or considering whither I was going. Chance at last conducted me to a pleasant Valley, surrounded with Trees; and, being tired with riding, I lighted, and tying my Horse to a Tree, walked forward, with an Intention to repose myself a few Moments under the Shade of one of those Trees, that had attracted my Observation: But while I was looking for the most convenient Place, I spied, at the Distance of some few Yards from me, a Woman lying asleep upon the Grass: Curiosity tempted me to go nearer this Person; and, advancing softly, that I might not disturb her, I got near enough to have a View of her Person: But, ah! Heavens! what Wonders did my Eyes encounter in this View!— The Age of this fair Sleeper seemed not to exceed Sixteen; her Shape was formed with the exactest Symmetry; one of her Hands supported her Head; the other, as it lay carelessly stretched at her Side, gave me an Opportunity of admiring its admirable Colour and Proportion: The thin Covering upon her Neck discovered Part of its inimitable Beauty to my Eyes; but her Face, her lovely Face, fixed all my Attention.

Certain it is, Madam, that, out of this Company, it would be hard to find any thing so perfect, as what I now viewed. Her Complexion was the purest White imaginable, heightened by the inchanting Glow, which dyed her fair Cheeks with a Colour like that of a new-blown Rose: Her Lips, formed with the greatest Perfection, and of a deeper Red, seemed to receive new Beauties from the Fragrance of that Breath, that parted from them: Her auburn Hair fell in loose Ringlets over her Neck; and some straggling Curls, that played upon her fair Forehead, set off by a charming Contrast the Whiteness of that Skin it partly hid: Her Eyes indeed were closed; and though I knew not whether their Colour and Beauty were equal to those other Miracles in her Face, yet their Proportion seemed to be large; and the snowy Lids, which covered them, were admirably set off by those long and sable Lashes that adorned them.

For some Moments I gazed upon this lovely Sleeper, wholly lost in Wonder and Admiration.

Where, whispered I, where has this Miracle been concealed, that my Eyes were never blessed with the Sight of her before? These Words, though I uttered them softly, and with the utmost Caution; yet by the murmuring Noise they made, caused an Emotion in the beauteous Sleeper, that she started, and presently after opened her Eyes: But what Words shall I find to express the Wonder, the Astonishment, and Rapture, which the Sight of those bright Stars inspired me with? The Flames which darted from those glorious Orbs, cast such a dazling Splendor upon a Sight too weak to bear a Radiance so unusual, that, stepping back a few Paces, I contemplated at a Distance, that Brightness, which began already to kindle a consuming Fire in my Soul.

Bless me! interrupted Sir *Charles*, confounded at so pompous a Description; who could this be?

The pretty Milk-maid, *Dolly Acorn*, replied Mr. *Glanville* gravely: Did you never see her, Sir, when you was at your Seat, at ——? She used often to bring Cream to my Lady.

Aye, aye, replied Sir *Charles*, I remember her: She was a very pretty Girl: And so it was from her Eyes, that all those Splendors and Flames came, that had like to have burnt you up, Sir *George*: Well, well, I guess how the Story will end: Pray let us hear it out.

I have already told you, Madam, resumed Sir *George*, the marvelous Effects the Sight of those bright Eyes produced upon my Spirit: I remained fixed in a Posture of Astonishment and Delight; and all the Faculties of my Soul were so absorbed in the Contemplation of the Miracles before me, that I believe, had she still continued before my Eyes, I should never have moved from the Place where I then stood: But the fair Virgin, who had spied me at the small Distance to which I was retired, turned hastily about, and flew away with extraordinary Swiftness.

When Love, now lending me Wings, whom Admiration had before made motionless, I persued her so eagerly, that at last I overtook her; and, throwing myself upon my Knees before her,

Stay, I conjure you, cried I; and if you be a Divinity, as your celestial Beauty makes me believe, do not refuse the Adoration I offer you: But if, as I most ardently wish, you are a Mortal, though sure the fairest that ever graced the Earth; stop a Moment, to look upon a Man, whose Respects for you as a Mortal fall little short of those Adorations he offers you as a Goddess.

I can't but think, cried Sir *Charles*, laughing, how poor *Dolly* must be surprised at such a rhodomontade Speech!

Oh, Sir! replied Mr. *Glanville*, you will find she will make as good a one.

Will she, by my Troth, said Sir *Charles*: I don't know how to believe it.

This Action, pursued Sir *George*, and the Words I uttered, a little surprised that fair Maid, and brought a Blush into her lovely Cheeks; but, recovering herself, she replied with an admirable Grace,

I am no Divinity, said she; and therefore your Adorations are misplaced: But if, as you say, my Countenance moves you to any Respect for me, give me a Proof of it, by not endeavouring to hold any further Discourse with me, which is not permitted me from one of your Sex and Appearance.

A very wise Answer, indeed! interrupted Sir *Charles* again: Very few Town Ladies would have disclaimed the Title of Goddess, if their Lovers had thought proper to bestow it upon them. I am mightily pleased with the Girl for her Ingenuity.

The Discretion of so young a Damsel, resumed Sir *George*, charmed me no less than her Beauty; and I besought her, with the utmost Earnestness, to permit me a longer Conversation with her.

Fear not, lovely Virgin, said I, to listen to the Vows of a Man, who, till he saw you, never learnt to sigh: My Heart, which defended its Liberty against the Charms of many admirable Ladies, yields, without Reluctance, to the pleasing Violence your Beauties lay upon me. Yes, too charming and dangerous Stranger, I am no longer my own Master: It is in your Power to dispose of my Destiny: Consider therefore, I beseech you, whether you can consent to see me die? For I swear to you, by the most sacred Oaths, unless you promise to have some Compassion on me, I will no longer behold the Light of Day.

You may easily conceive, Madam, that, considering this lovely Maid in the Character of a Shepherdess, in which she appeared, I made her a Declaration of my Passion, without thinking myself obliged to observe those Respects, which, to a Person of equal Rank with myself, Decorum would not have permitted me to forget.

However, she repelled my Boldness with so charming a Modesty, that I began to believe, she might be a Person of illustrious Birth, disguised under the mean Habit she wore: But, having requested her to inform me who she was, she told me, her Name was *Dorothea*; and that she was Daughter to a Farmer, that lived in the neighbouring Valley. This Knowledge increasing my Confidence, I talked to her of my Passion, without being the least afraid of offending her. And therein you was greatly to blame, said *Arabella*: For, truly, though the fair *Dorothea* told you, she was Daughter to a Farmer; yet, in all Probability, she was of a much higher Extraction, if the Picture you have drawn of her be true.

The fair *Arsinoe*, Princess of *Armenia*, was constrained for a while to conceal her true Name and Quality, and pass for a simple Country-woman, under the Name of *Delia*: Yet the generous *Philadelph*, Prince of *Cilicia*, who saw and loved her under that Disguise, treated her with all the Respect he would have done, had he known she was the Daughter of a King.[1] In like manner, Prince *Philoxipes*, who fell in Love with the beautiful *Policrete*, before he knew she was the Daughter of the great *Solon*; and while he looked upon her as a poor Stranger, born of mean Parents; nevertheless, his Love supplying the Want of those Advantages of Birth and Fortune, he wooed her with a Passion as full of Awe and Delicacy, as if her Extraction had been equal to his own.[2] And therefore those admirable Qualities the fair *Dorothea* possessed, might also have convinced you, she was not what she seemed, but, haply, some great Princess in Disguise.

To tell you the Truth, Madam, replied Sir *George*, notwithstanding the fair *Dorothea* informed me, she was of a mean Descent, I could not easily forego the Opinion, that she was of an illustrious Birth: And the Histories of those fair Princesses you have mentioned, coming into my Mind, I also thought it very possible, that this divine Person might either be the Daughter of a great King, or Lawgiver, like them; but, being wholly engrossed by the Violence of my new-born Affection, I listened to nothing, but what most flattered my Hopes; and, addressing my lovely Shepherdess with all the Freedom of a Person who thinks his Birth much superior to hers; she listened to my Protestations, without any seeming Reluctance, and condescended to assure me before we parted, that she did not hate me. So fair a Beginning, seemed to promise me the most favourable Fortune I could with Reason expect. I parted from my fair Shepherdess with a thousand Vows of Fidelity; exacting a Promise from her, that she would meet me as often as she conveniently could, and have the Goodness to listen to those Assurances of inviolable Tenderness my Passion prompted me to offer her. When she left me, it seemed as if my Soul had forsaken my Body to go after her: My Eyes pursued her Steps as long as she was in Sight; I envied the Ground she prest as she went along, and the Breezes that kissed that celestial Countenance in their Flight.

For some Hours I stood in the same Posture in which she had left me; contemplating the sudden Change I had experienced in my Heart, and the Beauty of that divine Image, which was now engraven in it. Night drawing on, I began to think of going home; and, untying my Horse, I returned the Way I had come; and at last struck into a Road, which brought me to the Place where I parted from the Company; from whence I easily found my Way home, so changed both in my Looks and Carriage, that my Father, and all my Friends, observed the Alteration with some Surprize.

CHAPTER II

In which Sir George, *continuing his surprising History,*
relates a most stupendous Instance of a Valour only to be
parallelled by that of the great Oroondates, Cæsareo,
&c. &c. &c.

FOR some Months, continued Sir *George*, I prosecuted my Addresses to the admirable *Dorothea*; and I flattered myself with a Hope, that I had made some Progress in her Heart: But, alas! this deceitful Fair-one, who only laughed at the Torments she made me endure, at the time she vowed eternal Constancy to me, gave her Hand to a Lover of her Father's providing, and abandoned me, without Remorse, to the most cruel Despair.

I will not trouble you, Madam, with the Repetition of those Complaints, which this perfidious Action drew from me for a long time. At length, my Courage enabling me to overcome the Violence of my Grief, I resolved to think of the ungrateful *Dorothea* no more; and the Sight of another Beauty completing my Cure, I no longer remembred the unfaithful Shepherdess, but with Indifference.

Thus, Madam, have I faithfully related one of those Infidelities, wherewith my Enemies slander me; who can support their Assertion, with no better Proof, than that I did not die, when *Dorothea* abandoned me: But I submit it to your Candour, whether an unfaithful Mistress deserved such an Instance of Affection, from a Lover she had betrayed?

Why, really, replied *Arabella*, after a little Pause, you had some Excuse to plead for your Failure in this Point: And though you cannot be called, the most perfect amongst Lovers, seeing you neither died, nor was in Danger of dying; yet neither ought you to be ranked among those who are most culpable: But pray proceed in your Story: I shall be better able to form a right Judgment of your Merit as a Lover, when I have heard all your Adventures.

My Passion for *Dorothea*, resumed Sir *George*, being cured by her Treachery towards me, the Love of Glory began again to revive in my Soul. I panted after some Occasion to signalize my Valour, which yet I had met with no Opportunity of doing; but, hearing that a mighty Army was preparing to march upon a secret Expedition, I privately quitted my Father's Seat; and, attended only by my faithful 'Squire, I took the same Route the Army had taken, and arrived the Day before the terrible Battle of —— was fought, where, without making myself known, I performed such Prodigies of Valour, as astonished all who beheld me. Without doubt, I should have been highly caressed by the Commander, who certainly would have given me the Honour of a Victory my Sword alone had procured for him; but, having unwittingly engaged myself too far in Pursuit of the flying Enemy, I found myself alone, encompassed with a Party of about Five hundred Men; who, seeing they were pursued only by a single Man, faced about, and prepared to kill or take me Prisoner.

Pray, Sir, interrupted Sir *Charles*, when did all this happen? And how came it to pass, that your Friends have been ignorant to this Moment of those Prodigies of Valour you performed at that Battle? I never heard you was ever in a Battle: Fame has done you great Injustice, by concealing the Part you had in that famous Victory.

The great Care I took to conceal myself, replied Sir *George*, was one Reason why my Friends did not attribute to me the Exploits, which the Knight in black Armour, who was no other than myself, performed; and the Accident I am going to relate, prevented my being discovered, while the Memory of those great Exploits were yet fresh in the Minds of those I had so greatly obliged.

Be pleased to know, therefore, Madam, that, seeing myself about to be encompassed by this Party of the Enemy, I disdained to fly; and, though I was alone, resolved to sustain their Attack, and sell my Life as dear as possible.

Why, if you did so, you was a Madman, cried Sir *Charles* in a Heat: The bravest Man that ever lived, would not have presumed to fight with so great a Number of Enemies. What could you expect, but to be cut in Pieces? Pooh! pooh! don't think any body will credit such a ridiculous Tale: I never knew you was so addicted to—

Lying, perhaps, the good Knight would have said; but Sir *George*, who was concerned he was present at his Legend, and could not blame him for doubting his Veracity, prevented his Utterance of a Word he would be obliged to take ill, by abruptly going on with his Story.

Placing my Back therefore against a Tree, pursued he, to prevent my being assaulted behind, I presented my Shield to the Boldest of these Assailants; who, having struck an impotent Blow upon it, as he was lifting up his Arm to renew his Attack, I cut it off with one Stroke of my Sword; and the same Instant plunged it to the Hilt in the Breast of another, and clove the Scull of a Third, who was making at me, in two Parts.

Sir *Charles*, at this Relation, burst into a loud Fit of Laughter; and, being more inclined to divert himself, than be offended at the Folly and Vanity of the young Baronet, he permitted him to go on with his surprising Story, without giving him any other Interruption.

These Three Executions, Madam, pursued Sir *George*, were the Effects only of so many Blows; which raised such Indignation in my Enemies, that they prest forward in great Numbers to destroy me; but, having, as I before said, posted myself so advantageously, that I could only be assaulted before, not more than Three or Four could attack me at one time. The Desire of lengthening out my Life, till happily some Succour might come to my Relief, so invigorated my Arm, and added to my ordinary Strength an almost irresistible Force, that I dealt Death at every Blow; and in less than a quarter of an Hour, saw more than Fifty of my Enemies at my

Feet, whose Bodies served for a Bulwark against their Fellows Swords.

The Commander of this little Body, not having Generosity enough to be moved with those prodigious Effects of my Valour in my Favour, was transported with Rage at my Resistance; and the Sight of so so many of his Men slain before his Face, served only to increase his Fury; and that Moment, seeing, that, with Two more Blows, I had sent Two of his most valiant Soldiers to the Shades, and that the rest fearing to come within the Length of my Sword, had given me a few Moments Respite,

Ah! Cowards! cried he, are you afraid of a single Man? And will you suffer *him* to escape from your Vengeance, who has slain so many of your brave Comrades before your Eyes?

These Words inspiring them with a Fierceness, such as he desired, they advanced towards me with more Fury than before: By this time, I had received several large Wounds, and my Blood ran down from many Parts of my Body: Yet was I not sensible of any Decay of Strength, nor did the settled Designs of my Enemies to destroy me daunt me in the least: I still relied upon the Assistance I expected Providence would send to my Relief, and determined, if possible, to preserve my Life, till it arrived.

I fought, therefore, with a Resolution, which astonished my Enemies, but did not move them to any Regard for my Safety: And, observing their brutal Commander, a few Paces from me, encouraging his Men, both with his Cries and Gestures, Indignation against this inhuman Wretch so transported me out of my Discretion, that I quitted my Post, in order to sacrifice him to my Revenge.

Seeing me advance furiously towards him, he turned pale with Fear, and endeavoured to shelter himself in the midst of his Men; who, more valiant than himself, opposed themselves to my Rage, to favour his Retreat: But quickly clearing myself a Way with my Sword, I pressed towards the barbarous Coward; and, ere he could avoid the Blow I aimed at him, it struck him senseless at my Feet.

My particular Revenge thus satisfied, I was sensible of the Fault I had committed in quitting my Post, by which I exposed myself to be surrounded by the Enemy. I endeavoured to regain it, but in vain: I was beset on all Sides, and now despaired of any Safety; and therefore only sought to die courageously, and make as many of my Enemies as I could, attend my Fall.

Exasperated by the Misfortune of their Commander, they pressed upon me with redoubled Fury. Faint as I was, with the Loss of Blood, and so fatigued with the past Action, and the obstinate Fight I had maintained so long with such a considerable Number, I could hardly any longer lift up my Arm; and, to complete, my Misfortune, having thrust my Sword into the Body of one of the forwardest of my Enemies, in my endeavouring to regain it, it broke in Pieces, and the Hilt only remained in my Hand.

This Accident completed my Defeat: Deprived of my Sword, I was no longer capable of making any Defence: Several of them pressed upon me at once; and, throwing me down, tied my Hands together behind me. Shame and Rage at this Indignity worked so forcibly upon my Spirits, weakened as I then was, that I fell into a Swoon. What happened till my Recovery, I am not able to tell; but, at the Return of my Senses, I found myself laid on a Bed in a tolerable Chamber, and some Persons with me, who kept a profound Silence.

CHAPTER III

A Love-Adventure, after the Romantic Taste

RECOLLECTING in a few Moments all that happened to me, I could not choose but be surprised at finding myself treated with so little Severity, considering I was Prisoner to Persons who had been Witnesses of the great Quantity of Blood I had shed in my own Defence. My Wounds had been dressed while I continued in my Swoon; and the Faces of those Persons who were about me, expressed nothing of Unkindness.

After reflecting some time longer on my Situation, I called to a young Man, who sat near my Bed side, and intreated him to inform me, Where I was, and to whom I was a Prisoner? But could get no other Answer to those Questions, than a most civil Intreaty to compose myself, and not protract the Cure of my Wounds by talking, which, the Surgeons had declared, would be of a bad Consequence; and had therefore ordered me to be as little disturbed as possible.

Notwithstanding this Remonstrance, I repeated my Request,

promising to be entirely governed by them for the future in what regarded my Health, provided they would satisfy me in those Particulars: But my Attendant did not so much as reply to those Importunities; but, to prevent the Continuance of them, rose from his Seat, and retired to the other End of the Chamber.

I passed that Day, and several others, without being able to learn the Truth of my Condition: All this time, I was diligently waited on by the two Persons I had first seen, neither of whom I could prevail upon to inform me of what I desired to know; and, judging, by this obstinate Reserve, and the Manner of my Treatment, that there was some Mystery in the Case, I forbore to ask them any more Questions, conceiving they had particular Orders not to answer them.

The Care that was taken to forward my Cure, in Three Weeks entirely restored me to Health: I longed impatiently to know, what was to be my Destiny; and busied myself in conjecturing it, in vain; when, one Morning, an elderly Lady entered my Chamber, at whose Appearance my Two Attendants retired.

After she had saluted me very civilly, and inquired after my Health, she seated herself in a Chair near my Bedside, and spoke to me in this manner:

I make no question, Sir, but you are surprised at the Manner in which you have been treated, and the Care there has been taken to prevent discovering to you the Place where you now are; but you will doubtless be more surprised, to hear you are in the Fortress of ——, and in the House of Prince *Marcomire*, whose Party you fought against alone; and whom you so dangerously wounded, before you was taken Prisoner by his Men.

Is it possible, Madam, said I, who, from the first Moment of her Appearance, had been in a strange Perplexity, is it possible, I am in the House of a Man, whose Life I endeavoured so eagerly to destroy? And is it to him, who oppressed me so basely with Numbers, that I am obliged for the Succour I have received?

It is not to him, replied the Lady, that you are obliged for the favourable Treatment you have had; but listen to me patiently, and I will disclose the Truth of your Adventure.

Prince *Marcomire*, who was the Person that headed that Party against which you so valiantly defended yourself, after the Loss of the Battle, was hastening to throw himself into this Place, where his Sister, and many Ladies of Quality, had come for Security:

Your indiscreet Pursuit engaged you in the most unequal Combat
that ever was fought; and—

Nay, Sir, interrupted *Arabella*, though I do not refuse to give
you all the Praises your gallant Defence of yourself against Five
hundred Men deserves; yet I cannot agree with that Lady, in saying, it was the most unequal Combat that ever was fought: For, do
but reflect, I beseech you, upon that which the brave Prince of
Mauritania sustained against twice that Number of Men, with no
other Arms than his Sword; and, you having been in Battle that
Day, was, as I conceive, completely armed. The young Prince of
Egypt, accompanied only by the valiant, but indiscreet, *Cepio* his
Friend, engaged all the King of *Armenia*'s Guards, and put them all
to Flight. The courageous *Ariobasanes* scorned to turn his Back
upon a whole Army; not to mention the invincible *Artaban*, whom
a thousand Armies together could not have made to turn.[1]

Be pleased to observe, Madam, said Sir *George*, that to the end I
may faithfully recount my History, I am under a Necessity of
repeating Things, which, haply, may seem too advantageous for a
Man to say of himself: Therefore I indeed greatly approve of the
Custom, which, no doubt, this Inconveniency introduced, of a
'Squire, who is thoroughly instructed with the Secrets of his
Master's Heart, relating his Adventures, and giving a proper
Eulogium of his rare Valour, without being in Danger of offending
the Modesty of the renowned Knight; who, as you know, Madam,
upon those Occasions, commodiously slips away.

It being, however, this Lady's Opinion, that no Man ever undertook a more hazardous Combat, or with greater Odds, against him,
she did not fail to express her Admiration of it, in very high Terms.

The Noise of this Accident, pursued she, was soon spread over
the whole Town; and the beautiful *Sydimiris*, *Marcomire*'s Sister,
hearing that her Brother was wounded, as it was though to Death,
and that the Person who killed him, was taken Prisoner; she flew
out to meet her wounded Brother, distracted with Grief, and
vowing to have the severest Tortures executed on him, who had
thus barbarously murdered her Brother. Those who bore that unhappy Prince, having brought him into the House, his Wounds
were searched; and the Surgeons declared, they were very dangerous.

Sydimiris, hearing this, redoubled her Complaints and Vows of
Vengeance against you: Her Brother having then the chief Author-

ity in the Place, she commanded, in his Name, to have you brought
hither, and to be most strictly guarded; determined, if her Brother
died, to sacrifice you to his Ghost.

Full of these sanguinary Resolutions, she left his Chamber,
having seen him laid in Bed; and his Wounds dressed; but passing
along a Gallery to her own Apartment, she met the Persons who
were bringing you to the Room that was to be your Prison: You
was not, pursued the Lady, yet recovered from your Swoon, so
that they carried you like one that was dead: They had taken off
your Helmet to give you Air; by which means your Face being
quite uncovered, pale, languishing, and your Eyes closed, as if in
Death, presented the most moving, and, at the same time, most
pleasing Object in the World.

Sydimiris, who stopt, and for a Moment eagerly gazed upon you,
lost all of a sudden the Fierceness, which before had animated her
against you: And lifting up her Eyes to view those Men that carried
you;

Are you sure, said she to them, that this is the Person who
wounded my Brother?

Yes, Madam, replied one of them; this must be he, since there
was no other in his Company; and he alone sustained the Attack of
Five hundred Men; and would probably not have left one of them
alive, had not his Sword, by breaking, put it into our Power to take
him Prisoner.

Carry him away, said *Sydimiris*; but let his Wounds be dressed,
and let him be carefully looked to, that, if my Brother dies, he may
be punished as he deserves.

Pronouncing these Words in a low and faltering Voice, she
turned her Eyes a second time upon you; then, hastily averting her
Looks, she hurried to her own Chamber, and threw herself into a
Chair, with all the Marks of a very great Disturbance.

The Affection I have for her, being the Person who had brought
her up, and most favoured with her Confidence, made me behold
her in this Condition with great Concern; and supposing it was her
Brother that disquieted her, I besought her not to give way to the
Violence of her Grief, but to hope that Heaven would restore him
to her Prayers.

Alas! my dear *Urinoe*, said she, I am more culpable than you can
imagine; and I grieve less for the Condition to which I see *Marcomire* reduced, than for that Moderation wherewith I am con-

strained, spite of myself, to behold his Enemy.

Yes, dear *Urinoe*, pursued she, blushing, and casting down her Eyes, the Actions of this Unknown appear to me in quite another Light, since I have seen him; and, instead of looking upon him as the Murderer of my Brother, I cannot help admiring that rare Valour, with which he defended himself against so great a Number of Enemies; and am even ready to condemn the furious *Marcomire*, for oppressing so brave a Man.

As I had never approved of those violent Transports of Grief and Rage, which she had expressed upon the first News of her Brother's Misfortune; and as I looked upon your glorious Defence with the utmost Admiration; so, far from condemning the Change of her Thoughts, I confirmed her in the favourable Opinion she began to entertain of you; and, continuing to make Remarks upon all the Particulars of the Combat, which had come to our Knowlege, we found nothing in your Behaviour, but what increased our Admiration.

Sydimiris therefore, following the Dictates of her own Generosity, as well as my Advice, placed Two Persons about you, whose Fidelity we could rely on; and gave them Orders to treat you with all imaginable Care and Respect, but not to inform you of the Place in which you was, or to whom you was Prisoner.

In the mean time, *Marcomire*, whose Wounds had been again examined, was declared out of Danger by the Surgeons; and he having understood the Excess of his Sister's Grief, and the Revenge she had vowed against you, gave her Thanks for those Expressions of her Tenderness; and also uttered some Threats, which intimated a violent Hatred against you; and a Design of prosecuting his Revenge upon you, as soon as he was in a Condition to leave his Chamber.

Sydimiris, who heard him, could with Difficulty dissemble her Concern.

Ah! *Urinoe*, said she to me, when we were alone; 'tis now, that I more than ever repent of that Excess of Rage, which transported me against the brave Unknown. I have thereby put him intirely into my Brother's Power, and shall be haply accessary to that Death he is meditating for him, or else a perpetual Imprisonment.

This Reflection gave her so much Pain, that I could not choose but pity her; and considering, that the only way to preserve you, was for her to dissemble a Rage equal to *Marcomire*'s against you, in

order to prevent being suspected of any Design in your Favour, I
persuaded her to join with him in every thing he said; while, in the
mean time, we would endeavour to get you cured of your Wounds,
that you might at least be in a Condition once more to defend yourself with that miraculous Valour Heaven has bestowed on you.

Sydimiris perceiving her Brother would soon be in a Condition
to execute his Threats, resolved to hazard every thing, rather than
to expose you to his Rage: She therefore communicated to me her
Design of giving you Liberty, and, by presenting a sufficient
Reward to your Guard, inducing them to favour your Escape.

I undertook to manage this Business in her Name, and have done
it so effectually, that you will this Night be at Liberty, and may
depart the Town immediately, in which it will be dangerous to stay
any time, for fear of being discovered.

Sydimiris forbad me to let you know the Person to whom you
would be obliged for your Freedom; but I could not endure, that
you should unjustly involve the Sister of *Marcomire*, in that Resentment you will questionless always preserve against *him*; and to keep
you from being innocently guilty of Ingratitude, I resolved to
acquaint you with the Nature of those Obligations you owe to her.

CHAPTER IV

The Adventure continued

Ah! Madam, said I, perceiving she had finished her Discourse,
doubt not but I shall most gratefully preserve the Remembrance of
what the generous *Sydimiris* has done for me; and shall always be
ready to lose that Life in her Defence, which she has had the superlative Goodness to take so much Care of. But, Madam, pursued I,
with an earnest Look, do not, I beseech you, refuse me one Favour,
without which I shall depart with inconceivable Sorrow.

Depend upon it, valiant Sir, replied she, that if what you will
require of me, be in my Power, and fit for me to grant, I shall very
willingly oblige you.

It is then, resumed I, trembling at the Boldness of my Request,
that you would condescend to intreat the most generous *Sydimiris*
to favour me with an Interview, and give me an Opportunity of

throwing myself at her Feet, to thank her for all those Favours I have received from her Compassion.

I cannot promise you, replied the Lady, rising, to prevail upon *Sydimiris* to grant you an Audience; but I assure you, that I will endeavour to dispose her to do you this Favour; and it shall not be my Fault, if you are not satisfied.

Saying this, she went out of my Chamber, I having followed her to the Door, with Protestations that I would never forget her Kindness upon this Occasion.

I past the rest of that Day in an anxious Impatience for Night, divided between Fear and Hope, and more taken up with the Thoughts of seeing *Sydimiris*, than with my expected Liberty.

Night came at last, and the Door of my Apartment opening, I saw the Lady who had been with me in the Morning, enter.

I have prevailed upon *Sydimiris* to see you, said she; and she is willing, at my Intreaty, to grant that Favour to a Person, who, she with Reason thinks, has been inhumanly treated by her Brother.

Then, giving me her Hand, she conducted me along a large Gallery, to a stately Apartment; and after traversing several Rooms, she led me into one, where *Sydimiris* herself was: Who, as soon as she perceived me, rose from her Seat, and received me with great Civility.

In the Transport I then was, I know not how I returned the graceful Salute the incomparable *Sydimiris* gave me; for most certain it is, that I was so lost in Wonder, at the Sight of the many Charms I beheld in her Person, that I could not unlock my Tongue, or remove my Eyes from her inchanting Face; but remained fixed in a Posture, which at once expressed my Admiration and Delight.

To give you a Description of that Beauty which I then contemplated, I must inform you, Madam, that *Sydimiris* is tall, of a handsome Stature, and admirably proportioned; her Hair was of the finest Black in the World; her Complexion marvelously fair; and all the Lineaments of her Visage were perfectly beautiful; and her Eyes, which were large and black, sparkled with so quick and piercing a Fire, that no Heart was able to resist their powerful Glances: Moreover, *Sydimiris* is admirably shaped; her Port is high and noble; and her Air so free, yet so commanding, that there are few Persons in the World, with whom she may not dispute the Priority of Beauty.[1] In fine, Madam, *Sydimiris* appeared with so many Advantages, to a Spirit prepossessed already with the most

grateful Sense of her Favours, that I could not resist the sweet
Violence wherewith her Charms took Possession of my Heart: I
yielded therefore, without Reluctance, to my Destiny, and resigned
myself, in an Instant, to those Fetters, which the Sight of the
Divine *Sydimiris* prepared for me: Recovering therefore a little
from that Admiration, which had so totally ingrossed all my
Faculties, I threw myself at her Feet, with an Action wholly composed of Transport.

Divine *Sydimiris*, said I, beholding her with Eyes, in which the
Letters of my new-born Passion might very plainly be read, see at
your Feet a Man devoted to your Service, by all the Ties of Gratitude and Respect. I come, Madam, to declare to you, that from the
First Moment you gave me Liberty, I had devoted that and my
Life to you; and at your Feet I confirm the Gift; protesting by all
that is most dear and sacred to me, that since I hold my Life from
the Divine *Sydimiris*, she alone shall have the absolute Disposal of
it for the future; and should she please again to demand it, either to
appease her Brother's Fury, or to sacrifice it to her own Security, I
will most faithfully perform her Will, and shed the last Drop of that
Blood at her Command, which I would with Transport lose in her
Defence.

A fine high-flown Speech indeed! said Sir *Charles*, laughing; but
I hope you did not intend to keep your Word.

Sure, Sir, replied *Arabella*, you do not imagine, that Sir *George*
would have failed in executing all he had promised to the beautiful
and generous *Sydimiris*: What could he possibly have said less?
And indeed what less could she have expected from a Man, whom
at the Hazard of her own Life and Happiness, she had given
Freedom to?

I accompanied these Words, Madam, pursued Sir *George*, with
so passionate a Look and Accent, that the fair *Sydimiris* blushed,
and, for a Moment, cast down her Eyes with a visible Confusion.
At last,

Sir, replied she, I am too well satisfied with what I have done,
with respect to your Safety, to require any Proofs of your Gratitude,
that might be dangerous to it; and shall remain extremely well
satisfied, if the Obligations you think you owe me, may induce you
to moderate your Resentment against my Brother, for the cruel
Treatment you received from him.

Doubt not, Madam, interrupted I, eagerly, but I shall, in the

Person of *Marcomire*, regard the Brother of the divine *Sydimiris*; and that Consideration will be sufficient, not only to make me forget all the Violences he committed against me, but even to defend his Life, if need be, with the Hazard of my own.

Excessively generous indeed! said Sir *Charles*: I never heard any thing like it.

Oh! dear, Sir, replied *Arabella*, there are numberless Instances of equal, and even superior Generosity, to be met with in the Lives of the Heroes of Antiquity: You will there see a Lover, whose Mistress has been taken from him, either by Treachery or Force, venture his Life in Defence of the injurious Husband who possesses her; and though all his Felicity depends upon his Death, yet he will rescue him from it, at the Expence of the greater Part of his Blood.[1]

Another, who after a long and bloody War, has, by taking his Enemy Prisoner, an Opportunity of terminating it honourably; yet, thro' an heroick Principle of Generosity, he gives his Captive Liberty, without making any Conditions, and has all his Work to do over again.[2]

A Third, having contracted a violent Friendship with the Enemies of his Country, through the same generous Sentiments, draws his Sword in their Defence, and makes no Scruple to fight against any Army, where the King his Father is in Person.[3]

I must confess, said Sir *Charles*, that Generosity seems to me very peculiar, that will make a Man fight for his Enemies against his own Father.

It is in that Peculiarity, Sir, said *Arabella*, that his Generosity consists; for certainly there is nothing extraordinary in fighting for one's Father, and one's Country; but when a Man has arrived to such a Pitch of Greatness of Soul, as to neglect those mean and selfish Considerations, and, loving Virtue in the Persons of his Enemies, can prefer their Glory before his own particular Interest, he is then a perfect Hero indeed: Such a one was *Oroondates*, *Artaxerxes*, and many others I could name, who all gave eminent Proofs of their Disinterestedness and Greatness of Soul, upon the like Occasions: Therefore, not to detract from Sir *George*'s Merit, I must still insist, that in the Resolutions he had taken to defend his Enemy's Life at the Expence of his own, he did no more, than what any Man of ordinary Generosity ought to do, and what he was particularly obliged to, by what the amiable *Sydimiris* had done for him.

I was so happy, however, Madam, continued Sir *George*, to find that those Expressions of my Gratitude wrought somewhat upon the Heart of the lovely *Sydimiris* in my Favour: Her Words discovered as much, and her Eyes spoke yet more intelligibly; but our Conversation was interrupted by the discreet *Urinoe*, who, fearing the Consequence of so long a Stay in her Chamber, represented to me, that it was time to take my Leave.

I turned pale at this cruel Sound; and, beholding *Sydimiris* with a languishing Look,

Would to Heaven, Madam, said I, that instead of giving me Liberty, you would keep me eternally your Prisoner; for though a Dungeon was to be the Place of my Confinement, yet if it was near you, it would seem a Palace to me; for indeed I am no longer in a Condition to relish that Freedom you bestow upon me, since it must remove me farther from you: But I beseech you, Madam, to believe, that in delivering me from your Brother's Fetters, you have cast me into your own, and that I am more a Prisoner than ever, but a Prisoner to so lovely a Conqueror, that I do not wish to break my Chains, and prefer the sweet and glorious Captivity I am in, to all the Crowns in the World.

You are very bold, said *Sydimiris*, blushing, to entertain me with such Discourse; yet I pardon this Offence, in Consideration of what you have suffered from my Brother, and on Condition that you will depart immediately, without speaking another Word.

Sydimiris spoke this so earnestly, that I durst not disobey her; and, kissing the Hem of her Robe, with a passionate Air, I left her Chamber, conducted by *Urinoe*; who having brought me to a private Door, which carried us into the Street, I there found a Man waiting for me, whom I knew to be the same that had attended me during my Stay in that House.

Urinoe having recommended to him to see me safe out of the Town, I took Leave of her, with the most grateful Acknowlegements for her Kindness; and followed my Conductor, so oppressed with Grief at the Thoughts of leaving the Place where *Sydimiris* was, that I had hardly Strength to walk.

CHAPTER V

An extraordinary Instance of Generosity in a Lover,
somewhat resembling that of the great Artaxerxes, *in*
Cassandra[1]

THE farther I went, continued Sir *George*, the more my Regret
increased; and, finding it would be impossible to live, and quit the
Divine *Sydimiris*, I all at once took a Resolution to remain in the
Town concealed; and, communicating my Design to my Guide, I
engaged him to assist me in it, by a Present of a considerable Sum,
which he could not resist: Accordingly he left me in a remote Part
of the Town, and went to find out a convenient Lodging for me;
which he soon procured, and also a Suit of Cloaths to disguise me,
my own being very rich and magnificent.

Having recommended me as a Relation of his, who was newly
arrived, I was received very civilly by the People with whom he
placed me; and, finding this young Man to be very witty and discreet, and also very capable of serving me, I communicated to him
my Intentions by staying, which were only to be near the Divine
Sydimiris, and to have the Happiness of sometimes seeing her,
when she went abroad.

This Man entering into my Meaning, assured me, he would
faithfully keep my Secret; and that he would not fail to bring me
Intelligence of all that passed in the Palace of *Marcomire*.

I could with Difficulty keep myself from falling at his Feet, to
express my Sense of his kind and generous Offers; but I contented
myself with presenting him another Sum of Money, larger than the
first, and assured him of my future Gratitude.

He then took Leave, and left me to my Reflections, which were
wholly upon the Image of the Divine *Sydimiris*, and the Happiness
of being so near the Object I adored.

My Confident came to me the next Day; but brought me no other
News, than that my Escape was not yet known to *Marcomire*. I
inquired if he had seen *Sydimiris*; but he replied he had not, and
that *Urinoe* had only asked him, if he had conducted me safe out of
Town: To which he had answered as we had agreed, that I had got
out safe and undiscovered.

A Day or two after, he brought me News more pleasing; for he
told me, that *Sydimiris* had sent for him into her Chamber, and

asked him several Questions concerning me: That she appeared very melancholy, and even blushed, whenever she mentioned my Name.

This Account gave sufficient Matter for my Thoughts to work upon for several Days. I interpreted *Sydimiris*'s Blush a Thousand different Ways; I reflected upon all the different Causes to which it might be owing, and busied myself with all those innumerable Conjectures, which, as you know, Madam, such an Incident always gives Rise to in a Lover's Imagination. At length I explained it to my own Advantage, and felt thereby a considerable Increase of my Affection.

A whole Week having elapsed, without another Sight of my Confidant, I began to be greatly alarmed; when, on the Eighth Day of this cruel Suspense, I saw him appear; but with so many Marks of Disturbance in his Face, that I trembled to hear what he had to acquaint me with.

Oh! Sir, said he, as soon as his Concern suffered him to speak, *Marcomire* has discovered your Escape, and the Means by which it was procured: One of those in whom *Urinoe* confided, has betrayed it to him; and the beauteous *Sydimiris* is likely to feel the most terrible Effects of his Displeasure: He has confined her to her Chamber, and vows to sacrifice her Life to the Honour of his Family; which he says, she has stained; and he loads that admirable Lady with so many Reproaches, that it is thought, her Grief for such undeserved Calumnies will occasion her Death.

Scarce had he finished these cruel Words, when I, who all the time he had been speaking, beheld him with a dying Eye, sunk down at his Feet in a Swoon; which continued so long, that he began to think me quite dead: However I at last opened my Eyes; but it was only to pour forth a River of Tears, and to utter Complaints, which might have moved the most obdurate Heart.

After having a long time tormented myself in weeping and complaining, I at last took a Resolution, which offered me some Alleviation of my Grief; and the faithful *Toxares*, seeing me a little composed, left me to myself, with a Promise to return soon, and acquaint me with what passed further in the Palace of *Marcomire*.

As soon as he was gone, I rose from my Bed; and, dressing myself in those Cloaths I wore when I was taken Prisoner, I went to the Palace of *Marcomire*; and, demanding to see him, I was told he was in the Apartment of *Sydimiris*; and, at my earnest Desire, they conducted me thither.

When I entered the Room, I beheld that incomparable Beauty stretched upon a Couch, dissolved in Tears; and *Urinoe* upon her Knees, before her, accompanying with her own, those precious Drops which fell from the bright Eyes of her Mistress.

Marcomire, who was walking furiously about the Room, exclaiming with the utmost Violence against that fair Sufferer, did not observe my Entrance; so that I had an Opportunity of going towards *Sydimiris*, who, lifting up her Eyes to look upon me, gave a loud Shriek; and, by a Look of extreme Anguish, let me understand, how great her Apprehensions were upon my Account.

I am come, Madam, said I, to perform Part of the Promise I made you, and by dying, to prove your Innocence; and, freeing you from the Reproaches you suffer on my Account, I shall have the Happiness to convince you, that my Life is infinitely less dear to me, than your Tranquillity. *Sydimiris*, who hearkened to me with great Emotion, was going to make some Answer, when *Marcomire*, alarmed by his Sister's Shriek, came towards us, and, viewing me at first with Astonishment, and then with a Smile of Cruelty and Revenge,

Is it possible, said he, that I behold my designed Murderer again in my Power?

I am in thy Power, said I, because I am willing to be so; and came voluntarily to put myself into your Hands, to free that excellent Lady from the Imputation you have laid on her: Know, *Marcomire*, that it is to myself alone I owed my Liberty, which I would still preserve against all the Forces thou couldst bring to deprive me of it; and this Sword, which left thee Life enough to threaten mine, would haply once more put yours in Danger, were I not restrained by a powerful Consideration, which leaves me not the Liberty of even wishing you ill.

Ah! Dissembler, said *Marcomire*, in a Rage, think not to impose upon me by thy counterfeited Mildness: Thou art my Prisoner once more, and I shall take care to prevent your escaping a Second time.

I am not your Prisoner, replied I, while I possess this Sword, which has already defended me against greater Numbers than you have here to oppose me; but, continued I, throwing down my Sword at *Sydimiris*'s Feet, I resign my Liberty to restore that Lady to your good Opinion, and to free her from those base Aspersions thou hast unjustly loaded her with, upon my Account.

It matters not, said the brutal Brother, taking up my Sword, whether thou hast resigned, or I have deprived thee of Liberty; but since thou art in my Power, thou shall feel all the Effects of my Resentment: Take him away, pursued he to some of his People; put him into the worst Dungeon you can find; and let him be guarded carefully, upon Pain of Death, if he again escapes.

With these Words, several Men offered to lead me out of the Room; but I repulsed them with Disdain; and, making a low Reverence to *Sydimiris*, whose Countenance expressed the Extremes of Fear and Anguish, I followed my Conductors to the Prison allotted for me; which, hideous as it was, I contemplated with a secret Pleasure, since I had by that Action, which had brought me into it, given a Testimony of my Love for the adorable *Sydimiris*.

CHAPTER VI

In which it will be seen, that the Lady is as generous as her Lover[1]

I Passed some Days in this Confinement, melancholy enough: My Ignorance of the Destiny of *Sydimiris* gave me more Pain than the Sense of my own Misfortunes; and one Evening, when I was more than usually disquieted, one of my Guard entered my Prison, and, giving me a Letter, retired, without speaking a Word: I opened this Letter with Precipitation, and, by the Light of a Lamp which was allowed me, I read the following Words.

Sydimiris, *To the most generous* Bellmour.

I t is not enough to tell you, that the Method you took to free me from my Brother's Severity, has filled me with the utmost Esteem and Admiration. So generous an Action merits a greater Acknowlegement, and I will make no Scruple to confess, that my Heart is most sensibly touched by it: Yes, *Bellmour*, I have received this glorious Testimony of your Affection with such a Gratitude, as you yourself could have wished to inspire me with; and it shall not be

long, before you will have a convincing Proof of the Effect it has
had upon the Spirit of

Sydimiris.

This Letter, Madam, pursued Sir *George*, being wholly calculated to make me hope that I was not hated by the Divine *Sydimiris*;
and that she meditated something in my Favour; I resigned myself
up to the most delightful Expectations.

What! cried I, transported with the Excess of my Joy: Does the
most admirable *Sydimiris* condescend to assure me, that I have
touched her Heart? And does she promise me, that I shall receive
some convincing Proof of her Acknowlegement?

Ah! too happy, and too fortunate *Bellmour*, to what a glorious
Destiny hast thou been reserved! And how oughtest thou to adore
these Fetters, that have procured thee the Esteem of the Divine
Sydimiris!—

Such, Madam, were the Apprehensions, which the Billet I had
received inspired me with. I continually flattered myself with the
most pleasing Hopes; and during Three Weeks longer, in which I
heard no more from *Sydimiris*, my Imagination, was wholly filled
with those sweet Thoughts, which her Letter had made me entertain.

At length, on the Evening of a Day which I had wholly spent in
reading over *Sydimiris*'s Letter; and interpreting the Sense of it a
thousand different Ways, but all agreeable to my ardent Wishes; I
saw the sage *Urinoe* enter my Prison, accompanied by *Toxares*,
whom I had not seen during my last Confinement. Wholly transported at the Sight of these Two Friends, and not doubting but
they had brought me the most agreeable News, I ran towards them;
and, throwing myself at *Urinoe*'s Feet, I begged her, in an Ecstacy
of Joy, to acquaint me with *Sydimiris*'s Commands.

Urinoe, in some Confusion at this Action, intreated me to rise.
'Tis fit, cried I, in a Transport I could not master, that in this
Posture I should receive the Knowlege of that Felicity *Sydimiris*
has had the Goodness to promise me. *Urinoe* sighed at these Words;
and, beholding me with a Look of Compassion and Tenderness,

Would to God, said she, that all I have to say, were as agreeable,
as the first News I have to tell you; which is, that you are free, and at
Liberty to leave the Town this Moment! *Sydimiris*, continued she,
has bought your Freedom, at the Expence of her own; and, to
deliver you from her Brother's Chains, she has put on others, haply

more cruel than those you have worn: In fine, she has married a Man, whom she detested, to procure your Liberty; her Brother having granted it to her upon that Condition alone.

Scarce had *Urinoe* finished these Words, when I fell, without Sense or Motion, at her Feet. *Toxares* and she, who had foreseen what might happen, having provided themselves with Cordials necessary to restore me, brought me to myself with infinite Trouble.

Cruel! said I to them, with a Tone and Look, which witnessed the Excess of my Despair, Why have you hindered me from dying, at once to prevent the thousand Deaths I shall suffer from my Grief? Is this the Confirmation of those glorious Hopes *Sydimiris* had permitted me to entertain? Is this that Proof of the Acknowlegements I was to expect? And is it by throwing herself into the Arms of my Rival, that she repays those Obligations she thinks she owes me?

Ah! inhuman *Sydimiris!* was it to make my Despair more poignant, that thou flatterest me with such a Prospect of Happiness? And was it necessary, to the Grandeur of thy Nuptials, that me Life should be the Sacrifice?

But, how unjust am I, cried I, repenting in an Instant of those injurious Suspicions; How unjust am I, to accuse the Divine *Sydimiris* of Inhumanity? Was it not to give me Freedom, that she bestowed herself upon a Man she hates? And has she not made herself miserable for ever, to procure me a fansied Happiness?

Ah! if it be so, what a Wretch am I? I, who have been the only Cause of that Misery, to which she has doomed herself? Ah! Liberty! pursued I, how I detest thee, since purchased by the Misfortune of *Sydimiris!* And how far more sweet and glorious were those Chains, which I wore for her sake!

My Sighs and Tears leaving me no longer the Power of Speech, I sunk down on my Bed, oppress'd with a mortal Grief.

Urinoe and *Toxares* drew near to comfort me, and said all that sensible and discreet Persons could think of to alleviate my Despair.

Though I have heard that *Sydimiris* is married, replied I, without dying immediately; yet do not imagine, that I will suffer this odious Life to continue long. If Sorrow do not quickly dispatch me, I will seek Death by other Means; for since *Sydimiris* is lost, I have no more Business in the World.

The charitable *Urinoe* and *Toxares* endeavoured in vain to divert me from this sad Resolution, when *Urinoe*, finding all their Reasonings ineffectual, drew a Letter out of her Pocket, and, presenting it to me, I had Orders, said she, not to let this Letter be delivered to you, till you had left the Town; but the Despair, to which I see you reduced, does, I conceive, dispense with my rigorous Observation of those Directions.

While *Urinoe* was speaking, I opened this Letter trembling, and found it as follows.

CHAPTER VII

Containing an Incident full as probable as any in Scudery's *Romances*

Sydimiris, *To* Bellmour.

I F that Proof of my Gratitude, which I promised to give you, fall short of your Expectations; blame not the Defect of my Will, but the Rigour of my Destiny: It was by this only Way I could give you Liberty; nor is it too dearly bought by the Loss of all my Happiness, if you receive it as you ought: Had I been allowed to follow my own Inclinations, there is no Man in the World I would have preferred to yourself. I owe this Confession to the Remembrance of your Affection, of which you gave me so generous an Instance; and the Use I expect you will make of it, is, to console you under a Misfortune, which is common to us both; though I haply have most Reason to complain, since I could not be just to you, without being cruel at the same time, or confer a Benefit, without loading you with a Misfortune. If the Sacrifice I have made of myself for your sake, gives me any Claim to the Continuance of your Love, I command you, by the Power it gives me over you, to live, and not add to the Miseries of my Condition, the Grief of being the Cause of your Death. Remember, I will look upon your Disobedience, as an Act of the most cruel Ingratitude; and your Compliance with this Request shall ever be esteemed, as the dearest Mark you can give of that Passion you have borne to the unfortunate

Sydimiris.

Ah! *Sydimiris*, cried I, having read this Letter, more cruel in your Kindness than Severity! After having deprived me of yourself, do you forbid me to die; and expose me by so rigorous a Command to Ills infinitely more hard and painful than Death?

Yes, pursued I, after a little Pause; yes, *Sydimiris*, thou shalt be obeyed; we will not dye, since thou hast commanded us to live; and, notwithstanding the Tortures to which thou condemnest us, we will obey this Command; and give thee a glorious Proof of our present Submission, by enduring that Life, which the Loss of thee has rendered truly wretched.

Urinoe and *Toxares*, somewhat reassured, by the Resolution I had taken, exhorted me by all the Persuasions, Friendship could put in their Mouths, to persevere in it; and, *Urinoe* bidding me Farewel, I endeavoured to prevail upon her to procure me a Sight of *Sydimiris* once more, or at least to bear a Letter from me to her; but she refused both these Requests so obstinately, telling me, *Sydimiris* would neither consent to the one nor the other, that I was obliged to be contented with the Promise she made me, to represent my Affliction in a true Light to her Mistress; and to assure her, that nothing but her absolute Commands could have hindered me from dying. Then, taking leave of me with much Tenderness, she went out of the Prison, leaving *Toxares* with me, who assisted me to dress, and conducted me out of that miserable Place, where I had passed so many sad, and also joyful Hours. At a Gate to which he brought me, I found a Horse waiting; and, having embraced this faithful Confidant, with many Expressions of Gratitude, I bestowed a Ring of some Value upon him to remember me by; and, mounting my Horse, with a breaking Heart, I took the first Road which presented itself to my Eyes, and galloped away, without knowing whither I went. I rode the whole Night, so totally engrossed by my Despair, that I did not perceive my Horse was so tired, it could hardly carry me a Step farther: At last the poor Beast fell down under me, so that I was obliged to dismount; and, looking about me, perceived I was in a Forest, without seeing the least Appearance of any Habitation.

The Wildness, and Solitude of the Place, flattered my Despair, and while my Horse was feeding upon what Grass he could find, I wandered about: The Morning just breaking, gave me Light enough to direct my Steps. Chance at last conducted me to a Cave, which seemed to have been the Residence of some Hermit, or unfortunate Lover like myself. It was dug at the Side of a Rock, the Entrance to it thick set with Bushes, which hid it from View. I descended by a few Steps cut rudely enough, and was convinced, it had formerly served for a Habitation for some religious or melancholy Person; for there were Seats of Turf raised on each Side of it, a kind of Bed composed of dried Leaves and Rushes, and a Hole made artificially at the Top, to admit the Light.[1]

While I considered this Place attentively, I all at once took up a Resolution, inspired by my Despair; which was, to continue there, and indulge my Melancholy in a Retirement so fitted for my Purpose.

Giving my Horse therefore Liberty to go where he pleased, and hanging up my Arms upon a Tree near my Cave, I took Possession of this solitary Mansion, with a gloomy Kind of Satisfaction, and devoted all my Hours to the Contemplation of my Misfortunes.

I lived in this manner, Madam, for Ten Months, without feeling the least Desire to change my Habitation; and, during all that time, no Mortal approached my Solitude, so that I lived perfectly secure and undiscovered.

Sir *George* pausing here to take Breath, the old Baronet said what will be found in the following Chapter.

CHAPTER VIII

A single Combat fought with prodigious Valour, and described with amazing Accuracy

GIVE me Leave, Sir, said Sir *Charles*, to ask, If you eat in all this Time?

Alas! Sir, replied Sir *George*, Sighs and Tears were all my Sustenance.

Sir *Charles*, Mr. *Glanville*, and Miss, laughing at this Answer, *Arabella* seemed greatly confused:

It is not to be imagined, said she, that Sir *George*; or, to say better, Prince *Viridomer*, lived Ten Months without eating any thing to support Nature; but such trifling Circumstances are always left out, in the Relations of Histories; and truly an Audience must be very dull and unapprehensive, that cannot conceive, without being told, that a Man must necessarily eat in the Space of Ten Months.

But the Food Sir *George* lived on, replied the Baronet, was very unsubstantial, and would not afford him much Nourishment.

I suppose, resumed *Arabella*, he lived upon such Provisions as the Forest afforded him; such as wild Fruits, Herbs, bitter Sallads, and the like; which, considering the Melancholy that possessed him, would appear a voluptuous Repast; and which the unfortunate *Orontes*, when he was in the same Situation, thought infinitely too good for him.

Sir *Charles*, finding *Arabella* took no Notice of the Historian's Hyperbole of living upon his Sighs and Tears, passed it over, for fear of offending her; and Sir *George*, who had been in some Anxiety how to bring himself off, when he perceived *Arabella* was reasonable enough to suppose he must have eat during his Abode in the Forest, went on with his Relation in this Manner.

I lived, as I before observed to you, Madam, in this Cave for Ten Months; and truly I was so reconciled to that solitary way of Life, and found so much Sweetness in it, that I believe, I should have remained there till this Day, but for the Adventure which I am going to recount.

It being my Custom to walk out every Evening in the Forest; returning to my Cave, something later then usual, I heard the Cries of a Woman at some Distance, who seemed to be in Distress: I stopped to listen from what Side those Cries proceeded; and, perceiving they seemed to approach nearer to me, I took down my Armour from the Tree where I had hung it; and hastily arming myself, shaped my Course towards the Place from whence those Complaints seemed to come, resolving to assist that unknown Person with all the Strength that was left me.

Having gone some Paces, I spied through the Branches of the Trees a Man on Horseback with a Lady, who struggled to get loose, and at times calling aloud for Succour.

This Sight inflaming me with Rage against that impious Ravisher; I flew towards him: And when I came within hearing;

Hold, Wretch! cried I, and cease to offer Violence to that Lady, whom thou bearest away by Force; or prepare to defend thyself against one, who will die, before he will suffer thee to prosecute thy unjust Designs.

The Man, without answering me, clapped Spurs to his Horse;

and it would have been impossible to have overtaken him, had not my own Horse, which had never quitted the Forest, appeared in my View: I quickly mounted him, and followed the Track the Ravisher had taken, with such Speed, that I came up with him in a Moment.

Caitiff! said I, release the Lady, and defend thyself. These Words, which I accompanied with a thundering Blow upon his Head-piece, obliged him to set down the Lady, who implored Heaven, with the utmost Ardour, to grant me the Victory: And, recoiling back a few Paces, to take a View of me,

I know not, said he, for what Reason thou settest thyself to oppose my Designs; but I well know, that thou shalt dearly repent of thy Temerity.

Saying this, he advanced furiously towards me, and aimed so heavy a Blow at my Head, that, had I not received it on my Shield, I might haply have no longer been in a Condition to defend the distressed Lady: But, having, with the greatest Dexterity imaginable, avoided this Blow, I made at him with so much Fierceness, and directed my Aims so well, that in a few Moments I wounded him in several Places; and his Arms were all dyed with his Blood.

This good Success redoubled my Vigour; and having, by a lucky Stroke with my Sword, cut the Strings of his Head-piece, it fell off: And his Head being bare, I was going to let fall a dreadful Blow upon it, which doubtless would have shivered it in a thousand Pieces, when he cried out for Quarter, and, letting fall his Sword, by that Action assured me my Victory was intire.

Live Wretch, cried I, since thou art base enough to value Life after being vanquished; but swear upon my Sword, that thou wilt never more attempt the Liberty of that Lady.

While I was speaking, I perceived he was no longer able to sit his Horse: But, staggering a Moment, he fell off, and lay extended without Motion upon the Ground. Touched with Compassion at this Sight, I alighted, and, supposing him to be in a Swoon, was preparing to give him some Assistance; but, upon my nearer Approach, I found he was quite dead.

Leaving therefore this mournful Object, I turned about, with an Intention to go and offer the distressed Lady my further Help; but I perceived her already at my Feet.

Valiant Knight, said she, with a Tone of Voice so bewitching, that all my Faculties were suspended, as by Inchantment, suffer

me, on my Knees, to thank you, for the Deliverance you have procured me from that base Man; since to your admirable Valour I
owe not only the Preservation of my Life; but, what is infinitely
dearer to me, my Honour.

The Astonishment, wherewith I beheld the miraculous Beauty
that appeared before me, kept me a Moment in such an attentive
Gaze, that I forgot she was at my Feet: Recollecting myself, however, with some Confusion at my Neglect,

Oh! rise, Madam, cried I, helping her up with infinite Respect,
and debase not such Perfection to a Posture, in which all the
Monarchs on the Earth might glory to appear before it.

That you may the better conceive the Alteration which the Sight
of this fair Unknown produced in my Soul, I will endeavour, to
give you a Description of her Beauty, which was altogether
miraculous.

CHAPTER IX

*In which the Reader will find a Description of a Beauty, in a
Style truly sublime*

THE new-fallen Snow, pursued Sir *George*, was tanned, in Comparison of the refined Purity of that White which made up the
Ground of her Complexion; and, though Fear had a little gathered
the Carnations of her Cheeks, yet her joy at being delivered seemed
to plant them there with such fresh Advantages, that my Eye might
shrink at the Brightness of that mingled Lustre: Her Mouth, as
well for Shape as Colour, might shame the Imitation of the best
Pencils, and the liveliest Tints; and though through some petty
Intervals of Joy, it wanted the Smiles, which Grief and Terror
sequestred, yet she never opened it, but like the East, at the Birth
of a beautiful Day, and then discovered Treasures, whose excelling
Whiteness made the Price inestimable: All the Features of her
Face had so near a Kindred to Proportion and Symmetry, as the
several Masters of *Apelles*'s Art might have called it his Glory to
have copied Beauties from her, as the best of Models: The Circum-
ference of her Visage shewed the Extremes of an imperfect Circle,
and almost formed it to a perfect Oval: And this Abridgment of

Marvels was tapered by a Pair of the brightest Stars, that ever were lighted up by the Hand of Nature: As their Colour was the same with the Heavens, there was a spherical Harmony in their Motion; and that mingled with a Vivacity so penetrating, as neither the firmest Eye, nor the strongest Soul, could arm themselves with a Resistance of Proof against those pointed Glories: Her Head was crowned with a prodigious Quantity of fair long Hair, which Colour as fitly suited the Beauty of her Eyes, as Imagination could make it: To these Marvels of Face were joined the rest of her Neck, Hands, and Shape; and there seemed a Contest between the Form and Whiteness of the two former, which had the largest Commission from Nature to work Wonders.

In fine, her Beauty was miraculous, and could not fail of producing a sudden Effect upon a Heart like mine.

Having passed in an Instant from the extremest Admiration, to something yet more tender, I reiterated my Offers of Service to the fair Unknown; who told me, she feared her Father had Occasion for some Assistance, her Ravisher having left his Men to engage him, and keep off his Pursuit, while he rode off with his Prize: Hereupon I begg'd her to direct me to the Place where she left her Father, assuring her I would gladly venture my Life a Second time, to preserve his; and she desiring to go with me, I placed her before me on my Horse, and had the exquisite Pleasure of supporting with my Arms the fairest and most admirable Creature in the World.

In less than half an Hour, which had appeared to me but a Moment, we got to the Place where she had been torn from her Father; whom we beheld with three of his Servants, maintaining a Fight against twice as many of their Enemies.

Having gently set down the beauteous Unknown upon the Grass, I flew to the Relief of her Father; and, throwing myself furiously among his Assailants, dispatched two of them with so many Blows: The others, seeing so unexpected an Assistance, gave back a little; and I took Advantage of their Consternation, to redouble my Blows, and brought Two more of them at my Feet.

There remained now but Four to overcome; and my Arrival having given new Vigour to those whose Part I had taken, they seconded me so well, that we soon had nothing more left to do; for the rest, seeing their Comrades slain, sought their Safety in Flight: We were too generous to pursue them, the Blood of such Wretches being unworthy to be shed by our Swords.

The fair Unknown, seeing us Conquerors, flew to embrace her Father; who, holding her pressed between his Arms, turned his Eyes upon me; then quitting her, came towards me, and, in the most obliging Terms imaginable, returned me Thanks for the Assistance I had brought him; and being informed by his Daughter, of what I had done for her Preservation, this old Gentleman renewed his Acknowlegements, calling me the Preserver of his Life, the valiant Defender of his Daughter's Honour, his tutelary Angel, and the Guardian of his House.

In fine, he loaded me with so many Thanks and Praises, that I could not choose but be in some Confusion; and, to put an End to them, I begged he would inform me, by what means he came into that Misfortune.

He told me, that, residing in a Castle at the Extremity of this Forest, the Charms of his Daughter had captivated a neighbouring Lord, whose Character and Person being disagreeable both to her and himself, he had absolutely refused to give her to him: Thereupon he had set upon them as they were going to visit a Relation at some Distance, and, dragging *Philonice* out of the Coach, put her before him on his Horse, and carried her away, leaving Eight of his Men to engage him, and his Servants; who, being but Four in Number, must inevitably have perished, had I not come to his Relief, and, by my miraculous Valour, vanquished all his Enemies.

Saying this, he desired me to go home with him to the Castle; and having led his Daughter to the Coach, insisted upon my placing myself next her; and, getting in himself, ordered them to return home.

This Accident having altered his Design of making the Visit which had been the Occasion of this Journey;

The Baron, for that I found was his Title, entertained me, all the Way, with repeated Expressions of Acknowlegements and Tenderness; and the incomparable *Philonice* condescended also to assure me of her Gratitude for the Service I had done her.

At our Arrival at the Castle, I perceived it was very large and magnificent: The Baron conducted me to one of the best Apartments, and would stay in the Room till my Armour was taken off, that he might be assured I had received no Hurts: Having rendered him the like Civility in his own Chamber, and satisfied myself he was not wounded, we returned to the beautiful *Philonice*;

and this second Sight having finished my Defeat, I remained so absolutely her Slave, that neither *Dorothea* nor *Sydimiris* were more passionately beloved.

At the earnest Intreaty of the Baron, I staid some Weeks in the Castle; during which, the daily Sight of *Philonice* so augmented my Flames, that I was no longer in a Condition to conceal them; but, fearing to displease that Divine Beauty by a Confession of my Passion, I languished in secret; and the Constraint I laid upon myself, gave me such Torments, that I fell into a profound Melancholy, and looked so pale and dejected, that the Baron was sensible of the Alteration, and conjured me in the most pressing Terms, to acquaint him with the Cause of my Uneasiness: But though I continued obstinately silent with my Tongue, yet my Eyes spoke intelligibly enough; and the Blushes which appeared in the fair Cheeks of *Philonice*, whenever she spoke to me on the Subject of my Grief, convinced me she was not ignorant of my Passion.

At length the Agitation of my Mind throwing me into a Fever, the Baron, who was firmly persuaded, that my Illness proceeded from some concealed Vexation, pressed me continually to declare myself; and, finding all his Intreaties ineffectual, he commanded his Daughter to endeavour to find out the Cause of that Grief which had put me into such a Condition.

For that Purpose therefore, having brought the fair *Philonice* into my Chamber, he staid a few Minutes, and, leaving the Room, under Pretence of Business, *Philonice* remained alone by my Bedside, her Women, out of Respect, staying at the other End of the Chamber.

This Divine Person, seeing herself alone with me, and remembring her Father's Command, blushed, and cast down her Eyes in such apparent Confusion, that I could not help observing it: And, interpreting it to the Displeasure she took in being so near me,

Whatever Joy I take in the Honour your Visit does me, Madam, said I, in a weak Voice; yet since nothing is so dear to me, as your Satisfaction, I would rather dispense with this Mark of your Goodness to an unfortunate Wretch, then see you in the least Constraint.

And why, replied she, with a Tone full of Sweetness, do you suppose that I am here by Constraint, when it would be more just to believe, that in visiting the valiant Defender of my Honour, and the Life of my Father, I only follow my own Inclinations?

Ah! Madam, said I, transported with Joy at so favourable a Speech, the little Service I had the Happiness to do you, does not merit so infinite a Favour; and tho' I had lost the best Part of my Blood in your Defence, I should have been well rewarded with your Safety.

Since you do not repent of what you have done, replied she, I am willing to be obliged to you for another Favour; and ask it with the greater Hope of obtaining it, as I must acquaint you, it is by my Father's Command I take that Liberty, who is much interested in my Success.

There is no Occasion, Madam, returned I, to make use of any Interest but your own, to engage me to obey you, since that is, and ever will be, all-powerful with me: Speak then, Madam, and let me know what it is you desire of me, that I may, once in my Life, have the Glory of obeying you.

It is, said she, blushing still more than before, that you will acquaint us with the Cause of that Melancholy, which has, as we imagine, occasioned your present Illness.

At these Words I trembled, turned pale; and, not daring to discover the true Cause of my Affliction, I remained in a profound Silence.

I see, said the beautiful *Philonice*, that you have no Inclination to obey me; and since my Request has, as I perceive, given you some Disturbance, I will prevail upon my Father to press you no farther upon this Subject.

No, Madam, said I, eagerly; the Baron shall be satisfied, and you shall be obeyed; though, after the Knowlege of my Crime, you doom me to that Death I so justly merit.

Yes Madam, this unfortunate Man, who has had the Glory to acquire your Esteem by the little Service he did you, has cancelled the Merit of that Service by daring to adore you.

I love you, divine *Philonice*; and, not being able either to repent, or cease to be guilty of loving you, I am resolved to die, and spare you the Trouble of pronouncing my Sentence. I beseech you therefore to believe, that I would have died in Silence, but for your Command to declare myself, and you should never have known the Excess of my Love and Despair, had not my Obedience to your Will obliged me to confess it.

I finished these Words with so much Fear and Confusion, that I durst not lift my Eyes up to the fair Face of *Philonice*, to observe how she received this Discourse: I waited therefore, trembling, for her Answer; but finding that in several Minutes she spoke not a Word, I ventured at last, to cast a languishing Glance upon the Visage I adored, and saw so many Marks of Disorder upon it, that I was almost dead with the Apprehensions of having offended her beyond even the Hope of procuring her Pardon by my Death.

CHAPTER X

Wherein Sir George *concludes his History; which produces an unexpected Effect*

THE Silence of *Philonice*, continued Sir *George*, pierced me to the Heart; and when I saw her rise from her Seat, and prepare to go away without speaking, Grief took such Possession of my Spirits, that, uttering a Cry, I fell into a Swoon, which, as I afterwards was informed, greatly alarmed the beautiful *Philonice*; who, resuming her Seat, had the Goodness to assist her Women in bringing me to myself; and, when I opened my Eyes, I had the Satisfaction to behold her still by me, and all the Signs of Compassion in her Face.

This Sight a little re-assuring me; I ask your Pardon, Madam, said I, for the Condition in which I have appeared before you, and also for that I am not yet dead, as is doubtless your Wish: But I will make Haste, pursued I, sighing, to fulfil your Desires; and you shall soon be freed from the Sight of a miserable Wretch, who, to his last Moment, will not cease to adore you.

It is not your Death that I desire, said the fair *Philonice*; and, after having preserved both my Father and me from Death, it is not reasonable, that we should suffer you to die, if we can help it.

Live therefore, *Bellmour*, pursued she, blushing; and live, if possible, without continuing in that Weakness I cannot choose but condemn: Yet whatever are your Thoughts for the future, remember that your Death will be a Fault I cannot resolve to pardon.

Speaking these Words, without giving me time to answer, she left my Chamber; and I found something so sweet and favourable in them, that I resolved to obey her, and forward my Cure as much as I was able: However, the Agitation of Spirits increased my Fever so much, that my Life was despaired of.

The Baron hardly ever left my Bedside. *Philonice* came every Day to see me, and seemed extremely moved at the Danger I was in. One Day, when I was worse than usual, she came close to the Bedside; and, opening the Courtain,

What *Bellmour*, said she, do you pay so little Obedience to my Commands, that you resolve to die?

Heaven is my Witness, Madam, said I, faintly, that nothing is so dear and sacred to me as your Commands; and since, out of your superlative Goodness, you are pleased to have some Care for my Life, I would preserve it to obey you, were it in my Power; but, alas! Madam, I strive in vain to repel the Violence of my Distemper.

In a few Days more, I was reduced to the last Extremity: It was then that the fair *Philonice* discovered, that she did not hate me; for she made no Scruple to weep before me; and those Tears she so liberally shed, had so powerful an Effect upon my Mind, that the Contentment I felt, communicated itself to my Body, and gave such a Turn to my Distemper, that my Recovery was not only hoped, but expected.

The Baron expressed his Satisfaction at this Alteration, by the most affectionate Expressions; and though the fair *Philonice* said very little, yet I perceived by the Joy that appeared in her fair Eyes, that she was not less interested in my Recovery, than her Father.

The Physicians having declared me out of Danger, the Baron, who had taken his Resolutions long before, came one Day into my Chamber; and ordering those who attended me, to leave us alone,

Prince, said he, for in recounting my History to him, I had disclosed my true Quality, I am not ignorant of that Affection you bear my Daughter; and am sensible it has occasioned the Extremity to which we have seen you reduced: Had you been pleased to acquaint me with your Sentiments, you would have avoided those Displeasures you have suffered; for though your Birth were not so illustrious as it is, yet, preferring Virtue to all other Advantages, I should have esteemed my Daughter honoured by your Love, and have freely bestowed her on you: But since to those rare Qualities wherewith Heaven has so liberally endowed you, you add also that of a Birth so noble, doubt not but I shall think myself highly favoured by your Alliance: If therefore your Thoughts of my Daughter be not changed, and you esteem her worthy to be your Bride, I here solemnly promise you to bestow her upon you, as soon as you are perfectly recovered.

I leave you to guess, Madam, the Joy which I felt at this Discourse: It was so great, that it would not permit me to thank him, as I should have done, for the inestimable Blessing he bestowed on me.

I saw *Philonice* a few Minutes after; and, being commanded by her Father to give me her Hand, she did so, without any Marks of Reluctance, and, having respectfully kissed it, I vowed to be her Slave for ever.

Who would have imagined, continued Sir *George*, with a profound Sigh, that Fortune, while she thus seemed to flatter me, was preparing to make me suffer the severest Torments? I began now to leave my Bed, and was able to walk about my Chamber. The Baron was making great Preparations for our Nuptials; when one Night I was alarmed with the Cries of *Philonice*'s Women; and, a few Moments after, the Baron came into my Chamber, with a distracted Air.

O! Son, cried he, for so he always called me, now *Philonice* is lost both to you and me: She is carried off by Force, and I am preparing to follow and rescue her, if possible; but I fear my Endeavours will be fruitless, since I know not which Way her Ravishers have taken.

Oh! Sir, cried I, transported both with Grief and Rage, you shall not go alone: Her Rescue belongs to me; and I will effect it, or perish in the Attempt.

The Baron, having earnestly conjured me not to expose myself to the Danger of a Relapse, by so imprudent a Resolution, was obliged to quit me, Word being brought him, that his Horse was ready: And as soon as he was gone out of the Room, in spite of all that could be said to prevent me, by my Attendants, I made them put on my Armour; and, mounting a Horse I had caused to be made ready, sallied furiously out of the Castle, breathing out Vows of Vengeance against the Wretch who had robbed me of *Philonice*.

I rode the whole Night without stopping. Day appeared, when I found myself near a small Village. I entered it, and made strict Enquiry after the Ravisher of *Philonice*, describing the fair Creature, and offering vast Rewards to any who could bring me the least Intelligence of her: But all was in vain, I could make no Discovery.

After travelling several Days, to no Purpose, I returned to the Castle, in order to know if the Baron had been more successful in his Pursuit then myself; but I found him oppressed with Grief: He had heard no Tidings of his Daughter, and had suffered no small Apprehensions upon my Account. Having assured him I found myself very able to travel, I took an affectionate Leave of him, promising him never to give over my Search, till I had found the Divine *Philonice*: But Heaven has not permitted me that Happiness; and though I have spent several Years in searching for her, I have never been able to discover where she is: Time has not cured me of my Grief for her Loss; and, though by an Effect of my Destiny, another Object possesses my Soul, yet I do not cease to deplore her Misfortune, and to offer up Vows for her Happiness.

And is this all you have to say? said *Arabella*, whom the latter Part of his History had extremely surprised; or are we to expect a Continuance of your Adventures?

I have faithfully related all my Adventures, that are worthy your Hearing, Madam, returned Sir *George*; and I flatter myself, you will do me the Justice to own, that I have been rather unfortunate than faithless; and that Mr. *Glanville* had little Reason to tax me with Inconstancy.

In my Opinion, resumed *Arabella*, Mr. *Glanville* spoke too favourably of you, when he called you only inconstant; and if he had added the Epithet of Ungrateful and Unjust, he would have marked your Character better.

For, in fine, Sir, pursued she, you will never persuade any reasonable Person, that your being able to lose the Remembrance of the fair and generous *Sydimiris*, in your new Passion for *Philonice*, was not an Excess of Levity: But your suffering so tamely the Loss of this last Beauty, and allowing her to remain in the Hands of her Ravisher, while you permit another Affection to take Possession of your Soul, is such an Outrage to all Truth and Constancy, that you deserve to be ranked among the falsest of Mankind.

Alas! Madam, replied Sir *George*, who had not foreseen the Inference *Arabella* would draw from this last Adventure, What would you have an unfortunate Man, whose Hopes have been so often, and so cruelly, disappointed, do? I have bewailed the Loss of *Philonice*, with a Deluge of Tears; I have taken infinite Pains to find her, but to no Purpose; and when Heaven compassionating my Sufferings, presented to my Eyes, an Object, to whom the whole World ought to pay Adoration, how could I resist that powerful Impulse, which forced me to love what appeared so worthy of my Affection?

Call not, interrupted *Arabella*, that an irresistible Impulse, which was only the Effect of thy own changing Humour: The same Excuse might be pleaded for all the Faults we see committed in the World; and Men would no longer be answerable for their own Crimes. Had you imitated the illustrious Heroes of Antiquity, as well in the Constancy of their Affections, as, it must be confessed, you have done in their admirable Valour; you would now be either sighing in your Cave for the Loss of the generous *Sydimiris*, or wandering through the World in Search of the beautiful *Philonice*. Had you persevered in your Affection, and continued your Pursuit of that Fair-one; you would, perhaps, ere this, have found her sleeping under the Shade of a Tree in some lone Forest, as *Philodaspes* did his admirable *Delia*,[1] or disguised in a Slave's Habit, as *Ariobarsanes* saw his Divine *Olympia*;[2] or bound haply in a Chariot, and have had the Glory of freeing her, as *Ambriomer* did the beauteous *Agione*;[3] or in a Ship in the Hands of Pirates, like the incomparable *Eliza*;[4] or——

Enough, dear Niece, interrupted Sir *Charles*; you have quoted Examples sufficient, if this inconstant Man would have the Grace to follow them.

True, Sir, replied *Arabella*; and I would recommend to his Consideration the Conduct of those illustrious Persons I have named, to the end that, pursuing their Steps, he may arrive at their Glory and Happiness, that is the Reputation of being perfectly constant, and the Possession of his Mistress: And be assured, Sir, pursued *Arabella*, looking at Sir *George*, that Heaven will never restore you the Crown of your Ancestors, and place you upon the Throne to which you pretend, while you make yourself unworthy of its Protection, by so shameful an Inconstancy.

I perhaps speak with too much Freedom to a great Prince; whom though Fortune has despoiled of his Dominions, is intitled to a certain Degree of Respect: But I conceive, it belongs to me, in a you are pleased to make me the Excuse; and, looking upon myself, as dishonoured by those often prostituted Vows you have offered me, I am to tell you, that I am highly disobliged; and forbid you to appear in my Presence again, till you have resumed those Thoughts, which are worthy your noble Extraction; and are capable of treating me with that Respect, that is my Due.

Saying this, she rose from her Seat, and walked very majestically out of the Room, leaving Sir *George* overwhelmed with Shame and Vexation at having conducted the latter Part of his Narration so ill; and drawn upon himself a Sentence, which deprived him of all his Hopes.

CHAPTER XI

Containing only a few Inferences, drawn from the foregoing Chapters

MR. *Glanville*, excessively delighted with this Event, could not help laughing at the unfortunate Baronet; who seemed, by his Silence, and down-cast Looks, to expect it.

Who would have imagined, said he, that so renowned a Hero would have tarnished the Glory of his Laurels, as my Cousin says, by so base an Ingratitude? Indeed, Prince, pursued he, laughing, you must resolve to recover your Reputation, either by retiring again to your Cave, and living upon bitter Herbs, for the generous *Sydimiris*; or else wander through the World, in search of the Divine *Philonice*.

Don't triumph, dear *Charles*, replied Sir *George*, laughing in his Turn; have a little Compassion upon me, and confess, that nothing could be more unfortunate, than that damn'd Slip I made at the latter End of my History: But for that, my Reputation for Courage and Constancy had been as high as the great *Oroondates*, or *Juba*.

Since you have so fertile an Invention, said Sir *Charles*, you may easily repair this Mistake. Ods-heart! It is pity you are not poor enough to be an Author; you would occupy a Garret in *Grub-street*, with great Fame to yourself, and Diversion to the Public.

Oh! Sir, cried Sir *George*, I have Stock enough by me, to set up for an Author Tomorrow, if I please: I have no less than Five Tragedies, some quite, others almost finished; Three or Four Essays on *Virtue, Happiness, &c.* Three thousand Lines of an Epic Poem; half a Dozen Epitaphs; a few Acrostics; and a long String of Puns, that would serve to embellish a Daily Paper, if I was disposed to write one.

Nay, then, interrupted Mr. *Glanville*, you are qualified for a Critic at the *Bedford* Coffee-house;[1] where, with the rest of your

Brothers, Demy-wits, you may sit in Judgment upon the Productions of a *Young*, a *Richardson*, or a *Johnson*. Rail with premeditated Malice at the *Rambler*; and, for the want of Faults, turn even its inimitable Beauties into Ridicule: The Language, because it reaches to Perfection, may be called stiff, laboured, and pedantic; the Criticisms, when they let in more Light than your weak Judgment can bear, superficial and ostentatious Glitter; and because those Papers contain the finest System of Ethics yet extant, damn the queer Fellow, for over-propping Virtue; an excellent new Phrase! which those who can find no Meaning in, may accommodate with one of their own; then give shrewd Hints, that some Persons, though they do not publish their Performances, may have more Merit, than those that do.

Upon my Soul, *Charles*, said Sir *George*, thou art such an ill-natured Fellow, that I am afraid, thou wilt be sneering at me when I am gone; and wilt endeavour, to persuade Lady *Bella*, that not a Syllable of my Story is true. Speak, pursued he, Wilt thou have the Cruelty to deprive me of my lawful Claim to the great Kingdom of *Kent*; and rob me of the Glory of fighting singly against Five hundred Men?

I do not know, said Sir *Charles*, whether my Niece be really imposed upon, by the Gravity with which you told your surprising History; but I protest, I thought you were in earnest at first; and that you meant to make us believe it all to be Fact.

You are so fitly punished, said Mr. *Glanville*, for that ill-judged Adventure you related last, by the bad Opinion Lady *Bella* entertains of you, that I need not add to your Misfortune: And therefore, you shall be Prince *Veridomer*, if you please; since, under that Character, you are obliged not to pretend to any Lady, but the incomparable *Philonice*.

Sir *George*, who understood his Meaning, went home, to think of some Means, by which he might draw himself out of the Embarrassment he was in; and Mr. *Glanville*, as he had promised, did not endeavour to undeceive Lady *Bella*, with regard to the History he had feigned; being very well satisfied with his having put it out of his Power to make his Addresses to her, since she now looked upon him as the Lover of *Philonice*.

As for Sir *Charles*, he did not penetrate into the Meaning of Sir *George*'s Story; and only imagined, that by relating such a Heap of Adventures, he had a Design to entertain the Company, and give a

Proof of the Felicity of his Invention; and Miss *Glanville*, who supposed, he had been ridiculing her Cousin's strange Notions, was better pleased with him than ever.

Arabella, however, was less satisfied than any of them: She could not endure to see so brave a Knight, who drew his Birth from a Race of Kings, tarnish the Glory of his gallant Actions by so base a Perfidy.

Alas! said she to herself, How much Reason has the beautiful *Philonice* to accuse me for all the Anguish she suffers? since I am the Cause, that the ungrateful Prince, on whom she bestows her Affections, suffers her to remain quietly, in the Hands of her Ravisher, without endeavouring to rescue her: But, Oh! too lovely, and unfortunate Fair-one, said she, as if she had been present, and listening to her, distinguish, I beseech you, between those Faults, which the Will, and those which Necessity, makes us commit. I am the Cause, 'tis true, of thy Lover's Infidelity; but I am the innocent Cause; and would repair the Evils, my fatal Beauty gives Rise to, by any Sacrifice in my Power to make.

While *Arabella*, by her romantic Generosity, bewails the imaginary Afflictions of the full as imaginary *Philonice*; Mr. *Glanville*, who thought the Solitude she lived in, confirmed her in her absurd and ridiculous Notions, desired his Father to press her to go to *London*.

Sir *Charles* complied with his Request, and earnestly intreated her to leave the Castle, and spend a few Months in Town. Her Year of Mourning being now expired, she consented to go; but Sir *Charles*, who did not think his Son's Health absolutely confirmed, proposed to spend a few Weeks at *Bath*; which was readily complied with by *Arabella*.

The End of BOOK VI.

BOOK VII

CHAPTER I

*For the Shortness of which the Length of the next shall
make some Amends*

SIR *George*, to gratify *Arabella*'s Humour, had not presumed to
come to the Castle for several Days; but, hearing that they were
preparing to leave the Country, he wrote a short Billet to her; and
in the Style of Romance, most humbly intreated her to grant him a
Moment's Audience.

Arabella being informed by *Lucy*, to whom Sir *George*'s Gentleman had addressed himself, that he had brought a Letter from his
Master, she ordered her to bring him to her Apartment, and as soon
as he appeared,

How comes it, said she, that the Prince your Master, has had the
Presumption to importune me again, after my absolute Commands
to the contrary?

The Prince, my Master, Madam, said the Man, excessively surprised.

Ay! said *Arabella*, Are you not Sir *George*'s 'Squire? And does he
not trust you with his most secret Thoughts?

I belong to Sir *George Bellmour*, Madam, replied the Man, who
did not understand what She meant: I have not the Honour to be a
'Squire.

No! interrupted *Arabella*; 'tis strange then, that he should have
honoured you with his Commission; Pray, what is it you come to
request for him?

My Master, Madam, said he, ordered me to get this Letter
delivered to your Ladyship, and to stay for your Commands.

You would persuade me, said she, sternly, being provoked that
he did not deliver the Letter upon his Knees, as was the Custom in
Romances, that you are not acquainted with the Purport of this
audacious Billet, since you express so little Fear of my Displeasure;

but know, presumptuous, that I am mortally offended with your Master, for his daring to suppose I would read this Proof at once of his Insolence and Infidelity; and was you worth my Resentment, I would haply make you suffer for your Want of Respect to me.

The poor Man, surprised and confounded at her Anger, and puzzled extremely; to understand what she meant, was opening his Mouth to say something, 'tis probable in his own Defence, when *Arabella*, preventing him,

I know what thou wouldst say, said she: Thou wouldst abuse my Patience by a false Detail of thy Master's Sighs, Tears, Exclamations, and Despair.

Indeed, Madam, I don't intend to say any such Thing, replied the Man.

No! repeated *Arabella*, a little disappointed, Bear back this presumptuous Billet then, which, I suppose, contains the melancholy Account; and tell him, He that could so soon forget the generous *Sydimiris* for *Philonice*, and could afterwards be false to that incomparable Beauty, is not a Person worthy to adore *Arabella*.

The Man, who could not tell what to make of this Message, and feared he should forget these two hard Names, humbly intreated her to be pleased to acquaint his Master, by a Line, with her Intentions. *Arabella*, supposing he meant to importune her still more, made a Sign with her Hand, very majestically, for him to be gone; but he, not able to comprehend her Meaning, stood still, with an Air of Perplexity, not daring to beg her to explain herself; supposing, she, by that Sign, required something of him.

Why dost thou not obey my Commands? said *Arabella*, finding he did not go.

I will, to be sure, Madam, replied he; wishing at the same time secretly, she would let him know what they were.

And yet, said she hastily, thou art disobeying me this Moment: Did I not bid you get out of my Presence, and to speak no more of your inconstant Master, whose Crimes have rendered him the Detestation of all generous Persons whatever?

Sir *George*'s Messenger, extremely surprised at so harsh a Character of his Master, and the Rage with which the Lady seemed to be actuated, made haste to get out of her Apartment; and, at his Return, informed his Master, very exactly, of the Reception he had met with, repeating all Lady *Bella*'s Words; which, notwithstanding the Blunders he made in the Names of *Sydimiris* and

Philonice, Sir *George* understood well enough; and found new Occasion of wondering at the Excess of *Arabella*'s Extravagance, who he never imagined would have explained herself in that Manner to his Servant.

Without endeavouring therefore to see *Arabella*, he went to pay his Compliments to Sir *Charles*, Mr. *Glanville*, and Miss *Glanville*; to the last of whom he said some soft things, that made her extremely regret his staying behind them in the Country.

CHAPTER II

Not so long as was first intended; but contains, however, a surprising Adventure on the Road

THE Day of their Departure being come, they set out in a Coach and Six, attended by several Servants on Horseback. The First Day's Journey passed off, without any Accident worthy relating; but, towards the Close of the Second, they were alarmed by the Appearance of three Highwaymen, well mounted, at a small Distance.

One of the Servants, who had first spied them, immediately rode up to the Coach; and, for fear of alarming the Ladies, whispered Mr. *Glanville* in the Ear.

Sir *Charles*, who was sitting next his Son, and had heard it, cried out with too little Caution, How's this? Are we in any Danger of being attacked, say you?

Mr. *Glanville*, without replying, jumped out of the Coach; at which Miss *Glanville* screamed out; and, lest her Father should follow, sprung into her Brother's Seat, and held him fast by the Coat.

Arabella, being in a strange Consternation at all this, put her Head out of the Coach, to see what was the Matter; and, observing Three or Four Men of a genteel Appearance, on Horseback, who seemed to halt, and gaze on them, without offering to advance;

Sir, said she to her Uncle, are yonder Knights the Persons whom you suppose will attack us?

Ay, ay, said Sir *Charles*, they are Knights of the Road indeed: I suppose we shall have a Bout with them; for it will be scandalous to deliver, since we have the Odds of our Side, and are more than a Match for them.

Arabella, interpreting these Words in her own Way, looked out again; and, seeing the Robbers, who had by this time taken their Resolution, galloping towards them, her Cousin and the Servants ranging themselves of each Side of the Coach, as if to defend them,

Hold, hold, valiant Men, said she, as loud as she could speak, addressing herself to the Highwaymen; do not, by a mistaken Generosity, hazard your Lives in a Combat, to which the Laws of Honour do not oblige you: We are not violently carried away, as you falsly suppose; we go willingly along with these Persons, who are our Friends and Relations.

Hey-day! cried Sir *Charles*, staring at her with great Surprize; what's the Meaning of all this? Do you think these Fellows will mind your fine Speeches, Niece?

I hope they will, Sir, said she: Then, pulling her Cousin, shew yourself, for Heaven's Sake, Miss, pursued she, and second my Assurances, that we are not forced away: These generous Men come to fight for our Deliverance.

The Highwaymen, who were near enough to hear *Arabella's* Voice, though they could not distinguish her Words, gazed on her with great Surprize; and, finding they would be very well received, thought fit to abandon their Enterprize, and galloped away as fast as they were able. Some of the Servants made a Motion to pursue them; but Mr. *Glanville* forbad it; and, entering again into the Coach, congratulated the Ladies upon the Escape they had had.

Since these Men, said *Arabella*, did not come to deliver us, out of a mistaken Notion, that we were carried away by Force, it must necessarily follow, they had some bad Design; and I protest I know not who to suspect is the Author of it, unless the Person you vanquished, said she to Mr. *Glanville*, the other Day in a single Combat; for the disguised *Edward*, you assured me, was dead: But perhaps, continued she, it was some Lover of Miss *Glanville's*, who designed to make an Attempt to carry her away: Methinks he was too slenderly attended for such an hazardous Undertaking.

I'll assure you Madam, said Miss *Glanville*, I have no Lovers among Highwaymen.

Highwaymen! repeated *Arabella*.

Why, ay, to be sure, Madam, rejoined Sir *Charles*: What do you take them for?

For Persons of Quality, Sir, resumed *Arabella*; and though they came questionless, either upon a good or bad Design, yet it cannot be doubted, but that their Birth is illustrious; otherwise they would never pretend either to fight in our Defence, or to carry us away.

I vow, Niece, said Sir *Charles*, I can't possibly understand you.

My Cousin, Sir, interrupted Mr. *Glanville*, has been mistaken in these Persons; and has not yet, possibly, believed them to be High-waymen, who came to rob us.

There is no Question, Sir, said *Arabella*, smiling, that if they did not come to defend us, they came to rob you: But it is hard to guess, which of us it was of whom they designed to deprive you; for it may very possibly be for my Cousin's sake, as well as mine, that this Enterprize was undertaken.

Pardon me, Madam, said Mr. *Glanville*, who was willing to prevent his Father from answering her Absurdities; these Men had no other Design, than to rob us of our Money.

How! said *Arabella*: Were these Cavaliers, who appeared to be in so handsome a Garb, that I took them for Persons of prime Quality, were they Robbers? I have been strangely mistaken, it seems: However, I apprehend there is no Certainty, that your Suspicions are true; and it may still be as I say, that they either came to rescue or carry us away.

Mr. *Glanville*, to avoid a longer Dispute, changed the Discourse; having observed with Confusion, that Sir *Charles*, and his Sister, seemed to look upon his beloved Cousin as one that was out of her Senses.

CHAPTER III

Which concludes with an authentic Piece of History

Arabella, during the rest of this Journey, was so wholly taken up in contemplating upon the last Adventure, that she mixed but little in the Conversation. Upon their drawing near *Bath*, the Situation of that City afforded her the Means of making a Comparison between the Valley in which it was placed (with the Amphitheatrical View of the Hills around it) and the Valley of *Tempe*.[1]

'Twas in such a Place as this, said she, pursuing her Comparison,

that the fair *Andronice* delivered the valiant *Hortensius*.[1] And really
I could wish, our Entrance into that City might be preceded by an
Act of equal Humanity with that of that fair Princess.

For the Gratification of that Wish, Madam, said Mr. *Glanville*, it
is necessary some Person should meet with a Misfortune, out of
which you might be able to relieve him; but I suppose the Benevolence of your Disposition may be equally satisfied with not finding
any Occasion, as of exercising it, when it is found.

Though it be not my Fortune to meet with those Occasions,
replied *Arabella*, there is no Reason to doubt but others do, who
possibly have less Inclination to afford their Assistance than myself: And it is possible, if any other than the Princess of *Messina*
had happened to pass by, when *Hortensius* was in the Hands of the
Thessalians, he would not have been rescued from the ignominious
Death he was destined to, merely for killing a Stork.

How! interrupted Sir *Charles*, put a Man to Death for killing a
Stork! Ridiculous! Pray, in what Part of the World did that
happen? Among the *Indians* of *America*, I suppose.

No, Sir, said *Arabella*, in *Thessaly*; the fairest Part in all *Macedonia*, famous for the beautiful Valley of *Tempe*, which excited the
Curiosity of all Travellers whatever.

No, not all, Madam, returned Sir *Charles*; for I am acquainted
with several Travellers, who never saw it, nor even mentioned it;
and if it is so famous as you say, I am surprised I never heard of it
before.

I don't know, said *Arabella*, what those Travellers thought
worthy of their Notice; but I am certain, that if any Chance should
conduct me into *Macedonia*, I would not leave it till I saw the
Valley of *Tempe*, so celebrated by all the Poets and Historians.

Dear Cousin, cried *Glanville*, who could hardly forbear smiling,
what Chance, in the Name of Wonder, should take you into *Turky*,
at so great a Distance from your own Country?

And so, said Sir *Charles*, this famous Valley of *Tempe* is in
Turky.[2] Why you must be very fond of travelling, indeed, Lady
Bella, if you would go into the *Great Mogul's* Country,[3] where the
People are all Pagans, they say, and worship the Devil.

The Country my Cousin speaks of, said Mr. *Glanville*, is in the
Grand Signor's Dominions: The Great Mogul, you know, Sir—

Well, interrupted Sir *Charles*, the Great Mogul, or the Grand
Signor, I know not what you call him: But I hope my Niece does
not propose to go thither.

Not unless I am forcibly carried thither, said *Arabella*; but I do determine, if that Misfortune should ever happen to me, that I would, if possible, visit the Valley of *Tempe*, which is in that Part of *Greece* they call *Macedonia*.

Then I am persuaded, replied Sir *Charles*, you'll never see that famous Vale you talk of; for it is not very likely you should be forcibly carried away into *Turky*.

And why do you think it unlikely, that I should be carried thither? interrupted *Arabella*. Do not the same Things happen now, that did formerly? And is any thing more common, then Ladies being carried, by their Ravishers, into Countries far distant from their own? May not the same Accidents happen to me, that have happened to so many illustrious Ladies before me? And may I not be carried into *Macedonia* by a Similitude of Destiny with that of a great many beautiful Princesses, who, though born in the most distant Quarters of the World, chanced to meet at one time in the City of *Alexandria*, and related their miraculous Adventures to each other?[1]

And it was for that very Purpose they met, Madam, said Mr. *Glanville*, smiling.

Why, truly, said *Arabella*, it happened very luckily for each of them, that they were brought into a Place where they found so many illustrious Companions in Misfortune, to whom they might freely communicate their Adventures, which otherwise might, haply, have been concealed, or, at least, have been imperfectly delivered down to us: However, added she, smiling, if I am carried into *Macedonia*, and by that means have an Opportunity of visiting the famous Vale of *Tempe*, I shall take care not to draw the Resentment of the *Thessalians* upon me, by an Indiscretion like that of *Hortensius*.

For be pleased to know, Sir, said she, addressing herself to her Uncle, that his killing a Stork, however inconsiderable a Matter it may appear to us, was yet looked upon as a Crime of a very atrocious Nature among the *Thessalians*; for they have a Law, which forbids, upon Pain of Death, the killing of Storks; the Reason for which is, that *Thessaly* being subject to be infested with a prodigious Multitude of Serpents, which are a delightful Food to these Sorts of Fowls, they look upon them as sacred Birds, sent by the Gods to deliver them from these Serpents and Vipers: And though

Hortensius, being a Stranger, was pardoned through the Intercession of the Princess *Andronice*, they made him promise to send another Stork into *Thessaly*, to the end that he might be reputed innocent.

CHAPTER IV

In which one of our Heroine's Whims is justified,
by some others full as whimsical

THIS Piece of History, with Sir *Charles*'s Remarks upon it, brought them into *Bath*. Their Lodgings being provided beforehand, the Ladies retired to their different Chambers, to repose themselves after the Fatigue of their Journey, and did not meet again till Supper was on Table; when Miss *Glanville*, who had eagerly enquired what Company was then in the Place, and heard there were a great many Persons of Fashion just arrived, prest *Arabella* to go to the Pump-Room the next Morning, assuring her she would find a very agreeable Amusement.

Arabella accordingly consented to accompany her; and, being told the Ladies went in an Undress[1] of a Morning, she accommodated herself to the Custom, and went in a negligent Dress; but instead of a Capuchin,[2] she wore something like a Veil, of black Gauze, which covered almost all her Face, and Part of her Waist, and gave her a very singular Appearance.

Miss *Glanville* was too envious of her Cousin's Superiority in point of Beauty, to inform her of any Oddity in her Dress, which she thought might expose her to the Ridicule of those that saw her; and Mr. *Glanville* was too little a Critic in Ladies Apparel, to be sensible that *Arabella* was not in the Fashion; and since every thing she wore became her extremely, he could not choose but think she drest admirably well: He handed her therefore, with a great deal of Satisfaction, into the Pump-Room, which happened to be greatly crouded that Morning.

The Attention of most Part of the Company was immediately engaged by the Appearance Lady *Bella* made. Strangers are here most strictly criticized, and every new Object affords a delicious Feast of Raillery and Scandal.

The Ladies, alarmed at the Singularity of her Dress, crouded together in Parties; and the Words, Who can she be? Strange Creature! Ridiculous! and other Exclamations of the same Kind, were whispered very intelligibly.

The Men were struck with her Figure, veiled as she was: Her fine Stature, the beautiful Turn of her Person, the Grace and Elegance of her Motion, attracted all their Notice: The Phænomena of the Veil, however, gave them great Disturbance. So lovely a Person seemed to promise the Owner had a Face not unworthy of it; but that was totally hid from their View: For *Arabella*, at her Entrance into the Room, had pulled the Gauze quite over her Face, following therein the Custom of the Ladies in *Clelia*, and the *Grand Cyrus*, who, in mixed Companies, always hid their Faces with great Care.

The Wits, and Pretty-Fellows, railed at the envious Covering, and compared her to the Sun obscured by a Cloud; while the Beaux dem'd the horrid Innovation, and expressed a Fear, lest it should grow into a Fashion.

Some of the wiser Sort took her for a Foreigner; others, of still more Sagacity, supposed her a *Scots* Lady, covered with her Plaid; and a third Sort, infinitely wiser than either, concluded she was a *Spanish* Nun, that had escaped from a Convent, and had not yet quitted her Veil.

Arabella, ignorant of the Diversity of Opinions, to which her Appearance gave Rise, was taken up in discoursing with Mr. *Glanville* upon the medicinal Virtue of the Springs, the Oeconomy of the Baths, the Nature of the Diversions, and such other Topics, as the Objects around them furnished her with.

In the mean time, Miss *Glanville* was got amidst a Croud of her Acquaintance, who had hardly paid the Civilities of a first Meeting, before they eagerly inquired, who that Lady she brought with her was.

Miss *Glanville* informed them, that she was her Cousin, and Daughter to the deceased Marquis of —— adding with a Sneer, That she had been brought up in the Country; knew nothing of the World; and had some very peculiar Notions, as you may see, said she, by that odd kind of Covering she wears.

Her Name and Quality were presently whispered all over the Room: The Men, hearing she was a great Heiress, found greater Beauties to admire in her Person: The Ladies, aw'd by the Sanction of Quality, dropt their Ridicule on her Dress, and began to quote Examples of Whims full as inexcusable.

One remembred, that Lady *J— T—* always wore her Ruffles reversed; that the Countess of —— went to Court in a Farthingale; that the Duchess of —— sat astride upon a Horse; and a certain Lady of great Fortune, and nearly allied to Quality, because she was not dignified with a Title, invented a new one for herself; and directed her Servants to say in speaking to her, *Your Honouress*, which afterwards became a Custom among all her Acquaintance; who mortally offended her, if they omitted that Instance of Respect.

CHAPTER V

Containing some historical Anecdotes, the Truth of which may possibly be doubted, as they are not to be found in any of the Historians

AFTER a short Stay in the Room, *Arabella* expressing a Desire to return home, Mr. *Glanville* conducted her out. Two Gentlemen of his Acquaintance attending Miss *Glanville*, Sir *Charles* detained them to Breakfast; by which means they had an Opportunity of satisfying their Curiosity; and beheld *Arabella*, divested of that Veil, which had, as they said; and 'tis probable they said no more than they thought, concealed one of the finest Faces in the World.

Miss *Glanville* had the Mortification to see both the Gentlemen so charmed with the Sight of her Cousin's Face, that for a long time she sat wholly neglected; but the Seriousness of her Behaviour, giving some little Disgust to the youngest of them, who was what the Ladies call a Pretty-Fellow, a dear Creature, and the most diverting Man in the World; he applied himself wholly to Miss *Glanville*, and soon engaged her in a particular Conversation.

Mr. *Selvin*, so was the other Gentleman called, was of a much graver Cast: He affected to be thought deep-read in History, and never failed to take all Opportunities of displaying his Knowlege of Antiquity, which was indeed but very superficial; but having some few Anecdotes by Heart, which he would take Occasion to introduce as often as he could, he passed among many Persons for one, who, by Application and Study, had acquired an universal Knowledge of antient History.

Speaking of any particular Circumstance, he would fix the Time, by computing the Year with the Number of the Olympiads.[1]

It happened, he would say, in the 141st Olympiad.

Such an amazing Exactness, had a suitable Effect on his Audience, and always procured him a great Degree of Attention.

This Gentleman hitherto had no Opportunity of displaying his Knowlege of History, the Discourse having wholly turned upon News, and other Trifles; when *Arabella*, after some more Inquiries concerning the Place, remarked, that there was a very great Difference between the medicinal Waters at *Bath*, and the fine Springs at the Foot of the Mountain *Thermopylae* in *Greece*, as well in their Qualities, as manner of using them; and I am of Opinion, added she, that *Bath*, famous as it is for restoring Health, is less frequented by infirm Persons, than the famous Springs of *Thermopylae* were by the Beauties of *Greece*, to whom those Waters have the Reputation of giving new Lustre.[2]

Mr. *Selvin*, who, with all his Reading, had never met with any Account of these celebrated *Grecian* Springs, was extremely disconcerted at not being able to continue a Conversation, which the Silence of the rest of the Company made him imagine, was directed wholly to him.

The Shame he conceived at seeing himself posed by a Girl, in a Matter which so immediately belonged to him, made him resolve to draw himself out of this Dilemma at any Rate; and, though he was far from being convinced, that there were no such Springs at *Thermopylae*[3] as *Arabella* mentioned; yet he resolutely maintained, that she must be mistaken in their Situation; for, to his certain Knowlege, there were no medicinal Waters at the Foot of that Mountain.

Arabella, who could not endure to be contradicted in what she took to be so incontestable a Fact, reddened with Vexation at his unexpected Denial.

It should seem, said she, by your Discourse, that you are unacquainted with many material Passages, that passed among very illustrious Persons there; and if you knew any thing of *Pisistratus* the *Athenian*, you would know, that an Adventure he had at those Baths, laid the Foundation of all those great Designs, which he afterwards effected, to the total Subversion of the *Athenian* Government.

Mr. *Selvin*, surprised that this Piece of History had likewise escaped his Observation, resolved, however, not to give up his Point.

I think, Madam, replied he, with great Self-sufficiency, that I am pretty well acquainted with every thing which relates to the Affairs of the *Athenian* Commonwealth; and know by what Steps *Pisistratus* advanced himself to the Sovereignty. It was a great Stroke of Policy in him, said he, turning to Mr. *Glanville*, to wound himself, in order to get a Guard assigned him.

You are mistaken, Sir, said *Arabella*, if you believe, there was any Truth in the Report of his having wounded himself: It was done, either by his Rival *Lycurgus* or *Theocrites*; who believing him still to be in Love with the fair *Cerinthe*, whom he courted, took that Way to get rid of him: Neither is it true, that Ambition alone inspired *Pisistratus* with a Design of enslaving his Country: Those Authors who say so, must know little of the Springs and Motives of his Conduct. It was neither Ambition nor Revenge, that made him act as he did; it was the violent Affection he conceived for the beautiful *Cleorante*, whom he first saw at the famous Baths of *Thermopylæ*, which put him upon those Designs; for, seeing that *Lycurgus*, who was not his Rival in Ambition, but Love, would certainly become the Possessor of *Cleorante*, unless he made himself Tyrant of *Athens*, he had recourse to that violent Method, in order to preserve her for himself.

I protest, Madam, said Mr. *Selvin*, casting down his Eyes in great Confusion at her superior Knowlege in History, these Particulars have all escaped my Notice; and this is the first time I ever understood, that *Pisistratus* was violently in Love; and that it was not Ambition, which made him aspire to Sovereignty.

I do not remember any Mention of this in *Plutarch*, continued he, rubbing his Forehead, or any of the Authors who have treated on the Affairs of *Greece*.

Very likely, Sir, replied *Arabella*; but you will see the whole Story of *Pisistratus*'s Love for *Cleorante*, with the Effects it produced, related at large in *Scudery*.

Scudery, Madam! said the sage Mr. *Selvin*, I never read that Historian.

No, Sir! replied *Arabella*, then your Reading has been very confined.

I know, Madam, said he, that *Herodotus, Thucydides,* and

Plutarch, have indeed quoted him frequently.

I am surprised, Sir, said Mr. *Glanville*, who was excessively diverted at this Discovery of his great Ignorance and Affectation, that you have not read that famous Historian; especially, as the Writers you have mentioned quote him so often.

Why, to tell you the Truth, Sir, said he; though he was a *Roman*; yet it is objected to him, that he wrote but indifferent *Latin*; with no Purity or Elegance; and—

You are quite mistaken, Sir, interrupted *Arabella*; the great *Scudery* was a *Frenchman*; and both his *Clelia* and *Artamenes* were written in *French*.

A *Frenchman* was he? said Mr. *Selvin*, with a lofty Air: Oh! then, 'tis not surprising, that I have not read him: I read no Authors, but the Antients, Madam, added he, with a Look of Self-applause; I cannot relish the Moderns at all: I have no Taste for their Way of Writing.

But *Scudery* must needs be more ancient than *Thucydides*, and the rest of those *Greek* Historians you mentioned, said Mr. *Glanville*: How else could they quote him?

Mr. *Selvin* was here so utterly at a Loss, that he could not conceal his Confusion: He held down his Head, and continued silent; while the Beau, who had listened to the latter Part of their Discourse; exerted his supposed Talent of Raillery against the unhappy Admirer of the antient Authors; and increased his Confusion by a thousand Sarcasms, which gave more Diversion to himself, than any body else.

CHAPTER VI

Which contains some excellent Rules for Raillery[1]

MR. *Glanville*, who had too much Politeness and Good nature to insist too long upon the Ridicule in the Character of his Acquaintance, changed the Discourse: And *Arabella*, who had observed, with some Concern, the ill-judged Raillery of the young Beau, took Occasion to decry that Species of Wit; and gave it as her Opinion, that it was very dangerous and unpleasing.

For, truly, said she, it is almost impossible to use it without being hated or feared; and whoever gets a Habit of it, is in Danger of wronging all the Laws of Friendship and Humanity.

Certainly, pursued she, looking at the Beau, it is extremely unjust to railly one's Friends, and particular Acquaintance: First, choose them well, and be as nice as you please in the Choice; but when you have chosen them, by no means play upon them: 'Tis cruel and malicious, to divert one's self at the Expence of one's Friend.

However, Madam, said Mr. *Glanville*, who was charmed to hear her talk so rationally, you may give People Leave to railly their Enemies.

Truly, resumed *Arabella*, I cannot allow that, any more than upon Friends; for Raillery is the poorest kind of Revenge that can be taken: Methinks, it is mean to railly Persons who have a small Share of Merit; since, haply, their Defects were born with them, and not of their own acquiring; and it is great Injustice to descant upon one slight Fault in Men of Parts, to the Prejudice of a thousand good Qualities.

For aught I see, Madam, said the Beau, you will not allow one to railly any body.

I am of Opinion, Sir, said *Arabella*, that there are very few proper Objects for Raillery; and still fewer, who can railly well: The Talent of Raillery ought to be born with a Person; no Art can infuse it; and those who endeavour to railly in spite of Nature, will be so far from diverting others, that they will become the Objects of Ridicule themselves.

Many other pleasing Qualities of Wit may be acquired by Pains and Study, but Raillery must be the Gift of Nature: It is not enough to have many lively and agreeable Thoughts; but there must be such an Expression, as must convey their full Force and Meaning; the Air the Aspect, the Tone of the Voice, and every Part in general, must contribute to its Perfection.

There ought also to be a great Distance between Raillery and Satire, so that one may never be mistaken for the other: Raillery ought indeed to surprise, and sensibly touch, those to whom it is directed; but I would not have the Wounds it makes, either deep or lasting: Let those who feel it, be hurt like Persons, who, gathering Roses, are pricked by the Thorns, and find a sweet Smell to make amends.

I would have Raillery raise the Fancy, and quicken the Imagination, the Fire of its Wit should only enable us to trace its Original, and shine as the Stars do, but not burn. Yet, after all, I cannot greatly approve of Raillery, or cease to think it dangerous; and, to pursue my Comparison, said she, with an inchanting Smile, Persons who possess the true Talent of Raillery, are like Comets; they are seldom seen, and are at once admir'd and fear'd.

I protest, Lady *Bella*, said Sir *Charles*, who had listen'd to her with many Signs of Admiration, you speak like an Orator.

One would not imagine, interrupted Mr. *Glanville*, who saw *Arabella* in some Confusion at the coarse Praise her Uncle gave her, that my Cousin could speak so accurately of a Quality she never practises: And 'tis easy to judge by what she has said, that no body can railly finer than herself, if she pleases.

Mr. *Selvin*, tho' he bore her a Grudge for knowing more History than he did, yet assur'd her, that she had given the best Rules imaginable for raillying well. But the Beau, whom she had silenc'd by her Reproof, was extremely angry; and, supposing it would mortify her to see him pay Court to her Cousin, he redoubled his Assiduities to Miss *Glanville*, who was highly delighted at seeing *Arabella* less taken Notice of by this gay Gentleman, than herself.

CHAPTER VII

In which the Author condescends to be very minute in the Description of our Heroin's Dress

THE Indifference of Mr. *Tinsel*, convincing Miss *Glanville*, that *Arabella* was less to be dreaded than she imagin'd, she had no Reluctance at seeing her prepare for her publick Appearance the next Ball Night.

Having consulted her Fancy in a rich Silver Stuff, she had bought for that Purpose, a Person was sent for to make it; and *Arabella*, who follow'd no Fashion but her own Taste, which was form'd on the Manners of the Heroines, order'd the Woman to make her a Robe after the same Model as the Princess *Julia*'s.[1]

The Mantua-maker, who thought it might do her great Prejudice with her new Customer, to acknowledge she knew nothing of the Princess *Julia*, or the Fashion of her Gown, replied at Random, and with great Pertness,

That, that Taste was quite out; and, she would advise her Lady-ship to have her Cloaths made in the present Mode, which was far more becoming.

You can never persuade me, said *Arabella*, that any Fashion can be more becoming than that of the Princess *Julia*'s, who was the most gallant Princess upon Earth, and knew better than any other, how to set off her Charms. It may indeed be a little obselete now, pursued she, for the Fashion could not but alter a little in the Compass of near two thousand Years.

Two thousand Years! Madam, said the Woman, in a great Surprize; Lord help us Tradespeople, if they did not alter a thousand Times in as many Days! I thought your Ladyship was speaking of the last Month's Taste; which, as I said before, is quite out now.

Well, replied *Arabella*, let the present Mode be what it will, I insist upon having my Cloaths made after the Pattern of the beautiful Daughter of *Augustus*; being convinced, that none other can be half so becoming.

What Fashion was that, pray, Madam, said the Woman? I never saw it.

How, replied *Arabella*, Have you already forgot the Fashion of the Princess *Julia*'s Robe, which you said was wore but last Month? Or, are you ignorant that the Princess *Julia*, and the Daughter of *Augustus*, is the same Person?

I protest, Madam, said the Woman, extremely confus'd, I had forgot that, till you called it to my Mind.

Well, said *Arabella*, make me a Robe in the same Taste.

The Mantua-maker was now wholly at a Loss in what Manner to behave; for, being conscious that she knew nothing of the Prin-cess *Julia*'s Fashion, she could not undertake to make it without Directions; and she was afraid of discovering her Ignorance by asking for any; so that her Silence and Embarrassment persuading *Arabella* she knew nothing of the Matter, she dismist her with a small Present, for the Trouble she had given her, and had Recourse to her usual Expedient, which was, to make one of her Women, who understood a little of the Mantua-making Business, make a Robe for her, after her own Directions.

Miss *Glanville*, who imagin'd she had sent for Work-women, in order to have Cloaths made in the modern Taste, was surpriz'd at her Entrance into her Chamber, to see her dressing for the Ball, in a Habit singular to the last Degree.

She wore no Hoop, and the Blue and Silver Stuff of her Robe, was only kept by its own Richness, from hanging close about her. It was quite open round her Breast, which was shaded with a rich Border of Lace; and clasping close to her Waist, by small Knots of Diamonds, descended in a sweeping Train on the Ground.

The Sleeves were short, wide, and slashed, fastned in different Places with Diamonds, and her Arms were partly hid by half a Dozen Falls of Ruffles. Her Hair, which fell in very easy Ringlets on her Neck, was plac'd with great Care and Exactness round her lovely Face; and the Jewels and Ribbons, which were all her Head-dress, dispos'd to the greatest Advantage.[1]

Upon the whole, nothing could be more singularly becoming than her Dress; or set off with greater Advantage the striking Beauties of her Person.

Miss *Glanville*, tho' she was not displeas'd to see her persist in her Singularity of Dress; yet could not behold her look so lovely in it, without feeling a secret Uneasiness; but consoling herself with the Hopes of the Ridicule she would occasion, she assum'd a chearful Air, approv'd her Taste in the Choice of her Colours, and went with her at the usual Hour, to the Rooms, attended by Mr. *Glanville*, Mr. *Selvin*, and the young Beau we have formerly mention'd.

The Surprize *Arabella*'s unusual Appearance gave to the whole Company, was very visible to every one but herself.

The Moment she enter'd the Room, every one whisper'd the Person next to them; and for some Moments, nothing was heard but the Words, the Princess *Julia*; which was eccho'd at every Corner, and at last attracted her Observation.

Mr. *Glanville*, and the rest of the Company with her, were in some Confusion at the universal Exclamation, which they imagin'd was occasion'd by the Singularity of her Habit; tho' they could not conceive, why they gave her that Title. Had they known the Adventure of the Mantua-maker, it would doubtless have easily occurr'd to them; for the Woman had no sooner left *Arabella*, than she related the Conference she had with a Lady newly arriv'd, who had requir'd her to make a Robe in the Manner of the Princess *Julia*'s; and dismiss'd her, because she did not understand the Fashions that prevail'd two thousand Years ago.

This Story was quickly dispers'd, and for its Novelty, afforded a great deal of Diversion; every one long'd to see a Fashion of such Antiquity; and expected the Appearance of the Princess *Julia* with great Impatience.

It is not to be doubted but much Mirth was treasur'd up for her Appearance; and the occasional Humourist had already prepared his accustom'd Jest, when the Sight of the devoted fair One repell'd his Vivacity, and the design'd Ridicule of the whole Assembly.

Scarce had the first tumultous Whisper escap'd the Lips of each Individual, when they found themselves aw'd to Respect by that irresistable Charm in the Person of *Arabella*, which commanded Reverence and Love from all who beheld her.

Her noble Air, the native Dignity in her Looks, the inexpressible Grace which accompany'd all her Motions, and the consummate Loveliness of her Form, drew the Admiration of the whole Assembly.

A respectful Silence succeeded, and the Astonishment her Beauty occasion'd, left them no Room to descant on the Absurdity of her Dress.

Miss *Glanville*, who felt a malicious Joy at the Sneers she expected would be cast on her Cousin, was greatly disappointed at the Deference which seem'd to be paid her; and to vent some Part of her Spleen, took occasion to mention her Surprize, at the Behaviour of the Company on their Entrance; wondering what they could mean by whispering the Princess *Julia* to one another.

I assure you, said *Arabella*, smiling, I am not less surpriz'd than you at it; and since they directed their Looks to me at the same Time, I fancy they either took me for some Princess of the Name of *Julia*, who is expected here to-Night, or else flatter me with some Resemblance to the beautiful Daughter of *Augustus*.

The Comparison, Madam, said Mr. *Selvin*, who took all Occasions to shew his Reading, is too injurious to you, for I am of Opinion you as much excel that licentious Lady in the Beauties of your Person, as you do in the Qualities of your Mind.

I never heard Licentiousness imputed to the Daughter of *Augustus Caesar*, said *Arabella*; and the most her Enemies can say of her, is, that she loved Admiration, and would permit herself to be beloved, and to be told so, without shewing any Signs of Displeasure.

Bless me, Madam, interrupted Mr. *Selvin*, how strangely do you mistake the Character of *Julia*: Tho' the Daughter of an Emperor, she was, pardon the Expression, the most abandon'd Prostitute in *Rome*; many of her Intrigues are recorded in History; but to mention only one, Was not her infamous Commerce with *Ovid*, the Cause of his Banishment?

CHAPTER VIII

Some Reflexions very fit, and others very unfit for an Assembly-Room

YOU speak in strange Terms, replied *Arabella*, blushing, of a Princess, who if she was not the most reserv'd and severe Person in the World, was yet nevertheless, absolutely chaste.

I know there were People who represented her Partiality for *Ovid* in a very unfavourable Light; but that ingenious Poet, when he related his History to the great *Agrippa*, told him in Confidence all that had pass'd between him and the Princess *Julia*, than which nothing could be more innocent tho' a little indiscreet. For, 'tis certain that she permitted him to love her, and did not condemn him to any rigorous Punishment for daring to tell her so; yet, for all this, as I said before, tho' she was not altogether so austere as she ought to have been, yet she was nevertheless a most virtuous Princess.[1]

Mr. *Selvin*, not daring to contradict a Lady whose extensive Reading had furnish'd her with Anecdotes unknown almost to any Body else, by his Silence confess'd her Superiority. But Mr. *Glanville*, who knew all these Anecdotes were drawn from Romances, which he found contradicted the known Facts in History, and assign'd the most ridiculous Causes for Things of the greatest Importance; could not help smiling at the Facility with which Mr. *Selvin* gave into those idle Absurdities. For notwithstanding his Affectation of great Reading, his superficial Knowledge of History made it extremely easy to deceive him; and as it was his Custom to mark in his Pocket-Book all the Scraps of History he heard introduced into Conversation, and retail them again in other Company; he did not doubt but he would make a Figure with the curious Circumstances *Arabella* had furnish'd him with.

Arabella observing Mr. *Tinsel* by his familiar Bows, significant Smiles, and easy Salutations, was acquainted with the greatest Part of the Assembly, told him, that she did not doubt but he knew the Adventures of many Persons whom they were viewing; and that he would do her a Pleasure, if he would relate some of them.

Mr. *Tinsel* was charm'd with a Request which afforded him an Opportunity of gratifying a favourite Inclination, and seating himself near her immediately, was beginning to obey her Injunctions, when she gracefully intreated him to stay a Moment; and calling to Mr. *Glanville* and his Sister, who were talking to Mr. *Selvin*, ask'd them if they chose to partake of a more rational Amusement than Dancing, and listen to the Adventures of some illustrious Persons, which Mr. *Tinsel* had promis'd to relate.

I assure you, Madam, said Mr. *Glanville*, smiling, you will find that a less innocent Amusement than Dancing.

Why so, Sir, replied *Arabella*, since it is not an indiscreet Curiosity which prompts me to a Desire of hearing the Histories Mr. *Tinsel* has promis'd to entertain me with; but rather a Hope of hearing something which may at once improve and delight me; something which may excite my Admiration, engage my Esteem, or influence my Practice.

'Twas doubtless, with such Motives as these, that we find Princesses and Ladies of the most illustrious Rank, in *Clelia* and the Grand *Cyrus*, listning to the Adventures of Persons, in whom they were probably as little interested, as we are in these around us. Kings, Princes, and Commanders of Armies, thought it was no Waste of their Time, in the midst of the Hurry and Clamour of a Camp, to listen many Hours to the Relation of one single History, and not fill'd with any extraordinary Events; but haply a simple Recital of common Occurrences: The great *Cyrus*, while he was busy in reducing all *Asia* to his Yoke, heard nevertheless, the Histories of all the considerable Persons in the Camp, besides those of Strangers, and even his Enemies.[1] If there was therefore any thing either criminal or mean, in hearing the Adventures of others, do you imagine so many great and illustrious Persons would have given in to such an Amusement?

After this *Arabella* turn'd gravely about to Mr. *Tinsel*, and told him, he was at Liberty to begin his Recital.[2]

The Beau, a little disconcerted by the Solemnity with which she requested his Information, knew not how to begin with the

Formality that he saw was required of him; and therefore sat silent for a few Moments; which *Arabella* suppos'd was to recall to his Memory all the Passages he propos'd to relate.

His Perplexity would probably have increas'd instead of lessening by the profound Silence which she observed, had not Miss *Glanville* seated herself with a sprightly Air on the other Side of him, and directing his Eyes to a tall handsome Woman that had just enter'd, ask'd him pleasantly, to tell her History if he knew it.

Mr. *Tinsel,* brought into his usual Track by this Question, answer'd smiling, That the History of that Lady was yet a Secret, or known but to a very few; but my Intelligence, added he, is generally the earliest, and may always be depended on.

Perhaps, said *Arabella*, the Lady is one of your Acquaintances, and favour'd you with the Recital of her Adventures from her own Mouth.

No, really, Madam, answer'd Mr. *Tinsel*, surpriz'd at the great Simplicity of *Arabella*, for so he understood it; the Lady, I believe, is not so communicative: And to say the Truth, I should not chuse to hear her Adventures from herself, since she certainly would suppress the most material Circumstances.

In a Word, said he, lowering his Voice, That Lady was for many Years the Mistress of a young military Nobleman, whom she was so complaisant to follow in all his Campaigns, Marches, Sieges, and every Inconveniency of War: He married her in *Gibraltar*, from whence he is lately arriv'd, and introduc'd his new Lady to his noble Brother, by whom she was not unfavourably receiv'd. 'Tis worth remarking, that this same haughty Peer thought fit to resent with implacable Obstinacy, the Marriage of another of his Brothers, with the Widow of a brave Officer, of considerable Rank in the Army. 'Tis true, she was several Years older than the young Lord, and had no Fortune; but the Duke assign'd other Reasons for his Displeasure: He complain'd loudly, that his Brother had dishonour'd the Nobility of his Birth, by this Alliance, and continued his Resentment till the Death of the young Hero, who gave many remarkable Proofs of his Courage and Fortitude upon several Occasions, and died gloriously before the Walls of *Carthagena*; leaving his disconsolate Lady a Widow a second Time, with the Acquisition of a Title indeed, but a very small Addition to her Fortune.[1]

Observe that gay, splendid Lady, I beseech you, Madam, pursued he, turning to *Arabella*; how affectedly she looks and talks, and throws her Eyes around the Room, with a haughty Self-sufficiency in her Aspect, and insolent Contempt for every Thing but herself. Her Habit, her Speech, her Motions, are all *French*; nothing in *England* is able to please her; the People so dull, so aukwardly polite, the Manners so gross; no Delicacy, no Elegance, no Magnificence in their Persons, Houses, or Diversions; every Thing is so distasteful, there is no living in such a Place. One may crawl about, indeed, she says, and make a shift to breathe in the odious Country, but one cannot be said to live; and with all the Requisites to render Life delightful, here, one can only suffer, not enjoy it.

Would one not imagine, pursued he, this fine Lady was a Person of very exalted Rank, who has the Sanction of Birth, Riches, and Grandeur for her extraordinary Pride; and yet she is no other than the Daughter of an Inn-Keeper at *Spa*, and had the exalted Post assign'd her of attending new Lodgers to their Apartments, acquainting them with all the Conveniences of the Place, answering an humble Question or two concerning what Company was in the Town, what Scandal was stirring, and the like.

One of our great Sea Commanders[1] going thither for his Health, happen'd to lodge at this Inn; and was so struck with her Charms, that he marry'd her in a few Weeks, and soon after brought her to *England*.

Such was the Origin of this fantastick Lady; whose insupportable Pride and ridiculous Affectation, draws Contempt and Aversion wherever she appears.

Did I not tell you, Madam, interrupted Mr. *Glanville*, that the Amusement you had chose was not so innocent as Dancing? What a deal of Scandal has Mr. *Tinsel* utter'd in the Compass of a few Minutes?

I assure you, replied *Arabella*, I know not what to make of the Histories he has been relating. I think they do not deserve that Name, and are rather detatched Pieces of Satire on particular Persons, than a serious Relation of Facts. I confess my Expectations from this Gentleman have not been answer'd.

I think, however, Madam, said Mr. *Glanville*, we may allow that there is a negative Merit in the Relations Mr. *Tinsel* has made; for, if he has not shewn us any Thing to approve, he as at least shewn us what to condemn.

The Ugliness of Vice, reply'd *Arabella*, ought only to be represented to the Vicious; to whom Satire, like a magnifying Glass, may aggravate every Defect, in order to make its Deformity appear more hideous; but since its End is only to reprove and amend, it should never be address'd to any but those who come within its Correction, and may be the better for it: A virtuous Mind need not be shewn the Deformity of Vice, to make it be hated and avoided; the more pure and uncorrupted our Ideas are, the less shall we be influenc'd by Example. A natural Propensity to Virtue or Vice often determines the Choice: 'Tis sufficient therefore to shew a good Mind what it ought to pursue, though a bad one must be told what to avoid. In a Word, one ought to be always incited, the other always restrain'd.[1]

I vow, Lady *Bella*, said Miss *Glanville*, you'd make one think one came here to hear a Sermon; you are so very grave, and talk upon such high-flown Subjects. What Harm was there in what Mr. *Tinsel* was telling us? It would be hard indeed, if one might not divert one's self with other Peoples Faults.

I am afraid, Miss, said *Arabella*, those who can divert themselves with the Faults of others, are not behind hand in affording Diversion. And that very Inclination, added she, smilingly, to hear other Peoples Faults, may by those very People, be condemned as one, and afford them the same Kind of ill-natur'd Pleasure you are so desirous of.

Nay, Madam, return'd Miss *Glanville*, your Ladyship was the first who introduc'd the Discourse you condemn so much. Did not you desire Mr. *Tinsel* to tell you Histories about the Company; and ask my Brother and me, to come and hear them?

'Tis true, reply'd *Arabella*, that I did desire you to partake with me of a pleasing and rational Amusement, for such I imagin'd Mr. *Tinsel*'s Histories might afford; far from a Detail of Vices, Follies, and Irregularities, I expected to have heard the Adventures of some illustrious Personages related; between whose Actions, and those of the Heroes and Heroines of Antiquity, I might have found some Resemblance.

For Instance, I hop'd to have heard imitated the sublime Courage of a *Clelia*, who, to save her Honour from the Attempts of the impious *Tarquin*, leap'd into the River *Tyber*, and swam to the other Side;[2] or the noble Resolution of the incomparable *Candace*, who, to escape out of the Hands of her Ravisher, the Pirate

Zenadorus, set Fire to his Vessel with her own Hands, and committed herself to the Mercy of the Waves:[1] Or, the Constancy and Affection of a *Mandana*, who, for the Sake of a *Cyrus*, refused the richest Crowns in the World, and braved the Terrors of Death to preserve herself for him.[2]

As for the Men, I hoped to have heard of some who might have almost equall'd the great *Oroondates*, the invincible *Artaban*, the valiant *Juba*, the renowned *Alcamenes*,[3] and many thousand Heroes of Antiquity; whose glorious Exploits in War, and unshaken Constancy in Love, have given them immortal Fame.

While *Arabella* was uttering this long Speech, with great Emotion, Miss *Glanville*, with a sly Look at the Beau, gave him to understand, that was her Cousin's Foible.

Mr. *Tinsel*, however, not able to comprehend the Meaning of what she said, listen'd to her with many Signs of Perplexity and Wonder.

Mr. *Selvin* in secret repin'd at her prodigious Knowledge of History; and Mr. *Glanville*, with his Eyes fix'd on the Ground, bit his Lips almost through with Madness.

In the mean Time, several among the Company, desirous of hearing what the strange Lady was saying so loud, and with so much Eagerness and Emotion, gather'd round them; which Mr. *Glanville* observing, and fearing *Arabella* would expose herself still farther, whisper'd his Sister to get her away if possible.

Miss *Glanville*, tho' very unwilling, obey'd his Injunctions; and complaining of a sudden Head-ach, *Arabella* immediately propos'd retiring, which was joyfully complied with by Mr. *Glanville*, who with the other Gentlemen attended them home.

CHAPTER IX

Being a Chapter of the Satyrical Kind

At their Return, Sir *Charles* told his Niece, That she had now had a Specimen of the World, and some of the fashionable Amusements; and ask'd her, how she had been entertain'd.

Why, truly, Sir, replied she, smiling, I have brought away no great Relish for a Renewal of the Amusement I have partaken of

To-night. If the World, in which you seem to think I am but new initiated, affords only these Kinds of Pleasures, I shall very soon regret the Solitude and Books I have quitted.

Why pray, said Miss *Glanville*? What Kind of Amusements did your Ladyship expect to find in the World? And what was there disagreeable in your Entertainment to Night? I am sure there is no Place in *England*, except *London*, where there is so much good Company to be met with, as here. The Assembly was very numerous and brillant, and one can be at no Loss for Amusements: The Pump-Room in the Morning, the Parade, and the Rooms, in the Evening, with little occasional Parties of Pleasure, will find one sufficient Employment, and leave none of one's Time to lye useless upon one's Hand.

I am of Opinion, replied *Arabella*, that one's Time is far from being well employ'd in the Manner you portion it out: And People who spend theirs in such trifling Amusements, must certainly live to very little Purpose.

What room, I pray you, does a Lady give for high and noble Adventures, who consumes her Days in Dressing, Dancing, listening to Songs, and ranging the Walks with People as thoughtless as herself? How mean and contemptible a Figure must a Life spent in such idle Amusements make in History? Or rather, Are not such Persons always buried in Oblivion, and can any Pen be found who would condescend to record such inconsiderable Actions?

Nor can I persuade myself, added she, that any of those Men whom I saw at the Assembly, with Figures so feminine, Voices so soft, such tripping Steps, and unmeaning Gestures, have ever signalized either their Courage or Constancy; but might be overcome by their Enemy in Battle, or be false to their Mistress in Love.

Law! Cousin, reply'd Miss *Glanville*, you are always talking of Battles and Fighting. Do you expect that Persons of Quality, and fine Gentlemen, will go to the Wars? What Business have they to fight? That belongs to the Officers.

Then every fine Gentleman is an Officer, said *Arabella*; and some other Title ought to be found out for Men who do nothing but Dance and Dress.

I could never have imagined, interrupted Mr. *Tinsel*, surveying *Arabella*, that a Lady so elegant and gay in her own Appearance, should have an Aversion to Pleasure and Magnificence.

I assure you, Sir, replied *Arabella*, I have an Aversion to neither: On the contrary, I am a great Admirer of both. But my Ideas of Amusements and Grandeur are probably different from yours.

I will allow the Ladies to be sollicitous about their Habits, and dress with all the Care and Elegance they are capable of; but such Trifles are below the Consideration of a Man, who ought not to owe the Dignity of his Appearance to the Embroidery on his Coat, but to his high and noble Air, the Grandeur of his Courage, the Elevation of his Sentiments, and the many heroick Actions he has perform'd.

Such a Man will dress his Person with a graceful Simplicity, and lavish all his Gold and Embroidery upon his Armour, to render him conspicuous in the Day of Battle. The Plumes in his Helmet will look more graceful in the Field, than the Feather in his Hat at a Ball; and Jewels blaze with more Propriety on his Shield and Cuirass in Battle, than glittering on his Finger in a Dance.

Do not imagine, however, pursued she, that I absolutely condemn Dancing, and think it a Diversion wholly unworthy of a Hero.

History has recorded some very famous Balls, at which the most illustrious Persons in the World have appear'd.

Cyrus the Great, we are inform'd, open'd a Ball with the divine *Mandana* at *Sardis*.[1] The renown'd King of *Scythia* danc'd with the Princess *Cleopatra* at *Alexandria*.[2] The brave *Cleomedon* with the fair *Candace* at *Ethiopia*;[3] but these Diversions were taken but seldom, and consider'd indeed as an Amusement, not as a Part of the Business of Life.

How would so many glorious Battles have been fought, Cities taken, Ladies rescu'd, and other great and noble Adventures been atchiev'd, if the Men, sunk in Sloth and Effeminacy, had continually follow'd the Sound of a Fiddle, saunter'd in Publick Walks, and tattled over a Tea-table.

I vow, Cousin, said Miss *Glanville*, you are infinitely more severe in your Censures than Mr. *Tinsel* was at the Assembly. You had little Reason methinks to be angry with him.

All I have said, reply'd *Arabella*, was the natural Inference from your own Account of the Manner in which People live here. When Actions are a Censure upon themselves, the Reciter will always be consider'd as a Satirist.

CHAPTER X

*In which our Heroine justifies her own Notions by some
very illustrious Examples*

MR. *Selvin* and Mr. *Tinsel*, who had listen'd attentively to this
Discourse of *Arabella*, took Leave as soon as it was ended, and went
away with very different Opinions of her.

Mr. *Tinsel* declaring she was a Fool, and had no Knowledge of
the World, and Mr. *Selvin* convinc'd she was a Wit, and very
learn'd in Antiquity.

Certainly, said Mr. *Selvin*, in Support of his Opinion, the Lady
has great Judgment; has been capable of prodigious Application,
as is apparent by her extensive Reading: Then her Memory is quite
miraculous. I protest, I am quite charm'd with her: I never met
with such a Woman in my Life.

Her Cousin, in my Opinion, reply'd Mr. *Tinsel*, is infinitely
beyond her in every Merit, but Beauty. How sprightly and free her
Conversation? What a thorough Knowledge of the World? So true
a Taste for polite Amusements, and a Fund of Spirits that sets
Vapours and Spleen at Defiance.

This Speech bringing on a Comparison between the Ladies, the
Champions for each grew so warm in the Dispute, that they had
like to have quarrell'd. However, by the Interposition of some other
Gentlemen who were with them, they parted tolerable Friends that
Night, and renew'd their Visits to Sir *Charles* in the Morning.

They found only Miss *Glanville* with her Father and Brother.
Arabella generally spent the Mornings in her own Chamber, where
Reading and the Labours of the Toilet employ'd her Time till
Dinner: Tho' it must be confess'd to her Honour, that the latter
engross'd but a very small Part of it.

Miss *Glanville*, with whom the Beau had a long Conversation at
one of the Windows; in which he recounted his Dispute with Mr.
Selvin, and the Danger he ran of being pink'd in a Duel, that was
his Phrase, for her Sake, at last propos'd a Walk; to which she consented, and engag'd to prevail upon *Arabella* to accompany them.

That Lady at first positively refus'd; alleging in Excuse, That she
was so extremely interested in the Fate of the Princess *Melisintha*,[1]
whose Story she was reading, that she could not stir till she had
finish'd it.

That poor Princess, continu'd she, is at present in a most terrible Situation. She has just set Fire to the Palace, in order to avoid the Embraces of a King who forc'd her to marry him. I am in Pain to know how she escapes the Flames.

Pshaw, interrupted Miss *Glanville*, let her perish there, if she will: Don't let her hinder our Walk.

Who is it you doom with so much Cruelty to perish, said *Arabella*, closing the Book, and looking stedfastly on her Cousin? Is it the beautiful *Melisintha*, that Princess, whose Fortitude and Patience have justly render'd her the Admiration of the whole World? That Princess, descended from a Race of Heroes, whose heroick Virtues all glow'd in her own beauteous Breast; that Princess, who, when taken Captive with the King her Father, bore her Imprisonment and Chains with a marvellous Constancy; and who, when she had enslaved her Conqueror, and given Fetters to the Prince who held her Father and herself in Bonds, nobly refus'd the Diadem he proffer'd her, and devoted herself to Destruction, in order to punish the Enemy of her House. I am not able to relate the rest of her History, seeing I have read no further myself; but if you will be pleased to sit down and listen to me while I read what remains, I am persuaded you will find new Cause to love and admire this amiable Princess.

Pardon me, Madam, said Miss *Glanville*, I have heard enough; and I could have been very well satisfy'd not to have heard so much. I think we waste a great deal of Time talking about People we know nothing of. The Morning will be quite lost, if we don't make Haste. Come, added she, you must go: You have a new Lover below, who waits to go with us; he'll die if I don't bring you.

A new Lover! return'd *Arabella*, surpriz'd.

Aye, aye, said Miss *Glanville*, the learned Mr. *Selvin*; I assure you, he had almost quarrell'd with Mr. *Tinsel* last Night about your Ladyship.

Arabella, at this Intelligence, casting down her Eyes, discover'd many Signs of Anger and Confusion: And after a Silence of some Moments, during which, Miss *Glanville* had been employ'd in adjusting her Dress at the Glass, addressing herself to her Cousin with an Accent somewhat less sweet than before.

Had any other than yourself, Miss, said she, acquainted me with the Presumption of that unfortunate Person, I should haply have discover'd my Resentment in other Terms: But, as it is, must inform you, that I take it extremely ill, you should be accessary to giving me this Offence.

Hey day! said Miss *Glanville*, turning about hastily, How have I offended your Ladyship, pray?

I am willing to hope, Cousin, reply'd *Arabella*, that it was only to divert yourself with the Trouble and Confusion in which you see me, that you have indiscreetly told Things which ought to have been bury'd in Silence.

And what is all this mighty Trouble and Confusion about then, Madam, said Miss *Glanville*, smiling? Is it because I told you, Mr. *Selvin* was a Lover of your Ladyship?

Certainly, said *Arabella*, such an Information is sufficient to give one a great deal of Perplexity. Is it such a little Matter, think you, to be told that a Man has the Presumption to love one?

A meer Trifle, reply'd Miss *Glanville*, laughing; a hundred Lovers are not worth a Moment's Thought, when one's sure of them, for then the Trouble is all over. And as for this unfortunate Person, as your Ladyship called him, let him die at his Leisure, while we go to the Parade.

Your Levity, Cousin, said *Arabella*, forces me to smile, notwithstanding the Cause I have to be incens'd; however, I have Charity enough to make me not desire the Death of Mr. *Selvin*, who may repair the Crime he has been guilty of by Repentance and Discontinuation.

Well then, said Miss *Glanville*, you are resolv'd to go to the Parade: Shall I reach you your odd Kind of Capuchin?

How, said *Arabella*, can I with any Propriety see a Man who has discover'd himself to have a Passion for me? Will he not construe such a Favour into a Permission for him to hope?

Oh! no, interrupted Miss *Glanville*, he does not imagine I have told your Ladyship he loves you; for indeed he don't know that I am acquainted with his Passion.

Then he is less culpable than I thought him, reply'd *Arabella*; and if you think I am in no Danger of hearing a Confession of his Fault from his own Mouth, I'll comply with your Request, and go with you to the Parade. But added she, I must first engage you to promise not to leave me alone a Moment, lest he should take Advantage of such an Opportunity, to give some Hint of his Passion, that would force me to treat him very rigorously.

Miss *Glanville* answer'd laughing, That she would be sure to mind her Directions. However, said she, your Ladyship need not be apprehensive he will say any fine Things to you; for I knew a young Lady he was formerly in Love with, and the odious Creature visited her a Twelve-month before he found Courage enough to tell her she was handsome.

Doubtless, reply'd *Arabella*, he was much to be commended for his Respect. A Lover should never have the Presumption to declare his Passion to his Mistress, unless in certain Circumstances, which may at the same Time in part disarm her Anger. For Instance, he must struggle with the Violence of his Passion, till it has cast him into a Fever. His Physicians must give him over, pronouncing his Distemper incurable, since the Cause of it being in his Mind, all their Art is incapable of removing it. Thus he must suffer, rejoicing at the Approach of Death, which will free him from all his Torments, without violating the Respect he owes to the Divine Object of his Flame. At length, when he has but a few Hours to live, his Mistress, with many Signs of Compassion, conjures him to tell her the Cause of his Despair. The Lover, conscious of his Crime, evades all her Inquiries; but the Lady laying at last a peremptory Command upon him to disclose the Secret, he dares not disobey her, and acknowledges his Passion with the utmost Contrition for having offended her; bidding her take the small Remainder of his Life to expiate his Crime; and finishes his Discourse by falling into a Swoon.

The Lady is touch'd at his Condition, commands him to live, and if necessary, permits him to hope.

This is the most common Way in which such Declarations are, and ought to be brought about. However, there are others, which are as well calculated for sparing a Lady's Confusion, and deprecating her Wrath.

The Lover, for Example, like the Prince of the *Massagetes*, after having buried his Passion in Silence for many Years, may chance to be walking with his Confidant in a retir'd Place; to whom, with a Deluge of Tears, he relates the Excess of his Passion and Despair. And while he is thus unbosoming his Griefs, not in the least suspecting he is overheard, his Princess, who had been listning to him in much Trouble and Confusion, by some little Rustling she makes, unawares discovers herself.

The surpriz'd Lover throws himself at her Feet, begs Pardon for his Rashness, observes that he had never presum'd to discover his

Passion to her; and implores her Leave to die before her, as a Punishment for his undesign'd Offence.[1]

The Method which the great *Artamenes* took[2] to let the Princess of *Media* know he adored her, was not less respectful. This valiant Prince, who had long loved her, being to fight a great Battle, in which he had some secret Presages he should fall, which however deceiv'd him, wrote a long Letter to the divine *Mandana*, wherein he discover'd his Passion, and the Resolution his Respect had inspir'd him with, to consume in Silence, and never presume to disclose his Love while he lived; acquainting her, that he had order'd that Letter not to be deliver'd to her, till it was certainly known that he was dead.

Accordingly he receiv'd several Wounds in the Fight, which brought him to the Ground, and his Body not being found, they concluded it was in the Enemy's Possession.

His faithful 'Squire, who had receiv'd his Instructions before the Battle, hastens to the Princess, who, with all the Court, is mightily affected at his Death.

He presents her the Letter, which she makes no Scruple to receive, since the Writer is no more. She reads it, and her whole Soul is melted with Compassion; she bewails his Fate with the most tender and affectionate Marks of Grief.

Her Confidant asks why she is so much affected, since in all Probability, she would not have pardon'd him for loving her, had he been alive?

She acknowledges the Truth of her Observation, takes Notice that his Death having cancell'd his Crime, his respectful Passion alone employs her Thoughts; she is resolv'd to bewail as innocent and worthy of Compassion when dead, whom living she would treat as a Criminal, and insinuates, that her Heart had entertain'd an Affection for him.

Her Confidant treasures up this Hint, and endeavours to console her, but in vain, till News is brought, that *Artamenes*, who had been carry'd for dead out of the Field, and by a very surprizing Adventure conceal'd all this Time, is return'd.

The Princess is cover'd with Confusion, and tho' glad he is alive, resolves to banish him for his Crime.

Her Confidant pleads his Cause so well, that she consents to see him; and, since he can no longer conceal his Passion, he confirms the Confession in his Letter, humbly begging Pardon for being still alive.

The Princess, who cannot plead Ignorance of his Passion, nor deny the Sorrow she testify'd for his Death, condescends to pardon him, and he is also permitted to hope. In like Manner the great Prince of *Persia*———[1]

Does your Ladyship consider how late it is, interrupted Miss *Glanville*, who had hitherto very impatiently listen'd to her? Don't let us keep the Gentlemen waiting any longer for us.

I must inform you how the Prince of *Persia* declar'd his Love for the incomparable *Berenice*, said *Arabella*.

Another Time, dear Cousin, said Miss *Glanville*; methinks we have talk'd long enough upon this Subject.

I am sorry the Time has seem'd so tedious to you, said *Arabella*, smiling; and therefore I'll trespass no longer upon your Patience. Then ordering *Lucy* to bring her Hat and Gloves, she went down Stairs, follow'd by Miss *Glanville*, who was greatly disappointed at her not putting on her Veil.

CHAPTER XI

In which our Heroine being mistaken herself, gives Occasion for a great many other Mistakes

As soon as the Ladies enter'd the Room, Mr. *Selvin*, with more Gaiety than usual, advanc'd towards *Arabella*, who put on so cold and severe a Countenance at his Approach, that the poor Man, extreamly confus'd, drew back, and remain'd in great Perplexity, fearing he had offended her.

Mr. *Tinsel*, seeing Mr. *Selvin*'s Reception, and aw'd by the becoming Majesty in her Person, notwithstanding all his Assurance, accosted her with less Confidence than was his Custom; but *Arabella* softning her Looks with the most engaging Smiles, made an Apology for detaining them so long from the Parade, gave her Hand to the Beau, as being not a suspected Person, and permitted him to lead her out, Mr. *Glanville*, to whom she always allow'd the Preference on those Occasions, being a little indispos'd, and not able to attend her.

Mr. *Tinsel*, whose Vanity was greatly flatter'd by the Preference

Arabella gave him to his Companion, proceeded according to his usual Custom, to examine her Looks and Behaviour with more Care; conceiving such a Preference must proceed from a latent Motive which was not unfavourable for him. His Discernment on these Occasions being very surprising, he soon discover'd in the bright Eyes of *Arabella* a secret Approbation of his Person, which he endeavour'd to increase by displaying it with all the Address he was Master of, and did not fail to talk her into an Opinion of his Wit, by ridiculing every Body that pass'd them, and directing several study'd Compliments to herself.

Miss *Glanville*, who was not so agreeably entertain'd by the grave Mr. *Selvin*, saw these Advances to a Gallantry with her Cousin with great Disturbance: She was resolved to interrupt it if possible, and being convinc'd Mr. *Selvin* preferr'd *Arabella*'s Conversation to hers, she plotted how to pair them together, and have the Beau to herself.

As they walk'd a few Paces behind her Cousin and Mr. *Tinsel*, she was in no Danger of being over-heard; and taking Occasion to put Mr. *Selvin* in mind of *Arabella*'s Behaviour to him, when he accosted her; she ask'd him, if he was conscious of having done any thing to offend her?

I protest, Madam, reply'd Mr. *Selvin*, I know not of any thing I have done to displease her. I never fail'd, to my Knowledge, in my Respects towards her Ladyship, for whom indeed I have a most profound Veneration.

I know so much of her Temper, resum'd Miss *Glanville*, as to be certain, if she has taken it into her Head to be angry with you, she will be ten times more so at your Indifference: And if you hope for her Favour, you must ask her Pardon with the most earnest Submission imaginable.

If I knew I had offended her, reply'd Mr. *Selvin*, I would very willingly ask her Pardon; but really, since I have not been guilty of any Fault towards her Ladyship, I don't know how to acknowledge it.

Well, said Miss *Glanville* coldly, I only took the Liberty to give you some friendly Advice, which you may follow, or not, as you please. I know my Cousin is angry at something, and I wish you were Friends again, that's all.

I am mightily oblig'd to you, Madam, said Mr. *Selvin*; and since you assure me her Ladyship is angry, I'll ask her Pardon, tho', really, as I said before, I don't know for what.

Well, interrupted Miss *Glanville*, we'll join them at the End of the Parade; and to give you an Opportunity of speaking to my Cousin, I'll engage Mr. *Tinsel* myself.

Mr. *Selvin*, who thought himself greatly oblig'd to Miss *Glanville* for her good Intentions, tho' in reality she had a View of exposing of her Cousin, as well as an Inclination to engage Mr. *Tinsel*, took Courage as they turn'd, to get on the other Side of *Arabella*, whom he had not dar'd before to approach, while Miss *Glanville*, addressing a Whisper of no great Importance to her Cousin, parted her from the Beau, and slackning her Pace a little, fell into a particular Discourse with him, which *Arabella* being too polite to interrupt, remain'd in a very perplexing Situation, dreading every Moment that Mr. *Selvin* would explain himself. Alarm'd at his Silence, yet resolv'd to interrupt him if he began to speak, and afraid of beginning a Conversation first, lest he should construe it to his Advantage.

Mr. *Selvin* being naturally timid in the Company of Ladies, the Circumstance of Disgrace which he was in with *Arabella*, her Silence and Reserve so added to his accustom'd Diffidence, that tho' he endeavour'd several times to speak, he was not able to bring out any thing but a preluding Hem; which he observ'd, to his extreme Confusion, seem'd always to encrease *Arabella*'s Constraint.

Indeed, that Lady, upon any Suspicion that he was going to break his mysterious Silence, always contracted her Brow into a Frown, cast down her Eyes with an Air of Perplexity, endeavour'd to hide her Blushes with her Fan; and to shew her In-attention, directed her Looks to the contrary Side.

The Lady and Gentleman being in equal Confusion, no Advances were made on either Side towards a Conversation, and they had reach'd almost the End of the Parade in an uninterrupted Silence; when Mr. *Selvin*, fearing he should never again have so good an Opportunity of making his Peace, collected all his Resolution, and with an Accent trembling under the Importance of the Speech he was going to make, began,

Madam, Since I have had the Honour of walking with your Ladyship, I have observed so many Signs of Constraint in your Manner, that I hardly dare intreat you to grant me a Moment's Hearing while I——

Sir, interrupted *Arabella*, before you go any further, I must inform you, that what you are going to say will mortally offend me. Take heed then how you commit an Indiscretion which will force me to treat you very rigorously.

If your Ladyship will not allow me to speak in my own Justification, said Mr. *Selvin*, yet I hope you will not refuse to tell me my Offence, since I——

You are very confident, indeed, interrupted *Arabella* again, to suppose I will repeat what would be infinitely grievous for me to hear. Against my Will, pursued she, I must give you the Satisfaction to know, that I am not ignorant of your Crime, but I also assure you that I am highly incens'd; and that, not only with the Thoughts you have dar'd to entertain of me, but likewise with your Presumption in going about to disclose them.

Mr. *Selvin*, whom the seeming Contradictions in this Speech astonish'd, yet imagin'd in general it hinted at the Dispute between him and Mr. *Tinsel*; and supposing the Story had been told to his Disadvantage, which was the Cause of her Anger, reply'd in great Emotion at the Injustice done him.

Since somebody has been so officious to acquaint your Ladyship with an Affair which ought to have been kept from your Knowledge; 'tis a Pity they did not inform you, that Mr. *Tinsel* was the Person that had the least Respect for your Ladyship, and is more worthy of your Resentment.

If Mr. *Tinsel*, replied *Arabella*, is guilty of an Offence like yours, yet since he has conceal'd it better, he is less culpable than you; and you have done that for him, which haply he would never have had Courage enough to do for himself as long as he lived.

Poor *Selvin*, quite confounded at these intricate Words, would have begg'd her to explain herself, had she not silenc'd him with a dreadful Frown: And making a Stop till Miss *Glanville* and Mr. *Tinsel* came up to them. She told her Cousin with a peevish Accent, that she had perform'd her Promise very ill; and whisper'd her, that she was to blame for all the Mortifications she had suffer'd.

Mr. *Tinsel*, supposing the Alteration in *Arabella*'s Humour proceeded from being so long depriv'd of his Company; endeavour'd to make her Amends by a Profusion of Compliments; which she receiv'd with such an Air of Displeasure, that the Beau, vex'd at the ill Success of his Gallantry, told her, he was afraid Mr. *Selvin*'s Gravity had infected her Ladyship.

Say rather, reply'd *Arabella*, that his Indiscretion has offended me.

Mr. *Tinsel*, charm'd with this beginning Confidence, which confirm'd his Hopes of having made some Impression on her Heart; conjur'd her very earnestly to tell him how Mr. *Selvin* had offended her.

'Tis sufficient, resum'd she, that I tell you he has offended me, without declaring the Nature of his Crime, since doubtless it has not escaped your Observation, which, if I may believe him, is not wholly disinterested. To confess yet more, 'tis true that he hath told me something concerning you, which——

Let me perish, Madam, interrupted the Beau, if one Syllable he has said be true.

How, said *Arabella*, a little disconcerted, Will you always persist in a Denial then?

Deny it, Madam, return'd Mr. *Tinsel*, I'll deny what he has said with my last Breath; 'tis all a scandalous Forgery: No Man living is less likely to think of your Ladyship in that Manner. If you knew my Thoughts, Madam, you would be convinc'd nothing is more impossible, and——

Sir, interrupted *Arabella*, extremely mortify'd, methinks you are very eager in your Justification. I promise you, I do not think you guilty of the Offence he charg'd you with; if I did, you would haply experience my Resentment in such a Manner, as would make you repent of your Presumption.

Arabella, in finishing these Words, interrupted Miss *Glanville*'s Discourse with Mr. *Selvin*, to tell her, she desir'd to return Home; to which that young Lady, who had not been at all pleas'd with the Morning's Walk, consented.

CHAPTER XII

In which our Heroine reconciles herself to a mortifying
Incident, by recollecting an Adventure in a Romance,
similar to her own

As soon as the Ladies were come to their Lodgings, *Arabella* went up to her own Apartment to meditate upon what had pass'd, and Miss *Glanville* retir'd to dress for Dinner; while the two Gentlemen, who thought they had great Reason to be dissatisfy'd with each other on Account of Lady *Bella*'s Behaviour, went to a Coffee-house, in order to come to some Explanation about it,

Well, Sir, said the Beau, with a sarcastick Air, I am greatly oblig'd to you for the Endeavours you have us'd to ruin me in Lady *Bella*'s Opinion. Rat me, if it is not the greatest Misfortune in the World, to give occasion for Envy.

Envy, Sir, interrupted Mr. *Selvin*; I protest I do really admire your great Skill in Stratagems, but I do not envy you the Possession of it. You have, indeed, very wittily contriv'd to put your own Sentiments of that Lady, which you deliver'd so freely the other Night, into my Mouth. 'Twas a Master-piece of Cunning, indeed; and, as I said before, I admire your Skill prodigiously.

I don't know what you mean, reply'd *Tinsel*, you talk in Riddles. Did you not yourself acquaint Lady *Bella* with the Preference I gave Miss *Glanville* to her? What would you propose by such a Piece of Treachery? You have ruin'd all my Hopes by it: The Lady resents it excessively, and 'tis no Wonder, 'faith, it must certainly mortify her. Upon my Soul, I can never forgive thee for so *mal a propos* a Discovery.

Forgive me, Sir, replied *Selvin*, in a Rage, I don't want your Forgiveness. I have done nothing unbecoming a Man of Honour. The Lady was so prejudiced by your Insinuations, that she would not give me Leave to speak; otherwise, I would have fully inform'd her of her Mistake, that she might have known how much she was oblig'd to you.

So she would not hear thee, interrupted *Tinsel* laughing, dear Soul, how very kind was that? 'Faith, I don't know how it is, but I am very lucky, without deserving to be so. Thou art a Witness for me, *Frank*, I took no great Pains to gain this fine Creature's Heart; but it was damn'd malicious tho', to attempt to make Discoveries. I see she is a little piqu'd, but I'll set all to rights again with a *Billet-doux*. I've an excellent Hand, tho' I say it, at a *Billet-doux*. I never knew one of mine fail in my Life.

Harky, Sir, said *Selvin* whispering, any more Attempts to shift your Sentiments upon me, and you shall hear of it. In the mean Time, be assur'd, I'll clear myself, and put the Saddle upon the right Horse.

Demme, if thou art not a queer Fellow, said *Tinsel*, endeavouring to hide his Discomposure at this Threat under a forc'd Laugh.

Selvin, without making any Reply, retir'd to write to *Arabella*; which *Tinsel* suspecting, resolv'd to be before-hand with him; and without leaving the Coffee-house, call'd for Paper, and wrote a Billet to her, which he dispatch'd away immediately.

The Messenger had just got Admittance to *Lucy*, when another arriv'd from *Selvin*.

They both presented their Letters, but *Lucy* refus'd them, saying, her Lady would turn her away, if she receiv'd such Sort of Letters.

Such Sort of Letters, return'd *Tinsel's* Man! Why, do you know what they contain, then?

To be sure, I do, reply'd *Lucy*; they are Love-Letters; and my Lady has charg'd me never to receive any more.

Well, reply'd *Selvin's* Servant, you may take my Letter; for my Master desir'd me to tell you, it was about Business of Consequence, which your Lady must be acquainted with.

Since you assure me it is not a Love-Letter, I'll take it, said *Lucy*.

And, pray take mine too, said *Tinsel's Mercury*; for I assure you, it is not a Love-Letter neither; 'tis only a *Billet-doux*.

Are you sure of that, reply'd *Lucy*; because I may venture to take it, I fancy, if 'tis what you say.

I'll swear it, said the Man delivering it to her. Well, said she, receiving it, I'll take them both up. But what did you call this, pursu'd she? I must not forget it, or else my Lady will think it a Love-Letter.

A *Billet-doux*, said the Man.

Lucy, for fear she should forget it, repeated the Words *Billet-doux* several Times as she went up Stairs; but entering her Lady's Apartment, she perceiving the Letters in her Hand, ask'd her so sternly, how she durst presume to bring them into her Presence, that the poor Girl, in her Fright, forgot the Lesson she had been conning; and endeavouring to recal it into her Memory, took no Notice of her Lady's Question, which she repeated several times, but to no Purpose.

Arabella, surpriz'd at her in-attention, reiterated her Commands, in a Tone somewhat louder than usual; asking her at the same Time, why she did not obey her immediately?

Indeed, Madam, reply'd *Lucy*, your Ladyship would not order me to take back the Letters, if you knew what they were: They are not Love-Letters; I was resolv'd to be sure of that before I took them. This, Madam, is a Letter about Business of Consequence; and the other——Oh dear! I can't think what the Man call'd it! But it is not a Love-Letter, indeed, Madam.

You are a simple Wench, said *Arabella* smiling: You may depend upon it, all Letters directed to me, must contain Matters of Love and Gallantry; and those I am not permitted to receive. Take them away then immediately. But stay, pursued she, seeing she was about to obey her, one of them, you say, was deliver'd to you as a Letter of Consequence; perhaps it is so: Indeed it may contain an Advertisement of some Design to carry me away. How do I know, but Mr. *Selvin*, incited by his Love and Despair, may intend to make such an Attempt. Give me that Letter, *Lucy*, I am resolved to open it. As for the other——yet who knows but the other may also bring me a Warning of the same Danger from another Quarter. The Pains Mr. *Tinsel* took to conceal his Passion, nay, almost as I think, to deny it, amounts to a Proof that he is meditating some Way to make sure of me. 'Tis certainly so: Give me that Letter, *Lucy*; I should be accessary to their intended Violence, if I neglected this timely Discovery.

Well, cried she, taking one of the Letters, this is exactly like what happen'd to the beautiful Princess of *Cappadocia*;[1] who, like me, in one and the same Day, receiv'd Advice that two of her Lovers intended to carry her off.

As she pronounc'd these Words Miss *Glanville* enter'd the Room, to whom *Arabella* immediately recounted the Adventure of the Letters; telling her, she did not doubt, but they contain'd a Discovery of some Conspiracy to carry her away.

And whom does your Ladyship suspect of such a strange Design, pray, said Miss *Glanville* smiling?

At present, reply'd *Arabella*, the two Cavaliers who walk'd with us to Day, are the Persons who seem the most likely to attempt that Violence.

I dare answer for Mr. *Tinsel*, replied Miss *Glanville*, he thinks of no such Thing.

Well, said *Arabella*, to convince you of your Mistake, I must inform you, that Mr. *Selvin*, having the Presumption to begin a Declaration of Love to me on the Parade this Morning, I reprov'd him severely for his Want of Respect, and threatned him with my Displeasure; in the Rage of his Jealousy, at seeing me treat Mr. *Tinsel* well, he discover'd to me, that he also was as criminal as himself, in order to oblige me to a severer Usage of him.

So he told you Mr. *Tinsel* was in Love with you, interrupted Miss *Glanville*?

He told it me in other Words, reply'd *Arabella*; for he said, Mr. *Tinsel* was guilty of that Offence, which I resented so severely to him.

Miss *Glanville* beginning to comprehend the Mystery, with great Difficulty forbore laughing at her Cousin's Mistake; for she well knew the Offence Mr. *Selvin* hinted at, and desirous of knowing what those Letters contain'd, she begg'd her to delay opening them no longer.

Arabella, pleas'd at her Solicitude, open'd one of the Letters; but glancing her Eye to the Bottom, and seeing the Name of *Selvin*, she threw it hastily upon the Table, and averting her Eyes, What a Mortification have I avoided, said she, that Letter is from *Selvin*; and questionless, contains an Avowal of his Crime.

Nay, you must read it, cried Miss *Glanville*, taking it up; since you have open'd it, 'tis the same Thing: You can never persuade him but you have seen it. However, to spare your Nicety, I'll read it to you. Which accordingly she did, and found it as follows.

MADAM,

'I Know not what Insinuations have been made use of to persuade you I was guilty of the Offence, which, with Justice, occasion'd your Resentment this Morning; but I assure you, nothing was ever more false. My Thoughts of your Ladyship are very different, and full of the profoundest Respect and Veneration. I have Reason to suspect Mr. *Tinsel* is the Person who has thus endeavoured to prejudice me with your Ladyship; therefore I am excusable if I tell you, that those very Sentiments, too disrespectful to be named, which he would persuade you are mine, he discover'd himself. He then, Madam, is the Person guilty of that Offence he so falsly lays to the Charge of him, who is, with the utmost Respect and Esteem,
Madam,
Your Ladyship's
most obedient, and
most humble Servant,
F. SELVIN.

How's this, cry'd Miss *Glanville*? Why, Madam, you are certainly mistaken. You see Mr. *Selvin* utterly denies the Crime of loving you. He has suffer'd very innocently in your Opinion. Indeed, your Ladyship was too hasty in condemning him.

If what he says be true, replied *Arabella*, who had been in extream Confusion, while a Letter so different from what she expected was reading; I have indeed unjustly condemn'd him. Nevertheless, I am still inclin'd to believe this is all Artifice; and that he is really guilty of entertaining a Passion for me.

But why should he take so much Pains to deny it, Madam, said Miss *Glanville*? Methinks that looks very odd.

Not at all, interrupted *Arabella*, whose Spirits were rais'd by recollecting an Adventure in her Romance, similar to this. Mr. *Selvin* has fallen upon the very same Stratagem with *Seramenes*;[1] who being in Love with the beautiful *Cleobuline*, Princess of *Corinth*, took all imaginable Pains to conceal his Passion, in order to be near that fair Princess; who would have banish'd him from her Presence, had she known he was in Love with her. Nay, he went so far in his Dissimulation, as to pretend Love to one of the Ladies of her Court; that his Passion for the Princess might be the less taken notice of. In these Cases therefore, the more resolutely a Man denies his Passion, the more pure and violent it is.

Then Mr. *Selvin*'s Passion is certainly very violent, reply'd Miss *Glanville*, for he denies it very resolutely; and I believe none but your Ladyship would have discover'd his Artifice. But shall we not open the other Letter? I have a strong Notion it comes from *Tinsel*.

For that very Reason I would not be acquainted with the Contents, reply'd *Arabella*. You see, Mr. *Selvin* accuses him of being guilty of that Offence which he denies: I shall doubtless, meet with a Confirmation of his Love in that Letter. Do not, I beseech you added she, seeing her Cousin preparing to open the Letter, expose me to the Pain of hearing a presumptuous Declaration of Love. Nay, pursued she, rising in great Emotion, if you are resolved to persecute me by reading it, I'll endeavour to get out of the hearing of it.

You shan't, I declare, said Miss *Glanville*, laughing and holding her, I'll oblige you to hear it.

I vow, Cousin, said *Arabella* smiling, you use me just as the Princess *Cleopatra* did the fair and wise *Antonia*.[2] However, if by this you mean to do any Kindness to the unfortunate Person who wrote that Billet, you are greatly mistaken; since, if you oblige me to listen to a Declaration of his Crime, you will lay me under a Necessity to banish him. A Sentence he would have avoided, while I remained ignorant of it.

To this Miss *Glanville* made no other Reply than by opening the Billet, the Contents of which may be found in the following Chapter.

CHAPTER XIII

In which our Heroin's Extravagance will be thought, perhaps, to be carried to an extravagant Length

MADAM,

'I Had the Honour to assure you this Morning on the Parade, that the Insinuations Mr. *Selvin* made use of to rob me of the superlative Happiness of your Esteem were entirely false and groundless. May the Beams of your bright Eyes never shine on me more, if there is any Truth in what he said to prejudice me with your Ladyship. If I am permitted to attend you to the Rooms this Evening, I hope to convince you, that it was absolutely impossible I could have been capable of such a Crime, who am, with the most profound Respect,

Your Ladyship's
most devoted, &c.
D. TINSEL.

Well, Madam, said Miss *Glanville* when she had read this Epistle, I fancy you need not pronounce a Sentence of Banishment upon poor Mr. *Tinsel*; he seems to be quite innocent of the Offence your Ladyship suspects him of.

Why, really, return'd *Arabella*, blushing with extreme Confusion at this second Disappointment, I am greatly perplex'd to know how I ought to act on this Occasion. I am much in the same Situation with the Princess *Serena*.[1] For you must know, this Princess—. Here *Lucy* entering, inform'd the Ladies Dinner was serv'd——I shall defer till another Opportunity, said *Arabella*, upon this Interruption, the Relation of the Princess *Serena*'s Adventures; which you will find, added she, in a low Voice, bears a very great Resemblance to mine.

Miss *Glanville* reply'd, she would hear it whenever she pleas'd, and then follow'd *Arabella* to the Dining Room.

The Cloth was scarce remov'd, when Mr. *Selvin* came in. *Arabella* blush'd at his Appearance, and discover'd so much Perplexity in her Behaviour, that Mr. *Selvin* was apprehensive he had not yet sufficiently justify'd himself; and therefore took the first Opportunity to approach her.

I shall think myself very unhappy, Madam, said he bowing, if the Letter I did myself the Honour to write to you this Morning——

Sir, interrupted *Arabella*, I perceive you are going to forget the Contents of that Letter, and preparing again to offend me by a presumptuous Declaration of Love.

Who I, Madam, reply'd he, in great Astonishment and Confusion, I-I-I protest—tho' I-I have a very great Respect for your Ladyship, yet—yet I never presum'd to—to—to—

You have presum'd too much, replied *Arabella*, and I should forget what I ow'd to my own Glory, if I furnish'd you with any more Occasions of offending me. — Know then, I absolutely forbid you to appear before me again, at least, till I am convinc'd you have chang'd your Sentiments.

Saying this, she rose from her Seat, and making a Sign to him not to follow her, which indeed he had no Intention to do, she quitted the Room, highly satisfy'd with her own Conduct upon this Occasion, which was exactly conformable to the Laws of Romance.

Mr. *Tinsel*, who had just alighted from his Chair, having a Glimpse of her, as she pass'd to her own Apartment, resolv'd, if possible, to procure a private Interview; for he did not doubt but his Billet had done Wonders in his Favour.

For that Purpose he ventur'd up to her Anti-Chamber, where he found *Lucy* in waiting, whom he desir'd to acquaint her Lady, that he intreated a Moment's Speech with her.

Lucy, after hesitating a Moment, and looking earnestly at him, replied, Sir, if you'll promise me faithfully, you are not in Love with my Lady, I'll go and deliver your Message.

Duce take me, said *Tinsel*, if that is not a very whimsical Condition truly——Pray, my Dear, how came it into thy little Brain, to suspect I was in Love with thy Lady? But, suppose I should be in Love with her, what then?

Why, then 'tis likely you would die, that's all, said *Lucy*, without my Lady would be so kind to command you to live.

I vow thou hast mighty pretty Notions, Child, said *Tinsel* smiling; hast thou been reading any Play-Book lately? But pray, dost think thy Lady would have Compassion on me, if I was in Love with her? Come, I know thou art in her Confidence? Hast thou ever heard her talk of me? Does she not tell thee all her Secrets?

Here *Arabella*'s Bell ringing, the Beau slipp'd half a Guinea into her Hand, which *Lucy* not willing to refuse, went immediately to her Lady; to whom, with a trembling Accent, she repeated Mr. *Tinsel*'s Request.

Imprudent Girl, cried *Arabella*, for I am loth to suspect thee of Disloyalty to thy Mistress. Dost thou know the Nature and Extent of the Request thou hast deliver'd? Art thou ignorant that the presumptuous Man whom thou sollicitest this Favour for, has mortally offended me?

Indeed, Madam, said *Lucy* frighted out of her Wits, I don't sollicit for him. I scorn to do any such Thing. I would not offend your Ladyship for the World: For, before I would deliver his Message to your Ladyship, I made him assure me, that he was not in Love with your Ladyship.

That was very wisely done, indeed, replied *Arabella*, smiling: And do you believe he spoke the Truth?

Yes, indeed, I am sure of it, said *Lucy* eagerly, if your Ladyship will but be pleas'd to see him, he is only in the next Room; I dare promise——

How, interrupted *Arabella*! What have you done? Have you brought him into my Apartment then? I protest this Adventure is exactly like what befel the beautiful *Statira*, when, by a Stratagem of the same Kind, *Oroondates* was introduc'd into her Presence. *Lucy*, thou art another *Barsina*, I think; but I hope thy Intentions are not less innocent than hers was.[1]

Indeed, Madam, reply'd *Lucy*, almost weeping, I am very innocent, I am no *Barsina*, as your Ladyship calls me.

I dare answer for thee, said *Arabella* smiling at the Turn she gave to her Words, thou art no *Barsina*; and I should wrong thee very much to compare thee with that wise Princess; for thou art certainly one of the most simple Wenches in the World. But since thou hast gone so far, let me know what the unfortunate Person desires of me; for, since I am neither more rigid, nor pretend to more Virtue than *Statira*, I may do at least as much for him, as that great Queen did for *Oroondates*.

He desires, Madam, said *Lucy*, that your Ladyship would be pleas'd to let him speak with you.

Or, in his Words, I suppose, replied *Arabella*, he humbly implor'd a Moment's Audience.

I told your Ladyship his very Words, indeed, Madam, said *Lucy*.

I tell thee, Girl, thou art mistaken, said *Arabella*; 'tis impossible he should sue for such a Favour in Terms like those: Therefore, go back, and let him know that I consent to grant him a short Audience upon these Conditions.

First, Provided he does not abuse my Indulgence by offending me with any Protestations of his Passion.

Secondly, That he engages to fulfil the Injunctions I shall lay upon him, however cruel and terrible they may appear.

Lastly, That his Despair must not prompt him to any Act of Desperation against himself.

Lucy having received this Message, quitted the Room hastily, for fear she should forget it.

Well, my pretty Ambassadress, said *Tinsel* when he saw her enter the Anti-Chamber, Will your Lady see me?

No, Sir, replied *Lucy*.

No, interrupted *Tinsel*, that's kind 'faith, after waiting so long.

Pray Sir, said *Lucy*, don't put me out so; I shall forget what my Lady order'd me to tell you.

Oh! I ask your Pardon, Child, said *Tinsel*. Come, let me hear your Message.

Sir, said *Lucy* adapting the Solemnity of her Lady's Accent—My Lady bad me say, that she will grant—No, that she consents to grant you a short Dience.

Audience you would say Child, said *Tinsel*: But how came you to tell me before she would not see me?——

I vow and protest, Sir, said *Lucy*, you have put all my Lady's Words clean out of my Head—I don't know what comes next—

Oh, no matter, said *Tinsel*, you have told me enough: I'll wait upon her directly.

Lucy, who saw him making towards the Door, prest between it and him; and having all her Lady's Whims in her Head, suppos'd he was going to carry her away—Possess'd with this Thought, she screamed out, Help! Help! for Heaven's Sake! My Lady will be carry'd away!

Arabella hearing this Exclamation of her Woman's, eccho'd her Screams, tho' with a Voice infinitely more delicate; and seeing *Tinsel*, who, confounded to the last Degree at the Cries of both the Lady and her Woman, had got into her Chamber he knew not how, she gave herself over for lost, and fell back in her Chair in a Swoon, or something she took for a Swoon, for she was persuaded it could happen no otherwise; since all Ladies in the same Circumstances are terrify'd into a fainting Fit, and seldom recover till they are conveniently carried away; and when they awake, find themselves many Miles off in the Power of their Ravisher.

Arabella's other Women, alarm'd by her Cries, came running into the Room; and seeing Mr. *Tinsel* there, and their Lady in a Swoon, concluded some very extraordinary Accident had happen'd.

What is your Business here, cry'd they all at a Time? Is it you that has frighted her Ladyship?

Devil take me, said *Tinsel* amaz'd, if I can tell what all this means.

By this Time Sir *Charles*, Mr. *Glanville*, and his Sister, came running astonish'd up Stairs. *Arabella* still continu'd motionless in her Chair, her Eyes clos'd, and her Head reclin'd upon *Lucy*, who with her other Women, was endeavouring to recover her.

Mr. *Glanville* eagerly ran to her Assistance, while Sir *Charles* and his Daughter as eagerly interrogated Mr. *Tinsel*, who stood motionless with Surprize, concerning the Cause of her Disorder.

Arabella, then first discovering some Signs of Life, half open'd her Eyes.

Inhuman Wretch, cry'd she, with a faint Voice, supposing herself in the Hands of her Ravisher, think not thy cruel Violence shall procure thee what thy Submissions could not obtain; and if when thou hadst only my Indifference to surmount, thou didst find it so difficult to overcome my Resolution, now that by this unjust Attempt, thou hast added Aversion to that Indifference, never hope for any Thing but the most bitter Reproaches from me.—

Why, Niece, said Sir *Charles* approaching her, what's the Matter? Look up, I beseech you, no-body is attempting to do you any Hurt; here's none but Friends about you.

Arabella, raising her Head at the Sound of her Uncle's Voice, and casting a confus'd Look on the Persons about her,

May I believe my Senses? Am I rescu'd, and in my own Chamber? To whose Valour is my Deliverance owing? Without doubt, 'tis to my Cousin's; but where is he? Let me assure him of my Gratitude.

Mr. *Glanville*, who had retir'd to a Window in great Confusion, as soon as he heard her call for him, came towards her, and in a Whisper begg'd her to be compos'd; that she was in no Danger.

And pray, Niece, said Sir *Charles*, now you are a little recover'd, be so good to inform us of the Cause of your Fright. What has happen'd to occasion all this Confusion?

How, Sir, said *Arabella*, don't you know then what has happen'd?—Pray how was I brought again into my Chamber, and by what Means was I rescu'd?

I protest, said Sir *Charles*, I don't know that you have been out of it.

Alas, replied *Arabella*, I perceive you are quite ignorant of what has befallen me; nor am I able to give you any Information: All I can tell you is, that alarm'd by my Womens Cries, and the Sight of my Ravisher, who came into my Chamber, I fainted away, and so facilitated his Enterprize; since doubtless it was very easy for him to carry me away while I remain'd in that senseless Condition. How I was rescu'd, or by whom, one of my Women can haply inform you; since its probable one of them was also forc'd away with me——Oh Heav'ns! cry'd she, seeing *Tinsel*, who all this while stood gazing like one distracted; what makes that impious Man in my Presence! What am I to think of this? Am I really deliver'd or no?

What can this mean, cried Sir *Charles*, turning to *Tinsel?* Have you, Sir, had any Hand in frighting my Niece?——

I, Sir, said *Tinsel!* Let me perish if ever I was so confounded in my Life: The Lady's Brain is disorder'd I believe.

Mr. *Glanville*, who was convinc'd all this Confusion was caus'd by some of *Arabella*'s usual Whims, dreaded lest an Explanation would the more expose her; and therefore told his Father, that it would be best to retire, and leave his Cousin to the Care of his Sister and her Women; adding, that she was not yet quite recover'd, and their Presence did but discompose her.

Then addressing himself to *Tinsel*, told him he would wait upon him down Stairs.

Arabella seeing them going away together, and supposing they intended to dispute the Possession of her with their Swords, call'd out to them to stay.

Mr. *Glanville* however, without minding her, press'd Mr. *Tinsel* to walk down.

Nay, pray, Sir, said the Beau, let us go in again; she may grow outrageous if we disoblige her.

Outrageous, Sir, said *Glanville*, do you suppose my Cousin is mad?

Upon my Soul, Sir, replied *Tinsel*, if she is not mad, she is certainly a little out of her Senses, or so——

Arabella having reiterated her Commands for her Lovers to return, and finding they did not obey her, ran to her Chamber-door, where they were holding a surly Sort of Conference, especially on *Glanville*'s Side, who was horridly out of Humour.

I perceive by your Looks, said *Arabella* to her Cousin, the Design you are meditating; but know that I absolutely forbid you, by all the Power I have over you, not to engage in Combat with my Ravisher here.[1]

Madam, interrupted *Glanville*, I beseech you do not——

I know, said she, you will object to me the Examples of *Arta-menes, Aronces*,[2] and many others, who were so generous as to promise their Rivals not to refuse them that Satisfaction whenever they demanded it—but consider, you have not the same Obligations to Mr. *Tinsel* that *Artamenes* had to the King of *Assyria*, or that *Aronces* had to——

For God's Sake, Cousin, said *Glanville*, what's all this to the Purpose? Curse on *Aronces* and the King of *Assyria*, I say——

The Astonishment of *Arabella* at this intemperate Speech of her Cousin, kept her for a Moment immoveable, when Sir *Charles*, who during this Discourse, had been collecting all the Information he could from *Lucy*, concerning this perplex'd Affair, came towards *Tinsel*, and giving him an angry Look, told him, He should take it well if he forbore visiting any of his Family for the future.

Oh! Your most obedient Servant, Sir, said *Tinsel*: You expect, I suppose, I should be excessively chagrin'd at this Prohibition? But upon my Soul, I am greatly oblig'd to you. Agad! I have no great Mind to a Halter: And since this Lady is so apt to think

People have a Design to ravish her, the wisest Thing a Man can do, is to keep out of her Way.

Sir, replied *Glanville*, who had follow'd him to the Door, I believe there has been some little Mistake in what has happen'd To-day—However, I expect you'll take no unbecoming Liberties with the Character of Lady *Bella*—

Oh! Sir, said *Tinsel*, I give you my Honour I shall always speak of the Lady with the most profound Veneration. She is a most accomplish'd, incomprehensible Lady: And the Devil take me, if I think there is her Fellow in the World——And so, Sir, I am your most obedient——

A Word with you before you go, said *Glanville* stopping him— No more of these Sneers as you value that smooth Face of yours, or I'll despoil it of a Nose.

Oh! Your humble Servant, said the Beau, retiring in great Confusion, with something betwixt a Smile and a Grin upon his Countenance, which he took Care however Mr. *Glanville* should not see; who as soon as he quitted him went again to *Arabella*'s Apartment, in order to prevail upon his Father and Sister to leave her a little to herself, for he dreaded lest some more Instances of her Extravagance would put it into his Father's Head, that she was really out of her Senses.

Well, Sir, said *Arabella* upon his Entrance, you have I suppose, given your Rival his Liberty. I assure you this Generosity is highly agreeable to me—And herein you imitate the noble *Artamenes*, who upon a like Occasion, acted as you have done. For when Fortune had put the Ravisher of *Mandana* in his Power, and he became the Vanquisher of his Rival, who endeavour'd by Violence to possess that divine Princess; this truly generous Hero relin- quish'd the Right he had of disposing of his Prisoner, and instead of sacrificing his Life to his just and reasonable Vengeance, he gave a Proof of his admirable Virtue and Clemency by dismissing him in Safety, as you have done.[1] However, added she, I hope you have made him swear upon your Sword, that he will never make a second Attempt upon my Liberty. I perceive, pursued she, seeing Mr. *Glanville* continued silent, with his Eyes bent on the Ground, for indeed he was asham'd to look up; that you would willingly avoid the Praise due to the heroick Action you have just perform'd—Nay, I suppose you are resolv'd to keep it secret if possible; yet I must tell you, that you will not escape the Glory due to it. Glory is as necessarily the Result of a virtuous Action, as Light is an Effect of the Sun which causeth it, and has no Dependence on any other Cause; since a virtuous Action continues still the same, tho' it be done without Testimony; and Glory, which is, as one may say born with it, constantly attends it, tho' the Action be not known.

I protest Niece, said Sir *Charles*, that's very prettily said.

In my Opinion, Sir, pursued *Arabella*, if any thing can weaken the Glory of a good Action, 'tis the Care a Person takes to make it known: As if one did not do Good for the Sake of Good, but for the Praise that generally follows it. Those then that are govern'd by so interested a Motive, ought to be consider'd as sordid rather than generous Persons; who making a Kind of Traffick between Virtue and Glory, barter just so much of the one for the other, and expect like other Merchants, to make Advantage by the Exchange.

Mr. *Glanville*, who was charm'd into an Extacy at this sensible Speech of *Arabella*'s, forgot in an Instant all her Absurdities. He did not fail to express his Admiration of her Understanding in Terms that brought a Blush into her fair Face, and oblig'd her to lay her Commands upon him to cease his excessive Commendations. Then making a Sign to them to leave her alone, Mr. *Glanville* who understood her, took his Father and Sister down Stairs, leaving *Arabella* with her faithful *Lucy*, whom she immediately commanded to give her a Relation of what had happen'd to her from the Time of her swooning till she recover'd.

CHAPTER XIV

A Dialogue between Arabella *and* Lucy, *in which the latter seems to have the Advantage*

WHY, Madam, said *Lucy*, all I can tell your Ladyship is, that we were all excessively frighted, to be sure, when you fainted, especially myself; and that we did what we could to recover you— And so accordingly your Ladyship did recover.

What's this to the Purpose, said *Arabella*, perceiving she stop'd here? I know that I fainted, and 'tis also very plain that I recover'd again—I ask you what happen'd to me in the intermediate Time between my Fainting and Recovery. Give me a faithful Relation of all the Accidents, to which by my Fainting I am quite a Stranger; and which no doubt, are very considerable——

Indeed, Madam, replied *Lucy*, I have given your Ladyship a faithful Relation of all I can remember.

When, resum'd *Arabella* surpriz'd?——

This Moment, Madam, said *Lucy*.

Why, sure thou dream'st Wench, replied she, Hast thou told me how I was seiz'd and carry'd off? How I was rescu'd again? And——

No, indeed, Madam, interrupted *Lucy*, I don't dream; I never told your Ladyship that you was carry'd off.

Well, said *Arabella*, and why dost thou not satisfy my Curiosity? Is it not fit I should be acquainted with such a momentous Part of my History?

I can't, indeed, and please your Ladyship, said *Lucy*.

What, can'st thou not, said *Arabella*, enrag'd at her Stupidity.

Why, Madam, said *Lucy* sobbing, I can't make a History of nothing.

Of nothing, Wench, resum'd *Arabella*, in a greater Rage than before: Dost thou call an Adventure to which thou was a Witness, and borest haply so great a Share in, nothing?——An Adventure which hereafter will make a considerable Figure in the Relation of my Life, dost thou look upon as trifling and of no Consequence?

No, indeed I don't, Madam, said *Lucy*.

Why then, pursued *Arabella*, dost thou wilfully neglect to relate it? Suppose, as there is nothing more likely, thou wert commanded by some Persons of considerable Quality, or haply some great Princes and Princesses, to recount the Adventures of my Life, would'st thou omit a Circumstance of so much Moment?

No indeed, Madam, said *Lucy*.

I am glad to hear thou art so discreet, said *Arabella*; and pray do me the Favour to relate this Adventure to me, as thou would'st do to those Princes and Princesses, if thou wert commanded.

Here, *Arabella* making a full Stop, fix'd her Eyes upon her Woman, expecting every Moment she would begin the desir'd Narrative—But finding she continu'd silent longer than she thought was necessary for recalling the several Circumstances of the Story into her Mind,

I find, said she, it will be necessary to caution you against making your Audience wait too long for your Relation; it looks as if you was to make a studied Speech, not a simple Relation of Facts, which ought to be free from all Affectation of Labour and Art; and be told with that graceful Negligence which is so becoming to. Truth.

This I thought proper to tell you, added she, that you may not fall into that Mistake when you are called upon to relate my Adventures——Well, now if you please to begin——.

What, pray, Madam, said *Lucy*?

What, repeated *Arabella*? Why, the Adventures which happen'd to me so lately. Relate to me every Circumstance of my being carried away, and how my Deliverance was effected by my Cousin.

Indeed, Madam, said *Lucy*, I know nothing about your Lady-ship's being carried away.

Begone, cried *Arabella* losing all Patience at her Obstinacy, get out of my Presence this Moment. Wretch, unworthy of my Confidence and Favour, thy Treason is too manifest, thou art brib'd by that presumptuous Man to conceal all the Circumstances of his Attempt from my Knowledge, to the End that I may not have a full Conviction of his Guilt.

Lucy, who never saw her Lady so much offended before, and knew not the Occasion of it, burst into Tears; which so affected the tender Heart of *Arabella*, that losing insensibly all her Anger, she told her with a Voice soften'd to a Tone of the utmost Sweetness and Condescension, that provided she would confess how far she had been prevail'd upon by his rich Presents, to forget her Duty, she would pardon and receive her again into Favour—

Speak, added she, and be not afraid after this Promise, to let me know what Mr. *Tinsel* requir'd of thee, and what were the Gifts with which he purchas'd thy Services; doubtless, he presented thee with Jewels of a considerable Value——

Since your Ladyship, said *Lucy* sobbing, has promis'd not to be angry, I don't care if I do tell your Ladyship what he gave me. He gave me this half Guinea, Madam, indeed he did; but for all that, when he would come into your Chamber I struggled with him, and cry'd out, for fear he should carry your Ladyship away——

Arabella, lost in Astonishment and Shame at hearing of so inconsiderable a Present made to her Woman, the like of which not one of her Romances could furnish her, order'd her immediately to withdraw, not being willing she should observe the Confusion this strange Bribe had given her.

After she had been gone some Time, she endeavour'd to compose her Looks, and went down to the Dining-Room, where Sir *Charles* and his Son and Daughter had been engag'd in a Conversation concerning her, the Particulars of which may be found in the first Chapter of the next Book.

The End *of the* Seventh B O O K.

BOOK VIII

CHAPTER I

Contains the Conversation referr'd to in the last Chapter of the preceding Book

MISS *Glanville*, who with a malicious Pleasure had secretly tri-umph'd in the Extravagances her beautiful Cousin had been guilty of, was now sensibly disappointed to find they had had so little Effect on her Father and Brother; for instead of reflecting upon the Absurdities to which they had been a Witness, Mr. *Glanville* artfully pursu'd the Subject *Arabella* had just before been expatiat-ing upon, taking notice frequently of some Observations of hers, and by a well contriv'd Repetition of her Words, oblig'd his Father a second Time to declare that his Niece had spoken extremely well.

Mr. *Glanville* taking the Word, launch'd out into such Praises of her Wit, that Miss *Glanville*, no longer able to listen patiently, reply'd,

'Twas true Lady *Bella* sometimes said very sensible Things; that 'twas a great Pity she was not always in a reasonable Way of thinking, or that her Intervals were not longer—

Her Intervals, Miss, said *Glanville*, pray what do you mean by that Expression?—

Why, pray, said Miss *Glanville*, don't you think my Cousin is sometimes a little wrong in the Head?

Mr. *Glanville* at these Words starting from his Chair, took a Turn a-cross the Room in great Discomposure, then stopping all of a sudden, and giving his Sister a furious Look——*Charlotte*, said he, don't give me Cause to think you are envious of your Cousin's superior Excellencies——

Envious, repeated Miss *Glanville*, I envious of my Cousin—I vow I should never have thought of that—Indeed, Brother, you are much mistaken; my Cousin's superior Excellencies never gave

me a Moment's Disturbance—Tho' I must confess her unaccountable Whims have often excited my Pity—

No more of this, *Charlotte*, interrupted Mr. *Glanville*, as you
value my Friendship—No more of it——

Why, really Son, said Sir *Charles*, my Niece has very strange
Whimsies sometimes. How it came into her Head to think Mr.
Tinsel would attempt to carry her away, I can't imagine? For after
all, he only prest rather too rudely into her Chamber, for which, as
you see, I have forbidden his Visits.

That was of a Piece, said Miss *Glanville* sneeringly to her
Brother, with her asking you if you had made Mr. *Tinsel* swear
upon your Sword, that he would never again attempt to carry her
away; and applauding you for having given him his Liberty, as the
generous *Atermens* did on the same Occasion.

I would advise you, *Charlotte*, said Mr. *Glanville*, not to aim at
repeating your Cousin's Words, till you know how to pronounce
them properly.

Oh! that's one of her superior Excellencies, said Miss *Glanville*.

Indeed, Miss, said *Glanville* very provokingly, she is superior to
you in many Things; and as much so in the Goodness of her Heart,
as in the Beauty of her Person——

Come, come, *Charles*, said the Baronet, who observ'd his
Daughter sat swelling and biting her Lip at this Reproach, personal
Reflections are better avoided. Your Sister is very well, and not to
be disparag'd; tho' to be sure, Lady *Bella* is the finest Woman I ever
saw in my Life.

Miss *Glanville* was, if possible, more disgusted at her Father's
Palliation than her Brother's Reproaches; and in order to give a
Loose to her Passion, accus'd Mr. *Glanville* of a Decrease in his
Affection for her, since he had been in Love with her Cousin; and
having found this Excuse for her Tears, very freely gave vent to
them—

Mr. *Glanville* being softned by this Sight, sacrificed a few
Compliments to her Vanity, which soon restor'd her to her usual
Tranquillity; then turning the Discourse on his beloved *Arabella*,
pronounc'd a Panegyrick on her Virtues and Accomplishments of
an Hour long; which, if it did not absolutely persuade his Sister to
change her Opinion, it certainly convinc'd his Father, that his
Niece was not only perfectly well in her Understanding, but even
better than most others of her Sex.

Mr. *Glanville* had just finish'd her Eulogium, when *Arabella* appear'd; Joy danc'd in his Eyes at her Approach; he gaz'd upon her with a Kind of conscious Triumph in his Looks; her consummate Loveliness justifying his Passion, and being in his Opinion, more than an Excuse for all her Extravagancies.

CHAPTER II

In which our Heroine, as we presume, shews herself in two very different Lights

Arabella, who at her Entrance had perceiv'd some Traces of Uneasiness upon Miss *Glanville*'s Countenance, tenderly ask'd her the Cause; to which that young Lady answering in a cold and reserv'd Manner, Mr. *Glanville*, to divert her Reflexions on it, very freely accus'd himself of having given his Sister some Offence. To be sure, Brother, said Miss *Glanville*, you are very vehement in your Temper, and are as violently carry'd away about Things of little Importance as of the greatest; and then, whatever you have a Fancy for, you love so obstinately.

I am oblig'd to you, Miss, interrupted Mr. *Glanville*, for endeavouring to give Lady *Bella* so unfavourable an Opinion of me——

I assure you, said *Arabella*, Miss *Glanville* has said nothing to your Disadvantage: For, in my Opinion, the Temperament of great Minds ought to be such as she represents yours to be. For there is nothing at so great a Distance from true and heroick Virtue, as that Indifference which obliges some People to be pleas'd with all Things or nothing: Whence it comes to pass, that they neither entertain great Desires of Glory, nor Fear of Infamy; that they neither love nor hate; that they are wholly influenc'd by Custom, and are sensible only of the Afflictions of the Body, their Minds being in a Manner insensible——

To say the Truth, I am inclin'd to conceive a greater Hope of a Man, who in the Beginning of his Life is hurry'd away by some evil Habit, than one that fastens on nothing: The Mind that cannot be brought to detest Vice, will never be persuaded to love Virtue; but one who is capable of loving or hating irreconcileably, by having, when young, his Passions directed to proper Objects, will remain fix'd in his Choice of what is good. But with him who is incapable of any violent Attraction, and whose Heart is chilled by a general Indifference, Precept or Example will have no Force—And Philosophy itself, which boasts it hath Remedies for all Indispositions of the Soul, never had any that can cure an Indifferent Mind—Nay, added she, I am persuaded that Indifference is generally the inseparable Companion of a weak and imperfect Judgment. For it is so natural to a Person to be carry'd towards that which he believes to be good, that if indifferent People were able to judge of Things, they would fasten on something. But certain it is that this luke-warmness of Soul, which sends forth but feeble Desires, sends also but feeble Lights; so that those who are guilty of it, not knowing any thing clearly, cannot fasten on any thing with Perseverance.

Mr. *Glanville*, when *Arabella* had finish'd this Speech, cast a triumphing Glance at his Sister, who had affected great Inattention all the while she had been speaking. Sir *Charles* in his Way, express'd much Admiration of her Wit, telling her, if she had been a Man, she would have made a great Figure in Parliament, and that her Speeches might have come perhaps to be printed in time.

This Compliment, odd as it was, gave great Joy to *Glanville*, when the Conversation was interrupted by the Arrival of Mr. *Selvin*, who had slipt away unobserv'd at the Time that *Arabella*'s Indisposition had alarm'd them, and now came to enquire after her Health; and also if an Opportunity offer'd to set her right with Regard to the Suspicions she had entertain'd of his designing to pay his Addresses to her.

Arabella, as soon as he had sent in his Name, appear'd to be in great Disturbance; and upon his Entrance, offer'd immediately to withdraw, telling Mr. *Glanville*, who would have detain'd her, that she found no Place was likely to secure her from the Persecutions of that Gentleman.

Glanville star'd, and look'd strangely perplex'd at this Speech; Miss *Glanville* smil'd, and poor *Selvin*, with a very silly Look— hem'd two or three times, and then with a faultring Accent said, Madam, I am very much concern'd to find your Ladyship resolv'd to persist in——

Sir, interrupted *Arabella*, my Resolutions are unalterable. I told you so before, and am surpriz'd, after the Knowledge of my

Intentions, you presume to appear in my Presence again, from whence I had so positively banish'd you.

Pray, Niece, said Sir *Charles*, what has Mr. *Selvin* done to disoblige you?

Sir, reply'd *Arabella*, Mr. *Selvin*'s Offence can admit of no other Reparation than that which I requir'd of him, which was a voluntary Banishment from my Presence: And in this pursu'd she, I am guilty of no more Severity to you, than the Princess *Udosia* was to the unfortunate *Thrasimedes*. For the Passion of this Prince having come to her Knowledge, notwithstanding the Pains he took to conceal it, this fair and wise Princess thought it not enough to forbid his speaking to her, but also banish'd him from her Presence; laying a peremptory Command upon him, never to appear before her again till he was perfectly cur'd of that unhappy Love he had entertain'd for her[1]—Imitate therefore the meritorious Obedience of this poor Prince, and if that Passion you profess for me—

How, Sir, interrupted Sir *Charles*, Do you make Love to my Niece then?——

Sir, replied Mr. *Selvin*, who was strangely confounded at *Arabella*'s Speech, tho' I really admire the Perfections this Lady is possess'd of, yet I assure you, upon my Honour, I never had a Thought of making any Addresses to her; and I can't imagine why her Ladyship persists in accusing me of such Presumption.

So formal a Denial after what *Arabella* had said, extremely perplex'd Sir *Charles*, and fill'd Mr. *Glanville* with inconceivable Shame—

Miss *Glanville* enjoy'd their Disturbance, and full of an ill-natur'd Triumph, endeavour'd to look *Arabella* into Confusion: But that Lady not being at all discompos'd by this Declaration of Mr. *Selvin*'s, having accounted for it already, replied with great Calmness,

Sir, 'Tis easy to see thro' the Artifice of your disclaiming any Passion for me—Upon any other Occasion questionless, you would rather sacrifice your Life, than consent to disavow these Sentiments, which unhappily for your Peace you have entertain'd. At present the Desire of continuing near me, obliges you to lay this Constraint upon yourself; however you know *Thrasimedes* fell upon the same Stratagem to no Purpose. The rigid *Udosia* saw thro' the Disguise, and would not dispense with herself from banishing him from *Rome*, as I do you from *England*——

How, Madam! interrupted *Selvin* amaz'd—

Yes, Sir, replied *Arabella* hastily, nothing less can satisfy what I owe to the Consideration of my own Glory.

Upon my Word, Madam, said *Selvin*, half angry, and yet strongly inclin'd to laugh, I don't see the Necessity of my quitting my native Country, to satisfy what you owe to the Consideration of your own Glory. Pray, how does my staying in *England* affect your Ladyship's Glory?

To answer your Question with another, said *Arabella*, Pray how did the Stay of *Thrasimedes* in *Rome*, affect the Glory of the Empress *Udosia*?

Mr. *Selvin* was struck dumb with this Speech, for he was not willing to be thought so deficient in the Knowledge of History, as not to be acquainted with the Reasons why *Thrasimedes* should not stay in *Rome*.

His Silence therefore seeming to *Arabella* to be a tacit Confession of the Justice of her Commands, a Sentiment of Compassion for this unfortunate Lover, intruded itself into her Mind; and turning her bright Eyes, full of a soft Complacency upon *Selvin*, who star'd at her as if he had lost his Wits——

I will not, said she, wrong the Sublimity of your Passion for me so much, as to doubt your being ready to sacrifice the Repose of your own Life to the Satisfaction of mine: Nor will I do so much Injustice to your Generosity, as to suppose the Glory of obeying my Commands, will not in some Measure soften the Rigour of your Destiny—I know not whether it may be lawful for me to tell you, that your Misfortune does really cause me some Affliction; but I am willing to give you this Consolation, and also to assure you, that to whatever Part of the World your Despair will carry you, the good Wishes and Compassion of *Arabella* shall follow you——

Having said this, with one of her fair Hands she cover'd her Face, to hide the Blushes which so compassionate a Speech had caus'd—Holding the other extended with a careless Air, supposing he would kneel to kiss it, and bathe it with his Tears, as was the Custom on such melancholy Occasions, her Head at the same Time turned another Way, as if reluctantly and with Confusion she granted this Favour.—But after standing a Moment in this Posture, and finding her Hand untouch'd, she concluded Grief had depriv'd him of his Senses, and that he would shortly fall into a Swoon as *Thrasimedes* did: And to prevent being a Witness of so

doleful a Sight, she hurry'd out of the Room without once turning
about, and having reach'd her own Apartment, sunk into a Chair,
not a little affected with the deplorable Condition in which she had
left her suppos'd miserable Lover.

CHAPTER III

The Contrast continued

THE Company she had left behind her being all, except Mr.
Glanville, to the last Degree surpriz'd at her strange Words and
Actions, continued mute for several Minutes after she was gone,
staring upon one another, as if each wish'd to know the other's
Opinion of such an unaccountable Behaviour. At last Miss
Glanville, who observed her Brother's Back was towards her, told
Mr. *Selvin* in a low Voice, that she hop'd he would call and take
his Leave of them before he set out for the Place where his Despair
would carry him.—

Mr. *Selvin* in spite of his natural Gravity, could not forbear
laughing at this Speech of Miss *Glanville's*, which shock'd her
Brother, and not being able to stay where *Arabella* was ridicul'd,
nor intitled to resent it, which would have been a manifest Injustice on that Occasion, he retir'd to his own Apartment to give
vent to that Spleen which in those Moments made him out of
Humour with all the World.

Sir *Charles*, when he was gone, indulg'd himself in a little Mirth
on his Niece's Extravagance, protesting he did not know what to do
with her. Upon which Miss *Glanville* observ'd, that it was a Pity
there were not such Things as Protestant Nunneries; giving it as
her Opinion, that her Cousin ought to be confin'd in one of those
Places, and never suffer'd to see any Company, by which Means
she would avoid exposing herself in the Manner she did now.

Mr. *Selvin*, who possibly thought this a reasonable Scheme of
Miss *Glanville's*, seem'd by his Silence to assent to her Opinion;
but Sir *Charles* was greatly displeas'd with his Daughter for expressing herself so freely; alledging that *Arabella*, when she was
out of those Whims, was a very sensible young Lady, and sometimes talk'd as learnedly as a Divine. To which Mr. *Selvin* also

added, that she had a great Knowledge of History, and had a most surprizing Memory; and after some more Discourse to the same Purpose, he took his leave, earnestly entreating Sir *Charles* to believe that he never entertain'd any Design of making his Addresses to Lady *Bella*.

In the mean Time, that Lady after having given near half an Hour to those Reflexions which occur to Heroines in the same Situation with herself, called for *Lucy*, and order'd her to go to the Dining-Room, and see in what Condition Mr. *Selvin* was, telling her she had certainly left him in a Swoon, as also the Occasion of it; and bid her give him all the Consolation in her Power.

Lucy, with Tears in her Eyes at this Recital, went down as she was order'd, and entering the Room without any Ceremony, her Thoughts being wholly fix'd on the melancholy Circumstance her Lady had been telling her; she look'd eagerly round the Room without speaking a Word, till Sir *Charles* and Miss *Glanville*, who thought she had been sent with some Message from *Arabella*, ask'd her both at the same Instant, What she wanted?——

I came, Sir, said *Lucy*, repeating her Lady's Words, to see in what Condition Mr. *Selvin* is, and to give him all the Solation in my Power.

Sir *Charles*, laughing heartily at this Speech, ask'd her what she could do for Mr. *Selvin?* To which she reply'd, she did not know; but her Lady had told her to give him all the Solation in her Power.

Consolation thou would'st say, I suppose, said Sir *Charles*.

Yes, Sir, said *Lucy* curtesying. Well, Child, added he, go up and tell your Lady, Mr. *Selvin* does not need any Consolation.

Lucy accordingly return'd with this Message, and was met at the Chamber-Door by *Arabella*, who hastily ask'd her if Mr. *Selvin* was recover'd from his Swoon: To which *Lucy* reply'd that she did not know; but that Sir *Charles* bid her tell her Ladyship, Mr. *Selvin* did not need any Consolation.

Oh Heavens! cry'd *Arabella*, throwing herself into a Chair as pale as Death—He is dead, he has fallen upon his Sword, and put an End to his Life and Miseries at once—Oh! how unhappy am I, cry'd she, bursting into Tears, to be the Cause of so cruel an Accident—Was ever any Fate so terrible as mine—Was ever Beauty so fatal—Was ever Rigour so unfortunate—How will the Quiet of my future Days be disturbed by the sad Remembrance of a Man whose Death was caused by my Disdain—But why, resum'd she after a little Pause—Why do I thus afflict myself for what has happen'd by an unavoidable Necessity? Nor am I singular in the Misfortune which has befallen me—Did not the sad *Perinthus* die for the beautiful *Panthea*[1]—Did not the Rigour of *Barsina* bring the miserable *Oxyatres* to the Grave[2]—And the Severity of *Statira* make *Oroondates* fall upon his Sword in her Presence, tho' happily he escap'd being kill'd by it[3]—Let us then not afflict ourselves unreasonably at this sad Accident—Let us lament as we ought the fatal Effects of our Charms—But let us comfort ourselves with the Thought that we have only acted conformable to our Duty.

Arabella having pronounc'd these last Words with a solemn and lofty Accent, order'd *Lucy*, who listen'd to her with Eyes drown'd in Tears, to go down and ask if the Body was remov'd—for added she, all my Constancy will not be sufficient to support me against that pitiful Sight.

Lucy accordingly deliver'd her Message to Sir *Charles* and Miss *Glanville*, who were still together, discoursing on the fantastical Turn of *Arabella*, when the Knight, who could not possibly comprehend what she meant by asking if the Body was removed, bid her tell her Lady he desired to speak with her.

Arabella, upon receiving this Summons, set herself to consider what could be the Intent of it. If Mr. *Selvin* be dead, said she, what Good can my Presence do among them? Surely it cannot be to upbraid me with my Severity, that my Uncle desires to see me— No, it would be unjust to suppose it. Questionless my unhappy Lover is still struggling with the Pangs of Death, and for a Consolation in his last Moments, implores the Favour of resigning up his Life in my Sight. Pausing a little at these Words, she rose from her Seat with a Resolution to give the unhappy *Selvin* her Pardon before he dy'd. Meeting Mr. *Glanville* as he was returning from his Chamber to the Dining-Room, she told him, she hop'd the Charity she was going to discover towards his Rival, would not give him any Uneasiness; and preventing his Reply by going hastily into the Room, he follow'd her dreading some new Extravagance, yet not able to prevent it, endeavour'd to conceal his Confusion from her Observation—*Arabella* after breathing a gentle Sigh told Sir *Charles*, that she was come to grant Mr. *Selvin* her Pardon for the Offence he had been guilty of, that he might depart in Peace.

Well, well, said Sir *Charles*, he is departed in Peace without it.

How, Sir, interrupted *Arabella*, is he dead then already? Alas! why had he not the Satisfaction of seeing me before he expir'd, that his Soul might have departed in Peace! He would have been assur'd not only of my Pardon, but Pity also; and that Assurance would have made him happy in his last Moments.

Why, Niece, interrupted Sir *Charles* staring, you surprize me prodigiously: Are you in earnest?

Questionless I am, Sir, said she, nor ought you to be surpriz'd at the Concern I express for the Fate of this unhappy Man, nor at the Pardon I propos'd to have granted him; since herein I am justified by the Example of many great and virtuous Princesses, who have done as much, nay, haply more than I intended to have done, for Persons whose Offences were greater than Mr. *Selvin*'s.

I am very sorry, Madam, said Sir *Charles*, to hear you talk in this Manner: 'Tis really enough to make one suspect you are——

You do me great Injustice, Sir, interrupted *Arabella*, if you suspect me to be guilty of any unbecoming Weakness for this Man: If barely expressing my Compassion for his Misfortunes be esteem'd so great a Favour, what would you have thought if I had supported his Head on my Knees while he was dying, shed Tears over him, and discover'd all the Tokens of a sincere Affliction for him?——

Good God! said Sir *Charles* lifting up his Eyes, Did any body ever hear of any thing like this?

What, Sir, said *Arabella*, with as great an Appearance of Surprize in her Countenance as his had discover'd, Do you say you never heard of any thing like this? Then you never heard of the Princess of *Media*, I suppose——

No, not I, Madam, said Sir *Charles* peevishly.

Then, Sir, resum'd *Arabella*, permit me to tell you, that this fair and virtuous Princess condescended to do all I have mention'd for the fierce *Labynet*, Prince of *Assyria*; who tho' he had mortally offended her by stealing her away out of the Court of the King her Father, nevertheless, when he was wounded to Death in her Presence, and humbly implor'd her Pardon before he died, she condescended as I have said, to support him on her Knees, and shed Tears for his Disaster[1]——I could produce many more Instances of the like Compassion in Ladies almost as highly born as herself, tho' perhaps their Quality was not quite so illustrious, she being the Heiress of two powerful Kingdoms. Yet to mention only these——

Good Heav'ns! cry'd Mr. *Glanville* here, being quite out of Patience, I shall go distracted——

Arabella surpriz'd at this Exclamation, look'd earnestly at him for a Moment—and then ask'd him, Whether any thing she had said had given him Uneasiness?

Yes, upon my Soul, Madam, said *Glanville* so vex'd and confus'd that he hardly knew what he said——

I am sorry for it, reply'd *Arabella* gravely, and also am greatly concern'd to find that in Generosity you are so much exceeded by the illustrious *Cyrus*; who was so far from taking Umbrage at *Mandana*'s Behaviour to the dying Prince, that he commended her for the Compassion she had shewn him. So also did the brave and generous *Oroondates*, when the fair *Statira*——

By Heav'ns! cry'd *Glanville* rising in a Passion, there's no hearing this. Pardon me, Madam, but upon my Soul, you'll make me hang myself.

Hang yourself, repeated *Arabella*, sure you know not what you say?—You meant, I suppose, that you'll fall upon your Sword. What Hero ever threatned to give himself so vulgar a Death? But pray let me know the Cause of your Despair, so sudden and so violent.

Mr. *Glanville* continuing in a sort of sullen Silence, *Arabella* raising her Voice went on:

Tho' I do not conceive myself oblig'd to give you an Account of my Conduct, seeing that I have only permitted you yet to hope for my Favour; yet I owe to myself and my own Honour the Justification I am going to make. Know then, that however suspicious my Compassion for Mr. *Selvin* may appear to your mistaken Judgment, yet it has its Foundation only in the Generosity of my Disposition, which inclines me to pardon the Fault when the unhappy Criminal repents; and to afford him my Pity when his Circumstances require it. Let not therefore the Charity I have discover'd towards your Rival, be the Cause of your Despair, since my Sentiments for him were he living, would be what they were before; that is, full of Indifference, nay, haply Disdain. And suffer not yourself to be so carried away by a violent and unjust Jealousy, as to threaten your own Death, which if you really had any Ground for your Suspicions, and truly lov'd me, would come unsought for, tho' not undesir'd—For indeed, was your Despair reasonable, Death would necessarily follow it; for what Lover can live under so

desperate a Misfortune. In that Case you may meet Death un-
undauntedly when it comes, nay, embrace it with Joy; but truly the
killing one's self is but a false Picture of true Courage, proceeding
rather from Fear of a further Evil, than Contempt of that you fly to:
For if it were a Contempt of Pain, the same Principle would make
you resolve to bear patiently and fearlessly all kind of Pains; and
Hope being of all other the most contrary Thing to Fear, this being
an utter Banishment of Hope, seems to have its Ground in Fear.

CHAPTER IV

In which Mr. Glanville *makes an unsuccessful Attempt upon* Arabella

Arabella, when she had finish'd these Words, which banish'd in
part Mr. *Glanville*'s Confusion, went to her own Apartment,
follow'd by Miss *Glanville*, to whom she had made a Sign for that
Purpose; and throwing herself into a Chair, burst into Tears,
which greatly surprizing Miss *Glanville*, she prest her to tell her the
Cause.

Alas! reply'd *Arabella*, have I not Cause to think myself extremely unhappy? The deplorable Death of Mr. *Selvin*, the Despair to which I see your Brother reduc'd, with the fatal Consequences which may attend it, fills me with a mortal Uneasiness.

Well, said Miss *Glanville*, your Ladyship may make yourself
quite easy as to both these Matters; for Mr. *Selvin* is not dead, nor
is my Brother in Despair that I know of.

What do you say, Miss, interrupted *Arabella*, is not Mr. *Selvin*
dead? Was the Wound he gave himself not mortal then?

I know of no Wound that he gave himself, not I, said Miss
Glanville; what makes your Ladyship suppose he gave himself a
Wound? Lord bless me, what strange Thoughts come into your
Head.

Truly I am rejoic'd to hear it, reply'd *Arabella*; and in order to
prevent the Effects of his Despair, I'll instantly dispatch my Commands to him to live.

I dare answer for his Obedience, Madam, said Miss *Glanville*
smiling.

Arabella then gave Orders for Paper and Pens to be brought her, and seeing Mr. *Glanville* enter the Room, very formally acquainted him with her Intention, telling him, that he ought to be satisfy'd with the Banishment to which she had doom'd his unhappy Rival, and not require his Death, since he had nothing to fear from his Pretensions.

I assure you, Madam, said Mr. *Glanville*, I am perfectly easy upon that Account: And in order to spare you the Trouble of sending to Mr. *Selvin*, I may venture to assure you that he is in no Danger of dying.

'Tis impossible, Sir, reply'd *Arabella*, according to the Nature of Things, 'tis impossible but he must already be very near Death— You know the Rigour of my Sentence, you know——

I know, Madam, said Mr. *Glanville*, that Mr. *Selvin* does not think himself under a Necessity of obeying your Sentence; and has the Impudence to question your Authority for banishing him from his native Country.

My Authority, Sir, said *Arabella* strangely surpriz'd, is founded upon the absolute Power he has given me over him.

He denies that, Madam, said *Glanville*, and says that he neither can give, nor you exercise an absolute Power over him; since you are both accountable to the King, whose Subjects you are, and both restrain'd by the Laws under whose Sanction you live.

Arabella's apparent Confusion at these Words giving Mr. *Glanville* Hopes that he had fallen upon a proper Method to cure her of some of her strange Notions, he was going to pursue his Arguments, when *Arabella* looking a little sternly upon him,

The Empire of Love, said she, like the Empire of Honour, is govern'd by Laws of its own, which have no Dependence upon, or Relation to any other.[1]

Pardon me, Madam, said *Glanville*, if I presume to differ from you. Our Laws have fix'd the Boundaries of Honour as well as those of Love.

How is that possible, reply'd *Arabella*, when they differ so widely, that a Man may be justify'd by the one, and yet condemn'd by the other? For Instance, pursued she, you are not permitted by the Laws of the Land to take away the Life of any Person whatever; yet the Laws of Honour oblige you to hunt your Enemy thro' the World, in order to sacrifice him to your Vengeance. Since it is impossible then for the same Actions to be at once just and unjust, it must necessarily follow, that the Law which condemns it, and that which justifies it is not the same, but directly opposite—And now, added she, after a little Pause, I hope I have entirely clear'd up that Point to you.

You have indeed, Madam, reply'd Mr. *Glanville*, proved to a Demonstration, that what is called Honour is something distinct from Justice, since they command Things absolutely opposite to each other.

Arabella without reflecting on this Inference, went on to prove the independent Sovereignty of Love, which, said she, may be collected from all the Words and Actions of those Heroes who were inspir'd by this Passion. We see it in them, pursued she, triumphing not only over all natural and avow'd Allegiance, but superior even to Friendship, Duty, and Honour itself. This the Actions of *Oroondates, Artaxerxes, Spitridates*,[1] and many other illustrious Princes sufficiently testify.

Love requires a more unlimited Obedience from its Slaves, than any other Monarch can expect from his Subjects; an Obedience which is circumscrib'd by no Laws whatever, and dependent upon nothing but itself.

I shall live, Madam, says the renowned Prince of *Scythia* to the divine *Statira*, I shall live, since it is your Command I should do so; and Death can have no Power over a Life which you are pleas'd to take Care of——[2]

Say only that you wish I should conquer, said the great *Juba* to the incomparable *Cleopatra*, and my Enemies will be already vanquish'd——Victory will come over to the Side you favour—and an Army of a hundred thousand Men will not be able to overcome the Man who has your Commands to conquer——[3]

How mean and insignificant, pursued she, are the Titles bestow'd on other Monarchs compar'd with those which dignify the Sovereigns of Hearts, such as divine Arbitress of my Fate, Visible Divinity, Earthly Goddess, and many others equally sublime——

Mr. *Glanville* losing all patience at her obstinate Folly, interrupted her here with a Question quite foreign to the Subject she was discussing, and soon after quitting her Chamber, retir'd to his own, more than ever despairing of her Recovery.

CHAPTER V

In which is introduc'd a very singular Character

MISS *Glanville*, whose Envy and Dislike of her lovely Cousin was heighten'd by her Suspicions that she disputed with her the Possession of Sir *George*'s Heart, she having been long in reality a great Admirer of that gay Gentleman, was extremely delighted with the Ridicule her absurd Behaviour had drawn upon her at *Bath*, which she found by Enquiry was thro' Mr. *Tinsel*'s Representation grown almost general.

In order therefore to be at Liberty to go to the Publick Places un-eclips'd by the superior Beauty of *Arabella*, she acquainted her Father and Brother with Part of what she had heard, which determin'd them to prevent that young Lady's Appearance in Publick while they staid at *Bath*; this being no difficult Matter to bring about, since *Arabella* only went to the Rooms or Parade in Compliance with the Invitation of her Cousins.

Miss *Glanville* being by these Means rid of a Rival too powerful even to contend with, went with more than usual Gaiety to the Assembly, where the Extravagancies of *Arabella* afforded a perpetual Fund for Diversion. Her more than passive Behaviour upon this Occasion, banishing all Restraint among those she convers'd with, the Jest circulated very freely at *Arabella*'s Expence. Nor did Miss *Glanville* fail to give new Poignancy to their Sarcasms, by artfully disclosing the bent of her Cousin's Studies, and enumerating the many Absurdities they had made her guilty of.

Arabella's uncommon Beauty had gain'd her so many Enemies among the Ladies that compos'd this Assembly, that they seem'd to contend with each other who should ridicule her most. The celebrated Countess of——[1] being then at *Bath*, approach'd a Circle of these fair Defamers, and listning a few Moments to the contemptuous Jests they threw out against the absent Beauty, declar'd herself in her Favour; which in a Moment, such was the Force of her universally acknowledg'd Merit, and the Deference always pay'd to her Opinion, silenc'd every pretty Impertinent around her.

This Lady, who among her own Sex had no Superior in Wit, Elegance, and Ease, was inferior to very few of the other in Sense, Learning, and Judgment. Her Skill in Poetry, Painting, and

Musick, tho' incontestably great, was number'd among the least of her Accomplishments. Her Candour, her Sweetness, her Modesty and Benevolence, while they secur'd her from the Darts of Envy, render'd her superior to Praise, and made the one as unnecessary as the other ineffectual.

She had been a Witness of the Surprize *Arabella*'s extraordinary Appearance had occasion'd, and struck with that as well as the un-common Charms of her Person, had prest near her with several others of the Company, when she was discoursing in the Manner we have related.

A Person of the Countess's nice Discernment could not fail of observing the Wit and Spirit, which tho' obscur'd, was not absolutely hid under the Absurdity of her Notions. And this Dis-covery adding Esteem to the Compassion she felt for the fair Visionary, she resolv'd to rescue her from the ill-natur'd Raillery of her Sex; praising therefore her Understanding, and the Beauty of her Person with a Sweetness and Generosity peculiar to herself, she accounted in the most delicate Manner imaginable for the Singularity of her Notions, from her Studies, her Retirement, her Ignorance of the World, and her lively Imagination. And to abate the Keenness of their Sarcasms, acknowledg'd, that she herself had when very young, been deep read in Romances; and but for an early Acquaintance with the World, and being directed to other Studies, was likely to have been as much a Heroine as Lady *Bella*.

Miss *Glanville*, tho' she was secretly vex'd at this Defence of her Cousin, was however under a Necessity of seeming oblig'd to the Countess for it: And that Lady expressing a Desire to be ac-quainted with Lady *Bella*, Miss *Glanville* respectfully offer'd to attend her Cousin to her Lodgings, which the Countess as respect-fully declin'd, saying, As Lady *Bella* was a Stranger, she would make her the first Visit.

Miss *Glanville* at her Return gave her Brother an Account of what had happen'd at the Assembly, and fill'd him with an in-conceivable Joy at the Countess's Intention. He had always been a zealous Admirer of that Lady's Character, and flatter'd himself that the Conversation of so admirable a Woman would be of the utmost Use to *Arabella*.

That very Night he mention'd her to his beloved Cousin; and after enumerating all her fine Qualities, declar'd that she had already conceiv'd a Friendship for her, and was solicitous of her Acquaintance.

I think myself extremely fortunate, replied *Arabella*, in that I have (tho' questionless undeservedly) acquir'd the Amity of this lovely Person; and I beg you, pursued she to Miss *Glanville*, to tell her, that I long with Impatience to embrace her, and to give her that Share in my Heart which her transcendent Merit deserves.

Miss *Glanville* only bow'd her Head in Answer to this Request, giving her Brother at the same Time a significant Leer; who tho' used to *Arabella*'s Particularities, could not help being a little confounded at the heroick Speech she had made.

CHAPTER VI

Containing something which at first Sight may possibly puzzle the Reader

THE Countess was as good as her Word, and two Days after sent a Card to *Arabella*, importing her Design to wait on her that Afternoon.

Our Heroine expected her with great Impatience, and the Moment she enter'd the Room flew towards her with a graceful Eagerness, and straining her in her Arms, embrac'd her with all the Fervour of a long absent Friend.

Sir *Charles* and Mr. *Glanville* were equally embarrass'd at the Familiarity of this Address; but observing that the Countess seem'd not to be surpriz'd at it, but rather to receive it with Pleasure, they were soon compos'd.

You cannot imagine, lovely Stranger, said *Arabella* to the Countess, as soon as they were seated, with what Impatience I have long'd to behold you, since the Knowledge I have receiv'd of your rare Qualities, and the Friendship you have been pleas'd to honour me with—And I may truly protest to you, that such is my Admiration of your Virtues, that I would have gone to the farthest Part of the World to render you that which you with so much Generosity have condescended to bestow upon me.

Sir *Charles* star'd at this extraordinary Speech, and not being able to comprehend a Word of it, was concern'd to think how the Lady to whom it was address'd would understand it.

Mr. *Glanville* look'd down, and bit his Nails in extreme Confusion; but the Countess who had not forgot the Language of Romance, return'd the Compliment in a Strain as heroick as hers.

The Favour I have receiv'd from Fortune, said she, in bringing me to the Happiness of your Acquaintance, charming *Arabella*, is so great, that I may rationally expect some terrible Misfortune will befall me: Seeing that in this Life our Pleasures are so constantly succeeded by Pains, that we hardly ever enjoy the one without suffering the other soon after.

Arabella was quite transported to hear the Countess express herself in Language so conformable to her own; but Mr. *Glanville* was greatly confounded, and began to suspect she was diverting herself with his Cousin's Singularities: And Sir *Charles* was within a little of thinking her as much out of the Way as his Niece.

Misfortunes, Madam, said *Arabella*, are too often the Lot of excellent Persons like yourself. The sublimest among Mortals both for Beauty and Virtue have experienc'd the Frowns of Fate. The sufferings of the divine *Statira* or *Cassandra*, for she bore both Names, the Persecutions of the incomparable *Cleopatra*, the Distresses of the beautiful *Candace*, and the Afflictions of the fair and generous *Mandana*, are Proof that the most illustrious Persons in the World have felt the Rage of Calamity.

It must be confess'd, said the Countess, that all those fair Princesses you have nam'd, were for a while extremely unfortunate: Yet in the Catalogue of these lovely and afflicted Persons you have forgot one who might with Justice dispute the Priority of Sufferings with them all—I mean the beautiful *Elisa*, Princess of *Parthia*.

Pardon me, Madam, reply'd *Arabella*, I cannot be of your Opinion. The Princess of *Parthia* may indeed justly be rank'd among the Number of unfortunate Persons, but she can by no means dispute the melancholy Precedence with the divine *Cleopatra*—For in fine, Madam, what Evils did the Princess of *Parthia* suffer which the fair *Cleopatra* did not likewise endure, and some of them haply in a greater Degree? If *Elisa* by the tyrannical Authority of the King her Father, saw herself upon the Point of becoming the Wife of a Prince she detested,[1] was not the beautiful Daughter of *Antony*, by the more unjustifiable Tyranny of *Augustus*, likely to be forced into the Arms of *Tyberius*, a proud and cruel Prince, who was odious to the whole World as well as to her?[1] If *Elisa* was for some time in the Power of Pyrates,[2] was not *Cleopatra* Captive to an inhuman King, who presented his Sword to the fair Breast of that divine Princess worthy the Adoration of the whole Earth?[3] And in fine, if *Elisa* had the Grief to see her dear *Artaban* imprison'd by the Order of *Augustus*, *Cleopatra* beheld with mortal Agonies, her beloved *Coriolanus* inclos'd amidst the Guards of that enrag'd Prince, and doom'd to a cruel Death.[4]

'Tis certain, Madam, reply'd the Countess, that the Misfortunes of both these Princesses were very great, tho' as you have shew'd me with some Inequality: And when one reflects upon the dangerous Adventures to which Persons of their Quality were expos'd in those Times, one cannot help rejoicing that we live in an Age in which the Customs, Manners, Habits, and Inclinations differ so widely from theirs, that 'tis impossible such Adventures should even happen.

Such is the strange Alteration of Things, that some People I dare say at present, cannot be persuaded to believe there ever were Princesses wandering thro' the World by Land and Sea in mean Disguises, carry'd away violently out of their Father's Dominions by insolent Lovers—Some discover'd sleeping in Forests, other Shipwreck'd on desolate Islands, confin'd in Castles, bound in Chariots, and even struggling amidst the tempestuous Waves of the Sea, into which they had cast themselves to avoid the brutal Force of their Ravishers. Not one of these Things having happen'd within the Compass of several thousand Years, People unlearn'd in Antiquity would be apt to deem them idle Tales, so improbable do they appear at present.

Arabella, tho' greatly surpriz'd at this Discourse, did not think proper to express her Thoughts of it. She was unwilling to appear absolutely ignorant of the present Customs of the World, before a Lady whose good Opinion she was ardently desirous of improving. Her Prepossessions in favour of the Countess made her receive the new Lights she held out to her with Respect, tho' not without Doubt and Irresolution. Her Blushes, her Silence, and down-cast Eyes gave the Countess to understand Part of her Thoughts; who for fear of alarming her too much for that Time, dropt the Subject, and turning the Conversation on others more general, gave *Arabella* an Opportunity of mingling in it with that Wit and Vivacity which was natural to her when Romances were out of the Question.

CHAPTER VII

In which if the Reader has not anticipated it, he will find an
Explanation of some seeming Inconsistencies in the
foregoing Chapter

THE Countess, charm'd with the Wit and good Sense of *Arabella*, could not conceal her Admiration, but exprest it in Terms the most obligingly imaginable: And *Arabella*, who was excessively delighted with her, return'd the Compliments she made her with the most respectful Tenderness.

In the midst of these mutual Civilities, *Arabella* in the Style of Romance, intreated the Countess to favour her with the Recital of her Adventures.

At the Mention of this Request, that Lady convey'd so much Confusion into her Countenance, that *Arabella* extremely embarrass'd by it, tho' she knew not why, thought it necessary to apologize for the Disturbance she seem'd to have occasion'd in her.

Pardon me, Madam, reply'd the Countess recovering herself, if the uncommonness of your Request made a Moment's Reflexion necessary to convince me that a young Lady of your Sense and Delicacy could mean no Offence to Decorum by making it. The Word Adventures carries in it so free and licentious a Sound in the Apprehensions of People at this Period of Time, that it can hardly with Propriety be apply'd to those few and natural Incidents which compose the History of a Woman of Honour. And when I tell you, pursued she with a Smile, that I was born and christen'd, had a useful and proper Education, receiv'd the Addresses of my Lord —— through the Recommendation of my Parents, and marry'd him with their Consents and my own Inclination, and that since we have liv'd in great Harmony together, I have told you all the material Passages of my Life, which upon Enquiry you will find differ very little from those of other Women of the same Rank, who have a moderate Share of Sense, Prudence and Virtue.

Since you have already, Madam, replied *Arabella* blushing, excus'd me for the Liberty I took with you, it will be un-necessary to tell you it was grounded upon the Customs of antient Times, when Ladies of the highest Rank and sublimest Virtue, were often expos'd to a Variety of cruel Adventures which they imparted in Confidence to each other, when Chance brought them together.

Custom, said the Countess smiling, changes the very Nature of Things, and what was honourable a thousand Years ago, may probably be look'd upon as infamous now—A Lady in the heroick Age you speak of, would not be thought to possess any great Share of Merit, if she had not been many times carried away by one or other of her insolent Lovers: Whereas a Beauty in this could not pass thro' the Hands of several different Ravishers, without bringing an Imputation on her Chastity.

The same Actions which made a Man a Hero in those Times, would constitute him a Murderer in These—And the same Steps which led him to a Throne Then, would infallibly conduct him to a Scaffold Now.

But Custom, Madam, said *Arabella*, cannot possibly change the Nature of Virtue or Vice: And since Virtue is the chief Characteristick of a Hero, a Hero in the last Age will be a Hero in this—Tho' the Natures of Virtue or Vice cannot be changed, replied the Countess, yet they may be mistaken; and different Principles, Customs, and Education, may probably change their Names, if not their Natures.

Sure, Madam, said *Arabella* a little moved, you do not intend by this Inference to prove *Oroondates, Artaxerxes, Juba, Artaban*, and the other Heroes of Antiquity, bad Men?

Judging them by the Rules of Christianity, and our present Notions of Honour, Justice, and Humanity, they certainly are, replied the Countess.

Did they not possess all the necessary Qualifications of Heroes, Madam, said *Arabella*, and each in a superlative Degree?—Was not their Valour invincible, their Generosity unbounded, and their Fidelity inviolable?

It cannot be denied, said the Countess, but that their Valour was invincible; and many thousand Men less courageous than themselves, felt the fatal Effects of that invincible Valour, which was perpetually seeking after Occasions to exert itself. *Oroondates* gave many extraordinary Proofs of that unbounded Generosity so natural to the Heroes of his Time. This Prince being sent by the King his Father, at the Head of an Army, to oppose the *Persian* Monarch, who had unjustly invaded his Dominions, and was destroying the Lives and Properties of his Subjects; having taken the Wives and Daughters of his Enemy Prisoners, had by these Means an Opportunity to put a Period to a War so destructive to his

Country: Yet out of a Generosity truly heroick, he releas'd them immediately without any Conditions; and falling in Love with one of those Princesses, secretly quitted his Father's Court, resided several Years in that of the Enemy of his Father and Country, engag'd himself to his Daughter, and when the War broke out again between the two Kings, fought furiously against an Army in which the King his Father was in Person, and shed the Blood of his future Subjects without Remorse; tho' each of those Subjects, we are told, would have sacrific'd his Life to save that of their Prince, so much was he belov'd.[1] Such are the Actions which immortalize the Heroes of Romance, and are by the Authors of those Books styl'd glorious, godlike, and divine. Yet judging of them as Christians, we shall find them impious and base, and directly opposite to our present Notions of moral and relative Duties.

'Tis certain therefore, Madam, added the Countess with a Smile, that what was Virtue in those Days, is Vice in ours: And to form a Hero according to our Notions of 'em at present, 'tis necessary to give him Qualities very different from *Oroondates*.[2]

The secret Charm in the Countenance, Voice, and Manner of the Countess, join'd to the Force of her reasoning, could not fail of making some Impression on the Mind of *Arabella*; but it was such an Impression as came far short of Conviction. She was surpriz'd, embarrass'd, perplex'd, but not convinc'd. Heroism, romantick Heroism, was deeply rooted in her Heart; it was her Habit of thinking, a Principle imbib'd from Education. She could not separate her Ideas of Glory, Virtue, Courage, Generosity, and Honour, from the false Representations of them in the Actions of *Oroondates, Juba, Artaxerxes*, and the rest of the imaginary Heroes. The Countess's Discourse had rais'd a Kind of Tumult in her Thoughts, which gave an Air of Perplexity to her lovely Face, and made that Lady apprehensive she had gone too far, and lost that Ground in her Esteem, which she had endeavour'd to acquire by a Conformity to some of her Notions and Language. In this however, she was mistaken; *Arabella* felt a Tenderness for her that had already the Force of a long contracted Friendship, and an Esteem little less than Veneration.

When the Countess took Leave, the Professions of *Arabella*, tho' deliver'd in the Language of Romance, were very sincere and affecting, and were return'd with an equal Degree of Tenderness by the Countess, who had concev'd a more than ordinary Affection for her.

Mr. *Glanville* who could have almost worship'd the Countess for the generous Design he saw she had entertain'd, took an Opportunity as he handed her to her Chair, to intreat in a Manner as earnestly as polite, that she would continue the Happiness of her Acquaintance to his Cousin; which with a Smile of mingled Dignity and Sweetness she assur'd him of.

CHAPTER VIII

Which concludes Book the Eighth

MR. *Glanville* at his Return to the Dining-Room, finding *Arabella* retir'd, told his Father in a Rapture of Joy, that the charming Countess would certainly make a Convert of Lady *Bella*.

Methinks, said the Baronet, she has as strange Whims in her Head as my Niece. Ad's-heart, what a deal of Stuff did she talk about! A Parcel of Heroes as she calls them, with confounded hard Names—In my Mind she is more likely to make Lady *Bella* worse than better.

Mr. *Glanville*, a little vex'd at his Father's Mis-apprehension, endeavour'd with as much Delicacy as he could, to set him right with Regard to the Countess; so that he brought him at last to confess she manag'd the Thing very well.

The Countess, who had resolv'd to take *Arabella* openly into her Protection, was thinking on Means to engage her to appear at the Assembly, whither she propos'd to accompany her in a modern Dress. But her good Intentions towards our lovely Heroine were suspended by the Account she receiv'd of her Mother's Indisposition, which commanded her immediate Attendance on her at her Seat in ——

Her sudden Departure gave *Arabella* an extreme Uneasiness, and proved a cruel Disappointment to Mr. *Glanville*, who had founded all his Hopes of her Recovery on the Conversation of that Lady.

Sir *Charles* having Affairs that requir'd his Presence in *London*, propos'd to his Niece the leaving *Bath* in a few Days, to which she consented; and accordingly they set out for *London* in *Arabella*'s Coach and Six, attended by several Servants on Horseback, her

Women having been sent away before in the Stage.

Nothing very remarkable happen'd during this Journey, so we shall not trouble our Readers with several small Mistakes of *Arabella*'s, such as her supposing a neat Country Girl who was riding behind a Man, to be some Lady or Princess in Disguise, forc'd away by a Lover she hated, and intreating Mr. *Glanville* to attempt her Rescue; which occasion'd some little Debate between her and Sir *Charles*, who could not be persuaded to believe it was as she said, and forbid his Son to meddle in other Peoples Affairs. Several of these Sort of Mistakes, as we said before, we omit, and will therefore if our Reader pleases, bring our Heroine without further Delay to *London*.

The End *of the* Eighth Book.

BOOK IX

CHAPTER I

In which is related an admirable Adventure

MISS *Glanville* whose Spirits were greatly exhilerated at their Entrance into *London*, that Seat of Magnificence and Pleasure, congratulated her Cousin upon the Entertainment she would receive from the new and surprizing Objects which every Day for a considerable Time would furnish her with; and ran over the Catalogue of Diversions with such a Volubility of Tongue, as drew a gentle Reprimand from her Father, and made her keep a sullen Silence till they were set down in St. *James*'s Square, the Place of their Residence in Town.

Sir *Charles* having order'd his late Lady's Apartment to be prepar'd for the Accommodation of his Niece; as soon as the first Civilities were over, she retir'd to her Chamber, where she employ'd herself in giving her Women Directions for placing her Books, of which she had brought a moderate Quantity to *London*, in her Closet.

Miss *Glanville* as soon as she had dispatch'd away some hundred Cards to her Acquaintance, to give them Notice she was in Town, attended *Arabella* in her own Apartment; and as they sat at the Tea she begun to regulate the Diversions of the Week, naming the Drawing-Room, Park, Concert, *Ranelagh*, Lady —— Assembly, the Dutchess of — Rout, *Vaux-Hall*, and a long *&c.* of Visits; at which *Arabella*, with an Accent that express'd her Surprize, ask'd her, If she suppos'd she intended to stay in Town three or four Years——

Law, Cousin, said Miss *Glanville*, all this is but the Amusement of a few Days.

Amusement, do you say, replied *Arabella*, methinks it seems to be the sole Employment of those Days: And what you call the Amusement, must of Necessity be the Business of Life.

You are always so grave, Cousin, said Miss *Glanville*, one does not know what to say to you. However, I shan't press you to go to Publick Places against your Inclination, yet you'll condescend to receive a few Visits, I suppose?

Yes, replied *Arabella*, and if among the Ladies whom I shall see, I find any like the amiable Countess of ——, I shall not scruple to enter into the most tender Amity with them.

The Countess of —— is very well, to be sure, said Miss *Glanville*, yet I don't know how it is, she does not suit my Taste—She is very particular in a great many Things, and knows too much for a Lady, as I heard my Lord *Trifle* say one Day: Then she is quite un-fashionable: She hates Cards, keeps no Assembly, is seen but seldom at Publick Places; and in my Opinion, as well as in a great many others, is the dullest Company in the World. I'm sure I met her at a Visit a little before I went down to your Seat, and she had not been a quarter of an Hour in the Room, before she set a whole Circle of Ladies a yawning.

Arabella, tho' she had a sincere Contempt for her Cousin's Manner of thinking, yet always politely conceal'd it; and vex'd as she was at her Sneers upon the Countess, she contented herself with gently defending her, telling her at the same Time, that till she met with a Lady who had more Merit than the Countess, she should always possess the first Place in her Esteem.

Arabella, who had from Youth adopted the Resentments of her Father, refus'd to make her Appearance at Court, which Sir *Charles* gently intimated to her; yet being not wholly divested of the Curiosity natural to her Sex, she condescended to go *incog.* to the Gallery on a Ball Night, accompanied by Mr. *Glanville* and his Sister, in order to behold the Splendor of the *British* Court.

As her Romances had long familiariz'd her Thoughts to Objects of Grandeur and Magnificence, she was not so much struck as might have been expected, with those that now presented them-selves to her View. Nor was she a little disappointed to find that among the Men she saw none whose Appearance came up to her Ideas of the Air and Port of an *Artaban, Oroondates,* or *Juba*; or any of the Ladies, who did not in her Opinion, fall short of the Perfections of *Elisa, Mandana, Statira,* &c. 'Twas remarkable too, that she never enquir'd how often the Princesses had been carried away by love-captivated Monarchs, or how many Victories the King's Sons had gain'd; but seem'd the whole Time she was there to have suspended all her Romantick Ideas of Glory, Beauty, Gallantry, and Love.

Mr. *Glanville* was highly pleas'd with her compos'd Behaviour, and a Day or two after intreated her to allow him the Honour of shewing her what was remarkable and worthy of her Observation in this great Metropolis. To this she also consented, and for the greater Privacy began their Travels in a hir'd Coach.

Part of several Days were taken up in this Employment; but Mr. *Glanville* had the Mortification to find she was full of Allusions to her Romances upon every Occasion, such as her asking the Person who shews the Armoury at the *Tower*, the Names of the Knights to whom each Suit belong'd, and wondering there were no Devices on the Shields or Plumes of Feathers in the Helmets: She observ'd that the Lyon *Lysimachus* kill'd, was according to the History of that Prince, much larger than any of those she was shew'd in the *Tower*, and also much fiercer.[1] Took Notice that St. *Paul*'s was less magnificent in the Inside, than the Temple in which *Cyrus*, when he went to *Mandana*, heard her return Thanks for his suppos'd Death:[2] Enquir'd if it was not customary for the King and his whole Court to sail in Barges upon the *Thames*, as *Augustus* used to do upon the *Tyber*,[3] whether they had not Musick and Collations in the Park, and where they celebrated the Justs and Tournaments.

The Season for *Vaux-Hall* being not yet over, she was desirous of once seeing a Place, which by the Description she had heard of it, greatly resembled the Gardens of *Lucullus* at *Rome*, in which the Emperor, with all the Princes and Princesses of his Court were so nobly entertain'd, and where so many gallant Conversations had pass'd among those admirable Persons.[4]

The Singularity of her Dress, for she was cover'd with her Veil, drew a Number of Gazers after her, who prest round her with so little Respect, that she was greatly embarrass'd, and had Thoughts of quitting the Place, delightful as she own'd it, immediately, when her Attention was wholly engross'd by an Adventure in which she soon interested herself very deeply.

An Officer of Rank in the Sea Service had brought his Mistress disguis'd in a Suit of Man's or rather Boy's Cloaths, and a Hat and Feather, into the Gardens. The young Creature being a little intoxicated with the Wine she had taken too freely, was thrown so much off her Guard as to give Occasion to some of the Company to suspect her Sex; and a gay Fellow, in order to give them some Diversion at her Expence, pretending to be affronted at something she said, drew his Sword upon the disguis'd Fair One, which so alarm'd her, that she shriek'd out, She was a Woman, and ran for Protection to her Lover, who was so disorder'd with Liquor, that he was not able to defend her.

Miss *Glanville* ever curious and inquisitive, demanded the Cause why the Company ran in Crouds to that particular Spot; and receiv'd for Answer, That a Gentleman had drawn his Sword upon a Lady disguis'd in a Man's Habit.

Oh Heav'ns! cry'd *Arabella*, this must certainly be a very notable Adventure. The Lady has doubtless some extraordinary Circumstances in her Story, and haply upon Enquiry, her Misfortunes will be found to resemble those which oblig'd the beautiful *Aspasia* to put on the same Disguise, who was by that Means murder'd by the cruel *Zenodorus* in a Fit of Jealousy at the Amity his Wife exprest for her.[1] But can I not see this unfortunate Fair One, added she, pressing in spite of Mr. *Glanville's* Intreaties thro' the Croud— I may haply be able to afford her some Consolation.

Mr. *Glanville* finding his Persuasions were not regarded, follow'd her with very little Difficulty: For her Veil falling back in her Hurry, she did not mind to replace it, and the Charms of her Face, join'd to the Majesty of her Person, and Singularity of her Dress, attracting every Person's Attention and Respect, they made Way for her to pass, not a little surpriz'd at the extreme Earnestness and Solemnity that appear'd in her Countenance upon an Event so diverting to every one else.

The disguis'd Lady whom she was endeavouring to approach, had thrown herself upon a Bench in one of the Boxes, trembling still with the Apprehension of the Sword, tho' her Antagonist was kneeling at her Feet, making Love to her in Mock-Heroicks for the Diversion of the Company.

Her Hat and Peruke had fallen off in her Fright, and her Hair which had been turn'd up under it, hung now loosely about her Neck, and gave such an Appearance of Woe to a Face, which notwithstanding the Paleness that Terror had overspread it with, was really extremely pretty, that *Arabella* was equally struck with Compassion and Admiration of her.

Lovely Unknown, said she to her with an Air of extreme Tenderness, tho' I am a Stranger both to your Name and History, yet your Aspect persuading me your Quality is not mean, and the Condition and Disguise in which I behold you, shewing that you are Unfortunate, permit me to offer you all the Assistances in my Power, seeing that I am mov'd thereto by my Compassion for your Distress, and that Esteem which the Sight of you must necessarily inspire.

Mr. *Glanville* was struck dumb with Confusion at this strange Speech, and at the Whispers and Scoffs it occasion'd among the Spectators. He attempted to take hold of her Hand in order to lead her away, but she disengag'd herself from him with a Frown of Displeasure; and taking no Notice of Miss *Glanville*, who whisper'd with great Emotion, Lord, Cousin, how you expose yourself! prest nearer to the Beautiful Disguis'd, and again repeated her Offers of Service.

The Girl being perfectly recover'd from her Intoxication by the Fright she had been in, gaz'd upon *Arabella* with a Look of extreme Surprize: Yet being mov'd to respect by the Dignity of her Appearance, and strange as her Words seem'd to be by the obliging Purport of them, and the affecting Earnestness with which they were deliver'd, she rose from her Seat and thank'd her, with an Accent full of Regard and Submission.

Fair Maid, said *Arabella*, taking her Hand, let us quit this Place, where your discovery may probably subject you to more Dangers: If you will be pleas'd to put yourself into my Protection, and acquaint me with the History of your Misfortunes; I have Interest enough with a valiant Person who shall undertake to free you from your Persecutions, and re-establish the Repose of your Life.

The kneeling Hero, who as well as every one else that were present, had gaz'd with Astonishment at *Arabella* during all this Passage, perceiving she was about to rob him of the disguis'd Fair, seiz'd hold of the Hand she had at Liberty, and swore he would not part with her.

Mr. *Glanville* almost mad with Vexation, endeavour'd to get *Arabella* away.

Are you mad, Madam, said he in a Whisper, to make all this Rout about a Prostitute? Do you see how every body stares at you? What will they think—For Heav'ns sake let us be gone.

What, Sir, replied *Arabella* in a Rage, Are you base enough to leave this admirable Creature in the Power of that Man, who is questionless her Ravisher; and will you not draw your Sword in her Defence?

Hey day! cry'd the Sea-Officer, wak'd out of his stupid Dose by the Clamour about him: What's the Matter here—What are you doing? Where's my *Lucy?* Zoons! Sir, said he to the young Fellow who held her, What Business have you with my *Lucy?* And uttering a dreadful Oath, drew out his Sword, and stagger'd towards his gay Rival, who observing the Weakness of his Antagonist, flourish'd with his Sword to shew his Courage and frighten the Ladies, who all ran away screaming. *Arabella* taking Miss *Glanville* under the Arm, cried out to Mr. *Glanville* as she left the Place, to take Care of the distress'd Lady, and while the two Combatants were disputing for her, to carry her away in Safety.

But Mr. *Glanville* without regarding this Injunction, hasten'd after her; and to pacify her, told her the Lady was rescu'd by her favourite Lover, and carry'd off in Triumph.

But are you sure, said *Arabella*, it was not some other of her Ravishers who carry'd her away, and not the Person whom she has haply favour'd with her Affection? May not the same Thing have happen'd to her, as did to the beautiful *Candace,* Queen of *Ethiopia*; who while two of her Ravishers were fighting for her, a third whom she took for her Deliverer, came and carry'd her away.[1]

But she went away willingly, I assure you, Madam, said Mr. *Glanville*: Pray don't be in any Concern about her——

If she went away willingly with him, reply'd *Arabella*, 'tis probable it may not be another Ravisher: And yet if this Person that rescu'd her happen'd to be in Armour, and the Vizor of his Helmet down, she might be mistaken as well as Queen *Candace*.

Well, well, he was not in Armour, Madam, said *Glanville* almost beside himself with Vexation at her Folly——

You seem to be disturb'd, Sir, said *Arabella* a little surpriz'd at his peevish Tone: Is there any Thing in this Adventure which concerns you? Nay, now I remember, you did not offer to defend the Beautiful Unknown. I am not willing to impute your In-action upon such an Occasion, to Want of Courage or Generosity; perhaps you are acquainted with her History, and from this Knowledge refus'd to engage in her Defence.

Mr. *Glanville* perceiving the Company gather from all Parts to the Walk they were in, told her he would acquaint her with all he knew concerning the disguis'd Lady when they were in the Coach on their Return Home; and *Arabella* impatient for the promis'd Story, propos'd to leave the Gardens immediately, which was

gladly comply'd with by Mr. *Glanville*, who heartily repented his
having carry'd her thither.

CHAPTER II

Which ends with a very unfavourable Prediction
for our Heroine

AS soon as they were seated in the Coach she did not fail to call
upon him to perform his Promise: But Mr. *Glanville*, excessively
out of Humour at her exposing herself in the Gardens, reply'd,
without considering whether he should not offend her, That he
knew no more of the disguis'd Lady than any body else in the Place.

How, Sir, reply'd *Arabella*, Did you not promise to relate her
Adventures to me? And would you have me believe you knew no
more of them than the rest of the Cavaliers and Ladies in the Place?

Upon my Soul, I don't, Madam, said *Glanville*; yet what I know
of her is sufficient to let me understand she was not worth the Consideration you seem'd to have for her.

She cannot sure be more indiscreet than the fair and unfortunate
Hermione, reply'd *Arabella*; who like her put on Man's Apparel,
through Despair at the ill Success of her Passion for *Alexander*—
And certain it is, that tho' the beautiful *Hermione* was guilty of one
great Error which lost her the Esteem of *Alexander*, yet she had a
high and noble Soul; as was manifest by her Behaviour and Words
when she was murder'd by the Sword of *Demetrius*. Oh! Death,
cry'd she, as she was falling, how sweet do I find thee, and how
much and how earnestly have I desir'd thee![1]

Oh Lord! oh Lord! cry'd Mr. *Glanville* hardly sensible of what
he said, Was there ever any Thing so intolerable?

Do you pity the unhappy *Hermione*, Sir? said *Arabella* interpreting his Exclamation her own Way? Indeed she is well worthy
of your Compassion. And if the bare Recital of the Words she
utter'd at receiving her Death's Wound affects you so much, you
may guess what would have been your Agonies, had you been
Demetrius that gave it to her.

Here Mr. *Glanville* groaning aloud thro' Impatience at her
Absurdities——

This Subject affects you deeply, I perceive, said *Arabella*. There is no Question but you would have acted in the same Circumstance, as *Demetrius* did: Yet let me tell you, the Extravagancy of his Rage and Despair for what he had innocently committed, was imputed to him as a great Imbecillity, as was also the violent Passion he conceiv'd soon after for the Fair *Deidamia*. You know the Accident which brought that fair Princess into his Way.

Indeed, I do not, Madam, said *Glanville* peevishly.

Well, then I'll tell you, said *Arabella*, but pausing a little:

The Recital I have engag'd myself to make, added she, will necessarily take up some Hours Time, as upon Reflexion I have found: So if you will dispense with my beginning it at present, I will satisfy your Curiosity To-morrow, when I may be able to pursue it without Interruption.

To this Mr. *Glanville* made no other Answer than a Bow with his Head; and the Coach a few Moments after arriving at their own House, he led her to her Apartment, firmly resolv'd never to attend her to any more Publick Places while she continued in the same ridiculous Folly.

Sir *Charles*, who had several Times been in doubt whether *Arabella* was not really disorder'd in her Senses; upon Miss *Glanville's* Account of her Behaviour at the Gardens, concluded she was absolutely mad, and held a short Debate with himself, Whether he ought not to bring a Commission of Lunacy against her, rather than marry her to his Son, whom he was persuaded could never be happy with a Wife so unaccountably absurd. Tho' he only hinted at this to Mr. *Glanville*, in a Conversation he had with him while his Dissatisfaction was at its Height, concerning *Arabella*, yet the bare Supposition that his Father ever thought of such a Thing, threw the young Gentleman into such Agonies, that Sir *Charles* to compose him, protested he would do nothing in relation to his Niece that he would not approve of. Yet he expostulated with him on the Absurdity of her Behaviour, and the Ridicule to which she expos'd herself wherever she went; appealing to him, whether in a Wife he could think those Follies supportable, which in a Mistress occasion'd him so much Confusion.

Mr. *Glanville*, as much in Love as he was, felt all the Force of this Inference, and acknowledg'd to his Father, That he could not think of marrying *Arabella*, till the Whims her Romances had put into her Head, were eraz'd by a better Knowledge of Life and

Manners. But he added with a Sigh, That he knew not how this Reformation would be effected; for she had such a strange Facility in reconciling every Incident to her own fantastick Ideas, that every new Object added Strength to the fatal Deception she laboured under.

CHAPTER III

In which Arabella *meets with another admirable Adventure*

OUR lovely Heroine had not been above a Fortnight in *London*, before the gross Air of that smoaky Town affected her Health so much, that Sir *Charles* propos'd to her to go for a few Weeks to *Richmond*, where he hir'd a House elegantly furnish'd for her Reception.

Miss *Glanville* had been too long out of that darling City, to pay her the Compliment of attending her constantly at *Richmond*; yet she promis'd to be as often as possible with her: And Sir *Charles*, having Affairs that could not dispense with his Absence from Town, plac'd his Steward in her House, being a Person whose Prudence and Fidelity he could rely upon; and he, with her Women, and some other menial Servants, made up her Equipage.

As it was not consistent with Decorum for Mr. *Glanville* to reside in her House, he contented himself with riding to *Richmond* generally every Day: And as long as *Arabella* was pleas'd with that Retirement, he resolv'd not to press her Return to Town till the Countess of —— arriv'd, in whose Conversation he grounded all his Hopes of her Cure.

At that Season of the Year *Richmond* not being quite deserted by Company, *Arabella* was visited by several Ladies of Fashion; who charm'd with her Affability, Politeness, and good Sense, were strangely perplex'd how to account for some Peculiarities in her Dress and Manner of thinking.

Some of the younger Sort from whom *Arabella*'s extraordinary Beauty took away all Pretensions to Equality on that Score, made themselves extremely merry with her Oddnesses, as they call'd them, and gave broad Intimations that her Head was not right.

As for *Arabella*, whose Taste was as delicate, Sentiments as refin'd, and Judgment as clear as any Person's could be who believ'd the Authenticity of *Scudery*'s Romances, she was strangely disappointed to find no Lady with whom she could converse with any tolerable Pleasure: And that instead of *Clelia*'s, *Statira*'s, *Mandana*'s, &c. she found only Miss *Glanville*'s among all she knew.

The Comparison she drew between such as these and the charming Countess of —— whom she had just begun to be acquainted with at *Bath*, increas'd her Regret for the Interruption that was given to so agreeable a Friendship: And it was with infinite Pleasure Mr. *Glanville* heard her repeatedly wish for the Arrival of that admirable Lady (as she always call'd her) in Town.

Not being able to relish the insipid Conversation of the young Ladies that visited her at *Richmond*, her chief Amusement was to walk in the Park there; which because of its Rural Privacy, was extremely agreeable to her Inclinations.

Here she indulg'd Contemplation, leaning on the Arm of her faithful *Lucy*, while her other Women walk'd at some Distance behind her, and two Men Servants kept her always in Sight.

One Evening when she was returning from her usual Walk, she heard the Sound of a Woman's Voice, which seem'd to proceed from a Tuft of Trees that hid her from her View. And stopping a Moment, distinguish'd some plaintive Accents, which increasing her Curiosity, she advanc'd towards the Place, telling *Lucy*, she was resolv'd if possible to discover who the distress'd Lady was, and what was the Subject of her Affliction.

As she drew nearer with softly treading Steps, she could distinguish through the Branches of the Trees, now despoil'd of great part of their Leaves, two Women seated on the Ground, their Backs towards her, and one of them with her Head gently reclin'd on the other's Shoulder, seem'd by her mournful Action to be weeping; for she often put her Handkerchief to her Eyes, breathing every Time a Sigh, which, as *Arabella* phras'd it, seem'd to proceed from the deepest Recesses of her Heart.

This Adventure, more worthy indeed to be styl'd an Adventure than all our Fair Heroine had ever yet met with, and so conformable to what she had read in Romances, fill'd her Heart with eager Expectation. She made a Sign to *Lucy* to make no Noise, and creeping still closer towards the Place where this afflicted Person sat, she heard her distinctly utter these Words, which however were often interrupted with her Sighs.

Ah! *Ariamenes*, whom I to my Misfortune have too much loved, and whom to my Misfortune I fear I shall never sufficiently hate, since that Heav'n and thy cruel Ingratitude hath ordain'd that thou shalt never be mine, and that so many sweet and dear Hopes are for ever taken from me, return me at least, ungrateful Man, return me those Testimonies of my innocent Affection, which were sometimes so dear and precious to thee. Return me those Favours, which all innocent as they were, are become Criminal by thy Crime. Return me, Cruel Man, return me those Reliques of my Heart which thou detainest in Despight of me, and which, notwithstanding thy Infidelity, I cannot recover.

Here her Tears interrupting her Speech, *Arabella* being impatient to know the History of this afflicted Person, came softly round to the other Side, and shewing herself, occasion'd some Disturbance to the sad Unknown; who rising from her Seat, with her Face averted, as if asham'd of having so far disclos'd her Sorrows in a Stranger's Hearing, endeavour'd to pass by her unnotic'd.

Arabella perceiving her Design, stop'd her with a very graceful Action, and with a Voice all compos'd of Sweetness, earnestly conjur'd her to relate her History.

Think not, Lovely Unknown, said she (for she was really very pretty) that my Endeavours to detain you proceed from an indiscreet Curiosity. 'Tis true, some Complaints which have fallen from your fair Mouth, have rais'd in me a Desire to be acquainted with your Adventures; but this Desire has its Foundation in that Compassion your Complaints have fill'd me with: And if I wish to know your Misfortunes, 'tis only with a View of affording you some Consolation.

Pardon me, Madam, said the Fair Afflicted, gazing on *Arabella* with many Signs of Admiration, if my Confusion at being overheard in a Place I had chosen to bewail my Misfortunes, made me be guilty of some Appearance of Rudeness, not seeing the admirable Person I wanted to avoid. But pursued she, hesitating a little, those Characters of Beauty I behold in your Face, and the Gracefulness of your Deportment convincing me you can be of no ordinary Rank, I will the less scruple to acquaint you with my Adventures, and the Cause of those Complaints you have heard proceed from my Mouth.

Arabella assuring her, that whatever her Misfortunes were, she might depend upon all the Assistance in her Power, seated herself near her at the Foot of the Tree where she had been sitting, and giving *Lucy* Orders to join the rest of her Women, and stay at a Distance till she made a Sign to them to advance, she prepar'd to listen to the Adventures of the Fair Unknown, who after some little Pause, began to relate them in this Manner.

CHAPTER IV

In which is related the History of the Princess of Gaul

MY Name, Madam, is *Cynecia*, my Birth Illustrious enough, seeing that I am the Daughter of a Sovereign Prince, who possesses a large and spacious Territory in what is now called Antient *Gaul*.

What, Madam, interrupted *Arabella*, Are you a Princess then?

Questionless I am, Madam, replied the Lady; and a Princess happy and prosperous, till the Felicity of my Life was interrupted by the perfidious *Ariamenes*.

Pardon me, Madam, interrupted *Arabella* again, that my Ignorance of your Quality made me be deficient in those Respects which are due to your high Birth, and which notwithstanding those Characters of Greatness I might read in the Lineaments of your Visage, I yet neglected to pay——

Alas! Madam, said the Stranger, that little Beauty which the Heavens bestow'd on me only to make me wretched, as by the Event it has proved, has long since taken its Flight, and together with my Happiness, I have lost that which made me Unhappy. And certain it is, Grief has made such Ravages among what might once have been thought tolerable in my Face, that I should not be surpriz'd if my being no longer Fair, should make you with Difficulty believe I ever was so.

Arabella after a proper Compliment in Answer to this Speech, intreated the Princess to go on with her History, who hesitating a little, comply'd with her Request.

Be pleas'd to know then, Madam, said she, that being bred up with all imaginable Tenderness in my Father's Court, I had no sooner arriv'd to my Sixteenth Year than I saw myself surrounded with Lovers; who nevertheless, such was the Severity with which I behav'd myself, conceal'd their Passions under a respectful Silence, well knowing Banishment from my Presence was the least Punishment they had to expect, if they presum'd to declare their Sentiments to me.

I liv'd in this Fashion, Madam, for Two Years longer, rejoicing in the Insensibility of my own Heart, and triumphing in the Sufferings of others, when my Tranquillity was all at once interrupted by an Accident which I am going to relate to you.

The Princess stopt here to give Vent to some Sighs which a cruel Remembrance forc'd from her; and continuing in a deep Muse for five or six Minutes, resum'd her Story in this Manner.

It being my Custom to walk in a Forest adjoining to one of my Father's Summer Residences, attended only by my Women, one Day when I was taking this Amusement, I perceiv'd at some Distance a Man lying on the Ground; and impell'd by a sudden Curiosity, I advanc'd towards this Person, whom upon a nearer View I perceiv'd to have been wounded very much, and fainted away through Loss of Blood. His Habit being very rich, I concluded by that he was of no mean Quality: But when I had look'd upon his Countenance, pale and languishing as it was, methought there appear'd so many Marks of Greatness, accompany'd with a Sweetness so happily blended, that my Attention was engag'd in an extraordinary Manner, and interested me so powerfully in his Safety, that I commanded some of my Women to run immediately for proper Assistance, and convey him to the Castle, while I directed others to throw some Water in his Face, and to apply some Linen to his Wounds, to stop the Bleeding.

These charitable Cares restor'd the wounded Stranger to his Senses; he open'd his Eyes, and turning them slowly to the Objects around him, fix'd at last their languishing Looks on me: When mov'd, as it should seem, to some Respect by what he saw in my Countenance, he rose with some Difficulty from the Ground, and bowing almost down to it again, by that Action seem'd to pay me his Acknowledgments for what he suppos'd I had done for his Preservation.

His extreme Weakness having oblig'd him to creep towards a Tree, against the Back of which he supported himself, I went nearer to him, and having told him the Condition in which I found him, and the Orders I had dispatch'd for Assistance, requested him to acquaint me with his Name and Quality, and the Adventure which had brought him into that Condition.

My Name, Madam, answer'd he, is *Ariamenes*, my Birth is Noble enough; I have spent some Years in my Travels, and was returning to my native Country, when passing thro' this Forest I was seiz'd with an Inclination to sleep. I had ty'd my Horse to a Tree, and retiring some few Paces off, stretch'd myself at the Foot of a large Oak whose Branches promis'd me an agreeable Shade. I had not yet clos'd my Eyes, when the Slumber I invited was dissipated by the Sound of some Voices near me.

A Curiosity, not natural to me, made me listen to the Discourse of these Persons, whom by the Tone of their Voices, tho' I could not see them, I knew to be Men.

In short, Madam, I was a Witness to a most horrible Scheme which they concerted together; my Weakness will not permit me to enter into an exact Detail of all I heard: The Result of their Conference was, To seize the Princess of this Country and carry her off.

Here, pursued *Cynecia*, I interrupted the Stranger with a loud Cry, which giving him to understand who I was, he apologiz'd in the most graceful Manner imaginable for the little Respect he had hitherto paid me.

I then intreated him to tell me, If he had any Opportunity of hearing the Name of my design'd Ravisher; to which he reply'd; that he understood it to be *Taxander*.

This Man, Madam, was one of my Father's Favourites, and had been long secretly in Love with me.

Ariamenes then inform'd me, that being enflam'd with Rage against these impious Villains, he rose from the Ground, remounted his Horse, and defy'd the two Traytors aloud, threatning them with Death, unless they abandon'd their impious Design.

Taxander made no Answer, but rush'd furiously upon him, and had the baseness to suffer his wicked Associate to assist him: But the valiant *Ariamenes*, tho' he spoke modestly of his Victory, yet gave me to understand that he had made both the Villains abandon their wicked Enterprize, with their Lives; and that dismounting in order to see if they were quite dead, he found himself so faint with the Wounds he had received from them both, that he had not Strength to re-mount his Horse; but crawling on, in Hopes of meeting with some Assistance, fainted away at last through Weariness and Loss of Blood.

While he was giving me this Account, the Chariot I had sent for arrived, and having made him such Acknowledgments as the Obligation I had received from him demanded, I caus'd him to get into the Chariot, and sending one with him to acquaint the Prince my Father with all that had happen'd, and the Merit of the valiant Stranger, I return'd the same Way I came with my Women, my Thoughts being wholly engross'd by this Unknown.

The Service he had done me fill'd me with a Gratitude and Esteem for him, which prepar'd my Heart for those tender Sentiments I afterwards entertain'd to the Ruin of my Repose.

I will not tire your Patience, Madam, with a minute Detail of all the succeeding Passages of my Story; it shall suffice to tell you, That *Ariamenes* was received with extraordinary Marks of Esteem by my Father; that his Cure was soon compleated; and that having vow'd himself to my Service, and declar'd an unalterable Passion for me, I permitted him to love me, and gave him that Share in my Heart, which I fear not all his Infidelities will ever deprive him of.

His Attachment to me was soon suspected by *Taxander's* Relations, who having secretly vow'd his Ruin, endeavour'd to discover if I had admitted his Addresses, and having made themselves Masters of our Secrets, by means of the Treachery of one of my Women, procur'd Information to be given to my Father of our mutual Passion.

Alas! what Mischiefs did not this fatal Discovery produce: My Father, enrag'd to the last Degree at this Intelligence, confin'd me to my Apartments, and order'd *Ariamenes* to leave his Dominions within three Days.

Spare me, Madam, the Repetition of what pass'd at our last sad Interview, which by large Bribes to my Guards, he obtain'd.

His Tears, his Agonies, his Vows of everlasting Fidelity, so sooth'd my Melancholy at parting with him, and persuaded me of his Constancy, that I waited for several Months with perfect Tranquillity for the Performance of the Promise he made me, to do my Father such considerable Services in the War he was engag'd in with one of his Neighbours, as should oblige him to give me to him for his Reward.

But, alas! two Years roll'd on without bringing back the unfaithful *Ariamenes*. My Father died, and my Brother who succeeded him, being about to force me to marry a Prince whom I detested, I secretly quitted the Court, and attended only by this faithful Confidant whom you behold with me, and some few of my trusty Domesticks, I came hither in Search of *Ariamenes*, he having told me this Country was the Place of his Birth.

Polenor, the most prudent and faithful of my Servants, undertook to find out the ungrateful *Ariamenes*, whom yet I was willing to find Excuses for, but all his Enquiries were to no Effect; the Name of *Ariamenes* was not known in this Part of the World.

Tir'd out with unsuccessful Enquiries, I resolv'd to seek out some obscure Place, where I might in secret lament my Misfortunes, and expect the End of them in Death. My Attendants found me out such a Retreat as I wanted, in a neighbouring Village, which they call *Twickenham*, I think, from whence I often make Excursions to this Park, attended only as you see; and here indulge myself in Complaints upon the Cruelty of my Destiny.

The sorrowful *Cynecia* here ended her Story, to which in the Course of her Relation she had given a great many Interruptions through the Violence of her Grief: And *Arabella*, after having said every thing she could think on to alleviate her Affliction, earnestly intreated her to accept of an Asylum at her House; where she should be treated with all the Respect due to her illustrious Birth.

The afflicted Lady, tho' she respectfully declin'd this Offer, yet express'd a great Desire of commencing a strict Amity with our fair Heroine, who on her Part, made her the most tender Protestations of Friendship.

The Evening being almost clos'd, they parted with great Reluctancy on both Sides; mutually promising to meet in the same Place the next Day.

Cynecia, having enjoin'd her new Friend absolute Secrecy, *Arabella* was under a Necessity of keeping this Adventure to herself. And tho' she long'd to tell Mr. *Glanville*, who came to visit her the next Day, that the Countess was extremely mistaken, when she maintain'd there were no more wandering Princesses in the World, yet the Engagement she had submitted to, kept her silent.

CHAPTER V

A very mysterious Chapter

Arabella, who impatiently long'd for the Hour of meeting the fair Princess, with whom she was extremely delighted, consulted her Watch so often, and discover'd so much Restlessness and Anxiety, that Mr. *Glanville* began to be surpriz'd; and the more, as she peremptorily commanded him not to attend her in her Evening Walk. This Prohibition, which, tho' he durst not dispute, he secretly resolv'd to disobey; and as soon as she set out for the Park with her usual Attendants, he slipp'd out by a Back-door, and keeping her in his Sight, himself unseen, he ventur'd to watch her Motions.

As he had expected to unravel some great Mystery, he was agreeably disappointed to find she continu'd her Walk in the Park with great Composure; and tho' she was soon join'd by the imaginary Princess, yet conceiving her to be some young Lady, with whom she had commenc'd an Acquaintance at *Richmond*, his Heart was at Rest; and for fear of displeasing her, he took a contrary Path from that she was in, that he might not meet her, yet resolv'd to stay till he thought she would be inclin'd to return, and then shew himself, and conduct her Home. A Solicitude for which he did not imagine she need be offended.

The two Ladies being met, after reciprocal Compliments, the Princess intreated *Arabella* to relate her Adventures; who not being willing to violate the Laws of Romance, which require an unbounded Confidence upon these Occasions, began very succinctly to recount the History of her Life; which, as she manag'd it, contain's Events almost as Romantick and Incredible as any in her Romances; winding them up with a Confession that she did not hate Mr. *Glanville*, whom she acknowledg'd to be one of the most faithful and zealous of Lovers.

Cynecia with a Sigh, congratulated her upon the Fidelity of a Lover, who by her Description, was worthy the Place he possess'd in her Esteem: And expressing a Wish, that she could see, unobserv'd by him, this gallant and generous Person, *Arabella*, who that Moment espy'd him at a Distance, yet advancing towards them, told her, with a Blush that overspread all her Face, That her Curiosity might be satisfy'd in the Manner she wish'd, for, yonder, added she is the Person we have been talking of.

Cynecia, at these Words, looking towards the Place where her fair Friend had directed; no sooner cast her Eyes upon Mr. *Glanville*, than giving a loud Cry, she sunk into the Arms of *Arabella*, who, astonish'd and perplex'd as she was, eagerly held them out to support her.

Finding her in a Swoon, she dispatch'd *Lucy*, who was near her, to look for some Water to throw in her Face; but that Lady breathing a deep Sigh, open'd her languishing Eyes, and fixing a melancholy Look upon *Arabella*,

Ah! Madam, said she, wonder not at my Affliction and Surprize, since in the Person of your Lover I behold the ungrateful *Ariamenes*.

Oh Heav'ns! my fair Princess, replied *Arabella*, What is it you say? Is it possible *Glanville* can be *Ariamenes*?

He, cried the afflicted Princess with a disorder'd Accent, He whom I now behold! and whom you call *Glanville*, was once *Ariamenes*, the perjur'd, the ungrateful *Ariamenes*. Adieu, Madam, I cannot bear his Sight; I will hide myself from the World for ever; nor need you fear a Rival or an Enemy in the unfortunate *Cynecia*, who if possible, will cease to love the unfaithful *Ariamenes*, and will never hate the beautiful *Arabella*.

Saying this, without giving her Time to answer, she took hold of her Confidant by the Arm, and went away with so much Swiftness, that she was out of sight before *Arabella* was enough recover'd from her Astonishment to be able to intreat her Stay.

Our charming Heroine, ignorant till now of the true State of her Heart, was surpriz'd to find it assaulted at once by all the Passions which attend disappointed Love. Grief, Rage, Jealousy, and Despair made so cruel a War in her gentle Bosom, that unable either to express or to conceal the strong Emotions with which she was agitated, she gave Way to a violent Burst of Tears, leaning her Head upon *Lucy*'s Shoulder, who wept as heartily as her Lady, tho' ignorant of the Cause of her Affliction.

Mr. *Glanville*, who was now near enough to take Notice of her Posture, came running with eager Heart to see what was the matter; when *Arabella*, rous'd from her Extacy of Grief by the Sound of his Steps, lifted up her Head, and seeing him approach,

Lucy, cried she, trembling with the Violence of her Resentment, Tell that Traitor to keep out of my Sight. Tell him, I forbid him ever to appear before me again. And, tell him, added she, with a Sigh that shook her whole tender Frame, All the Blood in his Body is too little to wash away his Guilt, or to pacify my Indignation.

Then hastily turning away, she ran towards her other Attendants, who were at some Distance; and joining her Women, proceeded directly Home.

Mr. *Glanville*, amaz'd at this Action, was making after her as fast as he could, when *Lucy* crossing in his Way, cry'd out to him to stop.

My Lady, said she, bid me tell you, Traitor——

Hey day! interrupted *Glanville*, What the Devil does the Girl mean?

Pray Sir, said she, let me deliver my Message: I shall forget if you speak to me till I have said it all—Stay, let me see, What comes next?

No more Traitor, I hope, said *Glanville*.

Nor, Sir, said *Lucy*; but there was something about washing in Blood, and you must keep out of her Sight, and not appear before the Nation——Oh dear! I have forgot it half: My Lady was in such a piteous Taking, I forgot it, I believe, as soon as she said it. What shall I do?——

No Matter, said *Glanville*, I'll overtake her, and ask——

No, no, Sir, said *Lucy*, Pray don't do that, Sir, my Lady will be very angry: I'll venture to ask her to tell me over again, and come back and let you know it.

But tell me, reply'd *Glanville*, Was any thing the Matter with your Lady? She was in a piteous Taking, you say.

Oh dear! yes, Sir, said *Lucy*; but I was not bid to say any thing about that. To be sure, my Lady did cry sadly, and sigh'd as if her Heart would break; but I don't know what was the Matter with her.

Well, said *Glanville*, excessively shock'd at this Intelligence, Go to your Lady; I am going Home—You may bring me her Message to my own Apartment.

Lucy did as she was desir'd; and Mr. *Glanville*, impatient as he was to unravel the Mystery, yet dreading lest his Presence should make *Arabella* be guilty of some Extravagance before the Servants who were with her, he follow'd slowly after her, resolving if possible, to procure a private Interview with the lovely Visionary, for whose Sorrow, tho' he suspected it was owing to some ridiculous Cause, he could not help being affected.

CHAPTER VI

Not much plainer than the former

Arabella, who had walk'd as fast as her Legs would carry her, got Home before *Lucy* could overtake her, and retiring to her Chamber, gave Way to a fresh Burst of Grief, and bewail'd the Infidelity of *Glanville* in Terms befitting a *Clelia* or *Mandana*.

As soon as she saw *Lucy* enter, she started from her Chair with great Emotion.

Thou comest, said she, I know, to intercede for that ungrateful Man, whose Infidelity I am weak enough to lament: But open not thy Mouth, I charge thee, in his Defence.

No, indeed, Madam, said *Lucy*.

Nor bring me any Account of his Tears, his Desperation, or his Despair, said *Arabella*, since questionless he will feign them all to deceive me.

Here *Glanville*, who had watch'd *Lucy*'s coming, and had follow'd her into *Arabella*'s Apartment, appear'd at the Door.

Oh Heav'ns! cry'd *Arabella* lifting up her fine Eyes, Can it be that this disloyal Man, unaw'd by the Discovery of his Guilt, again presumes to approach me!——

Dearest Cousin, said *Glanville*, What is the Meaning of all this? —How have I disoblig'd you?—What is my Offence? I beseech you, tell me.

* Ask the inconstant *Ariamenes*, reply'd *Arabella*, the Offence of the ungrateful *Glanville*. The Betrayer of *Cynecia* can best answer that Question to the Deceiver of *Arabella*. And the Guilt of the one can only be compar'd to the Crimes of the other.

Good God! interrupted Mr. *Glanville* fretting excessively, What am I to understand by all this? On my Soul, Madam, I don't know the Meaning of one Word you say.

Oh Dissembler! said *Arabella*, Is it thus that thou would'st impose upon my Credulity? Does not the Name of *Ariamenes* make thee tremble then? And can'st thou hear that of *Cynecia* without Confusion?

---

* This Enigmatical Way of speaking upon such Occasions, is of great Use in the voluminous *French* Romances; since the Doubt and Confusion it is the Cause of, both to the Accus'd and Accuser, gives Rise to a great Number of succeeding Mistakes, and consequently Adventures.

Dear Lady *Bella*, said *Glanville* smiling, What are these Names to me?

False Man, interrupted *Arabella*, Dost thou presume to sport with thy Crimes then? Are not the Treacheries of *Ariamenes* the Crimes of *Glanville*? Could *Ariamenes* be false to the Princess of *Gaul*, and can *Glanville* be innocent towards *Arabella*?

Mr. *Glanville*, who had never heard her in his Opinion, talk so ridiculously before, was so amaz'd at the incomprehensible Stuff she utter'd with so much Emotion, that he began to fear her Intellects were really touch'd. This Thought gave him a Concern that spread itself in a Moment over his Countenance. He gaz'd on her with a fix'd Attention, dreading, yet wishing she would speak again; equally divided between his Hopes, that her next Speech would remove his Suspicion, and his Fears, that it might more confirm them.

Arabella taking Notice of his pensive Posture, turn'd away her Head, lest by beholding him, she should relent, and treat him with less Severity than she had intended; making at the same Time a Sign to him to be gone.

Indeed, Lady *Bella*, said *Glanville* who understood her perfectly well, I cannot leave you in this Temper. I must know how I have been so unfortunate as to offend you.

Arabella, no longer able to contain herself, burst into Tears at this Question: With one Hand she made repeated Signs to him to be gone, with the other she held her Handkerchief to her Eyes, vex'd and asham'd of her Weakness.

But Mr. *Glanville*, excessively shock'd at this Sight, instead of leaving her, threw himself on his Knees before her, and taking her Hand, which he tenderly prest to his Lips,

Good God! my dearest Cousin, said he, How you distract me by this Behaviour! Sure something extraordinary must be the Matter. What can it be that thus afflicts you?—Am I the Cause of these Tears?—Can I have offended you so much?—Speak, dear Madam —Let me know my Crime. Yet may I perish if I am conscious of any towards you——

Disloyal Man, said *Arabella* dis-engaging her Hand from his, Does then the Crime of *Ariamenes* seem so light in thy Apprehension, that thou can'st hope to be thought innocent by *Arabella*? No, no, ungrateful Man, the unfortunate *Cynecia* shall have no Cause to say, that I will triumph in her Spoils. I myself will be the

Minister of her Revenge; and *Glanville* shall suffer for the Crime of *Ariamenes*.

Who the Devil is this *Ariamenes*, cry'd *Glanville* rising in a Passion? And why am I to suffer for his Crime, pray? For Heav'ns Sake, dear Cousin, don't let your Imagination wander thus. Upon my Soul, I don't believe there is any such Person as *Ariamenes* in the World,

Vile Equivocator, said *Arabella*; *Ariamenes*, tho' dead to *Cynecia*, is alive to the deluded *Arabella*. The Crimes of *Ariamenes* are the Guilt of *Glanville*: And if the one has made himself unworthy of the Princess of *Gaul*, by his Perfidy and Ingratitude, the other by his Baseness and Deceit, merits nothing but Contempt and Detestation from *Arabella*.

Frenzy, by my Soul, cry'd *Glanville* mutteringly between his Teeth: This is downright Frenzy. What shall I do?——

Hence, from my Presence, resum'd *Arabella*, false and ungrateful Man; persecute me no more with the hateful Offers of thy Love. From this Moment I banish thee from my Thoughts for ever; and neither as *Glanville* or as *Ariamenes*, will I ever behold thee more.

Stay, dear Cousin, said *Glanville* holding her (for she was endeavouring to rush by him, unwilling he should see the Tears that had overspread her Face as she pronounc'd those Words) hear me, I beg you, but one Word. Who is it you mean by *Ariamenes*?—Is it me? Tell me, Madam, I beseech you—This is some horrid Mistake—You have been impos'd upon by some villainous Artifice—Speak, dear Lady *Bella*—Is it me you mean by *Ariamenes*? For so your last Words seem'd to hint——

Arabella, without regarding what he said, struggled violently to force her Hand from his: and finding him still earnest to detain her, told him with an enrag'd Voice, That she would call for Help, if he did not unhand her directly.

Poor *Glanville*, at this Menace, submissively dropt her Hand; and the Moment she was free, she flew out of the Room, and locking herself up in her Closet, sent her Commands to him by one of her Women, whom she call'd to her, to leave her Apartment immediately.

CHAPTER VII

Containing indeed no great Matters, but being a
Prelude to greater

MR. *Glanville*, who stood fix'd like a Statue in the Place where *Arabella* had left him, was rous'd by this Message, which tho' palliated a little by the Girl that deliver'd it, who was not quite so punctual as *Lucy*, nevertheless fill'd him with extreme Confusion. He obey'd however immediately, and retiring to his own Apartment, endeavour'd to recall to his Memory all Lady *Bella* had said.

The Ambiguity of her Style, which had led him into a Suspicion he had never entertain'd before, her last Words had partly explain'd, if as he understood she did, she meant him by *Ariamenes*. Taking this for granted, he easily conceiv'd some Plot grounded on her Romantick Notions had been laid, to prepossess her against him.

Sir *George*'s Behaviour to her rush'd that Moment into his Thoughts: He instantly recollected all his Fooleries, his History, his Letter, his Conversation, all apparently copied from those Books she was so fond of, and probably done with a View to some other Design upon her.

These Reflections, join'd to his new awak'd Suspicions, that he was in Love with her, convinc'd him he was the Author of their present Mis-understanding; and that he had impos'd some new Fallacy upon *Arabella*, in order to promote a Quarrel between them.

Fir'd almost to Madness at this Thought, he stamp'd about his Room, vowing Revenge upon Sir *George*, execrating Romances, and cursing his own Stupidity for not discovering Sir *George* was his Rival, and knowing his plotting Talent, not providing against his Artifices.

His first Resolutions were to set out immediately for Sir *George*'s Seat, and force him to confess the Part he had acted against him: But a Moment's Consideration convinc'd him, that was not the most probable Place to find him in, since it was much more likely he was waiting the Success of his Schemes in *London*, or perhaps at *Richmond*.

Next to satiating his Vengeance, the Pleasure of detecting him in such a Manner, that he could not possibly deny or palliate his Guilt, was next his Heart.

He resolv'd therefore to give it out, that he was gone to *London*, to make Lady *Bella* believe it was in Obedience to her Commands that he had left her, with a Purpose not to return till he had clear'd his Innocence; but in reality to conceal himself in his own Apartment, and see what Effects his reputed Absence would produce.

Having thus taken his Resolution, he sent for Mr. *Roberts* his Father's Steward, to whose Care he had entrusted Lady *Bella* in her Retirement, and acquainting him with Part of his Apprehensions with Regard to Sir *George*'s Attempts upon his Cousin; he imparted to him his Design of staying conceal'd there, in order to discover more effectually those Attempts, and to preserve Lady *Bella* from any Consequence of them.

Mr. *Roberts* approv'd of his Design; and assur'd him of his Vigilance and Care, both in concealing his Stay, and also in giving him Notice of every Thing that pass'd.

Mr. *Glanville* then wrote a short Billet to *Arabella*, expressing his Grief for her Displeasure, his Departure in Obedience to her Orders, and his Resolution not to appear in her Presence, till he could give her convincing Proofs of his Innocence.

This Letter he sent by *Roberts*, which *Arabella* condescended to read, but would return no Answer.

Mr. *Glanville* then mounting his Horse, which *Roberts* had order'd to be got ready, rode away, and leaving him at a House he sometimes put up at, return'd on Foot, and was let in by Mr. *Roberts* at the Garden-door, and conducted unseen to his Chamber.

While he pass'd that Night and great Part of the next Day, meditating on the Treachery of Sir *George*, and soothing his Uneasiness with the Hopes of Revenge, *Arabella*, no less disquieted, mus'd on the Infidelity of her Lover, the Despair of *Cynecia*, and the Impossibility of her ever being happy. Then ransacking her Memory for Instances in her Romances of Ladies equally unfortunate with herself, she would sometimes compare herself to one Lady, sometimes to another, adapting their Sentiments, and making Use of their Language in her Complaints.

Great Part of the Day being spent in this Manner, the uneasy Restlessness of her Mind made her wish to see *Cynecia* again. She long'd to ask her a hundred Questions about the unfaithful *Ariamenes*, which the Suddenness of her Departure, and her own Astonishment prevented her from doing, when she made that fatal

Discovery, which had cost her so much Uneasiness.

Sometimes a faint Hope would arise in her Mind that *Cynecia* might be mistaken, thro' the great Resemblance that possibly was between *Ariamenes* and *Glanville*.

She remember'd that *Mandana* had been deceiv'd by the Likeness of *Cyrus* to *Spitridates*; and concluded that illustrious Prince inconstant, because *Spitridates*, whom she took for *Cyrus*, saw her carry'd away, without offering to rescue her.

Dwelling with Eagerness upon this Thought, because it afforded her a temporary Relief from others more tormenting, she resolv'd to go to the Park, tho' she had but little Hopes of finding *Cynecia* there; supposing it but too probable, that the Disturbance which the Sight, or fancy'd Sight of *Ariamenes* had given her, would confine her for some Days to her Chamber. Yet however small the Probability was of meeting with her, she could not resist the impatient Desire she felt of going to seek her.

Dispensing therefore with the Attendance of any other Servant but *Lucy*, she left her Apartment, with a Design of resuming her usual Walk, when she was met at her stepping out of the Door by Lady *L*—'s three Daughters, (who had visited her during her Residence at *Richmond*) and another young Lady.

These Ladies, who to vary the Scene of their Rural Diversions, were going to cross over to *Twickenham*, and walk there, prest Lady *Bella* to accompany them. Our melancholy Heroine refus'd them at first, but upon their repeated Importunity, recollecting that the Princess of *Gaul* had inform'd her she resided there, she consented to go, in Hopes some favourable Chance might bring her in their Way, or discover the Place of her Retreat, when she could easily find some Excuse for leaving her Companions, and going to her.

Mr. *Roberts*, who according to his Instructions, narrowly watch'd *Arabella*'s Motions, finding she did not command his Attendance as usual, resolv'd however to be privately of this Party. He had but just Time to run up and acquaint Mr. *Glanville*, and then follow'd the Ladies at a Distance, who taking Boat, pass'd over to *Twickenham*, which he also did as soon as he saw them landed.

CHAPTER VIII

Which acquaints the Reader with two very extraordinary Accidents

MR. *Glanville*, who did not doubt but *Roberts* would bring him some Intelligence, sat waiting with anxious Impatience for his Return. The Evening drew on apace, he number'd the Hours, and began to grow uneasy at *Arabella*'s long Stay. His Chamber Window looking into the Garden, he thought he saw his Cousin, cover'd with her Veil as usual, hasten down one of the Walks; his Heart leap'd at this transient View, he threw up the Sash, and looking out, saw her very plainly strike into a cross Walk, and a Moment after saw Sir *George*, who came out of a little Summerhouse, at her Feet. Transported with Rage at this Sight, he snatch'd up his Sword, flew down the Stairs into the Garden, and came running like a Madman up the Walk in which the Lovers were. The Lady observing him first, for Sir *George*'s Back was towards him, shriek'd aloud, and not knowing what she did, ran towards the House, crying for Help, and came back as fast, yet not Time enough to prevent Mischief: For Mr. *Glanville*, actuated by an irresistible Fury, cry'd out to Sir *George* to defend himself, who had but just Time to draw his Sword and make an ineffectual Pass at Mr. *Glanville*, when he receiv'd his into his Body, and fell to the Ground.

Mr. *Glanville* losing his Resentment insensibly at the Sight of his Rival's Blood, threw down his Sword, and endeavour'd to support him; while the Lady, who had lost her Veil in her running, and to the great Astonishment of Mr. *Glanville*, prov'd to be his Sister, came up to them, with Tears and Exclamations, blaming herself for all that had happen'd. Mr. *Glanville*, with a Heart throbbing with Remorse for what he had done, gaz'd on his Sister with an accusing Look, as she hung over the wounded Baronet with streaming Eyes, sometimes wringing her Hands, then clasping them together in an Agony of Grief.

Sir *George* having Strength enough left to observe her Disorder, and the generous Concern of *Glanville*, who holding him in his Arms, intreated his Sister to send for proper Assistance, Dear *Charles*, said he, you are too kind, I have us'd you very ill, I have deserv'd my Death from your Hand—You know not what I have been base enough to practise against you—If I can but live to clear your Innocence to Lady *Bella*, and free you from the Consequences of this Action, I shall die satisfy'd—

His Strength failing him at these Words, he fainted away in Mr. *Glanville*'s Arms; who tho' now convinc'd of his Treachery, was extremely shock'd at the Condition he saw him in.

Miss *Glanville* renewing her Tears and Exclamations at this Sight, he was oblig'd to lay Sir *George* gently upon the Ground, and ran to find out somebody to send for a Surgeon, and to help him to convey him into the House.

In his Way he was met by Mr. *Roberts*, who was coming to seek him; and with a Look of Terror and Confusion told him, Lady *Bella* was brought Home extremely ill—that her Life had been in Danger, and that she was but just recover'd from a terrible fainting Fit.

Mr. *Glanville*, tho' greatly alarm'd at this News, forgot not to take all possible Care of Sir *George*; directing *Roberts* to get some Person to carry him into the House, and giving him Orders to procure proper Assistance, flew to Lady *Bella*'s Apartment.

Her Women had just put her to Bed, raving as in a strong Delirium. Mr. *Glanville* approach'd her, and finding she was in a violent Fever, dispatch'd a Man and Horse immediately to Town, to get Physicians, and to acquaint his Father with what had happen'd.

Mr. *Roberts*, upon the Surgeon's Report that Sir *George* was not mortally wounded, came to inform him of this good News, but he found him incapable of listning to him, and in Agonies not to be exprest. 'Twas with Difficulty they forc'd him out of *Arabella*'s Chamber into his own; where throwing himself upon his Bed, he refus'd to see or speak to any Body, till he was told Sir *Charles* and the Physicians were arriv'd.

He then ran eagerly to hear their Opinions of his beloved Cousin, which he soon discover'd by their significant Gestures and half pronounc'd Words, to be very bad. They comforted him however, with Hopes that she might recover, and insisting upon her being kept very quiet, oblig'd him to quit the Room. While all the necessary Methods were taken to abate the Violence of the Disease, Sir *Charles*, who had been inform'd by his Steward of his Son's Duel with Sir *George*, was amaz'd to the last Degree at two such terrible Accidents.

She hung over the wounded Baronet with streaming Eyes

Having seen his Son to his Chamber, and recommended him to be patient and compos'd, he went to visit the young Baronet, and was not a little surpriz'd to find his Daughter sitting at his Bed's Head, with all the Appearance of a violent Affliction.

Indeed Miss *Glanville*'s Cares were so wholly engross'd by Sir *George*'s, that she hardly ever thought of her Cousin *Arabella*, and had just stept into her Chamber while the Surgeons were dressing Sir *George*'s Wound, and renew'd her Attendance upon him as soon as that was over.

Miss *Glanville* however, thought proper to make some trifling Excuses to her Father for her Solicitude about Sir *George*. And the young Baronet, on whom the Fear of Death produc'd its usual Effects, and made him extremely concern'd for the Errors of his past Life, and very desirous of attoning for them if possible, assur'd Sir *Charles*, that if he liv'd he would offer himself to his Acceptance for a Son-in-law; declaring that he had basely trifled with the Esteem of his Daughter, but that she had wholly subdued him to herself by her forgiving Tenderness.

Sir *Charles* was very desirous of knowing the Occasion of his Quarrel with his Son, but Sir *George* was too weak to hold any further Conversation, upon which Sir *Charles*, after a short Visit retir'd, taking Miss *Glanville* along with him.

That the Reader, whose Imagination is no doubt upon the Stretch to conceive the Meaning of these Two extraordinary Incidents, may be left no longer in Suspence, we think proper to explain them both in the following Chapter, that we may in the next pursue our History without Interruption.

CHAPTER IX

Which will be found to contain Information absolutely necessary for the right understanding of this History

OUR fair and afflicted Heroine, accompanied by the Ladies we have mention'd, having cross'd the River, pursu'd their Walk upon its winding Banks, entertaining themselves with the usual Topicks of Conversation among young Ladies, such as their Winnings and

Losings at *Brag*,[1] the Prices of Silks, the newest Fashions, the best Hair-Cutter, the Scandal at the last Assembly, &c.

Arabella was so disgusted with this (as she thought) insipid Discourse, which gave no Relief to the Anxiety of her Mind, but added a Kind of Fretfulness and Impatience to her Grief; that she resolv'd to quit them, and with *Lucy*, go in quest of the Princess of *Gaul*'s Retreat.

The Ladies however, insisted upon her not leaving them; and her Excuse that she was going in search of an unfortunate Unknown, for whom she had vow'd a Friendship, made them all immediately resolve to accompany her, extremely diverted with the Oddity of the Design, and sacrificing her to their Mirth by sly Leers, Whispers, stifled Laughs, and a thousand little sprightly Sallies, which the disconsolate *Arabella* took no Notice of, so deeply were her Thoughts engag'd.

Tho' she knew not which Way to direct her Steps, yet concluding the melancholy *Cynecia* would certainly chuse some very solitary Place for her Residence, she rambled about among the least frequented Paths, follow'd by the young Ladies, who ardently desir'd to see this unfortunate Unknown; tho' at *Arabella*'s earnest Request, they promis'd not to shew themselves to the Lady, who, she inform'd them, for very urgent Reasons, was oblig'd to keep herself conceal'd.

Fatiguing as this Ramble was to the delicate Spirits of *Arabella*'s Companions, they were enabled to support it by the Diversion her Behaviour afforded them.

Every Peasant she met, she enquir'd if a Beautiful Lady disguis'd did not dwell somewhere thereabout.

To some she gave a Description of her Person, to others an Account of the Domesticks that were with her; not forgetting her Dress, her Melancholy, and the great Care she took to keep herself conceal'd.

These strange Enquiries, with the strange Language in which they were made, not a little surpriz'd the good People to whom she address'd herself, yet mov'd to Respect by the majestick Loveliness of her Person, they answer'd her in the Negative, without any Mixture of Scoff and Impertinence.

How unfavourable is Chance, said *Arabella* fretting at the Disappointment, to Persons who have any Reliance upon it! This Lady that I have been in Search of so long without Success, may probably be found by others who do not seek her, whose Presence she may wish to avoid, yet not be able.

The young Ladies finding it grew late, express'd their Apprehensions at being without any Attendants; and desir'd *Arabella* to give over her Search for that Day. *Arabella* at this Hint of Danger, enquir'd very earnestly, If they apprehended any Attempts to carry them away? And without staying for an Answer, urg'd them to walk Home as fast as possible, apologizing for the Danger into which she had so indiscreetly drawn both them and herself; yet added her Hopes, that if any Attempt should be made upon their Liberty, some generous Cavalier would pass by who would rescue them: A Thing so common, that they had no Reason to despair of it.

Arabella construing the Silence with which her Companions heard these Assurances, into a Doubt of their being so favoured by Fortune, proceeded to inform them of several Instances wherein Ladies met with unexpected Relief and Deliverance from Ravishers.

She mention'd particularly the Rescue of *Statira* by her own Brother, whom she imagin'd for many Years dead; that of the Princess *Berenice* by an absolute Stranger,[1] and many others, whose Names, Characters and Adventures she occasionally run over; all which the young Ladies heard with inconceivable Astonishment. And the Detail had such an Effect upon *Arabella*'s Imagination, bewilder'd as it was in the Follies of Romances, that 'spying three or four Horsemen riding along the Road towards them, she immediately concluded they would be all seiz'd and carry'd off.

Possess'd with this Belief, she utter'd a loud Cry, and flew to the Water-side, which alarming the Ladies, who could not imagine what was the Matter, they ran after her as fast as possible.

Arabella stop'd when she came to the Waterside, and looking round about, and not perceiving any Boat to waft them over to *Richmond*, a Thought suddenly darted into her Mind, worthy those ingenious Books which gave it Birth.

Turning therefore to the Ladies, who all at once were enquiring the Cause of her Fright;

'Tis now, my fair Companions, said she, with a solemn Accent, that the Destinies have furnish'd you with an Opportunity of displaying in a Manner truly Heroick, the Sublimity of your Virtue, and the Grandeur of your Courage to the World.

The Action we have it in our Power to perform will immortalize our Fame, and raise us to a Pitch of Glory equal to that of the renown'd *Clelia* herself.

Like her, we may expect Statues erected to our Honour: Like her, be propos'd as Patterns to Heroines in ensuing Ages: And like her, perhaps, meet with Sceptres and Crowns for our Reward.

What that beauteous *Roman* Lady perform'd to preserve herself from Violation by the impious *Sextus*,[1] let us imitate to avoid the Violence our intended Ravishers yonder come to offer us.

Fortune, which has thrown us into this Exigence, presents us the Means of gloriously escaping: And the Admiration and Esteem of all Ages to come, will be the Recompence of our noble Daring.

Once more, my fair Companions, If your Honour be dear to you, if an immortal Glory be worth your seeking, follow the Example I shall set you, and equal with me the *Roman Clelia*.

Saying this, she plung'd into the *Thames*, intending to swim over it, as *Clelia* did the *Tyber*.

The young Ladies, who had listen'd with silent Astonishment at the long Speech she had made them, the Purport of which not one of them understood, scream'd out aloud at this horrid Spectacle, and wringing their Hands, ran backwards and forwards like distracted Persons, crying for Help. *Lucy* tore her Hair, and was in the utmost Agony of Grief, when Mr. *Roberts*, who, as we have said before, kept them always in Sight, having observ'd *Arabella* running towards the Water-side, follow'd them as fast as he could, and came Time enough up to see her frantick Action. Jumping into the River immediately after her, he caught hold of her Gown, and drew her after him to the Shore. A Boat that Instant appearing, he put her into it, senseless, and to all Appearances dead. He and *Lucy* supporting her, they were wafted over in a few Moments to the other Side: Her House being near the River, Mr. *Roberts* carry'd her in his Arms to it; and as soon as he saw her shew Signs of returning Life, left her to the Care of the Women, who made haste to put her into a warm Bed, and ran to find out Mr. *Glanville*, as we have related.

There remains now only to account for Sir *George* and Miss *Glanville*'s sudden Appearance, which happen'd, gentle Reader, exactly as follows.

Miss *Glanville*, having set out pretty late in the Afternoon, with a Design of staying all Night at *Richmond*, as her Chaise drove up

Kew-Lane, saw one of her Cousin's Women, *Deborah* by Name, talking to a Gentleman, whom, notwithstanding the Disguise of a Horseman's Coat, and a Hat slouch'd over his Face, she knew to be Sir *George Bellmour*.

This Sight alarming her Jealousy, and renewing all her former Suspicions, that her Cousin's Charms rival'd hers in his Heart, as soon as she alighted, finding *Arabella* was not at Home, she retir'd in great Anguish of Mind to her Chamber, revolving in her Mind every Particular of Sir *George*'s Behaviour to her Cousin in the Country, and finding new Cause for Suspicion in every Thing she recollected, and reflecting upon the Disguise in which she saw him, and his Conference with her Woman, she concluded herself had all along been the Dupe of his Artifice, and her Cousin the real Object of his Love.

This Thought throwing her into an Extremity of Rage, all her tenderest Emotions were lost in the Desire of Revenge. She imagin'd to herself so much Pleasure from exposing his Treachery, and putting it out of his Power to deny it, that she resolv'd, whatever it cost her, to have that Satisfaction.

Supposing therefore *Deborah* was now return'd, she rung her Bell, and commanded her Attendance on her in her Chamber.

The Stern Brow with which she receiv'd her, frighten'd the Girl, conscious of her Guilt, into a Disposition to confess all, even before she was tax'd with any thing.

Miss *Glanville* saw her Terror, and endeavour'd to heighten it, by entering at once into Complaints and Exclamations against her, threatning to acquaint her Father with her Plots to betray her Lady, and assuring her of a very severe Punishment for her Treachery.

The Girl, terrify'd extremely at these Menaces, begg'd Miss *Glanville*, with Tears, to forgive her, and not to acquaint Sir *Charles* or her Lady, with her Fault; adding, that she would confess all, and never while she liv'd, do such a Thing again.

Miss *Glanville* would make her no Promises, but urg'd her to confess: Upon which *Deborah* sobbing, own'd, That for the Sake of the Presents Sir *George* had made her, she consented to meet him privately from Time to Time, and give him an Account of every Thing that pass'd with Regard to her Lady; not thinking there was any Harm in it. That according to his Desires, she had constantly acquainted him with all her Lady's Motions, when, and where she

went, how she and Mr. *Glanville* agreed, and a hundred other
Things which he enquir'd about. That that Day in particular, he
had intreated her to procure him the Means of an Interview with
her Lady, if possible; and understanding Mr. *Glanville* was not at
Richmond, she had let him privately into the Garden, where she
hop'd to prevail upon her Lady to go.

What, said Miss *Glanville* surpriz'd, Is Sir *George* waiting for my
Cousin in the Garden then?

Yes, indeed, Madam, said *Deborah*: But I'll go and tell him to
wait no longer; and never speak to him again, if your Ladyship will
but be pleas'd to forgive me.

Miss *Glanville* having taken her Resolution, not only promis'd
Deborah her Pardon, but also a Reward, provided she would contrive it so, that she might meet Sir *George* instead of her Cousin.

The Girl, having the true Chamber-Maid Spirit of Intrigue in
her, immediately propos'd her putting on one of her Lady's Veils;
which as it was now the Close of the Evening, would disguise her
sufficiently; to which Miss *Glanville*, transported with the
Thoughts of thus having an Opportunity of convincing Sir *George*
of his Perfidy, and reproaching him for it, consented, and bid her
bring it without being observ'd, into her Chamber.

Deborah informing her, that Sir *George* was conceal'd in the
Summer-House, as soon as she had equipp'd herself with *Arabella's* Veil she went into the Walk that led to it; and Sir *George*,
believing her to be that Lady, hasten'd to throw himself at her
Feet, and had scarce got through half a Speech he had study'd for
his present Purpose, when Mr. *Glanville* gave a fatal Interruption
to his Heroicks, in the Manner we have already related.

CHAPTER X

A short Chapter indeed, but full of Matter

Richmond was now a Scene of the utmost Confusion and Distress.
Arabella's Fever was risen to such a Height, that she was given
over by the Physicians; and Sir *George's* Wounds, tho' not judg'd
mortal at first, yet by the great Effusion of Blood had left him in so
weak a Condition, that he was thought to be in great Danger.

Sir *Charles*, almost distracted with the Fears of the Consequences of Sir *George*'s Death, intreated his Son to quit the Kingdom; but Mr. *Glanville*, protesting he would rather die than leave *Arabella* in that Illness, he was oblig'd to give Bail for his Appearance, in Case Sir *George* dy'd: This Affair, notwithstanding all Endeavours to prevent it, having made a great Noise.

Poor Sir *Charles*, opprest as he was with the Weight of all these Calamities, was yet oblig'd to labour incessantly to keep up the Spirits of his Son and Daughter. The settled Despair of the one, and the silent swelling Grief of the other, cut him to the Heart. He omitted no Arguments his Paternal Affection suggested to him, to moderate their Affliction. Mr. *Glanville* often endeavour'd to assume a Composure he was very far from feeling, in order to satisfy his Father. But Miss *Glanville*, looking upon herself to be the Cause of Sir *George*'s Misfortune, declar'd, She should be miserable all her Life, if he died.

Arabella in her lucid Intervals, being sensible of her Danger, prepar'd for Death, with great Piety and Constancy of Mind, having solemnly assur'd Mr. *Glanville* of her Forgiveness, who would not at that Time enter into an Explanation of the Affair which had given her Offence for fear of perplexing her. She permitted his Presence often in her Chamber, and desir'd with great Earnestness the Assistance of some worthy Divine in her Preparations for Death. The Pious and Learned Doctor —— at Sir *Charles*'s Intimation of his Niece's Desire, came constantly twice a Day to attend her. Her Fever, by a favourable Crisis, and the great Skill of her Physicians, left her in a Fortnight; but this violent Distemper had made such a Ravage in her delicate Constitution, and reduc'd her so low that there seem'd very little Probability of her Recovery. Doctor ——, in whom her unfeign'd Piety, her uncommon Firmness of Mind, had created a great Esteem and Tenderness for her, took all Opportunities of comforting, exhorting, and praying by her. The Occasion of her Illness being the Subject of every body's Conversation at *Richmond*, he gently hinted it to her, and urg'd her to explain her Reasons for so extravagant an Action.

In the Divine Frame *Arabella* was then in, this Action appear'd to her rash and vain-glorious, and she acknowledg'd it to be so to her pious Monitor: Yet she related the Motives which induc'd her to it, the Danger she was in of being carry'd away, the Parity of her Circumstances then with *Clelia*, and her emulous Desire of doing as much to preserve her Honour as that renown'd *Roman* Lady did for hers.

The good Doctor was extremely surpriz'd at this Discourse: He was beginning to think her again delirious; but *Arabella* added to this Account such sensible Reasoning on the Nature of that Fondness for Fame, which prompted her to so rash an Undertaking, that the Doctor left her in strange Embarrassment, not knowing how to account for a Mind at once so enlighten'd, and so ridiculous.

Mr. *Glanville*, meeting him as he came out of her Chamber, the Doctor took this Opportunity to acknowledge the Difficulties *Arabella*'s inconsistent Discourse had thrown him into. Mr. *Glanville* taking him into his own Apartment, explain'd the Nature of that seeming Inconsistency, and expatiated at large upon the Disorders Romances had occasion'd in her Imagination; several Instances of which he recounted, and fill'd the Doctor with the greatest Astonishment and Concern. He lamented pathetically the Ruin such a ridiculous Study had brought on so noble a Mind; and assur'd Mr. *Glanville*, he would spare no Endeavours to rescue it from so shocking a Delusion.

Mr. *Glanville* thank'd him for his good Design, with a Transport which his Fears of his Cousin's Danger almost mingled with Tears; and the Doctor and he agreed to expect for some few Days longer an Alteration for the better in the Health of her Body, before he attempted the Cure of her Mind. Mr. *Glanville*'s extreme Anxiety had made him in Appearance neglect the repentant Sir *George*, contenting himself with constantly sending twice a Day to enquire after his Health, but had not yet visited him.

No sooner had the Physicians declared that *Arabella* was no longer in Danger, than his Mind being freed from that tormenting Load of Suspence under which it had labour'd while her Recovery was yet doubtful, he went to Sir *George*'s Chamber, who by reason of his Weakness, tho' he was also upon the Recovery, still kept his Bed.

Sir *George*, tho' he ardently wish'd to see him, yet conscious of the Injuries he had both done and design'd him, could not receive his Visit without extreme Confusion: But entering into the Cause of their Quarrel, as soon as he was able to speak, he freely acknowledg'd his Fault, and all the Steps he had taken to supplant him in *Arabella*'s Affection.

Mr. *Glanville* understanding by this Means, that he had brib'd a young Actress to personate a Princess forsaken by him; and had taught her all that Heap of Absurdity with which she had impos'd upon *Arabella*, as has been related, desir'd only by Way of Reparation, That when his Cousin was in a Condition to be spoken to upon that Subject, he would condescend to own the Fraud to her; which Sir *George* faithfully promising, an Act of Oblivion pass'd on Mr. *Glanville*'s Side for all former Injuries, and a solemn Assurance from Sir *George* of inviolable Friendship for the future. An Assurance, however, which Mr. *Glanville* would willingly have dispens'd with: For tho' not of a vindictive Temper, it was one of his Maxims, That a Man who had once betray'd him, it would be an Error in Policy ever to trust again.

CHAPTER XI

Being in the Author's Opinion, the best Chapter in this History[1]

THE good Divine, who had the Cure of *Arabella*'s Mind greatly at Heart, no sooner perceiv'd that the Health of her Body was almost restor'd, and that he might talk to her without the Fear of any Inconvenience, than he introduc'd the Subject of her throwing herself into the River, which he had before lightly touch'd upon, and still declar'd himself dissatisfy'd with.

Arabella, now more dispos'd to defend this Point than when languishing under the Pressure of Pain and Dejection of Mind, endeavour'd by Arguments founded upon Romantick Heroism, to prove, That it was not only reasonable and just, but also great and glorious, and exactly conformable to the Rules of Heroick Virtue.

The Doctor listen'd to her with a mix'd Emotion, between Pity, Reverence, and Amazement: And tho' in the Performance of his Office he had been accustom'd to accommodate his Notions to every Understanding, and had therefore accumulated a great Variety of Topicks and Illustrations; yet he found himself now engag'd in a Controversy for which he was not so well prepar'd as he imagin'd, and was at a Loss for some leading Principle, by which he might introduce his Reasonings, and begin his Confutation.

Tho' he saw much to praise in her Discourse, he was afraid of confirming her Obstinacy by Commendation: And tho' he also found much to blame, he dreaded to give Pain to a Delicacy he rever'd.

Perceiving however, that *Arabella* was silent, as if expecting his Reply, he resolv'd not to bring upon himself the Guilt of abandoning her to her Mistake, and the Necessity of speaking forc'd him to find something to say.

Tho' it is not easy, Madam, said he, for any one that has the Honour of conversing with your Ladyship to preserve his Attention free to any other Idea, than such as your Discourse tends immediately to impress, yet I have not been able while you was speaking, to refrain from some very mortifying Reflections on the Imperfection of all human Happiness, and the uncertain Consequences of all those Advantages which we think ourselves not only at Liberty to desire, but oblig'd to cultivate.

Tho' I have known some Dangers and Distresses, reply'd *Arabella* gravely, yet I did not imagine myself such a Mirror of Calamity as could not be seen without Concern. If my Life has not been eminently fortunate, it has yet escap'd the great Evils of Persecution, Captivity, Shipwrecks and Dangers to which many Ladies far more Illustrious both by Birth and Merit than myself, have been expos'd. And indeed, tho' I have sometimes rais'd Envy, or possible incurr'd Hatred, yet I have no Reason to believe I was ever beheld with Pity before.

The Doctor saw he had not introduc'd his Discourse in the most acceptable Manner; but it was too late to repent.

Let me not, Madam, said he, be censur'd before I have fully explain'd my Sentiments.

That you have been envy'd, I can readily believe: For who that gives Way to natural Passions has not Reason to envy the Lady *Arabella?* But that you have been hated, I am indeed less willing to think, tho' I know how easily the greater Part of Mankind hate those by whom they are excell'd.

If the Misery of my Condition, reply'd *Arabella*, has been able to excite that Melancholy your first Words seem'd to imply, Flattery will contribute very little towards the Improvement of it. Nor do I expect from the Severity of the Sacerdotal Character, any of those Praises, which I hear perhaps with too much Pleasure, from the rest of the World.

Having been so lately on the Brink of that State, in which all Distinctions but that of Goodness are destroy'd, I have not recover'd so much Levity, but that I would yet rather hear Instructions than Compliments.

If therefore you have observ'd in me any dangerous Tenets, corrupt Passions, or criminal Desires, I conjure you discover me to myself. Let no false Civility restrain your Admonitions. Let me know this Evil which can strike a good Man with Horror, and which I dread the more, as I do not feel it.

I cannot suppose that a Man of your Order would be alarm'd at any other Misery than Guilt: Nor will I think so meanly of him whose Direction I have intreated, as to imagine he can think Virtue unhappy, however overwhelm'd by Disasters or Oppression.

Keep me therefore no longer in Suspence: I expect you will exert the Authority of your Function, and I promise you on my Part, Sincerity and Submission.

The good Man was now compleatly embarrass'd; he saw his Meaning mistaken, but was afraid to explain it, lest he should seem to pay Court by a cowardly Retraction: He therefore paus'd a little, and *Arabella* supposed he was studying for such Expressions as might convey Censure without Offence.

Sir, said she, if you are not yet satisfy'd of my Willingness to hear your Reproofs, let me evince my Docility, by intreating you to consider yourself as dispens'd from all Ceremony upon this Occasion.

Your Imaginations, Madam, reply'd the Doctor, are too quick for Language; you conjecture too soon, what you do not wait to hear; and reason upon Suppositions which cannot be allow'd you.

When I mention'd my Reflections upon human Misery, I was far from concluding your Ladyship miserable, compar'd with the rest of Mankind; and though contemplating the abstracted Idea of possible Felicity, I thought that even You might be produc'd as an Instance that it is not attainable in this World, I did not impute the Imperfection of your State to Wickedness, but intended to observe, That though even Virtue be added to external Advantages, there will yet be something wanting to Happiness.

Whoever sees you, Madam, will immediately say, That nothing can hinder you from being the happiest of Mortals, but Want of Power to understand your own Advantages. And whoever is admitted to your Conversation, will be convinc'd that you enjoy

all that Intellectual Excellence can confer; yet I see you harrass'd
with innumerable Terrors and Perplexities, which never disturb
the Peace of Poverty or Ignorance.

I cannot discover, said *Arabella*, how Poverty or Ignorance can
be privileg'd from Casualty or Violence, from the Ravisher, the
Robber, or the Enemy. I should hope rather that if Wealth and
Knowledge can give nothing else, they at least confer Judgment to
foresee Danger, and Power to oppose it.

They are not indeed, return'd the Doctor, secur'd against real
Misfortunes, but they are happily defended from wild Imagina-
tions: They do not suspect what cannot happen, nor figure
Ravishers at a Distance, and leap into Rivers to escape them.

Do you suppose then, said *Arabella*, that I was frighted without
Cause?

It is certain, Madam, reply'd he, that no Injury was intended
you.

Disingenuity, Sir, said *Arabella*, does not become a Clergyman—
I think too well of your Understanding to imagine your Fallacy
deceives yourself: Why then should you hope that it will deceive
me?

The Laws of Conference require that the Terms of the Question
and Answer be the same.

I ask, if I had not Cause to be frighted? Why then am I answer'd
that no Injury was intended?

Human Beings cannot penetrate Intentions, nor regulate their
Conduct but by exterior Appearances. And surely there was
sufficient Appearance of intended Injury, and that the greatest
which my Sex can suffer.

Why, Madam, said the Doctor, should you still persist in so wild
an Assertion?

A coarse Epithet, said *Arabella*, is no Confutation. It rests upon
you to shew, That in giving Way to my Fears, even supposing
them groundless, I departed from the Character of a reasonable
Person.

I am afraid, replied the Doctor, of a Dispute with your Ladyship, not because I think myself in Danger of Defeat, but because
being accustom'd to speak to Scholars with Scholastick Rugged-
ness, I may perhaps depart in the Heat of Argument, from that
Respect to which you have so great a Right, and give Offence to a
Person I am really afraid to displease.

But, if you will promise to excuse my Ardour, I will endeavour to prove that you have been frighted without Reason.

I should be content, replied *Arabella*, to obtain Truth upon harder Terms, and therefore intreat you to begin.

The Apprehension of any future Evil, Madam, said the Divine, which is called Terror, when the Danger is from natural Causes, and Suspicion, when it proceeds from a mortal Agent, must always arise from Comparison.

We can judge of the Future only by the Past, and have therefore only Reason to fear or suspect, when we see the same Causes in Motion which have formerly produc'd Mischief, or the same Measures taken as have before been preparatory to a Crime.

Thus, when the Sailor in certain Latitudes sees the Clouds rise, Experience bids him expect a Storm. When any Monarch levies Armies, his Neighbours prepare to repel an Invasion.

This Power of Prognostication, may, by Reading and Conversation, be extended beyond our own Knowledge: And the great Use of Books, is that of participating without Labour or Hazard the Experience of others.

But upon this Principle how can you find any Reason for your late Fright.

Has it ever been known, that a Lady of your Rank was attack'd with such Intentions, in a Place so publick, without any Preparations made by the Violator for Defence or Escape?

Can it be imagin'd that any Man would so rashly expose himself to Infamy by Failure, and to the Gibbet by Success?

Does there in the Records of the World appear a single Instance of such hopeless Villany?

It is now Time, Sir, said *Arabella*, to answer your Questions, before they are too many to be remembered.

The Dignity of my Birth can very little defend me against an Insult to which the Heiresses of great and powerful Empires, the Daughters of valiant Princes, and the Wives of renowned Monarchs, have been a thousand Times exposed.

The Danger which you think so great, would hardly repel a determin'd Mind; for in Effect, Who would have attempted my Rescue, seeing that no Knight or valiant Cavalier was within View?

What then should have hinder'd him from placing me in a Chariot? Driving it into the pathless Desart? And immuring me in a Castle, among Woods and Mountains? Or hiding me perhaps in the Caverns of a Rock? Or confining me in some Island of an immense Lake?

From all this, Madam, interrupted the Clergyman, he is hinder'd by Impossibility.

He cannot carry you to any of these dreadful Places, because there is no such Castle, Desart, Cavern, or Lake.

You will pardon me, Sir, said *Arabella*, if I recur to your own Principles:

You allow that Experience may be gain'd by Books: And certainly there is no Part of Knowledge in which we are oblig'd to trust them more than in Descriptive Geography.

The most restless Activity in the longest Life, can survey but a small Part of the habitable Globe: And the rest can only be known from the Report of others.

Universal Negatives are seldom safe, and are least to be allow'd when the Disputes are about Objects of Sense; where one Position cannot be inferr'd from another.

That there is a Castle, any Man who has seen it may safely affirm. But you cannot with equal Reason, maintain that there is no Castle, because you have not seen it.

Why should I imagine that the Face of the Earth is alter'd since the Time of those Heroines, who experienc'd so many Changes of uncouth Captivity?

Castles indeed, are the Works of Art; and are therefore subject to Decay. But Lakes, and Caverns, and Desarts, must always remain.

And why, since you call for Instances, should I not dread the Misfortunes which happen'd to the divine *Clelia*, who was carry'd to one of the Isles of the *Thrasymenian Lake*?[1]

Or those which befel the beautiful *Candace*, Queen of *Ethiopia*, whom the Pyrate *Zenodorus* wander'd with on the Seas?[2]

Or the Accidents which imbitter'd the Life of the incomparable *Cleopatra*?[3]

Or the Persecutions which made that of the fair *Elisa* miserable?[4]

Or, in fine, the various Distresses of many other fair and virtuous Princesses: Such as those which happen'd to *Olympia*,[5] *Bellamira*,[6] *Parisatis, Berenice,*[7] *Amalazantha,*[8] *Agione,*[9] *Albysinda,*[10] *Placidia,*[11] *Arsinoe,*[12] *Deidamia,*[13] and a thousand others I could mention.

To the Names of many of these illustrious Sufferers I am an absolute Stranger, replied the Doctor.

The rest I faintly remember some Mention of in those con-

temptible Volumes, with which Children are sometimes injudici-
ously suffer'd to amuse their Imaginations; but which I little expected to hear quoted by your Ladyship in a serious Discourse.

And though I am very far from catching Occasions of Resentment, yet I think myself at Liberty to observe, That if I merited
your Censure for one indelicate Epithet, we have engag'd on very
unequal Terms, if I may not likewise complain of such contemptuous Ridicule as you are pleas'd to exercise upon my Opinions
by opposing them with the Authority of Scribblers, not only of
Fictions, but of senseless Fictions; which at once vitiate the Mind,
and pervert the Understanding; and which if they are at any Time
read with Safety, owe their Innocence only to their Absurdity.

From these Books, Sir, said *Arabella*, which you condemn with
so much Ardour, though you acknowledge yourself little acquainted with them, I have learnt not to recede from the Conditions I
have granted, and shall not therefore censure the Licence of your
Language, which glances from the Books upon the Readers.

These Books, Sir, thus corrupt, thus absurd, thus dangerous
alike to the Intellect and Morals, I have read; and that I hope without Injury to my Judgment, or my Virtue.

The Doctor, whose Vehemence had hinder'd him from discovering all the Consequences of his Position, now found himself
entangled, and reply'd in a submissive Tone,

I confess, Madam, my Words imply an Accusation very remote
from my Intention.

It has always been the Rule of my Life, not to justify any Words
or Actions because they are mine.

I am asham'd of my Negligence, I am sorry for my Warmth, and
intreat your Ladyship to pardon a Fault which I hope never to
repeat.

The Reparation, Sir, said *Arabella*, smiling, over-balances the
Offence, and by thus daring to own you have been in the Wrong,
you have rais'd in me a much higher Esteem for you.

Yet I will not pardon you, added she, without enjoining you a
Penance for the Fault you own you have committed; and this
Penance shall be to prove,

First, That these Histories you condemn are Fictions.

Next, That they are absurd.

And Lastly, That they are Criminal.

The Doctor was pleas'd to find a Reconciliation offer'd upon so very easy Terms, with a Person whom he beheld at once with Reverence and Affection, and could not offend without extreme Regret.

He therefore answered with a very chearful Composure:

To prove those Narratives to be Fictions, Madam, is only difficult, because the Position is almost too evident for Proof.

Your Ladyship knows, I suppose to what Authors these Writings are ascrib'd?

To the *French* Wits of the last Century, said *Arabella*.

And at what Distance, Madam, are the Facts related in them from the Age of the Writer?

I was never exact in my Computation, replied *Arabella*; but I think most of the Events happen'd about two thousand Years ago.

How then, Madam, resum'd the Doctor, could these Events be so minutely known to Writers so far remote from the Time in which they happen'd?

By Records, Monuments, Memoirs, and Histories, answered the Lady.

But by what Accident, then, said the Doctor smiling, did it happen these Records and Monuments were kept universally secret to Mankind till the last Century?

What brought all the Memoirs of the remotest Nations and earliest Ages only to *France*?

Where were they hidden that none could consult them but a few obscure Authors?

And whither are they now vanished again that they can be found no more?

Arabella having sat silent a while, told him, That she found his Questions very difficult to be answer'd; and that though perhaps the Authors themselves could have told whence they borrowed their Materials, she should not at present require any other Evidence of the first Assertion:

But allow'd him to suppose them Fictions, and requir'd now that he should shew them to be absurd.

Your Ladyship, return'd he, has, I find, too much Understanding to struggle against Demonstration, and too much Veracity to deny your Convictions; therefore some of the Arguments by which I intended to shew the Falshood of these Narratives may be now used to prove their Absurdity.

You grant them, Madam, to be Fictions?

Sir, interrupted *Arabella* eagerly, You are again infringing the
Laws of Disputation.

You are not to confound a Supposition of which I allow you only
the present Use, with an unlimited and irrevocable Concession.

I am too well acquainted with my own Weakness to conclude an
Opinion false, merely because I find myself unable to defend it.

But I am in haste to hear the Proof of the other Positions, not
only because they may perhaps supply what is deficient in your
Evidence of the first, but because I think it of more Importance to
detect Corruption than Fiction.

Though indeed Falshood is a Species of Corruption, and what
Falshood is more hateful than the Falshood of History.

Since you have drawn me back, Madam, to the first Question,
returned the Doctor, Let me know what Arguments your Ladyship
can produce for the Veracity of these Books.

That there are many Objections against it, you yourself have
allowed, and the highest moral Evidence of Falshood appears when
there are many Arguments against an Assertion, and none for it.

Sir, replied *Arabella*, I shall never think that any Narrative,
which is not confuted by its own Absurdity, is without one Argument at least on its Side; there is a Love of Truth in the human
Mind, if not naturally implanted, so easily obtained from Reason
and Experience, that I should expect it universally to prevail where
there is no strong Temptation to Deceit; we hate to be deceived,
we therefore hate those that deceive us; we desire not to be hated,
and therefore know that we are not to deceive. Shew me an equal
Motive to Falshood, or confess that every Relation has some Right
to Credit.

This may be allowed, Madam, said the Doctor, when we claim
to be credited, but that seems not to be the Hope or Intention of
these Writers.

Surely Sir, replied *Arabella*, you must mistake their Design; he
that writes without Intention to be credited, must write to little
Purpose; for what Pleasure or Advantage can arise from Facts that
never happened? What Examples can be afforded by the Patience
of those who never suffered, or the Chastity of those who were
never solicited? The great End of History, is to shew how much
human Nature can endure or perform. When we hear a Story in
common Life that raises our Wonder or Compassion, the first
Confutation stills our Emotions, and however we were touched

before, we then chase it from the Memory with Contempt as a Trifle, or with Indignation as an Imposture. Prove, therefore, that the Books which I have hitherto read as Copies of Life, and Models of Conduct, are empty Fictions, and from this Hour I deliver them to Moths and Mould; and from this Time consider their Authors as Wretches who cheated me of those Hours I ought to have dedicated to Application and Improvement, and betrayed me to a Waste of those Years in which I might have laid up Knowledge for my future Life.

Shakespear, said the Doctor, calls just Resentment the Child of Integrity,[1] and therefore I do not wonder, that what Vehemence the Gentleness of your Ladyship's Temper allows, should be exerted upon this Occasion. Yet though I cannot forgive these Authors for having destroyed so much valuable Time, yet I cannot think them intentionally culpable, because I cannot believe they expected to be credited. Truth is not always injured by Fiction. An admirable * Writer of our own Time, has found the Way to convey the most solid Instructions, the noblest Sentiments, and the most exalted Piety, in the pleasing Dress of a † Novel, and, to use the Words of the greatest ‡ Genius in the present Age, 'Has taught the Passions to move at the Command of Virtue.'[2] The Fables of *Æsop*, though never I suppose believed, yet have been long considered as Lectures of moral and domestic Wisdom, so well adapted to the Faculties of Man, that they have been received by all civilized Nations; and the *Arabs* themselves have honoured his Translator with the Appellation of *Locman* the Wise.

The Fables of *Æsop*, said *Arabella*, are among those of which the Absurdity discovers itself, and the Truth is comprised in the Application; but what can be said of those Tales which are told with the solemn Air of historical Truth, and if false convey no Instruction?

That they cannot be defended Madam, said the Doctor, it is my Purpose to prove, and if to evince their Falshood be sufficient to procure their Banishment from your Ladyship's Closet, their Day of Grace is near an end. How is any oral, or written Testimony, confuted or confirmed?

By comparing it, says the Lady, with the Testimony of others,

* *Richardson.*   † *Clarissa.*
‡ The Author of the Rambler.

or with the natural Effects and standing Evidence of the Facts related, and sometimes by comparing it with itself.

If then your Ladyship will abide by this last, returned he, and compare these Books with antient Histories, you will not only find innumerable Names, of which no Mention was ever made before, but Persons who lived in different Ages, engaged as the Friends or Rivals of each other. You will perceive that your Authors have parcelled out the World at Discretion, erected Palaces, and established Monarchies wherever the Conveniency of their Narrative required them, and set Kings and Queens over imaginary Nations. Nor have they considered themselves as invested with less Authority over the Works of Nature, than the Institutions of Men; for they have distributed Mountains and Desarts, Gulphs and Rocks, wherever they wanted them, and whenever the Course of their Story required an Expedient, raised a gloomy Forest, or overflowed the Regions with a rapid Stream.

I suppose, said *Arabella*, you have no Intention to deceive me, and since, if what you have asserted be true, the Cause is undefensible, I shall trouble you no longer to argue on this Topic, but desire now to hear why, supposing them Fictions, and intended to be received as Fictions, you censure them as absurd?

The only Excellence of Falshood, answered he, is its Resemblance to Truth; as therefore any Narrative is more liable to be confuted by its Inconsistency with known Facts, it is at a greater Distance from the Perfection of Fiction; for there can be no Difficulty in framing a Tale, if we are left at Liberty to invert all History and Nature for our own Conveniency. When a Crime is to be concealed, it is easy to cover it with an imaginary Word. When Virtue is to be rewarded, a Nation with a new Name may, without any Expence of Invention, raise her to the Throne. When *Ariosto* was told of the Magnificence of his Palaces, he answered, that the Cost of poetical Architecture was very little;[1] and still less is the Cost of Building without Art, than without Materials. But their historical Failures may be easily passed over, when we consider their physical or philosophical Absurdities; to bring Men together from different Countries does not shock with every inherent or demonstrable Absurdity, and therefore when we read only for Amusement, such Improprieties may be born: But who can forbear to throw away the Story that gives to one Man the Strength of Thousands; that puts Life or Death in a Smile or a Frown; that

recounts Labours and Sufferings to which the Powers of Humanity
are utterly unequal; that disfigures the whole Appearance of the
World, and represents every Thing in a Form different from that
which Experience has shewn. It is the Fault of the best Fictions,
that they teach young Minds to expect strange Adventures and
sudden Vicissitudes, and therefore encourage them often to trust
to Chance. A long Life may be passed without a single Occurrence
that can cause much Surprize, or produce any unexpected Consequence of great Importance; the Order of the World is so established, that all human Affairs proceed in a regular Method, and
very little Opportunity is left for Sallies or Hazards, for Assault or
Rescue; but the Brave and the Coward, the Sprightly and the Dull,
suffer themselves to be carried alike down the Stream of Custom.[4]

Arabella, who had for some Time listened with a Wish to
interrupt him, now took Advantage of a short Pause. I cannot
imagine, Sir, said she, that you intend to deceive me, and therefore
I am inclined to believe that you are yourself mistaken, and that
your Application to Learning has hindered you from that Acquaintance with the World, in which these Authors excelled. I have
not long conversed in Public, yet I have found that Life is subject
to many Accidents. Do you count my late Escape for nothing? Is
it to be numbered among daily and cursory Transactions, that a
Woman flies from a Ravisher into a rapid Stream?

You must not, Madam, said the Doctor, urge as an Argument
the Fact which is at present the Subject of Dispute.

Arabella blushing at the Absurdity she had been guilty of, and
not attempting any Subterfuge or Excuse, the Doctor found himself at Liberty to proceed:

You must not imagine, Madam, continued he, that I intend to
arrogate any Superiority, when I observe that your Ladyship must
suffer me to decide, in some Measure authoritatively, whether Life
is truly described in those Books; the Likeness of a Picture can
only be determined by a Knowledge of the Original. You have yet
had little Opportunity of knowing the Ways of Mankind, which
cannot be learned but from Experience, and of which the highest
Understanding, and the lowest, must enter the World in equal
Ignorance. I have lived long in a public Character, and have
thought it my Duty to study those whom I have undertaken to
admonish or instruct. I have never been so rich as to affright Men
into Disguise and Concealment, nor so poor as to be kept at a

Distance too great for accurate Observation. I therefore presume to tell your Ladyship, with great Confidence, that your Writers have instituted a World of their own, and that nothing is more different from a human Being, than Heroes or Heroines.

I am afraid, Sir, said *Arabella*, that the Difference is not in Favour of the present World.

That, Madam, answered he your own Penetration will enable you to judge when it shall have made you equally acquainted with both: I have no desire to determine a Question, the Solution of which will give so little Pleasure to Purity and Benevolence.

The Silence of a Man who loves to praise is a Censure sufficiently severe, said the Lady. May it never happen that you should be unwilling to mention the Name of *Arabella*. I hope wherever Corruption prevails in the World, to live in it with Virtue, or, if I find myself too much endanger'd, to retire from it with Innocence. But if you can say so little in Commendation of Mankind, how will you prove these Histories to be vicious, which if they do not describe real Life, give us an Idea of a better Race of Beings than now inhabit the World.

It is of little Importance, Madam, replied the Doctor, to decide whether in the real or fictitious Life, most Wickedness is to be found. Books ought to supply an Antidote to Example, and if we retire to a contemplation of Crimes, and continue in our Closets to inflame our Passions, at what time must we rectify our Words, or purify our Hearts? The immediate Tendency of these Books which your Ladyship must allow me to mention with some Severity, is to give new Fire to the Passions of Revenge and Love; two Passions which, even without such powerful Auxiliaries, it is one of the severest Labours of Reason and Piety to suppress, and which yet must be suppressed if we hope to be approved in the Sight of the only Being where Approbation can make us Happy. I am afraid your Ladyship will think me too serious.—I have already learned too much from you, said *Arabella*, to presume to instruct you, yet suffer me to caution you never to dishonour your sacred Office by the Lowliness of Apologies. Then let me again observe, resumed he, that these Books soften the Heart to Love, and harden it to Murder. That they teach Women to exact Vengeance, and Men to execute it; teach Women to expect not only Worship, but the dreadful Worship of human Sacrifices. Every Page of these Volumes is filled with such extravagance of Praise, and expressions

of Obedience as one human Being ought not to hear from another;
or with Accounts of Battles, in which thousands are slaughtered for
no other Purpose than to gain a Smile from the haughty Beauty,
who sits a calm Spectatress of the Ruin and Desolation, Bloodshed
and Misery, incited by herself.

It is impossible to read these Tales without lessening part of
that Humility, which by preserving in us a Sense of our Alliance
with all human nature, keeps us awake to Tenderness and Sympathy, or without impairing that Compassion which is implanted
in us as an Incentive to Acts of Kindness. If there be any preserved
by natural Softness, or early Education from learning Pride and
Cruelty, they are yet in danger of being betrayed to the Vanity of
Beauty, and taught the Arts of Intrigue.

Love, Madam, is, you know, the Business, the sole Business of
Ladies in Romances. *Arabella*'s Blushes now hinder'd him from
proceeding as he had intended. I perceive, continued he, that my
Arguments begin to be less agreeable to your Ladyship's Delicacy,
I shall therefore insist no longer upon false Tenderness of Sentiment, but proceed to those Outrages of the violent Passions which,
though not more dangerous, are more generally hateful.

It is not necessary, Sir, interrupted *Arabella*, that you strengthen
by any new Proof a Position which when calmly considered cannot
be denied; my Heart yields to the Force of Truth, and I now
wonder how the Blaze of Enthusiastic Bravery, could hinder me
from remarking with Abhorrence the Crime of deliberate un-
necessary Bloodshed.

I begin to perceive that I have hitherto at least trifled away my
Time, and fear that I have already made some Approaches to the
Crime of encouraging Violence and Revenge. I hope, Madam, said
the good Man with Horror in his Looks, that no Life was ever lost
by your Incitement. *Arabella* seeing him thus moved, burst into
Tears, and could not immediately answer. Is it possible, cried the
Doctor, that such Gentleness and Elegance should be stained with
Blood? Be not too hasty in your Censure, said *Arabella*, recovering
herself, I tremble indeed to think how nearly I have approached
the Brink of Murder, when I thought myself only consulting my
own Glory; but whatever I suffer, I will never more demand or
instigate Vengeance, nor consider my Punctilios as important
enough to be ballanced against Life.

The Doctor confirmed her in her new Resolutions, and thinking

Solitude was necessary to compose her Spirits after the Fatigue of
so long a Conversation, he retired to acquaint Mr. *Glanville* with
his Success, who in the Transport of his Joy was almost ready to
throw himself at his Feet, to thank him for the Miracle, as he called
it, that he had performed.

CHAPTER XII

In which the History is concluded

MR. *Glanville*, who fancied to himself the most ravishing Delight
from conversing with his lovely Cousin, now recovered to the free
Use of all her noble Powers of Reason, would have paid her a Visit
that afternoon, had not a moments Reflection convinced him that
now was the Time, when her Mind was labouring under the force
of Conviction, to introduce the repentant Sir *George* to her, who by
confessing the ridiculous Farce he had invented to deceive her,
might restore him to her good Opinion, and add to the Doctor's
solid Arguments the poignant Sting of Ridicule which she would
then perceive she had incurred.

Sir *George* being now able to leave his Chamber, and *Arabella*
well enough recovered to admit a Visit in hers, Mr. *Glanville* intreated his Father to wait on her, and get Permission for Sir *George*
to attend her upon a Business of some Consequence. Sir *Charles* no
sooner mentioned this Request, than *Arabella* after a little Hesitation complied with it. As she had been kept a Stranger to all the
Particulars of Mr. *Glanville*'s Quarrels with the young Baronet, her
Thoughts were a little perplex'd concerning the Occasion of this
Visit, and her Embarrassment was considerably increased by the
Confusion which she perceived in the Countenance of Sir *George*.
It was not without some Tokens of a painfully supprest Reluctance
that Sir *George* consented to perform his Promise, when Mr.
Glanville claim'd it, but the Disadvantages that would attend his
Breach of it, dejected and humbled as he now was, presenting
themselves in a forcible manner to his Imagination, confirmed his
wavering Resolutions. And since he found himself obliged to be his
own Accuser, he endeavoured to do it with the best Grace he could.
Acknowledging therefore to Lady *Bella* all the Artifices her Deception by Romances had given him Encouragement to use upon her,

and explaining very explicitly the last with relation to the pretended Princess of *Gaul*, he submissively asked her Pardon for the Offence it would now give her, as well as for the Trouble it had formerly.

Arabella struck with inconceivable Confusion, having only bowed her Head to his Apology desired to be left alone, and continued for near two Hours afterwards wholly absorb'd in the most disagreeable Reflections on the Absurdity of her past Behaviour, and the Contempt and Ridicule to which she now saw plainly she had exposed herself. The Violence of these first Emotions having at length subsided, she sent for Sir *Charles*, and Mr. *Glanville*, and having with a noble Ingenuity expatiated upon the Follies her vitiated Judgment had led her into, she apologized to the first, for the frequent Causes she had given him of Uneasiness; and, turning to Mr. *Glanville*, whom she beheld with a Look of mingled Tenderness and Modesty, To give you myself, said she with all my remaining Imperfections, is making you but a poor Present in return for the Obligations your generous Affection has laid me under to you; yet since I am so happy as to be desired for a Partner for Life by a Man of your Sense and Honour, I will endeavour to make myself as worthy as I am able of such a favourable Distinction.

Mr. *Glanville* kissed the Hand she gave him with an emphatic Silence, while Sir *Charles*, in the most obliging Manner imaginable, thanked her for the Honour she conferred both on himself and Son by this Alliance.

Sir *George*, entangled in his own Artifices, saw himself under a Necessity of confirming the Promises he had made to Miss *Glanville* during his Fit of Penitence, and was accordingly married to that young Lady, at the same Time that Mr. *Glanville* and *Arabella* were united.

We chuse, Reader, to express this Circumstance, though the same, in different Words, as well to avoid Repetition, as to intimate that the first mentioned Pair were indeed only married in the common Acceptation of the Word; that is, they were privileged to join Fortunes, Equipages, Titles, and Expence; while Mr. *Glanville* and *Arabella* were united, as well in these, as in every Virtue and laudable Affection of the Mind.

FINIS

TEXTUAL NOTES

1, 2: the first and second editions, both published in 1752.

VOLUME I

Page	Line	
17	39	the 2 : that *1*
20	4	For a Ravisher, interrupted *Arabella*, an impious Ravisher *2* : For a Villain, for a Ravisher, interrupted *Arabella 1*
24	26	sublime] *not in 1*
25	3	evil 2 : bad *1*
25	26	Facility 2 : Faculty *1*
26	26	a few Days after] *not in 1*
32	22	Action 2 : Notion *1*
37	15	by 2 : to *1*
38	7	desire 2 : design *1*
45	12	and] but *2*
45	14	Lover 2 : Lovers *1*
52	15	a little] *not in 1*
63	2	Fellows 2 : Heroes *1*
65	22	resolving to do 2 : doing *1*
75	32	she was several 2 : she was now several *1*
77	23	the 2 : her *1*
84	12	her Coach 2 : her Coach, which was waiting *1*
86	35	his Love 2 : the Love he felt for her *1*
88	39	reddening 2 : colouring *1*
91	26	settling 2 : setting *1*
105	18	Conversation 2 : Dispute *1*
105	27	said he] *not in 1*
106	13	again] *not in 1*
106	22ff.	The same Treachery which made the Palace of *Candace* the Place of her Confinement, may turn the Castle of *Arabella* into her Jayl.] *not in 1*
108	2	low-spirited 2 : low *1*
130	19	the] *not in 1*
137	33–4	a Favour, his Sickness, and the Terms upon which they now were 2 : a Favour, the Terms upon which they now were, and his Sickness *1*
141	32	reddening 2 : blushing *1*
144	22	says 2 : said *1*

Page	Line	
278	10	immortal Fame *2* : an immortal Fame *1*
280	36	was *2* : were *1*
282	15	had] *not in 1*
285	10	acquainting *1* : acquainted *2**
298	37	almost weeping *2* : excessively uneasy at her Lady's Words *1*
305	16	Stupidity. *2* : Stupidity, as she thought it. *1*
306	13	carried away. *2* : carried away. All I know is—— *1*
308	6	had just before *2* : just before had *1*
326	32	Lights *2* : Delights *1*
332	21	the Dutchess of —— Rout *2* : the Dutchess of *Rant 1*
333	11	*Trifle 2* : *Fribble 1*
333	22	the Countess *2* : the Countess possess'd *1*
333	39	love-captivated *2* : captivated *1*
338	20	murder'd *2* : run thro' *1*
340	17	some *2* : two or three *1*
341	5	Miss *Glanville*'s *2* : Miss *Glanville 1*
349	19	his *2* : this *1*
351	30	Credulity *1* : Incredulity *2**
380	18	give *1* : gives *2**
383	16	said she] *not in 1*

* Mistaken 'corrections'.

EXPLANATORY NOTES

ABBREVIATIONS

Artamenes: Madeleine de Scudéry, *Artamenes; or, the Grand Cyrus. That Excellent Romance,* 1690–91.

Cassandra: Gauthier de Costes de La Calprenède, *Cassandra: the fam'd Romance,* 1652.

Clelia: Madeleine de Scudéry, *Clelia, an excellent new Romance,* 1678.

Cleopatra: Gauthier de Costes de La Calprenède, *Hymen's Praeludia or Love's Master-peice. Being That so much admired Romance, intituled Cleopatra,* 1674.

Parthenissa: Roger Boyle, Earl of Orrery, *Parthenissa, That most Fam'd Romance,* 1676.

Pharamond: Gauthier de Costes de La Calprenède, *Pharamond: or, the History of France. A fam'd Romance,* 1677.

The numbering of parts, books, and pages in these editions is often inaccurate. Every effort had been made, by giving full references and indicating where paging is wrong, to enable the reader to find the passages referred to.

Page 1. To the . . . Earl of Middlesex: Even though Boswell was mistaken about when *The Female Quixote* was published, there seems no reason to doubt his statement that Johnson wrote the dedication (*Life of Johnson,* 1934, i. 367 and n. 1). Charles Sackville Earl of Middlesex (1711–69), later second Duke of Dorset, is described as 'a dissolute and extravagant man of fashion' (*D.N.B.*). But the fact that he had a passion for directing operas, and wrote some verse, suggests that the dedication was not wholly inappropriate; at his death the *Gentleman's Magazine* (xxxix (1769), 54) described him as 'a lover of learning, and a patron of learned men; author of several esteemed pieces in prose and verse'. In 1750 he presented to the Princess of Wales an ode written by Mrs. Lennox on the Princess's birthday (ibid., xx (1750), 519).

VOLUME ONE

BOOK I

Page 7. (1) *had not her whole Time . . . another Study:* Mrs. Lennox overstates her case. Arabella shows a good deal of 'useful knowledge', on topics as varied as antiquities (see for example her description of the Olympic Games, pp. 82–3), rhetoric (e.g. her discussion of satire, pp. 276–7), and moral philosophy (e.g. her discussion of indifference, pp. 310–11).

(2) *very bad Translations:* This was a common opinion, but not necessarily correct. See T. P. Haviland, *The Roman de longue haleine on English Soil*, 1931, pp. 28ff.

Page 8. (1) *Disappointments:* Lady Mary Wortley Montagu in a letter written in 1758 said that the character of Arabella was modelled on that of Lady Hertford, later Duchess of Somerset (1699–1754), 'a Poetical Great Lady who I realy think was the character of Lady Arabella in the Female Quixote (without the Beauty)' (*Complete Letters*, 1965–7, iii. 187). The cause of this remark was Lady Mary's anger that Dodsley in his *Collection of Poems* for 1758 had ascribed to 'Lady Mary W***' a poem by Lady Hertford, making rather bold advances to 'Dear Colin', when Lady Mary had written only the prim reply. There is no support for this identification. Lady Hertford's letters show her as serious, pious, and sententious; and while the earlier letters contain some entertaining references to the French romances, she refers far more often to poetry, history, and works of devotion. The literary pretensions that roused the scorn of Horace Walpole seem mild and harmless enough. It is possible that Charlotte Lennox drew Arabella from the life, but it is hard to think that Lady Hertford, middleaged, bereaved, and ailing when *The Female Quixote* was written, was the model.

(2) *the odd Whim . . . behind her:* Mr. Hervey would expect the servants to sit at the back of the church, and not to follow Arabella almost to her own seat.

(3) *Her Dress, though singular . . . :* Conventional church-going attire for a lady of Arabella's rank would at this date have consisted of a dress with a tight bodice and a hooped skirt, and a wide-brimmed hat, probably worn over a cap, and with the hair arranged 'somewhat close to the head, with one or two curls falling behind and others encircling the face' (Iris Brooke and James Laver, *English Costume of the Eighteenth Century*, 1931, p. 46. See also Iris Brooke, *A History of English Costume*, 3rd edn., 1949, pp. 133–41).

The veil was particularly out of fashion. It is referred to on numerous occasions in the novel (for example, pp. 84, 95, 262), and plays a part in the denouement. Arabella copies the fashion of the divine Mandana and other heroines of romance. Cf. *Artamenes*, I. ii. 117, II. iii. 379, and *Cleopatra*, IX. i. 195.

Page 10. *us:* I have observed only one heroine of French romance using the plural number of herself, and she was a queen—Thomiris Queen of the Massagetes in *Artamenes*. But Richardson in his *Familiar Letters* has it used by a girl who is laughing at and preparing to finish answering a love-letter described as 'a romantic Rhapsody in Courtship': 'Here she put on a royal air: We will conclude Our own letter ourself, said she . . .' (*Familiar Letters on Important Occasions*, ed. B. W. Downs, 1928, pp. 112–13). Arabella uses the plural of herself only occasionally (as on p. 316); Mrs. Lennox extends it to the hero of romance when Sir George Bellmour uses it of himself in the course of his 'history' (e.g., p. 238).

Page 20. *Hanger:* 'A kind of short sword, originally hung from the belt' (*O.E.D.*). It was specially used for the chase or travelling (cf. p. 157). See P. Carrington-Peirce, *A Handbook of Court and Hunting Swords 1660–1820*, 1937, Foreword and chap. 5.

Page 24. *with an Air very different from an Oroondates:* Oroondates, Prince of Scythia, is a leading character in La Calprenède's *Cassandra*. When Statira, whom he loves, is a prisoner of Alexander, Oroondates disguises himself as a gardener in order to be near her (*Cassandra*, I. iv. 87ff.). He was of course adorned with every perfection of mind and body, and seems to have typified the romance hero for English writers. E. A. Baker (*The History of the English Novel*, 1950, iii. 92) conjectures that Mrs. Behn's Oroonoko, himself an idealized character, got his name from Oroondates; and eighteenth-century authors often mention him casually as if expecting their readers to know who he is. See for example *The Spectator*, nos. 199 and 377; *The Tender Husband*, I. i.; and *Amelia*, VIII. 7. Cf. infra, p. 329.

Page 28. *saluting:* kissing. Cf. *Pamela*, 1929 edn., ii. 59: 'Sir *Simon* said, Good Neighbour, by your Leave; and saluting me, added, Now will I say, that I have kissed the loveliest Maiden in *England*.'

Page 29. *The Heroines . . . short Absence:* This is not so. In general, a heroine of romance embraces a hero only in circumstances where those most in favour of reserve would regard such a demonstration as appropriate. For example, when Coriolanus returns from the wars, and learns that Augustus opposes his marriage with Cleopatra, he goes sadly to greet her, 'and while he put his knee to the ground, and took her fair hand to kiss it, she let fall her head upon his, and laid her arm upon his shoulder, with an action full of sweetness and affection' (*Cleopatra*, II. iii. 127).

Page 39. *resent:* 'to feel or experience (joy, sorrow, pain, etc.)' (*O.E.D.*); in this sense very frequent in the English translations of the French romances, from which Arabella has picked it up. The italics draw the reader's attention to this peculiarity of her speech. Contrast 'Resentment' in the previous paragraph.

Page 44. Statira, Parisatis, Clelia, Mandana: Statira and Parisatis were sisters, daughters of Darius King of Persia, in La Calprenède's *Cassandra* (the name 'Cassandra' is adopted by Statira during the course of the book). Clelia is the heroine of Madeleine de Scudéry's novel of that name; Mandana is the princess beloved by Artamenes in Mlle de Scudéry's *Artamenes; or, The Grand Cyrus.*

Page 45. (1) *Oroondates, Artaxerxes, and the illustrious Lover of Clelia:* For Oroondates see p. 24, note. Artaxerxes Prince of Persia is a leading character in *Cassandra.* Clelia had several noble and virtuous lovers; Aronces, who finally won her, is referred to here.

(2) *Tiribases, Artaxes:* The ambitious and treacherous Tiribasus, a typical romance villain, figures in the story of Candace Queen of Ethiopia (*Cleopatra,* Part III. Books i. and ii.). Artaxes is a villain who works by bribery and treachery to destroy Artamenes (*Artamenes,* I. i. 53ff. and III. ii. 207f.).

Page 47. Thus Mazares . . . his adored Mistress: Mazares, one of Mandana's abductors, repents and is bidden by Mandana to join Cyrus, thereby to 'express some convincing testimonies of his real penitency' (*Artamenes,* V. ii. 299f.), and recover her esteem. Mazares remains a faithful follower of Cyrus till the end of the romance.

Page 48. Oroondates, to punish himself . . . to live: Though Persia and Scythia are at war, Oroondates Prince of Scythia comes for love of the Princess Statira to the Persian court. He passes as Orontes Prince of the Massagetes, a guise in which he had earlier spared the life of the princess and saved that of her brother Artaxerxes. When his secret love for Statira makes him fall ill, and she asks him to tell her the cause of his illness, he obeys; furious at his presumption (for Orontes is a mere vassal prince), she orders him never again to entertain her with such follies. At this he swoons, and his illness becomes increasingly grave; here he utters the words on which Glanville's eye lights (p. 49); see *Cassandra,* I. ii. 28 for the original, which Mrs. Lennox has quoted with substantial accuracy. Finally, Oroondates having revealed to Artaxerxes both who he is and why he is ill, that prince passes on the information to Statira, entreating her to have mercy on her lover. She bids Oroondates live; he replies, '*Oroondates* would live, Madam, if she for whom he both will and ought to die, did but consent unto his life. The Princesse answered him in hast, *She not onlie consents to it, but also entreats, and if she have anie power commands it*' (ibid., p. 34). This episode is one of those that later, when Glanville is ill, persuade Arabella that a visit from her will cure him.

Page 54. Artimisa, Candace . . . Daughter of Cleopatra: All these heroines have lovers who are imprisoned and under sentence of death, and all express their readiness to die with them in terms which Arabella imitates when faced with the dreadful prospect of marrying Mr. Glanville. See *Cleopatra*, IV. ii. 307, XII. i. 487, and XII. iii. 531.

Page 55. (1) *I'll burn . . . Hands upon:* The Marquis's intention emphasizes the parallel between this episode and the burning of Don Quixote's books; that the intention is unfulfilled emphasizes the contrast between the purely comic character of Mrs. Lennox's novel, and the strong element of the tragic in Cervantes'.

(2) *the brave Orontes:* Probably Arabella has in mind the real Orontes, Prince of the Massagetes and lover of Thalestris Queen of the Amazons. Their story is an important one in *Cassandra*.

BOOK II

Page 61. (1) *The Great Sysigambis . . . that Posture:* Sysigambis was the mother of Darius. She behaves thus when told that her *two* granddaughters Statira and Parisatis have been killed by Roxana (*Cassandra*, II. ii. 236).

(2) *Menecrates . . . her Ashes:* Though there are in *Artamenes* two minor characters called Menecrates, Arabella seems to be referring to another called Menesteus. When his wife died he built two tombs, buried her in one, and himself lived for years in the other (*Artamenes*, VIII. ii. 173ff.).

Page 62. (1) *But for the inimitable Pen . . . Scudery:* The following passage implies two serious misconceptions about the French romances: (i) that Georges de Scudéry and not his sister Madeleine was chiefly responsible for the romances that appeared under his name, though a look at the dedication to Part V of the 1661 translation of *Clelia*, or at Bishop Huet's treatise on the origin of romance published in 1670 as the preface to Mme de La Fayette's *Zaÿde*, would have shown Arabella her mistake; (ii) that 'Scudery' wrote *Cassandra* (in which Oroondates is a character) and *Cleopatra* (in which figure Juba, Artaban, Cleopatra herself, and the historical persons associated with her), as well as *Clelia* (of which Aronces is the hero). The difference between the romances of La Calprenède and those of Mlle de Scudéry is so great that one can excuse the error only by remembering the youth of Arabella, and of her creator.

(2) *that Action of Clelia's . . . in the Camp:* The story of Clelia's swimming the Tiber at the head of a band of hostages is told or mentioned by many ancient writers. None gives any reason for the deed beyond her desire to escape from the power of Porsena. Mlle de Scudéry's version of the episode is in *Clelia*, V. ii. 691ff. and V. iii. 736. The statue and other honours awarded Clelia are described in the closing sentences of the romance, which no doubt helped to impress on Arabella's mind the aquatic exploit by which they were won.

(3) *the inimitable Poetess Sappho . . . Brother's Affection:* For 'The History of Sapho' see *Artamenes*, Part X, Book ii. The description of Sapho is a 'portrait' of Mlle de Scudéry herself.

(4) *that Cleopatra was really married to Julius Caesar: Cleopatra*, I. ii. 42f.

(5) *or that Caesario . . . took Refuge: Cleopatra*, I. iii. 49ff. The survival of Caesario and his love for Candace Queen of Ethiopia form one of the main stories of that romance.

Page 63. *the History of Jack the Giant killer:* Fielding in the first chapter of *Joseph Andrews* mentions among biographies 'the History of *John* the Great, who, by his brave and heroic Actions against Men of large and athletic Bodies, obtained the glorious Appellation of the Giant-killer'; he indicates an attitude very like that of Sir Charles.

Page 68. *Quadrille:* a card-game played by four persons.

Page 72. (1) *Who would have thought . . . his adored Princess: Cleopatra*, IV. i. 285ff.

(2) *the Contrivance of Orontes . . . in their Court: Cassandra*, II. iii. 251ff. and II. iv. 19ff.

Page 73. *and yet this Prince . . . accused her of:* When Spitridates, who resembles Artamenes so closely as to be almost his double, is killed and his head is shown to Mandana, she believes that Artamenes is dead, and is grief-stricken. Suddenly, however, and without, as it seems, any possibility that she has learned of her mistake, her grief is reported to be alleviated, and Artamenes, hidden in the enemy camp, actually sees her smile for a moment as she rides by his place of concealment. He feels violent anger and jealousy at her apparent infidelity (*Artamenes*, X. iii. 414ff.).

Page 78. *do you think . . . those of Clelia:* It is Lysimena Princess of the Leontines to whom Celeres, friend and confidant of Aronces, tells 'The History of Aronces and Clelia' at the beginning of *Clelia*. Much later, she allows Aronces to pretend love for her, in order to prevent his father Porsenna from forcing him into a distasteful marriage, and while Clelia feels unfounded jealousy, Lysimena remains loyal to both lovers.

Page 81. *do not these Races . . . ride in Chariots:* The country races resemble the Olympic Games quite as closely as does the description of them from *Clelia* on which Arabella's expectations are based. There they are transformed, as part of 'The History of the Princess Elismonda', into a tournament; the ladies are the spectators and one of them awards the crowns; the contestants wear their favours; and there appears a mysterious stranger who, after the events, rides away without divulging his identity. Only the chariot-races are described. Elismonda has the felicity to crown 'her secret Admirer' Hortensius, who defeats, among others, the mysterious stranger, as well as two princes who were acknowledged aspirants for her hand. But he receives only one crown (*Clelia*, IV. i. 454ff.).

Page 82. *They were a kind of School . . . Justs and Tournaments:* Arabella may have neglected the reading of history in favour of romance, but Mrs. Lennox had read Temple Stanyan's *Grecian History*. This paragraph is quoted with insignificant alteration from a passage in his account of the Olympic Games (2nd edn., 1739, i. 162). It is interesting that the analogy between the Games and 'Justs and Tournaments' is not Mrs. Lennox's invention, but is made by a serious historian, who ignores the tradition that women were not allowed to watch the Games.

Page 83. I remember . . . entered the Lists: Wherever Arabella read this— Alcibiades' successes in the chariot-races are recorded by Thucydides, Plutarch, and most subsequent historians—she is referring to the usual practice whereby a rich man was not required to drive his chariot. This was not of course how Mlle de Scudéry described the Games in *Clelia*, where the chariots are driven by the heroes of the romance.

Page 84. the Haste and Negligence . . . lovely and genteel: Heroines of romance unite a graceful indifference to their appearance with exquisite beauty and perfect taste in dress.

Page 86. (1) *as Hortensius did . . . at those Games:* Arabella is mistaken. Hortensius was well known to all present at the Games. The mysterious stranger was later discovered to be Attalus, from whose attempt to abduct her Hortensius had previously rescued the Princess Andronice (*Clelia*, IV. i. 423, 455ff.).

(2) *surprised at so uncommon a Civility:* Boundless hospitality to chance-met strangers was an established convention of romance, but not of polite society in eighteenth-century England.

Page 87. Adventures: Misunderstandings between Arabella and Miss Glanville often arise from the different meanings they attach to such words as 'adventure', and (later in this chapter) 'favour'. Compare the cross-purposes between Arabella and her 'Protector' over the word 'servant' (pp. 100–1); between Sir Charles Granville and the rest of the company over 'Divine Things' and Sir George Bellmour's 'infidelity' (p. 206); and between Arabella and Sir George's servant over the word 'squire' (p. 255).

Page 88. (1) *Pray do you remember . . . run away with:* Cf. Boileau's *Les Héros de roman* (English translation, 1713, p. 121):

> *Diog.* But for all that can you tell me why *Cyrus* conquer'd so many Provinces, travers'd *Asia, Media, Hyrcania, Persia,* and in short ravaged more than half the World?
>
> *Pluto.* A fine Question! 'Twas because he was an ambitious Prince, who had a Mind to have all the World under his Subjection.
>
> *Diog.* Not at all. 'Twas to deliver his Princess who had been run away with.
>
> *Pluto.* What Princess?

Diog. Mandana.

Pluto. Mandana?

Diog. Yes. And do you know how often she was run away with?

Pluto. How shou'd I know?

Diog. Eight Times.

In Gabriel Guéret's *Le Parnasse reformé* (1671), one of the charges brought by Cyrus against Mlle de Scudéry is her giving him a mistress who has been so often run away with, and whose chastity he does not believe to have stood so hard a test: 'Vous deviez, ce me semble, mettre sa pudeur à d'autres épreuves; Celles-là sont un peu trop fortes pour une chose si fresle' (p. 136). Cf. infra, p. 328: a beauty in the present age 'could not pass thro' the Hands of several different Ravishers, without bringing an Imputation on her chastity'.

(2) *She was no Jew . . . she asked:* Arabella remembers, not quite accurately, the episode in which Artamenes (whose other name is Cyrus) frees the Jews who had been captives in Babylon, and gives money towards rebuilding the temple. Mandana applauds but does not instigate this action (*Artamenes*, VIII. ii. 346ff.).

(3) *she refused . . . on his Knees: Artamenes*, I. ii. 210f. Arabella characteristically invents the detail, 'he begged it on his Knees'.

Page 89. *you put me in mind . . . in private:* Antonia, described as 'having a dis-inclination to love, and an aversion for whatever had but the least appearance of gallantry', says to a respectful suitor, 'I should sooner pardon an affect of Hatred in my enemies, then an expression of Love in those that call themselves my Friends' (*Cleopatra*, IX. ii. 206 and 211). On the whole matter of 'favours', see the discussion between Ovid and other characters in *Cleopatra*, XI. i. 376f.

Page 90. *inconsiderate:* careless, thoughtless. For La Calprenède's (still idealized) account of Augustus's daughter Julia, see *Cleopatra*, II. i. 94f. and iii. 132; 'The History of Marcellus and Julia' (*Cleopatra*, Part V, Book iii); and 'The History of Ovid, Cipassis and Julia' (ibid., Part VII, Book iii).

Page 93. *Ah! had Cylenia and Martesia . . . their Captivity:* Concerning the comfort given to Berenice by her confidant Cyllenia, Arabella is slightly confused; it was while immured by her father because she refused to marry the man of his choice that Berenice was allowed to have Cyllenia with her (*Cassandra*, IV. iv. 12). During her abduction by Arsacomes Berenice was alone, except for a woman of his providing, and bewailed the absence of Cyllenia (ibid., IV. vi. 62ff.). Martesia is the favourite waiting-woman of Mandana, 'the Divine Princess of *Media*'. Again, Arabella does not remember quite accurately. When the King of Assyria's minions were carrying Mandana off, she cried, 'Ah *Martesia*, do not forsake me!'

Martesia clung so hard to her mistress's clothes that they had to take her too (*Artamenes*, II. i. 184).

Page 96. she was not to be found: Had Lucy and her brother been as well read as her mistress, they would not have been astonished. Nothing is more common in the romances than for a person, left wounded or supposedly dead, to have disappeared by the time the rescue party arrives.

Page 99. Did not the wicked Arianta . . . insolent Lover: Arianta, or Arianita, was a waiting-woman to Mandana, and by her treachery helped the King of Assyria to carry her mistress off (*Artamenes*, II. i. 183 and ii. 252).

Page 102. like Philidaspes . . . for his Wife: Philidaspes is the name by which the King of Assyria is known at the court of Ciaxares, Mandana's father. Before leaving Assyria to avoid marrying the bride chosen for him by his mother, he tries in vain to get several men to take her off his hands, including one to whom he suggests he should carry her away (*Artamenes*, II. ii. 245 and VIII. i. 34ff.).

Page 105. (1) Mandana, Candace, Clelia: Mandana was carried away by the King of Assyria, Mazares Prince of Saces, the King of Pontus, and Prince Ariantes. Candace was carried away by the pirate Zenodorus, and was threatened with the same fate on a later occasion. Clelia was carried away by Horatius, by the minions of Tarquin, and by Sextus.

(2) *Parthenissa, or Cleopatra:* The heroine of Roger Boyle's romance was kept for some months in a castle by an importunate suitor, then carried away into Media, whence she was rescued by her lover Artabanes. Cleopatra (and Artemisa with her) was carried away by the King of Armenia and kept prisoner on his ship till rescued by Coriolanus, Alexander, and Marcellus. Though the period of their captivity was long enough for several 'histories' to be related, it is explicitly stated by Coriolanus to have lasted 'not many dayes' (*Cleopatra*, IX. iv. 269), and not the 'some months' of Arabella's version. The gentleman of course confuses Cleopatra Queen of Egypt with her daughter, the heroine of the romance.

Page 106. The same Treachery . . . her Jayl: When the traitor Tiribasus got control of the Ethiopian army, Queen Candace was not allowed to show herself in public (*Cleopatra*, III. ii. 193).

Page 107. like the poor Prince Thrasybulus . . . restored: Thrasibulus, dispossessed of his inheritance, sails round the Mediterranean in search of adventure. At the Isthmus of Gnides, he is welcomed by Euphranor, and falls hopelessly in love with his daughter Alcionida. One day, while he entertains her and other ladies on his ship, 'Love in an Instant, seducing both my Generosity, and my Reason', as he describes it, made him agree to the suggestion of his friend Leosthenes to cut the cable and away. He repents just in time to prevent the action (*Artamenes*, III. iii. 407ff.).

Book III

Page 111. And truly . . . concealed Torments: Mandana says this when she learns that the King of Assyria is planning to carry her away, crying: 'But that a Lover should manifest his Love by a raping way, is a thing without Example, and above my Patience: Mine, I say, (added she, in all disorder) who could not indure a Declaration of Love from one of the greatest Princes upon Earth, after ten Years Service, Respects, Sighs, and Submissions!' (*Artamenes*, II. i. 76).

Page 115. (1) *The valiant Coriolanus* [p. 114] . . . *aimed at him:* Cleopatra, IX. iv. 265ff. Arabella touches up La Calprenède's account of Coriolanus' exploits by adding a few vivid details, such as his being covered with wounds, and that he 'for several Hours, continued fighting alone with near Two hundred Men'.

(2) '*Go, therefore, Glanville . . . in your behalf' :* The original of Cleopatra's speech, which Arabella quotes here and continues on p. 116, is: 'Go, Coriolanus, *said she to him,* go, and endeavour your justification, I desire you should effect it, no lesse than you do your self. 'Tis possible you might be sufficiently justified in my apprehensions by the things you have done for my deliverance, by the probability which I find in your discourse, and by the good opinion I have of you, were it not requisite to make your innocence apparent, that so it might be lawfull for *Cleopatra* to readmit you, with honour, into her former favour and affection' (*Cleopatra*, IX. iv. 280).

Arabella makes three significant changes. She adds the offer to pray for Glanville's success in redeeming himself; Glanville's *anxiety* for her safety replaces the *things done* by Coriolanus for Cleopatra's deliverance; and she substitutes the cooler *Esteem and Friendship* for the original *favour and affection.*

Page 125. You know, I suppose . . . injurious Suspicion: The exact nature of the 'injurious Suspicion' is that Thalestris Queen of the Amazons has sought Alexander to make him, in accordance with Amazon custom, father of a child who shall be her successor (*Cassandra*, III. vi. 55). Orontes had 'some Shadow of Reason for his Jealousy and Rage', having been given this information by a leading Amazon. When convinced of his error, he retires to the melancholy solitude described by Arabella, emerging only to save Thalestris' life on several occasions during the siege of Babylon which forms the climax of *Cassandra.*

Page 126. But, Madam . . . Siege of Troy: Glanville, having no doubt enjoyed the benefits of a classical education, remembers that the Amazons were allies of the Trojans, and that their queen Penthesilea was slain by Achilles.

Page 127 (1) *Juba :* the other name of Coriolanus, lover of Cleopatra in the romance of that name.

(2) *Artaban :* also a character in *Cleopatra.* Though not a prince, he turns out to be the posthumous son of Pompey the Great, and finally marries Elisa Princess of Parthia.

Page 128. (1) *The Law has no Power over Heroes :* Cf. Don Quixote's words, when he is in danger of being arrested for freeing the galley-slaves: 'What Blockhead of a Justice durst issue out a Warrant to apprehend a Knight-Errant like me? Could not his Ignorance find out that we are exempt from all Courts of Judicature? That our Valour is the Bench, our Will the Common-Law, and our Sword the Executioner of Justice. Could not his Dullness inform him that no Rank of Nobility or Peerage enjoys more Immunities and Priviledges? Has he any President that a Knight-Errant ever paid Taxes, Subsidy, Poll-mony, or so much as Fare or Ferry? What Taylor has ever had Mony for his Clothes, or what Constable ever made him pay a Reckoning for his Lodging in his Castle? What Kings are not proud of his Company, and what Damsels of his Love? And lastly, Did you ever read of any Knight-Errant that ever was, is, or shall be, that cou'd not with his single force cudgel four hundred such Rogues as you to pieces, if they have the Impudence to oppose him' (I. iv. 18; Motteux's translation).

The account of Artaban which follows is characterized by the same kind of hyperbole as Don Quixote uses (cf. a similar statement on p. 210 below), and is part of the whole attack, to culminate at the end of the book, on a certain idea of the 'heroic'.

(2) *the Noise and Bustle . . . her Charms :* The idea that a lady's reputation depends upon the noise she makes in the world is contrary to eighteenth-century notions of decorum, and to Arabella's own taste for retirement. The blood that the heroine of romance could have on her conscience is indicated by Mandana's summary of Artamenes' career, who for her sake 'hath beaten the King of *Assiria,* taken *Babylon,* surprized *Synope,* subdued *Armenia,* won the Battel of *Thybarra* against *Cressus,* taken *Sardis,* put the King of *Pontus* to flight, . . . delivered me by taking *Cumes* . . . vanquished *Thomyris* and *Ariantes,* and gloriously brought me home to *Ecbatane*' (*Artamenes,* X. iii. 492).

But more than one heroine expresses her sorrow at the deaths she causes; cf. the story of Melisintha Princess of Jutland: 'How, (*said the Princess, full of sorrow*) must I be the incendiary to set all my native Country in a combustion? Must the blood of thousands be shed for me?' (*Pharamond,* VI. iii. 176).

Page 130. (1) *being a very accurate Critic . . . in that Romance :* Gerard Langbaine in *An Account of the English Dramatick Poets,* 1691, p. 132, says of *The Conquest of Granada* that 'all the Characters of that Play are stollen from the French', and discusses Scudéry's *Almahide* as its chief source. Of this there seems no doubt; and Dryden would have agreed with Sir George about Artaban. For in his essay 'Of Heroic Plays' he writes that the character of Almanzor is taken from those of Achilles, Rinaldo, and the Artaban of M. Calprenède. Almanzor and Artaban resemble each other particularly in their obscure birth, in their success as warriors, and in their habit of changing sides.

But concerning the story of Ozmyn and Benzayda Sir George seems to be muddled; whether it was taken by Dryden, as Langbaine asserted, from Mlle de Scudéry's *Ibrahim*, or, as a modern writer thinks, from *Almahide* (see Jerome W. Schweitzer in *Modern Language Notes* lxii (1947), 262-3), it was not based on 'The History of Sesostris and Timareta' (not 'Timerilla') in *Artamenes* (Part VI, Book ii). As Langbaine said, that story was used by Dryden to form the serious part of the plot of *Marriage à la Mode*, and this must be what Sir George has confusedly in mind.

About the character of Melantha in this latter play, N. B. Allen says (*The Sources of John Dryden's Comedies*, 1935, pp. 121-2) that its originality has not yet been successfully questioned. Berisa is a character in 'The History of the King of Assiria, of Intaphernes, of Atergates, of Istrina, and of the Princess of Bythinia' (*Artamenes*, Part VIII, Book i). The resemblance between her and Melantha seems to me slight. For a description of Berisa, see *Artamenes*, VIII. i. 88ff.

(2) *the Ridicule*: that which is ridiculous; a common use at this time. Cf. p. 267.

Page 131. *As she conceived . . . Passion for her*: On Arabella's notion of the cause and cure of a lover's sickness see p. 284 below, and p. 48, note.

Page 132. (1) *as it happened . . . to visit him*: *Artamenes*, I. ii. 172. Arabella does not mention that Mandana was conducted on her visit to Artamenes, recovering from wounds received in battle, by her father, nor that the invalid was well out of danger before the visit, which was indeed 'to congratulate his recovery'. Still, the narrator does say that it 'wrought a wonderful effect in *Artamenes*; so that in a few days after, his Wounds healed extraordinarily; such power, it seems, has the Soul over the temper of the Body'.

(2) *A few kind Words . . . of Death*: See p. 48, note.

(3) *one Line . . . to obey her*: When he has conquered Persia, Alexander determines to marry the Persian Princess Parisatis to his favourite Hephestion. Lysimachus attacks Hephestion, and, put in prison as a punishment, determines to starve himself to death. He is prevented from doing so only by a letter from Parisatis, ordering him to live; she writes him a similar letter after he has defeated a lion intended to be the means of his execution (*Cassandra*, II. ii. 217 and 220). Arabella refers to the episode again on p. 193.

BOOK IV

Page 141. the brave Caesario . . . in Ethiopia: For Caesario's assumption of
the name 'Cleomedon', and his exploits, see *Cleopatra*, Part III, Books i
and ii.

(2) *the unequalled Prince of Mauritania:* Coriolanus, the hero of *Cleopatra*.

Page 142. what she did for Alexander: See 'The History of Alexander and
the Princess Artemisa' (*Cleopatra*, Part IV, Books i and ii). Artemisa is
exceptional among heroines of the French romances for at last having run
away with the hero; and this is the action which some have not scrupled to
condemn.

Page 143. Imbecillity: weakness of character.

Page 148. (1) the Two celebrated Beauties: The reading of the first edition,
'the Two Sister Beauties', makes it clear that Mrs. Lennox refers to Mary
(or Maria) and Elizabeth Gunning, who had come with their mother from
Ireland to England in 1749 and made a tremendous stir. Early in 1752
Elizabeth married the Duke of Hamilton, and Maria the Earl of Coventry.

(2) *the Siren Frasi:* for an account of this celebrated singer, see Grove's
Dictionary of Music and Musicians.

Page 149. those numerous and long Conversations: Especially in *Clelia*, the
conversations Mlle de Scudéry incorporates in her romances are of great
importance. Arabella is correct when she says that conquerors and heroes
take part in these discussion of 'questions'; for example, those present at
the most famous, that on tenderness, include Aronces and Horatius, the
noble rivals for Clelia's love. The *carte de tendre*, drawn by Clelia on this
occasion, favours Aronces, who not unnaturally finds it exquisite (*Clelia*,
I. i. 41ff.). I have not found an instance of 'the Superiority of fair and brown
Hair' being controverted, except casually in the conversation which en-
quires why most women are greedy of praise, and also unjust. This injustice
is shown by women who express their views of 'the fair and brown in
general' in accordance with their own particular colouring (ibid., p. 34).
For a list (not quite complete) of the topics discussed in *Artamenes* and
Clelia, see T. F. Crane's Introduction to his edition of Boileau's *Les Héros
de roman*, 1902, pp. 126 and 129f.

Page 150. (1) The great Oroondates . . . his Divine Princess: Princess Roxana,
of close kin to the Persian royal family, was in love with Oroondates, and
contrived by cunning to convince the Princess Statira that he was unfaithful (*Cassandra*, Part I, Books iv. and v.).

(2) *the valiant and unfortunate Artamenes . . . Inconstancy:* This came
about when Mandana, deceived by the extraordinary likeness between
Artamenes and Spitridates, cried to the latter for help as she was being

carried off by the King of Assyria; she is pardonably suspicious and enraged when he takes no notice (*Artamenes*, VI. iii. 430ff.).

(3) *the irresistible Juba . . . Mistress and Friend:* Juba—Coriolanus—has the common experience of being traduced by his enemies, who are believed by Cleopatra, his mistress, and Marcellus, his friend (*Cleopatra*, II. iv. 146f. (really p. 156), and V. ii. 398f.).

Page 152. (1) *I said once before . . . Inclinations:* Arabella refers to the not too flattering comparison between Miss Glanville and the Princess Julia (p. 90).

(2) *her Beauty may . . . win her a Sceptre:* Arabella is not quite accurate. Elisa, Artaban's 'Princess', was recognized by the Parthians as their queen in her own right, though the people were anxious for her to marry Artaban. I have not found the words which Arabella quotes as Artaban's. He several times expresses the general sentiments they convey, as in this speech to Elisa: 'Madam, my birth is noble, 'tis all I can say of it, and my fortunes are now so low, but I hope my sword may one day raise them to an equal pitch with theirs that openly pretend to the glory of your service: First Courage and Vertue should lead the way, then Crowns must follow to deserve you; and Madam I will seek for Crowns before I vow the boldness to demand you; To that of *Parthia* which you are born to, I'le join the *Median* Diadem, and then the accession of others shall strengthen my claim . . .' (*Cleopatra*, III. iii. 233f.).

(3) *the great Artaban . . . successively:* The three great princesses loved by Artaban are Candace Queen of Ethiopia, Arsinoe Princess of Armenia, and finally Elisa Princess of Parthia. Arabella is correct in saying that this is very unusual behaviour for a hero of romance.

Page 155. *But as it happened . . . their Defence:* Apparently a confused recollection of an episode in *Cleopatra* (I. iv. 66ff. (really p. 68)). Candace and her woman Clitie, not Cleopatra and Candace (the 'Princesses' of Juba and Cleomedon respectively), watch while Coriolanus (Juba) and Caesario (Cleomedon), aided by Artaban and three others, are set on by 'fifteen or twenty Horse-men' (p. 73). As they watch, the pirate Zenodorus, captain of the assailants, and an accomplice carry Candace and Clitie away. The only significant departure from fact is the transmogrification of 'fifteen or twenty' into 'some hundred Men'.

Page 164. (1) *Olympia . . . enamoured of her:* See 'The History of Olympia' (*Cleopatra*, Part VI, Book i).

(2) *Did not the Divine Clelia . . . adore her:* Arabella's memory betrays her. Maherball is briefly Clelia's suitor at Carthage, but it is the supposed Adherbal Prince of Numidia who is later revealed as her lost brother Octavius. The mistake is made also by Aronces (*Clelia*, II. ii. 225).

(3) *was not the Uncle . . . in his Power:* see 'The Historie of Alcione' (*Cassandra*, Part II, Book vi). The lustful Bagistanes is actually the uncle

of Alcione's husband Theander; both La Calprenède and Mrs. Lennox are of their time in not distinguishing the relationship by marriage from the relationship by blood.

VOLUME TWO

BOOK V

Page 180. *the History of the fair Amalazontha: Pharamond*, Part V, Books iii and iv describes the love of Ambioner, to all appearances a mere knight, for the haughty Princess of the Thuringians. She resists his suit, even though her father favours it, and the visit she pays the wounded and languishing hero is at her father's express bidding (V. iv. 90).

Page 183. (1) *the fair and witty Doralisa:* For her portrait, see *Artamenes*, V. i. 24f. Arabella is not quite correct about her. At the end of the romance we learn that 'since certainly tender and passionate expressions were not her custom: all that she was able to do, was to let the Prince *Myrsiles* use them' (X. i. 488). She listens to his talk of love, and marries him.

   (2) *the Virtue of the divine Mandana:* For Mandana's visit to the bedridden Artamenes, see p. 132, note (1).

   (3) *the haughty Amalazontha:* See p. 180, note.

   (4) *the fair Statira:* See p. 48, note.

   (5) *the cold and rigid Parisatis:* See p. 189, note (3).

Page 184. (1) *These chaste Ladies* [p. 183] . . . *their Husband:* Arabella is too sweeping. Statira and Oroondates, for example, kiss each other enthusiastically when their marriage, though agreed on, is known by them to be at best very distant. On one occasion Oroondates 'surpris'd her lips with his, and seal'd them with so much fervidness, or rather forgot himself with so much sweetness, that he seem'd as if he never would have parted from them, if the Princess had not gently thrust him back . . .' (*Cassandra*, I. iv. 88). On the other hand, Lysimachus only once kisses Parisatis's hand during his long wooing, and the princess blushed to see him take such a liberty (*Cassandra*, II. ii. 223); and the heroines of Mlle de Scudéry are very reserved.

   (2) *Mandana . . . Two powerful Kingdoms:* Cappadocia and Media.

   (3) *the fair Cleonice . . . his Bed:* This seems a mistake; there is no such episode in 'The History of Ligdamis and Cleonice' (*Artamenes*, Part IV, Book iii).

Page 187. *the jealous Transports of an enraged Orontes:* See p. 125, note.

Page 189. (1) *the great Actions . . . the Cilicians:* Orontes, disguised as the Amazon Orithia, led the forces which rescued Thalestris when she was captured by Neobarzanes, and finally overthrew him (*Cassandra*, II. iv. 8ff.).

(2) *Did not the brave Memnon . . . a Visit*: Had Glanville read *Cassandra*, he would have been able to answer 'No' to Arabella's rhetorical question. When Prince Oxyatres falls ill and is like to die for love of Barsina, Memnon, the favoured suitor, resigns his pretensions for the sake of his prince. Moved to equal generosity, Oxyatres decides to conquer his passion. This rivalry in generosity is probably in Arabella's mind, but Memnon does not actually persuade Barsina to visit Oxyatres (*Cassandra*, V. iii. 83ff.).

(3) *And the complaisant Husband . . . her sake*: Lysimachus, describing the nearly fatal illness which he suffered after the marriage of Parisatis to Hephestion, says: '. . . *Hephestion* was he who behaved himself the handsomeliest in that occasion; hee was not satisfied with being every day at my bedside, nor with showing himself next *Ptolomeus* the most diligent of all my friends; neither did he think it enough that the Princess his wife came many times to see me, but he accused her himself of ill nature, and sollicited her to visit me oftner; he brought her divers times himself, and going away without her, gave me as much liberty to entertain her as I could wish' (*Cassandra*, II. ii. 226).

Page 193. *Remember . . . insupportable Misfortune*: See p. 132, note (3).

Page 194. *like the unfortunate Agilmond . . . my Eyes*: Agelmond King of Lombardy loves and is loved by Gilismene Princess of the Sarmatians. But wicked intriguers poison her mind against him; when he forces his way into her presence she accuses him of perfidy, whereupon he throws himself on his sword. He survives (*Pharamond*, X. ii. 526).

Page 195. *and since . . . the fair Parisatis*: Though determined to obey her grandmother and marry Hephestion, Parisatis does not conceal from Lysimachus that she esteems him as much as she does her future husband, if not more.

Page 205. *offered her the chief Command of their Forces*: During a generous conflict among the leading warriors whose forces had gathered to rescue Statira and Parisatis from their Babylonian captivity, Thalestris was one of those pressed to take the command, but she excused herself by reason of her sex (*Cassandra*, III. iii. 164).

Page 206. *some little Infidelities he was accused of*: See p. 152 and note (3).

Page 207. *She has too much . . . Infidelity*: Cf. pp. 90 and 152.

BOOK VI

Page 216. (1) *The fair Arsinoe . . . a King*: See 'The History of Philadelph' (*Cleopatra*, Part IV, Books iii and iv).

(2) *In like manner . . . his own:* See 'The History of Philoxypes and Poli-
crite' (*Artamenes*, Part II, Book iii).

Page 223. For, do but reflect . . . to turn: Typical of Arabella's exaggeration.
Her first example of valour seems to be the defence of Cleopatra and
Artemisa by Coriolanus ('the brave Prince of *Mauretania*') on board the
ship of Artaxus; he is armed only with his sword, but the number of his
opponents is not stated (*Cleopatra*, IX. iv. 265ff.). And on an earlier
occasion he had failed to prevent the carrying off of these ladies by a mere
ten or twelve armed horsemen (ibid., V. ii. 394ff.). Alexander ('The young
Prince of *Egypt*') and Cepio did engage the King of Armenia's guards, but
despite their prowess Cepio was killed and Alexander recaptured (*Cleopatra*, IV. ii. 308 (really 306) ff.). Ariobarzanes does the deeds of a hero, but
even a partial narrator, his mistress Olympia, says when describing his
defence of Byzantium that he was not 'in a condition with a Body of Six or
seven thousand men, to fight an Army of above Thirty thousand', nor able
'with an handful of men to drive out a puissant and victorious Army' (ibid.,
VII. i. 24). For the exaggeration of Artaban's exploits, cf. p. 128.

La Calprenède at least once seems aware that the reader's disbelief in a
hero's powers must be allayed, saying that Coriolanus himself 'had some
reason to think it strange, that a Prince born of a barbarous King, Enemy
to the People of *Rome*, not exceeding the age of 21, should command a
Roman army, at a time when *Rome* abounded with so many famous Cap-
tains of her own . . .'. His success is attributed to 'the bounteous distribution
of Natures favour, signally stamp'd in his Face, Language, and Actions'
(*Cleopatra*, II. iii. 120).

Page 227. To give you a Description . . . of Beauty: It would not escape the
attention of Sir George's audience that the description of Sydimiris might
well be a 'portrait' of Arabella.

Page 229. (1) *You will there see . . . his Blood:* I have failed to identify this
episode.

(2) *Another, who . . . over again:* Artabenes King of Media, having led an
army against Surena to force the latter to release Parthenissa, and having
captured his enemy, promptly released him. The man ordered to send
Surena home reports himself as being 'as much astonisht at this Command
as *Surena* was when I went to obey it' (*Parthenissa*, IV. iv. 578). Sure
enough, Surena refuses to let Parthenissa go, and all is to do again.

(3) *A Third . . . in Person:* Oroondates Prince of Scythia who for love of
Artaxerxes and Statira fights with the Persians against his own people, led
by his own father. This is a striking and rather crude realization of that
conflict between love and duty which is a main theme of heroic romance.
The squire Araxes, who relates the story of Oroondates, outlines the
possible courses of action open to his master, and ends with the simple

statement: 'These considerations held him for some time in uncertainty; but in the end, paternall duty, and the protection of his Countrey, yeilded to the love of *Statira*, and to the friendship of *Artaxerxes* . . .' (*Cassandra*, I. ii. 39).

Page 231. An extraordinary Instance . . . in Cassandra: The heading of this chapter in Sir George's narrative must refer to the episode wherein Arsaces (really Artaxerxes Prince of Persia) gives himself up to the King of Scythia, hoping thereby to divert the anger which makes the king force his daughter Berenice to wed the loathed Arsacomes. This act of generosity is analogous to that whereby Bellmour gives himself up to 'Prince Marcomire', hoping to take upon himself the guilt imputed to 'Sydimiris', and so divert her brother's anger from her. See *Cassandra*, IV. v. 39ff.

Page 234. In which . . . her Lover: Sir George has perhaps modelled this instance of a lady's generosity on the way in which Statira and Parisatis save the life of Lysimachus from the fury of Alexander; they make it the price of their marrying respectively Alexander himself, and his friend Hephestion. As Lysimachus is in love with Parisatis, the analogy is quite close. See *Cassandra*, II. ii. 220ff.

Page 239. Chance at last . . . the Light: There is a general resemblance between this cave and that to which Orontes retired to work out his penance for misjudging Thalestris (Cf. supra, p. 126. See also *Cassandra*, V. ii. 48f.).

Page 251. (1) *have found . . . admirable Delia: Cleopatra*, IV. iii. 318f.

(2) *or disguised . . . Divine Olympia: Cleopatra*, VI. iii. 513.

(3) *or bound . . . beauteous Agione: Pharamond*, IX. i. 404.

(4) *or in a Ship . . . incomparable Eliza: Cleopatra*, III. iv. 264ff.

Page 252. the Bedford Coffee-house: Those who frequented this celebrated coffee house, situated near Covent Garden Theatre, included Garrick, Quin, Foote, Macklin, Murphy, Churchill, Collins, Fielding, Pope, Sheridan, and Horace Walpole. See Bryant Lillywhite, *London Coffee Houses*, 1963, p. 114.

Page 259. See supplementary note on p. 417.

BOOK VII

Page 260. (1) *'Twas in such a Place* [p. 259] *. . . Hortensius:* In 'The History of the Princess Elismonda' Mlle de Scudéry describes the Vale of Tempe; here occurred the incident Arabella goes on to relate, when Andronice Princess of Messina rescued Hortensius from being punished for killing a stork (*Clelia*, IV. i. 421ff.).

(2) *And so . . . in Turky:* Macedonia was in 1752 part of the Ottoman Empire.

(3) *the Great Mogul's Country:* India. The Great Mogul was the designa-

tion of the emperor of Delhi. As Mr. Glanville points out, his father is confusing him with the Grand Signior, Sultan of Turkey.

Page 261. *a great many beautiful Princesses . . . each other:* So many indeed that at the end of *Cleopatra* Augustus had eleven of them married off in one grand ceremony at the temple of Isis.

Page 262. (1) *Undress:* the term used to describe any clothing 'that fell short of full dress. . . . Undress was worn in the morning, indoors and outdoors. To discard one part of a full dress, such as a hoop, a cravat or periwig, a coat or long gown, was to be "undressed"' (Iris Brooke, *Dress and Undress,* 1958, p. vii).

(2) *Capuchin:* a kind of soft hood, very commonly worn at this time.

Page 265. (1) *the Number of the Olympiads:* An Olympiad was 'A period of four years reckoned from one celebration of the Olympic games to the next, by which the ancient Greeks computed time' (*O.E.D.*).

(2) *the famous Springs . . . new Lustre:* The Springs of Thermopylae, Pisistratus, his rivals Lycurgus and Theocrites, the fair Cerinthe and the beautiful Cleorante all occur in 'The History of Pisistrates' (*Artamenes,* Part IX, Book iii).

(3) See supplementary note on p. 418.

Page 267. *Which contains . . . for Raillery:* Arabella's sage remarks on raillery are taken from a conversation on the subject in 'The History of Pisistrates' (*Artamenes,* IX. iii. 325ff.). She selects from and modernizes words spoken by the grave Euridamia, who leads the conversation; the two remarks made by Mr. Glanville are adapted from those made by Pisistratus. Arabella adds two ideas of her own: raillery directed against 'Persons who have a small Share of Merit' (p. 268) is deprecated, because 'haply, their Defects were born with them, and not of their own acquiring' (in the original such raillery is just 'never handsom'); and at the end of her discourse she extends the simile of wit shining as the stars do, without burning, by going on to compare people who have the talent of raillery with comets (p. 269).

Page 269. *a Robe . . . the Princess Julia's:* How the mantua-maker was to carry out this task, even had she read *Cleopatra,* is hard to say. For though there is much conspicuous consumption in La Calprenède's world, he makes only occasional and slight references to women's clothes, nowhere giving a description that could possibly be copied. What Arabella may have had in mind was the account of 'a magnificent Assembly at the Princess Julia's Lodgings' in Alexandria: 'Julia indeed was the most glorious object there, as well by reason of her natural beauty, as the ornaments whereby she had advanc'd it, and adding to the lustre of her countenance the sprightliness of her eyes, the freedom, gallantry and insinuation of her action and deportment, she for a long time inhanc'd to her self the observance of the whole Assembly' (*Cleopatra,* XI. ii. 418 (really p. 410)).

Page 271. She wore no Hoop ... greatest Advantage: The most striking thing about Arabella's ball-dress was the absence of the hoop, an essential part of full dress at this date. The low-cut breast was perhaps a little outmoded; like other modest women, Arabella wore lace to cover her breast. The absence of a head-dress was remarkable, at a time when 'Few ladies appeared in public without some sort of lacy nonsense pinned in their hair' (Iris Brooke, *Dress and Undress*, p. 87). See p. 108 for evidence of the universal wearing of caps.

Page 273. I know ... virtuous Princess: Ovid's story of the relationship between him and Julia is given in *Cleopatra*, Part VII, Book iii, 'The History of Ovid, Cipassis, and Julia'.

Page 274. (1) The great Cyrus ... his Enemies: Concerning Cyrus' patience as a listener, Mlle de Scudéry at least once shows some misgivings. After hearing 'The Sequel of the History of Aglatidas and Amestris', he has to talk business with a group of kings and princes. He goes 'with so much Majesty as it can hardly be imagined that a Prince of so high a Soul should be so sweet as to hearken unto a long amorous Discourse, in which he had no other interest, than as relating unto a Man whom he loved, unless it were by comparing the Torments which other Lovers suffer, with those which he endured for *Mandana*' (*Artamenes*, IV. ii. 257).

And in Gabriel Guéret's *Le Parnasse reformé* (1671) Cyrus complains to Mlle de Scudéry that she makes him listen to 'mille petites nouvelles indifferentes, lors même quand je suis prest à combattre' (p. 137).

(2) *his Recital:* Mr. Tinsel's 'Recital' may owe something to a passage early in the tenth part of *Artamenes*. Mrs. Lennox has twice in the preceding few chapters referred to the third book of part nine, and may have been re-reading this section of the romance as she wrote. In *Artamenes*, a character at a ball 'had a lash at every one in the company', impugning variously the clothes, birth, and morals of those present. The following is typical: 'I beseech you (said *Pelinthes*, seeing a Lady of a good presence and quality) tell me who that Lady is? If you should judge of her by the Grandure of her air (replyed she) you would think her to be some kin to the gods, and to say the truth (added she, to palliate her scandal) she is a very admirable Lady, for every action and word of hers speaks her of a royal race; yet heavens know, her grandfather was no better than a poor stranger, whose Original the gods do know and none else, and those who are acquainted with her can tell you, she smells of the business of her ancestors in all her inclinations, and though she looks more like a Queen than a Subject, yet she speaks as if her education were amongst the basest sort of pesants: her carriage also displeaseth, she cannot as much as make a curtesy as others do, and has a most ill favoured gate: Yet truly, to speak truth, she is a very good woman' (X. i. 78).

Page 275. the Marriage of another of his Brothers . . . her Fortune: It seems possible that Mrs. Lennox, like Mlle de Scudéry, drew some of her characters from the life. The details in this account of the marriages made by two brothers of a duke not only give it an air of authenticity, but fit the history of Lord George and Lord Aubrey Beauclerk, brothers of the second Duke of St. Albans. According to *Collins's Peerage of England* (1812, i. 249f.), Lord Aubrey married the daughter of Sir Henry Newton, Knight, and widow of Colonel Francis Alexander. This lady, whose Christian name is not given, may well be 'the Widow of a brave Officer, of considerable Rank in the Army'. The date of the marriage is not stated. Lord Aubrey lost his life at Carthagena on 24 March 1740/41. It does then look as if this might be the marriage Mr. Tinsel refers to, as having been disapproved of by 'the Duke'. Of the Duke's other brothers, only Lord George, also a soldier, made what seems to have been an even more obscure marriage, to 'Margaret, daughter of . . . Bainbridge' (ibid. p. 249). Again, no date is given. This may be the lady whose 'History' Mr. Tinsel is relating. Lord Aubrey's death at Carthagena happened during the years when Charlotte Lennox was in America; this may be an instance of her drawing for material on her life in New York province, where the details of the engagement would be well known.

Page 276. One of our great Sea Commanders: Perhaps Admiral (later Sir) Charles Knowles. The *Dictionary of National Biography* says that in July 1750 at Aix-la-Chapelle (which is near Spa) he married, as his second wife, Maria Magdalena Teresa, daughter of the Comte de Bouget. Debrett's *Baronetage* (6th edn., 1828, p. 344) on the other hand describes the lady as Maria-Magdalena Theresa Bouquet, born in Germany, and makes no mention of her parentage. The discrepancy suggests that the lady's origin was open to speculation, and that Mr. Tinsel is repeating malicious gossip about her.

Page 277. (1) The Ugliness of Vice . . . always restrain'd: The view expressed by Arabella in this paragraph, that literature should on the whole avoid representing vice, may be compared with that expressed by Johnson in the *Rambler*, no. 37 (24 July 1750); in all writing 'chastity of sentiment ought doubtless to be observed, and purity of manners to be represented'.

(2) *the sublime Courage of a Clelia . . . other Side:* See p. 62, note (2). In fact it is Sextus, not his father Tarquin (they are so distinguished in the romance), whom Clelia flees.

Page 278. (1) the noble Resolution . . . the Waves: Cleopatra, III. ii. 210f.

(2) *the Constancy . . . for him:* Mandana for the sake of Cyrus refused the kings of Assyria and Pontus, as well as several princes, and underwent all the usual trials of a heroine.

(3) *the renowned Alcamenes:* See 'The History of Alcamenes and Melanippa' (*Cleopatra*, Part VIII, Books ii–iv).

Page 280. (1) *Cyrus the Great . . . at Sardis:* a slip. Mandana was whipped away from Sardis by the King of Pontus before Cyrus could deliver her. They do dance together at a wedding, however, after her ultimate rescue (*Artamenes,* VIII. iii. 434); and dancing is a common pastime of characters in French romances.

(2) *The renown'd King of Scythia . . . at Alexandria:* For Alcamenes King of Scythia see p. 278, note (3). Arabella must be thinking of the evening of Augustus' arrival in Alexandria, where dancing took place. Alcamenes and Cleopatra had a long conversation, though it is not clear that they danced together (*Cleopatra,* XI. ii. 418 (really p. 410)–414).

(3) *The brave Cleomedon . . . at Ethiopia:* Again, while Cleomedon (Caesario) was the darling of the Ethiopian court, replete with accomplishments and refined qualities, I find no mention of his dancing with Candace. See 'The History of Caesario, and the Queen Candace' (*Cleopatra,* Part I, Book iii, and Part III, Book i).

Page 281. *the Fate of the Princess Melisintha:* Melisintha escaped the flames with the help of her father, who broke prison, killed the importunate bridegroom, and got his daughter away while the palace burned down (*Pharamond,* VI. ii. 134ff.).

Page 285. (1) *The Lover* [p. 284] *. . . undesign'd Offence:* Arabella does not remember quite accurately. Orontes Prince of the Massagetes betrays his love for Thalestris not by revealing it to a confidant but by the equally common convention of an overheard soliloquy. In all other respects Arabella's description fits the episode. The supposed Orithea (Orontes disguised as an Amazon) speaks in a voice interrupted with sighs and sobs, relates his passion and despair, and realizes he is overheard when Thalestris 'could not forbeare making a little noise'. He throws himself at the feet of his angry mistress, says he is not fit to ask her pardon, and avers his readiness to die in expiation of his guilt (*Cassandra,* II. iii. 257ff.).

(2) *The Method which the great Artamenes took . . . :* See *Artamenes,* II. i. 23ff., for these events.

Page 286. *In like Manner the great Prince of Persia:* The homage paid by Artaxerxes, 'the great Prince of *Persia*', to the incomparable Berenice is long silent, and when at last he declares himself, revealing his identity as well as his love, it is in the spirit of the following typical statement: 'That perfect knowledge I had of her admirable qualities, check'd my aspiring hopes, and I could not consider Berenice, in that sublime degree of perfection to which the Gods had raised her, without remembring my self to be but a man, and therefore utterly unworthy to serve her' (*Cassandra,* IV. ii. 117).

Page 293. *the beautiful Princess of Cappadocia:* Mandana. But the plots to carry her off seem to come singly, not in pairs.

Page 295. (1) *Seramenes:* There is no Seramenes in 'The History of Cleo-buline Queen of Corinth' (*Artamenes*, Part VII, Book ii), nor is there any character who plays the part given to him here.

(2) *you use me . . . wise Antonia:* For the episode where Cleopatra per-suades Antonia to read a lover's letter, see *Cleopatra*, IX. ii. 213.

Page 296. *I am much . . . Princess Serena:* The resemblance does not seem close. Serena, niece of the Emperor Theodosius, has three real—not imagined—suitors, two of whom intrigue against the one she favours. One of their devices is to show Serena letters written by him to a long-forgotten mistress, thus convincing her for a while that he is unfaithful. But when she reads them, and his own letter of justification, she is not at all perplexed about how she should act (*Pharamond*, VII. iii. 273ff.).

Page 298. *I protest . . . than hers was:* The parallel is not very close. Statira comes to visit Barsina, where, unknown to the princess, Oroondates is staying. He is in Barsina's closet when Statira is announced, overhears her conversation with Barsina in the next room, and runs in to cast himself at her feet. While the intentions of both Lucy and Barsina are innocent, Lucy in no other way resembles this high-born and gracious lady—as Arabella is well aware. See *Cassandra*, I. vi. 156ff.

Page 302. (1) *but know . . . Ravisher here:* The redundant 'not' possibly arises from confusion with the construction, already obsolete, of 'forbid' with a personal object and a negative clause.

(2) *the Examples of Artamenes, Aronces:* Artamenes promises his rival the King of Assyria not to marry Mandana, even though she and her father should consent, 'before the Fate of Arms has rendred me a Conqueror in Combat with you' (*Artamenes*, I. i. 17). He is ready to keep his word, but Mlle de Scudéry protects her hero from the odium of killing a generous rival, and makes the King of Assyria die, instead, in the attempt to rescue Mandana from yet another ravisher (ibid., IX. i. 18ff.). Aronces and Horatius both try to rescue Clelia when she is being carried off for the last time; Aronces succeeds where Horatius fails, but needs the latter's protec-tion for Clelia's journey back to Rome. The rivals exchange promises: Horatius, if Aronces should die in the war to which he must return, will put no constraint on Clelia to marry him, while Aronces undertakes not to marry Clelia till he has offered to win her in single combat with Horatius. His obligations to Horatius are those of one honourable and generous rival to another (*Clelia*, V. iii. 732f. and 736).

Page 303. *And herein you imitate . . . have done:* Artamenes spares the King of Assyria, the ravisher of Mandana, when he has him in his power (*Arta-menes*, I. i. 15ff.). This is a typical act of 'generosity'; Mandana speaks with rare common sense when she later calls it 'over-generosity' (ibid., VIII. i. 6).

Book VIII

Page 312. than the Princess Udosia ... for her: Thrasimond (not Thrasi-medes) Prince of the Vandals visits the court of Constantinople, where he falls hopelessly in love with Eudoxia. When she learns of this she banishes him (*Pharamond*, VII. ii. 237ff.). He later dies of grief. Eudoxia is an empress—the Eudocia of history, wife of Theodosius II; this analogy altogether marks one of Arabella's more overweening moments.

Page 316. (1) Did not the sad Perinthus ... Panthea: For the hopeless love and death of Perinthus, see 'The History of Abradates and of Panthea' (*Artamenes*, Part V, Book i).

(2) *Did not the Rigour of Barsina ... Grave:* The illness of Oxyatres, who had failed to detach Barsina from the suitor to whom she had first given her heart, was exactly of the kind that Arabella believes proper to a rejected lover. He was 'seaz'd with a violent Feaver', and 'he sometimes fell into ravings' in which 'hee talked of nothing but Barsina, and by all his actions made those that were about him judge, that nothing but his love had caused his sickness' (*Cassandra*, V. iii. 83).

(3) *And the Severity of Statira ... kill'd by it:* When Statira, now the wife of Alexander, reminds Oroondates of her virtue and the strict rules of her duty to her husband, he approves them, but, asserting that all that is left for him is to die, runs on his sword. Barsina knocks it aside, and he is not hurt (*Cassandra*, I. vi. 161).

Page 317. the Princess of Media ... his Disaster: *Artamenes*, IX. i. 20f. The Princess of Media is Mandana.

Page 320. The Empire of Love ... any other: With this discussion of the law of love and honour, and its pre-eminence over the law of the land, compare p. 128 and note (1).

Page 321. (1) the Actions of Oroondates, Artaxerxes, Spitridates: All these face a conflict between love on the one hand and their duty to family and country on the other. For the conduct of Oroondates see p. 229, note (3). Artaxerxes Prince of Persia, son of King Darius, loves the Scythian princess Berenice. For her sake he disguises himself, lives unknown at the Scythian court and fights the Scythians' battles, while his own country, Persia, is overrun by the Macedonian army. La Calprenède expresses some mis-givings about this, saying in the introduction to the fourth part of *Cassandra*, 'I have been put to it, as many others would have been, to make Darius his son pass his time handsomly in Scythia, whilest his Countrey was laid desolate, and his father deprived of his Empire, and of his life, by Alex-anders victorious forces.'

Spitridates is a prince of Bithynia, in love with Araminta Princess of Pontus; their countries have long been at war. Spitridates reflects upon his dilemma: '... I must resolve upon one way, I must either go unto *Heraclea*, or *Chalcedonia*: If to the first, then I lose my Honour, but satisfy my Love: if to the last, then I shall satisfy my Ambition, but ruin my Self in the Opinion of my Princess, which I prefer before all things, even my very Life' (*Artamenes*, III. ii. 275).

In the end, 'Love was the most predominate in his Heart'; but Mlle de Scudéry, much more skilful in this respect than La Calprenède, contrives to keep him from actually fighting against his country, which Oroondates is made to do.

(2) *I shall live . . . take Care of:* I have not been able to find this passage in *Cassandra*.

(3) *Say only . . . to conquer:* The nearest I have found to these words is part of a speech made by Juba (Coriolanus) as he leaves Rome to win back his father's kingdom: 'Now let *Augustus, cry'd he,* display all the puissance of his *Empire* against me, and let the whole world assist him in his aims at my overthrow, I brave them all, *my Princess,* in the estate to which your goodness has exalted me...' (*Cleopatra*, II. iv. 143f.).

Page 322. The celebrated Countess of——: Lady Mary Wortley Montagu, writing to her daughter in 1754, conjectures that *The Female Quixote* is by Sarah Fielding, and asks: 'Tell me who is that accomplish'd Countess she celebrates. I left no such person in London...' (*Complete Letters*, 1965-7, iii. 67). This suggestion, that the character of the countess is founded on fact, would occur to Lady Mary the more readily because Charlotte Lennox in *The Life of Harriot Stuart* had in the character of Lady Cecilia represented a real person, Lady Cecilia Isabella Finch. Lady Mary had been furious about this (*Complete Letters*, iii. 8).

Page 325. If Elisa . . . she detested: Elisa is a character in *Cleopatra*. Her father tries to make her marry Tigranes King of Media.

Page 326. (1) *was not the beautiful daughter of Antony* [p. 325] *... to her:* The desire of Augustus that Cleopatra should marry Tiberius is foiled only at the end of the romance, when Tiberius renounces his claim.

(2) *If Elisa ... of Pyrates:* See p. 251 and note (4).

(3) *was not Cleopatra ... whole Earth:* Cleopatra was kept captive on his ship by Artaxus King of Armenia, who held back her rescuers by putting his sword to her breast and threatening to kill her (*Cleopatra*, IX. iv. 276).

(4) *And in fine ... cruel Death:* The climax of *Cleopatra* comes when two of the three most important of the male characters, Coriolanus and Caesario, are imprisoned by Augustus and threatened with death. As Cleopatra here seems about to see her lover and brother executed, while the life of Elisa's lover Artaban is not immediately threatened, Arabella has the best of the argument (*Cleopatra*, XII. iv. 564ff.).

Page 329. (1) *Oroondates ... was he belov'd:* See p. 229, note (3).

(2) *very different from Oroondates:* See p. 24, note.

BOOK IX

Page 334. (1) *She observ'd ... much fiercer:* Arabella is using her imagination here, for La Calprenède does not, in his vivid sketch of the lion's appearance, mention its size at all. But he certainly stresses its ferocity (*Cassandra*, II. ii. 219).

(2) *the Temple ... suppos'd Death:* The magi having foretold that Cyrus would one day conquer the throne of Media, the news of his supposed death is an occasion for rejoicing among the Medes. So it happens that when Cyrus, disguised as Artamenes, first sees Mandana, she is offering sacrifices of thanks to the gods for his death. But as regards the temple Arabella is drawing on her imagination, for all that is said of it is that it is 'stately', and 'magnificently adorned' (*Artamenes*, I. i. 115).

(3) *to sail in Barges ... upon the Tyber:* In *Cleopatra* there is described a divertissement upon the Tiber, in which occur barges, collations, a little sea-fight, and much gallantry (*Cleopatra*, IX. ii. 220ff.).

(4) *the Gardens of Lucullus ... Persons:* La Calprenède describes how Augustus entertains Terentia, Maecenas' wife, 'with a Comedy, Musick, and Walking, in the fair and famous Gardens of *Lucullus*' (*Cleopatra*, IX. ii. 209). The walking gave an opportunity for lovers to hold 'gallant Conversations', not on the more abstract topics of the conversations in Mlle de Scudéry's romances, but about themselves.

Page 335. *her Misfortunes ... exprest for her:* Artesia, not Aspasia, disguised herself as a man when fleeing the adulterous advances of Phraates King of Parthia (*Cleopatra*, IX. iii. 256). This device, so frequent in comedy, is very unusual in French romances.

Page 337. *May not the same ... carry'd her away:* This seems to be based on the same confused recollection of an episode in *Cleopatra* as are Arabella's words on p. 155 (see note) about Candace and Cleopatra.

Page 338. *She cannot sure ... desir'd thee:* Demetrius Prince of Phrygia, fighting against the forces of Roxana, is attacked by a feeble warrior who inflicts no injury on him but runs on his sword. 'O Death! (cried hee as hee was falling) how sweet do I finde thee, and how much have I desired thee' (*Cassandra*, III. iii. 168). The warrior turns out to be a woman; her wounds are mortal, though she lives long enough to win the love of Demetrius, and in 'The History of Hermione' (twenty-two folio pages) to tell her passion for Alexander. The 'Agonies' felt by Demetrius, and 'the Extravagancy of his Rage and Despair' are described at the end of Hermione's story (ibid., III. iv. 26, 30f., 37f.). But soon he encounters the fair Deidamia, herself bewailing the loss of Agis, and falls in love with her. 'All the remembrance of *Hermione* was dissipated in his soul by the charms of *Deidamia*' (ibid., V. i. 6). While the first meeting of Demetrius and Deidamia is not specially dramatic, Arabella no doubt felt that to describe it effectively she must give in detail the earlier history of both characters. This would indeed have taken up 'some Hours Time'.

Page 361. Brag: a card-game, closely resembling poker.

Page 362. She mention'd ... absolute Stranger: For the rescues of Statira and Berenice, see *Cassandra,* IV. v. 52 and IV. vi. 73.

Page 363. What that beauteous Roman lady ... Sextus: See p. 62, note (2).

Page 368. Being in the Author's Opinion ... this History: The theory that Dr. Johnson wrote this chapter of *The Female Quixote* was put forward by the Rev. John Mitford, editor of *The Gentleman's Magazine* (N.S. xx (August 1843), 132, and xxi (January 1844), 41). In the second discussion, he alluded briefly to the external evidence of Johnson's long-continued interest in Mrs. Lennox, which has been fully discussed by Mr. Duncan Isles in *The New Rambler,* Serial No. C.III (June 1967), 34–48.

A further bit of external evidence is that at least twice in earlier chapters of the novel Mrs. Lennox borrowed from other writers passages which she put into the mouth of Arabella, to support her character as unusually sensible and well-informed on all subjects except romance (see pp. 82 and 267ff., and notes). I suspect that originals could be found for other speeches made by Arabella, as for example her disquisitions on glory, indifference, and suicide (pp. 303f., 310f., and 318f.), in which the style seems different from that of most of her conversation. If Mrs. Lennox was not wholly confident of her ability to invent intelligent conversation for her heroine, she was still less likely to trust herself when it came to doing the same for the Doctor who must argue Arabella out of her folly.

As for internal evidence, the style of the chapter does show many qualities singled out as characteristic by W. K. Wimsatt in *The Prose Style of Samuel Johnson* (1941), and not characteristic of the style of *The Female Quixote* in general. Particularly obvious is the large number of what Wimsatt calls doublets, triplets, and so on—parallelism of single words, phrases, clauses or sentences. These range from the simple parallelism of two words, sometimes emphasized by alliteration ('Sincerity and Submission' (p. 370), 'Tenderness and Sympathy' (p. 381)), through more complex examples ('introduce his Reasonings, and begin his Confutation' (p. 368), 'dangerous Tenets, corrupt Passions, or criminal Desires' (p. 370)), to what we might call compound effects, such as '... these Books soften the Heart to Love, and harden it to Murder ... they teach Women to exact Vengeance, and Men to execute it ...' (p. 380), or '... they have distributed Mountains and Desarts, Gulphs and Rocks, wherever they wanted them, and whenever the Course of their Story required an Expedient, raised a gloomy Forest, or overflowed the Regions with a rapid Stream' (p. 378). In these latter examples, the parallel is elaborated by antithesis or chiasmus.

Other characteristics of Johnson's style found in this chapter are the high proportion of abstract words and phrases (such as 'the Severity of the Sacerdotal Character' (p. 369), 'The most restless Activity in the longest Life' (p. 373)); the use of rather unusual words, often of classical and learned origin ('Sacerdotal' (p. 369), 'Casualty' (p. 371), 'uncouth' (p. 373), 'Spectatress' (p. 381)); some 'literary' verb forms (like the future perfect of 'when it shall have made you equally acquainted with both' (p. 380); but note 'you was speaking' (p. 369)); and inversion of the usual order of clauses or phrases ('That you have been envy'd, I can readily believe' (p. 369); 'To the Names of many of these illustrious Sufferers I am an absolute Stranger' (p. 373)).

On the other hand, the sentences are on average not long—32.8 words, compared with 43.1 in *The Rambler* (Wimsatt p. 88; he takes the figure from Warner Taylor, 'The Prose Style of Johnson', *University of Wisconsin Studies in Language and Literature*, No. 2, 1918, p. 35). And while the number of nouns in the chapter, just over 1,000, is too small to be an adequate sample, it is perhaps worth saying that the proportion of monosyllabic nouns to the total occurrences of all nouns, 27.6 per cent, while almost exactly the same as in *The Rambler* (see S. Krishnamurti in *Journal of the University of Bombay*, N.S. xix (September 1950), Part 2, 7), is actually a little higher than that in a sample taken from elsewhere in *The Female Quixote*. For this sample I chose Book I Chapters 11–13 and Book VIII Chapters 6–7, because they include some dialogue of a serious kind, just comparable with that in the chapter Johnson may have written, and because the total occurrences of nouns in them were fairly close to those in the chapter being discussed. The proportion of monosyllabic nouns to total occurrences of all nouns in these chapters was 26.9 per cent.

As far as the content of the chapter is concerned, its marked and sustained sententiousness has no parallel elsewhere in the book. The sentiments range from statements about 'the great Use of Books' (p. 372) and 'The great End of History' (p. 376), to statements about logic ('The Laws of Conference require...' (p. 371), 'Universal Negatives are seldom safe...' (p. 373)). With these compare the analysis of apprehension into terror and suspicion, and the statement of its origin on p. 372, another example of an abstract logical way of thought characteristic of Johnson but not of the rest of *The Female Quixote*.

Finally, the chapter not only lays great stress on reason and morality as criteria by which to judge a work of fiction, views implicit in the novel as a whole, but also embodies some typically Johnsonian and 'very mortifying Reflections on the Imperfection of all human Happiness' (p. 369), which are not.

None of this evidence, however, is conclusive, and the attribution of the chapter to Johnson remains a plausible theory. For a statement of the contrary view, see Mr. Isles's Appendix, p. 418.

Page 373. (1) *the divine Clelia ... Thrasymenian Lake: Clelia* opens with the heroine's abduction by Horatius, who holds her captive on an island in Lake Trasimene.

(2) *Or those which befel the beautiful Candace ... Seas: Cleopatra,* III. ii. 204ff.

(3) *Or the Accidents ... Cleopatra:* These are the typical sufferings of the romance heroine, and are of two main kinds: those which come from interference with the course of true love, through parental pressure or false report, and those which come from the unwelcome attentions of undesirable admirers. Augustus wants Cleopatra to marry first Marcellus and then Tiberius, rather than Coriolanus whom she loves; Coriolanus suspects her fidelity when he sees Tiberius wearing her scarf during a tournament; Tiberius sows in her mind suspicions of the fidelity of Coriolanus; Artaxus King of Armenia carries her off, and Tiberius tries to do the same.

(4) *Or the Persecutions ... fair Elisa miserable:* These included capture in war and by pirates, being married against her will to Tigranes King of Media, and a long separation from Artaban, whom she believed to be dead.

(5) *Olympia:* In addition to the regular sufferings of a heroine, Olympia had the misery of being loved by her brother and sold as a slave (see p. 164 and note (1)).

(6) *Bellamira:* an outstandingly harassed heroine from *Pharamond.* Her distresses included being three times carried away, a long period of imprisonment in a castle, the necessity to pull from its sheath the sword of a would-be ravisher, whom she forthwith kills, and nearly being burnt to death in the place of her third incarceration.

(7) *Parisatis, Berenice:* The sufferings of Parisatis included capture in war; the loss, either in war or through natural causes, of grandmother, both parents, and (apparently) her brother; marrying one man when she loved another; loss of this husband; and long delays before a final union with the man of her choice.

Berenice, also a character in *Cassandra,* is carried away, and though rescued is almost forced by her father into a hateful marriage.

(8) *Amalazantha:* or Amalzontha. She is twice carried away; but her chief distress is her hopeless love for Pharamond (who loves and is loved by Rosamond). Though she at last conquers this passion and turns to the faithful Sunnon, the effort would seem to be too much for her, and she dies soon after.

(9) *Agione:* a comparatively lucky heroine. Her only great distress is referred to on p. 251 (and see note (3)). She is carried away by Mundisic, who has her tied to her chariot while he fights her would-be rescuers.

(10) *Albysinda:* a character in *Pharamond.* Her distresses include the importunities of unwanted suitors, the thwarting of her love for Marcomire by her father, and being imprisoned in Cologne.

(11) *Placidia:* a character in *Pharamond.* Sister of the Roman Emperor

Honorius, she loves and is beloved by Constance, but is captured when Rome falls to Alaric, and forced to marry his brother Autalphe. When Autalphe dies, however, she is able to marry Constance.

(12) *Arsinoe*: See p. 216 and note (1).

(13) *Deidamia*: See p. 338 and note.

Page 377. (1) *Shakespear . . . Integrity:* Malcolm (*Macbeth*, IV. iii. 115) describes as 'Child of integrity' the 'noble passion' of rage with which Macduff attacks his prince for the many black vices to which he has confessed. What Macduff expresses is not, however, just resentment at a wrong done to himself.

(2) *'Has taught the Passions to move at the Command of Virtue'*: Johnson used these words to introduce Richardson's contribution to the *Rambler*, no. 97, 19 February 1751.

Page 378. When Ariosto . . . very little: Ariosto's son Virginius tells us that the poet could not afford to adorn his house as he wished; and 'when men told him that they wondered that he did not make a fine house, as he was a person who depicted palaces so well, he answered that he made these latter fine without money' (Edmund G. Gardner, *The King of Court Poets*, 1906, p. 236).

Page 379. It is the Fault . . . of Custom: Cf. Lady Mary Wortley Montagu's judgment of *Tom Jones*, *Amelia*, and similar novels: 'All these sort of Books have the same fault, which I cannot easily pardon, being very mischeivous. They place a merit in extravagant Passions, and encourrage young people to hope for impossible events to draw them out of the misery they chuse to plunge themselves into, expecting legacys from unknown Relations, and generous Benefactors to distress'd Virtue, as much out of Nature as Fairy Treasures' (*Complete Letters*, iii. 66).

This was written in 1754, after Lady Mary had read *The Female Quixote* (see p. 322, note). To attack novels for placing a merit in extravagant passions was common enough, but the charge that they encourage young people to form illusory expectations was not. Moreover, the legacies that rescue Tom Jones and Captain Booth from the consequences of their follies do not come from unknown relations or against the course of nature. Perhaps Lady Mary had some recollection of this passage in her mind.

Supplementary Notes for World's Classics Edition
(*Margaret Anne Doody*)

Page 259. Valley of Tempe: now as in antiquity a celebrated beauty spot in Thessaly, a vale between the mountains of Olympos and Ossa through which flows the Peneios river. Once a centre of the worship of Apollo,

Tempe is noted by many classical authors and has historical associations. Arabella's male companions seem equally ignorant of geography, history, and literature: they may not have obtained their ideas through the false medium of romances, but part of the joke is that they have no information at all. Sir Charles is sure the place cannot exist since he knows no one who has seen it, and young Glanville can only smile at Arabella's desire to go into 'Turky' (p. 260). All of Greece was under Turkish rule in the eighteenth century, but Arabella is certainly not wrong in her reference to Greece and Macedonia.

Page 265 (3). no such Springs at Thermopylae: Mr. Selvin's learned reading does not seem to have assisted his study of etymology; he might have guessed from the words that make the name of Thermopylae that the place must be a site of hot springs. Modern hydropathic establishments have been set up there; according to the *Blue Guide* for 1988, 'The waters... are impregnated with carbonic acid, lime, salt, and sulphur, and are said to be efficacious in the cure of sciatica.' Madeleine de Scudéry was not altogether unreasonable or arbitrary in her use of a site more customarily associated with the gallant defence of the pass by Leonidas and his Spartans against the Persians in 480 BC.

APPENDIX

JOHNSON, RICHARDSON, AND *The Female Quixote*

WHEN she was writing *The Female Quixote*, Mrs. Lennox was fortunate in receiving both literary and practical assistance from Samuel Johnson and Samuel Richardson. Johnson had already played an active part in furthering her career.[1] By introducing her to Richardson,[2] he provided her with a particularly valuable new ally, who helped her in at least three distinct ways: as a novelist, he gave her literary advice; as a printer, he printed the first edition of *The Female Quixote*; as one of London's most prominent men of letters, he used his influence in the literary world on her behalf. Several letters written by both Johnson and Richardson in connection with *The Female Quixote* have recently been discovered.[3] Two of Richardson's contain detailed criticism of Mrs. Lennox's manuscript, and her answer to one of these has survived.[4] These letters enable us to follow the pre-publication history of *The Female Quixote* in some detail. In particular, Richardson's criticisms improve our understanding of the finished novel by indicating some of the problems that arose while it was being written.

The following discussion is divided into two sections. The first contains an account of the writing of *The Female Quixote*, with particular reference to the involvement of Johnson and Richardson. The second begins by reproducing Richardson's criticisms of Mrs. Lennox's manuscript, and her reply, mentioned above. It then dis-

---

[1] See D. Isles, 'Johnson and Charlotte Lennox', *The New Rambler*, June 1967, pp. 41–2.

[2] Details of the introduction (date unknown) are given in Charlotte F. Barrett ed., *Diary and Letters of Madame D'Arblay* (1842–6), I, 91.

[3] The letters used here are: Richardson to Johnson, 2 Nov. 1751; Richardson to Mrs. Lennox, c. Nov.–Dec. 1751 and 13 Jan. 1752; Johnson to Mrs. Lennox, 4 Feb. and 12 Mar. 1752 (all in the Houghton Library, Harvard). For further details of the Houghton collection, see D. Isles, 'Unpublished Johnson Letters' and 'Other Letters in the Lennox Collection', *T.L.S.*, 29 July and 5 Aug. 1965.

[4] Mrs. Lennox to Richardson, c. Nov.–Dec. 1751 (Pierpont Morgan Library, New York).

cusses the significance of these criticisms, and concludes by summing up the nature of Richardson's contribution, and of Mrs. Lennox's reaction to it.

(i) The Writing of The Female Quixote

Mrs. Lennox's desire to ridicule the French heroic romances, and to point out their potentially harmful effects on the minds of inexperienced readers, is seen in her earliest writings. Mockery of romance conventions is found in 'Shallum to Hilpah',[5] one of the best of her 1747 *Poems*. More important, the dangers of romance-reading play a prominent part in her first novel, *The Life of Harriot Stuart*. Harriot, who at one point sees herself as 'nothing less than a Clelia or Statira', is in many ways an early version of Arabella. Her friend Mrs. Villars and a clergyman who woos her 'in the stile of Alexander the Great' have been corrupted by heroic romances and heroic drama respectively, and her mother claims that 'these horrid romances has turned the girl's brain'.[6] In *The Female Quixote*, then, Mrs. Lennox chose to subject an already-familiar topic to deeper and more comprehensive treatment, examining the general relationship between fiction and history, and emphasizing the positive value of good fiction, as well as ridiculing the romances themselves.

Mrs. Lennox would have been free to devote herself to *The Female Quixote* after the completion of her *Memoirs of the Duke of Sully*, published in March 1751. On 23 April, Johnson's *Rambler* no. 115 contained a brief sketch of a deluded romance-reader called Imperia.[7] This lady's circumstances and foibles are so similar to Arabella's that coincidence can be ruled out. Mrs. Lennox's previous interest in the topic makes it unlikely that Imperia inspired her to write *The Female Quixote*. We can therefore assume that by early April Mrs. Lennox had discussed her idea with Johnson, who paid it the compliment of imitation.

By October 1751 Mrs. Lennox had completed a draft approxi-

[5] Based on Addison's 'The Story of Hilpa' (*Spectator* nos. 584–585), an Eastern tale described by Robert Mayo as 'a kind of mock-heroic romance' (*The English Novel in the Magazines 1740–1815*, 1962, p. 40).

[6] *Harriot Stuart*, I. pp. 8, 11, 29–30; II. p. 25.

[7] Johnson, *Works*, ed. Sir John Hawkins (1787), VI. 283–4.

mating to Books i–iv (that is, Vol. I) of the final version. At this point, Richardson became involved in the undertaking. Although Mrs. Lennox may already have been introduced to him, they could not have known each other well at this stage, for Johnson acted as an intermediary. The most likely course of events is that Johnson persuaded Richardson to read Mrs. Lennox's manuscript, lent it to him and took Mrs. Lennox to see him at Salisbury Court. In a letter to Johnson dated 2 November 1751, Richardson reported that he had not finished reading 'Mrs. Lennox's Piece', but very much liked it. He apologized for being out when Johnson and Mrs. Lennox had visited him together, and asked if they were to come again. Successful visits must indeed have taken place, for within a very short time Mrs. Lennox knew Richardson well enough to discuss her manuscript with him, in the company of two of his friends—one each of the Misses Fielding (Patty and Sarah, Henry's sisters) and Collier (Jane and Margaret).

Meanwhile, the pace of Mrs. Lennox's writing appears to have increased. A continuation of her manuscript, the equivalent of Books v, vi, and the first two chapters of Book vii, was shown to Richardson either later in November or—less likely—early in December. Before he had time to read it, he was involved in the more mundane task of trying to persuade Andrew Millar, a leading London bookseller, to accept Mrs. Lennox's unfinished manuscript for eventual publication. According to Mrs. Lennox herself (who had a particularly suspicious mind in such matters), Millar's literary advisers were maliciously conspiring against her, and had succeeded in prejudicing him against her and her work. In any event, Millar was obviously reluctant to accept *The Female Quixote*, and Mrs. Lennox's well-wishers—including the Earl of Orrery as well as Johnson and Richardson—were exerting their considerable influence in its favour. Richardson visited Millar on a certain Thursday evening, soon after receiving the continuation. He gave Millar a glowing report of the novel, left him at eight, went home and hurriedly read the continuation, making critical notes as he went along. The notes were sent to Mrs. Lennox on Friday morning, along with an optimistic account of the meeting with Millar. Mrs. Lennox, in a bitter and agitated mood, replied by return, at four o'clock in the afternoon. Apart from discussing Richardson's notes, she told him that further discussion of her novel had taken place at Millar's after his departure, as a result of which she feared that Millar would not publish it.

Her fears proved to be premature; Millar soon agreed to publish —a decision which her friends no doubt helped to influence. She continued to write rapidly. By the beginning of January 1752 she was struggling with the final Book. In a letter dated 13 January, Richardson attempted to help her out of her difficulties. By the end of the month, Mrs. Lennox's share of the writing was apparently complete, and the novel ready for publication. Johnson contributed the Dedication. Apart from this, we can assume that Mrs. Lennox had discussed at least the conclusion with him. She obviously had him in mind when she created Arabella's eventual saviour, 'the pious and learned Doctor ——', and was heavily influenced by his ideas and phraseology in the penultimate chapter (Book ix, Ch. 11). In fact, it is usually claimed that Johnson wrote this chapter—wholly or in part—himself. I would suggest, however, that this claim is by no means adequately supported. It rests largely on internal stylistic evidence. Against this, there is absolutely no contemporary suggestion of his having written it; linguistically, there appears to be nothing in it that a good writer familiar with Johnson's style could not have achieved; structurally, the dialogue and argument are far below Johnson's standard. On the whole, it would seem best to regard the chapter, with all its faults, as wholly Mrs. Lennox's until definite evidence to the contrary is found.[8]

As soon as *The Female Quixote* was complete, a final practical problem arose concerning its date of publication. Some misdemeanour of Richardson's (presumably in his role as the novel's printer) threatened to delay publication considerably—so much so that on 4 February Johnson advised Mrs. Lennox to postpone it until the following year, rather than publish at an unprofitable time. In the same letter, he condemned Richardson, comforted her, and assured her of his future assistance whenever possible. As it happened, the delay must have been shorter than had been anticipated. Johnson received his presentation copy no later than Thursday 12 March, and the novel was officially published on the following day, Friday 13 March.

[8] The claim was originally made by John Mitford (*Gentleman's Magazine*, N.S. XX, 1843, pp. 132–3). Cf. Miriam Small, *Charlotte Ramsay Lennox* (1935), pp. 79–82.

(ii) Richardson's Criticisms of *The Female Quixote* Manuscript.

The relevant sections of the correspondence read as follows :[9]

(1) *Richardson to Mrs. Lennox, 'Friday Morn', c. November–December 1751* (Houghton Library)
(a) *Postscript of the letter :*

I have ventured a few Lines, written as I read. You will excuse the Liberty. Excuse Haste.

(b) *Separate sheet sent with the letter :*

As you seem'd, Madam, to be apprehensive of Matter falling short for two Vols. I have taken the Liberty by these Marks, in the beginning Pages [[to suppose New Paragraphs, which will, in the whole Work, greatly and properly help you

I am quite charm'd with the lovely Visionary's Absurdity (and the Perplexity which follows it, to Sir Charles to Glanville and her self) on her supposing Sir Charles in Love with her.

But I think, that Sir Georges's [*sic*] Story, and his Pretensions to the Kingdom of Kent, is carried too far. He ought not at least to have made his Claim so recent—He might have made a Discovery of his Genealogy from the Saxons and the Heptarchy, without so immediately interesting his Father and Grandfather in it. It is impossible, but she must know, that there had not been a Kingdom of Kent for many Generations. And it was too gross for Mr. Glanville to bear, who had been sollicitous that Sir George should not play upon Arabella.

Omit, I beseech you, Madam, the middle Name in the first Line of p. 238 ['a Young, a Richardson, or a Johnson'; Book vi, Ch. 11, p 253]—Utterly unworthy of a Rank, or Mention, with the two others—

The story of the Highway-Men, and Arabella's Absurdity on their Appearance, very pretty—

You have very pretty Scenes before you, Madam, at Bath and London.

(2) *Mrs. Lennox to Richardson, answering (1). 'Friday 4 o clock'* (Pierpont Morgan Library)

. . . I am extreamly happy in the approbation you have been

---

[9] This correspondence is published by kind permission of the Houghton and Pierpont Morgan libraries. The spelling and punctuation of the originals are retained, and editorial additions are enclosed in square brackets.

pleased to express of my second Vol and am perfectly Convinced of the justice of your exceptions, I return you my thanks for them, and shall not fail to make the alterations you point out to me—

You must excuse me Sir if I do not comply with your injunction concerning the second Name—in this particular I can never be of your opinion, since my own is supported by the united Voice of the World, which has agreed in giving your inimitable performances a universal applause.

(3) *Richardson to Mrs. Lennox, 13 January 1752* (Houghton Library)

Dear Madam,

It is my humble Opinion, that you should finish your Heroine's Cure in your present Vols. The method you propose, tho' it might flatter my Vanity, yet will be thought a Contrivance between the Author of Arabella, and the Writer of Clarissa, to do Credit to the latter; and especially if the Contraste will take up much Room in the proposed 3d Volume. If it will not take up much, it may be done, if you *will* do it, that way (which I beg you to consider, and to consult Mr. Johnson before you resolve) at the latter End of the Second Volume. You are a young Lady have therefore much time before you, and I am sure, will think that a good Fame will be [in?] your Interest [*sic*]. Make therefore, your present Work as complete as you can, in two Volumes; and it will give Consequence to your future Writings, and of course to your Name as a Writer; And without a Complement I think you set out upon an admirable Foundation.

Excuse Haste. I write while a Friend is with me. And have hardly time for Reperusal. I am, Madam, Yours most sincerely S. Richardson

The problems revealed by the correspondence bear an illuminating relationship to subsequent critical opinion. Mrs. Barbauld's criticism that *The Female Quixote* is 'rather spun out too much, and not very well wound up' has recently been intelligently supplemented by Ronald Paulson. He sees a marked deterioration in the quality of the last three Books; whereas in Books i–vi 'the focus appears to be on the heroine's mind', from Book vii onwards 'the intense psychological scrutiny of Arabella . . . is replaced by a rather

clumsy attempt at the rapid satiric survey of society'.[10] It appears to
me that spinning-out (particularly in the form of excessive reference
to the romances) accompanies the psychological scrutiny from Book
ii onwards, and that the Bath section (Books vii–viii) has more merit
than Paulson allows. Paulson's general argument, however, seems
valid, and the deterioration he complains of is particularly noticeable in the concluding Book. It is therefore especially interesting to
discover from the letters that for Mrs. Lennox herself the two most
troublesome aspects of *The Female Quixote* were the concluding
section and the general problem of length, in the sense of adjusting
her content to fill either two or three volumes. The problem of
length was no doubt aggravated by her failure to plan the novel
carefully in advance. Initially, her apparent problem (like her
financial situation) resembled that of Edwin Reardon—in Gissing's
New Grub Street—when writing *Margaret Home*; she felt com-
mercially obliged to produce at least two volumes, but thought she
would have to spin her material out in order to achieve the desired
length.[11] Having done so with Richardson's assistance, however,
she later discovered that she had overdone it, and would now need
a third volume to enable her to conclude her novel as she wished.
As a needy professional writer, the alternative solution—complete
revision—was a luxury beyond her means. When Richardson
decisively condemned the idea of a third volume, she made do with
two, and telescoped her last Book accordingly. The final effect of
this uncertainty was to give *The Female Quixote* the worst of both
worlds; both the prolixity of the earlier Books and the relatively
summary nature of the last (as seen, for example, in the brief dis-
missal of the London section in Book viii, Ch. 8–Book ix, Ch. 2)
detract from Mrs. Lennox's achievement.

The more important problem of Arabella's 'Cure' is closely
linked to the question of length. As originally planned, the cure
would seemingly have been more leisurely, and impossible to contain in the second volume. The other factor against it was that
Richardson had doubts about its very nature. Although we cannot
be surprised at Mrs. Lennox's decision to follow Richardson's
advice, we cannot help questioning its wisdom. The stilted and

---

[10] Paulson, *Satire and the Novel in Eighteenth-Century England* (1967), p. 277.

[11] *New Grub Street* (1891), Vol. I, Ch. ix ('Invita Minerva'), pp. 220, 224, 239–240,
and *passim*. Reardon, of course, has three volumes to fill.

unconvincing conclusion of the final version has a decidedly make-shift appearance. Under the circumstances, it is tempting to speculate on the nature of the conclusion originally planned. As we have only Richardson's comments, and the novel itself, to go on, any reconstruction must remain highly speculative. It could, for example, be conjectured that Mrs. Lennox intended to emulate *Don Quixote* and *Clarissa* simultaneously by giving Arabella a fatal illness, a consequent realization of the follies of romances, and an exemplary, virtuous death. My guess, however, is that the cure was to have been gradual, and based on a continuation of the Countess's attempt to cure Arabella, which begins so promisingly and yet is abandoned so abruptly and oddly (Book viii, Chs. 5–8). Mrs. Lennox, as opposed to most other anti-romance writers, was interested in constructively recommending good fiction as well as destructively condemning romances. The Countess is shown as well read. The original preface to the fourth volume of *Clarissa* condemns romances,[12] and *Clarissa* itself is the outstanding contemporary example of 'natural' and moralistic fiction. What, then, would be more appropriate than for the Countess to culminate her curative efforts by bringing Arabella and *Clarissa* together? This conjecture at least accounts for both the involvement of *Clarissa* in the original ending and the curious abandonment of the Countess in the final one. As it happens, a similar approach was used fifty years later in Maria Edgeworth's 'Angelina; or, L'Amie Inconnue' (in *Moral Tales for Young People*, 1801) which is strongly influenced by *The Female Quixote*. Angelina (née Anne Warwick) has been corrupted by novels of sensibility, and has 'a striking resemblance to the female Quixote'. Lady Frances Somerset, modelled on Mrs. Lennox's Countess, befriends Angelina in Bristol, and, as part of her cure, makes Angelina read *The Female Quixote* itself.[13]

When we compare Richardson's work on *The Female Quixote* with, say, his later work on Edward Young's *Conjectures on Original Composition*—which he discussed so thoroughly and minutely as to

---

[12] 'The Editor to the Reader,' *Clarissa*, 1st edn. (1748), IV. i–vi, especially ii–iv. This preface appears to have been omitted from later editions.
[13] *Moral Tales for Young People* (3 vols., 1802), II, 147–255, esp. pp. 220 and 242.

become virtually its co-author[14]—we are reminded that his involvement with the former is not as deep as it might have been. His
written comments are hasty jottings, and it is unlikely that he had
the time to think long and deeply about *The Female Quixote* as a
whole. If he had, he would surely have noticed Mrs. Lennox's
talent for 'intense psychological scrutiny' in the earlier Books, and
his advice about the conclusion might well have been different. As
it stands, even allowing for hindsight, this advice seems to be the
least helpful of his comments. Another minor flaw is the way in
which his habitual and irritating false modesty (as in his objection
to the use of his name) intrudes on his criticism. These two short-
comings, however, count for comparatively little compared with
the positive advantages which Mrs. Lennox must have derived
from Richardson's assistance. Allowing for his haste, his comments
are those of a perceptive reader and an experienced writer, who is
keenly aware of the practical as well as the artistic aspects of the
profession of letters. His objection to Sir George's 'Pretensions to
the Kingdom of Kent' is particularly sound, whereas his expedient
of re-arranging the paragraphs to spin out the length demonstrates
his practicality. Above all, the most outstanding characteristic of
his comments is his desire to encourage Mrs. Lennox. He praises
her lavishly whenever he can, and is gentle in his adverse criticisms.
In itself, this encouragement from Europe's most widely-respected
living novelist was one of the most valuable assets that a young and
largely unknown writer could ever hope to have.

Mrs. Lennox's known reactions to Richardson's advice are
appropriately deferential and generally sensible. As already suggested, it is perhaps unfortunate that she did not conclude the
novel in her own way, notwithstanding Richardson's qualms. Apart
from this, her common sense is shown in both what she accepts and
what she rejects. We have one example of her modifying his advice
with regard to the inclusion of his name.[15] In the case of Sir
George and the Kingdom of Kent, on the other hand, we see her

---

[14] See the Richardson-Young correspondence in the *Monthly Magazine*, XLII–
XLVII (1816–19), *passim*, and Alan D. McKillop, 'Richardson, Young and the
Conjectures', *M.P.*, XXII (1925), 391–404.

[15] In spite of her vehemence on this point in excerpt (2) above, Mrs. Lennox
compromised in the first edition by including only Richardson's initial ('a *Young*, a
R——, or a *Johnson*', II. 119). His full name was given in the second and subsequent
editions. See p. 253.

following his suggestion very carefully; in the final version, although Sir George's grandfather retains the title of Prince Veridomer, he is left with only a 'small pittance of ground', and the period in which his ancestors lost their kingdom is left deliberately vague (Book vi, Ch. 1).

Our examination of Johnson's and Richardson's involvement in the writing of *The Female Quixote* has demonstrated Mrs. Lennox's indebtedness to their advice, assistance, and encouragement. This indebtedness now extends to us, in that their letters preserve a record of Mrs. Lennox's progress and problems which contributes considerably towards our understanding of her greatest novel.

Birkbeck College   Duncan Isles
University of London